AGE OF FORGED STEEL

RISE OF MANKIND 5

JEZ CAJIAO

TABLE OF CONTENTS

THANKS

Hi everybody! So, I don't know about you all, but this last few months has been a rollercoaster for me, my team's increased in size and complexity, as has the job, but I'm loving it!

So, as is tradition; I need to thank a few people!

First, as always is Chrissy. My moon-and-stars, my sun-and-similar-romantic-type-shenanigans. You make all this possible, and I love you. I can't say it better than that.

To my boys, Max and Xander. You two rock my world in different ways on different days, but damn I'm so proud of you, and I love you both so much. No matter what else happens and anything else that may come along, you will always be that which I am most proud of.

I usually thank a lot more people than this, mainly because so many help me along the way, but this time? This is all about my little family.

I hope you all understand, and I hope you enjoy the book!

-Jez, 4th April, 2023

PROLOGUE

"Fucking…hills…" Nick Pots gasped, finally reaching the top of the cracked asphalt. "Why are…there so…many…fucking…hills…?!"

"Scotland, mate." Ivarsson grunted laconically, cracking his back and twisting around, searching for threats without thinking. "That's what happens when you go to Scotland. It fuckin' rains, you get jumped by the locals, and it's all a fuckin' hill, goin' up or down."

"Shit." Nick leaned over the handles of the wheelchair he was pushing and tried to catch his breath. "Tell me…it's your turn…"

"Nope," Steve "Napalm" Higgs interrupted cheerfully. "I distinctly remember you promising six hills, as long as we covered your watch last night…"

"Aye, fuckin' *hills*," Nick whispered, shaking his head and watching sweat drop from the tip of his nose to the road below. "What's…the difference…between a mountain…an' a hill again?"

The hill the platoon had just topped was the last for a while, or as near as they could tell, a gradual decline down to the reservoir ahead and to the border.

The captain was approaching fast, even as one and two section split off, running for the trees on either side of the road.

"Fall in!" Blake called, jogging back to the group, waving a hand as they straightened automatically at the captain's presence.

"Sir?" Ivarsson asked, squinting down at the dip in the road that currently hid the group that had been seen moving closer. "Those our boys then?"

"Not sure," Blake replied, coming to a halt with the others. "All we know is they're wearing our gear and heading for us. Usually, that'd be a comforting sign. Not anymore, though. First and second sections are in the woods on either side of the road, ready to pincer just in case, or should they not be friendly, hammer them on our anvil."

"Fair enough, sir," Ivarsson agreed. "Gather up, lads and lasses. Let's look like we have a right to be here."

The remainder of the troop spread out quickly, pulling off their ponchos to clear weapons. Nick wheeled the stolen wheelchair to the side of the road and secured it. The two ammo cases it held were as valuable as gold to the severely depleted troop.

There was a general muttering as soldiers checked their gear, making sure their guns were loaded, their fire lanes clear, and that they were as ready as could be.

In deference to the fact that the approaching group wore their uniforms and displayed no outward signs of aggression, the survivors of the third and fourth sections stood ready to meet the newcomers on the road, rather than spread out, blatantly ready to fight.

Anyone who thought that meant they weren't ready to kill, though, had never met Royal Marines before. Even before the fall, the commandos were known for kicking shit out of anyone who crossed them, and it was generally accepted that the most elite of the elite fighting forces around the world paid through the nose to hire the ex-commandos to train them.

The US Marine Corp were far larger, more diverse, and had little luxuries like dedicated transport and even *air support*. The Royal Marines, on the other hand, made do, essentially, with just their guns, pure insanity, and a very loose definition of "theirs" and "ours" being applied to everything.

Namely, that if a Royal Marine needed something to complete a mission, then it therefore "belonged" to the Royal Marines…regardless of who had previously believed—in error—they were the owners of that item.

The remaining two sections spread out, weapons held ready, not pointed at the approaching soldiers, but not exactly pointing away either.

"Looks like they're out of Otterburn, sir," Ivarsson muttered to the captain, getting a grunt of agreement as Blake stared at them through his binoculars. "Never thought I'd see the day I'd be wishing we had a sneaky-beaky with us."

"Me neither." Blake lowered the glasses and passed them to his right for Ivarsson. "They'd still be wrong, though. You know what they say about the intelligence corps…"

"That military intelligence is an oxymoron?"

"That's the one. But I'd even take the sneaky's crap info over nothing. Check out their skin…I'm not liking that mottling."

Ivarsson squinted through the glasses and nodded.

The incoming soldiers were soaked through, their outdoor gear looking like they'd run up a waterfall. They plodded along the road as one, thirty or so men spread out, carrying their guns at the ready. But…

"I don't like this," Ivarsson said slowly. "Not one bit."

"Me neither. Hold the boys here. I'll—"

"Let me, sir," Ivarsson said, passing the glasses back and moving in front of his superior. "It's an NCO's role to make contact and an officer's to evaluate and lead, you know that."

Blake paused, then nodded. He'd come up through the ranks, an NCO who'd made the fatal mistake of being promoted to an officer, and then, by sheer dint of capability, the bastards had kept promoting him.

He was still an NCO at heart, though, and would rather lead from the front than be a regular Rupert.

"Heads on a swivel, lads," he called out, squinting at the group closing on them, then spreading the team out even as Ivarsson jogged forward, ready to make contact.

"Hold there, lads!" Ivarsson slowed to a walk a hundred meters from the approaching soldiers. They gave no sign they'd heard and kept moving as a single unit. Ivarsson swallowed hard, the feeling of subtle "wrongness" getting stronger.

The troop had been in the far north of Scotland, training for a deployment when all hell had broken loose, and the camp CO had decided that nothing could be done without more information.

The marines and another troop had been broken loose and sent out on recon. The first had turned back once it became clear just how widespread the loss of power was, while the marines had been detailed to head for London and report.

A full troop had set off, and although they'd not lost many, losing any of their friends, highly trained and experienced commandos all, was a blow to them.

Now they'd finally made it through the wilderness, running up and down the goddamn mountains of Scotland until the border with England came distantly into view through the curtains of rain and low scudding clouds.

They'd made it this far, and the two forests on either side of the road that ran in close now held the first and second sections, seven and five men respectively, each ready to fight if they were needed.

The scrub bush and gorse that covered the sides of the road were thick at this time of the year, having recently had the first frost of the year, and the way they rustled was enough to raise thoughts of creatures creeping up, no matter the situation.

The troop would be damn glad to get back to normal life, or even a decent sneaky-beaky—or intelligence debriefing—that could fill them in on what had been happening.

"That's close enough, lads!" Ivarsson called out again, louder this time, and with the bite of command that only a born NCO could manage. "Stop right there."

They didn't.

The entire platoon looked scruffy, as if they'd marched the length of the country, rather than from the Otterburn garrison, maybe fifteen or twenty miles at most away.

Their gear was soaked through, rainwater dripping from the barrels of their guns, from their bone domes—helmets—and more. Boots were battered, as if they'd marched a hundred miles. The soldiers themselves…

They were buried in their gear, faces almost hidden under helmets and goggles that looked filthy. The little skin that was on display, though, looked pale, with sick-looking red and purple markings.

"OI!" Ivarsson barked, shouldering his rifle and pointing at the advancing group, sure now that no matter how exhausted they might have been, there was no way they could have missed his order. "Stop and drop, or I'll fuckin' *drop* you! Where's yer CO?"

Silence.

Ivarsson swallowed hard again, sighting down his rifle as they kept marching, guns held ready, toward him.

What the fuck was he supposed to do now? If he opened fire, so too would the others. It'd be a slaughter, and they were British Army! Sure, the army might be fucking useless compared to a real combat unit like the marine commandos, but they were still a *team*. They were like distant cousins you knew were shit useless but you had to look after, and separate from the occasional farm animal.

They were *family*.

If they didn't stop, though…Should he shoot? *Could* he actually shoot? He'd be up on charges, at the least, if they killed these men, but…

Movement.

Movement in the trees.

The two sections they'd sent into the trees to arc around and encircle the incoming team were moving out into the open.

"What the hell?" Ivarsson muttered, glancing from them to the advancing force, before turning slightly and calling out behind him. "Orders, sir?"

"Fall in!" Blake barked. "Rifles up! Draw a line, lads...ten meters out. Anything crosses it, we fire!"

Ivarsson backed up as fast as he could, and for the first time, there was a reaction from the incoming soldiers...

They moved faster, rifles lifting as if to stop him backing away.

"Sir?!" he shouted, his blood running cold.

"DOWN!" Blake bellowed, and Ivarsson obeyed, dropping prone, rifle raised, sighting in on the closing forces, desperately glancing from the unknowns on the road, and the two sections that had entered the woods.

First section had seven men in it. They'd lost Si, a good marine, to some snake bite that had rotted him from the inside out in a handful of minutes, but the rest of the section were good men. They'd not have left their spot without a reason, but here they were, marching out into the open, rifles held ready. But they faced their friends instead, trooping closer and closer.

"Last chance!" the captain bellowed, before going on. "On three! One, two..."

"H...old..." a voice called out, warbling, cracking, and full of alien harmonics, as one of the soldiers moved forward ahead of the other, hand slipping from bracing his rifle and lifting in a "wait" gesture...as they continued to close. "Ho...ld...there...la...ds..."

Ivarsson froze, seeing what was happening a second before anyone else as they drew close.

"They're mimics!" he shouted, and opened fire, even as the one that had spoken tried again.

"That...s...clo...se...enough..." the same voice gurgled out, as the bullets started to fly.

Ivarsson aimed as he was taught: center of mass, three-round burst, tightly controlled. The one that was repeating his own words was smashed from his feet, and the others let loose a weird hiss, lifting their own rifles into place.

Most of them pulled their triggers over and over, aiming for the prone marine...and had no luck. Their magazines were empty, used already, with the controlling sentience having no understanding of reloading or more.

Some, though, notably the two marine sections that had entered the forest, had full magazines loaded, and the few of their number who had already flicked the safety off opened fire.

Bullets flew, even as the last two sections under Captain Blake poured out controlled fire, taking down the soldiers with surprising ease. Their own marines, though, marching closer, rifles raised to their shoulders and firing over and over, were a different story.

Still, the two small sections that stumbled and staggered through the gorse, making no attempt to hide, against Royal Marines in full control of their bodies, lying prone on the road, sighting carefully, didn't last long.

In less than two minutes, the survivors of the marine troop slowly regained their feet and stood stunned, staring at the bodies and trying to make sense of what had just happened.

The survivors worked automatically, triaging wounds, reloading rifles, and generally doing anything to avoid thinking about what the hell had just happened.

Those who were least injured quickly spread out to check on the two sections that had moved into the trees, trying to figure out how someone had taken them down that quickly and silently, then had dressed in their gear in time to turn on them.

Most of the survivors had taken at least one hit, and they quickly checked each other, and themselves, when the first shout rang out.

"Sir!" Ivarsson croaked, one hand pressed to the bleeding hole in his shoulder as he nodded to a nearby body. "He's alive…"

"So's that one…" came a call from off to one side.

"And this…" In seconds, all the bodies that had been taken down were twitching.

"Put them out of their misery, boys!" Blake barked, stepping up and switching to his handgun, firing a single round into the back of a neck here and an exposed head there. "I don't know who or what they are, but they've got our ammo, and we need it back. Ivarsson, take two and check out the forest, see where our lads went…"

"These are our lads, sir," Ivarsson called back.

"I…What?"

"These are our lads," he repeated, having already started to move toward the other section, ready to check, but already knowing what he was going to find.

Blake moved up quickly, jogging across to the nearest body, crouching and rolling him over, seeing the twitching eyes, the shaking body as it tried to move again.

He backed away quickly, eyes going wide as a bullet hole in the forehead of the commando before him slowly filled in. Blood that had still been streaming from the wound stopped and a flattened round was pushed up and out. Black fragments mixed with the white of bones, and the pink brain slid free…and then something black moved in the wound.

"What the hell…" Blake whispered, shaking his head and backing up as the body twitched, fingers closing around the rifle grip. "Get the guns!"

He stomped on the wrist and fired another round into the man's face, then reached down and stripped the gun from unresisting fingers. "Guns, ammo, then boot it!" he ordered.

"Sir!" another shouted, *shrieked*, almost after a minute. "The ground!"

Blake backed up fast, arms full of rifles, handguns, and mags, when he glanced down, seeing nothing.

"What's up?" he shouted.

"Leeches…or something like it!" a marine shouted, stamping down hard on something only he could see. "There's loads of them!"

"Back!" Ivarsson barked, hurrying from the bushes and breaking for the road. "Everyone back on the road!"

The survivors moved automatically. Any weapons they already had in hand were taken with them, but anything left on the ground was abandoned as they hotfooted it back.

"What is it…" Blake started to ask his NCO, until the nearest bodies moved again. "Fuck's sake, what does it take to kill them!"

"We need to move, sir…hoof it south right goddamn now." Ivarsson moved in close. "We need to get the hell out of here with what we have. I don't know what happened to our lads, but they looked like the others, and I'm betting they moved through those leeches like I nearly did."

"Point—fuck!" Blake cursed, torn between a need to check his dead—to recover their tags, at least—and his duty to the living.

"We need to move, sir, *now*."

Blake nodded, gesturing to Ivarsson to give the order.

"Pots!" he yelled, turning to the man who'd been stuck with the wheelchair the last few miles. "Ammo!" He pointed, getting a nod; then he barked out other orders. The survivors fell in and gathered their gear as fast as they could.

By the time the ponchos and the two ammunition containers in the wheelchair had been recovered, it was clear all the bodies were moving, several already back on their feet. Gunfire rang out again, putting them back down.

A minute later, the remainder of the troop was off again, this time moving at a steady dogtrot: a run for ten minutes, followed by a fast walk for ten, then a run again.

They'd covered almost three miles when the first of the marines collapsed, falling facedown, unresponsive.

Rolling him onto his back, the others pulled back instinctively, as they saw the telltale grey of the skin and the bruising that marked the passage of something moving up under the skin.

It was the marine who'd first seen the leeches, or whatever they were, and had stomped on them. Ten seconds after collapsing, he opened his eyes again…and went for his gun, both eyeballs as pitch black as if they'd been filled with oil.

Blake did the deed himself, putting the marine out of his suffering, before stripping him of his ammunition, weapon, and tags, then rolling him off the road. The body picked up speed as it bounced and rolled down a short hill to a narrow but deep river…and was grabbed by a thin tentacle and yanked into its depths in seconds.

"Eyes up and out!" Blake called, checking to make sure they were clear as he moved into the middle of the group. Most of the force stared out, keeping them safe as he quickly checked himself over…any flesh that he could see, anyway.

It was healthy, pink skin on the arms, his stomach—lifting his gear so that Ivarsson could check quickly—and his ankles, rolling his pants up and socks down.

"Good enough," the NCO assured, stepping into the middle of the ring in his place.

Three more were confirmed as clean, before the first was found.

"Jameson…" Ivarsson saw the grey skin as soon as the marine lifted his top. "Armor off, son."

"What?" The young marine grunted, shocked. "I'm fine, Sarge."

"Just need to be sure, son. Top off, *now*."

The flesh that was exposed once he'd stripped his body armor and clothing off was a mottled mess of healthy pink and a greying, bruised mess.

Prodding at the skin made him shake his head.

"Nothing, sir," he said, "I can't feel nothin', sir, thought I was just cold…"

It took seconds to locate them; three of the small black leeches were slowly inching their way up the body, headed for the brain, presumably.

"Deep breath, son." Ivarsson dragged his blade free, then stepped in as soon as he nodded he was ready. Two swift cuts, forming an X over the slowly moving mass, and then a shucking motion, flicked the unwelcome passenger free.

An uncomfortably invasive search followed and two more cuts later, Jameson was bandaged up, and the next marine was in the center of the ring.

"Gotta say, sir...I thought all the rumors about the navy making you get naked for lads was bullshit," one of the marines tried to joke, only to have it fall flat as another of the team was found to be infected.

Ten minutes later, they were moving again, but this time the mood was even more subdued as they considered that they might all be infected.

"Why are some more advanced than others, then, you think?" Blake quietly asked Ivarsson.

"Thinking they're like the leeches or worms they look like, sir. Numbing bite, then they need to move up the body. If they're on the ground and make it past your boots, then they've got a long way to climb. They fall off a tree onto your neck? It's over fast."

"Think the trees were full of them?" The pain in the captain's voice made it clear he thought he'd fucked up and sent those men to their deaths.

"Probably," Ivarsson agreed bluntly. "No way you could have known that, though, sir. I sure as shit didn't."

"I know, but if the trees aren't safe, and the river sure as shit isn't safe..."

"Nothing is, sir."

"Yeah, but—"

"No," Ivarsson snapped, his voice low and hard. "Get this into your head, Blake...*nothing* is fucking safe. Whatever's happened out there..." He gestured with the barrel of his rifle up and about, ahead of where they ran side by side. "Whatever happened, we're in a different world now. I don't know if it's a different reality, if monsters slipped through, or if we're all in a fucking hospital bed with nurses pumping us full of random shit as a tester for the Ruperts. All I know is that *everything* is dangerous now. You need to get that in your head."

"I know. I—"

"Seriously! You stay out of everything else. Just plan...just get a plan in place, 'cos we're not gonna make it down to headquarters, nor London. Get your head around that now. I'll take care of the lads. You just...you just do the officering shit."

"Aye, Sarge." Blake forced a smile, nodding as he stared into the rain that swept across the moors toward them. "I'll do that..."

They kept running, crossing up and down the hills as they got smaller, until in the distance they could see an army checkpoint closing the road off, and the sign by the side of the road that proclaimed 'Welcome to Otterburn'.

One more dip in the road and they'd be running straight to the base they'd been aiming for, and that they now feared almost as much as the open road.

"Do we go around...?" Blake muttered to himself before shaking his head as Ivarsson looked at him questioningly. "It was a rhetorical question, Sergeant. We go ahead, but before we do..."

"Yes, sir?"

"Break the wheelchair ammo down, spread it out and reload. Anything that's left? Stash it by the side of the road once we're out of sight of them."

"You expecting trouble, sir?" one of the other marines asked, and he nodded.

"Those soldiers had to come from somewhere. Chances are the base is that place. If it's infected with more of those fuckers? We run on. Otherwise, we stop and get a medic…"

CHAPTER ONE

Sunrise was a cold one, made even more so for our people because the magic they'd all come to rely on, and take for granted, wasn't there.

The dungeon was always a steady, pleasant temperature. The changes that had been made since the others moved in, like the lighting and the secure doors, were all things I'd grown used to as well. Not to mention little things like being able to summon food and drink with an idle thought.

As it was now, after I'd been out of action apparently for a little over a day, the dungeon was a strange place. Normally, even at this hour—a little after seven in the morning, I guessed—there'd be a hum of activity filling the dungeon.

Instead, it was more or less silent, not to mention cold and dark.

I sat on the roof, having explained to a reluctant Kelly that I needed a little space and time, and I stared out over the frost-coated buildings, doing my best to ignore the increasing numbness invading my arse from the damn stone I sat on.

"That'll give you piles, you know," Chris called from behind me, and I turned, looking over at him with a hint of annoyance at the intrusion. "Sitting on hard stone, I mean."

"Bollocks," I muttered.

"Aye, they'll catch a cold as well," he agreed, as if that made sense, walking over and sitting on the wall next to me, dangling his legs over the side. "So, what's the crack?"

"What's that?" I frowned.

"What's going on?" he said, slowly and clearly. "Fuck me, I know you're a Yank, but I thought you'd have picked a few things up by now."

"Fuck off, Chris," I snapped. "I knew what you meant. I mean what bit! You want to know about the dungeon being fucked up? How unbelievably I screwed up? About how I've a fucking soul-bound passenger now? About how people might starve and lose their home because of me? Or how about—"

"All of it," he said, ignoring my black mood.

"Yeah, well, that'll take a while."

"Do I look like I'm going anywhere?" He nudged me gently with his shoulder. "Come on, you damn colonial…cheer the fuck up."

"Fuck off." I picked up a loose bit of stone and flicked it over the side as he grinned, clearly knowing my heart wasn't in it.

"Okay, so the dungeon's fucked." He nodded, going right to the heart of things. "Is it fixable, or are we looking to move on?"

"I don't know," I admitted. "And 'move on'? Fuck's sake, you idiot, where would we go?"

"I always liked the Greek islands," he replied calmly. "Fuck freezing our balls off here…If the dungeon's borked, then we pack up our gear, tell the others to look after each other and we'll be back soon, then we head off, find a boat and we're outta here."

"What, and abandon everyone?" I asked, stunned he'd even consider it.

"Nah. We start scouting, find another dungeon." He exhaled. "You said this one was number a hundred and something, right? That means there's more than a hundred out there. We just need to find another one and bish-bosh-boom, Bob's your uncle, Fanny's your aunt…"

"*Or she was till she died*," we chorused, mimicking a guy we'd worked with years ago who loved that saying.

"And then we send for the others. Build a fleet of fucking boats. I don't know." He shrugged. "We'll sort it out."

I looked at him, seeing the simple faith that radiated off him like ginger kids from a nuclear reactor.

"You really believe that, don't you?" I asked him after a few seconds, feeling touched. "Not us fucking off to Crete or wherever, but that we'll sort it out?"

"Aye." His shoulders slumped. "Dude, we've literally fought a god of the dead, we've battled weird-ass creatures that shouldn't exist, and had giant orc dongs shook at us. We've fought fucking steampunk robots and vampires, and we've even both gotten insanely hot girlfriends. All of that and considering it's us and who we *really* are? I don't know what the weirdest bit is."

"Clearly that you got laid without paying," I responded unthinkingly, before sighing and nudging him back with a shoulder. "But thanks, man."

"It's all right." He shook his head. "Seriously, you just need a kick up the arse now and then, that's all."

"Dude, I don't know where to fucking start," I said, my voice dropping to a whisper. "We've not been storing food. We've got practically fuck all, and if I can't fix the dungeon…"

"Then let's start at the beginning," he suggested. "You said you fucked the dungeon. How exactly?"

"We overtaxed it. We fucking hammered it, over and over. Forced it to upgrade insanely fast, and never gave it time to actually adjust, then forced it to produce literally hundreds of living creatures, constantly."

"So, it needs what? Rest? A blanket and a teddy, made to chill out for a few days?"

"I don't know. I need to check it out, the core I mean, but even me sinking into it uses its power…I could shatter the fucking core just by examining it."

"Can you fix it without doing that?"

I shook my head. "I need to find the issues and make sure I understand them…I don't know if the way the dungeon started shutting down is the first level of a reaction or the last. For all I know, it's beyond fixing—"

I broke off as something shifted inside me.

That wasn't right. My fuckin' spleen hadn't just migrated to see what the view was like on the other side but it shifted inside me, nevertheless. Discomfort, and maybe hope? Reassurance?

I hesitated, still unsure about this, about my "passenger" and what the hell that meant for me. I'd tried speaking internally to her, and externally when I first came up here, but there was nothing.

No hint that she was listening and would or even *could* respond, and yet...she'd definitely heard that. I had a feeling—no, a *sense*—that I could fix it, and that was the first ray of hope I'd had in long hours.

When I'd first woken up, when she'd first joined with me, I'd felt that there was a good chance we could fix things, that it just required a bit of work, some understanding about limits and, fuck, some research into systems that could stabilize things.

After all, the buggers that had kicked the end of the world off had a plan and wanted us to build things as fast as possible.

We'd earned boons because...

Boons.

We'd earned special boons that the fairy could make happen.

That was it...Maybe one of them could...

No.

I felt the negation as soon as I considered that, and somehow knew that the boons were out of reach...for now, at least.

Once the fairy had been fully bonded into me, sealing my soul shut again from the damage I'd done, she'd felt the dungeon through my bond, and that had been the hammer that killed my mood.

Literally.

Bleak despair had filled me, and no matter how hard I tried, I just couldn't shake it.

That was why I'd come up here originally, to sit and try to figure shit out without people bugging me or trying to cheer me up.

Some might have said I was wallowing in my shitty mood, but I'd have told them to fuck right off. They'd never soul-bonded a dead dungeon fairy, and until they did? They could go eat a barrel of dicks.

"You've got a plan," Chris said softly.

"Yeah...well, no." I shook my head. "But it's time to get to work, if that helps?"

"Is you getting to work going to sort the dungeon out?"

"Hopefully."

"Thank fuck, man." He shook his head in relief. "You've no idea how much we need the lights back on and no more fucking candles..."

"Why?" I asked, sudden suspicion rearing its head.

"Look, let's just say that first and foremost, I don't want the risk of people being hurt, you know, fire and shit..."

"Bollocks, but go on. I know you, dickhead."

Chris bit his lip, then shrugged. "Fine, look...Becky likes candles, all right?"

"Right...?"

"Like she really LIKES candles...or more to the point, candle *wax.*"

"Right...oh." I winced. "You mean..."

"I mean I'm fuckin' tender. I had to use some of her special cream to get rid of my hair because there's that much wax clogging it together..."

"Okay," I said, unable to help myself and smiling at him.

"No, man, it's not okay. It's not even *slightly* okay, all right?" he hissed. "That cream had details on it that are REALLY important, all right?"

"Like…?"

"Like DON'T use it on sensitive areas!"

"And you did."

"And I did."

"Why?"

"I'm a fucking badass Druid!" he almost wailed. "I've thrown tanks around, I've been shot, I've been burned and flayed and tortured and…"

"And you've cooked your nuts," I finished for him, trying to stifle a smile.

"Not just my fucking nuts! The…" He looked around to make sure nobody was close enough to hear before going on. "The chocolate starfish, all right? The rusty sheriff's badge…the chutney tunnel…"

"Dude!" I burst out laughing and shook my head, lifting my hands and covering my ears. "Too much information, man!"

"Seriously, Matt, it's like Satan's stuck his fucking tongue up there!" he hissed. "I mean it. I've eaten shit from dodgy kebab shops. I've told them at the curry house to 'show me what they can do.' I've—"

"You've fucking shared too much, mate!" I told him seriously, chuckling. "You've got a healing spell. Why—"

"I've used it!" he snapped. "You think I'm stupid? I've used it loads!"

"And you want me to fix stuff so this doesn't happen again, right? Fuck everything else, just don't give Becky an excuse to get all kinky with the wax?"

"No, you stupid fucker! I need the damn ice cream! And yeah, no more wax would be great, but there's no hair left right now, and I can, *you know*, 'put up' with a bit of kinky shit for a few weeks!"

"I see." I shook my head, clambering to my feet and stepping back from the edge as I clapped him on the shoulder. "I'll go see what I can do. For now? Well, there's a lot of frost on the tiles around here…I suppose you could always sit on them?"

He nodded slowly, and I stifled a smile, before hoping that nobody saw the imprints before the day warmed up enough to get rid of them.

"Thanks, man, and, uh…keep this to yourself, all right?" he half begged.

"Of course!" I assured him and grinned. We shared a look, and he growled, knowing damn well I had such no intention. "Seriously, though…" I hesitated before heading off. "Are you okay?"

"Besides my literally toasted undercarriage?" he asked, before sighing. "Yeah, man."

"What you did in the fight, when you—"

"I don't want to talk about it." He cut me off sharply, and I paused. It was important, and he knew it, but whatever he'd done, he'd still been linked to Simo, and it'd clearly opened a wound that wasn't healed yet.

"Okay, mate…but soon though, okay?"

He nodded.

"Thanks, Chris," I said, meaning it for more than I said.

"Anytime." He turned and looked back out over the dungeon, squirming uncomfortably, as it was, in the rear.

I headed inside, feeling a bit shit. He'd come to cheer me up, and I'd hurt him by bringing up Simo. I hesitated, seriously considering going out to him and sitting down again, but the feeling I had coming from inside made me promise myself that I'd make the time soon instead.

Besides, he'd probably have his pants down and his balls on a frozen tile by now, and I really didn't need to see that. I needed to fix the dungeon, or at least figure out what the hell I'd done to it.

I jogged down the stairs, squinting as I passed the candles that sat in bowls here and there, glad that someone hadn't absorbed them all before now.

It didn't take long to reach the ground floor, and a minute after that to reach our private and secluded floor below it. The doors opened with a firm push of my hand rather than the normal magical sensors or whatever.

Kelly stood, having been sitting, talking quietly with Aly, Mike, and Patrick, and I waved her down, pausing before moving on.

Patrick had been shot a handful of times in the escape from the QE hospital recently, and although Jo had gotten him sorted out while I was basically brain-dead, he still looked pretty fucked.

"You all right?" I asked him, getting a tired smile.

"Yeah, I'm good, man. Lost a lot of blood. Just tired now that I've been all fixed up. Going to take a few hours before I get to work and…"

"Patrick," I said bluntly, shaking my head. "You were shot, then hidden in a fucking bush and had to drag yourself miles home. Take some time and recover, okay?"

"I—" He broke off when Finn reached out, squeezing his forearm, and he smiled, nodding and seeming to relax. "I will, thanks, Matt. Are you okay?"

"No," I admitted. "No, I'm pretty fucked right now, but I need to do something with the dungeon core. Once things are back on track, though, I'm going to be taking a little goddamn time to relax and recover as well. So don't any of you feel bad about needing to stop and rest."

I made a point of making eye contact with all of them as I said it, but it was Kelly who stood, stepping around the chairs and reaching out to me. I hugged her, feeling the relief coming off her in waves that I was okay, more or less, and that I had a plan.

I didn't dare share just how concerned I was with her about the dungeon, so I kissed the top of her head and gently disentangled myself, smiling around and speaking quickly.

"Mike? We'll have a catch-up soon. Okay, mate?"

He nodded, and then I moved off, the pull from the fairy strong enough that I was almost dragged down the corridor regardless.

The passageway that led to our room was set slightly back from the others, literally just a short corridor that ended with our bedroom door on the right-hand side.

It probably looked a little weird to others who weren't in the know if they came down here for whatever reason, considering everyone else simply had a door in the wall of the main area that led to their room. But there was a damn good reason that no outsider was aware of.

The core was here.

The core was hidden behind the wall that lay directly ahead, and I reached out to it, feeling the yearning that came from the fairy, even as I felt the cold stone of the wall.

I focused. The dungeon core pulsed dangerously in my mind as I reached out and dissolved the wall using its power, wincing at the light that shone free.

The core had changed massively from the small crystal ball I first brought here. It still hung suspended between two spikes of silvery metal that rose and fell from the ceiling, the core slowly shivering between them.

The smaller core had rotated, spinning gently; the filaments that led off it twisted around and around, causing them to move slowly along their paths. This one shook gently instead.

What had changed, though, besides the size—the original had been about as big as my thumbnail and probably crystal; the Steel core was the size of a basketball—was the light that it gave off. Rather than the gentle blue glow, there was now a frantic striation of colors that raced back and forth, tiny fracture points lit by internal light, and then sealed over again and again.

I reached out before I even knew I was doing it, the need to help the core as much a part of me as the need to pull my hand from a blisteringly hot radiator or more.

As soon as my fingers closed around the core, though…the world vanished in a burst of multicolored light.

I was in the dungeon sense again, but similar to the first time I'd placed the core, the outside world seemed frozen to me.

I could see my body, hand pressed to the core as my physical mouth opened— oh so slowly—to scream in pain. Fingers of mana-driven flames burst to life across the core, racing out to destroy the offending limb, even as Kelly and the others started to turn, seemingly racing through treacle to come to my aid.

I saw it all happening, but from a distance, as if watching it through a VR headset. I could twist and turn the image, examining it from every angle, even as the flames crept a fraction of an inch closer to my wrist.

Seconds to the outside world were minutes to me, possibly longer, as I stared at the world around me, seeing the shiver that shook the core replicated here as well.

The walls, the floor, everything that existed in here was part of the core, and it pulsed and shook as I stared in shock, seeing just how bad things were.

I sensed the dungeon fairy alongside me, reaching out through me and into the core.

Focusing on her, I winced. The higher functions that I'd seen, that had bonded with me and sealed my leaking soul, were gone. The personality, the knowledge, memories, and more I guessed to have actually been her, were lost.

They'd been part of the energy matrix that made her up, part of her soul, and she'd burned them all when she'd used that energy to stabilize me, so that I could stabilize the dungeon.

I still felt the need to help the dungeon, as well as faint, vague hints about how to help it. But the actual knowledge that the fairy had before? The fairy, or more accurately the *soul* of the fairy, was almost entirely lost.

I experienced a surge of regret at that. She'd literally burned away what I suspected was her immortal soul to save me, and yet…I was relieved as well. I didn't want to share my soul, to have a third party in there besides me and the dungeon. Yes, I'd accept it, if it meant saving her, and saving the dungeon itself. But like it? No.

What was left was a little twisting in the pattern of my soul, a subtle addition that was more in the nature of a bond to the dungeon, with a few additional instincts thrown in, rather than a sentient partner.

The core shivered again, and I moved, ignoring the thoughts as I banished the distant pain from the core. Moving forward, I could see the frantic work of the core as it attempted to seal the cracks, hauling back on the energy that flowed back and forth, the desperate spurts of mana that escaped through the cracks.

As the cracks spread, mana burst free, and the core lost energy—the energy needed to hold the core together and to maintain the dungeon. As each crack was sealed, another would shatter.

I frowned, trying to make sense of what was going on. The cracks were being sealed by the dungeon's rudimentary sentience, but the work it was doing? It was botched, panicked work: each time it focused on one area, it released the greater whole, and the cracks spread again.

I wasn't sure what I could do. All my abilities to "do" anything in the dungeon were down to me telling the dungeon what to do, and it just

did it. But fuck it, I had to do something, or we were down to the last hours of the core's existence.

I moved in closer to the core, seeing it growing larger and larger…until a fresh crack appeared before me.

Before the core had time to react, I reached out mentally and pressed the edges of the crack together, feeling a pull on my own mana as it seemed to form a plaster over the crack.

There was a split-second feeling of relief, a slight sag in the desperate battle to contain itself; then that was gone as a second crack appeared.

This time the core didn't respond, leaving it to me, and I moved as fast as I could, sticking that down, and then the next.

Each time the core flashed and pulsed, the sealed-over areas appeared to hold together—just—as I moved on and on. Seconds turned to minutes of internal time, making me think that maybe, just maybe we were winning, that I was doing the right thing…

Until I saw the rest.

The cracks had stopped. My patch up job had done the trick—for now—but as I watched? The mana intake, which had been steady until now, was dropping by the millisecond.

I searched frantically, trying to figure out what I'd done, and then cursed as I fell inward. The core grew larger and larger until I hovered before a curved wall the size of a house that arced up and over me.

The core, once smooth and glistening, now looked to be a mass of patches, seals that were sloppily slapped down over the damaged areas.

The core below the patches was suffocating as the mana it needed to live was denied it. I reached out, laying one spiritual hand against the core itself, and smoothed the surface slowly, my mana draining by the second as I did it.

I couldn't explain it any better than that, mainly because I didn't understand what I was doing any more than that the core was sentient and could direct me, or the fairy was alive.

This was an amalgamation of the three of us working together to figure the needs out. I worked slowly but steadily, and the pain that had surged up distantly began to die away.

I looked back, seeing my physical body collapse to the floor, Kelly and the others running in slow motion toward me. I nodded, knowing they'd look after me, and got back to work.

It was like scar tissue. The clagged-over patch I'd slapped onto the core was a patch in truth, like when you were cut and the skin sealed over. No longer was the life—blood in that case, and mana in this—leaking out. Instead, it was kept inside, as it should be. But also like a scar, the original form was damaged.

I could sense how the mana that flowed through the core underneath was being twisted by the plastered-over cracks, breaking up the smooth passage, and I nodded to myself.

The immediate problem—the cracks and leaking mana—had been dealt with, but only in the most basic of ways. The core had glowing stress lines, sections that would become fractures in the future. I'd forced the dungeon core to grow at an insane rate, and rather than taking the time to strengthen it with each level, I'd thrown it at the next upgrade and the next.

Reaching out again, I closed my "eyes," stopping the image that was being fed to me by the dungeon, and instead I "felt" the core itself, pushing my mana out and sensing the way it slid and seeped into the core under my fingers.

Some places, essentially where neither the cracks nor the patches had been, the mana sank in like water on sand, flowing through the surface easily and sinking inside. The core stripped the various aspects from it and broke it down and down until it was pure.

Other sections, notably worse, my patches were laid over the top of the dungeon's sealed cracks. There, where the mana could enter at all, it seemed to catch and bunch up, finding weak spots that let a small amount through, while the majority was lost.

I'd managed to "smooth" a section of the core already, sinking my mana into it and focusing on the change I wanted to see, making my mana permeate the shell of the core as I'd permeated things I'd wanted to accept into it before.

This time, instead of absorbing it, I focused on what it should be like, smoothing the damage away, sealing the cracks as if they'd never been, and reducing the scar tissue that existed. Like in my own wounds where deep scarring had led to hitches in the muscles, or weakness that had been healed by mana literally stitching the damaged sections back together, I did that with the crystalline core of the dungeon now.

An area the size of my palm seemed to take ages, and to free up a section that was almost as large as I was? Literally hours.

By the time my brain was fogged with exhaustion, and I'd managed to seal, heal, and fix a section that was roughly three meters by three, I gave in, and left the dungeon sense, flashing back to my body.

I blinked slowly, barely able to speak through the exhaustion and the pain of my burnt and blackened skin, but the conversations around me cut off as soon as I did.

"For now? Only you two have access, but the doors can be controlled again, and some light and food can be summoned," I whispered, turning my head to look at Kelly, seeing Aly not far from her.

I'd healed a fraction of the core, literally a tiny one, but in doing that, I'd seen the difference. No longer was the dungeon fighting against itself as it worked. The mana flowed in and out, and although it had precious little mana compared to the insane amount it'd held recently, it was climbing again.

CHAPTER TWO

I woke sometime later, my eyes opening cautiously in the darkness of our bedroom, shifting slightly and feeling the flow of the duvet across my naked body, as well as hearing the gentle in and out of Kelly's breathing next to me.

Lifting my right hand, I tested the way my fingers flexed and moved without issue, and I had Jo to thank for that. I'd been able to distantly sense the damage that was done to my damn hand and arm from touching the core, and it'd not been small. Despite that, though, I was whole and hale again, and I felt the pull of the dungeon's need.

I took a deep breath, then surrendered to it, floating free of my body and passing through the wall to the core outside our room.

Aly was there, waiting for me, and I forced a feeling of thanks for her, sensing she'd been waiting for me in spiritual form.

"Can I help?" she asked, and I sent a mental shake of my head.

"No, unfortunately. I'm sorry, Aly. I know you would if you could, and I certainly trust you to do it if you could, but I don't think you can."

"Is there anything I can do to help you then?" She sent me a mental image of how fucked I'd been before, the burned and blackened remains of my hand and arm, then the utterly exhausted state of me a few hours earlier.

"No," I said, knowing instantly why I looked like shit there. "It's the mana. I'm powering the core repairs with my own mana. It doesn't take a huge amount, but the way I'm using it, it's literally using my life force to work the core."

"Is it dangerous?"

"Yeah," I admitted, seeing how easily I could accidentally give too much, but I didn't have a choice. "I need to recover my mana. The more mana I have, the less dangerous this will be for me. But the time I need to recover it? I need to spend it on the core for now."

"We've got limited food, light, and we can open and close the doors now," Aly pointed out. "We can survive like this for a few days while you recover. Hell, we've all lived with a lot less…"

"You could," I agreed. "If it was just us, I'd do it as well, but we need the core back online. We can't summon any reinforcements yet. Hell, we've hardly got any of the dungeon-born creatures left. We've no backup, no heating, no stability, and after everything everyone's been through, they need that.

"The core will be able to function again soon, at a lower level than before, admittedly, but that's fine. A few days of a gradual repair and growth will do for now, and it'll remind people that all power has limits."

"It'll certainly make them more thankful for the core, put it that way," Aly agreed. "People are shitting themselves that this is the end, and the dungeon is dying."

"No." I shook my head. "It's what, the middle of the night?"

"Early morning."

"I'll work as hard as I can and get as much of the core operational again. Make the canteens a priority, make them warm and bright, get them producing real food, not subsistence. It'll help people relax, and I'll work my ass off."

"What about meditating?" she suggested. "A few hours of meditating might help you fix the dungeon faster in the long run?"

"It will, but I need to make it stable first. Once I've done that, I'll sleep again, then I'll meditate."

She hesitated, clearly wanting to help, until I sent a none-too-subtle push her way, indicating her own quarters.

"Go," I said firmly. "I'll need you and Kelly to be ready in the morning. We need people to know the dungeon is okay, but it's going to be out of action for a few more days, and I'll be, well, I won't be around. It's going to be you two doing the hand-holding for them all."

"Okay…so with the weapons and ammo…"

I shook my head, sending her another push to her quarters. "I don't care," I said frankly. "You're part of my little leadership team for a reason. You and the others sort this shit out. I can't focus on anything right now but the core. That has to be the utmost priority. You do what you need to do. I trust you."

"I…okay." She sent me a feeling of nervous pride. "I'll sort it," she assured me, before sending an exasperated sense of giving up, as I mentally shoved at her again.

She left, vanishing from the dungeon sense, and I sighed in relief, finally giving in and moving in closer. The side of the dungeon core grew larger as I moved in, until I finally found the area I'd been working on.

Where most of the core was currently a milky grey and brown, feeling subtly wrong, this section was the iridescent flowing pattern of Damascus steel, pearlescent and gleaming.

As I moved in, examining the edges where I'd worked, the contamination was slowly breaking down, and the closer I went, the clearer it became.

Shrinking down and down, I saw the edges of the clean and good section fuzzing as something so utterly tiny I couldn't focus on it crept out, fixing and adjusting the contamination.

Nanites, or something like it, I assumed, but they worked tirelessly. I sighed with relief, even if something happened to me right this very second, eventually the core would repair itself.

Moving back slightly, I reached out, focusing in, and began to work again.

The minutes became hours, and unlike last night when I'd been working as frantically as I could, and the dungeon had somehow slowed the world down, or more likely increased my perception of time's passage, now I worked at the same rate as the outside world.

I smoothed away the mess, gaining a sense of the dungeon core's structure as I did so. The outer layer moved and was malleable, the inner far less so.

There was an impression that made me think of Fabergé eggs I'd seen on TV, or those Russian dolls where one was inside the other. Each core was still there. I grunted as I reached out more, sinking my Perception in closer…only to be firmly rebuffed.

I'd sensed the cores layered one atop the other, sections that existed between the layers set aside for technological upgrades, and I realized, finally, that this was why we had to do the research before we could make things.

It was in part that the designers didn't want us just leapfrogging all the way to the end, and not actually growing in power. But it was also because the dungeon core needed to work these things out. It needed to build the relevant sections that could control the things we built.

The layers we had so far…they were mostly *empty*.

When I'd strained the core, it'd had massive sections that were layered atop empty places, like making a hexagon, then a bigger one, then another, each time laying the upper levels over the lower, but then missing entire sections of supports.

The topmost layer looked strong, it really did, but if you kept going? A single misplaced blow could shatter the entire structure.

That had been what I'd done, in forcing mana into the structure repeatedly, making it swell to bursting at the seams, and then ripping all the mana—and life— free in a fast burst to build shit, then doing it again and again.

I winced at the thought of how many other dungeons around the world might have been lost. After all, they seemed to want us to bond, or ally with the dungeons.

Maybe the dungeons were fine, that the fairies were keeping them from growing too fast, but the first—and only—other dungeon I'd met had been multiple steps ahead of mine in loads of places.

The thought of the human sacrifices that it'd used to leapfrog the usual methods brought a rage to the boil in both me and my fairy soul fragment, and I had to pause, focusing in on the process to stop my rising anger.

Minutes passed again as I concentrated. My mana ebbed and flowed as I smoothed it into the rough edges of the section I was working on.

Layers of rough patches blurred as I worked, softening and sinking back, their structure converting into mana as I moved on. Inch by inch, a structure the size of a four-bed house was polished and fixed. My mind felt like I was trying to do squats with a jumbo-jet on my back.

All too soon, I was sliding free of the dungeon, blinking around blearily as I found our room surrounding me again. I heard the tinkle of running water, and the soft tones of Kelly's voice as she sang to herself quietly in the shower.

I rolled over, intending to look, wanting to see the wonderful image of the woman I loved, naked and wet…and finding that I'd been tucked in when she'd gotten up.

The duvet was arranged around me *perfectly* and I let out a little groan, determined I'd move and see her in just a second…just one…more…

My eyelids closed of their own volition, and I slid deep into an exhausted sleep again.

It was hours later when I woke next, and it was to the welcome sensation of warmth in the room, along with the smell of food!

Kelly was there again, this time sitting on the edge of the bed, stroking my hair back from my face and smiling down at me.

"Hey…" she whispered. "I thought you might need some food."

I looked at her, the wonderful smile, the way she'd tucked her hair back behind one ear, those amazing eyes…and then I saw the food she'd set on the bedside table, and my stomach growled loudly.

I nodded, struggling upright, and she helped me, kissing me quickly and then pressing a bacon and sausage sandwich into my hands, making sure I could see the can of energy drink.

Both were virtually inhaled. The plate and can were set aside as I took her in my arms, blinking and lying back, propped up with a pillow.

"How's it going?" she asked, and I forced a smile.

"It's working," I assured her. "But it's a hell of a job."

"How long do you think?" she asked softly. "Until you're actually out and can be with us all again? And can I help at all?"

"Honestly, I don't think you can. And not long. One more session, I think, and it'll be more or less stable enough that I can take some time and meditate. Once I've got a decent amount of mana again, I should be able to work faster."

"Aly said she'd spoken with you…You could have woken me, you know," she said reproachfully. "I was worried about you. You grabbed the core, blew yourself up, then we couldn't wake you and—"

"I know. I'm sorry." I was, but I'd do it again in an instant. "I don't know why I had to touch the core…but I did. Since doing it, I've been able to interact with the core more directly."

That wasn't entirely true, but "I bonded my soul to an alien fairy, and she made me touch the shiny rock" probably wouldn't go down well.

I was finding it easier to interact with the core, though, and I realized that once again, without consciously trying this time, I was starting to sense details about the core.

The structure was uneven, that was true, and there was frankly fuck all I could do about that, but…but I could form a stronger layer *now*, before it was too late and the damage was irreparable.

The core was a sphere, more or less, one that was currently layered deep in certain areas, and empty under others. How we fixed that, and provided the layers yet to come with a stable foundation, was the same.

We needed to work on research and upgrades.

I'd already intended on not leapfrogging my way through the next core, mainly because at Steel, we had a chance to develop usable, real technology.

Everything from guns to relays, cameras and more.

In theory, everything that humanity had should be available in this core, or the next. That meant that everything I needed to turn our little hamlet into a functional city was finally within reach. Adding magic to that should mean that we could truly make wonders available for our people.

Everything from cars to aircraft *should* be possible, but then the gulf between what was possible and what could be achieved was still massive.

Before we could build a motorbike, we required every single tech that led up to it. Everything from the batteries or internal combustion engine, all the way up to the lights and electrical relays. The cushioning for the seat to the damn locks would need to be researched, and either replaced with a new mana-friendly version or the old rebuilt.

Some sections could be ignored. After all, absorb the cushioning and as long as it was inside the right range, we could develop it. We didn't need to reinvent the wheel…but there was so much that needed to be done the right way now…

"Matt?"

I blinked, jerking awake, and looked around, feeling Kelly as she moved, sitting next to me and smiling.

"You were drifting off," she told me softly, adjusting the pillows, an amused smile on her lips. "Go on, get some more sleep."

I wanted to refuse, there was so much damn work to do with the core, but instead of speaking, I struggled with a massive yawn.

"I'm sorry." I'd had no idea I'd been slipping back into sleep, but she cut me off with a kiss, climbing to her feet.

"Matt, it's okay. Seriously. You've ran a marathon, you've spent months constantly fighting for your life, and you did…I don't even know what you did back there. You cast magic that's *not* your normal, and you literally almost killed yourself to fix our mistakes. You've earned a little time to rest and recover."

"I'll have an hour," I mumbled. "Just an hour's sleep, then I'll work on the core again. After that—" I yawned hugely, and she leaned in, pushing me back, rearranging my pillows again and tucking me in.

"After that, we can talk," she promised. "We've got hot food and water, the dungeon is up and running again, and people are okay. Just relax…"

I nodded, eyes sliding closed…when a memory surged up and I jerked, suddenly awake.

"The park!"

"What?" Kelly gasped, startled from watching me slip into sleep.

"The park. When we were out, we saw something flying around it!" I explained. My words tumbled over themselves, until Kelly stopped me, shaking her head and pressing her fingers to my lips.

"It's okay. We don't know what they are, not yet, but people have been seeing them for a while, apparently. They killed the creatures that were picking people off…the flying ones, I mean. Barry doesn't know what the other ones are, but when Chris went to warn them, they apparently shrugged and just said they do it all the time—fly around the park and watch people but they don't attack."

"Thank fuck," I whispered, sagging back, before cursing. If they were watching but not attacking that could mean two things.

One, they were sapient and were planning something, or two, they were sentient at least and were watching the park, looking for something.

It might be as innocent as they just liked to watch people…or it could be that they were looking at the park as their private hunting reserve. According to Barry, people disappeared on a fairly regular basis. He thought they were moving on to join others, or giving up and walking out into the night prior to us taking over. It might be a case of they'd been poached by our flying visitors.

That, in turn, begged the question: why did they circle the park? Why not the dungeon? After all, we had a lot of lights as well.

I blinked, my mind racing as I tried to think of everything and nothing, trying to decide what and where and…

"Matt?" Kelly said softly. "It's okay. We're watching them. Don't worry. We're treating them as hostile until they prove they're not, so just sleep."

I nodded, forcing a smile, my heart pounding. But at the mention of sleep, despite everything, my jaw cracked again, another massive yawn making my eyes tear up.

"An hour," I mumbled, worried still, but trusting her as I settled back. "Just an hour."

"Okay." Kelly smiled and leaned in, brushing my hair back and kissing my forehead as if I were a child.

This time I didn't last until she was even to the door, before I was deep asleep.

It was a handful of hours later when I woke again. I knew from the steady thrum that echoed down from above, the noise distant but carried by the various cracks and air vents, that somewhere overhead a meal was in progress in the canteen.

Stretching, I fought another yawn, then took care of nature's needs, before settling back in bed and getting to work. Reaching out, I sank into the dungeon sense, and seconds later, I stood before the core, looking at the slowly spreading healing.

I was overjoyed that it was happening, but damn, it looked weird, like it was rusting but in reverse. The surface buckled as the mass beneath healed; the "scar tissue" over the core broke up and fragmented, reducing down to mana and sinking into the core.

Each time, the shape that was left behind made me shake my head in wonder at the beauty of the pearlescent metal. The way that looking at it from a slightly different perspective made it seem to flow like oil on water, the colors changing subtly, and yet, I knew the core was solid.

I reached out and started to work, smoothing a section and sliding sideways. Instead of making an entire block clean and smooth, I moved around the outside. It cost more mana working like this, but it should be worth it. My hope was to create a thin line all the way around the diameter of the core, leaving it to hopefully spread up and down from that line and speed up the healing.

Unfortunately, I ran out of mana again after a short while.

Sighing, and wincing from the mana-induced migraine, I forced myself out of the dungeon sense, and to my feet, dressing in regular clothing, considering my armor needed both a damn good clean and a comprehensive repair.

Wearing my jeans and a simple top in place of the body armor I was usually dressed in, I slipped past people on the stairwells, passing the canteen level and more, reaching the roof without having to have any conversations with anyone.

The few people who had seen me in my abnormal clothing had nodded respectfully or just left me alone.

Striding out onto the roof, I hesitated, hearing the low hum of conversation nearby and cursing internally at the handful of wannabe mages sitting around the converters I was headed for.

I sighed, annoyed at their presence, even though I shouldn't be. These weren't off-limits, and I usually encouraged people to come and meditate. I needed a fuckload of mages more than anything else, after all.

I strode through the outskirts of the group. My mood blackened even more when I spotted—of all fucking people—Gerald and whatever that sow-in-a-dress he'd married was called.

They sat in the center of the converters, chairs pulled round, and blathered on to a handful of people. "These people don't know what he's like, not really…not like we do."

Silence fell as I stopped in the middle of them, and I looked around. By the fear on a few faces and the rising redness here and there, the conversation I'd just interrupted was *exactly* what it'd sounded like.

They were slagging me off, while living under my roof, and from the last I'd heard, they were even refusing to work.

"Are you here to meditate?" I asked coldly.

"To what?" Gerald whined.

"To meditate." I forced my voice to remain even. "This area is set apart to meditate."

"We don't hold with all that nonsense." His wife sneered, and a memory finally kicked in, supplying her name. Sharon.

"Well, considering this area is reserved for those who are meditating, either get with it, or move on," I said bluntly, glaring at her.

"You can't intimidate *us*!" She struggled to her feet and stared at me with a mix of contempt and hatred in her tiny piggy eyes. "We've got as much right to be here as you! This is part of the city…even if you've been *stealing*."

"Stealing?" My voice dropped, my rising anger moving from hot to cold.

"That's right!" she crowed triumphantly. "*Stealing!* We know the truth." She moved quickly, stepping to the side and pointing to a thin, scruffy little man who was swallowing repeatedly, clearly scared, but scowling at me as well. "Come on, Councilor Merriman, you tell him!"

"Y…yes!" he stammered. "You…you've no right!" He ended with a squeak as I glowered at him.

"No right to what?" I was genuinely fucking confused as to what this little turd of a man was getting at. "What are you on about?"

"STEALING," Sharon called loudly, nodding in satisfaction at the expressions on people's faces, especially the clearly annoyed looks on a few people who seemed to have been genuinely trying to meditate.

"Stealing fucking what?" I sighed, rubbing at my face and reminding myself that I had a mana migraine, and there were people who could see me. I had to meditate and help the dungeon. I couldn't just summon an orc and have it beat her to death with a giant rubber dick.

She'd probably enjoy it and do things that would traumatize the poor fucking orc.

"THE CITY!" she screeched, waving her arms around. "Councilor Merriman…"

"Yes, *yes,* I know," he assured her, smiling. He took a deep breath, clearly trying to show some patience as he turned back to me. "Now then, young man, this isn't how I wanted to *start* this conversation…but it's all true."

"What is?" I groaned. "Look, I'm not in the mood for this shit. I need to meditate, so…"

"You've stolen city property." He frowned at me as he drew himself up and tried to be intimidating. "Listen here, I'm Councilor Merriman, and *unlike you*, I was elected to serve the public here as part of the council!"

"And?" I tried to remain calm, while imagining taking a hammer to all three of them, and banning the handful of dickheads who stood around them like nodding dogs.

"*And* as such, I am the legally elected representative of the people. I, and *I alone*, have the right to make decisions that affect the people and property of the city!"

"You got a point?" I forced myself to not summon a ghast.

"I require you to hand control of the dungeon over to the new council of Newcastle immediately," he squeaked. Sweat broke out on his tiny bald head. "I accept that you took the steps you felt you needed to, at the time, to protect people, and I'll bear that in mind when the time comes to discuss your future and any punishments—"

"Get out," I said flatly.

"And rest assured, the council will...What?" he asked, his ears finally catching up with his mouth.

"Get out of the dungeon," I repeated, my voice a low growl that promised violence, and damn soon. "Get out of my sight and forget this shit, or get out of the dungeon, right fucking now."

"I don't think you understand..." He blustered, shaking his head and forcing a chuckle. "I'm a *councilor*...Councilor Merriman—"

"I don't think *you* understand. The old world is gone. Ended. Over. This is the new one now, and I don't give a shit. I lost friends the last few days fighting to keep you shits safe, and where were you? How were you helping?"

"I've been finding out exactly what you've been up to, and what kind of person you are!" he snapped, pushing his chest out. Intimidation clearly wasn't something that came easily to him, although the desire obviously did.

To be intimidating, you generally needed physical mass, overt desire to use violence, or a position of petty power and a clear willingness to abuse that position. He clearly fell into that final category, pre-fall.

Thing is, this wasn't the pre-fall world anymore.

"I. Don't. Care," I growled, hand going to my hip unconsciously for either a gun or my hammer. It was the touch of my hip through the jeans that reminded me that I was unarmed and unarmored. Not that I needed either for this, but it made it clear to both of us what I'd been thinking.

"You were going for a weapon!" He gasped. "You see this?! Everyone! You see this? He's a thug, relying on violence rather than respectful discussion...Is this really the man you want leading you?"

"Yes."

Silence fell as everyone turned to the man who stood at the back of the group, scarred, battered, and clearly annoyed to all hell.

"Yes, he damn well is!" The man stepped forward, glaring around. "He's the man who fought to save my damn life, and yours! He's the one who's been trying to teach people to use magic, to fight and who's been making damn sure that we're all safe and we've got food."

"The food wasn't here for long, though, and neither was the light!" Sharon snapped, getting in on the conversation. "I'm lactose intolerant—where's the thought about my situation? There's no care given to those of us who need special diets, not here!"

"It's the end of the fucking world!" another voice called out as an older, grey-haired woman stalked around the side of a converter to yell at her. "I'm a vegetarian, or I was! I can eat meat now because it's never actually been alive. It's literally magically summoned. And you know what? I LOVE BACON! There! I said it!"

There was a moment of silence as I grinned at the rage and joy on her face at that wondrous declaration.

"*Years* I lived without it, and now? Now I get to eat it because it's *magic* bacon! If it wasn't? I'd eat normal bacon, although I'd be fighting with myself over it. I'd eat it because it's the end of the world! I'd eat it because there's only so much we can do. And to complain about that? That's the sign of someone with too much time on their hands!"

"I'm—" Sharon started.

"I work with the gatherers, and I work damn hard. I work so that everyone's safe and everyone can eat! I carry and I fetch crap because it's a hell of a lot better doing that, than fighting with fucking demons and the crazed lunatics that try to kill us. But you...?"

"Me?"

"Where do you work?" the woman snapped. "I've never seen you in the gathering teams, or the canteens, but you're always eating, and always complaining!"

"I work as hard as any of you!" Sharon hissed in outrage, not noticing as her husband subtly moved, trying to sidle out of sight.

"Where?" the little woman seethed, stalking forward and jabbing a finger at the other. "What do you do? How do you help?"

"I've got chronic..." Sharon blustered, only to squeal as the older—and smaller—woman grabbed her by the ear and twisted it, dragging her to one side, before pausing and looking back at me, hesitating and bobbing her head.

"Apologies, milord...I'll take care of this one!" she promised.

"Thank you." I smiled at her. "The rest of you, if you're not meditating, you can go with..." I hesitated, looking at the woman in question.

"Pat."

"You can all go with Pat," I finished, smiling again, then fumed at the way Gerald and the councilor were still backing away and trying to pretend they weren't involved. "And you two can go with her as well!"

Councilor Merriman started to protest, drawing himself up and glaring around, until a fast-moving hand clamped on his ear as well.

"Bloody stupid is what you are," I muttered, ignoring the gasps and squeals as the pair were marched off by the little old lady, with Gerald sulking along at the back as she glowered at him. "Right, if you're not here to meditate, you've got three seconds to fuck off. If you're here past that, I'll take it that you want to join the conversation with Pat."

By the end of my count to two, the last complainers were hurrying from the roof, leaving half a dozen clearly amused people who were actually trying to better themselves.

"Sorry about that," I said to them all. "And thank you for stepping in." I nodded to the older man.

"Anytime, son," he replied with a little smile and a gruff clearing of the throat. "You saved my damn life an' that 'o my family. Least I could do is stand up to that sack 'o shite."

"What's your name?" I took the hand when he offered it.

"Isaac." He grunted. "Isaac Templar."

"I'm Matt."

"Aye, I've seen you around a time or two." He snorted. "Now then, seems you came here for a reason, and it weren't to get grief from that useless wanker nor 'is friends. You need anything from me?"

"Nope, I just need to meditate."

He nodded. "Does it make a difference?" he asked nervously, jerking his head toward the converters. "A real one?"

"It does. Have you found your core yet?"

"None of us have," he admitted, looking ashamed, and I looked around at the half dozen people sitting there, looking at me hopefully.

I hesitated for a long minute. I wanted to work on my own meditation, not teach a goddamn class, but he had helped me, as had Pat. And we always needed mages.

"Okay then, let's see if I can help you get started." I forced a smile, grabbing the various chairs and more that were cluttering up the space and tossing them aside so that I could sit on the floor at the base of the Storm converter.

"So, have you looked at your affinities yet?"

CHAPTER THREE

Two hours later, I was sinking deeper into my own meditation. One of the group had managed to find their core, and was now trying to guide the others. I slid into my own core, feeling the shivers of mana as they in turn spiraled into me, drawn in close, as I focused, staring…and finally sighing as I accepted that it was damn well time to read my notifications.

My core was *glowing*.

It'd always glowed, more or less. The steady light of mana gleamed somewhere deep inside of me, the flare of the various forms of mana being dragged down their respective spires and out of the constant river of mana.

This wasn't that, though.

My core beat with a steady golden light now. The thousand spires that extended out seemed to quiver with each beat of my heart, even as I fell in closer, entranced by the hypnotic rhythm.

I resolved to look over my notifications as soon as I was done. Most of the important stuff had been dealt with already—and the change of my species to a Soul Titan had been made clear.

It wasn't like there was going be any other change of that magnitude waiting for me, and the dungeon fairy had been focused to an insane degree on the core itself. I'd accepted that and decided I'd look at the minor notifications later.

The core was far more important, but…

My core was fucking glowing.

I could feel the difference in it, and my mana…I looked at it in shock. The core was dragging that fucker up like it was nobody's business.

I moved in closer, seeing the tattered remains of the gates and rings that had constrained my mana before, that had compressed and sped up the flow around my body.

They were all destroyed.

Every single compression trick that I'd managed to achieve, the weeks of work and I had no clue how many hours of meditation it'd taken…all lost.

I stared at them in horror, seeing how the damaged sections flapped weakly as mana flowed past them. And yet…?

I'd created them this way, compressing the mana and somehow creating these mana gates with Thor's help, and all to speed up the mana inside me.

I'd done it to create a kind of vacuum in my core, one that had slowly pulled more and more mana in, meaning that despite my loss of access to most mana forms, I'd been able to draw mana back in *slightly* faster than I would have been able to unaided.

Now, though, I was pulling mana in faster than I would usually, and I was still doing it despite losing the gates.

I sensed a sudden presence and opened my eyes, unsurprised to find the furry shit-biscuit sitting calmly before me.

"You're back," I whispered, getting a flick of the tail as my only response. "I'll not embarrass myself by asking where you've been, you fluffy turd. So, if you're here now…I assume there's a reason?"

Again, a flick of the tail as he stared at me, head cocked slightly to one side, making me wonder whether the fucker was even listening, or if he'd developed some weird feline tic.

"Different. Wrong."

That was it. We were back to one-word descriptions and speeches.

"Yeah, I had to use other mana because you weren't there, you little—" I realized that my voice was rising, and I took a breath, muttering my apologies to the others. "So…you gonna help me?"

"No."

I stared at him, trying to keep my cool, trying to relax, and then glared at the furry shite as he stood up and sauntered off.

"WELL, FUCK YOU VERY MUCH!" I shouted after him, before taking a deep breath and looking around at the stunned faces of those around me. "Sorry, *sorry*! I know, meditation…*Fuckinfurrylittlebastard…*" That last bit was muttered under my breath as I forced myself to take it easy, closing my eyes and focusing on my breathing again.

I sank down into my body, the cold air around me crisp as the wind picked up. The stone under me was rough, and I squashed a curious thought about the leather padding I'd summoned to sit on before, and where it'd ended up.

All of these things I banished, sinking deeper and deeper, focusing on my core, and then the flow of my mana. Rather than dropping all the way, I slid into the fast-moving river of mana, riding it around my body, sensing the pulse as I went.

It was definitely my heartbeat, even though the mana channels and bloodstream were separate. I could feel the beat of my heart as I lifted my left hand and pressed my fingertips to my sternum.

Each beat sent my mana flaring. I flashed around and around, passing through my body again and again, building up a picture of the state of my "system."

The gates, or rings or whatever they were, had constrained my mana before, compressing it and speeding it up. But now that they were all shredded…?

Whatever the pure mana had done when I'd torn it through me and out to kill the Red Queen and I'd shattered my own soul, it'd also fucked my mana system well and truly.

For some reason I couldn't understand, though, it'd also increased my mana regeneration. I finally gave in, sinking through the river of mana and floating free of its pull at the core. Staring upward at the huge central spire, and the hundreds of others, possibly thousands, I couldn't help but be awed.

Whatever this thing was, be it a mental construct or a sub-space link that somehow existed elsewhere in the galaxy and inside my body at the same time— no fucking clue how that worked, but that was what it felt like—it was amazing and different every time I saw it.

I could feel the constant push and pull of the tides of mana as well. The flow that was unique to me, the way that some of the various spires called out, seeming to sing inside me, drew me closer, while others repulsed me.

I could feel a need, a desire to float to the central core, to reach out and draw its power into me. And before I knew what I was doing, I'd alighted on the spire.

As always, when I knelt, pressing my bare hands against it, the reality seemed to shift until I was both human and incorporeal spirit. I sighed as the power pulsed through me.

There was an answering beat in the stonelike surface under my hands, a yearning to subsume myself in the river of pure mana just ahead. And yet that would be a terrible mistake.

There was a draw to it that I'd never sensed from Lightning or the Storm. They seemed to be part of me, to complete me. They were dangerous and destructive, but they made no apology for what they were.

There was no desire, no pull beyond to use the Storm and to be a part of it.

The pure mana, though? It seemed…alien still: alive with purpose, a need and a desire—like hunger—and urged me to pull on it again, that I should fill myself, take that power and use it to cleanse the world…

I could remake it in my image; I could *fix* it. People like that asshole councilor would never understand. They weren't fit to wield power, not real power. They should step aside for their betters.

The mana pulsed faster as I nodded unconsciously.

They didn't deserve to be here, not really. I'd *saved* them. I'd saved *everyone* here, and what did I get from it, really? I got grief from assholes who should be on their knees *worshipping* me.

Power flooded me as I contemplated using it, the rise of the pure mana in my body, how it somehow reacted. It wasn't like the other mana I'd had access to. It *wanted* to be used!

The power flowed through me, building steadily and picking up speed. Even as more and more mana flooded into me, every second I held this power, it grew. My mana didn't feel like this. Not normally.

Yeah, Lightning wanted to be free, and the Storm wanted to rise, to spread out and glory in its evolution, but this…this power was desperate to be used.

It wanted to be set free, go out into the world to spread. It wanted to be used, to evolve, to change and to spread. It needed to be used. Every use of pure mana increased the mana in the universe, I somehow knew, as it became other forms.

Each point, for want of a better term, of pure mana that became, say, Fire mana, also became other kinds of mana. I'd felt it before with the strands of Air. They might be mostly Fire or Air, but they were also other things.

Earth might be Mud, Water, Air, and Fire. It might have hints of Metal or a thousand other variants. It might be a million things, and every single fragment of mana grew over time.

What started as one point of mana might be fifty-one percent Air, and—I don't know—thirty percent Water, some Earth and more. The more that Air interacted with Water though, in a thunderstorm, say, the more the percentage of Water would increase.

The Air would never become liquid, though; it would simply split, becoming two points of mana, one Water mana with some Air and more in it, and the other one being Air mana with some Water in there.

The mana would increase regardless, continuing to spread and to fill the cosmos. Pure might start as a single point, but it ended as billions, given enough time, and all those fragments of pure could be absorbed back into the dungeon.

They could be used to make anything and everything, increasing all the life that filled the universe.

I didn't understand it all—gods, I was an insane distance from understanding it—but as I felt the truth of that, a soft chime rang out, reverberating through my soul.

Congratulations!

Through careful examination of reality and the logical progression through study of your soul, you have increased your understanding of your own mana, mana in general, and the secrets of its manipulation. Your evolution has taken a step again.

Continue to study to raise this affinity further!

Your current evolutionary position is: Thunderstorm: 29%

Increase your understanding of mana to reach the next level of Evolution.

29% > 34%...

I didn't know what had changed, and why that notification overrode my wishes to pop up, but the mana was rising inside me, then a pair of furry feet pressed against my shoulders.

I opened my eyes slowly, as though everything was an effort, locking them onto the glowing blue eyes of the Raiju.

"Wrong."

I took a deep breath, focusing on it and reaching out to the mental connection we shared. I'd rarely used it, preferring to swear openly at the damn cat, but this felt important, and the connection tended to convey things more accurately.

"What's wrong?" I stared into those bright-blue eyes, and wondered whether I was actually mad, talking with my mind to a cat.

"You."

"Well, fuck you very much."

"Wrong."

"Anything in particular? Anything I can do to fix it?" I asked flippantly, then winced as the damn cat extended its claws! The damn things slid effortlessly through my clothing and into the skin.

"Fix it."

"HOW? I don't know what's wrong."

That was true as well. If anything, I was pretty damn pleased about my mana and what was going on. I was getting my mana back at a hell of a speed compared to before and...

A horrible image leapt into my mind: the Storm Bolt I'd used against the undead, somehow converting the much more manageable Lightning Bolt into that.

I'd not been able to cast that spell since, not until I was full of pure mana, anyway. Then I'd channeled it into the damn thing, and it hadn't been a bolt at all; it'd been some kind of insane laser beam shit.

That didn't mean it wasn't awesome, but the desperate flashing of the notifications told me there was something about it to read yet.

The point that concerned me right now, though, was that I'd tried to cast that spell later on and had failed miserably. I'd needed the power of that bolt, and I'd not been able to use it.

I was a *Lightning* mage. The whole Storm Titan and First Lord of the Storm kinda gave that away. I'd been able to cast Storm Bolt when I was filled with pure mana, and when I wasn't, I couldn't use it…So did that mean…?

"Wrong."

"I can't use my abilities when I'm full of pure mana?" I asked, and the Raiju seemed to sigh, looking at me as if to say that even a fucking kitten could have gotten this before me.

"Bad mana."

"Why?" I asked. *"What's wrong with pure—"*

"Bad," he repeated. ***"Soulburn."***

"What's a Soulburn?"

"Bad. Damage. Ghoul."

I focused on that. The words might not have meant much, but the feelings? There was something bad there, something terrible, and the goddamn cat knew what it was.

I intended to ask more, when Thor shifted, and I frowned. There was a spark of something in his eyes, a light that seemed to grow as I fell toward it. Images floated up as the words repeated.

Soulburn: Creatures of a thousand variations walked, stood, and flew; they swam through liquid nitrogen, and they farted methane. Creatures I knew were alive and not just shining crystal glimmered in my mind, and along with each of them, there was a spark, a collection of energy that grew and dimmed.

They stabilized as they aged, sometimes growing dark and dim, fragmenting and falling apart. Others grew brighter, reaching out to draw others in close.

They interacted with people, the way they led and cared. The dark ones hid and schemed, and I saw murders committed by those whose soul had dead fragments, and I understood that wasn't a random thing, but a genuine pattern.

Each was unique, but as they grew and faded, I saw the changes that brought. The great people—or beings, anyway—lifted others up. Their souls spread out, energy fields that touched others, freely sharing their energy, helping them to heal, and to rise in turn.

I saw the way that these people shared a tiny bit of their soul, and their life, almost always unconsciously, and unknowing. They helped others, and those they helped rose up in turn. Their souls did the same, creating a wave of light that could spread across an entire civilization.

Then I saw the opposite.

"Damage."

Fragmented souls, creatures that worked against the collective. I saw murders, thefts and worse, tortures of sentients and sapients.

I saw the rise of serial killers, torturing small animals, then larger, then their own species and more. I saw the dead sections of their soul skein, and I understood.

These beings weren't inherently evil, not in the way I understood it, or thought I did anyway. This pattern was them: it represented their choices, their lives, and who and what they were.

The dead sections could be made to breathe and live again, and the bright living sections could die and dim.

In this way, our experiences could drive anyone, or almost anyone, to be a serial killer, or a saint.

The dead sections could be repaired. I watched a broken one, a being that was on the path to murders and worse, being surrounded by a loving family.

They worked together, uplifting this person, healing them, and I saw the difference that caring and love made.

For a split second, I thought that Thor was showing me that anyone could be redeemed, that anyone could be good, and I forced myself to examine that, and not just dismiss it as touchy-feely-tree-hugger crap.

Then I saw it.

"Ghoul. Soulburn."

The images that flowed up now were different. One of the good ones, a paragon of knightly virtue, someone who fought for their worlds, went out again and again, facing nightmares and worse for their fellows, and was being worshipped for it.

He grew in power, rising higher and higher until he was almost a different species to their fellows, he'd grown that much.

His power changed them—a little bit here, a little there—as glowing sections faded slowly, across centuries and millennia.

He made decisions that haunted him, at first. I saw him sacrifice one or two to save the majority—decisions that were undoubtably the best that could be made…but that led inevitably to the loss of innocents.

The deaths climbed as the knight fought on, as a tiny step here and a tiny step there was taken. Each time, another fragment, another tiny section died, until eventually those who had worshiped the knight feared his return.

They hid from him; they begged to be left alone, and the knight grew angry.

He'd done so much for these ungrateful creatures, and this was how he was repaid?

The step from defender to conqueror was a short one, and more and more of the surrounding souls grew darker. An empire that had shone like a golden sea, bringing peace and protection to a thousand worlds, sank into barbarism. A new and evil empire grew in its place.

Finally, the gold wave began again as a new soul rose up. They were winning; they were bringing back the light, and I felt the insane urge to cheer for them…until they unleashed a power that looked horrifyingly familiar.

A bright light that sang to me flowed out, cutting the souls of those they faced apart. The golden light of hope turned grey and solid.

The soul grew cold, and hard.

They didn't turn to the dark, not truly, but they didn't like the light much either. Their soul grew darker with each use of the power, as something was taken from them to feed the pure mana, and I understood at last.

I could use this power, and I would be powerful. Horrifically, wonderfully so. But the cost? It was…it was *everything* that I was.

That was why I'd been so fucked up before. I'd done what most of the others had done, and I'd somehow torn my soul open, letting it fall apart. It was also why, when I was holding the mana, that I felt such contempt for those around me.

I hesitated, as the world seemed to flow back up from the depths of that furry bastard's eyes…and I swallowed hard.

The power I'd somehow gained wasn't evil; it just wasn't good. It was power, pure and simple, and absolute power, as the saying went, absolutely corrupted.

I could use it—I felt that proviso; I *could* use it, and more or less safely— but it'd have to be small amounts of the power, and I'd have to be very, very fuckin' careful.

No more using the power of literal creation to scour my enemies from the universe. That, of course, left me with a single option, as that goddamn cat knew.

I was filled with pure mana, and I needed rid of it, I needed rid of it all, and to not let myself refill with it. I needed my own mana, that of the Storm, of Lightning and more.

I was a creature of balance. The majority of me was, indeed, the Storm, but the rest? I had an affinity for a shitload of different forms of mana, and I damn well needed to raise them all.

First, though…

I took a deep breath, and I focused in tight.

I felt him there, watching, waiting, as I started, not entirely understanding what I was doing, as I worked to convert my power. Lightning was Air and Fire, in equal measure, but before I could mix them to make Lightning, I needed to make them.

Fire was at seventy-six percent, and Air was at seventy-two. That was great. I was highly compatible with them both…*yay, go me*. Only one issue, though.

Anything over a hundred percent, and you stopped taking damage from that element, instead being healed by it. That was wonderful, and yeah, being able to be healed by Fire would be frankly awesome.

The issue was that under a hundred? It was actively damaging. You just had a resistance to it. Water had been really low for me, making it much more effective when it was used on me.

Now that I'd managed to raise it over fifty percent, I could use it without fear…but that was still using my normal, corrupted mana.

When our mana regenerated, it regenerated into a mélange of mana forms. I wasn't always full of Lightning; I was full of *mana*. Most of it was Lightning or Storm, or could be converted to it, but it certainly wasn't *pure* normally.

For me to change myself again, for me to make it so that I was able to be who and what I was, and to have access to my spells again?

I needed to convert my mana to Fire, which would burn me, and Air, which would…I didn't know, in all honesty. Make me lighter? Make me float away?

Fuck if I knew.

I needed to do it, though, or I'd be *fucked*. Every usage of my spells would mess me up, and massively so. I'd become a worse monster than any I'd fought so far.

I was about to start the conversion process, essentially setting fire to the mana inside me, when ten fresh bursts of pain rose in me. I blinked, glaring at the goddamn cat...before seeing what he was trying to show me, and internally berating myself for being a fucking idiot.

I'd been about to set fire to the mana in my core and throughout my body. I'd been about to fuck my mana channels even more, hoping that I could keep the Air mana that I'd also need to create separate.

Instead of, you know, letting the damn Fire use the Air as fuel.

Thor, however, showed me a single complex image. That of me casting a spell, or not, with the mana raising to my hands, and then sinking back again.

"Idiot cub."

I winced, then sighed. "Sorry...and thank you," I whispered, seeing the self-satisfied smug little bastard cat nod his head, before releasing me and strolling off.

I could feel more people around me, more than there'd been earlier, and I knew they were watching me. But I didn't have the time to fuck about with this.

"You need to move back...give me room..." I ordered them, not even bothering to see whether they'd obeyed. If they hadn't? What was coming would either convince them to move, or they'd never be a problem again.

The dungeon's need grew stronger. The fairy wanted me to go to the core, to help it, and every second that ticked by was a second that whatever unnamed enemy we'd be facing next grew stronger.

Taking a deep breath, I lifted both palms, turning my hands so they were facing up, and I started. Pulling the mana from deep in my core wasn't hard; hell, it was insanely easy. This mana desperately wanted to be used: the pure mana flowed like a tap had been turned.

I focused, creating a dual spark of energy, balancing them both just above each palm. I felt the glow on my closed eyelids and heard the collective gasps as the power built. My manapool dipped slowly as more and more mana seemed to want to take its place inside me.

I pulled it faster and faster, hearing people moving backward quickly as the twin gleaming suns of pure mana hovered above my palms.

For a handful of seconds, I pulled and built them, feeling the vacuum that was developing inside me as the power bottomed out, and I solidified my channels without knowing how.

I forced the mana to stay out, and kept only a small amount inside me, suddenly seeing that this would have been a hell of a lot easier had I just used the mana first...Thankfully, I'd not had time to recover a huge amount since I'd last bottomed out.

But that would have defeated the object, injuring my damn soul further.

Instead, and before I could think better of it, I began the next phase, twisting the mana in my left hand and compressing it, even as I allowed the right to swell, and to change.

The left flickered for a second, then grew from a flickering spark, sending people scrabbling backward in a rush of heat, even as the right shifted, spinning faster and faster, creating a tiny hurricane atop my palm.

Both grew stronger. The left moved from a joyous flame to a roaring inferno, as the right went from a tiny spinning blur to a barely constrained rush of fast-moving air.

"You might…want to back…up…" I hissed through clenched teeth, straining as I brought my palms closer together, feeling the resistance as both forms tried to stay as they were.

I almost pressed them together as one. For just a split second, I was there, then a spark of warning from the cat, and I felt a burst of Fire increase. It was almost unnoticeable, but it was enough.

Fire needed to be in ascendence; Fire and Air made Lightning, instead of Air and Fire making…Inferno!

I'd almost summoned a raging maelstrom of nuclear fire atop the rooftop, but as soon as the knowledge appeared, it was gone.

Pressing the two forms together and flexing mental and soul muscles, I shifted them again, feeding them into each other as the world changed around me.

A resistance sprung from deep within me, as the fairy soul tried to rebel, wanting the pure unaspected mana for the dungeon…but it was too late.

A crackling blue-white burst of light flooded the rooftop, and I opened my eyes.

It was a crackling bolt of lightning.

An actual bolt, not a spell I'd hurled. This was *pure lightning*. It glowed, and I could feel the potential in the glory I held.

I rose to my feet and followed my instincts, converting the last of my mana into Earth and Water. I fed them into the bolt, seeing them unbalanced and all, but surging forward. Other mana in the area flooded inward, drawn by the roiling bolt of power in my hands.

I pulled more, I *demanded* more, dragging it from the elements around me, creating something that Zeus himself would have been proud of.

Moisture was drained from the air, wind roared, and the ground shivered. The temperature dropped as it was all fed into the single bolt, and I held it aloft, bathing everyone present in the light and glory of a true *thunderbolt*.

CHAPTER FOUR

I hissed in wonderful agony. The pain of my mana being utterly bottomed out spread through me, even as the thunderbolt in my hands bathed me in its glory. The power flowed and spit; arcing lightning played across its surface as I lifted the bolt high, its power increasing.

Mana crackled through the air around me as I pulled on the thunderbolt. I wanted to absorb it, to pull the mana in its new complete form into myself, to refill my mana channels with it, to bond myself back with the storm.

The thunderbolt didn't want that, though.

The thunderbolt wanted to be *used*. The storm wanted to spread, to grow, to rage and to bring about renewal of the world. The storm was destruction and sheer, unbridled joy. Life was scoured away and saved by the storm as the world was cleansed by its power.

The world around me responded to the spell, as first the converters beside me, and then others farther away thrummed with the contained power.

The Lightning and Storm converters shivered next to me. I reached out to them; lightning arced from the bolt I held to link to them, then set their converted mana free.

Water was next, then Air. There were more converters around the buildings of the dungeon, but they were mainly Life and Nature. They could be converted, but they would take as much mana as it was worth.

Air, Water, Storm, and Lightning, though? They poured their converted mana out, flooding the bolt that I held upright before me. Magic rolled through me, and I felt amazing.

Where Lightning healed me and pure seared me from the inside out, the Storm…was me.

I felt complete as I let the power arc upward. The air around me got heavier and heavier as the storm developed; clouds formed and rolled around the central rod of power that I was creating. The air grew close as the charge built. The mana that I held between my hands was more than I'd ever thought I could withstand, and still, as the converters released their hold, more and more flooded the world around me.

I cried out in pain, the terrible migraine building. I'd be blind if my eyes were open. And even with them shut, the light that bled through was awful. The flaring, surging headache made me want to be sick, to throw up everything I'd ever eaten.

I also wanted to scream in triumph. I wanted to dance and to drink, to fuck and to laugh my ass off as the power built between my fingers.

It was there, and it was wild, growing more and more powerful by the second. I needed to absorb it. I knew that as soon as I did, this pain would stop…or at least, I hoped it would. The world would be made right again: my soul filled with my own mana again, rather than the terrible, wonderful pain of pure mana.

But something tiny told me not to, that it wasn't time yet.

Everything that was in me screamed for me to take it, to absorb it all, to flood myself and fix myself, to heal the terrible wounds I had in me. But a tiny, insistent part kept whispering to me to wait.

For every second I held off, the storm grew. More and more of the loose and unaffiliated mana that was just merrily spreading out, that just floated and existed, was being changed.

The thunderbolt grew stronger, reaching higher...

"Soon. Wait. Help soon."

I gritted my teeth. I was literally seconds away from blacking out and losing control, but it was that little furry fucker, I knew. The feeling had been him, him guiding me.

I kept going, though, clutching to the spell, frantically holding it tight and channeling each and every point that I could get into it.

It wouldn't be enough, though...not for long.

I could feel it slipping, the thunderbolt beginning to unravel.

I could feel more than that as well. I felt...

I felt *hands*.

I felt hands reaching out, laid atop my shoulders. A hiss of pain and a burst of sudden relief, as mana poured into me, a cupful compared to the ocean that I felt all around me, but it was enough.

That single cupful of mana was enough to give me a second's relief, and in that second, I saw it all.

I saw dozens of people, maybe hundreds.

They were in a ring around me, all of them pushed back a handful of meters by flickering, arcing lightning that danced around me.

I saw three people in close, as two more hands were laid on me. Kelly, Chris, and Mike were there, and they reached out, their hands resting on others, forming a link. Behind them, Aly rested a hand on her husband's shoulder. I saw Finn and Patrick, Jo and John, Becky and more. Dozens were there, their hands outstretched—one resting on the shoulders of those before them, one on the person next to them, while more and more reached out to join the link.

Mana flooded into me again. It went from a few points, to hundreds, then thousands. Tens of thousands of points of mana poured like a river. Groans rose all around as I pulled on the links, and I gloried in the sudden power.

Most people had a few hundred to a thousand mana, but those who wanted to be mages had gone all out. Some had higher manapools than *I* did, which stunned me, but I wasn't complaining.

As soon as the mana entered, the cooling, soothing touch of "normal" mana flooding me, I altered it, converting it and feeding it to the thunderbolt in my hands.

I felt the changes: where Lightning grew too strong, I dialed it back, adding Earth and Air, more Water here, a touch of Fire there. Voices rose around me as I worked; links in my mind weakened as individuals shifted, about to give up.

Other voices rose, telling them to stand strong. They encouraged where I couldn't, lost to the wonder of the spell...and I shifted one more link, then another, adding a touch of Water here.

We were seconds from failing, from the net we were weaving collapsing, when the Raiju, Thor, joined us.

Whatever else he might be, he was definitely not just a cat, that was for sure. The storm that was rumbling around us broke all at once. A dozen bolts of lightning flashed from the heavy clouds as the downpour began.

Each of the bolts that fell were met by an arcing finger from the thunderbolt, and the world went white as the circuit was completed. Then the thunderbolt dissolved, and the power roared into me.

Pain, and terrible, wonderful heat flowed through me as my mana channels were reformed. Every cell in my body screamed with power, before it tore out of me, and into the others.

Screams rose as the power of the storm flooded us all, pain clear as people clung to one another. And then, as quickly as it'd begun, it was over, the pain a memory as the links collapsed.

I was alone again, kneeling. Smoke rose from me as I opened my eyes. My notifications flashed with madness, all over again, even as my manapool pulsed that it was once again full, and this time of pure Lightning mana.

A sudden, stray thought wondered what it'd take to break the system, and if I was close to that limit with the desperate way it was flashing now.

I read it all as soon as I was sure the others were okay, because I certainly was now. I took a deep breath, straightening up and looking around, stunned at just how many people were climbing to their feet.

They all had utter shock on their faces as they stared around, many lifting hands and looking at them as I blinked in confusion.

Why had they all come? And the screams? I'd hurt them—somehow. The mana that I'd accepted had roared around me, and then out into all of them? If I'd been capable of thought at the end, I'd never have let them do that. Hell, I could have killed them if they had too low a Lightning affinity!

I stared in shock as I realized the utterly insane risk I'd run.

I could have burned the ability to touch their mana out of them at the very least! I'd not even considered it. Hell, I'd not been operating on any kind of thought process; I'd been going on instinct all the way.

Instinct...

Literally, it was *all* instinct. I'd not known that there were others helping me until the last few seconds, and only after Thor had bade me to wait.

Had he known? He was...no. I was thinking, again, as I always goddamn did, that he was just a fucking *cat*. He was not a cat—he wasn't even close to that. He was a goddamn Lightning affinity-aligned beast that seemed to have the one guiding principle of making damn sure I was on my way to Storm Titan as quickly as possible.

Considering that the rest of the creatures of the dungeon rarely had a driving impetus beyond "survive" for most of them—and "be a complete dick" for the orcs—that was another confusing issue.

Either way, though, the damn Raiju was doing its best to make sure I survived and was as powerful as I could be.

The fact that so many people were here, and that, as near as I could tell, while they'd all felt the pain of the mana, they'd also survived it?

That wasn't down to chance. It couldn't be.

"What…happened?" I husked, coughing, my mouth dry as the Sahara.

"Thor rounded us up," Kelly said. "He stopped some people joining us, but he was…everywhere. People were appearing and saying he'd just dragged them from their rooms and meals, while others were coming in the opposite direction, and saying the same thing." She shook her head, bewildered.

"I've no idea how he did it, but that furry little bastard made it clear I was needed, and damn well now." Chris shrugged. "He arranged us, pushing some in closer and others farther out, or stopping them joining in…"

"How?" I asked, and they both hesitated, clearly not able to say.

"He just…did?" Chris finished lamely.

"I didn't know, but he was in and out of the crowd, separating people," Mike said after a few seconds thinking about it. "He stopped Ashley, but left Dante in. Might be an idea to compare the two of them?"

"It was worth it, though." Dante squeezed through the milling people to stand next to us, grinning from ear to ear.

"What was?" I asked. "No, wait, before you tell me, what happened? How did Thor gather you all? And why push Ashley out?"

"Her affinity was too low," he said, as if that answered everything, glancing from one of us to another, then shaking his head as if in disbelief anyone could be so stupid. "Seriously, people, do none of you look at your affinities?"

"Not really…" was the general comment.

"I do, but that's because I need to improve mine," I said. "You're saying that all of these people had decent Lightning affinity?"

"That's not right," Kelly said. "Mine's shit, twenty-six percent."

"You sure?" Dante asked, his eyes unfocused as he read something on his screens. "Because I just earned a handful of points in my magical research skill. That only happens when I test a theory and have it proved right."

"What magical research skill?" I groaned, looking around. "Look, every goddamn time I turn around, there's something new! What the hell just happened?"

"Have you checked your notifications?" Dante countered, banishing his, I assumed, as he suddenly focused on me again. "Seriously, Matt, this is important."

"No," I admitted. "I've not had time and didn't want to start that yet." I caught the look he was giving me, and I growled in annoyance and shook my head. "I need to get back to working on the core. Fuck's sake, I haven't even looked at my own mana and shit yet…"

I paused, glancing at my manapool and sighed as I saw the steady, normal glow of my mana, and the comforting, bone-deep warmth of Lightning.

I knew I'd gained more notifications—fucking things—and that I needed to read through them all and soon. But I had to sort this out before I got distracted, again.

"Right," I said after a few seconds, taking a deep breath and looking around at everyone. "I'll read the goddamn notifications soon. I need to get to the core and get back to work on healing it, but before I do? You." I pointed at Dante. "Explain."

"Thor came to me, or he didn't…it was his spirit, maybe. I don't know how but he was just there, then gone. I knew I was needed and right now, that there wasn't time to waste, so I got up and ran, thinking you'd summoned us all. It wasn't until Ashley started asking me questions that I realized it *wasn't* all of us. When I got here, she saw Thor and stopped. I didn't even see him, but she said that she'd seen him, and she wasn't allowed to come."

He paused, rubbing at one cheek as he thought about it. "It was weird. I knew, as she said it, that it was about magic, and when she asked me if she should come? I didn't doubt it. I just told her that it was all right."

"Okay, but that doesn't explain why…"

He shook his head, going on. "Ashley's Lightning affinity is four percent. We compared them last night. We've been working to increase them all, focusing on meditation."

"And she's only got it to four?" I asked.

"No, she's been working on Light," he said excitedly. "We have a theory that Light will enable her to—"

"Focus!" Kelly growled at him. "Dante, seriously, stay on topic!"

"Oh…right, sorry. So, her Lightning affinity is insanely low, but if I was to guess? All of us here will have a high affinity for a core mana strain. So, I have Fire. Kelly, you've got…?"

"Fire as well." Kelly sighed. "I was at sixty-eight for Fire, and I've been working on increasing it whenever I've got any kind of bonuses. I'm at seventy-nine now."

"Cool. We should have a talk some time about spells then. But Mike?" he asked.

Mike shrugged. "Air is my highest, sixty-six."

"Chris?"

"Water," he said. "My Nature is highest, but if you mean, like Air, Fire, Water, and Earth? Water is mine, sixty-six."

"That's what I mean," Dante said. "Basically, Lightning and Storm mana are both made up of simple combinations of the first four elements. They have Light and Darkness in there, as well as Life and Death, but they're not major parts. If anything, I'd say those elements are contaminations. So anyone who has really high levels of those first four were summoned here."

"Then we all knew you needed us." Mike took over. "No clue how, just that you did, that you needed mana." The big soldier looked around a bit self-consciously before grinning. "I didn't expect to get soaked, though, I'll admit."

"Soaked…?" I muttered, looking up at the storm that was still spreading overhead, the rumble and crash of thunder, the flash of lightning lighting the clouds.

"You didn't even notice, did you?" Kelly shook her head. "There's a hundred and more of us up here, watching you literally making a storm, and you had no clue. What was that all about? And can we go inside? I'm freezing!"

I hesitated, not wanting to leave the storm, feeling the wonderful twinning of my power and the storm all around me. I looked over, seeing that most people were hanging around, standing in the downpour in case they were still needed.

I winced, raising my voice. "Thank you all!" I called. "You can go inside now…if you want!"

"Oh, thank God." Aly shook her head and pushed her hair back from her face. "You can explain it all later, but right now I could etch glass with my nipples. I need a shower and warm, dry clothes."

I barely stopped myself looking, well aware that it wasn't an invite, and that if I did, Mike may very well shoot me in the face. But I stole a glance at Kelly, who I was more or less allowed to look at whenever I wanted in that way, as she'd assured me.

Yup.

The girls were definitely cold, or they were trying to point out the local tourist attractions.

"Okay…" I muttered a few seconds later. "So basically everyone up here had an affinity to an element, and a high one?"

"I think so, yeah," Dante said. "And I got a boost to my Lightning and Storm affinity. They both went up by ten percent."

"Shit, really?" I gasped, making the fatal mistake of pulling up my own notifications. There was an instant barrage, literally dozens popping up, and I glared at them all.

Most of this stuff was needed—hell, I'd already cut most of the time-wasting notifications out! For there to be this many even now?

I scowled and mentally filtered them, condensing and twisting them until they were down to a handful, rather than replicating the same data over and over.

Congratulations, Titanborn!

You have successfully blended your Soul Titan and Storm Titan branches into a unique path, giving birth to a new profession in the process. As you have rejected the Soul Titan evolution, and yet still hold significant specific bonuses and attributes of this species, you have been reclassified as TITANBORN.

As a Titanborn, you have two specific evolutionary lines that are competing for dominance: Storm and Soul. Yet no creature can reach transcendence as both species.

You must choose one as the dominant trait line, and will henceforth receive bonuses related to this line ONLY. Please select one line, and as always, be true to yourself.

This is the only path to true power.

I hesitated, genuinely concerned. The change to Soul Titan had been worrying. I loved the storm, and when I'd initially ascended to First Lord of the Storm, it'd felt right in a way that being a Soul Titan just didn't.

But…

It was apparently a path to an insane level of power, although it'd damage my soul as I used it.

It'd regenerate, evidently, as long as I only used a small amount of the power? And I rested between uses? I sighed, seeing the options before me and cursing, shaking my head.

I knew what I was doing. Regardless, I just didn't like it much.

I'd gained a much higher mana regeneration level when I'd changed to Soul Titan, because I was channeling pure mana, and although all mana out and around me was contaminated, it meant that every single point that existed around me contained some of the mana I wanted, and so could draw in that but more and faster. Frankly, though, I was freaking out a little at the whole thing, every use of my powers risked killing me, or turning me into something I didn't want to be.

Yeah, I might be able to stop the Orakai invasion thanks to this, but at what cost?

The two options hovered before me, and I selected what was right for me, hoping that I wasn't making a terrible mistake.

Congratulations Titanborn!

You have chosen to turn aside from the path of the reaper, abandoning, untrodden, the path to soul mastery, in favor of that of the storm.

As a Thunderstorm, your path to Storm Titan is returned to thus:

Thunderstorm > Cyclone > Storm Titan

HOWEVER: as the first of your species to share a soul with another, your evolutionary path was altered permanently, and although a choice has been made, the past cannot be altered!

You are Titanborn, and will forever more have the gifts of both evolutionary lines.

Although your species is not irrevocably tied to this path of evolution, your innate capabilities in the manipulation of the Soulfire have given you access to a new ability.

Soul Forge:
The soul of a sentient or sapient is the highest form of compressed energy known to the universe, layered over and over and imprinted into the soul of all of those that have ever lived, are their experiences and their knowledge.

This results in all souls, including your own, having certain alignments that are fixed and unalterable. The energy pattern that holds this knowledge, however, is anything but indestructible.

You may choose to use your own soul, or that of others to imbue devices and creations *THAT YOU PERSONALLY MAKE* with those alignments.

BEWARE: Using the souls of sapients has long been outlawed in this way, and the use of unwilling souls to power weapons of destruction will result in your being marked as a pariah. You have been warned.

I stared at that, working it through in my mind repeatedly. Basically, I'd made the choice to revert to the Storm, which yeah, I felt was right, but I'd also lost access to pure mana, and the ability to draw it from the central spire when I was really in need.

Sure, I'd had no intention of doing it again. The first time had fucked me up and cost me access to the Lightning Bolt spell, and the second time had pretty much shredded my soul, but…

I moved on quickly, wanting it all over as quickly as I could, and dismissing that "pariah" bit. I didn't give two fucks about what the intergalactic community might think of me; they'd killed most of my species.

Congratulations!

You have made progress in your class quest!

You have successfully created your first signature ranged spell. Continue to research, investigate, and create to benefit from the wonders of your class.

Remember, only you can decide your destiny…

Complete this quest to receive a boost to your selected affinities.
- Melee spell: 1/1
- Ranged spell: 1/1
- Defensive spell: 0/1

*

Congratulations!

You have created your first signature class spell!

Through what is assuredly a highly unwise series of decisions, you managed to link your soul to your manapool! Congratulations! You are now one of an extremely small number of beings that have both linked their soul to anything else, and survived!

You have gained the following spell:

Soul Beam:
At a cost of your entire manapool, as well as a minimum of 1000 health per second, you can share the reality of your soul with another…through the cleansing heat of destruction! Now you too can reduce your friends and enemies to drifting gaseous impurities at will!

Note: This ability requires pure mana, and will sear your soul to ashes as well, if channeled excessively.

*

WARNING!

You have lost progress in your class quest!

You have lost access to your first signature ranged spell. Continue to research, investigate, and create to benefit from the wonders of your class.

Remember, only you can decide your destiny…

Complete this quest to receive a boost to your selected affinities.
- Melee spell: 1/1
- Ranged spell: 0/1
- Defensive spell: 0/1

Fuck. There was no better word for what I'd just done. I'd chosen the species that I wanted to be, sealing myself to it, and fucked up massively.

I still felt the knowledge of that Soul Beam spell sitting there. I understood it, and I knew how to cast it. And I also knew I had as much chance of casting it now as I did catching a fish and teaching it fucking algebra.

"Fuck!"

I ignored the questions from people around me, sagging to the floor and sitting on the soaking wet roof with a squelch from my pants.

The deluge all around me and overhead wasn't letting up, and I could sense the others moving away, as Kelly crouched next to me, putting a hand on my shoulder.

"Matt…?" she whispered.

"I'm fine," I assured her. "I fucked up. My goddamn kingdom for a wiki!"

"It's okay." She hesitated, then went on. "It…it is okay, right?"

"It is. The dungeon will be fine, and so will we. I just lost access to a spell, that's all. Look, I need to finish this, then go and work on the core. We'll talk soon, okay?"

"Okay, Matt," she whispered, squeezing my shoulder, before leaning in and pressing a soft kiss to my wet cheek.

Then she was gone, and the others were moving off as well, chivvied along by her as Dante tried to ask questions. A few minutes later, the roof was almost empty. The heavy rain made even the most terminally curious accept that there were better places to be.

"I can hear you breathing, you know," I said after a few seconds, getting a snort of amusement as Chris moved out of the shadows, striding across the rooftop to stand nearby. "I don't need a minder, either."

"Nope," he agreed. "You didn't just nearly fuck yourself up casting something you needed a hundred more people to help with."

"I didn't know I needed help."

"And you won't know if you need more."

"No, I won't, but I can't concentrate with you watching me, you prick," I shot at him.

"Ah, so it's like wanking, is it?" he asked. "Bit of performance anxiety?"

"What the hell is so wrong with your sex life that you feel the need to wank with people watching you, to even develop that?" I asked, then spoke quickly. "No, don't answer that please, mate."

"Hey, as long as everyone's having fun." He shrugged, and I glared at him, banishing the screen and catching a glimpse of him before the next one popped up.

Congratulations!

Through careful study and manipulation, both of internal structures and through the alignment of your soul, you have increased your understanding of your own mana, mana in general, and the secrets of its manipulation. Your evolution has begun again.

Continue to study to raise this affinity further!

Your current evolutionary position is: Thunderstorm: 39%

Increase your capacity to reach the next level of Evolution.

34% > 39%…

I needed to work on my magic. Damn, I seriously needed to work on my magic, and stop fucking around with things! I vowed to skip through these notifications as fast as possible, get the core fixed, then have a full day of sleep, before getting myself back on track while Aly and Kelly and the others get the dungeon back on target.

The next notification wasn't so bad, at least.

Congratulations, Dungeon Lord!

As stated before, you have climbed to the height of the mighty rank of Steel, and your dungeon is now named as the Second Steel Dungeon.

The process of linkage is now nearly complete, but the six Primary Nexus Gates cannot activate until all are in alignment. Please bring your dungeon core back to standard functionality as soon as possible. You have three solar revolutions before you are automatically excluded from the Primary Nexus and a new dungeon is elected to take your place.

Please speak to your Dungeon Fairy for more details and to make the necessary arrangements.

Note: Due to the impressive speed of your evolution, you were granted both a 10,000 xp bonus and an additional bonus over the standard for the dungeon. Please speak to your Dungeon Fairy to attempt access to this reward.

Whatever the "Nexus Gates" were, I had a few more days to get them sorted out. I'd totally forgotten about them, in all honesty, dismissing them from my mind as I was focused on fixing the dungeon. And as the fairy itself wasn't exactly talkative, well...I'd dismissed the bonuses as well for now, although "attempt access" was concerning.

That was probably a mistake, though, and I damn well needed to sort it out.

First things first: finish the notifications, then fix the dungeon, then look at the nexus gates or whatever the hell they were.

I took a deep breath, pulling up the next in line.

Congratulations!

You have killed the following:
- 1x Asuras Red Queen, Level 17, 6,100 XP
- 2x Asuras Heavy Exterminator (AHE), various levels, for 325 XP
- 1x Asuras Champion, level 1, 5000 XP

Total XP earned: 11,425 XP

A party under your command killed the following:
- 11x Asuras Termination Drone, level 1, 770 XP
- 1x Asuras Mobile Extermination Platform (AMEP), level 1 for 100 XP
- 4x Asuras Heavy Exterminator (AHE), various levels, for 675 XP
- 2x Asuras Guardians, various levels for 12,250 XP

Total Party XP earned: 13,795 XP

As party leader, you receive 25% of all XP earned.

Total XP awarded 11,425+(13,795x0.25=3,448.75)=14,873.75 XP

Partial XP is lost to the ether.

Current XP to next level stands at 26,053/45,000

*

Congratulations!

You have completed a Quest:

Defend the Dungeon (4)
The defeat of the asuras queen and her fragments has been achieved, the latest threat to the dungeon vanquished, and although there was severe damage inflicted, the dungeon has survived. You have completed the latest stage of this quest and receive the following bonuses:

- +5 to top three Attributes
- +1 Spell
- +2 Class Skill Points
- 10,000 XP

*

Current XP to next level stands at 36,053/45,000

*

You have gained additional Stat Points in the following areas through constant effort.

- +1 Constitution
- +1 Intelligence
- +1 Luck
- +1 Strength
- +1 Wisdom

Continue to work hard to increase these or other stats…

*

You have made progress in your Quest!

Quest!
Checkmate! (II)

The asuras Green Queen has survived the attack of the Red Queen, albeit through no actions of her own. She is now highly aware that not only are you the master of the local dungeon, and able to provide her with all she requires to rebuild and evolve herself, you have also killed any and all attackers that threaten her.

Use the current situation to form a more permanent alliance with the asuras queen to complete this quest and receive the following bonuses:

- +3 to top three Attributes
- +1 Class Skill point to allocate
- Additional forces (Access to)
- 10,000 XP

Damn. That was a hell of a lot of notifications. As the last one fell away, I was bloody glad to see it go, even if there had been no mention of a magical research skill like Dante had mentioned.

I resolved to look at that later, and I wasn't far off my next level either, which was nice to see. But either way, I'd earned a few nice bonuses with the last few days, and as usual, they didn't show up until I actually acknowledged them.

I had two class skill points to assign now, and a single spell to choose, which was a relief, as well as both the five earned points and the fifteen free points from the quest. I pulled up my stat screen, seeing immediately where they'd been assigned and groaning as the pain rippled through my body as the changes took hold.

Name: Matt, First Lord of the Storm				
Host Powers: 1 (Enhanced Regeneration)				
Species: Thunderstorm		**Bonus**: None		
Level: 25		**Progress to next level**: 36,053/45,000		
Stat	**Current Points**	**Description**	**Effect**	**Progress to Next Level**
Agility	34	Governs dodge and movement	Heightened chance to dodge attacks 68%+20%= 88%	56/100
Charisma	26	Governs likely success to charm, seduce, or threaten	35% more likely to succeed in events that require seduction, persuasion, or threats (10%+ (16x2) = 35)	71/100
Constitution	49	Governs Health and Health Regeneration	HP: 49x50 = 2450	14/100
Dexterity	37	Governs ability with weapons and crafting	+37% Increased chance of improved result +13 to melee damage	89/100
Endurance	36	Governs Stamina and Stamina Regeneration	Stamina: 36x40 = 1,440	54/100
Intelligence	58	Governs base manapool, standard intellectual capacity	Mana: 58x60=3480	16/100
Luck	39	Governs overall chance of bonuses and critical hits	+58% increased chance of positive outcome	24/100
Perception	36	Governs ranged damage and chance to spot hidden items/traps	+26 to all ranged attacks	98/100
Strength	33	Governs damage with melee weapons and carrying capacity	+46 to all damage with Melee weapons	11/100
Wisdom	47	Governs mana regeneration	76 mana regenerated per hour (internal improvements destroyed)	14/100

Five points had been added to my Constitution—no surprise there, really—and another five points to my Intelligence. Okay, yeah, I got that, and it wasn't exactly a shock. It was down to the constant channeling, I guessed, the use and focus of my magic, rather than any sign of actual intelligence on my part, but okay.

The surprise was that the third set of five weren't in pure goddamn Luck, which was where I felt they were most deserved. It was in *Perception*, which made no sense at first.

I paused, thinking that over, before finally grunting as I saw the connection. *Mana.* I'd been examining the data and had been discovering more about mana and its place in the world. I'd used sheer bloody determination and ignored pain to tear myself half apart in using magic I shouldn't. In the process, I'd seen how things interacted.

I had taken that and the secrets I'd seen hidden in mana to kill the Red Queen by channeling pure mana. How had I found that I could? By perceiving the reality around me.

I'd examined my own core and the way mana reacted with the universe, and it'd been that, looking and actually *seeing*, that had made all the difference.

No wonder my Perception had increased.

I banished the last screen and sat there for a long minute before a detail caught my eye. And in the way that these things happen, it became all I could see.

"Chris…" I said slowly. "Why in the name of all that's fucking holy, are you trying to cover yourself with a bacon seed umbrella?"

CHAPTER FIVE

"**A** what?" He frowned and then grinned at the children's cartoon character that was jumping in a muddy puddle on his umbrella. "Oh…bacon seed…yeah, good one."

"Seriously, you're like seven foot and the same across the shoulders. I've seen you transform into a fucking tiger-man, and you're hiding under a kids' umbrella from a little rain. Man up." I shook my head, staring at him.

"Hey, I don't need to catch a cold, all right? I'm secure enough in my own manhood that I can hold a pink umbrella. Sorry you're not in yours." He grinned.

"I could say a lot about your manhood, starting with the fact it's been a disappointment to every lady you've ever shown it to. But I won't." I climbed awkwardly to my feet and took a deep breath of the stormy air. "I'm your friend, though, so I won't bring that up," I assured him. "God that feels good…"

"That's what she said," he quipped, and I grunted.

"Yeah, just not about anything you were doing," I finished for him, winking.

"Anyway, is there a point to this delightful repartee, or can we go inside now? Some of us have a sex life we'd like to get back to."

"Dame Wrist and her five lovely daughters will be there when you get back to your room, don't worry." I snorted.

"Hey, just because your ex was called Palmela…" He tried to recover. "I heard you put lipstick around your thumb and everything…"

"Sad." I shook my head and moved up to the edge of the wall, staring up and glorying in the feeling of the air. "Tell me that you can feel that?"

"That's what she said you said…"

"Chris…" I sighed, gesturing him closer and to shut the fuck up. "Seriously. Can you feel that? The air…"

"Dude, seriously, I'm in danger of *drowning*. That's all I can feel. Even under here, I'm almost drowning, there's so much fuckin' water in the air."

"And the lightning?" I asked. "The potential?"

"Nope," he said after a minute, shaking his head. "Can we go inside now?"

"Okay, mate," I agreed sadly. "Thanks for trying."

We headed inside, and I tried to make sense of the fact that not only had I *not* gained any increase in my affinities when I'd used so much mana and created the storm, but the others had, apparently.

Somehow the person sharing or guiding the magic didn't gain from it, but everyone else had.

Just knowing that it was possible was a massive boost. Hell, knowing that there were multiple ways to increase your mana affinities was crazy, and I resolved to work on it some more. But first?

I stomped—or squelched—down the stairs after Chris, passing the umbrella he'd left for anyone who needed it. The door behind us banged closed. I sighed as the sense of wonder the storm always engendered dissipated slightly.

There was something about the storm that I absolutely loved, and it made me just want to sit and enjoy it. Failing that, I wanted to feed the dungeon on it, to reach up into the sky again, to set free my Lightning and call the Storm to me, now that it'd had time to develop a bit.

The world could do with the rain and the glory, I knew, but I also knew I'd created a damn building and I'd done a fuckload of research the last time I'd drained a storm, and I wanted to do that now.

I wasn't *that* stupid, though.

The dungeon was damaged, wounded, even if no longer terminally, and I doubted that powering a few thousand megawatts or whatever into it would be a good idea until it was fixed up properly.

Reaching the canteen level, Chris paused, and I went straight past him, headed for the basement and the dungeon private area, along with the core.

"Wait up." He jogged to catch up, and I paused, looking back to him.

"What's going on?"

"Hey, a man can't spend some time with a friend these days?" he replied innocently.

"Yeah, but why?" I said bluntly. "I know you, Chris, and I know that look on your face." I leveled a finger at him before going on. "It means you're going to lie, and you think looking innocent will help."

"I don't know what…"

"Seriously, it didn't work when we were kids, and it's not gonna work now. Just say it," I growled.

"Fine, fuck you very much." He sighed. "We decided that one of us should be with you for the next few days, keep an eye on you and make sure you're all right."

"Why?"

"Because you nearly died."

"Chris, I nearly die on a daily basis," I pointed out. "So do you."

"Yeah, from fighting, from monsters, from whatever. You just…stopped." He shrugged. "I can't say it any other way. I don't know the words, but you were slipping away because you stopped giving a fuck. I could see that much. So we're watching over you."

"It's an intervention. You all think I'm a risk to myself somehow and you're watching over me in case I decide to do something stupid."

"Want me to be honest or blow sunshine up your arse?" Chris asked, and I glared at him. "Honest it is then. Which is a relief, I can tell you."

"Go on."

"You're my best mate, and you look like shit. You keep nearly dying and you're the glue that holds this place together. I really like having hot food and a shower that works, not to mention a hot girlfriend who I can have lots of sex with, not to mention it turns out I like killing shit. You die, I lose my best mate, my new home, the hot food and the showers. Maybe I'll keep the girlfriend, but let's face it, if we're both reeking, the sex won't be as much fun."

"So you're saying that you need me alive so that your girlfriend doesn't smell?" The ghost of a smile tugged at the edges of my lips.

"Well, you said it, not me. I mean, I smell magnificent, even after I've been working out."

I snorted. "I can smell you from here, even after that deluge and you've had access to the showers."

"That's the point," he assured me. "I still smell magnificent, despite the fact that none of us have had showers. We're still trying to use as little mana as possible, so…"

"So fuck off and fix everything so you can have sex," I finished for him, and he nodded.

"I wasn't going to put it quite that bluntly, but yeah."

"Fine, that's where I'm going." I turned away, only to hesitate when he followed. "Why are you still following me?"

"Because you're my mate, and I want to see what you're going to do."

"It's going to be boring."

"Probably."

"And it'll take hours. You won't enjoy it."

"Enough about your sex life," he quipped, before sighing and reaching out as we paused on the landing, looking at each other. "Matt, you're my mate, and I'm worried about you, all right?" He squeezed one shoulder. "I don't know what you're going through most of the time, I know that, and frankly I'm glad it's you and not me who's ended up in charge of this shitshow."

"But?"

"But you need someone to watch your back. Even if it's just so you can tell me I smell, and I can point out how Kelly walks around fine after you two get it on, while poor Becky walks like John Wayne."

We stared at each other for a brief moment. Smiles twitched at the corner of our lips, before we gave in and grinned openly. I shook my head and set off again, him hurrying along behind me as I moved down the steps, still soaking wet.

"You're a dickhead," I called back to him, quietly.

"Takes one to know one," he replied, the old line from school making us both smile.

"Love ya, man," I said, feeling it, and knowing that it was true. Despite being an only child, I'd had a brother all my life, and it'd always been Chris.

"I know. I'm awesome, and I love ya too, you ugly bugger…"

I snorted, the two of us continuing down to our floor and splitting up to go and get changed. It didn't take long, peeling the soaking wet clothes off and dumping them in the shower area, letting the water drain out and run away, even as I roughly toweled myself dry and dressed again.

Fresh clothes did make a difference, and I'd not realized in the glory of the storm just how cold I'd been getting. But as I shivered, dressing quickly, I resolved that I'd fix as much as possible of the dungeon core this time around.

A handful of minutes later, I was out of mine and Kelly's room, Chris a heartbeat behind, strolling to the end of the corridor and looking down as I gestured at him to bugger off and leave me to work.

He grunted and dragged a chair down for me, setting it in place, and then moved back along the corridor to sit on a comfy settee and watch me from a distance.

I ignored him, already absorbed in the core's repairs. The remnants of the fairy wanted me to use pure mana, utterly unaspected, despite the damage that would cause to me, but that was because that was what was best for the dungeon.

The dungeon fed on corruption and released pure mana. Using pure mana on it meant there was a lot less effort required on its part. It didn't need to strip the impurities from the corrupted mana that was used on it; it could just accept it.

That was great, but I was a Lord of the Storm, and frankly, I got bonuses for my creatures thanks to that, so why the hell was the dungeon itself not able to make the most of the mana I had?

I got myself comfy and reached out, beginning the process all over again. My mana flowed out, sinking into the dungeon's core and was drunk down greedily. The tarnished edge of the repaired and cleansed area showed just how far I still had to go to restore it.

Seconds became minutes, minutes became hours, as I worked, shrunken down to a fraction of my size, mentally seeing the massive core hanging before me, shaping and smoothing the problems away.

All too soon, I felt the warning tingle of an incoming mana migraine, and I forced myself to stop, leaning back and releasing the mental image of the core, along with the constant drain that came from using my mana in such a way, hour after hour.

The core was at seventy-eight percent now. The soul of the fairy inside me was far less stressed and concerned, falling quiescent as I sagged in relief as well.

Seventy-eight percent of the core as it was now, considerably larger as it was, provided a hell of a lot more power and potential than we'd ever had as an Iron core. I forced myself to my feet, moving down the corridor to the main room to spread the good word.

Chris was gone, having been replaced on "Matt-watch" by Aly, who was casually thumbing through a book when I paused, looking at me over the top of it.

"Yes?" she asked, as if wondering what the issue was.

"The core is up and running," I said. "We're at nearly eighty percent, and can use it normally again, more or less. No heavy builds, no mass summoning of creatures, but food, hot showers, heat, and light I know we've said are fine. Well, all the rest of it? Go for it, just keep it slow, okay? And keep it at just community leaders for now, you guys, Barry and so on, not everyone, not yet."

"You're sure?" She climbed to her feet, staring at me. "What about research?"

I paused, thinking about it, then nodded. "It should be fine."

"Should or…"

"I don't know. There's no wiki, there's no warning lights, and there's no goddamn magical help desk letting us know there's a problem. I'll be monitoring the core. If any problems come up? I'll step in. Otherwise, just stick to those rules for today, all right?"

"Okay." She smiled, setting the book down and stretching.

"So, how are—"

"I'm fine. I'm no more stressed than normal, I'm less depressed than I was in my previous life, and I don't need to speak to anyone about it," I said. "I know you're all watching me in case I freak out, but seriously, don't worry. I'm fine."

"Goddamn it, Chris!" She cursed under her breath, shaking her head when I snorted in laughter. "I knew he'd not keep it quiet that we were worried."

"He tried," I admitted. "But seriously, he's been my closest mate my entire life. I've seen things no therapist can help me get over…" I shook my head when I saw the flash of concern in her eyes and went on quickly. "I mean him running around the halls of the hotel in Malia, bare-ass naked, an inflatable chicken on his head and condoms on all his fingers, shouting 'anal probe' at people."

"What did he…?"

"Mezcal," I explained. "A pint of mezcal downed for a bet, as well as some recreational substances. We used to have photos of him somewhere. Me and the lads used to mail them to him anonymously with notes like 'we know…' attached to it."

"Male bonding rituals." Aly sighed, shaking her head in bewilderment. "How any of you survive until you get a wife is beyond me."

"Yeah, well, my point was that if you're trying to hide something from me, don't let Chris in on it. I know all his giveaways."

"I'll remember that. So, seeing as we're talking openly, what happened?"

"I tore my soul apart, lost a lot of the energy that keeps our body and soul as one, and bonded a fairy creature that was genetically engineered to run the dungeon," I said calmly, watching her face.

"Oh." She nodded. "I guess that makes sense. So how's this fairy doing now?"

"More or less dead." I sighed. "She'd been dead for months. Her soul's energy field held together more through determined devotion to the dungeon than anything else. Turns out it was her who led me to the dungeon and bound me to it. She basically gave up her life in exchange for saving me."

"Her soul," she clarified. "She was already dead, right?"

"Yeah. Turns out there's a lot of the things we take for granted that's just not right."

"Like?"

"We're surrounded by the dead." I shrugged. "If you're strong enough in yourself, then you don't dissipate on death, you just…go on."

"Like, to an afterlife?" she asked. "I don't believe I'm asking this, but is there a God? Did you meet them as well?"

"Oh, I know God." I nodded, unable to help myself as I channeled a crazy old hermit from the dune sea. "He's me."

"Oh fuck…" she whispered, rubbing at her face, before shaking her head firmly. "Matt, bullshit aside, are you serious? Did you just solve one of the age-old mysteries, 'is there life after death' and you tossed it off as nothing?"

"Maybe…?" I winced. "Look, I saw a shitload of weird things, some of which I sort of understand, others I don't. But the asuras? They're like these space souls that have been wiping out entire species, turning suns nova forever. You know that theory about all life being weird in the galaxy, like there should be more, but there isn't?"

"Yeah…" Aly whispered, staring at me in horror. "You mean the Fermi Paradox?"

"Could be." I nodded. "Anyway, apparently it's—"

"Stop," Aly snapped, putting one hand over my mouth and glaring at me. "In a few days, you've figured out why there are missing civilizations in the galaxy, and that there is life after death, as well as proof that we have immortal souls. Is that right?"

"Well, not immortal. They can be destroyed and—"

"We have souls?" she growled. "You know this for sure?"

"Well, yeah?"

"Fuck. The religious crowd are going to go nuts…"

I winced, having not even thought about that, and opened my mouth to suggest we keep it to ourselves, as she started to speak, her other hand over her eyes as her thumb and forefinger massaged her temples.

"I know you're *not* going to suggest we hide one of the most important discoveries of all of human history, Matt, so you're going to suggest something else…right?" She took the hand away and glared at me.

"Yes." I closed my mouth and swallowed those traitorous words. "Never crossed my mind," I lied.

"So what were you going to say?" she asked sweetly.

"Ummm…that we get our people together and I explain?" I suggested hesitantly, and she nodded.

"Not just our people. If by 'our' you mean the leadership cadre. I think it's important enough that we all have a good meal, and then we go to the council chambers; we tell Clarissa and let her bring a few of her most sensible. We make sure that when this comes out, it does so because we've shared it, not hidden it, and someone's overheard."

"But—"

"Matt, are you a leader or a politician?"

"Aly!" I gasped, hurt. "That's a fucking hell of an insult!"

"Exactly, Matt. Either you lead these people, and us, obviously, or you lie to them. You need to pick, as you can't do both."

"Then we tell them the truth, I guess." I winced at the thought of the conversation that was going to be.

"When do you want to do it?"

I sighed. "I don't," I admitted flatly, before rolling my shoulders and stretching. "We do it as soon as I've eaten, though. No sense in putting it off. What time is it?"

"Late evening. Most people have finished eating. I swapped with Chris so he could go get dinner."

"Then let's go eat, and we can have people start gathering in the council chamber while we do it."

The meal was a quick one. We'd bumped into Amy—Aly and Mike's daughter—and Tulio's son Guido apparently totally innocently "going for a walk" and Aly had grabbed them both, whispering something into their ears, before sending them off.

"What's up?" I saw the way she watched the pair as they raced away.

"Nothing," she said shortly.

"Aly, that's the same as me saying that I was totally going to tell everyone the truth."

She looked at me and snorted, before nodding. "Okay, fine. I just don't like how close they're getting."

"Aly, she's ten years old…it's not like she's sixteen."

"I know. I gave them a job to find the others and get them to the council chambers but…Oh, fuck it, you'll understand when you and Kelly have your first."

I froze, turning to her with eyes opening wide in horror. "She's not…?"

"Who, Kelly?" Aly smiled quickly. "Not as far as I know, no, but it'll probably happen if you two aren't being careful. Life generators and all that, remember?"

"We're being careful, and one of the top priorities of the Steel dungeon just became a pharmaceutical system. We need a fuckload of contraceptive pills making," I said very definitely, doing my best to totally forget about the times we'd certainly *not* been as careful as we should have been.

"And condoms?"

"Fuck yes. We need a lot of those too."

"Glad to hear it." Aly grinned. "I don't want any more kids either, certainly not for a while at least. Maybe once the world is sorted out and everything. But until then? No."

That was an easy agreement to make, and the next half an hour, as I ate quickly, downed energy drinks and thought, giving the others time to gather while I planned, passed quickly.

All too soon, I stood in the main private council chambers, looking around the room. There were public council chambers here as well, set out farther to the front and below us in the Parthenon building.

That was where people could come and meet with the ostensible council that was Clarissa and her people. They dealt with all the day-to-day shit for me: interactions between people, arranging jobs, dealing with complaints, and all that kind of crap.

This room, however, was where the actual work got done.

The chamber was circular, and big enough that we could all move around easily as we took our chairs. There was fortunately no need for things like coffee-making equipment, not when the dungeon could supply everything we needed.

That meant that the room was straightforward in its layout. A large map of the local area was built into a round table before us and on the wall, and it could be brought up and zoomed in easily. It was easy to track in and out to a degree that we could examine individual rooms in a building, or back out to see the area from above for several miles.

The areas near the influence generators and towers, or the constructions we'd made, were updating in real time, while farther out were set as they had been at the increase from Iron to Steel. Clearly there was some kind of mapping system that sent a pulse—or something else…magical pixies taking pictures maybe…fuck knew, really—to see what was out there.

I'd found I could go up in the system on my own, floating like a ghost up and up and I could see far farther. But the major advantage of this system as it was?

It showed the world as it had been a few days ago.

Zooming in and out, we could see, for example, that the army base on the outskirts of the area, the battalion headquarters, was not only still there, but it was sealed up tight. The parade ground had been torn apart and the ground over a serious percentage of the base had been turned over to crops.

I stood at my spot. The big table still had a few empty spots for others to join us, if we decided to invite them. But for now, my "council" was here and waiting, more or less patiently.

I had Kelly to my left, and Aly to my right. Mike sat next to Aly, and Clarissa and Markus sat side by side to Kelly's left. Next to them were the Sikh, Catholic, and Muslim religious leaders, all of them looking damn confused as to why they were involved in a meeting like this.

Next were Chris and Becky, Jo and John, Finn and Patrick, with Rhodes and Griffiths opposite them next to Mike. Then on that side were Sarah, Ashley, Dante, and Ramnik, and that was it for this meeting.

I took a deep breath, then got started.

"Okay then, people, the last few days, things have been hard, I know, but they're getting sorted now. I've also come across some information that I think is important that I share with you all…"

CHAPTER SIX

Some two hours later, I slammed my palm down hard on the table. The loud bang brought a shocked silence to the room.

"That's enough!" I snapped, glaring at the people who had been engaged in a shouting match. "I'm happy you all have opinions on what we should be doing with the asuras, and I've listened to them all, but it seems I have to remind you, *this isn't a democracy.*"

I snarled that last bit. Several people had been getting out of control over what should be done. It was ranging from torturing and killing the asuras, to trying to design a soul-destroying weapon and deploying it against them. As well as using the Green Queen as a test subject.

The prevalent opinion was that they were soul eaters, and so we should kill them right now.

"Mike, you've been surprisingly quiet." I looked at him. As the conversation had gone on, most people had made their feelings clear, but he'd kept silent.

"Not much I can add." He shook his head. "As Aly says, we could learn a shitload from them, and they could be massively helpful. Also, as Jo says, they're a massive threat."

"They are," I agreed. "If it was a case of this is the only one of them here? I'd be inclined to kill them and get it over with. They might be trying to play nice, after all, but they've been responsible for the deaths of probably trillions."

"Thank you!" Jo said heatedly, gesturing to me as she sat back. "So we should—"

"IF!" I corrected. "*If* it was just them, I said. *It's not.* They're a single fragment or individual part of the 'one' that is the asuras. There are tens of thousands more up there. Hell, I don't know how many there are! Well over two hundred thousand of them at least in total. If we kill this one? The others might not even notice, or they might send our star nova immediately."

"You said they didn't like mana?" Griffiths asked musingly. "Could that be an advantage against them?

"They don't. They can't use it. The touch of it is deadly to them, and it's everywhere. That's why they need to seal themselves up into a 'sleeve' or body. This one, the one that wants to be our 'friend,' had basically bonded with a scientist who had been helping it. It's learning about the consequences of its actions, and it can help us. The other alternative, given that we can't trust it to behave if we tell it to fuck off, is that we kill it."

I looked around the room again, making eye contact with as many as I could. "That means we kill it, and we wait and see what happens. We lose access to it as an ally, and instead gain a possible target on our species' back from a group that regularly turn stars nova and feels utterly no guilt over it."

"What use could it be to us?" Clarissa asked, and I smiled.

"That's a very good question, Clarissa, thank you. First and foremost, it can speak on our behalf should we encounter any others of its species, meaning there's a chance for allies, rather than enemies. Remember, this one was disgusted by the actions it was forced to take, as were the majority, according to it. We're back to the fairy issue with the dungeons.

"The fairy we met who was running the Gateshead dungeon was a murderous psychopath, because she was trying to raise the level of the dungeon as fast as she could. She was doing that to try to save lives in the area. I don't like her methods, but I can understand them. The asuras send stars nova to release the soul essence of sapients. That massive surge of energy allows them to split and birth new ones of their kind. Again, I don't like it, but it is what it is.

"The next dungeon we meet might be fine. It might ally with us, or it might immediately declare war. *We don't know.* All we know is what we have in front of us. We know that this creature wants our help and is, frankly, desperate to get it. It can help us to build and design systems, and it can speak on our behalf to others of its species. More to the point, it can construct metal and mechanical bodies."

"Do they need fuel?" Rhodes asked, and I pointed a finger at her.

"Another good question! No, as far as I understand it, they don't. So let's be clear: a self-repairing, upgrading mechanical system, that requires no maintenance from us, nor fuel, and is willing to speak to its species on our behalf as a friend, is asking to ally with us." I paused, holding one hand up as Jo started to speak and I cut her off.

"Yes, it could be homicidal. Yes, it could be personally responsible for the death of entire civilizations. I don't deny that. It could be a terrible monster, and that's why it'll never be allowed into the dungeon proper. It'll never be allowed anywhere near the core, and should it try to get there, we kill it. It's also highly susceptible to Lightning and electrical weapons." I looked around the room, making eye contact as I went on.

"I don't trust it, not at all, but we damn well need what it's offering. If it can build us a land train or a jet or something? We can copy the design. We can make our own, just obviously based on mana systems. We can have it make a fuckin' walker from the movies and we can all sit our asses down and drink beer as it carries us down south, so we can get your families and bring them back."

"It'd be a mobile platform," Griffiths mused. "A working tank, or hell, we could make anything…"

"Exactly, but more importantly, and because I don't trust the fucker, we could build something between us. We build a tank or dreadnought or something, and we get them to make the parts that we have issues with. Robotic limbs that are a pain in the ass to develop? We have them make those bits, then we copy it. We use the Asuras, and we protect them. If they prove to us that they can be trusted? Great. If they can't?" I looked at Aly, and she took the hint.

"I'll have the Lightning-based weaponry ready," she agreed.

"Thank you. Listen, people, I don't like this any more than you do, but the simple truth is, we need them, and they need us. Marriage of convenience situation here, so like it or lump it. If you feel I'm in the wrong with this, and you want to try to convince me of it, see me at the end. We need to get a move on." I straightened up. "Right, you now know that we have immortal souls, that there are species out there eating other civilizations, and that, as usual, we're a bit more fucked than we thought we were."

The three religious types had been sitting silent for some time, stunned, despite their entire belief structure being built around a part of what I'd told them I'd seen, and I shrugged at the shell-shocked look on their faces.

"Now, the third and final thing we need to discuss," I said firmly, looking around the room, "is the dungeon."

The change in people was massive, tearing them from the internal speculation and clearly deep metaphysical considerations, into "this actually affects me right the fuck now."

I smiled slightly, seeing I had everyone's utmost attention again, and I went on.

"So, the dungeon is a living organism, as well as a constructed entity, apparently. It's not fully sapient, but it is sentient, more or less. Does everyone understand the difference between those?" I glanced around. "Be honest…I know I didn't."

"Sapient, as I understand it, is a real, thinking, and active brain." Griffiths smiled. "Where a cat, a dog, or a horse might be sentient, in that it's aware of the world around it, can feed and breed and so on, understands pain, etc., a sapient understands more. A sense of self and awareness, planning for the future and more."

"So the difference between a cat or a rat and a human?" Markus asked, glancing around and smiling when I nodded.

"Literally that. I'd say between a horse and Chris, but we all know that there's not that much difference," Becky quipped, and Chris grinned.

"That's what she said." He looked around proudly, and seemed to wonder why nobody was offering a high five. "What?" he asked, confused.

"Don't worry about it, dear." Becky tried to hide her smile as Kelly instead gave her the high five.

"Okay, I don't care about the rest. You all heard me compared to a horse. You all know I'm just that well…argh!"

"We all heard it, Christopher, and we all knew what your good lady was *actually* saying," Clarissa said, holding onto one of his ears and giving it a little twist. "Now you need to learn to be quiet and take a compliment, rather than rubbing it in."

"Okay…okay!" he cried out, jerking back when she released him, rubbing at his ear as sniggers rang out.

"Now, you were saying, Matt?" Clarissa asked pointedly, folding her hands one atop the other on the table before her.

"Yeah…okay." I hid a smile. "So, the dungeon is alive in a sense, and like anything alive, it can be worn out. Essentially, what's happened is we were forcing it to grow so quickly, and shoving in and pulling out so much mana so frequently that we strained it. Massively so.

"I've spent the last day or so rebuilding the core. It's intact, and usable again now." I made eye contact with everyone as I spoke. "But, we need to be more careful. One of the things that I discovered when I worked on the core is that each level of the core is a separate technological layer. Think of a sphere." I held up my left hand and clenched my fist, looking at it.

"This is the original core, solid and layered over and over with crystal and whatever the hell else is in there." I gestured to it, providing a visual version as I spoke. "So let's say there's a second level that goes over this, a shell that forms the next level. That shell sits atop the constructions we've made on this layer. If there's a lot all the way around, then the shell is bigger, and stronger. If there's a lot of construction on just one area, though?"

I slapped my hand on the top of the balled fist, deliberately making an uneven bulge there.

"You put a shell over this, and while some of the shell is built atop a solid structure…"

"The rest isn't," Aly said quietly. "It's an empty shell that just needs a little tap and it'll shatter. Like an eggshell."

"Exactly," I agreed. "If instead we'd built all the way around it, though?"

"Then it'd been able to withstand the demands we placed on it." Kelly spoke up this time.

"Exactly," I repeated. "So, the core is more or less repaired. I should be able to fix the last lingering issues tomorrow, and get it all back to full. As it is, though, its current capacity, even while not fully repaired, is greater than it ever was at Iron level. So, as of now, the dungeon is fully open for business again."

The wave of relief that went through the room was palpable, and I smiled despite myself.

"That's right—hot showers, lights, and real food. I know Kelly and Aly spread the word about being available again, but only a select few were able to do the summoning while I watched over the system. Well things look to be fully stable and we can open all the way up now. Kelly, Aly, if you can start permitting access to everyone again at the end of this meeting, I've removed the lockouts. We need to start to rebuild our forces again. *But…*"

The room froze; the low murmurs that had started to spring up cut off sharply.

"Part of the strain on the core was summoning so many living beings. Remember that each and every one of these summoned dungeon creatures has the potential to be fully aware. To have a soul of their own. The energy that takes to create isn't something I fully understand, and it's not entirely mana dependent, either. I suspect that's one of the reasons that the advanced kobolds are so much more expensive, because they're sapient rather than sentient."

"Some of the others are as well, I think," Jo said. "Beta, for example. I think she's more aware than any of the others."

"And that's true," I agreed. "It might be down to blind luck, it might be that I'm totally wrong, or that she evolved differently due to her level choices and more. I don't know. I can just tell you what I feel and the hints I get from being tied into the system."

"And into the fairy…" Chris shook his head. "Man, should we start calling you Tinkerb—"

"You finish that thought, and you'll get the sewage water rerouted to your shower." He winced as Becky slapped her hand over his mouth. "Good boy," I said when he held his hands up to either side, protesting his innocence.

"So. From now on, we need to build the core a lot more carefully," I clarified. "We need research in all areas, more or less, and make sure we're a hell of a lot more 'rounded' than we have been. And we make sure the core itself is solid before we even consider moving on to Glass."

"We need to work on the core itself and its facilities as much as the creatures and specific tech forms," Aly suggested, and I nodded.

"Very much so," I agreed. "You said you thought you had figured out the rail guns?"

"What?" Griffiths asked, stunned, jerking upright.

"Yeah." Aly shot him a grin. "I figured out a low-powered version, more than powerful enough for what we need, but it needs a lot of refinement yet. Think of a rifle—I've developed that, and can probably construct it—but I need to research the individual parts and improve on them to make a functioning version. What I've got for now? It's more like a super-shotgun."

"If it's anything like she's been telling me?" Mike said to Griffiths and Rhodes. "You're going to love it."

"Can we make it now or does it need work?" I asked.

"I'd prefer a day or two to work on the outstanding issues," she said. "It'll work as it is, but don't expect to get many shots off before the barrels are fucked. In the last stages of the fight with the Red Queen? That wouldn't matter. In normal life? It'll massively matter."

"Okay, then make that your priority, *after* we've got the research team up and running again. I'm sure that Griffiths will have one or two soldiers who have an interest in helping design their new guns if you need help?"

Lots of nods from both Griffiths and Rhodes there.

"I'm good, unless they can do 3D design," she replied with a tired smile. "Honestly, a day, maybe two, and I'll have the first generation ready. We need to talk about that, though. The next generation of weapons are going to be rifles and shotguns, that kind of weaponry. What should we be looking at for the loadout for our people now?"

"Armor stays," I said firmly. "While I know it's not going to be great against others with rail guns, especially if they have proper ones, most of the enemy we'll be facing are still monsters. Think claws and teeth."

"I agree." Mike said, leaning on the table and looking from his wife to me. "Mostly we'll be fighting monsters, yeah, some assholes with guns as well, and when we face things like the asuras, we need better stopping power. Frankly, though, as much as I want a decent sniper rifle, I think swords and shields are still valid weapons. Considering the world we live in, as well as the fact that if I get in the shit out there? I want a weapon that doesn't need to reload."

Griffiths and Rhodes nodded along, as did Chris and I.

"Okay, so for now, we need to upgrade the armor again, maybe going more toward ballistic body armor now that we've a higher tech base, but it also needs to be resistant to edged weapons and more."

I winced as I realized the number of issues having something that could address all of those concerns would cause, when Finn spoke up.

"I'll take that one," he offered to Aly. "You showed me some of the systems, but I think that if we're going to go all out on research and developing the dungeon, then me and my team will be getting used a lot more? We might as well make a joint project with this, provided we can get access to the design systems?"

"You'll get it," I promised, Aly nodding in relief as well. "I'll be joining you in the crafting side soon, I think…I've got some ideas I need to work on."

"Really?" Finn asked, clearly surprised. "Well, I won't complain. I'd imagine all sorts of new upgrades will be available when you see their need."

He winced when he realized what he'd just said and facepalmed. "Shit. Engage brain, *then* speak, Finn. Come on, man."

He took a deep breath, then forced a smile. "What I meant was that when you, as the boss, see the difference the crafting teams could make directly, I think you'll see that we're ready for a serious investment."

"I'm sure," I murmured, frowning at him, and deliberately not saying anything else.

"He's teasing you," Kelly assured Finn, before squeezing the pressure points on either side of my knee and making me yelp.

"Okay, okay!" I laughed. "I am. Don't worry, mate. Okay, so we need to work on a lot more research and we're going to be consolidating our gains for a bit now; what else do we need to discuss?"

"The future," Clarissa said firmly. "What's our intentions for the short-term? What about my teams? We've enclosed the section you asked for, and we've been focusing in on claiming all the land inside the walls now, but that won't last my people much longer."

"Fine." I reached out, drawing the map up from the local area to the city of Newcastle from above, or what was left of it. "Here…" I gestured to the river and the bridge over it.

The bridge ran from near to our south wall, across the river, and then we'd constructed a straight line all the way up to the park, more or less.

Instead of following that, though, I traced a second line, from the carpark that we'd gathered in a few days ago, when we'd been hunting the asuras, and back from that point to the small industrial estate that was nestled by the river in that direction.

"Now this, as far as we knew, was just a collection of offices and so on, some random businesses and nothing else."

"Right," Mike agreed, looking at it. "I've ran through there in the past, doing PT. There's some fenced-off areas, but nothing unusual."

"This is where the Green Queen came from," I said. "I saw her memories, and there's a high-tech lab in here somewhere, working on physics issues. I don't know much more than that, but there was enough high-tech shit that a single scientist was able to craft a body for her, as well as containment systems. That means there's some decent tech at least. I'd like a line sent out in this direction. If all else fails, and there's nothing left? We can set up an early warning system here to watch over the area or something."

"Okay, I can do that," Clarissa agreed. "Anything else?"

"Hmmm," I murmured, looking at the map. "Okay, people, this is a 'vote' situation. I need your advice.

"We can set off and reach out to the army contingent, first of all. That's one option. Yes, I know we're going to be doing that, one way or another, but the question is, do we extend our influence in that direction?"

"Why would we?" Kelly asked, and I shrugged.

"Truthfully, it depends on how we view them. If as we hope, we think they'll be allies, or possible recruits, then we'd be in a position to help them if they need us much sooner. If we view them as possible enemies? If, as Griffiths says, they decide that I'm a threat and decide to take me down? We can fight them a lot farther from here, and force them to fight for every step to come after us."

I held up my hand quickly, one finger raised as I looked from Mike to Griffiths and to Rhodes.

"To be clear, I don't think it's likely, and I certainly don't want that outcome, but the way our lives have been of late? It's a solid risk."

"I don't want to be fighting our own people," Griffiths said. "I'm here, as are our people, and I say 'our' because this is looking more and more like our home. But I seriously advise against approaching them with a threat instead of a friendly face."

"I'm in favor of a friendly face," I agreed. "As we discussed last time, I was planning on sending Ashley…there's no friendlier face here." I quirked a smile as she snorted, and I went on. "I'm just looking at possibilities here, mate. So, show of hands: who thinks we should extend toward the battalion headquarters?"

"To assist or to set up fallback positions and plan for a fight?" Mike asked.

"Both," I said. "One doesn't mean we can't do the other. I'm really hoping that we can all be friends here, like seriously hoping." I lifted a hand and looked around.

"What's between there and here?" Kelly traced a finger along the river and grunted as she answered her own question. "Basically nothing. A load of housing and the occasional small industrial section. Fine, yeah, I'd say extend along, use it to drop converters and extend our warning system if nothing else."

"Anyone else?" I looked around.

"I'd say extend in that direction, *but…*" Griffiths said forcefully, "we stop here." He marked a collection of industrial buildings half a mile from the base. "This is close enough it's useful, and far enough out that it's not a blatant threat. It'd also be close enough to them that you could create food and so on here as a gesture of goodwill, without us having to shlep it all the way on our backs."

"Makes sense," I agreed. "Anyone else?" With that agreement reached, everyone happily raised a hand. "Then that's fine." I nodded. "Next, we need to look at the future."

"In what way, lad?" Markus said curiously.

"Essentially, we've been on a mad scramble to demolish the local area and make as many converters as possible. We've reached the point where we need to consider the next stage. Primarily, do we use that as our standard method from now on? Do we keep stripping the area and building converters, or once we've got a decent cleared area around each of our centers, do we stop?"

I held my hand up at the frowns on people's faces.

"Yes, I know we've had this discussion already, and we agreed we need to make converters and so on, but I mean are we winding down the absorption of the outer areas right now, or continuing a bit longer?"

"Why would we stop now?" Patrick asked, only for John to answer him.

"Because once we demolish something, it's gone," John said. "Regardless of the loss of a possible emergency resource we could call upon for the future, we're also demolishing buildings that were made sometimes hundreds of years ago. Yes, I approve of demolishing the new build housing estates. Most of them are little better than slums with pretty paint jobs. But the rest?"

"There are some beautiful buildings around," Kelly agreed softly. "Buildings that are literally our history as a culture and a species. We should protect them if we can."

"Also, our people are finite," I pointed out. "We might have the next Einstein currently breaking bricks up for essence, when they could be helping with research. Do we clear the area, push it back and then keep going, or do we invest more heavily in our people?

"We can either have our people working day in and day out, breaking the houses down, absorbing bricks and more, or we start to build a community. This is going to be a hell of a lot harder, mainly because I don't even know what we need. First because we don't need as many of the traditional roles filled. Plumbers, tilers, and carpenters? At first thought, we don't need any of them. We can create rooms with everything we need, after all."

I looked around. Some of the group nodded, even as Finn firmly shook his head.

"Thing is, the plumber understands water and sewage systems, pressure and blocks and all that shit better than anyone else. They could create some amazing systems that we don't even know we need yet. The carpenter could be making everything from normal chairs and shit, to..." I shrugged. "Honestly? I don't know. They might make magic fucking wands, or just really comfy toilet seats. Your guess is as good as mine."

"So we keep some," Mike suggested. "We switch out a handful of plumbers and all the other trades—some work in the research teams, develop shit we might need, work on their own plans, while others are involved in the community; they address issues as they come up. Maybe we have a primary and secondary team. One works on research and development; the other is on call to deal with issues?"

"That works," I agreed. "But skilled tradesmen are a small percentage of the overall we have. What about farmers and pharmacists? Nurses and nail technicians? All of them need a reason to get out of bed, and some of their skill sets, some of the jobs they spent their life working on getting really skilled at, are utterly fucked now. We need to get the ball rolling with retraining."

"You're not just talking about jobs, though. You need to talk about classes as well," Finn said after a few seconds. "Getting people up to a level where they get access to their class skills is a massive undertaking, and not least because we have so few combat classes, or production centers. *We...*" He pressed a hand to his chest as he spoke passionately.

"We, as crafters, get less chances to earn Experience than combat classes do, but we gain a little with everything we create. If I made a handful of new designs, I could hit my class choice easily. But I need to know the basics first. I can't just go 'Oh, I can sew, so I'll make some leather armor.' I had to learn step by step. You're talking about a tiny handful of us trying to teach hundreds of people to unlock their classes."

"And they'll be offered classes that are in direct response to their actions," I agreed. "So if someone wants to be, I don't know, a chef, say, and they spend all their time learning to craft armor to reach their class choice? They'll only be offered leatherworking classes."

"So we need to work logically," Clarissa said, undeterred. "We don't take everyone off the line. We leave the majority working on the demolition and absorption teams, and we ask for a hundred or two hundred volunteers who want to learn skills we can teach. We split them into those you can train for the army, and those who are to be crafters. We focus on training them, teaching them the basics, and then once they're trained, they can help to train the next generation. I'll look into that with Finn."

I nodded my thanks to her, as Markus spoke as well.

"Also..." Markus winced. "Most of our frontline fighters, well, they were lost. We have a decent team of archers now. They've gradually grown more and more experienced, but they're also becoming more and more useless, as bad as that sounds."

"They're not useless," Kelly said. "They've learned their craft and they're bloody good at it. The issue is that the world moved on, and so they're..." She paused, clearly thinking of a nice way to put it.

"Useless." Markus snorted. "They know this, Kelly, or that they will be soon. You might say obsolete or any one of a dozen nice terms, but there's been talk for some time about them being disbanded. They know that eventually there won't be a need for archers."

"Are their skills necessarily locked to bow and arrow, or are they generally ranged?" Rhodes asked, making notes as she spoke. "If they're general ranged fighters, then they may be able to transition to soldiers much easier than the frontline fighters..."

"Mainly they've been specializing in single hits. Where, as a soldier, I was taught to aim center of mass and take down the enemy in a hail of gunfire, preferably without wasting any ammunition, as crazy as that sounds..." He snorted. "Our archers have mostly been specializing in areas that might be problematic to carry over. 'Imbue,' for example, May recently unlocked. It enables her to channel her mana into her arrows, making each significantly more damaging. But..."

"There's always a but," John muttered, sighing.

"But it's down to single shots. She channels the mana into the bow and then into an arrow one at a time. She might be able to retrain as a sniper, but I don't see a way to use that skill with an assault rifle. It uses half of her manapool with each use. The higher her manapool, the more destructive. There's no option at this point, she says, for less mana and more shots."

"What about scouts?" Griffiths suggested. "We could always do with more scouts. Their bows are quieter than our guns, after all. Or hunters? What about training them in stealth?"

"That would work," I said. "Eventually, as you said, Clarissa, it'll be the army, rather than frontline and ranged, but for now we're talking about how we use weapons we don't even have. It's important, and yes, we need to plan for it, but it's not something we have to fix right now."

"We need to talk about the future with regard to the forces," Griffiths disagreed. "I know you want to look at this later, but it's important."

"Go on." I sighed, sitting back and trying not to frown.

"You said before that you plan to use mainly dungeon forces, with humans in the fight when you need quality over quantity. Is that still the plan?"

"Why?" I asked, deliberately not correcting him on the "quality over quantity" bit. The new advanced kobolds were literally the equal of our best; we'd just been using them as disposable shock troopers because of the ease of it and because they'd not had the time to train as more yet.

"You've just told us that we need an army, and that the souls that all living creatures have cost a lot to the dungeon. Basically, it's not a good idea to go all out on trying to make ten thousand goblins and have them overrun the enemy each time because it could fuck up the dungeon, right?"

I nodded, and he went on.

"So, what about the advanced goblins? If you're saying that creating too many souls too fast was in part responsible for the issues, then what if we do the research as you say, and try to build a much better, well-rounded force?"

"You don't know goblins," Mike said. "They're horrible little bastards."

"Then not goblins. Fuck's sake, Mike, my point is do we stop aiming for quantity and start focusing on quality? Do we research the advanced goblins and advanced orcs—"

"Not the orcs," I said. "Never the orcs."

"I know you don't like them, and they're a force we'll need to fight eventually, but what about—"

"No." I cut Griffiths off. "I'll accept using orcs in the training dungeons and arenas, because they're aggressive lunatics and we need the Experience, but fuck no. I'm not using them in any other situations that doesn't include cannon fodder. As soon as they're summoned, they start acting up. They're aggressive and unpleasant to their fellow dungeon creatures. They enjoy inflicting pain and basically being dicks. That doesn't even include the fact they'll challenge *me* given the chance. So you, as a normal human? They'll happily kill you."

"Okay, well, realistically, we need to practice against them. What if we upgrade them to the uncommon version then? Use that as a basic level for the dungeon to train against?" Griffiths suggested, holding one hand up as he spoke quickly. "I'm not being a dick about this, Matt. I'm serious. There's no point in everyone learning to fight the most basic and stupid versions. They'll grow complacent, believing that orcs are dumb beasts and easily outwitted if we do that. The greatest enemy any soldier has is themselves. Believe that you can face anything and win easily, and you'll be dead in seconds. Fear is a hell of a friend to a soldier."

"Provided it's kept under control, and you train them to leash it," Mike pointed out, getting a glare from Griffiths. "Sorry, mate, but you know the line you have to walk: too little fear and they're dead from their arrogance, too much fear and they die from cowardice and kill their friends as well."

"Point." He sighed, nodding.

"Okay, fine, I get it, and yeah, I was thinking along the same lines for the forces moving forward. Essentially, the kobolds, as they are, are ready to be more heavily integrated into the dungeon. Mike, Griffiths, and Rhodes, I want you to pick a handful of the survivors from the advanced kobolds and train them."

"Train them to be what, sir?" Rhodes asked, still making notes.

"Soldiers. I want kobold NCOs." I waited with a smile as all three stared at me in shock.

CHAPTER SEVEN

"You mean NCOs to lead the kobolds or…" Griffiths asked slowly, and I shook my head.

"I mean NCOs. We need a non-commissioned officer core. The advanced kobolds have higher stats than we do as baseline humans. Yes, we're anything but baseline now, but that's the point. They have the potential to be at least as intelligent as we are. Leaving them to be dumb soldiers holding a pike is bloody stupid."

"Okay, I'll just say it," Mike said. "Can they rebel against us and displace us? And while I'm sure I know the answer, I think we all need to hear it: are you looking to replace humans with your creatures?"

"They could, if they were pushed into it, but they'd have to be really pushed to overcome their inbuilt conditioning, and no, I'm not," I said, resolute. "But if we're being realistic, although I can, I think, kill all the dungeon creatures if I need to, I know that improving my class skills like Monster Master will make it impossible for them to rebel. Also, no, definitely not looking to supplant us as the top of the food chain. I'm not even considering going to the next level of kobold at this point."

"That's a relief then. So why NCOs?" Griffiths asked. "And I take it you mean for the general NCO core to be mixed, human and dungeon creatures, and the soldiers under them to be mixed as well? As in a kobold NCO leading a mixed human and kobold team?"

"Yes, frankly." I nodded. "I know there'll always be a certain difference. For one, they come into the world as adults—we take a little longer to be useful…"

"That's an understatement," Mike muttered.

"But at the end of the day, they have souls, just as we do and—"

"Do they know God?" the Catholic priest asked suddenly.

I paused, looking at him, then shrugged. "No clue, Father," I said, not particularly interested. "Feel free to ask them. Anyway, they've got souls so—"

"Souls are given by God." The priest interrupted again, frowning. "This is important. Souls differentiate us from the beasts of the field and the monsters out there. Knowing that souls are finally proved to you to exist is a wonder that the old world sorely missed. But to say that these creatures are our equals before God?" He shook his head. "I know blasphemy is not your intention, Matt, but this is an important point. We are made in God's image, and God was not a reptile."

Silence fell as we all looked at one another, unsure where to go from that. The priest, along with his religious companions, had been quite happy to go along with things and help people so far. There'd been no demonstration of possible issues; they'd just asked that we permit their faithful to pray as they will.

I had no issue with that, and I'd said so. Hell, I'd invited them to this meeting because if souls were real, they might have some kind of insight that was useful.

Instead, I recognized the light of zeal in the priest's eyes, and I forced myself to keep a polite smile on my face.

"Well, I'm sure the gods have a plan for us all—"

"GOD," he stated, determined. "Not gods, plural. There is one God. He has many faces. His prophets have come again and again, and there have been mixed messages due to man's inability to understand. We have agreed that this is likely, but to say that a lizard is—"

"Thank you." I cut him off in turn, mentally cursing the decision to bring them along to this. "I appreciate that you've been dealing with things, and helping your followers make sense of the situation. This is a council meeting, though. We deal with what affects the dungeon and this world. You want to talk about theology? That's great. Fuck off somewhere else and do that shit. If you want to stay? Don't interrupt me and don't tell me shit as a fact, not when an hour ago you'd no clue about it."

I took a deep breath, forcibly calming myself. I'd been trying to be patient, but clearly a little of my irritation had slipped through, judging from the look on people's faces. Some, like Finn and Chris, grinned openly. Others, like Clarissa and Markus, were clearly torn, glaring at the priest and me equally.

Others, like Kelly, simply sat, a faint and obviously forced smile on their faces, and they were probably plotting to murder me in my sleep later.

I sighed and shook my head. Better to bite the bullet now and get it over with.

"I don't think you understand—" the priest began hotly, and I cut him off again, speaking over him as he'd done to me.

"I don't think *you* do, Father. They have souls, and so do we. I know that to be a fact. I'm not going to treat the sapient and advanced ones as second-class citizens. They have souls, and some of them, at least, are our equals. As far as I know, they have their own galactic fucking civilizations out there. The system referred to the High Grenai, for example, a variant of goblins that are so beautiful and intelligent they don't bother to interact with most of the species of the galaxy.

"They have souls, the kobolds have souls, the fucking orcs have souls, and when we raise up the other species, and they learn to interact and improve their skills? We'll have researchers from each of the races; we'll have doctors and crafters…Hell, Starr—I don't even know for sure if Starr survived—but Starr the kobold was making his own potions." I looked around the room, seeing considering faces as they put two and two together.

"If an uncommon kobold can teach *himself* to make potions, then an advanced one certainly can. At what point do we treat them as citizens? At what point do we accept that if they have souls, they have rights?"

"They are beasts!" the priest snarled, and I glared at him.

"I'm sorry, Father, but the simple truth is I have to be a realist about the world. If I can't touch it and can't interact with it? I have to leave it be. You say God has a plan for us all? Great. Well, if that's the case, He or She clearly planned for me to say this as well. If these beings have souls, then they are citizens of the dungeon. Treating them as 'less' is the same as treating humans of different skin tones or backgrounds as 'less.' This is the first point at which for us specism replaces entrenched racism, so I'll make it fucking clear to everyone. This dungeon has not, nor will it ever have, space for racists, speciesists or whatever sexuality people are, nor anti-gender-ists and all that shit. Hell, I don't even know the words for it, but fuck it!

"Anyway, religion has no place in politics, nor in defending the dungeon. I'll make sure there's a place you can all lead services, and you'll always be allowed to teach your various religions, provided you're not hurting anyone, nor trying to cause issues for me. But as of now, your part in this council is ended. Thank you for your time and fuck off." I gestured to the door.

More people winced as the priest and his two companions stood, but for many of those in the room, I'd just made their day.

I'd owe the priest and the others an apology later, but that idiot had just made it clear that he was going to be an issue moving forward, and I didn't need them showing up to meetings in the future, just to be turned away. Better to make it clear right now.

"God has a plan," the priest said, clearly trying to be polite, and I nodded. "It includes you, and all that you have done. But God also gave us free will. He gives us the chance to turn our face from him, lest we be slaves—"

"And I appreciate that," I said firmly. "I have no issue with you or your God. I have a lot to do, though, and religious matters take place after defending our people, feeding and clothing the kids, and keeping everyone alive."

"I'll pray for you," the priest said grimly, striding toward the exit, his back straight and clearly offended.

"That's nice." I glared at Chris, raising one finger in warning to refrain from making a sarcastic comment, already regretting the way this had gone. But I kept my mouth shut, and so did the others. The imam paused as he shuffled past to pat me on the shoulder, letting me know that he, at least, understood.

I shot him a relieved smile, then waited until the room was empty before speaking again.

"Well, that was a clusterfuck, but it needed to be done."

"Matt?" Finn said softly, and I looked at him in question. "Thank you," he finished. "We're neither of us religious, but…it's nice to know where the dungeon stands."

Patrick nodded, silent as he so often was, but laying his hand over his partner's and squeezing.

"It's fine." I smiled easily, glad that not everyone was angry with me. "Seriously, I'm not putting up with that shit. I'm sorry, Clarissa, for kicking them out, but they need to understand that as leaders of the religious scene, they're not invited to the council normally. When he made his position clear, well, I had to make mine as well."

"Why are you apologizing to me?" Clarissa asked, and I frowned.

"I thought you'd be pissed at me?" I suggested.

"I am."

"Well then…"

"Why did you apologize, Matt?" she repeated, and I paused before answering this time.

"I apologized because I thought you'd be pissed, but—"

"But you did what you had to do as the Dungeon Lord," she said. "I don't like it, and I would have done it differently, but I'd have done many things differently in your place. We'd also all be dead by now, all things considered, or hiding in the lowest floors of the dungeon. Just because you do something I don't like doesn't mean you need to apologize. You're the Dungeon Lord, boy. Accept it." She folded her arms and glared at me.

I snorted, shaking my head before nodding. "You're right," I agreed. "Thank you."

I reached out, rolled my hand to the right then back again, summoning a cold can of my favorite energy drink and catching it as it fell from nothingness to land in my hand, grinning around the room.

"Oh, and you're all good to start summoning fun drinks and so on again, and just relaxing with it now, I know you'll all have been limiting yourselves."

The room erupted in clinking chinaware, the smell of tea, of coffee, and the cracking of soft drink cans. I pointedly ignored the glasses for the cola that were being blatantly topped up from a hip flask as well.

"So. As I was saying, no racism, speciesism, or any of that shit, all right?" I said. "If we're going to be summoning the various species and upgrading the plans for them all the way to advanced, then there needs to be an understanding that they're people."

"Except the orcs," Chris pointed out.

"Except the orcs," I agreed. "They're dickheads."

"And the goblins blatantly fiddle with themselves all day long," Chris added.

"So do you." Patrick grunted, and Chris looked at him in shock.

"Dude! You're not supposed to be watching…and we don't talk about making adjustments in public…"

"It's not making an adjustment if it's every other minute, Chris." Patrick groaned. "Either you need new pants, or you need to see a doctor, okay?"

"Okay, so what we're agreeing on here," I said quickly, grinning, "is that we treat them as equals in most cases, and in the case of the lower-caste goblins, we just don't summon them until we can do uncommon or advanced, all right?"

"Or we treat them like Chris," Becky suggested. "As barely house-trained?"

"Yeah, if for some reason we have to summon them, we make sure they don't piss in the corners." I nodded.

The room in general was grinning at the look Chris was wearing, clearly supposed to be hurt and disappointed, despite that we all knew perfectly well he was playing up to the crowd.

"Okay, so if we can get this back on track…" Griffiths said. "We look at summoning the various species and forming our new army from both humans and the other minions you have access to. We make a dedicated force with their various skills. The kobolds will make excellent soldiers. They're brave, strong, and intelligent. What do the other races bring to the table, and what other races are there?"

I opened my mouth to run through them, then shook my head, reaching out to the table before us, concentrating. I could make it project images and a map, after all; why not this?

Grunts and gasps rose around the room as the table began to project the details for each of us, showing an image alongside the creature that slowly rotated in the air.

Monsters

Fey: The Fey, or Tuatha De Danann, are an unusual group, sub-divided into many species. The Fey as a group are often misunderstood. From the playful sprites to the solemn dryads, to the capricious Daoine Sidhe and the thousands of variations in between, the Fey are as likely to hinder as to help, usually anyway.

Beware, Dungeon Lord:

While the Fey have donated their essences to be included in the core, they may yet take issue with your use of this…no two Fey regard their inclusion in the dungeon core program the same way. Some "wild" or "free" Fey may ignore your dungeon-born variants, others may include them joyfully…while some may declare war on you for your effrontery in summoning such as they.

You have been warned.

Fey: The most common of the Fey is the fairy, and while the common variant is somewhat unreliable in many ways, they grow more advanced and powerful with each evolutionary level.

Cost: Fairy (Common): 100 Nature, 400 Pure Mana, 5 Control points. Maintenance is 5 mana point per day, per individual.

Current Level: Common.

Already existing research boost detected!

The Fey "Fairy" class has already been absorbed into the dungeon with integrated cybernetics and nanite upgrades. Although cybernetic and nanite upgrades still require numerous prior technologies to be researched to make them available for general production, the original variant is available now.

Dungeon Fairy: [Enhanced] This specifically augmented dungeon variant of the fey designated [fairy] can greatly improve on the dungeon's reliability, production, and expansion rates.

Cost: Dungeon Fairies spawn individually for 250,000 pure mana each. Maintenance is 500 mana points per day, per individual; control points are not required.
Current Level: Advanced.

Fey: Dryads are less common than the fairy folk, but are still plentiful in the universe. A literal Nature elemental, the dryad is uninterested in anything beyond land entrusted to its care, but it will defend said land with its life should any seek to despoil it.

Note: Be wary in harvesting land cared for by a Dryad.

Cost: *Dryad (Common):* 400 Nature, 1600 Pure Mana, 10 Control points. Maintenance is 15 mana points per day, per individual.
Current Level: Common.

Fey: The Daoine Sidhe, or "people of the mounds," as many refer to them due to their preference for underground halls and homes, are often also referred to as the "lords and ladies." A graceful and glamorous creature, the Daoine Sidhe live for their revels, their pranks and parties, but this is not to say that they are useless to a Dungeon. The Daoine Sidhe are rogues and infiltrators without compare. Their natural affinity with glamours and mind-altering magics have firmly established them as some of the most powerful—and hated—rogues in the cosmos.

Cost: *Daoine Sidhe (Common):* 300 Light, 1200 Pure Mana, 15 Control points. Maintenance is 40 mana points per day, per individual.

Current Level: Common.

Mammal: Goblins as a species have multiple variations, ranging from the lowest caste, who are barely sentient, to the High Grenai, a race that suffers little interaction with "lesser" species, due to the enormous gulf of grace and beauty between those races and their own. The most basic can be spawned as Dungeon Monsters. Utilizing their species' polymorphic tendencies results in greater enhancements than are commonly available.

Cost: Goblins spawn individually for 5-30 mana each. Maintenance is 2-25 mana points per day, per individual.

Current Level: Common.

Mammal: Orcan, or as they are more commonly known, orcs, are a muscular, thick-skinned race. Similar to the goblinoid races in that they share a highly polymorphic tendency, resulting in as many versions of the Orcan as there are worlds, the gift of life to Orcans is a costly and highly risky decision that few Dungeons are willing to make lightly.

Note: The Orakai sub-species is blocked from reproduction by any and all Dungeons due to treaties and enforced by magical interference.

Cost: Orcan spawn individually for 25 mana each. Maintenance is 25 mana points per day, per individual.

Current Level: Common.

Mammal: Scepiniir are rarely seen, and are proud warriors. Only through a life debt were the Scepiniir convinced to permit their essence to be given to the dungeon core program. The conditions were made clear, and are passed onto you here as well:

- No Scepiniir may be forced into a bonded pairing against its will.
- No Scepiniir may be sacrificed to another species, nor consumed by any through any bond or partnership with the Dungeon.
- No Scepiniir can be forced into servitude, nor arenas for the purpose of entertainment.

Any breaking of the Three Edicts will constitute a declaration of war by the Scepiniir Empire.

Cost: *Scepiniir (Common):* 400 Nature, 1600 Pure Mana, 10 Control points. Maintenance is 15 mana points per day, per individual.

Max Number of Scepiniir you can summon: 4 per hut.

Current Level: Common.

Monster: The Lesser Ghast is a misnomer, considering the reality of the breed. Whereas most "monsters" are simply scared or confused members of races other than the one observing and identifying—example, goblins—certain species are quite rightly defined as monsters through their excessive bloodlust and violent natures.

Cost: Lesser Ghasts spawn individually for 100 Shadow mana, 400 Pure Mana each. Maintenance is 40 mana points per day, per individual, and requires 7 points of control.
Current Level: Uncommon.

Monster: Harpies are rarely used in dungeon settings, mainly due to their unpredictable and violent natures. Harpies will happily feast on their fellow dungeon-born unless forced to leave them be and are one of the most aggressive and antagonistic of the dungeon's innate catalog.

Cost: Harpies are 100 Storm mana, or 400 Pure Mana each. Maintenance is 40 mana points per day, per individual, and requires 7 points of control.
Current Level: Common.

Reptilian*:* Kobolds are a common, highly structured, caste-driven species. Semi-sentient kobolds are a standard sight in Dungeons, due to their advanced trap-making skills and low cost.

Cost: Advanced Kobolds spawn individually for 2,500 mana each, 25 control points. Maintenance is 100 mana points per day, per individual.
Current Level: Advanced.

Dinosauria: The Triceratops Horridus is an ancient herbivore, specifically evolved to be as unpalatable and difficult to consume as possible. Where many herbivores are peaceful, and even cowardly creatures, the Triceratops evolved with a slightly different design. Be this through nature or nurture, the Triceratops, through its many variations, became a highly feared sight in the late Cretaceous era.

Cost: Triceratops spawn individually for 12,500 mana each, 50 control points. Maintenance is 150 mana points per day, per individual.
Current Level: Common.

Avian: Impai are simple creatures, easily distracted by their own hungers and difficult to control, but they excel in two areas: randomized destruction and threat detection. The Impai as a species are widely viewed as unreliable and unstable, resulting in repeated attempts to eradicate their species.

Despite this, they remain a popular choice for lower-level Dungeons and lower-scale conflicts.

Cost: Impai spawn in packs of three for 25 mana each. Maintenance is 10 mana points per day, per individual.
Current Level: Common.

Undead: The various forms of the undead are as numerous as grains of sand or stars in the sky; they are matched only by their antithesis, the forces of Life. Undead can be split into two simple categories, Sentient and Non-Sentient, with the simple Skeletons, Zombies, Ghouls, and so on beginning with non-sentient forms, while the average Wraith, Vampyr, or Banshee begins with a form of rudimentary Intelligence and awareness.

Cost: Variable.

Skeletons (Uncommon): 10 Unlife, 40 Pure Mana, 1 Control point.

Maintenance is 1 mana point per day, per individual.

Zombies (Basic): 20 Unlife, 70 Pure Mana, 1 Control point.

Maintenance is 2 mana points per day, per individual.

Wraiths (Basic): 100 Unlife, 400 Pure Mana, 5 Control points.

Maintenance is 5 mana points per day, per individual.

Corpse Lord (Uncommon): 500 Unlife, 2,000 Pure Mana, 10 Control points.

Maintenance is 250 mana points per day, per individual.

Special: Due to your Lightning affinity and the effect that your species change has on your Dungeon, you may summon a single Raiju at a time. Raiju are exceedingly rare beasts, and as such cannot be summoned in large numbers. Their playful nature means that many underestimate them, to their peril.

Cost: 150 mana per summon, 50 mana per day, 10 control points.
Current Level: N/A.

Vermin: Rats are a common pest that are ubiquitous across the universe. Vermin of this type vary in size and limb count, but often conform to similar local design.

Note: Flying variants have now been unlocked…cost remains identical.

Cost: Vermin spawn in packs of three for 5 mana each. Maintenance is 1 mana point per day, per individual.
Current Level: Common.

The room was silent for a few minutes as we all read over the details. People occasionally muttered to the person next to them about details, such as how ugly the ghast was and the strangely preening look that the Daoine Sidhe showed, their wide smile radiating out of the projection.

"I'm just gonna say it now: fuck trying for the dungeon fairy," I declared. "If we summoned one of those, it might be able to boot us all out." There was a general grumble of agreement and approval, as we all went back to the screens.

Where the fairies showed pretty much as they were expected to, as tiny people with wings and an almost human face, eyes being a little too large and their chins small, the Daoine Sidhe were the opposite end of the scale.

They looked as if they could walk off the screen and onto a catwalk in Paris. Hell, their almost inhuman good looks and the way they stared at—and through—you, it made me wonder.

"That looks a hell of a lot like Amile, Corrine's friend. You remember her?" Chris called to me, and I snorted before I could help myself, nodding to him over the projection.

"Who's that?" Kelly asked.

"We both used to work together in a bar." I took Kelly's hand in mine.

"Our first jobs, we worked the bar, Corrine worked the manager," he corrected, and I pointed a finger at him in agreement.

"Basically she refused to actually do any 'work' and was focused on 'promotions'…only, she was hired as a barmaid, and never even pulled a pint."

"She pulled Ronny a lot, though!" Chris shook his head in disgust. "Literally, she never did a damn thing. Spent all her time on her phone 'promoting' the bar. Except it was always calls to her mates and selfies an' shit. Her and a bunch of her pretty mates would come in and get free cocktails, post reviews and take turns posing for their social media shit."

"A handful of us said we were going to quit if she didn't start working." I took over the narrative. "She was hired as a barmaid because we needed the help, too many customers and not enough staff. She never pulled a pint, but took up the slot in the bar's rota, and Ronny refused to hire anyone else."

"His dad owned the place," Chris pointed out.

"Yeah, so when we threatened to quit, he promised to sort it out…" I shook my head. "Corrine went into the office for him to talk it over with her, then she came out literally two minutes later, and got two of her slutty mates. All three went in, and half an hour later, me and Chris were summoned to the office. The girls went and sat in the corner of the bar, doing fuck all and drinking more cocktails, while Ronny told us that they were more valuable to the bar than we were, and we either put up and shut up, or we were fired."

"We quit on the spot." Chris grinned. "I mean, we totally understood. She'd blatantly fucked him, along with her mates, or something happened between the four of them anyway, considering the state of him when we went in."

"He didn't think we'd actually quit," I finished. "We walked out and left, straight down the stairs and into the bar next door. Ten minutes later, Ellie, the unofficial assistant bar manager, came and sat with us, she'd quit as well, and she showed us a photo of him being slapped after telling Corrine that as they were now short-staffed she had to work the bar after all."

"This is a fascinating story," Clarissa said coldly. "But what does it have to do with—"

"Amile was one of their friends, always in the center of things, but always subtly weird," I said placatingly. "Trust me, there's a point," I assured the rest of the room.

"So, basically, Amile used to barely speak, had a weird accent that wasn't French or anything we could guess, but was definitely from somewhere far off. She never so much as carried a bag. No phone, nothing like that, and when she was with the girls, none of them had their phones either. If people tried to take their photos, like friends who they'd normally be posing with, the entire lot would go nuts," Chris said.

"They'd all hang around Amile like flies round shit. Seriously, they worshipped her. She was some fashion model. She'd vanish for weeks at a time, then turn up and everyone bought her drinks. Guys went from being interested in one of the other girls, even dating them, to being with Amile. And so long as she was there? Nobody cared."

"Never saw the attraction myself," I lied. "I mean, yeah, she was pretty, beautiful even, in this weird way that these are as well, but not that amazing."

"When she was interested in someone, everyone backed off?" Ashley frowned. "And the person she was after was up for it, while whoever they were with would just accept it?"

"Yeah," I agreed, nodding to her. "Sound familiar?"

"Sounds like something I could pull off if I invested in the right skills," Ashley agreed.

"Yeah, but seriously, Ash…" Chris shook his head. "You're like, amazing, right, but you've got magic. She didn't, and she wasn't even that hot."

"I think she did," I said softly, looking at Ashley, who nodded.

"But this was *before*," Chris pointed out.

Surprisingly, it was Markus who spoke up.

"There are tales of the Daoine Sidhe or similar fey folk in most lands," he said slowly. "In my home, there were the Moss People, the Moosfräuleins. They were said to be friendly, usually. If you were kind and respectful to them, then they would reward you. But if you crossed them? They would curse you and your family. This is old folklore, yes, but knowing the world as we do now? Knowing that there is magic elsewhere? Perhaps there was some here?"

"It would make sense," Kelly suggested, squeezing my hand. "What if they'd been alongside us all this time? You did say that the various creatures existed somewhere out there…" She gestured at the roof vaguely.

"It'd explain why so many of the names match," Aly added. "If they exist, and they've been just wandering the cosmos? Spreading tall tales and basically laughing their asses off at us?"

"You mean Amile might have been an alien?" Chris stared at Aly, grinning.

"Maybe. Now what's got you so happy?"

"Oh, nothing." He smiled at me as I shook my head slowly, mouthing *Don't you dare.*

"You didn't?" Kelly asked me, staring, and I groaned, knowing it was too late.

"I'm going to kill you, Chris." I sighed.

"Nah, he didn't. Don't worry," Chris said. "But he liked her, tried chatting her up once, and she shot him down." He lifted one hand and mimicked a plane falling from the sky. "Seriously, down in *flames!*"

"She looked at me like I was a bug when I tried to buy her a drink," I admitted. "I never so much as spoke to her again."

"Seriously, though, she refused to have anything that wasn't gold. Like, all her boy-toys had to bring her stuff. I remember hearing that she wanted sparkles from them, and they never lasted more than a few days. She hated cameras…"

"That doesn't mean she's one of these fey creatures, though," Griffiths disagreed. "Yes, she'd apparently been a strange person, but…"

"But look at this thing and think about the catwalk models," I said softly. "Some of them are just naturally hot people, men and women. But sometimes? They look so fucking weirdly 'wrong.' What if they're these?"

"You think the Daoine Sidhe have been working the catwalk in Paris?" Rhodes asked, clearly amused.

"I think there's a good chance," I said, serious. "If they are these fey folk, and they can be anything they want, use their glamour and whatever, and they're basically as shallow and self-centered as all the tales say? Why wouldn't they?"

"I don't see how they'd exist," Griffiths said after a few seconds. "Without magic, without mana, I don't think they could do all of this. And if we didn't have it before…"

"Maybe we did," I whispered, staring at the screen. "Maybe we just had so little that it was shit. Like how certain areas have loads of mana now, and others have fuck all, maybe this is the same. Maybe those places had a tiny bit before, and now they've just got masses more? Like the stream of mana was always here, but there was a dam built somewhere upstream. The aliens tore the dam down and now we're here?"

"It's possible, but regardless…" Rhodes shrugged. "Do you think these creatures could be trusted to work with us?"

"The wild ones?" I snorted back a laugh. "If Amile was one of them and even a fraction of the tales are true, fuck no. If you were having a heart attack, she's the kind of person who'd be rifling your pockets because you were dead soon anyway, so she might as well help herself."

"There is a kind of cold logic to that, but yes, I agree." John spoke for the first time in a while. "If it's the same person, then I know exactly who you mean. There was a young lady who a few of my colleagues were suspended for. They caught her helping herself to some jewelry in a store, and instead of arresting her, they let her go."

"They just…let her go?"

"Yeah, basically." He nodded. "There were cameras farther down from the shop that caught them going in, them coming out and getting in their van and driving off. They both denied having ever been there, but the footage was clear."

"Did it show her?" I asked, and he nodded.

"It did, but we couldn't get a positive ID, the quality was that crap. It matched a few other incidences, though. The officers caught on camera ended up responding to an emergency 'all officers' call, and the union used that and the footage to show that they were distracted and worried about their friend rather than a thief. They both swore blind off the record it never happened; they watched the recording and swore it was a fake. It never made any sense, but maybe…" He sighed, sitting back. "There's a couple of people high up in the force who tend to turn up when shit like this happens. They have a word, and the case is quietly closed. No muss, no fuss."

"Weird. Well, it's possible, I guess." I frowned, before dismissing it as something to ask about another time. "Now, we're getting new species with each level of core. We didn't bother to check the new creatures when we went from Iron to Steel—frankly, we were too busy—but looking at it, we've now got Harpies, who are apparently dicks. Three types of Fey, who are apparently all dicks, and the Scepiniir, who look awesome, but are apparently 'proud warriors,' whatever the fuck that means."

It was true. Where most of the images were basic—the goblin, for example, showed a pathetic little fucker that I half expected to start sniffing its finger at any second—the common Scepiniir looked as if it'd murder us all given half a chance.

It was a lion—or tiger-man, complete with the mane and built like he should be fighting minotaurs and bench-pressing small buildings. He was dressed in simple clothes, where most of the various creatures that could be summoned normally were naked, and I could summon four of them per "hut," whatever that was.

Focusing on the word, I got a pop-up informing me that the Scepiniir required a communal "hut" and that the designs were included with the Scepiniir. I looked it over and couldn't help but whistle.

The hut was ten meters on a side, with a fucking private whirlpool and half a dozen things that looked to be a cross between a torture rack or a sex toy. I had to assume they were for personal cleaning or massages or whatever, because I didn't want the mental images.

The hut was a massive luxurious construction that had specific temperature controls and all sorts of contraptions, making me grunt and dismiss the fuckers out of hand.

If all the other species had given their approval to use their "essence" or design or whatever because they were facing possible annihilation, and these guys had given it only on terms of the luxuries they expected even their poor clone cousins to get?

Assholes, clearly.

"Okay, so obviously we're going to try to summon all of these at some point," I said, rubbing my chin and trying to be an adult and to not stick my fingers up at the list of rules and regs.

"Which ones?" Sarah asked, and I sighed.

"Frankly, I don't see a use for most of them, but we'll summon them all and see what we get."

"And the goblins and so on?" Aly asked.

"Research," I said decisively. "We need to get the entire set up to advanced, and quickly. I know most are common, so that won't be a quick process."

"It'll be expensive," she agreed absently, searching through screens. "Okay, got it. The goblins are the same as the kobolds, ten thousand mana to go from common to uncommon…so that's no stress. But from uncommon to advanced is two hundred and fifty thousand. Do you just want them…?"

"No," I said after a few seconds' thought. "The impai to advanced as well, and…" I wrestled with myself for a minute, then sighed. "The orcs to uncommon. I'm not going all the way to advanced, not until we damn well know we can control them."

"Anything else?"

"We'll check out the other species first, print a few up and see if there's an actual use for them. But I do want the ghasts up to advanced."

"Those things?" Mike asked, surprised.

"Hell yes," Kelly said. "You didn't see how well they took down the asuras. If it wasn't for the asuras being linked to the queen and her adjusting tactics on the fly? We'd have won easily."

"Okay, but are they intelligent?" He tapped his coffee cup on the table. "Will they do as we tell them? If I end up away from the dungeon's influence, I trust the kobolds would keep going as we'd trained them. The goblins? Maybe. Those creatures?"

"You're worried they'd go feral?" I asked, and he nodded.

"It's a valid concern." Griffiths shifted on his seat, making himself more comfortable. "If we're out, away from you and the dungeon's influence, these are literally described as monsters. I'd not be comfortable with them as allies, put it that way."

"Harpies are the same," I agreed, nodding. "The way it's mentioned, the harpies and ghasts are evil, basically; the impai are more of little dipshits, and the goblins are well, goblins."

"I'd say we focus on the goblins, see how they do for now," Aly suggested. "We've got a lot to be working on, after all."

"What about the ship?" Patrick suddenly blurted, and we all looked at him. "Sorry guys, but that was a massive focus a few days ago. And yeah, getting the dungeon back on its feet is a priority over that, but…"

"But we need to recover it," I agreed. "That and actually deal with the asuras Green Queen. Okay, the ship was dumped in the hospital when it all kicked off. I don't know why it got taken there, if it was part of some plan or not, but the asuras identified it as being there. Once this meeting is over—"

"Tomorrow," Kelly interrupted. "Please, Matt. You've been throwing the power of the gods around and you've not slept unless you've been unconscious for days. Trust me—either send someone else, or wait until tomorrow."

"I can take a small team," Griffiths volunteered, and I hesitated, knowing damn well he wanted to poke around inside it.

I knew it, but he'd earned my trust and I needed to show that.

"Okay. It's in the hospital, that's all I know. Take the trikes and a small team. Did we recover much ammo from the assholes who had the green asuras captive?"

"Some. They definitely hit a transport convoy. Too much ammunition for them to have it any other way."

"Sorry, mate." For them to be using so much army gear, it had to have been an army transport, and that meant a lot of possible friends of his and Mike's were laid cold in the mud somewhere.

"It is what it is," he said philosophically. "The amount of ammunition they had, I was getting concerned they'd taken the battalion headquarters down, to be honest. Seeing that it's intact on here? It makes it less likely at least."

"Okay, do you have enough ammunition for this? Considering any survivors might be holed up there?"

"Matt, they're professional soldiers. If there are local scumbags hiding there with guns? Believe me, they'll be back with more ammo than they left with." Mike smiled.

"Fair enough. 'Make it so.'" I waved my hand dramatically and grinned at the wave of groans that I got for that. "Ah, you're no fun. Okay, so we've got a rough plan in place for the dungeon creatures. I'll sit with Aly after this, and we'll go through the research screens more in-depth, just because I know it'll be boring as hell for most of you fuckers."

"Oh, thank you God…" Chris muttered, deliberately loud enough for everyone to hear.

"And while we're doing that"—I ignored Chris—"and Griffiths and his team are retrieving the ship, does anyone else have anything they need to raise?"

"Crafting," Finn said firmly.

"Go on?" I looked at him.

"Your hunch about Tim, the Blacksmith, was right." Finn grinned; he'd clearly been looking forward to telling me this. "He spent the full forty-eight hours trying to improve his affinity to Metal, and by the end of it, he'd gone from fifty-seven to seventy-three. It took much longer for each point than the last, but he did it."

"That's a hell of a jump," Aly said, stunned. "I mean, if he managed that much in two days…"

"Each point increase costs more time than the last to gain," I reminded her, before taking a deep breath. "Okay, this is more important than I thought. Ramnik, you and Dante will want to be in on this, Finn obviously, and anyone else is welcome to stay. But if you need to leave and get on with things? This is as good a chance for you to go as you're going to get."

"One quick point, then I'll take the opportunity and escape," John said, even as Jo settled back, clearly getting comfy for this discussion.

"Go for it," I said, nodding.

"One enterprising young man found a work-around, and prior to the dungeon shutdown, had started up his own drug trade," John said candidly. "I need an official ruling on the law of the dungeon with regard to drugs. He's selling them to people, and considering he's literally printing them for free, and getting them hooked…I know my feelings but…"

"What drugs?"

"Hard ones," John said flatly. "He's somehow managed to get the dungeon to accept a certain white powder as 'sugar substitute' and is able to create it by the kilo, then he's using it to set himself up as a drug kingpin. People who had been, by necessity, facing their own demons and were getting over their addictions, are now sliding back, especially when he's offering it on 'credit' for some."

"Credit?" My heart sunk.

"Let's just say that young, attractive ladies have other means of paying their debt to him, and to his friends. It's not been used, as far as I know, but he's offering it, and trying to set himself up as a criminal mastermind. He was making a good start on taking over the underside of the park, when they were all kicked out of the system. Once he's back in? I expect him to be moving quickly."

"Okay, official ruling time. I'm fine with weed. Don't like it much myself, don't give a shit about people who use it, so long as they don't endanger anyone else. They want to have it? Fine. We'll see if we can get it refined a bit, though…less mental issues and more fun times. We treat it as booze: they fuck up and someone gets hurt because they're drunk or stoned? They're punished.

"Coke and more? The hard shit? Banned. I know some people can function well on it, and hell, I've done plenty over the years…" I saw the look on his face and went on quickly. "But I don't think that it's a good idea in the apocalypse," I finished lamely.

"And punishment?" he asked.

"For using, as long as nobody has been hurt and so on, then a punishment detail. They work their arse off for a week per incidence." I looked over at Griffiths, Mike, and Rhodes, who'd stood ready to leave when John had raised this point. "I'm thinking army-style punishment: heavy exercise, long hours, screaming drill instructor…all that good shit."

"Works for me," Griffiths said. "It might even get us some more recruits. But I'd suggest two tiers. First is a one-week punishment drill; second offense and any from then on are a month sentenced to full army life. First week is them working their ass off drill-style, the second week is them integrating into a unit, and third and fourth are serving with them, sentry duty and more. They'll get a taste of the army. It'll leave them with more respect for the soldiers and like I said, hopefully we'll get some recruits out of it as well."

"There we go," I agreed.

"And for the enterprising dealer?"

"He knows it's wrong, and he's trying to set himself up as a pimp, taking advantage of others as well," I said. "Banishment."

"I'll take care of it." John nodded. "Bag of crap supplies and boot up the arse?"

"Definitely. Make it public as well. And I'll find the loophole in the system and erase it."

"Will do."

"Who was it?" I asked, wondering whether it was anyone I'd met before.

"A kid called Flash Drake…His parents mustn't have liked him much to call him that." John shook his head. "Naming him something like that was never going to be fun for a young lad."

"He wasn't. His parents called him Francis," Dante muttered, looking pissed.

"Oh?" John looked over. "You know him?"

I noted the way Ashley took Dante's hand and the look on Dante's face, before jerking as Kelly started to laugh.

"The guy from the bridge?" she asked, and he nodded after a second, the corner of his mouth quirking into a smile.

"What's this?" I asked.

"When we were coming to help, and Dante first joined us, you remember that a load of people came along and refused to fight? They just fucked off?" Kelly asked.

"Yeah?" I agreed, frowning.

"Well, Flash was one of them, a right little shit, and he stole the club Dante made." Kelly smiled. "Dante was one of a handful of people who stayed, but Starr took a liking to him, and when Flash started waving his club and being an arse, Starr hit him with a spell, made him all confused and sick. He ended up smacking himself in the face with the club."

"Well, no loss there then!" I said. "If he's that much of a dickhead, we're better off without him. And, for the record, Dante?"

"Yeah?" He straightened up.

"Thank you again. You're a damn brave man, and I'm glad you're one of us." It was true, but seeing the effect the words had on him? It was worth it.

"Thank you." He beamed.

"Right. I'll deal with that kid, and let you all get on with things," John said, kissing Jo, then moving around the table.

Several of the others left.

Kelly kissed my cheek and spoke quietly. "I'll be here, but I'm going to start granting people access again. So if you need me, nudge me. I'll try to pay attention, but people need to know the dungeon is open for business again. Then I'll find that loophole, if you want?"

"Yes, please." I nodded, smiling my thanks to her, seeing the way she sat back in her chair, curling her legs up under her and summoning another cup of steaming hot chocolate. She took a sip, then set it down with a clink, her eyes drifting out of focus as she pulled up screens, sinking into the dungeon sense.

Clarissa stayed, but Markus left. Becky, Chris, and Jo stayed, as did Patrick and Finn, Dante, Ashley, and Ramnik. Mike, Sarah, Griffiths, and Rhodes left, Aly promising to go over the details with Mike and the others later if they wanted.

Now that the room had shrunk a little, we all got fresh drinks, as Finn, who'd clearly been desperate to spread the good news, started to speak.

"So, Matt had the idea that our affinities might be more meaningful than we knew." He looked around the group. "Basically, those of us with certain affinities for things like Tim had for Metal? He was always supposed to be working with it. He's naturally clumsy, breaks stuff all the time, drops things and is crap at almost everything—"

"Sounds like the perfect guy to make sharp weapons..." Ashley quipped, blushing as I looked over at her. "Sorry."

"No, you're right." I smiled. "Basically, when I started thinking about it, I wondered why some of us are just naturally good at things. Like Chris and I had a friend Dave. He was a chef. Never measured anything in his life, just tossed stuff in a bowl when he made cakes and Yorkshire puddings and stuff. They always came out, like every goddamn time, no effort. If I tried that? Clouds of black smoke and the fire brigade ended up visiting."

"Man, I miss his cookin'," Chris muttered. "Hope he's all right."

"We'll go looking for the others soon," I assured him. The thought had been in the back of my mind for a while. "Anyway, the point was that some of us just do it without thinking; we just know how to do certain things. Is that down to a naturally occurring and unspoken affinity? Is that why we have particular skills?"

"I was always fascinated by fire," Dante admitted, and I nodded.

"Exactly. You're our very own pyromancer, and you've got the burns to prove it, I bet. Jo wanted to be a healer, and that's what she ended up as. Her Life affinity is what?" I looked over.

"Seventy-three," she said. "It's my highest by far."

"For me, it was lightning and storms," I said. "I was always fascinated by them, loved them. Now I'm working toward being a literal god of the Storms and Lightning."

"So we all focus on what we're good at naturally?" Clarissa asked, and I smiled.

"Yes and no. What I was wondering, was if we could increase our natural affinity for something by focusing on it. So for Tim, as Finn said, a clumsy as fuck Blacksmith, I set him up with a Metal converter and got him to start working on his affinities."

"And it worked?" Ashley sat forward, smiling. "It's possible to increase your affinities and learn to do something else?"

"Very much so," Finn agreed. "He's basically spent two days working his ass off to increase his affinity, and each and every point he increased it by was harder than the last. *But…*" He looked around at us all, a wide smile trying to break out as he forced himself to be serious.

"It worked. Like, it really worked. The spears he'd been making were shit, let's be clear. He was trying to improve on the design we had, working to learn a little and to gradually improve, but understanding that what he was making was essentially a shitty copy."

"And?" I asked.

"And his latest one is nearly as good as the ones you produce through the dungeon." Finn grinned. "For those of you who haven't been involved in this, the issue is that the dungeon makes things the same every time. There's never a variation. The spear is a spear—it's not bad, but it's not good either. A spear that a master craftsman could make would be many times better than the basic one that the dungeon can produce."

"I tried," Aly muttered, and Finn shook his head quickly.

"That's not to say your work wasn't good, Aly, but you make a hundred things a day; you can't really focus on making this one perfect. If Tim spends a week on something, though? He can improve it noticeably. The spear he makes will be much better than the standard one."

"That's all great and all, but we're talking about making rail guns." Chris shook his head. "Sorry, Finn, mate, but I don't think him spending a week making a spear is much use if, by the time that's done, we've already moved up in the tech levels and the spear is obsolete."

"True, but the things he's learned?" Finn countered. "He can use that knowledge to make improvements to the next weapon!"

"Also, we need spears still, for now at least," I agreed. "So it worked? He's noticeably better as a Blacksmith from this?"

"Definitely." Finn nodded. "He's amazed by the change, and now I've got to put up with constant pestering from the others. They all want converters, and they're bugging him to teach them to work on their affinities, which slows him down in crafting as well."

"Well, he can put up with that," I muttered, my mind already miles away as I thought quickly. "Okay, we were always going to be working on the crafting stations, weren't we…"

"We need to upgrade them, and the gathering facilities," Aly said pointedly. "The crafting facilities as they are…well, they're botched-together shite."

I looked at her in surprise at the way she'd said it. Usually she was reasonably subtle.

"We've got the ability to make the higher-tier crafting setup," she clarified. "But we've been so busy with everything else, and you didn't have a need for it until now. We've done the research on both the common and uncommon crafting facilities, but this is where we come across the first problem."

As Aly spoke, she drew up the systems before us, flashing through the research system until she came to the section she wanted.

Dungeon Specialist Structures are sub-divided into the following forms, with each area being further researchable, and gaining improvable bonuses.

1) **Production***:* To produce any item entirely from mana is a costly endeavor. Instead, producing smaller, more specialized production facilities, that in turn can drive larger and more generalized facilities, is the accepted norm.

   Completed:
   - Level two: Common Gathering Facility.
   - Level three: Uncommon Crafting Facility.

   Currently available for research:
   - Uncommon Gathering Facility (3)
   - Advanced Crafting Facility (4)
   - Individual Basic Crafting Facility (Specialized) (1)

2) **Agriculture**: In order to maintain advanced populations, dungeons would be required to either entirely produce the needed sustenance on site, loot the required items, or turn the full production of sustenance products over to the mana collectors. The accepted norm is to produce mana-enhanced farming facilities.

   Completed:
   - Level one: Basic Farm (1)

   Currently available for research:
   - Common Farm (2)

3) **Detection**: Any location that includes an active Dungeon is by necessity a dangerous one. Producing basic sensors to increase the detection range, as well as the information available is common practice.

   Completed:
   - Level one: Basic Sensors (1)
   - Basic Sensors Visual Upgrade (1)

   Currently available for research:
   - Common Sensors (2)
   - Visual Upgrade (2)
   - Seismic Sensors (1)

Further research will unlock greater detection systems…

4) **Capacity:** All Dungeon creatures require Control Points to enable them to function as living creatures; however, without the entire levelling system of the Host/Fairy/Dungeon Lord dedicated to the Dungeon's staffing needs, this would result in considerably smaller facilities. Instead, the accepted method is to create Control Capacity Generators. These specialist facilities will increase the control limit of your Dungeon.

Completed:
- Level one: Basic Control Capacity Generator (BCCP) (1)

Currently available for research:
- Common Control Capacity Generator (CCCP) (2)

BEWARE

Should a Control Capacity Generator be destroyed and the Dungeon be taken under the current maximum threshold for Control Points, the excess creatures will be terminated at random.

5) **Lure:** Certain areas become overrun by pest, vermin, and monsters. In order to deal with these unwanted intruders, a Lure can be set, drawing the attention of all those inside its radius, enabling traps and termination facilities to be used efficiently.

Currently available:
- Basic Lure (1)

6) **Medical Facility:** The simple truth is that life in a Dungeon environment can be dangerous, so a simple solution to this is a medical facility. Even at its most basic level, the Medical Facility increases healing speed inside its AOE (Area of Effect) by a minimum of 10%, as well as increasing the speed at which medical staff gain levels and Experience and finally, removing all biological infections.

Note*:* Higher levels of the Medical Facilities can be used to upgrade/stabilize/remove nanite systems.

Completed:
- Level one: Basic Medical Facility (1)

Currently available for research:
- Common Medical Facility

I read the details over, nodding at the simple layout I remembered.

"Okay, so we've got the uncommon crafting facility there as an option. What's the problem?" Aly sighed and looked at Finn. "What?" I asked, confused.

"Matt, I've been working laid on a sofa most of the time, because we've not got the right facilities. These are customizable to a certain degree, but the basic version? The one that it starts at? It's a fucking table, basically."

"Okay…"

"How many films have you seen where people forge a sword at a table?" Aly asked. "Or they blow glass while sitting on a sofa with a table to work on? Or they—"

"Okay, I'm getting that tables are bad, I get that, but seriously, what…?"

"They're normal tables, Matt," Finn explained. "Like seriously, most of the gear you saw in the crafting 'hall'?"

I nodded.

"We *made* that. That's not what the crafting setup provided. They're tables and chairs we nicked from the pile of crap that was getting destroyed."

"Wait, you mean…?" I finally saw their point, and almost facepalmed. "Fuck's sake…by tables you mean, the system gave you a fucking table and left you to it?"

"Some very basic tools, and that's it," Finn agreed, pleased I was finally understanding.

"But we can make it at uncommon level…You're telling me it's shit?"

"No." Aly shook her head. "We only built the basic version. If we replace it with the uncommon? It should be a massive upgrade, but there's a problem."

"When is there *not* a fucking problem?" I growled, putting my face in my hands, my elbows resting on the table. "Go on," I ordered, my voice muffled. "I'm ready."

"The gear that a Glassblower or a Blacksmith needs can be set up together, or an Alchemist and a Herbalist, but you put a Leatherworker or Clothier next to a Glassblower and Blacksmith? There's going to be fights."

"Why?" I asked, staring out between my fingers at Finn.

"Because basically they fucking stink." He shook his head. "Yeah, leatherworkers used to, I mean they used literal piss to tan the hides, and thank fuck we don't need to do that, but they fill the room with smoke. You think anyone wants to wear gear that reeks of hot sweat and smoke?"

"It's not just that," Aly said quickly, leaning in. "Stray sparks, the backwash of heat, the smoke in the air…all these things cause issues and damage to others' projects. That's something that you can adjust. I've looked over the uncommon setup, and it provides solutions to all of that, but…"

She looked at me, and I nodded I was ready for the bad news.

"But…it's a limited functionality, and it has to be set up when the facility is constructed." Aly took a deep breath, then smiled. "The solution, though, is simple. We research the other facilities, and we build a unique one for each, or we make multiple uncommon ones."

"Go on."

"We build the uncommon facility, and we select the layout for clothing, leatherwork, and general. I know it sounds like a cop-out, but we set it up that way. Then we build a separate facility, a second crafting hall, but dedicated to Armorers, Mechanists, and Blacksmiths…"

"And the Glassblowers," Finn added in, and Aly nodded, shooting him a thumbs-up.

"Thanks, Finn. Okay they all need heat and extraction, as well as naturally being the kind of creators who can help one another. We make them their own section, and then we make a third one, that specializes in Alchemy, Herbalism, and Cooking."

"Which is more efficient?" I asked after a few seconds thought, and Aly smiled.

"That's kinda the issue."

"Fuck."

"The uncommon crafting facility is definitely the best, most efficient way to set these all up. We need to know what each requires, so we need to research at least the common one of each, then we set the uncommon facilities with those systems in place. If we don't specify? We end up with the most general crafting setup possible."

"And it's shit," Finn said firmly.

"Double fuck," I muttered. "You're telling me we need to research all of them before we can really do anything?"

"No. We can do things straightaway, but it'd be a waste. Look, trust me on this, Matt—we need at least the common version of each working out and as soon as possible. I've looked over the options, and there's so much we've ignored because we've been so busy."

"Okay, how much is it going to cost?" I saw the winces on their faces.

"Fifty-five thousand mana," Aly said. "Five for the basic, fifty for the common."

"Oh." I relaxed slightly. "That's not so b—"

"Each."

"Fuck."

CHAPTER EIGHT

An hour later, I was banging my head on the table before me.

"So let me get this right. Before we can build a better crafting facility, which we need to realistically train any new crafters, and especially for making things like the focal orb—which we need for teaching mages and so on much easier—we have to research every goddamn single crafting facility up to common at least?"

"Not all of them," Finn said cheerfully, and when I glowered at him, he grinned even more. "Only the ones we want to use."

"Which do we want?" I asked, and Aly counted them off on her fingers.

"Blacksmithing, Glassblowing, Herbalism, Alchemist, Leatherworker, Armorer, Mechanist, Arcanist, Clothier, Jeweler, Weaver, Tinker, Potter, and Cook."

"You're fucking kidding, right?" I glared at Aly and Finn. "Why the hell do we need all of those?"

"We'll need all of them and more," Aly said definitively. "Blacksmiths will create anything in metal of course, and Tinkers, Armorers, Mechanists, and Jewelers will all sort of share the same spaces. Oh, and Glassblowers."

"And the rest?"

"The problem is that everyone will do a little of other people's jobs, and we can get by with that, but the real technical roles?" Aly said. "They need somewhere to work, and these will need research systems built into it as well. Think about the rail guns I've been making. They're test bed systems. I can make them, and the system says they *should* work…but if we can get someone who's good at making these kinds of things? They can upgrade the individual systems, replace them one by one, working in concert with the Blacksmith, the Tinkers— hell, maybe the Glassblowers can make shit, I don't know. But the thing I do know is that the most I can make is the basic version."

"You can research higher levels, right?" I asked, and she nodded.

"We can. It'll take a hell of a lot longer, and the end product will be good, but it'll never be great. Imagine we get a Gunsmith to work in there, one of the guys Mike talks about…the army armorers. People who live and breathe guns. They could take a normal rifle, replace each part with a section that was a masterpiece of crafting, and create a rifle that could practically kill God."

"Then we could reproduce that," Finn pointed out. "Look at your armor. It's great and all, but with some skilled crafters, I could make you something that would blow your mind. We need to be sensible about this."

"And nothing can be done until we get these things ready?" I sighed in relief as Aly shook her head.

"No, we can bumble along as things stand, but we need all of these things, Matt. We need a plan for what we upgrade and when, because the last month all we've done is run from fire to fire. Yes, we've been fighting every day, we've been saving lives, but now we're at a place where we can capitalize on this."

"Okay…" I groaned, scrubbing at my face with both hands. "We need to do this right, I know. We're getting what, eighty-five thousand mana a day, thereabouts?"

"Near enough." Aly shrugged. "It's a little higher. The conduits are collecting mana from people in the park and visitors here, I think, as we're at eighty-seven thousand, one hundred and…twelve currently, but that peaks and dips."

"Okay, where are we with conduit research?"

"Each level of the core has its own level for them," she reminded me, pulling up the relevant details, and nodding. "There. We're at zero for this level, out of six levels. Basic, as it is right now, gives us five points per conduit. There's—"

She stared at the number of conduits, before turning her shocked expression at me, making me feel as if I'd just been taken under the sights of a destroyer's main gun.

"Matt. An explanation please?" she said calmly.

It was that "fun" calm that was just a hair off screaming and beating people with something, so I moved to answer quickly.

"You know how we couldn't figure out why the mana intake was higher?" I asked her. "Well, I figured it out!"

"And it's because…?" she asked slowly, clearly waiting for me.

"You remember the core fragment we got from the Gateshead dungeon, and how we didn't want to use it for most things because it was basically dodgy as fuck?"

"It'd been boosted over and over through blood sacrifices, so yes."

"Well, I didn't like the other options we got with it, but the last one was to basically break the core fragment down into its high-tech materials and use that to boost the conduits." I smiled winningly.

"I had no idea it'd make so many, but it sent hundreds out, worming around the area. Thing is, it took ages to come online, so I'd forgotten all about it. Then, when I went looking? Oh, hell yeah."

"Okay…" Aly said, nodding. "Well, that explains why the conduit research cost is so high. Level one is a hundred thousand mana."

"Yeah, but if I'm right? It'd take us from five points per conduit, which is…uh…Five points times two hundred and twenty-eight mana…"

"It's twenty-seven thousand, three hundred, and sixty mana a day, or one thousand, one hundred, and forty mana an hour." Aly ran the numbers faster than I could.

"Right! So, it went to five last time. Working it out quickly, if it went to ten next? Doubling or so each time?"

"A little out—it went from zero point five, to zero point seven-five, to one point five, then two point two-five, then five."

"Okay, so it might be a little more, or a little less than double, but if it hits ten points per level? That's more than fifty thousand points a day. That gives us a single level of the crafting we need *per day*."

"And we'd still have the needed mana from the converters," Aly agreed, nodding. "Okay, so how many are we doing? Do we do this one at a hundred thousand and then what?"

"We've got…twelve thousand mana and change in the dungeon's storage at the minute," I pointed out. "We need to get the park working again. As it is, it'll be at least a day to get that sorted out. But as soon as it is? I think we need to look at the next level of mana converters. What's the cost of that now?"

"Two hundred and fifty thousand." She winced. "Damn, we could nearly work out five of the…"

"We could, but if it doubles the mana that the converters are pulling in?" Aly added.

"Then that's another fifty thousand a day at least," I agreed, sighing. "Okay, do it. Spend the mana as we need it. Keep ten thousand in the tank at all times, just in case, though, please. People are going to go a bit wild when they can summon any food and drink they want today. Let them enjoy it, but tomorrow we're back to work."

"That works," Aly agreed. "So, to be clear, we've got a plan for the mana absorption conduits first, then the converters. Once they're done, I recommend we start producing the forge setup. Maybe we redo a building as the crafting hall? Build the forge on the ground floor?"

"I'd like to suggest something, if you don't mind?" Ashley lifted a hand almost like she was at school. Both Aly and I looked at her, grinning, and she lowered it sheepishly.

"Go on," I said, still smiling.

"How about we set up the Herbalist and Alchemist together, and next to the farms?" She shrugged. "The farms aren't producing much in the way of food at the minute, but the occasional herbs I've found I need? They're pretty busy with them right now."

"How's that going?" I asked, knowing damn well that the farms we were using were the most basic entry-level ones.

"They're growing well," she said. "The real issue is that I've not got a clue what the ingredients I need are, so we're basically growing a load of weeds and I'm trying to make potions, all with pretty low levels of success, if any at all."

"Shit," I muttered, nodding as I saw the problem. First, Ashley was a Courtesan, so yeah, she'd gotten a little information when it came to Alchemy, but that was it. Secondly, we were all from the city. There were a few farmers mixed in amongst us all, but they were used to producing rapeseed oil and wheat when I'd spoken to them.

We needed a damn Herbalist. The Herbalist could then provide herbs to the Alchemy team, who could experiment and learn as they went.

We were back to the whole research and development side. We needed to find the herbs, but until we knew what was an herb and what was a weed—when it came to Alchemy, anyway—we were back to trial and error.

Unless…

"Ashley, have you got any herbs with you?" I asked, and she frowned, shaking her head. "Damn. Okay, are the herbs you've been using in the cooking system?"

"Some of them are," she agreed. "Black mint, for example, is—"

"Black mint." I nodded. "Perfect." I reached out a hand and used the dungeon to summon the mint to me. A small sprig appeared in my right hand.

I grinned at it, then focused, and cast Examine.

Black Mint	Herb
This common ingredient smells pleasant and offers a light and refreshing infusion to anything it is added to. **Known Alchemical Uses:** 1) ???? 2) ???? 3) ???? 4) ????	
Strength: 1:10	**Quality**: Poor

"Fuck yes!" I exulted. "Okay, so I can examine this. I don't know what you use it for, beyond Alchemy, obviously, but I can see that it's an ingredient and that it has four alchemical uses."

"It's used in healing potions," Ashley said, and I checked the details, casting the spell again and nodding.

"It's showing that now as a use," I agreed. "Okay, so what we need to do is hammer our way through the ingredients, see what we can find, and make sure it's not just a case of everything is an ingredient or whatever."

I summoned a half dozen different ingredients from the kitchen's lists, finding that although they were all listed as ingredients, only two of them were marked as having alchemical uses.

Garlic	Herb
This common ingredient smells strongly, and is often a popular addition to meals. **Known Alchemical Uses:** 1) ???? 2) ???? 3) ???? 4) ????	
Strength: 3:10	**Quality**: Average

Nutmeg	Herb
This common ingredient smells strongly, and is often a popular addition to drinks, occasionally to make an abomination that includes pumpkin, cloves, and cinnamon. **Known Alchemical Uses:** 1) ???? 2) ???? 3) ???? 4) ????	
Strength: 2:10	**Quality**: Poor

I grinned reading the last one, feeling that at least there was another upside to the damn end of the world: no more pumpkin-spiced fucking lattes.

I hated those things. As soon as they appeared, my wait in a coffee shop for a perfectly reasonably chai tea latte went from a few minutes to half a bloody hour as random people filled the air with so much perfume and high-pitched giggling that I ended up having to avoid my usual haunts for an entire season.

"Okay, all three of these are ingredients…Did you know that?" I asked Ashley, and she shook her head.

"I know about the garlic and the black mint, not the nutmeg, but it makes sense. I'll need to try to work with cloves and cinnamon—"

"And pumpkin?" I asked her, my heart dipping.

"Oh, good God no. I do have standards." She shook her head firmly. "No fluffy boots, no big fluffy coats, and no fake fingernails ever again. Pumpkin-spiced lattes can be one of the casualties of the apocalypse."

"Oh, thank G—" I started, as Dante spoke up.

"Damn, I always loved them," he murmured, looking off into space as I glared at him in disgust.

I might hate racists with a passion, I might be willing to die to defend the innocent, but the eternal damnation of pumpkin-spiced lattes and the right to take the piss out of gingers were rights I'd never relinquish.

"Okay, so we're going to work on the research first, get both the conduits and converters upgraded to pull in more mana, and then work on researching the various designs we need. We've already got the Alchemist setup done, but not the Herbalist. So if we do that first, then we can build the uncommon Herbalist and Alchemy sections together."

I nodded to Ashley, who grinned widely, obviously loving the idea of the upgraded systems she'd have access to.

"You want it next to the farms?" I asked, and she nodded quickly.

"It just makes sense. That way, we can grow the herbs, make changes, and even nip out into the farm and grab more of something when we need it."

"Okay, well, that works," I agreed. "You don't have any issues with kobolds, do you?" I stared into the distance as I searched through the dungeon, going floor by floor and building by building.

"No, why?" she asked, and I smiled to myself as I found him.

I'd been worried that Starr had been killed, but apparently not. He sat, legs folded under him, by Beta's side. The pair of them looked over a small collection of stones in the tiny graveyard behind the old cathedral.

I winced, seeing that once again most of her team had been lost, and that Beta was mourning them.

"Starr," I said simply. "I was worried that we'd lost the kobold shaman, but he's with Beta. I can't see the rest of the team, though…"

"They were lost, all of them," Jo said sadly. "I managed to save Starr, but the others were killed outside when the Red Queen turned up. Starr was badly hurt, but I was lucky to save him."

"Thank you," I said, meaning it. "They've gone through the wringer of late, losing people left and right."

"Starr can help me?" Ashley interrupted, and I nodded, smiling.

"I hope so. He's made a few rudimentary potions of his own, and that's without access to the equipment. I think between you, you'll be able to make some progress."

"That would be wonderful," Ashley agreed but frowned, clearly getting her head around working on Alchemy with a kobold that couldn't speak.

"Got it!" Kelly interrupted, sitting upright and making everyone jump. "What did I miss?"

"Starr is alive, and I'm going to send him to work with Ashley, making potions." I got a frozen stare for a second as Kelly caught up, before she nodded slowly.

"I can see that working, yeah. What about Beta?"

"What about her?"

"She's lost almost all of her team, and now you're taking her only surviving member to work on potions. What about her? Does she get a choice? Is she fighting forever? An NCO?"

"I…I had been planning on offering her any trade she wanted, or possibly adding her to my personal team—we need to sort that out. But the NCO slot might be a better idea."

"Talk to her and see if she wants to do it, then see where you end up," Kelly suggested.

"I will," I promised. "Okay, you wanted the alchemy area in the same building as the farms, and that works well. They're on the roof and the top floor of the training dungeon. What we need to do is change the layout of the dungeon up a little more. We've got the 'main' dungeon over at the civic center now, so I think we need to stick with that. We'll use that as our primary training dungeon and keep this one as a low-level trainer. Use it to introduce our people to combat."

"And the other one for advanced?" Kelly suggested, getting a nod from me.

"If we stock the other one with the best we have, disposable obviously, we open it to anyone who wants to try it from our teams. Building things like the various loot generators was always because it'd increase the value of the loot that the various creatures dropped. Now, for whatever reason, the dungeon creatures don't drop loot outside of the dungeon when they're killed. When they're inside, they usually do. They didn't during the battle for the civic center, but I'm going to put that down to the dungeon failing and breaking, essentially."

"That's a point." Dante sat up. "There's a lot of people who want to get practice in, and the only way we can really grow at the minute is in fighting. That's been useful so far, because, let's admit it, there's been plenty of people for us to fight. But if we can use the dungeon regularly? That'd really help us."

"It will. Whatever the issue was with the loot drops, we need to fix it, because we need to start earning spellbooks and shit," I clarified, looking around. "We've already confirmed that through meditation we can increase our affinities, and I'm improving mine at a fairly constant rate, working on improving my Storm and Lightning powers. However, what I didn't make clear before, mainly because there was no reason to, as most people don't need to know, is that it's possible to draw directly on the mana in our cores, and through that, from the spires."

"The spires in the core?" Ramnik asked, and I nodded. "That shouldn't be possible."

"Probably not," I agreed. "I've done it twice, though, and each time only on pure mana. Important safety tip here—don't fucking do that."

"I don't think I'm emotionally ready for this," Ramnik whispered, pressing one hand over her eyes and taking a deep breath, before straightening up, rolling her hand and conjuring a full tea set into being.

"Clarissa?" She offered the older lady a cup, and Clarissa smiled, climbing to her feet and moving around the table to sit next to the young mage. The pair of them summoned biscuits and tea as everyone else refilled their drinks as well.

"So, what happened is this…" I started, before going over the basic details of souls, as we'd discussed them before, but this time, with those left in the room mainly having an understanding of the affinity system and magic, I went a lot more in-depth.

An hour later, the meeting was finally over. We had plans for the next few days, and Kelly and I were walking out of the council building, arm in arm.

"That went well," I said slowly.

"Really?" she asked. "Which bit? Where you threw the priests out, where you made it even clearer you're a god, or where you decided to redo almost everything we've been working on for the last few months?"

"Yeah," I muttered. "Okay, so maybe there were a few minor issues…"

"Matt, they're really trying to be okay with everything, you know," Kelly said softly, pulling on my arm and shaking me slightly as we walked. "I know the priest has been a bit rude, but he's old school, that's all, and we're not married. That alone is a sin in his eyes. He genuinely worries that we're going to hell for the things we've done, and he's trying to help."

"The things we've done in that bedroom…" I winked at her. "We're probably going to hell anyway."

"And we'll do a lot more." She grinned at me. "I'm feeling very neglected right now. But the point is that we need to be a little more understanding and we need to play the part a bit."

"How do you mean?"

"The Dungeon Lord, and the Mistress of the Dungeon." She smiled up at me. "We *are* the dungeon now, you obviously a lot more than me. Most people don't know who I am, beyond that I'm sleeping with you."

"They'll learn," I said. "Mainly because…" I took a deep breath, thinking things through and making sure I was sure about it, before I went on.

"Yeah?"

"I want you to run the council and more of the dungeon," I said quickly. "Start leading the groups and holding a daily meeting with them."

"But…" She frowned. "Matt, they need to see you, to understand that…"

"I'm the Dungeon Lord," I agreed, nodding. "I'm not trying to abdicate or anything, but I'm also literally a god. A baby one, but still. I'm starting to feel the edge of my powers, to see what I'm really capable of, and it's fucking terrifying."

"Are you okay?" Kelly asked, worried, and I nodded, putting my arm around her shoulders and hugging her close.

"I am," I assured her. "But, Kelly, the dungeon is what will enable us to grow as a settlement. Hell, it might be what lets us win the war. But me? As a Storm Titan? I have abilities I've never used before. I can use my soul, *literally* to forge things. I can fly and channel the storm. I somehow managed to use an evolution of one of my lowest powered spells, Lightning Bolt, to carve through the Red Queen like a hot knife through butter.

"I'm not evolving any more, because I've plateaued in my understanding. I can see the edges of things. I'm feeling an elephant's ear in the dark and deciding what the whole thing looks like from just that. I *need* to spend some time on this, and uninterrupted."

"And you want me to hold the meetings in your absence?" She looked up at me.

"Basically, yeah." I sighed. "I know it's a shitty job, and I'm sorry for that, but honestly? I need to do this. I need to work on my affinities, and I need to work on figuring out who and what I am. I've been fighting close range and far back, magic and steel, fists and feet. I need to figure out who, and what, I am," I repeated, looking at her and waiting for her to refuse and call me a lazy bastard for trying to dump the crap jobs onto her.

"Matt…" Kelly took a deep breath, nodding as if to herself. "Okay. If we're going to do this, then there need to be a few changes. And you're still going to be involved, okay? I…I can't tell you how much this means to me, that you trust me to this degree."

I blinked, convinced I had been giving her the shitty jobs. I hated the council meetings and dealing with people, but I loved her, and I trusted her with my back and my heart. How could asking her to be more publicly in charge of things mean so much to her?

"I'll prove that you can trust me, though, and that I can do this. And I'll make sure that people understand that you're the real boss."

"It's…fine?" I tried, only to have her shake her head firmly.

"No, Matt. It's the end of the world, or near enough. We're the one place that anyone can go as far as we know to have any old-world luxuries, let alone safety and a chance to really live and love. For you to name me to do all of this?" She paused, staring up at me in the cold night air. "Matt, you're giving me a lot of power, do you realize this?"

"I do," I said quickly. "Look, Kelly, I need someone to deal with all of this. I need to train. I started to with John, Markus, and Patrick awhile back. It feels like forever ago, and it was what, last week? The week before? I don't even know anymore."

"But Matt…"

"Kelly, I'm not abdicating," I repeated. "I don't think I could even if I wanted to, and I *don't* want to. I'll still be in charge of the dungeon. I'll still have the final say in everything, and the creatures of the dungeon will still be bonded to me first and foremost. I'll help with research priorities, and I'll make the decisions on how we expand.

"What will be changing is that as the dungeon grows, as more and more people join us, either I need to be a full-time administrator, and be that kind of a leader, or I can be a fighter. If my powers as a god, literally as a Storm Titan, are as rare and important as they seem? Then I have to focus on them. I have to learn more and evolve."

I paused, rubbing at my mouth as I thought, trying to make her understand.

"I keep making little steps along the path, finding out little details and realizing that I'm still at the 'baby steps' stage. I had the power to walk out of the dungeon when I woke up and just cut the Red Queen into sushi. I had no clue, though. And not only that…using it, I nearly killed myself. I tore my *soul*…"

"And now you need to actually start working on you, rather than the dungeon." She nodded. "Matt, I understand. I agree, even. I love you, I really do, and *I* know I'd never do anything that wasn't in our best interests, and that I believed was what you wanted me to do, but you need to understand, this is a *lot* of power."

"I do," I said, remembering the feeling toward the end of the fight for the civic center dungeon against the Red Queen. I'd felt lesser, demeaned almost, because I wasn't running the fight.

It'd been a fucking stupid way to feel, but I had, and it'd made me take a good hard look at myself. The dungeon was me to some degree, but the thing I knew in my heart was that I wanted the dungeon to survive more than I wanted me to do so.

That sounded stupid, even when I said it to myself, but it was true.

I might be able to turn the tide of the fight, if I could learn enough. Hell, if I could grow powerful enough, I might be able to take the orcs and more out myself. I had no fucking clue, really. What I did know was that even if I did manage to do all of that, and even survive afterward?

What humans, and hell, any other races that were here afterward, would need wasn't a living god who could set off storms whenever he felt like it. What they needed was the dungeon to provide medicine, food, alcohol, and fucking hot water and showers.

"I promise you, Kelly. I know what I'm asking. Please, run the council meetings and more, help me and give me the time I need."

She grinned as if I'd given her a diamond necklace, or maybe a pearl one. She stood on her tiptoes, and I lowered my head, kissing her deeply.

"Okay…" she said a few seconds later, a bit breathlessly. "In that case, you need to be seen more by your people, if you're not going to attend the meetings. You need to still be here, and to be seen improving and growing. All the stuff with the magic, like earlier on when you're literally summoning giant thunderstorms?"

"Yeah?"

"Do it more."

"You usually tell me not to."

"This is different. If you're not going to be running all the dungeon, and are *finally* accepting that you need to be seen as the hero we all know you are? You need to be doing things like that."

"Okay…well, I'll be experimenting with magic, so, you know, generally I'm just trying to learn when I do the shit you all complain about. Or I'm getting my ass kicked, so we'll see what happens."

"That's fine." Kelly smiled. "Right then…it's cold and it's dark, but we need some food, and you need to work on the core, is that right?"

"Yeah, some of my mana has regenerated. It's been hours. I can go and use that, then meet you for food?"

"Food and then the pool," Kelly said.

"The pool?" I asked, surprised.

"Yes, you know, you might not have noticed it, but that tiny pool..." Kelly sighed, rolling her eyes and pointing to the massive outdoor pool that was making a significant difference to the local area, there was that much of a temperature differential.

It'd been a reward, a plan for the dungeon that Kelly wouldn't explain beyond that it was useful as an outdoor pool for everyone to relax. It clearly hadn't been intended as one originally, or she would have just said that, but regardless, it was nice.

It was essentially a giant outdoor pool that had hotter and colder areas, differing depths, areas with cushioning and more. It was also in the middle of the dungeon area. So unless something flew in from above, it was totally secure thanks to how high the walls were on all sides.

Kelly and Aly had added little touches like changing rooms near to the pool, and covered walkways leading from the accommodation and main dungeon building to and from the pool. That meant that people were getting used to the idea gradually, and frequently changed in their room and walked down to the pool in dressing robes.

It was still also new enough that it was a bit weird, though. It was Newcastle, after all: it was cold enough to freeze a witch's tit in winter, and basically rained for fun from September till March. You didn't have an outdoor pool here, mainly because you'd freeze when you tried it, and most likely you'd go out to find unidentified animals floating in it, random shits and possibly a drunk who'd mistaken your private hot tub for his bath and was scrubbing himself in ways that would haunt you forever.

That meant that the only time that most people here had experienced outdoor pools was in nice hot countries when they were on holiday—and drinking constantly—or when they'd gone somewhere like a private cabin in the woods for a weekend of sex-filled shenanigans.

These little details meant there was a hell of a good chance that there would be a baby boom soon, as people were using it as a place to meet outside of surviving, working, and fighting.

They were bringing alcohol, and a number had already been given warnings that it was a pool, not a private sex pond, and that if they didn't put their clothes back on, they were banned.

We'd not ban anyone permanently, not for consensual fun, but they didn't know that, and there were a lot of older people and several small children who spent a lot of time in there.

An hour later, I was merrily hanging up my robe on a hook, not really paying attention to which one it was, as I'd just summon another if I needed to, before wading out into the pool.

I made it a few feet, before cursing, remembering that I needed to not be so cavalier about using the dungeon's abilities all the time, then I promptly forgot about it.

It was late—hell, it was after midnight now—and the rain was a steady drum on the surface. Wisps of steam clouded the air, and I groaned at the welcome heat as I moved in deeper. I let out a sharp breath as the water lapped over my shorts, and I hesitated.

It was cooler than elsewhere. I'd deliberately entered at the coolest place, wanting to really enjoy it, and despite the water being markedly warmer than the air around me, the feeling of the water cradling my nether region still made me gasp.

I took a deep breath, then sat, sinking down into the water up to my chin, eyes widening uncontrollably as I gasped again.

Kelly's low laugh floated on the air as she hung her robe up as well. She'd hung back to exchange a few words with someone, and I got to admire her as she walked out into the water toward me.

Long legs, a hell of a body barely hidden beneath a very nicely designed plain black—and low cut—swimsuit, and her long blonde hair tied up in a bun behind her head. As she walked out to me, she reached up, undoing it and shaking her hair out.

She sighed in relief, obviously glad to relax, but I just shook my head in wonder that she was wasting her time with a bugger like me, and reached out one hand as she moved closer.

I stood, water cascading off me as she smiled, wrapping her arms around my neck and kissing me as I lifted her. I rested one hand on her ass to support her, enjoying the feeling of the wet swimsuit that barely existed between us. She kissed me even deeper, making me spring to attention as she wrapped her legs around me.

I turned, wading deeper into the water as we kissed, moving quickly away from the side and where we could be easily observed, to a deeper part of the pool. The clouds of steam obscured the world around us as we kissed.

Our hands were exploring within seconds, and I groaned at the feeling as she gripped me, squeezing gently but firmly, before she lifted up and practically stuffed my face into her cleavage. She looked around, checking to see just how many people were, in fact, in sight.

She sighed and slid back, pulling her breasts from my face before I could free a nipple, and grinning at me as she pumped her hand once, twice and then a third time under the water, before releasing me.

"Later," she promised breathily. "Too many people around here right now, and we should make an effort to lead by example…"

"So we're making pornos now?" I groaned, staring at her, filled with need.

"HA!" She laughed. "No, I don't need anyone else seeing the things you do for me, or that I'm going to do for you later!" She grabbed my hands, making sure they couldn't roam, and moved in quickly, kissing me once more hard, then backed up, shaking her head and grinning at the look in my eyes.

"You're cruel…" I accused her.

"Just in love," she whispered, before freeing her hands and swimming back a bit, moving her arms and legs in slow, smooth circles. "Now, you need to calm down, and we can go and join the others."

"The others?" I groaned, not wanting to do anything but take her back to our room and try to break each other right then.

"Some of them are here, or are coming out. Don't worry, there won't be many of them or lots of other people here, but you need to actually relax a bit, and you need to be seen as well."

"We're playing the game?" I sighed. "I'd much rather be playing with…"

"And so would I!" she assured me as I moved closer. "I'd much rather be playing other games, but this is important. Okay, come on then…"

Before I could reach her, she was off, stroking across the pool and into the steamy mists. I grumbled a little under my breath, then started after her, deliberately thinking calming thoughts.

Life was so much easier for women when you'd been fooling around, especially when the air was cold. At worst, people might notice her nipples, and they'd chalk that up to the cold air, and hopefully look away.

It wasn't that easy for a guy. Tease us a little and for the next ten minutes, we were trying to think calming thoughts, especially when we're in wet swimming shorts. Walk out of the water and we might as well be providing a private landing platform for an eagle.

Or, you know, a cockatiel.

CHAPTER NINE

I made it through the middle of the pool. The shadowy figures of people off to the sides and scattered around appeared and vanished, and I shook my head in amazement.

I knew it was big—hell, it was the size of an Olympic swimming pool, one side to the other, mainly circular, with pillared columns rising on all sides,—but I'd never seen it as *this* big.

There were small private sections with shallow water, presumably for kids to roam in safety. Others had much higher temperatures, like a sauna and steam room combined. Something to do with the magic kept the majority of the steam contained, as well as most of the heat, but that same effect made damn sure you couldn't see far once you were inside.

I followed Kelly, seeing the dim shape of her as she waded on ahead. I caught up to her a few seconds later, spotting Chris with Becky, and Dante with Ashley in a shallow area. Drinks were passed around as Dante huddled in the water, clearly unsure of the protocol in a place like this.

I could understand it as well, considering he was with his first real girlfriend, as well as sitting next to Chris. Chris had always been a fairly imposing guy, not so much physically as he was now. Hell, these days he was a regular Adonis. Back in the old world, he'd have been modelling on the front of bodybuilder magazines if he'd been built like this then.

No, he'd been imposing because he was a good-looking guy, filled with self confidence and good at talking to the ladies. He could hold his own in a fight, and as much as he was enjoying playing "big dumb Chris" right now, he was actually really intelligent.

He was the kind of guy who would have been described as an alpha by most people in most groups, and that was before he added on several inches and an insane level of muscle.

I slowed as I moved closer, seeing them all with new eyes, and thinking, really *thinking* about what Kelly had said.

Chris was the most overt, mainly because he'd been my best mate all my life, and while I'd seen him changing gradually, just as I had? That meant that I'd just sort of ignored the changes until now.

He was built like a brick shithouse, could command the beasts, and conjure magical plants and more, and judging from the quiet conversation I could make out as I moved in closer, he'd been putting off a change of class as well.

"Well, it's there, you know?" Chris was saying. "Druid is all well and good, but it's not very versatile as things stand. Animals are either mental and attacking us, or they're boring. I need to go out and see what I can find, like really *need* to, to make a new bond with something, but I also need to make a class choice. I've been putting it off because I need to decide if I'm doubling down, or if I want to respec, you know?"

"Definitely!" Dante replied, shuffling in a bit and seeming to relax a little, clearly happier talking about something like this than making polite conversation with a man twice his size, despite him knowing Chris fairly well.

Dante was the other side of the coin, in that he was physically much as he had been before the world went to shit. Instead, he'd invested over and over into his mind and skills.

His choices were demonstrated ably as he lifted his right hand out of the water and conjured a simple flame, making it dance in his palm, then across the backs of his knuckles as he turned his hand over, rolling it back and forth.

"See, that's the kinda shit I mean," Chris said quickly. "You can conjure fire. Hell, you literally cut through steel and more like butter the other day. I saw that, and I'm making fuckin' weeds sprout."

"Chris..." Kelly waded up to the shallow section, then stepped down into a whirlpool and let out a sigh of relief at the heat and bubbles. "You do more than grow weeds. You've boosted the growth of the farms on your own. You've been healing constantly with your AOE heals, and you fight on the front line."

"And you turn into a giant tiger-man and flip tanks when you lose your temper, so there's that too." I stood and waded in a little closer to the group. The water was deep enough where I was to conceal the obvious issue I had.

"Hey man." Chris forced a smile. "Yeah well, that's not exactly something I can do very often, you know?"

"I saw Dante's spell," I pointed out. "He killed three of them and collapsed."

"I...yeah, I know," Dante apologized. "I put too much mana into the spell, and I just...I should have worked out the issues before..."

"Whoa, dude." I shook my head and held one hand up. "I wasn't complaining. You cut three of that fucker's 'elite' forces apart. They were bad-asses, and you took down three of them."

Ashley smiled and reached out, taking Dante's hand and whispering something to him, then kissed his cheek, before standing and wading up and out of the water. She moved to the little bubble pool and dropped into the deep section where Kelly was relaxing now.

The conversation faltered for a few seconds as for the first time I saw Ashley's swimsuit. She'd been next to Dante, her knees drawn up to her chest and one arm around them, holding a cocktail glass in the other.

Chris and I exchanged a long look that carried everything that needed saying as we shook our heads. Dante stared after her.

Ashley had won the genetic lottery in many respects: highly intelligent, exceedingly pretty, and sharp enough to be able to tell the difference between how intelligent she was and how many things she didn't know. She was both humble in her mind, and confident in her body and outlook.

She was also smart enough to know that no matter how hard she worked, people who didn't know her would see a pretty girl and assume that was all she was.

She'd been quick to stress that she'd never been a "whore," as she put it. In fact, she'd had very few partners, and had realized at a young age that she could either hide and be a victim of her looks or use them to her advantage.

When she'd ended up in the dungeon and I'd asked for volunteers to fight by my side with a sword, she'd jumped at the chance. Not only would she make a possibly powerful ally—me—but she'd have a sword and know how to use it.

She'd battled and leveled, earned my trust and she'd made friends, deciding to stay and make a new life as a citizen of the dungeon, as long as her sister was given the right to stay as well.

The class she'd been given was Courtesan, and far from the glorified hooker she'd worried that it was, she'd been overjoyed to realize it was a diplomatic and spy class, combining whispered breathy promises and poison, overt threats and hidden daggers, blackmail and bribery into a single class that she was growing to love.

The result was a slim, stunningly beautiful woman, who was used to wearing very little and was totally unselfconscious about it, body confident in a way that most models weren't, and she wore a tiny bikini that was under tremendous pressure as she literally bounced back to the surface in the heated pool, before almost snapping and flying free.

Chris and I looked at each other again, and then at Dante, regarding him as even luckier than he thought he was.

I moved up to the pair of them, keeping the water at waist level, and sitting when it got a little too shallow, still trying to calm myself after Kelly's promises, hands, and the feel of her in my arms. It was also *not* helped by the sight of Ashley in a bikini.

Becky kissed Chris's cheek and stood, dressed in the most chaste swimsuit of all three of the ladies, meaning she'd only have had a dozen complaints for inappropriate dressing at a normal pool pre-fall.

She was beautiful as well, a redheaded, wide-smiling woman who, although generally quiet in a lot of the meetings we had, never failed to add something that the rest of us had missed.

She was also a Fey Wrangler, which was apparently some kind of magical deal maker with the various weird species, and could tear people's souls out of their ass, banish it to a nether realm, and somehow feed off it.

Where Kelly was slim-waisted, reasonably busty, smart and sexy, and Ashley wore the persona of a sex kitten and porn star half the time, and then kicked people's ass the rest of it, Becky was well muscled and smarter than the average bear, able to survive for weeks in the wilderness with just Chris as a companion; they'd rescued kids and he'd come looking for help.

By the time we got back, she had a small community going and was kicking the crap out of a couple who were the only ones in the building, besides us, who were armed.

All in all, as I joined Chris and Dante, all three of us looking from Kelly to Ashley to Becky and relaxing in the pool, we were simultaneously reminded that we were incredibly lucky, and each of us possessed both a lower degree of intelligence, and were punching above our weight.

"Guys, all I'm gonna say is, if we could get those three naked and mud wrestling, we'd have been billionaires on pay-per-view before the fall," Chris quipped.

"Kelly would have been up for it." I snorted, summoning a beer and taking a swig.

"Don't say shit like that, man. I'll never be able to stop dreaming now." Chris sighed. "I don't suppose Ashley is up for a gangbang, is she?" he asked Dante, who went bright red.

"I...I..."

"Don't worry, dude. You're invited as well," Chris said quickly. "Do you want to go first, or hold the camera?"

"C...camera?" Dante squeaked, making Chris snort with laughter, even as I chuckled and took another swig from the bottle.

"He's winding you up," I assured Dante.

"Yeah, man, we can't get a camera working, but—"

"Chris, dude, that's enough." I sighed. "If Becky hears you, you're a dead man."

"You kidding? She's said she'd happily have invited Ashley to our bed if she was single..." Chris hung his head. "Man, even the thought..."

"Behave," I said sternly, before moving in closer to the shallow end, lying half submerged on my front. The other two joined me, our beers resting on a shelf nearby as we all relaxed.

"So...what's the plan then?" Chris asked quietly after a few minutes.

"Dude, you were in the fucking meetings...you still don't know?" I asked.

"Well, let's be clear. First of all, no. I stopped listening after a while...I got bored. Secondly, that's the overall plan for the dungeon, not the plan for us."

"Us?" Dante asked, then cleared his throat nervously as we both looked at him. "I mean...if you don't want to say, or if I'm not involved...it's okay...Do you want me to go?"

"Dante, relax." I smiled. "It's fine, man. Okay, to be fair, yeah, we discussed the dungeon's direction. We didn't really discuss what we're doing as individuals."

"I'm going to go and look for some fucking dinosaur bones," Chris said sternly. "You're going to bring them back to life, and I'm going to be the first Druid with a frickin' T. rex as my companion."

"First, I don't even know how I did it with the trikes, so I make no promises. Second? How many fucking T. rex's are you expecting to be lying around? There's no chance there's one of those there!"

"Actually, two points," Dante said quickly. "First, there is a T. rex skeleton in the Hancock—"

"Fuck yes!" Chris crowed. "Damn, man, if we get a move on, we could have it here and I could be riding it by morning. Come on..."

He started to stand up, opening his mouth to call to the girls, only for Dante to speak quickly.

"It's a fake!"

"What?" Chris said, confused, and I snorted, shaking my head.

"Man, you remember the conversation we had when we were making the trikes up? About how most of them are fake? Just replicas?" I asked him, and he visibly sagged.

"Matt, don't piss in my cereal like this." He sat back down, the water barely covering his junk as he faced me. "I need a dino, man. I'm a Druid, for fuck's sake, and…"

"And we'll see what we can do," I promised. "But dude, seriously, they're rare as fuck. You might have to wait till we can get to London or America if it's a T. rex you want…"

"Fuck." Chris groaned. "Matt…"

I paused, hearing the seriousness in his voice. He rubbed at his head, then opened his mouth, about to speak, before glancing at Dante and shutting up.

"I can go…" Dante offered, starting to get up. "I'll just go join the girls in the hot tub."

"Man, how wrong is it that the nerdy guy is the first of us to suggest joining the girls?" Chris asked, clearly changing whatever he was about to say.

"He can go or stay, Chris. If you want to talk, brother, then let's talk," I offered, feeling a lot more solemn, only to have him shake his head.

"Not right now. I need to think a bit, but…I'll need your help and soon, mate. Dante, you, too. I need to bond another animal. It's that or I change classes. It's…it's like an itch, you know? Like when I did a load of coke a few years back, and then I stopped?"

"An addiction?" I asked softly.

"Yeah, but not," he clarified unhelpfully. "It's really not the same."

"Chris…" I growled, and he grinned.

"Nah, sorry, man. Okay, look." He blew out a long breath, dropping his voice so the girls wouldn't be able to overhear us. "It's like that, that itch to have a line or whatever, but it's not as well. It's not because it's not addictive. It's not like I need to scratch my skin off as a distraction or go get off my face or something. It's a part of my class. Like, if you lost the dungeon, but you still had your class as a Dungeon Lord? You'd keep going to do things, things you should be able to do, but you'd not be able to do them anymore."

"So it's like you're missing something. You said that before, but…"

"It's getting worse," he said softly. "Look, I know I've been playing the fool a bit of late—" He looked at me, and then at Dante, clearly having difficulty saying it with him there.

"I'm going to go," Dante said quickly, standing up. "I've not heard anything, okay? Come join us when you're ready."

He moved off, wading out of the water and dropping down into the hot tub with the girls, getting a kiss from Ashley as she cuddled up to him, and Chris sighed.

"He's a good kid."

"That 'kid' is what, six years younger than us, seven?" I asked, smiling.

"Yeah, well, it's not the years, it's the mileage," Chris retorted.

"Come on then, spill," I said. "And you might as well tell me about that transforming spell as well, get it all out in the open."

"It's an essence transformation," he whispered. "It burns essence and mana, but it needs a physical conduit. So, for me to do things, like shape shift, I need a fuckload of mana, stamina, and a token of the beast I want to become. I'd taken the class skill awhile back, but you know…Until Simo died, I didn't have anything to use. It's a tooth of his I used."

"So, if you had more teeth?"

"I could change into more creatures," he admitted. "It's a class thing, like a specialist sub-class called Skin-Walker. I've been looking at it, but it'd mean I don't get much in the way of magic in the future. For me to use it, it takes all my mana, so no spells if I change."

"Do you want to sling spells around?"

"I don't know." He flicked the surface of the gently rolling water. "It sounds cool, but you know."

"Chris, you stupid fuck." I splashed a load of water at him, surprising him.

"What the…" He growled, glaring at me as he wiped the water off his face.

"You need to sort your head out, mate. I can't help you if you don't know what you want. You want magic? I need to work on mine; we can try to figure it out together. You want to meet an animal? We can fix that. I've got some class points to spend. I was considering saving them 'til later, when I get my next class choice, but we can use them to up the pets' classes."

"The what?" He blinked.

"Look." I sighed. "You know how we had the dogs for the goblins, and for Beta? The way that the other dungeon was making goblin riders?"

"Yeah?"

"One of my skills was supposed to help with that. It was all about helping me to find some pets for the dungeon creatures. It was vague as fuck, like it'd help them to find things that they wanted to keep as a pet, so it might be a dog to pet or one to ride, you know? A gerbil or whatever those furry little bastards are."

"A hamster?"

"Yeah, whatever. Same difference." I shrugged. "It warned me that different creatures viewed different things as pets, and that might cause problems."

"I bet. I don't want to know what a goblin or an orc considers cute."

"You, probably," I quipped, shrugging. "Fuck, it's getting colder," I muttered, shifting around and drawing back into the deeper water a little, Chris following me. "What I did, though, when I upgraded to Arcanist, and Arcane Dungeon Lord, was to get access to a new version of most of my class skills. I got Arcane Pets instead of normal ones."

"Shit, what kind of…?"

"No clue." I shook my head. "Seriously, man, I've got no clue. The first level is 'magical' creatures. The last, six levels up? 'Legendary.'"

"Dragons and shit. I bet it's dragons," he breathed.

"Now it's your turn," I said. "You want me to take that? I will…the first level only, though, for now. I need to spend my points carefully—they're for the whole dungeon, not just me. But it's your turn."

"To do what?"

"To fucking explain, you dick!" I growled, punching him lightly on the shoulder. "You said it's getting worse."

"It is." He turned from me and staring out across the wisps of steam that rose from the water. "I'm playing the fool a lot, but it's not always playing," he admitted. "The longer I go without a bond, the worse the itch gets, and the more

I need it. Sometimes it's all I can think about. And my senses? I keep smiling at people and not speaking because I can't hear them."

"You're deaf?" I asked, then shook my head as my brain caught up with my mouth. That was ridiculous; we were talking now.

"Not exactly. It's like when you're tuning a radio, you know how you, like, turn the dial and the signal comes and goes?"

I nodded.

"It's like that. I'll be listening fine and it's all good, and suddenly I can hear someone else that's only muttering, and it's like they're shouting in my ears, and the entire rest of the room is quiet. I thought at first it was my senses going, you know, that I was going deaf and blind a little…my senses in general dulling."

"Right? I remember you saying that."

"Yeah, it's not," Chris whispered. "It's my control. Without Simo, or a replacement bond, my soul is empty, and I can't control things the way I did before. It was effortless, you know? I just focused and boom. Now? I have to really work at it, and sometimes no matter what's happening, other senses flare. Like I was joking about me and Becky needing a shower…"

"But you weren't," I finished for him, and he nodded.

"But I wasn't," he agreed. "It's literally mad. I could smell us both, like we'd not washed for a month and been fighting and fucking all day, every day. One minute, I'd not notice it; the next, I'm trying to smile at her, pretending to just be too tired out to fool around, because the smell of my own goddamn body makes me want to vomit."

"And now that there's clean hot water?"

"It's a relief like you'll never know, bro," he confessed. "Look, don't worry about the class point. You need to save that for—"

"It's done." I pulled the system up and slotted it as I spoke. I'd look at the rest later on to use any other points, but for now I needed to help my friend, and it was something that would be useful, anyway.

"What?"

"I confirmed the point," I said decisively. "It's spent."

It was true. The point was gone, and I bit my cheek as new data downloaded. I could feel the dungeon having systems unlock as well.

The data was weird: a mix of a live data stream, or so it seemed, and a file in the dungeon being unlocked and offered up. The systems that were available there, though?

It was a serious upgrade to the "lure" system that I'd seen was available before, like a massive one. It made it possible to select magical beasts over mundane, and even provided a selection of recommended specialty lures for magical creatures…four of them to start with, I knew.

I'd have to unlock the lures, but that was fine. It was a token cost—well, it was these days, anyway. A thousand mana was practically free compared to the normal numbers we'd been dealing in.

"We'll get it up and running in the next day, dude," I assured him, before hesitating as more data unlocked, and I grunted.

There were four main lure styles, and each of them were exclusive, meaning that if I chose the one for flying creatures, it was of no use to the other three.

That wasn't a big issue, though, considering that the systems were still cheap: five thousand mana each to build. The Water one was probably best to leave alone; we already had a load of Water converters in the river. We didn't need to attract extra sea creatures.

I paused for a second, thinking that it might be a good idea actually. *Then we could train them to guard the converters...* And then banished the thought.

I'd seen some of the horrible shit that lived at the bottom of the sea pre-fall. The thought of that, mutated and much more powerful? Fuck, I was never going on a boat again.

The other three options were airborne, predator, and prey.

Airborne sounded cool as fuck, but terrifying as well, while predator or prey was fairly self-explanatory. After all, the lure for a predator was the prey, or so I assumed.

I considered it, not really sure why the airborne one wasn't as specific as the other, and decided that I'd do both airborne and predators. The prey could be sorted out later, but we'd need them all, for meat for the predators if nothing else.

"Chris..." I asked slowly, banishing the screen, and looked around, then blinking in confusion when I saw he was gone.

"Matt, over here!" Kelly called.

I shook my head. I must have been staring at the details longer than I thought. Everyone else was in the hot tub area, waving over at me.

I grunted then waded up and out, strode through the ankle-deep water to the pool, then groaned as I stepped down into the deeper hot tub.

It was circular, with a two-level design, although it was concealed by the bubbling water. The first level that everyone was sitting in was the outer ring, with a deeper ring in the middle for those who wanted to stand, and damn it was a lot hotter than the surrounding water.

"Remind me again what this place was meant to be used for?" I asked Kelly, settling into place beside her and shaking my head at the heat. "Damn, I could boil my balls in here."

"Stay away from the heaters," Chris said. "There's two separate jets of water. One's hot, one's warm. If you ever intend on having kids, don't sit on a hot jet. Nobody wants that kinda heat down there."

"Oh, I don't know," Becky said slowly, grinning at him. "I liked the noise you made when you sat down."

"The moan, you mean?" Ashley replied to Becky. "'Oh, my balls...'" she mimicked in a high-pitched falsetto.

"I think he liked it really," Dante said, joining in, and I grinned at him, glad to see he was trying.

"Well, Chris always was a sexual degenerate." I shifted back and let out another groan. "Okay, so whatever it was intended for, it's a damn godsend," I admitted, feeling a dozen different jets pummeling my back.

"So, what were you looking at?" Kelly asked me.

Eyes still closed, I spoke.

"We've talked before about the various creatures, and making use of them all, but one of the areas we're weakest—as a dungeon and a fighting force, I mean—is speed and recon. We can bring insane power to bear when we need to, and looking at the tech steps we're taking, the disparity between us and most of the locals is going to get worse and worse. Soon, if we've got rail guns and decent body armor, they're going to have no chance."

"Better, I think you mean." Chris took a swig from his bottle.

"Yeah, whatever," I agreed. "You knew what I meant. Anyway, the issue is that we're slow as shit. We need to move faster, and for that we need cavalry. Until we can make speeder bikes or whatever, it's going to have to be a biological version, and the trikes, awesome as they are, are slow as shit."

"So?" Kelly asked. "You'd not be talking about it now unless you had a solution in mind."

"The lures," I said. "I've used one of my class skill points to unlock magical animal taming for the dungeon. Part of it is to lure in magical creatures. We've got the options of marine, airborne, predator, and prey. They're a thousand mana to unlock each of them, and five thousand to build the basic lure, as well as…*damn*."

I shook my head as a final detail bobbed to the surface of my brain.

"*Aaaand* fifteen thousand to build the kennels and training area for the animals." I sighed, reaching up and rubbing at one side of my face. "Okay, I didn't think about that, but hey. *Anyway*…I'm thinking predators and airborne. We don't need to attract more marine animals near the Water converters…that's just asking for trouble."

"I still say we need a T. rex," Chris said sadly, shaking his head as he vanished his empty beer bottle, summoning a fresh one in its place.

"And I told you, mate, I'd love that," I said. "You get me a viable skeleton and I'll damn well make them. Until then? You've got the trikes."

"Dude, they're crap," Chris said, and Kelly glared at him.

"They're *awesome*, I think you meant to say," Kelly growled, trying to pretend to be annoyed. "They're amazing. They're literally living tanks. And if we can improve on them, they'll be utterly unstoppable."

"Well, can we?" Chris asked, unfazed by Kelly's teasing.

"We can, but I'm not even looking to see how much that'll cost," I said. "The fuckers cost as much as five advanced kobolds to summon, and they're thick as mince. Basically, they were an experiment that I thought would be useful for moving large things about, and also if anyone tries shit with big creatures as well."

"Why didn't you use them with the asuras?" Ashley asked Kelly, genuinely curious.

"They're too slow," Kelly admitted, shrugging and totally distracting me again. "They're awesome, but they're literally level zero. Their stamina is crap, as is their speed. With some armor? They'd be amazing, especially once they're built up a few levels. But as they are now? I've got them on the field to the north, up near where we fought Daedalus—"

"Dickless," I corrected.

"He probably was as well. I mean, a lich? Bet he kept it in a little jar. Like that dude who made himself into a half fly in the movies, you remember? After a few days, his dick fell off," Chris agreed.

"Well, regardless, they're up on the fields there, roaming wild. I can reach out and summon them, but they're eating all the weeds and they're quite happy.

The occasional creatures that try to attack them get stomped flat, giving them some Experience. There's a kobold watching over them, and Jack includes them in his sweeps each day."

"SO!" I said loudly, flicking some water at Chris. "The plan is, we'll get lures built over the next week or so, build a few and spread them out, see what we catch and then see what we can absorb into the dungeon. Chris gets first pick, as I know you'd rather bond with a 'real' creature, right?"

"Definitely," he said forcefully. "Part of the bond with me would break them free of the dungeon, anyway, I think, so if they need the dungeon to survive? They'd just die."

"Okay," I agreed, taking a swig from a bottle I conjured and relaxing. "So, to finish, there's the lures…Chris gets to check out what they catch and see if he wants them, and if not, no harm, no foul. We kill the creature and absorb its pattern into the dungeon. Even if it's just a fucking goat or sheep or whatever, add them into the dungeon."

"This might not come across very well, I'm trying to think of the best way to put it, but listen to the idea, rather than the words…okay?" Dante said, and I frowned, nodding at him.

"What about an arena?"

"We've got the training dungeon," I answered, and he shook his head.

"No, I mean an arena for the animals."

"Bit barbaric, isn't it?" I asked, not liking the idea.

"It is," he agreed. "But these are summoned creatures. How's it any different to run them through a dungeon to fight each other? You're summoning them and deciding these ones get to fight through the dungeon, these ones have to defend it. We're letting some of them die regardless, so why not take the next logical step? Have an arena for the beasts, set them off, make—I don't know—ten wolves or something, and send them in against goblins or orcs or whatever.

"Whoever lives gets healed and they go again until they've got a few levels under their belt. Then you redo them into the dungeon as new creature templates. They're more experienced and people get to cheer and drink beer," Dante finished, looking around at how everyone was looking at him.

"Look, I know the way it sounds, all right?" he said quickly. "But think about it…is it really that different? Take away the people watching aspect, which, yeah, is a bit barbaric, even though they do that in the dungeon. It's literally the same as the dungeon: you're killing living creatures, creatures with a soul, we now know, for Experience and practice…"

"Oh, well, thank you so much for *that*." I groaned, rubbing at my eyes. "Kelly, make a note please. Undead and orcs in the dungeon only, I think. Undead I don't think develop souls—if they do, I don't need to know—and orcs are assholes, so fuck them."

"We need to train," Kelly disagreed, knowing I wasn't being serious. "We summon for the dungeon, and we deliberately set them out in patterns in there with mainly lower intelligence and leveled creatures."

"I think I see what you mean," Ashley said, backing her boyfriend up, but the frown gave away how little she liked it.

"We'll look at it," I promised, glancing at Kelly, who shook her head.

"We'll be better off keeping it as it is, use the local 'training dungeon' as either a low, or high, level exclusive zone, one we adjust depending on who will be running it. That way we can keep an eye on things, so the real rank amateurs can use it to get to their class, for example."

"Right, and the high level?" Becky asked.

"We swap out the inhabitants," Kelly said. "For the low levels, we use pretty much all low-level creatures, little variations and no traps. For the higher end, we have the surviving low-end ones troop out and wait somewhere, maybe head to the other dungeon. Then we fill this one with all new higher-end mixed enemies, all set to a maximum level of aggression."

"Keep it secret from the higher-end teams what they'll face," I muttered in agreement. "We go in and use it to train, like train properly. Have Markus and Patrick set the rules. Like, for me, I need to work on my magic, so I can't use any weapons maybe?"

"All martial arts and magic, no hammers and shit," Chris agreed. "Send people in in teams for the less experienced, and then for the more experienced, they get to run it alone."

"Means we can claim the stuff we get from the reliquaries as well. I noticed they didn't spawn in the fight for the civic center dungeon. I should have seen that as a warning sign that something was wrong, but I didn't."

"Well, it is what it is." Kelly ducked under my arm and moved in for a cuddle. Her back pressed against my side and chest, my left arm down across her shoulder and under the water.

She surreptitiously moved my hand that had come to rest—utterly unintentionally, of course—on her tit, and held it in one of hers.

"So, you're going to be doing dungeon runs?" Kelly asked me, and I nodded.

"I need to. I've stepped back from all of this so I can focus on my powers, on learning to control them and develop them, so that I'm ready for the next time, and I don't damn well nearly kill myself."

"I agree with it." Kelly smiled up at me over her shoulder. "I just wanted to be sure."

"I'll be training a lot over the next few days and weeks," I told the others. "I'll be leaving the running of the dungeon to Kelly and Aly and others more and more. Magic and martial arts will be my focus in the short-term, then more and more using my magic."

"Patrick is becoming a real terror in his training." Dante shook his head. "I keep seeing people join his classes and quit after only a few sessions."

"Then I'll look at it—"

"I will," Chris said, cutting me off. "Dude, you need to train, yeah?"

"Yeah, I do."

"Then let me damn well help. I know I've been a bit scatterbrained of late, but..."

"It'd help you to have a job," Becky said softly, looking up at her boyfriend and then across at me. "Seriously, Chris needs a focus, or he mopes around."

"I do *NOT*," Chris hissed, scandalized. "Fuck's sake, I'm trying to help my friend and—"

"I'd appreciate it, Chris," I interrupted. "Get with Markus and Patrick and the others who are doing training…Jeffrey and so on. You were always awesome at organizational crap. Look into what's happening with the trainees. If Patrick's pushing them too hard, or if there's a problem, see if we can get things moving along, a bit more structured."

"I'll talk to Mike and Griffiths as well. Don't worry, we'll look at the training and see what we can come up with."

He seemed pleased I was asking him to do something, and I realized that besides being my right-hand man in a fight, of late I'd been ignoring him.

He'd been staying out of the way, and then acting a bit of a fool with me, distracting me and being there to talk whenever I needed it. He'd been wrestling with his own demons, and instead of leaving and dealing with them as he needed to, he'd been here, fighting to help me, and never saying a word about it.

I suddenly felt like a really shitty friend, and I looked at Chris, seeing the look in his eyes as he glanced back.

I raised my beer to him, silent, and he nodded, knowing what I was thinking, and more as he returned the gesture.

We'd been friends for so long there was no need for words; we both knew what was going on, and just like that, it was all dealt with.

The next half hour in the pool was a comfortable one. As I planned to use the training dungeon, Kelly had said firmly that I didn't need to be involved in any of the discussions about the layout of the training dungeon from then on. That way I'd not know what was in there, so I'd have to pay attention to everything as I went.

The civic center dungeon was briefly discussed, but only in an "it'll be the main training dungeon" way, and that was it. People from the park and here could learn the basics in the dungeon here, where there'd be help if something went wrong.

Then, once they were able to fight and probably survive with a reasonable level of competence, they'd go to the civic center dungeon, and fight and practice there.

Only once they'd completed both, and had been evaluated as ready by one of the trainers, would they be permitted into the upper training dungeon.

What would for now be the normal dungeon, just restocked with new and different creatures, would eventually be replaced with an entirely new level. It'd be filled with the most lethal of all the creatures we'd managed to get, and they'd all be set to maximum aggression, no mercy.

With that sorted, the last of my to-do jobs had suddenly evaporated. Finn and Clarissa were handling crafting and people, figuring out the training and more, Kelly was working with Aly to run the dungeon itself, and Aly would make sure all the research was done.

The dungeon was being sorted, the exterior was continuing to be claimed, and the various systems worked on. There was a million and one jobs to be done, as there always were, but they were all handed out to others.

I was suddenly more or less jobless. I still had to handle the magical evolutions—nobody else could—and I would have a single council meeting each day where we'd make sure things were going in the right direction, but…

I was now free for the rest of the day.

Free to train, to learn, and to finally, *finally* get to work on my Arcanist class quest. Free to learn to grow as a Storm Lord, and to achieve the higher ranks.

I was free to learn what the hell a Soul Forge was, and what the hell it meant in the real world. I could use my soul to make things, or I could imbue my soul into them, apparently.

I was also, I decided, smiling to myself, free to continue a little discussion I was having earlier with Kelly. She was laughing, Ashley doing impressions of a guy who had tried to seduce her earlier, when I leaned down and put my lips to her ear, whispering so that nobody else could overhear.

"Want to go play 'hide the sausage'?" I asked her, the utter soul of seduction, making her snort as she took a drink, spraying liquid all over, before wiping her face and looking up at me in disbelief.

"You are just so subtle, you know that?"

"Oh yeah." I nodded, bouncing my eyebrows suggestively.

"Fuck me…" She groaned.

"Okay, you've talked me into it!" I said loudly. "See you fuckers later!"

There was never a good way for a guy who's been considering any form of sexual liaison to leave a hot tub, especially one filled with attractive ladies, and that required you literally climb up and out, so I just went for it, ignoring the cockatiel landing perch that stood out proudly, my shorts laminated to it.

I took Kelly's hand and helped her out, like any gentleman would, and the two of us strolled to the side, summoning fresh robes rather than fucking around finding the ones we'd worn to come in.

"You're terrible," Kelly breathed as we stopped for a kiss outside, the cold stone floor icy and making us both summon flip-flops at almost the same time.

"You love it!" I assured her, getting a naughty grin from her as she nodded.

"You know what I do love?"

"What's that?"

"You remember when I had my ankles over your shoulders the other night," she purred, slipping her hand into the front of my robe and taking hold of me by a convenient handle. "I want more of what you did then."

"Oh…" I groaned, being "tugged" along the path by her, and trying to keep my robe closed for the few people who were still out and about. "Oh well, guess I'll be brave…"

CHAPTER TEN

The next morning was a cold one, even here in the dungeon, underground. We'd both discovered we liked it cold to sleep, probably because we tended to build up a lot of warmth when we were awake and in private.

As such, we'd set the dungeon to drop the temperature in our room to a few degrees below the temperature outside when we'd been all hot and bothered last night.

Wrapped in our blankets, as the temperature plummeted, we'd slept like the dead. Waking up, though, was a sobering experience. Kelly was cuddled into my side, one arm across my chest, with me laid on my back, one of my arms around her.

When I blinked, waking up slowly, I realized just how goddamn cold I was. Kelly had pulled the duvet in her sleep, tucking it in around her neck and exposing my chest and shoulder.

My skin was cold enough that it actually hurt, and great plumes showed in the air as I blew out a long breath. Looking to the glass of water I always summoned on my bedside table, ready for during the night when I wanted a drink—a habit I'd maintained since being a small child—the glass was frosted. A thin layer of ice across the top made it clear that I'd really fucked the pooch with the temperature controls.

I slid into the dungeon, searching and resetting the temperature to a more reasonable one, as well as accepting that I would not be getting up anytime soon.

It was a little before 0500, the cold having woken me, and Kelly was shaking too. Waiting for the temperature to adjust, my mind fully awake despite my fervent desire to go back to sleep, I shifted around, rolling Kelly onto her side.

That done, I cuddled up to her, tucking the duvet back in and spooning her, finally able to get my damn arm and chest out of the cool air.

"Cold…" Kelly whispered, shifting against me.

"I know. It's warming up now," I assured her, wrapping my arms around her under the duvet.

She snuggled against me, her bare ass rubbing slowly, half asleep, and I let out a long breath, holding her close to me.

"Warm me up…" she whispered, looking over her shoulder, smiling and reaching for a kiss, even as my hand found her hard nipple, and her fingers curled around me, guiding me into her.

The cold was forgotten as we worked on raising both our internal temperatures, and that of the entire world, or so it seemed.

An hour and more later, we were laid there, sweaty, the blanket kicked off, the room dimly lit as we liked it—more than enough to be able to see everything, without being bright—and we tried to catch our breath.

"Is this a bad time to tell you we're getting low on contraceptive pills?" she asked me, and we both looked down, then back up. Her finger pressed to my lips as I opened my mouth, and she went on quickly.

"Don't worry, I'm not pregnant, and we've got a month's supply. But after that, we either need to get more pills on the go, or start making condoms."

"I'd prefer the pill," I admitted, shrugging. "I mean, I'll wear them. It's just…"

"It's just not as nice, and they taste horrible." Kelly nodded. "You want me to put it in my mouth, then we need flavored ones, or none at all."

"None it is," I said firmly.

"We'll need them still, for other people," Kelly mused, idly stroking her fingertips across the skin of my stomach, enjoying the feeling of the solid muscle. "Some girls prefer the pill, others not, and it's not our place to decide that for them. Hell, there's a load of different pills, because some react badly to some formulas…"

"I probably don't want to hear this, but what have they been doing up to now?" I asked.

"No idea. I've spoken about it with Becky and Ashley, Aly and Jo, but not really anyone else. Even between the five of us, there's two different pills, and one of them prefers condoms all the way."

"Who…" I started to ask, then I shook my head. "You know what, I don't need to know."

"And I'm not telling you about our conversations," Kelly assured me, kissing me.

"I've heard that as bad as you all make guys out to be, you're worse," I offered.

"Depends on the conversation." She lifted one hand and wobbled it to and fro. "We're not so much into the crude things I've heard guys say when they think they're not being overheard, but also…well, more detailed than you'd enjoy hearing, I bet!"

"I did so not need to know that," I said. "Just tell me I compare favorably."

"You just keep telling yourself you do." She grinned, lifting herself up and straddling me, sitting on my stomach and looking down as she fixed her hair into a quick ponytail. "Now. I have a lot to do today. I'm Mistress of the Dungeon, don't you know. I can't lie around being serviced by my boy-toy all day."

I'd reached up automatically, my hands on the outside of her thighs, and I slowly drew my nails down her skin, how she liked it, before reaching up and pulling her down to kiss me.

Our arms went around each other, the kisses gentle, then repeated, each one with a little more fire. One hand stroked down her back, fingernails drawing fanciful designs along her skin. My other hand reached down, cupping her ass and squeezing gently, even as she shifted, moving forward and presenting one nipple to my lips, reaching back with a hand and making sure I was waking fully to the task ahead.

"Well…" She pushed my head back from her nipple as she lifted up, turning around, top to tail, and lowering herself back down. "I guess I *could* put things off a *little* longer…"

I groaned, and took advantage of the position we were in, making sure the morning was *very* well spent.

The sun was well up by the time we left our room, despite the lateness of the late autumn/early winter sunrise, and we walked hand in hand up to the canteen level to grab breakfast. Most of the others had long since been in and gone, so we sat at a small table, just the two of us, me with a good size fry-up, her with a bacon and sausage sandwich, and talked about little things.

We'd both needed the morning, and the night before, more than we'd realized. The stress of the fights, of nearly losing each other again, and my "solution" almost going so badly wrong for us all had made us value this more than we had before.

We talked about everything and nothing, before she finally rose, leaning in for a long kiss, and making me promise I'd leave the dungeon to them to manage until tonight when they'd give me a full report.

I agreed, knowing I was bad for jumping in and dealing with things without thinking about it, and kissed her one last time. I then asked her to factor me into the dungeon for a solo run tomorrow, and got a smile and a nod, before a final, extra, "one last kiss," and then she was gone, striding from the room, exchanging smiles and waves with people as she went.

I sat back, my usual energy drink in my hand, as I took a swig and contemplated where to start. Realistically, I needed to get my mana back up—I'd bottomed it out last night before going to join the others—and although the core was nearly up to full capacity again, it wasn't quite there.

I hesitated a few seconds, drinking and thinking, before setting the can on the table before me, tapping the rim of the base idly against the tabletop as I stared into the distance.

I *should* have enough mana to finish up the repairs now. I was literally only a handful of percent off, but that would leave me empty. Unless there was a damn good reason, I saw no point in enduring a mana migraine.

Fuck that shit.

I nodded to myself, setting the empty can down and absorbing it into the dungeon with a thought, along with the rest of the remains of our breakfast, leaving the table pristine as I stood.

Meditation first, then magic.

I set off, nodding to a few people as I passed them, speaking when I needed to, but miles away mentally, as I thought about my magic.

I paused at the door as someone hurried up to pass through, rather than waiting, and then glared at me for apparently not stepping back and out of their way.

Frowning, I recognized the self-proclaimed "Councilor Merriman" as he paused, waiting for me to step back. It was a dick move. I'd been closest to the door, and he'd seen it and hurried up, deliberately stepping in front of me so I had to step aside for him, or be rude and either order him, or shove him aside.

It was clearly a test, and just as clearly, one I wasn't interested in having in the slightest.

"You're blocking the door," he complained in his nasal voice.

"I was wondering where you're working," I replied, unaware until just that second that I *had* been wondering it, but the effect on his face was clear. "I think I'll ask Pat." I smiled and stepped back, gesturing to the canteen.

Pat was the older woman who had dragged him and his little coterie of friends off for a talking-to about not carrying their weight. At the mention of her name, he blanched, before speaking quickly.

"I'll be reporting that woman to the police! She *assaulted* me!"

"Really?" I asked, unconcerned. "Looked to me that your ear attacked her hand."

"My ear…what?"

"Viciously, in fact." I nodded. "I think speaking about this to the judge would be a good idea."

"A judge?" he whined. "Which one? I knew the judges and—"

"John." I smiled. "Now, I'm busy, so are you going to fuck off and find him yourself, or do I need to summon some creatures to take you to him?"

"I'll find him," Councilor Merriman snapped. "I'll find him, and we'll discuss this little criminal enterprise you've set up! You've no rights to—"

I pushed past him, starting up the stairs and banishing him from my mind as I called over my shoulder.

"He's in the park then. Best to run there while it's daylight…less monsters about."

"Outside?!" He gasped. "You expect me to put myself at risk out *there*?"

"What the hell are you doing then?" I asked, hesitating on the landing, about to walk up out of sight. "I damn well know you're not in the dungeon system, not really. If you're not part of the work details, and you're not helping with the dungeon, how are you earning your place here?"

"I am Councilor Merriman!" he snarled, drawing himself up to his full height and glaring at me. "I'm a part of the council, and as this dungeon is inside the boundaries of the City of Newcastle, it falls under my direct control!"

"There's no council anymore—"

"There is now," he said smugly. "And more to the point, they were democratically elected."

"What are you talking about?" I asked, confused. "There's been no damn election."

"We held it last night. When *some* people were frolicking in public and being a drunken nuisance, *exposing* themselves and practically *fornicating in public*, other, more responsible people, were working."

"Oh, fuck off." I grunted, shaking my head and walking away. The little bastard was well on his way to ruining my good mood, and I wasn't interested.

"We'll be talking again about this…" he called up after me, and I waved a finger at him, ignoring the little shit stain.

I dismissed it, jogging up the stairs and reaching the roof in short order, pushing the door open and wincing at the sudden blast of wintery cold air.

The rooftop was deserted. A handful of footprints showed that a few hardy souls had come up and had gone to the converters, in the hope of meditating, but they'd clearly given up with the temperature.

It was baltic.

Walking out, the ice crystals crunched underfoot—an unseasonably early snowfall had come at some point—and now, after what I guessed to have been a sleet shower after it, the entire roof was coated in glistening, ice-bound snow.

It was only half an inch or so deep, which made it worse, not better, because the bloody thing was too shallow to get a grip, and too icy to ignore, making me walk slowly and carefully over to the converters.

Reaching them easily enough—I only slipped once—I focused, summoning a comfy chair and a sleeping bag, stepping into it and sitting down.

Then, well aware that I couldn't make a structure around me, because one of the reasons that the Air converters produced so much was the constant stream of air across them, I summoned a handful of small tarps that Griffiths had asked me to make copies of.

They were part of the British Army "foul weather" gear he'd brought with him: totally waterproof, or as close as anything could be. They were easily set out, breaking the wind and forming a neat little cocoon around me.

Being able to control the dungeon as I could, it was child's play to summon a brace here, a stick there, all from within my sleeping bag, and I grinned to myself as within a minute, I was out of the wind, on a comfy chair, and surrounded by the converters.

I might not be working "in" the dungeon with the others, but I sure as shit wasn't giving up my abilities to manipulate things, just because I wasn't doing my usual job.

I closed my eyes, breathing deeply, and began.

Flowing down and into myself, being drawn along by the rolling tides of my mana, the great river that rolled back and forth, I groaned. I was down to an even lower level of mana regeneration now. I went back, searching my stat sheet and let out a low growl as I saw the point it'd changed.

When I'd had access to pure mana, even though my internals—the rings and more that had been slowly building through my body—had been destroyed, I'd had access to even more mana than normal.

Now?

I had less mana regen than I'd had in forever.

Well, that was part of the point of this time. I was here to fix this, here to work on my issues.

I hesitated, thinking about it, forcing myself to plan rather than just going for it. I needed to improve my magic, that was a major part of this, but I also needed to build my physical stats as well.

If I could work on them both at once, that would be the best way.

I'd managed a kind of Zen mindset a good few times at the gym, zoning out with the music blasting, working on cardio more than anything else.

That'd been easy because apart from the occasional attractive lady to stroll into the gym in Lycra, there was nothing else to do in there. There was no running track to pay attention to, or people to talk to.

When I was on one of my admittedly infrequent trips to the gym, I'd block everything out and focus on the action. I'd stick my brain in neutral and just keep going, over and over.

The treadmill was the best for that.

I couldn't do that here, obviously, but I'd learned to put my body on autopilot when I was working in the dungeon sense. I could stumble along, at least.

Could I do that with this? Could I meditate and exercise at the same time?

I couldn't do weights and stuff; that was just daft. Lifting a heavy weight over my head and not paying attention was asking to be hurt. As was trying to run on an icy roof, admittedly.

No. I needed something I could do on autopilot, though.

I needed a rowing machine.

They were generally electric, or the screens were anyway. The chain and pulley system they used internally, though? They should be good still. I could get one of them up here…

Or better yet, considering that this was only late autumn, early winter and we had literally months of this snowy bullshit to go, I could put it inside somewhere. Somewhere with other converters.

Life maybe?

I promised myself I'd discuss it with Kelly and Chris later on. Kelly because she was the person I always wanted to talk shit through with, and Chris, because if he was going to help sort out training issues, then arranging a gym would kinda fall under his remit.

Or Mike's.

Fuck it. I'd tell them what I wanted and leave them to make it work. *For now? Meditation.* I'd banished the thoughts about working out at least, so it was one less annoying detail buzzing around in my squirrel brain.

I settled back, closing my eyes, and sank into myself, feeling the crackling warmth of the Lightning flowing along inside me. It used to flood the specific channels that my mana poured along, the dancing, comforting blue-white light of Lightning filling me.

The mana was all kinds and none, generally, but with my own affinities being so high for Lightning and Storm, the real-world effect was that my mana was usually about fifty-fifty, half being Lightning and Storm, and the rest being a mix of all mana.

It resulted in a wave of comforting light flooding my mana channels, the river of "normal" mana filled with resounding bursts of bright light and warm, rolling cloud-like surges.

Looking at my mana now? Instead of it being constrained into my mana channels and flowing faster and faster around my body, hitting the spires of the star, or my mana core, at speed and being sucked up, a load of it was diffused throughout my body.

I rolled through the river of mana, finding it expanding the closer I sank into it, until I was a tiny speck of consciousness riding on an ocean of mana, lit from below by the Lightning.

I reveled in the flow, just relaxing and for long minutes actually doing nothing, just allowing myself to be carried, feeling the differences in my system.

Then I started to work.

Not by focusing as I normally did on the star at my core, or by coaxing the mana along, compressing it and trying to make it flow faster. Instead, I rode the stream, eyes closed. The vision of infinite darkness was above me, and a glowing, racing sea all around.

Colors came and went; tiny sparks of light flared and vanished, as if I rode a sea of incandescent fireflies having a rave. But here and there, as I went, I felt the old gates or rings.

I felt their remains as the mana that had been compressed and shaped by them now somehow flowed over their sunken remains.

The mana was slower here now, constrained by the fallen sections of ring. Like the river flowing over a collapsed bridge, it crashed and surged, tidal rolls creating whirlpools and eddies that had never existed before.

I felt them, and each time I passed one, I understood them a little more.

The structures were my will made solid, mana constrained into a solid form, made that way by my subconscious desire alone. Helped by that furry shit-biscuit, but made by me.

That, in turn, meant that if I could do it unconsciously, I could damn well rebuild them intentionally. I could make them better as well.

Racing along, I sensed one of them approaching, and I sank into the mana vanishing below the surface and reaching out. In my mind's eye, I saw the ring as a shattered mass of stone, fluted like old Roman columns, worn and weathered by time and the flow of water.

Reaching out, I gripped the largest fragment, feeling it stir beneath my hands. A gout of trapped mana that had been somehow kept there by this fragment suddenly released.

There was a layer of "sludge" at the bottom of my mana channels, I realized, like sediment in a river—mixtures that were "wrong" and broken, that couldn't be absorbed in the usual ways. Disturbing it sent a great "cloud" of this into my mana channel, floating downstream and making me feel sick as it clogged the channels.

I sensed it was possibly dangerous, and that if I accidentally filled my channels with it properly? It could fuck my mana up for a long time. I vaguely recognized it as a small but significant contributory factor in why I'd been so fucked up when I'd taken the pure mana into myself and torn my mana channels apart, releasing a great wash of this sludge into my body. I'd need to be careful.

I examined the patterning, the breaks, and lifted it, almost effortlessly, sliding it aside to where another fallen section was dimly visible. The breaks at one end roughly matched this one, and I slid them together. A burst of bright light flooded the section when I held them against each other.

The broken section knitted together. I laid my hand over it, a tugging sensation manifesting as more mana was gently pulled free.

Releasing the mana into the break, it sealed in seconds, forming a solid section again, the cracks clear, but filled mainly. Small, shattered sections had come free, and I scoured the bed of my mana channels, finding them and twisting, checking them and slotting them in, like a jigsaw puzzle.

More great sections were laid nearby, where they'd fallen. They'd been torn apart by the concentrated blast of pure mana, I knew, and I got to work. Sections lifted and spun as I proceeded, fixing each bit, pulsing as more sections connected, always moving slowly and carefully to avoid stirring up more sediment than I could avoid.

Soon I was ready, unable to find any more of this mass, and I reached out, finding the fracture nearby where the section of the ring that was buried below the channel sheared off.

Lifting the repaired mass, I floated it along, sliding it back into place and feeling the mana that was being drawn from me change.

I had a choice to make, I suddenly knew, as the ring began to glow. Sections of it brightened and dimmed, as the breaks healed over and spiderwebbed cracks were inundated with healing mana.

I was a Storm Titan, or I would be eventually.

I'd been pulling all mana in, breaking it down, fragmenting it and absorbing the mana I could from the basic four elements more recently, and before that Air and Fire.

Now, though, I had a ring that I'd remade myself.

The rings were something that you normally developed as you were much older, and more experienced, I knew…somehow. Thor had guided me toward them as part of his "make a titan out of the idiot" plan or goal or whatever he did when he wasn't fucking other cats and making life miserable for anything smaller than him.

These rings compressed and sped up my mana system. The faster it flowed, the more of a drag was created—a vacuum, almost, that sucked in more mana, improving my mana regeneration almost by accident.

They didn't just do that, though.

I could feel the possibilities.

The rings were powerful and advanced techniques. They could compress and speed up as they did currently, or had done before, but they could also act as filters, with a little pushing and a few minor changes.

They were currently comprised of every mana and none, generalists in the true sense of the word, and masters of nothing.

If instead I was to rebuild them, and do it right? I could massively boost my mana. Admittedly, I was doing everything as I always did, mixing half-seen and sensed information and instincts with my beliefs that this was what a cat wanted me to do.

I might explode.

I might block all mana from myself except for this one form. That was a serious risk.

Hell, I was specializing a section of my body with a certain form of mana. I might end up converting that section to Fire or Earth, have my hand drop off as the wrist it was attached to suddenly converted to Water.

It could do anything, but I had to risk it. I couldn't accept that I was plateaued with my growth. Not as I had been. No, I needed to get things moving, and I needed to understand my goddamn mana to do that.

I warred with myself, worrying that this could be fucking insanely stupid, but…

"Matt!"

A hand shook my shoulder roughly, and I opened my eyes, blinking up through frost-encrusted eyelashes at Kelly, who stood over me, looking panicked. The structure I'd been holding together with my mind and mana, but that wasn't fully fixed, collapsed again.

My mana channels shook as I groaned. A fresh burst of hitherto suppressed crap mana burst up to the surface and made me want to vomit as it clogged my mana streams.

"Matt, we've got problems," Kelly said, before grabbing me as I fell off the chair, disturbing my carefully set up windbreaks and I started to retch on the floor.

"Matt?" She gasped, rolling me onto my side and helping me by asking me a million stupid goddamn questions, even as I tried to get control again.

I eventually managed to free my hand from the confines of the sleeping bag and reached up, putting it over her mouth.

"Stop," I wheezed, shaking my head slowly as the world began to settle at last. The entire time she'd been there, she'd been talking, asking me questions, panicking that I'd been poisoned or something worse.

It'd all been a wash of noise, a sensory overload as I was already dealing with the sediment mana flooding my system and contaminating my core.

I blinked, groaning, and blew out an extended breath, focusing on the icy-cold layer of frost across the tiles before me, and took a long, shuddering breath in, before lowering my hand and looking at a very worried Kelly.

"I'm sorry," I whispered. "It was too much…the noise, the questions…"

"I'm sorry, I wouldn't have woken you, but—"

"But what?" I swallowed hard and forced a fresh, if weaker, wave of nausea down. "For the record, if I'm that deep in meditation, never, *ever* wake me like that," I said, refusing to let free a burp that I just knew would end badly.

"There's a portal being built in the dungeon," Kelly said quickly, getting it all out in a rush. "And we've got less than an hour before it opens!"

I pulled up the frantically blinking notification, seeing the real-time countdown ticking away as I read.

To all Inhabitants of the Second Steel Dungeon!

Congratulations!

You have climbed to the height of the mighty rank of Steel, and the issues that had prevented your core from fully unlocking have now been resolved!

The Nexus Gate is undergoing construction and in a little over 47 of your minutes, it will complete the process of linkage. Soon, additional dungeons will be connected to your own.

The Primary Nexus Gates will all unlock at the same time, allowing the inhabitants of the six primary dungeons to interact. Speak to your Dungeon Fairy for more details and to make the necessary arrangements.

> **Note:** Due to the impressive speed of your evolution, you gained an additional primary bonus for the dungeon, and both of these are outstanding still. Please speak to your Dungeon Fairy to attempt to access this reward!

"Well, fuck." I groaned, facepalming. In all the shit that had been going on, I'd forgotten about the nexus gates.

CHAPTER ELEVEN

"What do we do?" Kelly asked, helping me as I stood, kicking the sleeping bag free and standing, quickly gathering up all the crap I'd set out and carrying it toward the door to the stairs.

"We dump this in the first room we come to and sort it out later," I said. "Then we get ready. They might all be friendly, or we might be under attack in an hour. Get Aly, Mike, Griffiths, Ashley, and Ramnik, as well as any of the council you can. We need to get a move on."

I clattered down the stairs and into the first room. It was bare apart from an empty bottle of vodka, some burned patches where some cigarettes had been put out, and a handful of chairs.

Clearly they'd been looted from somewhere else and brought here by someone, and I dumped my gear by the door, not really caring. I'd get to it later, but if I was going to sit up there regularly until the gym or whatever was constructed, it seemed wasteful to just absorb it all back into the dungeon and recreate it each time.

I shrugged and turned my back on the mystery of who was using the room, jogging back up to the roof, and running straight across to the edge.

I leapt off, pulling my Storm mana into primacy and burning a little as I flew…only to develop a little wobble as the sudden thought that as screwed-up as my mana channels were after that little fuck-up, I might have discovered I couldn't use them, while plunging over the side and falling toward the ground.

Thankfully, I didn't. Instead I flew fast through the air toward the Parthenon reproduction council building, landing lightly and pushing open the nearest door.

I hesitated, waving back behind me at a couple of distant cheers that rang out. Clearly the sight of me flying was still working for some of the inhabitants. I strode in, tugging the door closed behind, barely noticing the wash of heat that rolled over me.

This building had been designed as both a refuge and proof of who we were and what we would be. It was a massive marble creation, laid out to mirror the original Greek Parthenon at the peak of its glory, with half of the building dedicated to open spaces for the inhabitants of the dungeon, and half to the actual business of the dungeon.

The front was all coffee stands and bakeries, play areas for the kids and areas for people to relax. A library had started up, with all the books we'd found so far available to be summoned at any time. The ones that had been created were returned here when people were done with them, set on shelves so people could wander through them and pick something that was clearly another's most favored book.

There were rooms that could be used to meditate or to have meetings, places you could go that were neither your rooms nor the canteen, and where you could just "be," without any stress.

The back half of the building was devoted to the real dungeon: research sections, council chambers, and a war room. It included areas that Clarissa and her people—all elderly to say the least—could relax and interface with the dungeon to spread its influence, with a Life generator next to their recliners. The wonders of pure Life mana flowed through them as they worked, growing healthier by the second.

It was a place of happy madness, of kids running around in safety, and of adults drinking coffee and relaxing…the trust that we were all working to better the dungeon, and therefore each other's lives. If someone was wandering around in here and doing nothing? That was totally fine, because they'd clearly been helping and working, and just needed a break.

That was the intention of it, anyway.

As soon as I strode in, I was met with the sight of my former neighbors and the wonderfully cheery face of that fucker "Councilman" Merriman.

They saw me, my jeans and a top, clearly disheveled, hair and beard a mess and overgrown, partially coated in frost, and they all broke into a round of loud complaints, demands, and mutterings, along with at least thirty other people behind them.

The peace and chaotic tranquility of the Parthenon was shattered by their uproar, and I could see dozens of other people all glaring at them. Clearly this had been going on awhile.

"What the hell is this?" I snapped, seeing a harassed-looking Michelle behind them, clearly relieved that I was there, and annoyed that I'd seen her having so much stress.

She was one of the original inhabitants who had come with Becky from the sports stadium, moving in with Jo and the group and her husband Ian. They had a ten-month-old baby girl, and she was pretty much ready to drop their second child any day now. She was a hell of a worker, kind and polite with everyone, and seeing the harassed and relieved expression on her face made my blood boil.

"Dungeon Lord!" Michelle greeted me, using my title in an effort to make it clear I wasn't someone to fuck with, as if me being damn near seven foot of solid muscle that could fly and use magic, not to mention a willingness to shoot people in the face at minor provocations, didn't. "I was explaining to these people that—"

"She's refusing to allow us access to the council chambers!" the sow-in-a-dress who used to live below me trumpeted indignantly.

"Of course she is," I agreed, frowning at her. "Why the hell would any of you be allowed in there?"

"We're the new council!" she proclaimed proudly.

"And unlike the previous council, we were democratically elected," Complete Dickhead Merriman added in quickly, stepping forward and folding his arms across his chest. "We demand—"

"No." I snorted, pushing past him and sending him staggering. "None of you are on my council, and I don't give two shits what you want. As to the previous council not being democratically elected, yeah. I lived in Newcastle most of my life—I heard some of the backhanded shit you were all pulling to get votes, but I don't care."

"The previous council of Newcastle WAS democratically elected!" Merriman spat, lunging forward and grabbing at me. "Unlike you and your band of thieves…"

"Thieves!" Sharon, the pig in a dress screeched, storming forward.

"Remove your hand," I growled, glaring at Merriman's hand on my arm.

"I'm a councilor!" Merriman threatened me, reaching up to wave one perfectly manicured finger at my face. "You don't know what you're…"

"Thieves!" The shout rang out again.

"Stealing!" Gerald's voice echoed from somewhere behind the planet he normally rotated.

"It's not right!" another older man complained.

"Disgrace!"

"Shame!"

Merriman, clearly buoyed up by the crowd, jabbed his finger into my chest, even as Sharon shoved forward, drunk on her own delight at some perceived power, and knocked poor Michelle off her feet.

She hit the side of her desk and bounced; as close to giving birth as she was, she was unbalanced and staggered. The marble floor went out from under her as she fell from sight to my left.

Sharon dismissed her as she screeched something about me "Getting what was coming to me."

I snapped.

More accurately, Merriman's finger, where I grabbed it as he stabbed it at me, snapped.

I'd gripped it full on in the palm of my right hand, and I yanked it sideways, even as I let loose the bonds on my usually carefully controlled rage.

Lightning washed out across me. My body flooded with mana that cried out for release as I stared daggers at Sharon. Her face went from red-faced indignation to white-faced terror at the literal lightning that filled my eyes and the screams coming from Merriman.

I'd almost torn his finger off, snapping the bone and dislocating it; the connections had torn as the blood ran free. The Lightning that flooded my body after that point?

For him, it was like having his half-severed finger jammed into a vise while he was being Tasered. His legs went out from under him as he collapsed, screaming and chewing on his own tongue, pissing himself.

I released him to collapse, forgotten, on the floor. "*MOVE!*" I thundered.

And of all the possible places for the terrible excuse for a human being to go, my former neighbor staggered back and to her right, standing on and tripping over Michelle, who'd been trying to get to her feet.

She was knocked down again. This time, the mass of another human not just trampling her, but actually falling on her, made her scream.

I grabbed Sharon by the arm and front of her dress, lifting her and throwing her bodily through the air a good ten meters. She crashed into a chair and toppled over the far side of it, screeching in pain and fear.

I reached out, shoving everyone else back in a great wave of outrage and anger, before stepping forward and crouching by Michelle.

She held her swollen bump protectively, her eyes screwed shut against the pain and biting her lip, trying to keep tears in. I suppressed my mana, feeling the Lightning tamp down so that I wouldn't hurt her as I took her hand.

"I'm here," I assured her. "How bad?"

"The baby…" She gasped, clutching at herself. Tears flooded her cheeks as she looked to me, fear clear on her face, not just pain.

"What happened?" Kelly gasped, staggering in through the door, and I twisted to look at her in relief.

"Get Jo!" I barked at her. "Her and all her people, NOW!"

Kelly had seen the way Michelle cradled herself, and the screaming and crying remnants of the mob all around me. She heard the rising complaints as many of them tried to deny any responsibility, and the horrified look on her face said it all.

She spun, shouting out an order to someone behind her, and then she was moving in, the door swinging as Griffiths and Rhodes followed her.

"We need to get her somewhere private," Kelly told me.

I nodded, gently scooping Michelle up, forcing a smile for Michelle as she gasped her thanks, wincing in pain.

I carried her through the outer areas, toward the private offices, twisting to glare at Griffiths as I went.

"Those fuckers," I growled to him. "Every single one of the assholes who caused this? I want them in a cell. We'll deal with them later."

"Do we have a cell?" Griffiths asked, then held his hands up. "We'll sort it." He twisted to Rhodes, and bellowed orders.

Kelly opened the door ahead of me, leading the way into one of the large meeting rooms, and I cursed, realizing that one of the many things on that list of "to be done" was a proper medical suite.

It'd not been a priority, despite its obvious benefits, because we could heal people with magic. Hell, apart from me in the last few weeks, anyone who was injured was back on their feet in minutes and told to get some rest if they needed it—that was the level of magic we were working at these days.

That meant that the medical suite that was supposed to be built in here, somewhere, was always put off in favor of other buildings.

"No more," I grumbled, focusing and reaching through the dungeon.

The dungeon didn't want to make the changes at first, not with us being there, but it wasn't a hard-coded thing, not like not changing the layout when enemies were there was.

The room around us blurred. The clean lines of the Spartan room with its chairs and tables ready for a meeting vanished. A great wash of light rolled over us as the medical suite was born.

It was crude compared to what we could build—it was common class, the same as the one that we'd built on the other side of the road in the dungeon building on the floor above the canteen.

That wasn't the point, though. It was clean, reassuringly "medical" in design, all antiseptic and sterile, and more to the point, it was right here, rather than carrying her to the medical facility over the road, across the ice and out into the cold.

It was also where we had discussed moving the medical facility anyway, so fuck it. I was the boss and at the end of the day, I was spending *my* dungeon's mana.

I laid Michelle on a bed, shaking my head as she tried to apologize for what had happened outside. I brought Kelly up to date, even as she checked Michelle over, her basic medical training obvious as she worked.

"I'm disappointed you didn't kill anyone." Kelly paused and looked at me, before jerking her head to the side for me to follow her. "Michelle, I'll be back in a minute. We're getting Ian, and I'll make sure you've got some privacy. Just let me talk to Matt."

"I'm sorry…" Michelle started again, and I reached out, squeezing her hand.

"No, Michelle, this happened because you were mobbed by assholes. I'm sorry I didn't put a stop to this before now. Rest and look after yourself and your little one. I'll take care of everything out there."

She nodded as she laid back, tears filling her eyes as she cradled her bump protectively, clearly wishing for the medical facilities of the modern era that could have told her the baby's condition easily.

We moved back. Kelly tugged a curtain around Michelle and drew me across the room. Glancing out the door, I could see disruption by the main doors, which hopefully signified Jo's arrival.

"Matt, we've got less than half an hour before portals to other dungeons might open up. You need to deal with this and right now."

"Oh, I will," I growled. "Griffiths is banging them all in a cell while the medics get a look at Michelle. If she or the baby is hurt? Or—gods forbid—the baby is…isn't—" I shook my head. "They're all on the boundary of banishment. It's only if they live long enough to leave now."

"Make an example of a few of them, maybe the rest will fall back into line. But if not? Get rid of them however you want. Just make damn sure that you're ready for whatever walks out of that portal. I'll deal with this. And Matt?"

"Yeah?"

"Keep Ian with you once he's seen Michelle. He'll only be in the way here."

"What? But he's—"

"He'll go straight to the cells, wherever they are, and cause more problems."

"Fine. Send him to me once he's seen her." I nodded, then let out a sigh of relief as Jo and the others ran down the hall.

I stepped out, holding the door open for them and closing it after as they barreled in, then strode down the hall toward the group angrily refusing to listen to Griffiths because he was "just a soldier" and had "no right to order us about."

I walked into the room, my anger building. I put my hand out into the middle of the rabble, seeing Griffiths's hand resting close to the butt of his gun as he tried to reason with these people.

"Guilty!" I barked, grabbing the shouting figure of one of those I'd recognized screaming into my face earlier. Then I released the restraints on my Lightning.

He screeched as the power of a supercharged Taser flooded through my fingers. I reached out quickly, grabbing all of those within reach, shocking them and sending them to the floor. The others rushed out of reach, looking at the glowing demonic figure in their midst.

"You forget!" I bellowed at the room in general. "You all live here at *my invitation and sufferance*! None of you have a single fucking right in these walls that I don't grant to you. And you *dare* to make demands of me?"

I glared around at them all, well aware of all the innocent people at the back of the room, and the terrifyingly mercurial figure I must appear to some of them now.

"You've a choice to make!" I barked. "You leave, right now! Run to the gate and it'll open for you. You get out of my lands and you never, ever return. If I see you again, I'll kill you myself! That's your first option!"

I turned back, staring at my former neighbors as they sat on the floor with Complete Dickhead Merriman.

"You assaulted a citizen of the dungeon," I spat. "You, who were a guest, permitted to stay here, in safety, eating my food, sleeping in my beds, and complaining all the while that it wasn't good enough. I fought and bled for everything you turned your nose up at. Well, now you decide. You leave right now, and your lives are forfeit if we ever see each other again, or you go quietly to the cells. You'll stand trial for the assault on Michelle. And if she loses her baby? By my word, I'll hang every single fucking one of you personally!"

Sharon went to speak, her mouth opening and flapping as her world of carefully constructed lies and privilege crashed down around her ears.

I raised a hand, one that was suddenly wreathed in crackling lightning. "The gate, or the cell. Any other word out of your mouth, and you die here and now." My cold voice carried in the sudden hush that followed, made even worse when I dismissed the lightning and instead reached out my hand and summoned a fresh hammer into it. The weight was solid and reassuring as I held it up in a warning to all, even as I selected them all in the dungeon sense, blocking them from any access to the system, each and every one.

"Decide quickly."

With that, I turned and marched up the wide marble steps to the upper floor. Griffiths and Rhodes moved quickly, as did their soldiers who had heard the uproar.

People were separated out. A surprising number chose to stay and face the trial rather than be booted out of the gate. Only a handful of the most feral and self-important decided to take that route.

I reached the top of the stairs and pushed through the doors before me. They opened at my presence, as they would for any of the dungeon's inner circle, but until now I'd not felt the real need to enforce the rules.

I silently swore that would change.

People would damn well learn there were limits to my patience, and the fact that Michelle's baby might have been lost to bring things to this point? I was trying to maintain my temper, trying to be calm, but I could feel the danger signs.

I teetered along the edge, dancing on a razor blade of control. My calm was an insanely fragile thing, and I needed to keep it together.

Before me was the main council room, a corridor here leading right and left, and a single set of stairs to the side of the council chamber.

It led up to the final floor, the private one that held the war room and the most secure, "real" council chambers.

I walked into the war room, sensing the incorporeal presence of Aly as she studied something on the main table. It showed, much as the council chamber's table did, the surrounding area in real time.

The difference was, the council chamber was built around a large circular table, one that was designed to sit and discuss things around. It was a nice room to plan things from.

The war room had much the same facilities, but it was standing room only, a handful of chairs pushed to the outside of the room as the wall and table maps were within reach.

I could see maps on the walls of each floor of the dungeon, or the buildings that were inside of its walls. I could pick a building and blow it up into a 3D version, flick through layers and see the people moving through it in real time.

It was a general's dream, permitting perfect access to the entirety of the land we held, able to summon our dungeon creatures and send them exactly where they were most needed.

For now, though, I needed to see the area that Aly already had on the table, zoomed in.

The training dungeon held the nexus gate as it steadily grew. Unlike the usual appearing from hard light, seemingly printed from the ether by an invisible 3D printer of light, this was a bubbling process. The rock and more around it seemed to convert at a molecular level to form the structure, flowing upward as great discs of floating light hovered on three sides, each equidistantly laid out.

The gate was growing, and I looked at the timer, cursing as I saw the time remaining.

27.03…27.02…27.01…

"How much mana do we have?" I asked Aly, glancing at her as she started, having been oblivious to my arrival.

"What? Oh…" She flicked a finger, and a counter appeared on the wall.

Sixteen thousand and eleven points. The counter bounced like an ass on social media, up and down with incredible speed as some added to the pot, and others used it.

"Where are we with research?" I asked bluntly. "Are the ghasts upgraded yet?"

"No…we're working on the mana absorption conduit research," Aly reminded me. "We've kept a decent reserve in the pot, and we're halfway through research now, a little bit more actually. Forty-eight thousand and three points left to go."

"I'm going to the dungeon," I said after a few seconds' thought. "Send Beta, Ashley, and Mike to me. I'll summon a handful of the ghasts once I'm there. They can be ready, just in case."

"Where's Kelly?" Aly suddenly asked, realizing she wasn't with me.

"She's with Michelle, and—"

The door banged open, Ian storming in and glaring round.

"Matt, I want their fucking heads!" he snapped at me, one finger jabbing down the stairs toward where the others were being rounded up and shuffled out by Griffiths and his people.

"I mean it! 'Chelle could have lost the baby! We—"

"What?" Aly practically shrieked, and I held my hands up in the middle of the room as Ashley and Dante hurried into sight at the top of the stairs.

"ENOUGH!" I barked. "Ian, you've got a choice to make, mate. You can come to the dungeon where I can keep an eye on you, or you can wait in the medical rooms. If you're there, you'll damn well stay there and only leave when Aly, Kelly, or I say you can. I'll not have you murdering some idiot because they didn't know to stay out of the way."

"Matt, they could have—"

"I know!" I thundered. "Fuck's sake, Ian, I know, all right! The doctors are working on her. Hopefully it's nothing, but that's why I panicked and got her there. As it is? I don't want you anywhere near the idiots who caused this until the trial because—"

"Because they might get off on some technicality?" Ian spat, rolling his shoulders and clearly getting ready for a fight. "I'm not having some lawyer—"

"Do you see any fucking lawyers?" I asked him grimly. "If the baby is hurt or gods forbid…if there's anything bad? I don't want you getting your hands on them before the trial because you'll kill them too fast!"

"What?"

"If they did what we're afraid of?" I asked him. "They're dead. It'll just not be a short, fast death. Now, choose—with me or sitting outside the medical wing?"

"The…the medical wing," he said gruffly, before seeming to deflate as he nodded at me. "I'm sorry, Matt. I thought…"

"Ian, they're guilty as fuck. I saw it, and I'll damn well be judge, jury, and executioner if this goes badly. Put that out of your mind. Go be with your family…But you damn well stay there. If I find out you've abused my trust by leaving her side…"

I gestured quickly behind him, and he nodded, turning and running back down the stairs, as Ashley and Dante entered, looking worried. Kelly hadn't wanted him there, and she'd chew my ear off over it later, no doubt, but he was the father of that child, and he had the right to decide where he'd be.

I brought all three up to date, starting again when Chris and Mike arrived, then leading the little procession down the stairs and back outside, jogging across the open ground to the training dungeon. Ramnik caught up to us, and the others brought her up to speed.

By the time the six of us were hightailing it through the dungeon, Beta caught up, falling into step beside me.

I wasn't in armor, which I was very much regretting, but then neither were the others. And, frankly, with what we had left in the tank, we couldn't afford to fix that for everyone. Better that we were all armed.

Chris and Mike had gotten their guns reloaded and stood on the wings of the group. Ashley stood by my side as our diplomat, and Dante and Ramnik were behind us and to the sides, ready to let loose with magic if it was needed. Beta was hidden off to one side, the only one of us who was fully armed and actually ready for a fight.

I used a small amount of mana, eight thousand points, to summon twenty ghasts. Then I spread them about the room, stealthed and ready to attack anything I ordered them to.

We were as ready as we could be as the timer counted down, clicking over the last few numbers and then flatlining at 00.00.

TO ALL INHABITANTS OF THE SECOND STEEL DUNGEON!

Congratulations!

Your Nexus Gate is now complete, and the process of linkage has begun! As all six primary dungeons are created equal in the eyes of the Nexus controller, each gate will link to the Nexus platform, opening into a dedicated Safe Zone.

As your Dungeon Fairy will have confirmed to you, no weapons nor aggression is permitted in the Safe Zone. Breach of these rules will result in your expulsion from the Nexus, and a dungeon from the secondary stratum will be elevated in your place.

As a neutral ground for dungeons, you will be permitted access to your five fellow Dungeon Lords, Ladies, and system controllers. Trade is encouraged, as is forming alliances. But beware! The pact of non-aggression only extends to the Nexus Platform itself!

In time, other dungeons will create their first gates, and some will further more choose to link to the Nexus. But unlike your own positions as the Primary Six, they will be housed both in the rung below your own, and will pay a fee for each transportal linked and used.

Final note: Trading hubs may be constructed and offered for 1 premium grade Mana crystal per solar cycle, discounted per your position as a member of the Primary Six. Current position in random rotation: 4th.

Speak to your Dungeon Fairy for more details and to make the necessary arrangements.

> **Note:** Due to the impressive speed of your evolution, you gained an additional primary bonus for the dungeon, and both of these are outstanding still. Please speak to your Dungeon Fairy to attempt to access this reward!

I read it all over, and to my massive relief, instead of linking us to another dungeon directly, this system was linking us to a neutral ground. One that was apparently a "one strike" for any form of aggression, which sort of made sense. After all, the whole point of this was to make us into living weapons to defeat the Orcan. They didn't want us wasting our energies fighting each other.

The trading hubs sounded like it'd be useful, but fuck knew what the hell we could trade. The dungeons could produce anything we wanted, and the Nexus was a link between dungeons that had reached Steel, so it wasn't like the others could give me lasers and shit.

There was the matter of wealth as well. What the hell did we buy shit *with*? What was a "Premium Grade Mana crystal," when it came down to it? I knew I could create mana stones, but no clue as to the grade. I shrugged. I had no way of knowing what lay on the other side.

I couldn't guess what the grade of the stones would be, nor what the intentions of the other dungeons would be until I reached them. Hell, I had no idea what I was walking into, but there was one thing I was damn sure about.

They'd not be expecting a Storm Titan trainee in a foul fucking mood.

"Ashley, you're with me. I'll need diplomatic options," I said grimly. "The rest of you be ready. Just because it says there's a non-aggression situation doesn't mean shit. We'll leave our weapons, but that means fuck all with magic. If we're not back in two hours, assume we've been fucked with. If we're not back in a day, bury this fucking chamber and go on with your lives as best you can."

With that, I dropped my hammer to the floor, shaking my head over how many hammers must be lying around these days thanks to me, and I glanced at Ashley. "You ready?"

"Not even slightly," she said. "Give me five minutes." With that, she ran to the other side of the gate, calling out that we'd "better not be watching." Dante hurried after her, taking up station where he was clearly supposed to be watching us…but was just staring goggle-eyed at his girlfriend.

Chris and I looked at each other. Mike sighed and walked over to join us; Ramnik moved to stand closer to the other side of the gate, watching us to make sure we weren't trying to sneak a peek.

"You know," Chris whispered, looking away and covering his mouth to be sure that neither Dante nor Ramnik could see or overhear him. "A quick look in the dungeon sense…"

"And if Aly, Becky, or Kelly or the others are in and watching us?" Mike shook his head. "A good way to be stabbed in your sleep, mate."

"That's a point." I groaned. "Ashley, I don't know if anyone else is in the dungeon sense…Wait a minute while I…"

"Too late!" Ramnik called. "Better make them leave if they are now!"

"Fuck's sake," I growled, sliding into the dungeon sense and being very careful not to shift around to see the other side of the portal. There were hints of someone being there recently—a sense of motion, of disturbance—but there was nobody now.

I hesitated, honest enough with myself to admit I was tempted to "accidentally" look…but didn't. It would be a shitty thing to do to any friend, let alone someone I trusted and who trusted me so much.

I watched the room, waiting, until Ashley stepped out from behind the portal and hurried over to meet us. Dante was at her side, his arms full of her previous clothing.

"Hope it's not cold where you're going." Mike shook his head at Ashley, even as she adjusted herself for maximum effect.

"If it is, I'll just distract them more." She shrugged, grinning at the response that simple movement had on everyone.

Before, she'd been dressed normally, more or less. Combat trousers that seemed to fit her slightly better than anyone else, and a plain, long-sleeved black top, her hair up in a bun, dagger on one hip, handgun on the other, sword across her shoulders and down her back.

She'd looked like the kind of woman who would have made Conan propose on the spot.

Now, she looked far more sex kitten than warrior goddess, especially at the way that she was about to fall out of her top, in a very low-cut red halter neck and a matching skirt, high heels that made her sway with every step as she quickly applied a few extra touches to her makeup, before smiling and handing the makeup compact to Dante, kissing his cheek and whispering something in his ear.

"Okay." She shook her hair out. "Give me one more second..."

She seemed to shiver, as if a ripple of water across a pond had flowed down her, passing over her entirely from head to toe, and suddenly my mouth was dry.

I could barely focus on anything. My need to not look—after all, she was both a subordinate and a friend—was overshadowed by my raging need and...

She clicked her fingers and winked at me, making me feel sick for a split second as the world around me swam back into focus. Just like that, she was back to normal, and she smiled at me as even Ramnik continued to gaze at her lustfully.

"Sorry, Matt," she said. "I recently leveled, and I put an extra point into Distraction. I was thinking it'd hide the kink in my hair from it being tied up, but..." She looked around and grinned. "Maybe we should go...you know, *before* Chris starts humping my leg?"

I looked at him, seeing the look of utter carnal lust on his face, and I nodded. "Yeah, let's go."

"I can't keep this active long. It uses mana and stamina, but when we step through, I'll keep it up for a few seconds. I excluded you from the field, so you'll be able to look about while they're distracted," Ashley said calmly, pushing her shoulders back and tits up, making a dozen tiny adjustments that reminded me of me settling my armor right before a fight.

"Good plan," I agreed, remembering that for her, this *was* her armor. The pair of us moved to the portal and hesitated unconsciously on the step, before I offered her my arm automatically.

I might be a Storm Titan trainee, I might be a god ascending—hell, I was a Dungeon Lord and a goddamn sexual tyrannosaurus—but Mama Aurelia did her best to drum some manners into me.

As Ashley and I stepped across the portal threshold, travelling across possibly time and space, for a split second, I was the gentleman that wonderful woman had tried to raise.

Chapter Twelve

The world seemed to lurch to one side. The event horizon of the portal between *there* and *here* slid from our skin as we stepped down on the far side.

It'd felt like a statically applied covering had been peeled from us, like you used to get on all the high-tech items when you bought them, protecting the metal from fingerprints and so on.

There was that feeling of dragging, of something pulling in every direction, but backward as we stepped through into this new world.

I blinked, stunned by the sudden wash of civility. There was low music playing—a piano, I guessed—somewhere nearby, the lights were warm but low, the floor carpeted deeply enough that I could feel it through my boots.

I was suddenly and uncomfortably aware that Ashley had donned her "armor" for this meeting and looked amazing, while I was wearing jeans and a plain, long-sleeved black top.

Admittedly, it could barely contain me. I stretched the soft material in all sorts of ways that would have gotten me a modelling contract pre-fall, or at least a cover slot on the front of a romance novel.

I was seriously underdressed compared to her, though, and as I looked around the room, I stifled an oath. I was seriously underdressed compared to the others as well.

The room we were in was a large one, circular, with large portal style windows. The floor was covered with a dark and deep shag carpet; the walls gently curved, and here and there a potted plant stood beneath a glowing light. The ceiling overhead was a good ten feet up and had obvious reinforcing as metal beams crossed over to meet in the center.

The others who were here already stood on the far side of the room, drinks in hand, having been staring out of a window at something that seemed to be brightly lit below us.

There were three distinct groups: one Asian, wearing what looked to be an old style of formal robes; one as dark-skinned as I'd ever seen, covered in gold. The final pair were different again, an American I guessed straightaway, both by the cowboy hat and boots, as well as the empty gun holsters on either hip. He was on his own, or at least when it came to a human partner.

All three had a fairy with them.

Each fairy was entirely different. The one with the African couple was jet black, the one with the American looked like a porn version of Tinker Bell, complete with stockings and suspenders, and the Asian...

They had a tiny Chinese dragon that was draped across the shoulders of the woman, its mouth close to her ear as they all regarded us both.

"No skills, spells nor abilities may be in use here!" the porno-fairy snapped, flashing through the air to hover close to us, glaring at Ashley. "Stop the glamour or…"

"My lord?" Ashley asked me, turning and looking up, clearly making our positions clear to everyone that we weren't a couple; instead, ours was a more formal relationship.

"That's fine." I nodded and patted her arm, before releasing it.

The shift from the glamour spell, or the Distraction ability that she'd been using, was obvious, and yet not. The five humans around the room all seemed to shake and come awake, but when you looked at Ashley, there wasn't any one thing you could point to as different.

The fairy swept in closer, glaring at her, opening her mouth to say something, then hissed in dislike and zipped back across the room.

She landed on the American's shoulder and whispered into his ear, as the two dark-skinned individuals strode forward. They were as tall as I was, if not taller, seriously heavily muscled. And damn.

Their skin was that deep blue-black that spoke of a life in the sun, combined with model good looks, ridiculously fit bodies, and plain black silken trousers.

Then add in the gold and the beautiful deep-red silken top that the woman wore? They were stunning, the pair of them. She wore three golden chains leading from her nose to her right ear, and her head trimmed so close she was almost bald, him with a head shaved and clearly recently polished as well.

The pair of them were intimidating, both as brawn and beauty, and they moved to stand before me quickly. Their fairy hovered between them, looking as if she'd been dipped in that ultra-black paint. Two tiny pinpricks of bright-white light for her eyes gave the only hint she was watching.

"Be welcome," the man said suddenly, extending a hand in greeting.

I jerked, a little surprised, then took his hand, covering my surprise as best I could. "Thank you." I smiled, pleased that he didn't go for the "me big man crush your hand" that so many tried.

"This is my wife, Akuba, and I am Kaatachi." He introduced them, and I nodded, introducing Ashley first as my assistant and friend, leaving that deliberately open-ended, as I wondered about Kaatachi.

"And I'm Matt," I said. "Kaatachi, I have to ask, your accent?"

"We met in London." He nodded to his wife, who smiled. "People tend not to expect either of us to speak any outside language, I know."

"It wasn't that…" I lied, then shook my head. "Okay, yeah, I was expecting an African dialect, sorry."

"Don't be." He smiled. "It's our nature to expect certain things when we meet people for the first time. I have grown used to it."

"I was an exchange student studying economics; he was there on a nuclear track," she explained, and I cocked an eyebrow at him.

"Nuclear?"

"Engineering," he admitted, his smile wide and brilliant. "I was studying to be a nuclear engineer, but that's not important now. Please, come and we will introduce you." He moved to the side, gesturing to the others who'd remained by the window, and I nodded my thanks.

"Your fairy…" a new voice said softly, and I glanced to the jet-black fairy who hung there in the air, wings blurring as she regarded me. "Did you kill her to assume control of the dungeon?"

"Onyx!" Akuba said quickly, shaking her head. "Now is not the—"

"We must know." The fairy, named Onyx apparently, slowly circled me. "To be one of the first to reach Steel, he must have had help, or be responsible for many deaths."

"Our ally raises an interesting point," Kaatachi agreed, nodding. "But before we ask such a question, it is good manners to at least greet our fellow guests. This is—"

"Bryan!" the American boomed, stepping forward and grabbing my hand, pumping it once and then clearly dismissing me, as he focused on Ashley. "Ah'm Bryan Martin, little lady, an' ah'm a Dungeon System Controller! It's one o' the highest—and rarest—classes out there! An' what, may ah ask, is *your* class?"

"I'm a Courtesan," Ashley replied honestly, smiling brilliantly at him.

He stepped in close, presenting his back to me and offering his arm to her in a way that was clearly intended to provoke me, and to get her attention. And she honest to fucking God *giggled*, taking his arm and walking to stand next to him.

I played the part, glaring at him, while internally I was laughing my arse off. Damn, she'd just singled out the lecherous fool of the group and was by his side in seconds. His fairy landed on her shoulder and tried to speak, only to be gestured away by Bryan.

The fairy took off and glared daggers at Ashley, even as the Asian couple stepped forward, glancing from one side to the other, and introducing themselves to the room at large.

"I am Kai." The man bowed sharply at the waist, then introduced his partner, who stood behind and slightly to one side of him. "And this is Leilani, my sister."

"We are the Dungeon Lord and Lady of the Hainan Province," Leilani said proudly. "Our family has taken responsibility for the island and its surrounding area."

"They mean they're conquering it," Bryan drawled loudly to Ashley.

"We are returning control of the province to those who know it best," Kai said, clearly uninterested in arguing with the American.

"And where are you from?" I asked Akuba and Kaatachi.

"Tulawe in Ghana," Akuba answered. "A small town, but when the dungeon grew, we met Onyx and she offered us sanctuary, provided we could learn to work for the betterment of our species."

"Ah, that's just bull-shit." Bryan snorted. "Fuck the betterment of the species. We need to be workin' toward survival! You know it's possible to make guns with the right tech? Ah've got a dungeon that's right on the brink of becomin' the first armory for the planet!"

"Really?" Ashley squeaked, her eyes wide as she pressed her chest to his arm, making his eyes almost fall out, they were that deep into her cleavage. "You'll have to tell me all about it…Matt's dungeon isn't so big yet…"

"Ah well, ya see missy…" Bryan started, grinning at me and rolling his shoulders. He obviously loved the effect that he appeared to be having on Ashley.

I glanced at Akuba, who shook her head in amazement at how the pair were acting.

"Matt, have you seen the wonder that lies below us?" Kai asked, and I shook my head, moving over to the window…and grunting as if I'd just been punched in the dick.

Before and below us was the Earth, slowly rotating with the sun lighting one side, the nighttime terminator rolling across the other.

I could see great swathes of green. The lands below us took a few seconds to resolve for me, before they finally matched up, and I blinked rapidly.

"That's South America," I whispered, stunned. "We're in orbit?"

"We are," Kai said. "We appear to be locked into a regular orbit, with the Earth passing below us…"

"Geostationary orbit!" Bryan called out, before going back to trying to whisper in Ashley's ear, one arm snaking around behind her back.

"It is not," Leilani said to the rest of us quietly. "We have been observing the orbit for the last few minutes. The position of the world below us changes relative to us. The day/night terminator line remains constant. We are in sun-synchronous orbit."

"Fair enough," I agreed, shrugging. "So, nobody asked their fairies?"

"Asked us what?" the Chinese dragon asked me coldly.

"Why we're here and why we're in space?" I replied.

"You are here, because despite your actions as a murderer, you remain in control of a dungeon. For now," Onyx replied grimly.

"I love that you all make the same assumption." I shook my head in disbelief. "I mean, not that I really have to explain myself, but you fairies always jump to the same conclusion, that I murdered my fairy to gain control."

"And you didn't?" The Chinese dragon flowed around behind Leilani's head and leapt from her shoulder to land on Kai's.

"No. She was dead when I found the dungeon," I replied. "The ship had crashed, and the dungeon core was damaged, hanging out of the wreckage. The fairy was killed in the crash, I assume."

"Then why do you share her soul?" Onyx asked, and I glared at her.

"That's none of your business," I snapped.

"You said that we 'always jump to the same conclusion.' You have had meetings with another dungeon then?" the dragon asked.

I nodded, well aware that the others were judging me on this and listening. "Yeah, my dungeon wasn't supposed to be where it was, I think. There was another one about a mile from where I set it up—"

"That is far too close!" Onyx growled. "You literally set up inside of another's territory?"

"I didn't know," I snapped back at her. "It's not like you fuckers come with a manual, is it! I didn't even know that dungeon was there until it fucking attacked me!"

"It was defending itself." She sniffed, and I glared at her.

"I was drawn by the soul of the dead fairy and made to touch the dungeon core," I said calmly and coldly. "Once I did? I was almost killed by the core, and told I had to set it up as soon as possible in a high mana area, or I'd die."

"So you set it up in the same area as an existing dungeon, and attacked it?" the dragon asked coolly.

"No, it attacked me. No warning, no negotiation. And it didn't just attack me. It was collecting the locals. It set up in a supermarket and was spawning goblins, using them to imprison the locals and sacrifice them on an altar."

"Did you discuss this with the fairy?" The dragon reared up and regarded me thoughtfully as the humans watched.

"Yeah, she was doing it for 'the greater good,'" I said grimly. "Sacrificing a smaller number of humans now to fuel the technological growth of the dungeon to enable her to save more in the future. Supposedly that was a good excuse for genocide."

"It wasn't genocide," Onyx said slowly, but she shook her head as I opened my mouth to argue. "No, I apologize. I understand why you would feel aggrieved at your treatment by a dungeon pairing that choose that path."

"What did you do with the secondary dungeon?" Leilani asked me, and I shrugged.

"I fractured the core and absorbed it."

"What did you gain?" Onyx asked quickly, and I smiled.

"Nothing I want to share right now." I looked around. "No offense, but I've just met you and…"

Another portal suddenly flared to life, drawing all our eyes. Then a pair of non-humans stepped through, glaring around.

Instantly the atmosphere in the room changed as all of us drew together, and the pair stalked across to face us.

"I am Orish," the larger of the two growled at us.

"I am Ornet," the second echoed.

"We claim this structure in the name of the Enlightened One," they said in unison.

The entire room chimed loudly, before we all received a fresh pop-up.

Welcome Dungeon Lords, Ladies, System Controllers, and Guests.

This structure is currently neutral territory and cannot be claimed by any one faction unless all remaining factions relinquish their claim upon it.

>***Steel Dungeon #1: Do you relinquish your claim?***

>***Steel Dungeon #2: Do you relinquish your claim?***

>***Steel Dungeon #3: Do…***

"Fuck no," I snapped.

I spoke as my dungeon, the second one, was asked, and as soon as I'd said it aloud, the prompt stopped. Kai spoke directly after me as well, Leilani echoing him and making me assume they were Dungeon #3.

"You challenge me?" the big fucker growled.

I opened my mouth, ready to tell him to get fucked, but Ashley spoke before I could.

"This is neutral territory, and we do not accept nor approve of your challenge," Ashley said clearly, and I grunted, remembering the details of entry into here.

"I challenge you all!" Orish snarled, thrusting his chest out and glaring round.

He—I assumed it was a he, anyway, by the deeper voice—he, or she or it, or whatever, was a little bigger than I was at nearly eight foot, but it was markedly alien.

The pair of them were wide of face, scaled, and bald apart from a stripe of bright-green hair that ran from their foreheads down their backs. Their scales made me think of a frog or a toad's skin: not quite flesh, but bumpy as fuck, though there were spiked tips of bones showing through here and there as well.

They were a dull grey/green over most of their bodies, with a wide section from their lower jaw down to the armor they wore that was a lighter yellow in color.

Small stubby horns atop their head made it look as though they were diseased or something. A dozen little lumps and bumps created a pattern that was clearly for something, though I didn't have a fucking clue what it was.

I'd also noticed they didn't have a fairy with them.

"No," I said clearly, and just like that, everyone shifted. Kai and Leilani were behind me and to the right, Bryan was backing up and seemed to be trying to hide behind a fucking potted plant, and Akuba and Kaatachi were behind me and to the left.

Ashley stood to the side, but level with me, directly opposing Ornet, while I faced Orish. The others were mainly close enough to help, but making it clear they were separate as well.

I could hear the low murmur of the fairies advising their allies, but I only had eyes for the big fucker.

"No?" He huffed, lowering his head and staring into my eyes, as if waiting for me to elaborate. "You are a weak, malformed thing…you refuse my challenge?"

"I refuse your challenge," I said loudly. "This is neutral territory."

"Coward," it hissed, showing its teeth, but also, I noticed, not attacking. It balled a fist, as if about to strike and out of the corner of my eye, Ashley shook her head gently.

It might be just her flipping her hair back or something, but it made me think, and I gave the smallest of nods, letting her know I'd seen it.

We'd been warned not to fight, that we would be banned. For us to have been warned, these fuckers had to have been as well. And there was no way that someone too dumb to know that they couldn't start a fight here was going to have made it to ruling one of the top six dungeons.

That meant they either knew something I didn't…or they were bluffing.

A thought sprang up then. If I was attacked, regardless of why, in neutral territory, I should have the right to claim recompense at the very least, if it was truly monitored.

I was being fucking set up.

"You're talking a lot for someone that wants a fight," I said, my mouth moving before my brain was sure. "We can all see who the coward is."

I shrugged and turned my back on him, waiting and torn between wanting him to attack, and being damn sure it was going to fucking hurt.

I managed a single step before he roared, fury evident, and I stiffened, knowing this was needed, that I had to let a blow fall before I could defend myself, and just fucking pray they didn't go for my throat or anything.

Nothing.

I took another step, then looked back over my shoulder, seeing him standing in the same spot, glaring at me.

I did the only sensible thing I could do, when confronted with a giant frogman that wanted to kill me.

I blew him a kiss.

That did it.

He'd gone pale before, his partner hissing something to him, clearly trying to keep him in check, but the kiss, well, it passed all species boundaries. A bit like lobbing my dick out and pissing on him probably would have.

He lunged for me, claws extending from sheathes hidden in the fingers, and the room went suddenly cold.

WARNING:

WEAPON DETECTED.

HOSTILE INTENT CONFIRMED.

The ground under the fucker vanished suddenly, and he and his partner were yanked downward as the seemingly solid floor, coated in carpet, was revealed to be nanotech that had been waiting for a command.

The pair of them screeched in fury, outrage, and fear as they were dragged downward…smacking into the edge of the floor where it was still solid, before being yanked backward and out of sight. Then there was a screech of pain, and a second later, silence as the floor reformed.

We all stared at one another in shock, as a new notification arrived before us all.

REGRETFULLY, A REPRESENTATIVE OF THE FIFTH STEEL DUNGEON HAS BREACHED THE AFOREMENTIONED NEUTRAL TERRITORY. THE OFFENDING PARTIES HAVE BEEN REMOVED, AND REPARATIONS WILL BE ENFORCED. THE FIFTH STEEL DUNGEON HAS BEEN RECONFIRMED AS THE LOWEST STEEL DUNGEON, AND WILL REMAIN SO, UNTIL IT REACHES THE NEXT EVOLUTIONARY STAGE.

ALL OTHER DUNGEONS BELOW FIFTH HAVE BEEN MARKED UP ONE LEVEL, AND THE NEWLY CONFIRMED SIXTH STEEL DUNGEON WILL BE OFFERED ACCESS TO THIS NEUTRAL TERRITORY.

I nodded, banishing the screen, then smiled at the next one that popped up.

APOLOGIES, DUNGEON LORD OF THE SECOND STEEL DUNGEON. THE ATTACK UPON YOU, WHILE NOT ENTIRELY FAULTLESS ON YOUR PART, WAS CLEARLY ORCHESTRATED BY ANOTHER. AS SUCH, YOU WILL BE COMPENSATED.

PLEASE CHOOSE FROM THE FOLLOWING OPTIONS:

1) RANDOM DESIGN UNLOCK

2) RANDOM SPECIES UNLOCK

3) RANDOM RESEARCH BOOST

I grimaced, looking them all over. I'd had hopes for something specific, but fuck it, all right. My guess, and Ashley's quick thinking, had paid off. Now to the nitty-gritty.

The random design unlock was a possibility. Although it was possible I'd get a toenail clipper, it was equally possible that said toenail clipper would be legendary in level as basic.

It was random, after all.

A legendary toenail clipper would probably be able to kill a fucking dragon if it was low-leveled enough.

I shrugged and moved on, leaving that on the back burner.

Random species unlock was tempting as well. After all, a troll or a dragon could be amazing. Again, it was just as likely as it was that I'd get an earthworm.

Last of all was a research boost. That…that was the shittiest option, and the most directly useful. For it to be a research option, I had to get it, and if it was far enough down the line that I'd have never gotten it otherwise, well, it had to be unlocked for me to get it.

It'd be like unlocking nuclear weapons or some shit. I couldn't do that without the other techs leading up to it, so it might include them, or it might not, and I'd have just wasted the fucker.

I dismissed that one, narrowing it to two choices.

A random design, or a species.

Logically, these were things from all of space and more, anything the dungeons had access to. If I took a species, I was much more likely to end up with a species that couldn't survive here than I was to get one that could.

There were space-born civilizations, after all. I seriously doubted all of them came from planets like Earth.

If I chose wrong, I might get a species that farted liquid nitrogen or something and that would kill us all in seconds, entirely accidentally.

No, at least if it was a design, and it was shit or lethal to us, I could not build it, and we might still be able to use parts of the design.

I reached out mentally and tagged that one, feeling a little tingle as a new bit of information was shared instantly with both me and the dungeon.

APOLOGIES, DUNGEON LORDS, LADIES, SYSTEM CONTROLLERS, AND GUESTS. A BREACH OF THE PEACE HAS BEEN DETECTED AND DEALT WITH, THE OFFENDING PARTIES DISCIPLINED, AND MATTERS HAVE BEEN RESOLVED TO THE SATISFACTION OF THE OFFENDED PARTY.

PLEASE RETURN TO YOUR PREVIOUS ACTIVITIES.

"You are brave," Kaatachi said softly once I banished my screens.

"Stupid, more like it!" Bryan snorted. "Hey, little lady, let's get back to that conversation we wus havin'."

"I take it there was an offer of compensation?" Onyx floated forward and hovered before me.

"There was," I admitted. They could see that much on the notification they must have all gotten, so there was no point in denying that.

"You have no dungeon fairy to guide you," she said after a few seconds, and I nodded, noting the way that Ashley had deliberately moved Bryan away from the conversation, clearly trusting him about as far as a cling film condom, just as I did.

There was a gasp a second later, and we all looked at the window, following Ashley's pointing finger as the two assholes floated past, clearly asphyxiating.

We watched them for a few more seconds, until they drifted out of sight, then looked at each other, more than a little unnerved.

The others were waiting, though, all listening and not being shy about it, but I wasn't giving shit away unless I needed to. Nothing they couldn't guess, anyway.

"Do you know the purpose of the dungeons?" Onyx asked, and I shrugged.

"I think so."

"What do you 'think' it is?" she asked more firmly.

"I think your masters wanted Earth to provide a galactic peacekeeping force," I said flatly, staring into her pinprick bright eyes. "I think they were willing to kill us all if it got them their soldiers, and they don't give a shit beyond that."

"That is...not entirely incorrect." The Chinese dragon moved forward and floated through the air as if weightless. "We were augmented by the Cinthian technicians to provide access to the less obvious dungeon systems, and we were tied to them.

"There were changes wrought in us, and amongst them was the need to provide and guide the dungeons. We must raise them as safely, and yet quickly, as is ethically possible. Once this is done, we are to search out allies for the dungeon, forming positive pair bonding between the dungeon and local inhabitants.

"You are unique in that, as far as I know, you are the only local variant humanoid to have bonded to a dungeon in the long-term. You grew your core from Stone, all the way till now?"

"I did."

"Then you have made tremendous advances, regardless of how these were achieved. You will, however, have made errors. You will have erroneous information that you have acted upon. You may believe some things that are incorrect, simply because you were never able to discuss them with another who had any of the answers."

"I can see that."

"I offer counsel," the Chinese dragon said. "Uncharged for advice, honestly given, in exchange for questions honestly answered."

"That sounds a lot like you answer my questions, I'll answer yours." I frowned. "That's charging for it. Information has value, after all."

"See it as you will. I offer it freely." The little dragon floated forward again, closer. It opened its mouth and extended its tongue, showing a tiny, triangular, glossy golden scale sitting there.

It offered it, and I reached out and took it, glancing over it curiously.

"Should you have questions, press the token to the portal, and it will attempt a link between our portals. You may ask any questions you wish."

"Thank you." I nodded slowly. "I can't give you one of these in return..."

"I understand." The little dragon shared a sharp-toothed grin, before floating back to Kai and landing on his shoulder. "I'm Lysander, by the way."

"Nice to meet you," I said politely, before glancing at Onyx as she floated forward as well.

"I will offer the same. Freely given advice, in exchange for questions answered, and possibly an exchange of technology?" She offered a black scale, one that shone with an incandescent light as I tilted it this way and that.

"Thank you," I said softly. "You mentioned tech?"

"That is why we are all here, is it not?" Kaatachi stepped forward. "This is neutral territory. The traditional uses for such is for trade between those who cannot trust each other elsewhere, and to discuss diplomatic offers that cannot be made publicly."

"Each of us are too far apart currently for any realistic form of assistance beyond technological," Kai agreed. "While we have many hands in our province, those who would be of most assistance to others…we would not wish to part with. If anyone should be looking for cheap, unskilled labor, however? Perhaps a deal could be made."

"We've got plenty of people," I said. "I'd take weapons though, or…"

"Or?" Akuba asked.

I snorted. "Dinosaur bones," I said. "And any form of magical animals, preferably that could be used as cavalry."

"Well, hell boy, ah've got plenty of horses…" Bryan started, and I looked at him, waiting.

"Are they magical?" I asked after a minute of silence.

"You ever met a magic horse?" he countered.

"Well, considering I asked for magical animals…I'd say that's a prerequisite," I tried to hide my annoyance as he tucked his fingers behind his belt and grinned at me.

"Well, maybe they're magic, maybe they ain't. All ah know is they're *fast*."

"I don't suppose you've got any…?" I asked Kai and Leilani, who both shook their heads.

"We have several museums, however. I shall look into the bones, and thank you for that idea," Kai said with a faint smile. "Should we have any success, I shall provide you with a template, or sample, if possible."

"Thank you." I figured that was probably the very best I could reasonably expect.

"As to technology," Akuba said, looking at Kaatachi. "What would you all be interested in?"

"And what do you have to trade?" I asked, quickly, grinning as a series of chairs boiled up from the ground around a small table, clearly designed with this in mind.

"As to what we can trade, I think we can all agree that mana crystals should be the only accepted form of payment…beyond barter for other tech, of course?" Leilani said smoothly, taking a seat and tapping the table.

Lysander sprang from Kai's shoulder, landing lightly on the table and tapping it with a single claw, bringing up a handful of different devices.

"As you can all see, we have been busy," Kai began. A smooth sales presentation began, showing off a variety of weapons, from a sword staff that looked just cool as fuck, to a small thrower, similar in design to the ones that the asuras had used.

I leaned forward, watching the screens as they populated with various details, range, number of shots before reload, reliability…

They were all shit, which was a bit of a relief, seeing the gaps where data would have been if they had much confidence in their creation.

"That's dogshit," Bryan said. "Yer don't want a toy gun, yer want a real one! That's what ah've got—rifles, shotguns. Hell, ah've got missile launchers!"

"Do they work?" Kai asked him bluntly.

"Some of 'em," he admitted, grinning. "Lower tech, the better. RPGs? They still work, 'specially the ones that come from the Middle East. No tracking, no complex shit, but they pack a punch!"

"And are they reproducible?" Kaatachi sighed. "These designs…" He gestured to the ones Kai had been going over. "They are easily reproduced. Explosives, not so much."

"Yeah well, ya can buy more from me, can't ya!" Bryan smiled widely, then reached down and put his hand on Ashley's leg, high up…before sliding it considerably higher.

That was a step too far even for Ashley's flirty persona, and she reached down, smiling at him, then took his middle finger and bent it right back, sending him to his knees with a cry of pain.

"You don't touch a girl like that unless she asks you to," she explained sweetly.

"Assault!" He cried out, "Ah fuck, yer crazy, bitch! Leggo!"

"Ask, *before* you touch," Ashley repeated grimly. Then she released him, glaring and sitting back in her chair.

She looked to the widely smiling Akuba and Leilani, who'd both clearly been on the wrong end of handsy men before and smiled. "So, what else do you have for us?" she asked them.

"Ah wus attacked!" Bryan shouted, holding his hand up for emphasis and glaring around at the roof and walls.

"You touched another of the group in a rude and possessive way," Onyx said. "You were the aggressor, not the victim. Do you really wish for arbitration? If so, then I stand witness."

"I stand witness," Lysander declared formally.

Bryan gaped at the two fairies, then spun to look at his own, who'd been hovering nearby, noticeably remaining silent and sulking after the way he'd dismissed her in favor of lusting over Ashley.

There was a long exchange of looks, before Bryan stood and glared at the fairy.

"Yer not on ma' side? Fine! Yer can fuck off! Ah'm t' system controller now, not yer! Ah'll just get a new fairy! One with better tits an'…"

"I apologize." The little fairy sighed, and he grinned at her, clearly thinking he'd won, until she blurred, suddenly dressed in a simple pair of trousers and a polite top, no longer facing Bryan. She drifted forward through the air to face us all. "I was forced by necessity to seek out a partnership with a local variant human to begin the next phase of the dungeon's development. Clearly, I chose poorly."

"Whut the fuck are you…" Bryan snarled, lifting his hand warningly as if to hit her. "Yer better remember yer place, yer little…"

"Overmind. I dissolve my alliance with this individual and refuse him return to my bonded dungeon. He is showing signs of aggression, and has already assaulted another of the Six. I bear witness," she said formally, and we all received a prompt, popping up before us.

THREE DUNGEON-BONDED FAIRIES HAVE DECLARED AN ASSAULT UPON ONE OF THE SIX NEXUS-ALIGNED DUNGEON REPRESENTATIVES. DUE TO SOCIETAL NORMS, NOT ALL ASSAULTS WILL MATCH THE PREREQUISITES THAT I AM PROGRAMMED WITH.

AS SUCH, I REQUIRE A MINIMUM OF ONE ASSENTING VOTE MORE THAN DISSENTING FROM A LOCAL VARIANT HUMAN.

PLEASE RESPOND ALOUD WITH THE FOLLOWING:

ASSENT, DISSENT, OR ABSTAIN.

I looked around the room. Ashley was remaining silent, and I didn't blame her. Yes, she was the one he'd grabbed, but she was also well aware that in this room, where everyone else was a Dungeon Lord or Lady, or otherwise bonded to the dungeon, she was a guest in many ways.

"Assent," I said resolutely, looking from Ashley to Bryan and back again, seeing the look of relief on Ashley's face that I was backing her, and how quickly she buried it.

"Abstain," Kai said after a few seconds, then he spun, staring in shock at his sister as she spoke.

"Assent," Leilani said firmly.

"Assent," Akuba said, followed by Kaatachi.

"Assent," he agreed, glancing from one of the ladies to the other, and shrugging as he made eye contact with Bryan.

"Now yer just fuckin'…wait a goddamn…" Bryan snarled, his face going white, until the sudden vanishing of the floor under him and his own horrified scream as he was yanked downward cut him off.

In under a second, he was gone; the floor reformed, and we all looked at one another in the silence of the room.

APOLOGIES, DUNGEON LORDS, LADIES, AND GUESTS. A BREACH OF THE PEACE HAS BEEN DETECTED AND DEALT WITH, THE OFFENDING PARTIES DISCIPLINED, AND MATTERS HAVE BEEN RESOLVED TO THE SATISFACTION OF THE OFFENDED PARTY.

PLEASE RETURN TO YOUR PREVIOUS ACTIVITIES.

"Well, that was…refreshing," Leilani said into the silence. "Tell me, did you set that up deliberately?" she asked Ashley.

"No," Ashley said firmly. "I was willing to distract and to encourage, nudging him to show his true self. The hand on my knee, I would have ignored. It's not the first time some asshole has groped me, after all. But when he tried to slip it up my skirt? No."

"Shit." I shook my head. "I'm sorry. I saw him touch your leg, but didn't think he would…"

"Yeah," Ashley said grimly, "let's just say he had long fingers, and I have small thighs. I'll need a shower after this."

"Do you want to go back…" I asked, pushing myself up.

"No," Ashley said. "No, thank you, Matt. The others are all honest people, more or less. It'd be better to actually get to know them a little."

"If you're sure." I nodded to her.

"I could do with a drink, though." She looked around the room.

"I can help with that." The little, formerly very sluttily dressed fairy said with a smile, landing in his chair and gesturing to the table. "Rest your hand on the table and think of the drink you wish. The link between this safe refuge, your own dungeons, and your mind will do the rest."

We all moved fairly quickly, reaching out and summoning everything from a can of my usual energy drink to an ornate tea set and a huge steaming mug of what smelled like hot chocolate. As we did so, the last fairy produced a scale of her own, passing one to each of us, with murmured apologies and hopes that we'd not judge her dungeon on the basis of her former representative.

We all nodded, accepting it, and it made me smile a few seconds later when Kaatachi was revealed as the one with the hot chocolate fetish, and Akuba summoned herself a tiny cup of espresso.

"So…who needs high-tech prosthetics and armor?" I asked, enjoying the look of curiosity and interest we got for that.

CHAPTER THIRTEEN

Half an hour later, we stepped back through the portal, me helping Ashley again, as she walked down the step.

As soon as we were on level ground and the portal had closed, Ashley let out a relieved sigh, bending at the waist to reach down and flick the clasps on her shoes, then kicking her feet free of them with a groan of pleasure.

"You've no idea how uncomfortable those damn things are," she complained, bracing herself against me and reaching down and rubbing her feet.

"No, but seriously, you need to not bend over like that, or you need to change your top." I looked away, and saw the look on Chris's face, as he hurried over with the others. "You're going to give Chris a heart attack."

"If I sit on the floor in a skirt this short, he'll be able to see what I ate for breakfast," she replied uncaringly. "Better he gets an eyeful of my tits than anything else."

"I…" I shook my head. "You know what, I'm sorry," I said. "Not my place to say it."

"I know it's coming from a good heart." She smiled as she straightened up and summoned a far too large hoodie, tugging it on over her head as Chris and the others reached us. "Don't worry, I know you're looking after me. It's sweet."

"First time I've been called that," I muttered, shrugging and turning to Kelly as she ran across the stone floor of the dungeon, leaping into my arms and hugging me. Ashley straightened up and held her arms out to Dante, who hugged her.

"Where the hell have you been?" Kelly asked me after a few seconds of hugging, and I smiled, enjoying the reality of where we'd been.

"We just went into orbit," I said casually. "We watched the world go by beneath us."

"You did what?" Kelly asked me slowly.

"We sat and drank coffee and talked shit in a special lounge on an orbital platform," I repeated. "Literally, we watched the Earth beneath us."

"That's not all we watched pass beneath us." Ashley snorted.

"Yeah, that's true," I added, taking Kelly's hand and kissing it, then reached out to the portal through the dungeon and locked it.

It'd been one of the things Onyx and the other fairies had shared with me. Leave the portal open and unsecured, and literally anyone could connect to it and walk through. And when they said "anyone," they meant it.

They'd automatically locked theirs down to local access only—meaning the local planet—and then set it to chime when an access request was made, but to stay locked unless instructed to open.

As it'd been before, basically if someone had found it was open? They could have marched straight through.

That sounded like it'd have caused a fight or something normally, but when you considered that although we were, according to the fairies, a "frontier" world, and "wild," we weren't considered overly dangerous. Not yet. We'd also had mana available for a matter of months.

Some of the worlds that had portals available had been marked as extremely hostile and had mana for centuries.

When I'd asked why they weren't being set on the Orcan, instead of us, the response was a withering "You don't want their attention."

Now the portal was locked down, I led Kelly and the others from the room, heading to the council chambers.

"We'll bring everyone up to date at once," I said. "Then it's time for…What time is it?"

I checked the dungeon, the dungeon sense having updated at some point to include a clock, and I grunted. It was early afternoon, that was all—1513.

It felt a lot later.

"How's Michelle?" I shook my head in disbelief at how much had happened today.

"She's okay, and so are the babies…"

"Babies, as in more than one?"

"Twins, we think." Kelly smiled. "It's a bastard of a job to be sure without any of the gear we used to have, but we've got stethoscopes still. There're definitely three heartbeats. Hers and two others, maybe three."

"Fuck…" I dropped my head. "We need to get her and Ian a nicer apartment…somewhere on the other side of the fucking dungeon. With soundproof walls."

"Well, we can sort out somewhere later. Right now, I need to know what happened and why you ended up on a space station and what the hell else you saw!"

"Three assholes broke the rules," I said simply. "There's a non-aggression pact in place to be on the space station. You break it, you get ejected."

"Literally." Ashley grinned. "Two creatures from another dungeon tried to start things with Matt. He didn't bite, and when they were obviously really close to attacking, he did something, and it pushed them over the edge. Next thing we know, they're floating past a window and their dungeon is banned from the meetings."

"You blew them a kiss, didn't you?" Chris asked me, and I shrugged.

"Matt, why do you always have to push?" Kelly snorted , and I winked at her.

"There was also an asshole American, the handsy type. I took him off to one side, see what kind of information I could pump out of him, and you do *not* want to know the kind of things he was saying to me." Ashley sighed, tossing her hair as she forced a smile. "Then he grabbed at me, though, and the others all agreed it was an assault…Thank you for backing me on that, Matt. I know some men see me dressing like this as meaning I deserve whatever happens to me."

"Yeah, you wear whatever the fuck you want," I said firmly. "If anyone touches you like that without your permission, you fucking kill them."

"I appreciate that." She smiled, and I winced, realizing that she damn well didn't need my permission, but…it was a fucked-up situation, really. She was dressing like that to entice men and women in, after all; she was literally what they used to call a honey trap.

She dressed and acted like that for our benefit, so really, I'd felt that I needed to make it clear it was her choice to deal with things. But…

Fuck it. I'd given her permission, she knew where I stood, and I trusted her. Hopefully nobody else would take her flirting like that as an offer to make a finger puppet out of her in public.

We jogged down the stairs and out across the road, passing some kids playing and adults taking a break. I saw smiles and happy faces, people who looked well fed and for the first time in ages, almost stress free, and I felt a little of the burden lifting.

"Are you really going to make me wait?" Kelly growled.

"It's neutral ground," I explained as we went. "I'll explain it all properly when we've got the others together, but it looks like they didn't just set us up to work independently. The station is neutral ground, but if we united behind a leader, the six of us in the first level of the Nexus, then that leader could claim the station. It's set up as neutral ground so we can trade and negotiate things somewhere that we know is safe. Then it's a jump start on production in space, if we ally and set up a uniform group."

"That's…convenient?" Chris suggested. "You sure they're not fucking us over? Setting us up or something?"

"No," I replied honestly. "But don't forget, they want us to win. They want us to be as strong as possible, to grow and be able to fight the Orcan. Basically, they're giving us the tools to do it."

"How do we claim the station then?" Kelly asked, clearly determined.

"We don't, not yet." I shook my head. "The others…fuck's sake, this is gonna take some explaining." I jogged up the last few steps, then hurried along the corridor to the council chamber; Chris peeled off to pull a few of the others from the war room and more. "We really need phones or something. Hell, a fucking pager would work."

"We need you to stop upending the damn world every day," Kelly pointed out. "Then we can have a meeting every other day and just catch up."

"Oh, what's gone wrong with my life that a meeting every other day sounds so amazing?" I muttered as the others filed in. Most of my council was here. The news of the portal had spread quickly, and they'd been hanging around, waiting.

The only three who weren't were Jo, who Kelly quickly explained was with Michelle, John, who was dealing with the "prisoners," and Markus, who was out leading a weapons drill with the spear and shield combo for a mixed group of humans and kobolds.

"This will do," I said. "Anyone not here can be brought up to date later. So, what happened was…"

An hour it took.

An entire hour to discuss what happened in an hour and a bit. It seemed ridiculous that it took so long, but between the stupid questions, the repeats, Dante's outrage at the American dude's actions and then John arriving with Jo, then Markus a few minutes later?

It just took time.

"So it's a neutral ground called the Nexus?" Clarissa asked, making notes. "It has a single 'main floor,' which you and the other five all have direct access to. Others who manage to connect later on will connect to the lower floors and will have to come up onto that floor to make deals and sell things and so on. You can have a stall or something like that, for one premium grade mana crystal per day, but just going there and sitting, drinking and making deals is free."

"It is, but if you piss off the Overmind, it'll kick you out into space," I pointed out. "That kinda makes me a bit uncomfortable about the place. Plus, it killed Bryan on the grounds we all agreed he'd assaulted Ashley. Taking that to the next logical conclusion, if we go there and two other representatives say we assaulted them by breathing on them, as long as their votes outnumber ours? We'd be killed. Not a place to go to lightly."

"Point," Kelly agreed. "Let's not go there without a good reason."

"We've made contact with three other dungeons, though—two with representatives, and one that happily had hers killed when he crossed a line. Don't get me wrong, he was an asshole and I'm glad he's dead, but the point remains: the dungeon fairies really don't give a shit."

"And we're back to the dungeon fairy in the list of creatures we can summon," Kelly said musingly.

"Are you nuts?" I asked her, aghast. "Seriously, as soon as I tried to absorb that dead one, the dungeon asked if I wanted to cede control to it. It was *dead*, and yet still the dungeon was willing to pass it control. What does that tell you?"

"Well, it doesn't suggest the dungeon has a lot of respect for your mental capacity," Chris joked, and I flicked the finger at him before going on.

"Seriously, I think it'd be a terrible idea to summon a dungeon fairy unless there's a desperate need," I said. "Why would you even consider it?"

"Because then we can send the dungeon fairy to the meetings," she said simply. "If the fairy wants what's best for the dungeon, then we need to convince it that's you. Then we can use it to maintain the dungeon and keep things together, rather than us stumbling around in the dark. We can send it to bargain at the Nexus and more."

"Nope," I said, undeterred. "Seriously, I'm always willing to listen, but to me, this is a far greater risk than we need."

"Okay, well, we'll consider it for the future. What if instead of a specific dungeon fairy, we get a standard one?"

"Why would you want to?" I asked her, confused.

"Because they're fairies!" she answered, shaking her head in wonder. "Genuine magical creatures, ones we've had legends about forever. They could be amazing."

"Or they could be dicks," I finished for her. "Aly, how's research going?" I asked, making it clear I was done with this conversation for now.

"Conduit research is still in progress." Aly looked up from the table and the screens she'd been looking over. "We've gotten a little over halfway, and we've enough in the bank from today that we could finish it early. But considering how things went? I decided to hold that back."

"Just in case we needed our forces?"

"Exactly."

"Good plan," I agreed, shifting and rubbing at my chin as I thought about it.

"Matt?" Kelly asked, and I looked at her questioningly. "Do you want to run this, or do you want us to do it?" She smiled.

"Sorry." I laughed, sitting up and shaking my head. "I'm so used to…"

"To doing it all yourself. Yes. Don't worry, we know. We've all got our jobs in place and we're all working on it. Is there anything you want us to focus on?"

"If the research is sorted, just spread the mana out." I sighed, sitting forward and resting my forearms on the table, looking around at the people I trusted most in the world these days. "We need our forces back up to strength, we need the kobold researchers, and we need the actual research doing. We need those rifles. Even if they're the shittiest version of them possible, the kobolds can learn to use them. And when we've got better versions, it'll be quicker for them to learn to use them."

"Anything else?" Kelly asked, and I smiled, knowing she was being polite. All this had been covered already, after all.

"The dungeons," I said. "Spread the mana out between the training dungeon and the civic center and our public forces. I need to train, as do our people. As soon as the conduit research is done, go to the converters, get us as much mana coming in as possible, then we start moving people through the dungeon. We need to grow."

"We'll handle it," she assured me.

"Here." I put three scales on the table before me. Black, red, and gold, they represented the other three dungeons. "These three dungeons each offered to trade, or to discuss things with us if we needed. I'll only lose them. Aly, you keep them. They're 'tokens' and represent destinations for the portals. We need to figure out how to do our own at some point, I guess."

I slid them across the table to Aly, who picked them up thoughtfully, examining them and passing them around so everyone could see what they looked and felt like.

"Okay, one last point to clarify." Aly collected them together a few minutes later. "The rest of us all know what we're doing. Research is in progress, and I'm spreading things out, with the majority going to research and development. The dungeon is working on conduits, and then it'll be converters, and upgrading the ones in place. I'd estimate those will be about three days, provided I continue with the current plan of me working on the rail guns mainly, and the dungeon and my assistants working on the conduits and so on."

She looked across at Clarissa and nodded to her. "I'll interview the first batch of hopefuls for research posts tomorrow morning, if that works for you?" Aly asked the older woman.

Clarissa nodded, making another note, and Kelly took over.

"I'll be summoning creatures for the dungeon. Apart from bringing one to you each day for you to try to evolve, we're all going to leave you out of the planning and day-to-day working of the dungeon as agreed, okay?"

"I…" I hesitated, having been thinking about this off and on, and then I just went for it. "I'm not going to come to the evening meetings either for a few days. I know how important they are, but I need to focus in my meditation today. I was on the verge of something…"

"I'm sorry, Matt, but with the portal—" Kelly apologized.

"No, you were right to, and it was important. Hell, you needed to get me—it was right to do so—but I *need* to sort this out. Until the research is done and you actually need me to decide on the direction for the dungeon? I'm going to meditate and exercise. I need to figure some shit out, and frankly, I need peace to do it."

"We'll make sure you have that then," Aly agreed, exchanging a brief look with Kelly.

"Thank you." I smiled. "Two things left to sort then, and then I'm going back to meditate. First and foremost, those dickheads and their actions." I turned to look at John. "You heard about it all, I assume?"

"I did," he said, settling back and looking at me. "Basically, they're the remains of the old city council of Newcastle: a single councilor, several of his desperate local friends who think they've been overlooked in their personal pursuit of power and can't let go of the old world, and your former neighbors."

"That's them."

"They're the kind of people I dealt with far too often as a copper." He sighed, scratching at the back of his head. "Self-righteous pricks who complain that everyone needs to follow the rules, but would think nothing of breaking them if it helped their cause. That would be fine, though, because it's 'just them' or 'just this once.'"

"Fuckers." I grunted. "As soon as they moved into the flat below me, I got a letter, a really shitty, blatant knockoff attempt pretending to be from the council advising me that due to the number of complaints about my aggressive driving and poor parking, I had to hand in my parking permit."

I snorted in disgust, shaking my head as I remembered reading it, seeing the shitty and obviously added imitation stamp, the lack of contact details and more.

It looked as though a child had done it and I'd tossed it on a table, thinking nothing of it, until I'd seen the looks the new assholes downstairs were giving me.

Rolling it up that night when I got back in from work, I stuffed it up the exhaust of their car and moved the fuck on with my life, laughing my arse off when a copper came to talk to me about "criminal damage" to their car.

He'd taken great pleasure in forcing them to move their car when I pointed out that it was a permit-only parking area, and they couldn't prove that it was me who had done it, nor could they provide a real permit. Theirs was obviously fake.

They got a warning, and I made sure to laugh my arse off loudly near the fireplace, knowing that the old connection pipes meant they'd hear me.

"Did you do it?" John asked me, and I shook my head, explaining quickly. "Yeah, seems about right. I dealt with a few like that."

"So what's the plan?" I asked him.

"Honestly, we've got a problem, and I know you've made your mind up." He shifted and summoned a coffee, then sipped from it and looked at me over the rim of his cup. "I thought they were being banished, and that was it."

"As long as the babies are born healthy and so on, yeah," I agreed. "They mobbed poor Michelle when she wouldn't give them access to the main public council rooms below. They—"

"I heard about that, but it presents a small problem," he said, setting his coffee cup down with a clink.

"Oh?"

"They were elected as the dungeon's council."

"No they fucking weren't," I said, confused.

"They were, actually." He pulled a sheaf of documents out of a bag and set them down on the desk. Literally hundreds of pages. "These were found in Merriman's rooms, right where he said they'd be. Fifty-one percent of the dungeon's inhabitants voted for them."

"What is this?" I picked a handful of the pages up and glanced them over.

There was a half dozen names on the carefully drawn brochure, details for Merriman and others, and the changes they were going to bring to the dungeon as the first democratically elected council.

Notably things like stopping humans having to fight at all, and banning most of the dungeon creatures from even being within the walls.

There was a plan for expansion, and bringing the surrounding area under the dungeon's control, of dealing with the gangs "compassionately" and a proper police force and more.

Each name on the list and the carefully drawn picture next to it, I could identify as one of the assholes I'd had thrown in a cell.

Each and every page asked people to sign their name at the bottom, and confirm they were happy with their "choice" to be on the council. The only names on it were these assholes, though, and each had a tick box next to them, meaning that any vote that people made was for one of the dickheads.

"So…they had someone make these up, then they got people to 'vote' on it and sign that they wanted them as their representatives…" I guessed.

"Yeah, except they had no authority to stage a vote, and they basically rigged it so the only people who were voted in were these assholes."

"How'd they do it?" I asked, bemusedly, flicking through the signatures, not recognizing any of the names.

"As near as I can tell, they went around the groups when none of us were there, and pretended you'd sent them. Nobody reported it, because why would they?" John shrugged.

"So they set up a fraudulent election, then when they 'won,' they expected me to just step aside and let them run things?" I shook my head. "This seems…I don't know, amateurish?"

"Stupid, certainly." Kelly flicked through several of the pictures. "Well, that's dealt with, I guess…"

"Not entirely," John said. "As far as everyone knows, this was an honest election, remember? They won. Now you're saying they hurt your friend and you're banishing them all."

"It's bullshit." I shook my head in disbelief and chucked the papers on the table.

"It is, and we all know it. I'm making you aware that, as the Judge here, there was no law against them doing this. Legally, if we're using the rules about assault that we've discussed? Only a few of them actually injured Michelle directly, and so only a few of them can be punished for it. Yes, the majority of them are guilty of fraud, as they misrepresented themselves to hold the election, but…"

He shrugged and held his hands out to the sides. "This is the law, Matt. We haven't got anything against them, so you need to be very careful here. Remember, I *need* to uphold the law as part of my class. If I don't? I'll lose my class. I…*we* need to tread carefully."

"I need to introduce laws that cover this?" I asked, and he nodded, but clearly wasn't happy about it.

"Yeah, but the problem, again, is that you didn't have these laws. I can't retrospectively punish them."

"You better not be suggesting what I think you are," I growled.

"We need to let them off with a warning." Kelly groaned, burying her head in her hands. "That's what you mean, isn't it, John?"

"Oh, for fuck's sake…" I growled, before twisting and looking at Markus. "You remember when Chris and I told you they'd be trouble?"

"I do," he admitted, sighing. "But I stand by what I said as well, Matt. They're unpleasant, not evil. You can't kill people because of what they might do in the future, nor for being greedy little rats."

"The hell I can't," I growled, my mind turning over quickly. "Fine. You say I have to limit it to punishing them, and I can't make it harsh and banish them, right?"

"Not for the first offense when there's no law in place to prevent it happening." John sighed. "Matt, I've spent time talking to them, and yeah, I see what they're doing. They're scum, plain and simple. I *have* to follow the *law*, though. Make it a law, and I can act. Otherwise…I have to let them go, and you're lucky there's no false imprisonment law that could punish you."

"Fine," I said, before grinning as a new plan slid into the forefront of my mind. "Then we get to trial the punishment system. First offense, they get a choice. A week with the army on shit detail, and I mean *shit* detail. They get to collect up the literal shit around the dungeon, like go out to the north fields and clean up from the trikes and more. They can spread that on the farms or whatever."

"What's the choice?" John asked, making a note and nodding as Kelly promised to make the law a bit clearer, as well as the punishment.

"The choice is they do it, or they leave," I growled. "We give them a…what do you call it? A bad mark on their record?"

"A demerit?" Dante asked.

"That's it." I nodded. "Two demerits and you're out of the dungeon here. You can go to the park and—"

"Won't work," Kelly interrupted. "If you're using the park as punishment, what about everyone else who lives there? Are they all punished? They'll resent you, and it'll cause issues."

"Fuck's sake!" I snarled. "Fine, *three* demerits, regardless of what they're for, and they're banished. Two, they get to do shit detail for a month at night, and work with the army as a trainee during the day. One demerit is a week. They always have the choice. Follow the rules or they get the choice of that or fuck off."

"So, you're okay with me letting them out of the cell?" he asked, and I glared at him. "I need you to say it, Matt."

"Fine," I growled. "I want the entire population of the dungeon gathered tonight in the training dungeon. There's a main hall on one of the floors, right? A large central area beyond the one that portal was in?"

"There is, but we've already started changing the dungeon, so you don't know what's in it, and it'd be a pain for everyone getting to that central room. How about the crafting area instead? It's big enough."

"Fine. We'll meet in the crafting area in…two hours?" I suggested. "Is that enough time for everyone to get the message?"

"Should be." John nodded. "I'll spread the word, and I'll bring them along last."

"I'll set up an area where everyone can see me, and we'll have that little group off to the side. Make it clear that they're on my shit list."

"I'll take care of that," Aly said. "I'm making a few small changes to the crafting area for Finn anyway."

"Great, thank you." I sighed. "The other thing is that we need a gym."

"A…gym?" Aly smiled. "Really?"

"Gods, yes," Kelly said, nodding as Ashley jumped in as well.

"Yes, please."

"Okay, I wasn't thinking of a gym for everyone…" I said, wincing. "I need somewhere I can work out, and not be interrupted and bothered, as I'm going to be doing it while meditating."

"So you want a private gym?" Aly asked, looking from me to Kelly and Ashley, whose faces had dropped when they heard that.

"We could definitely do with a gym as well," Griffiths said. "It was on the list of things I needed to discuss with you."

"List?" I groaned, putting my head in my hands. "Okay, fine, I'm totally good with the idea of everyone having a gym, but I need a quiet place to meditate, and weights and machines and shit for while I'm there."

"What about a proper gym for everyone else?" Kelly suggested. "A large one, that we can use to train our forces as well, and then a small box room for you?" She grinned at me as she said it, and I fixed her with a stare.

"I'll need converters as well." I shook my head. "All eight of the basic elements."

"That's literally tens of thousands of mana," Aly pointed out.

"I know," I said softly. "I feel guilty for asking for this, and this isn't a case of I want a nice private place for me and all the nice toys. I'm happy to share the shit with everyone, you know that, but—"

"But you can't meditate with others interrupting you," Kelly agreed. "Look, how about we try it? We don't have enough mana to build everything, so how about we build the gym on the top floor of the dungeon main building for now. We put in rules that for say, the morning, it's a silent gym. People aren't allowed to speak in there. The rest of the day? They can make as much noise as they like."

"That gives you the morning to exercise and meditate at the same time. After that, you can still use the gym, but you accept that other people will be as well," Aly agreed. "Try it for a week, okay, Matt? Give me a week to get things back on track, and we'll build a proper gym in the military building."

"Military…?" I started, then shook my head. "Of course, sorry." I'd not really thought about it. We'd spoken about building a barracks before, and we had a small armory, but mainly we'd just been making do. A proper gym with a proper barracks and armory, not to mention all the shitty bits that came with it? It was just common sense.

"Right, so you'll build a small gym with the converters in it over the next few days, though, right?" I asked Aly, and the look I gave her made it clear there was only one correct answer.

"Of course." She smiled. "I'll start a couple of converters now, and then a simple set of weights. After that, I'll get to working on it over the course of the next three days."

"And a rowing machine," I said quickly. "I'm sorry, but I need something I can do on autopilot with my eyes closed, that's not a normal weight rack or whatever…"

"Because you'd end up killing someone if you slip. Okay, a rowing machine as well." She agreed, but the glare was clear.

I got her hint as well. Basically, I was getting weights, the rower, and converters for now; beyond that, fuck all for a day at least while they worked on everything else, and I'd get it to myself for a bit, but then I'd have to share and like it.

"Okay, two hours from now, full dungeon meeting, right?" I agreed, rising to my feet. "Shit, we need to tell Barry, see if he can send someone…"

"I'll go to the park," Chris offered, standing and cracking his back. "I need to get a run in anyway."

"I'll join you," Rhodes said. "For now, better if nobody is outside the walls on their own until we've got the patrols back up and running."

"Thank you. I'll leave it all to you then." I nodded and moved around the table. That people actually let me go, without bugging me with "just one more thing," honestly meant the world.

CHAPTER FOURTEEN

I left them all to it, heading up to the top floor of the dungeon. I was hungry—gods, I was starving in fact, or I felt like it—but I needed to get back to my meditation. The effect before of being so deep in it and being startled out of it by Kelly was a killer.

I needed to fix the damage I'd taken then, and I couldn't afford to wait any longer.

Summoning a quick bacon sandwich to take the edge off the hunger, I jogged up the steps, gnawing on it as I went.

Five floors later, I was on the top floor of the dungeon proper, directly below the roof, and looked around at the room I was in.

The stairs that led up to this point were fairly wide. These rooms had been used as commercial offices for years, and the rooms were reasonable. This one, a "small" office, was about four meters by six, with high, lead-lined windows that had been long since painted shut.

Someone had been hard at work cutting around the paint, and had even broken part of the casement in an attempt to open the window, with a filthy ashtray overflowing with dead cigarettes underneath it.

The room next door, on the other side of the stairwell, was the one that others had been using a lot more, so I'd decided to leave that one to them.

This would be my new meditation space.

I hesitated, then smiled as I felt a tingle from a nearby presence in the dungeon. Sitting down, I slid into the dungeon sense, finding Aly there waiting for me.

"Hey, Matt," she said, clearly uncomfortable.

"Aly? Everything okay?" I asked, and she forced an image of a smile.

"Matt, look I'm sorry," she said quickly. "I talked with Kelly, and, yeah, look. This is *your* dungeon. We're all deciding that you can have this little bit of mana, and no more, because we've got our plans for the things that are our responsibility. Like I do for the research. But this is *your* dungeon and I think we forget that. I'm sorry that—"

"Aly, ALY!" I called, stopping her. "Seriously, it's okay. I asked you to run things like the research because it needs to be done, not neglected the way I get distracted. It's fine."

"Well…I'm sorry, anyway," she rushed out. "Look, Kelly and I spoke. The converters, as they are, the first-tier elemental ones, they're two thousand mana each, and there's eight of them. We've never made them all, mainly because it didn't make sense. Why make one like a Fire converter when it's cold—it'd barely earn the ten per hour we usually get—when putting an Air one would get twenty. But for a meditation room?"

"It makes sense," I agreed. "I know eventually we'll need to make them up as we keep talking about doing, fill an entire floor of the dungeon with them, each room holding a load of the same kind of converters for people to practice and work on improving their affinity levels."

"But for now, one of each in here is a lot more do-able," she agreed, nodding. "Kelly is working on absorbing stuff now, as are a few of the others who didn't have immediate jobs. We figured the least we could do is get you these, considering how little you ask for yourself."

"I...thank you," I said after a second, feeling oddly touched by her words.

"It's nothing," Aly said, shaking her head. "Matt, we've had these discussions before, and you really don't get it. But you rescued Amy and me. You saved Mike's family, and Kelly's. The rest of the dungeon is the same—you came out of nowhere most of the time, killed whatever was threatening us, and gave us a home. For us to give up half an hour and absorb some stuff so you can grow stronger and therefore protect us better? It's not a hard choice."

"Thank you," I repeated, really meaning it.

"The gym equipment, well, what do you want? We've absorbed a few things over the last few months. There's not much, but the hotel had a few little things in it, I think. We can hit an actual gym easily enough. I think there are some only a few streets outside of our usual zone..."

"That's a point," I agreed, grinning evilly. "Well, we've got some soldiers who need some exercise and some civilians who are on my shit list for them to 'teach.' I think a trip outside of the walls to carry a full gym's worth of gear here should help, right?"

"Oh, you're cruel!" Aly said, pretending to be horror-struck.

"Too much?"

"Oh fuck no." She snorted. "I think we need a lot of things from the other side of town, in fact. Heavy, heavy things..."

"Like what?" I asked, amused.

"I've not decided yet," she said. "But Michelle is a wonderful woman, and I think she deserves some nice things, like cots and baby furniture. Now there *might* be somewhere close that we could get that, but I really like that big department store on the other side of the city."

"I think you should have her give you a very big list. Her and any other expectant mothers. Anything they need? Well, those kids are our future. Got to start things off right."

"Oh, I will. I think we'll need all the furniture they have, in every color and style, just for a start." She sent a mental image of an evil smile, before I nodded and slid out of the dungeon sense.

I focused, looking around the room now that the converters were growing. I marked two spots, then slid back into the sense.

I tagged a battered old multigym that I'd seen when I'd looked in the dungeon's memory, and I set that on one side of the gym, and a rowing machine in the center.

Then I finished it off with a set of weights on the far wall between space reserved for two other converters, and I nodded in satisfaction.

Or I was.

Even odds, really.

Anyway, what I was going to do, I decided, forcing my squirrel brain back on track, was specialize every *other* ring to break out the mana I needed, then the next ring along to make it into something I could use more easily.

As a starter, and because it was one of the forms I was most confident in using, I sealed the ring before me to work with Air. I needed that most of all, so breaking that out of the mana forms that it was in could only help me.

I pressed my palms into the ring as it solidified fully. Sections that were filled with cracks sealed over as the substance they were made of regrew.

Air.

I focused on the air, on air as it was with mana, the feeling of it, the sense of space, of speed and stillness. My mind didn't dwell on any one part, but instead tagged sensations and images: The cold air seen from a plane's window above the mountains. The warm, muggy air in the tropics. The life-giving air that I sucked through a rebreather when I was swimming with an ex on holiday once in Egypt.

I saw it, I tasted it, and I felt the way that the Air mana enveloped me, lifting me up and buoying me along, like the sea had on holiday, and yet not.

Seeing and sensing all the little details, even the bits that were at contradiction here with there, and yet all together were the mental image for air for me.

I held onto it all, and I somehow poured those sensations and identifiers into the ring before me, feeling it changing as it accepted the use it was being tuned to.

Once it was done, and the ring felt perfect, solid, and as if it could take nuclear bombardment, I finally backed off, sliding into the stream of mana, panting as I looked up at the glowing circle.

It began with a simple pulse. A flash that was too weak for me to be sure I'd definitely seen what I thought I had. A second later came another, and another, then dozens as the ring began to spin in place, revolving at terrible speed, creating a vortex as it pulled on the mana that streamed through it again.

The stream twisted. Tiny fragments of brightly colored mana tore free and broke up, tugged to the edges and the Air being stripped from them.

For a split second, I grinned, thinking I'd managed something wonderful. Then the slight rumble of nausea reached me, and my eyes opened wide.

"Oh shit!" I groaned, flinging myself down the stream and frantically searching for the next ring along, hoping I could fix the imbalance before it really got bad.

It didn't take long, three or four seconds, then I was almost blasting past it. Reaching out, I snagged a section that overhung the stream and yanked myself around and down into the depths, frantically collecting all the bigger bits that I could.

Every second I spent, the nausea increased, and as the larger sections broke free of the silt of discarded mana, they set free great clouds of sediment.

The morass flowed downstream, dragged from sight at great speed, and increasing my nausea.

"Oh, gods no…" I whimpered, letting loose a liquid burp that tasted and felt terrible.

The converters were mushrooming up around the room, spaced out well, but the fields they'd generate would overlap to an insane degree in such a small space, and I positioned the rowing machine to sit in the middle of that space.

I felt Aly stepping back, giving me some mental and physical space, and I let out a long, deep breath.

I knew some of the dungeon wanted to use the gym. It was common sense to have our fighters using the gym as well, day in and out, and working to get our people as strong and fast as physically possible.

All of that was a good reason for me to share the gym, and for us to have already done this. To have already gotten the gym up and running, rather than wasting time on anything else.

But I needed to meditate. That wasn't a fucking spectator sport, and every gym I'd ever been in, in my entire life, apart from the times I was literally on my own? There'd been nutters screaming as they lifted weights that were too big for them.

There'd been girls talking about dates on the treadmills, and guys staring at their asses, or trying to chat them up.

There were people making calls too, which wouldn't happen now, but there were always people encouraging their friends. Weights being slammed down hard or let slip. There'd been the clank of metal and the whir of pulleys, the crash of slipped putdowns and the laugh of friends.

All of that had been fine for the gym, when the whole point was to distract yourself from the pain of muscle fibers tearing, from the dullness of steady plodding and more.

It was helpful, even.

But it damn well wouldn't be when you were trying to meditate.

I cheated as Aly left the room, and I knew she felt the change I made. It was a minor one, as I reached out and simply extended the stone of the wall, across the lock of the door.

There was no way anyone was opening that door this time. Not without a sledgehammer, or control of the dungeon equal to my own, which was to say none.

I'd share the gym with people tomorrow, but right now I needed some goddamn peace.

With that done, I dumped my drink and more on one side of the room, and sat in the rowing machine, giving it a little roll back and forth to make sure it was set in place and wouldn't catch, and that the castors or whatever were working.

That done, I slid my feet into the grips and locked the straps over them, securing myself in, before setting the resistance to medium, and starting to pull.

It was easy—hell, it was insanely easy—and I paused, moving it up to a higher level. It was now at the level I'd have expected for medium before all of this—the difference in my strength was insane—and I settled into the rhythm.

I'd never been a real gym bunny. I went fairly regularly, but I did it because I liked to eat good food and drink beer, I liked to be able to get laid, and it was frankly easier and less effort to carry round a fit body than it was a mountain of fat.

I was lazy; I was just tactical about it. That meant I had a fair amount of experience with the machines, but no actual training.

As far as I knew, I was using things right: a steady pull, starting upright, legs in tight, shins at about ninety degrees and finishing with my arms in close to my chest and legs at full extension, back angled back a bit.

Essentially, I was heaving the fuck out of the machine, but that was just to warm up. Once I got up to speed, and I settled into a comfortable row, I relaxed a little, my body repeating the same action over and over again.

As the minutes passed, I worked my mind as well, splitting my attention, keeping my body moving steadily and working hard, but sinking into myself.

The mana stream was steady. If anything, it looked like it was running faster than before, driven by the constant motion and exertion of the body.

I sank deeper, searching for my core, and flowing along the river of mana, losing focus a dozen or more times before I found the secret to maintaining my movements comfortably and being lost in myself in meditation.

Finding the structure I'd been repairing before, I recognized the ring that had been mainly rebuilt, reformed, and that was waiting on only a few final touches before it'd be complete again.

I lifted it, a strange mix of being there, in a simulacrum of my body and physically lifting the sections into place, as if I stood chest-deep in a river of liquid light, lifting sections into place…and the realization that it was all mental, as I was—after all—literally inside my own arm at the minute.

I thought about it and quickly dismissed it as too fucking "meta" for me. The structure slid into place easily enough, though, and I grunted unconsciously as I hesitated, still not sure whether this was a massive mistake.

The gates in my mana stream were there to compress the stream, to force it, like it was being fed through a fire hose, to move faster and to draw more mana in as a consequence, feeding my mana regeneration.

What if this wasn't all the gates could do, though?

I damn well knew that furry-arsed shit-biscuit knew more than he was letting on. I suspected they could be used to purify and align mana as well, judging from the way they interacted with the mana that streamed past.

I worked through it in my mind.

As a Storm Titan, I would grow much stronger if I chose to align the gates with the correct form of mana. Essentially, they could act as a sort of internal magical converter. Each aspect of mana that ran through the rings could be tweaked, adjusted, and realigned.

I could make it so that any Air and Fire mana that passed through was automatically converted into Lightning, or Air and Water to the Storm.

That would help, and it'd probably massively boost me in the short-term, which was awesome, but…it felt like that would be a mistake. Like I was cutting off potential gains, and gambling with it, effectively fucking myself if I was somewhere that didn't have any of the relevant kinds of mana to absorb.

Plus, once you took Storm and Lightning mana aside, there was all that mana that wouldn't be touched.

There were hundreds of kinds of mana in me that were being filtered and absorbed into the core, literally hundreds that were being worked on. But, thinking logically, what would happen if I focused on converting all that was available of a specific form of mana like that?

I had a minute, maybe less before I knew I'd be unable to work, doubled over with debilitating nausea, and I needed to make the changes I could, and damn fast.

I reached out, working more on instinct than anything else, as I lifted great sections from the stream; mana cascaded off it as more sediment filled the streams.

I needed to work in pairs, I'd suspected before, and now I damn well knew it. As the first ring broke out the primary element ready for easier absorption, the remaining fragment was dumped into the stream, floating away to sink into the depths.

Normally that wasn't a problem; it happened constantly, naturally. The problem was I had all this sediment in the channels already, and I'd just added to it.

I had to get the sediment purifying as fast as I could. The broken parts of mana were sinking into the depths as they tried to seal together again. Some of it managed to re-bond—hell, most of it was. As the broken links sank through the mass of streaming mana, more and more of these broken sections met fragments that could be used, and they joined, forming more complex—or simpler—mana forms.

The fraction that didn't, that missed it all and sank to the bottom, was the issue.

That and the fact I'd just accelerated the speed that this was happening, anyway.

I slammed sections back together, pressing fragments into gaps and forcing the mana that was streaming past to pour into those gaps and fill them.

In a matter of seconds, a reformed ring was there, holding in place. It wasn't as strong, nor as efficient as the first ring. It was solid, but really needed a fuckload of work. But for now? It was in place.

Taking heart from that, and gritting my teeth at the way my stomach and inner ear were combining forces to pick a fight with me, I dove into the stream, sinking through and aiming for the sediment that had been stirred up by my actions.

There was a mass of crap down here, I saw. Mana that tore in whirlpools and vortexes, actively damaging my channels as they did so.

This wasn't going to be a short-term thing.

I needed to massively work on my mana channels. And it'd take months, if not years to get them sorted out. For now, though? I needed to make a change before I vomited all over myself.

Searching the mana around me, feeling the broken links, I searched for a commonality. My first instinct was to look for Earth. I'd started stripping the Air out, after all, so it'd make sense if the imbalance was made worse by Air's opposite.

I worked as fast as I could, searching frantically for any of the fragments that stood out.

There was a tiny fraction less Air than anything else, mainly because the last ring was tearing it free, and I cursed over and over.

The mélange of mana, all this sediment and crap that filled my mana channels, was just that. It was a mess, and as much as I tried to fix it, to make it cleaner and to find a pattern I could make the rings focus on, to purify the stream…

There wasn't one.

There was just too much fucking mana streaming through, and in making the last gate focus on Air, a form I could manipulate the most efficiently?

I'd made the problem *worse*.

I held on a few more seconds, hoping, desperately searching. Then, as a fresh wave of nausea ripped through me, I cursed and surrendered to what I knew I had to do. Kicking off, I streaked through the stream, looping around the outer pattern, avoiding my core and rolling back to the first ring, the Air one I'd made work so much more efficiently.

Landing on it again, I coughed and gagged, then reached out and frantically unwound the specializations I'd somehow enforced on the ring.

It was slow; the twisting vortex that dragged the stream through and sped it up slowly rolled back inch by inch as the pull faded.

I couldn't hold on any longer. Releasing it all, I blinked my eyes open and promptly fell off the rowing machine, crashing to the floor and vomiting everywhere.

CHAPTER FIFTEEN

The next forty minutes or so were utterly miserable.

I spent them curled up on the floor, alternately vomiting, shaking, and slipping into the dungeon sense and absorbing the mess back up.

At one point, I summoned fresh clothing, depositing it off to one side, and resolving to ride it through, sipping at ice-cold water and generally feeling sorry for myself.

I did manage to distract myself with one thing, though: I'd been on the right path. My mana regeneration had risen slightly when I'd created the rings, and then again when I'd made the ring "spin up" and start absorbing the crap.

Sitting, shaking, and feeling sorry for myself, I came up with a better plan.

I was on the right path, but I'd clearly tried to do things in the wrong order, trying to do it all in one go. I took a deep breath, blew it out, and stared at my mana system in my mind.

The rings were needed. Clearly each ring I had in place would increase my mana regeneration, and that was the first step.

Where I'd gone wrong was to try to break all the mana up, setting all that crap loose into my mana channels, and just hoping to weather the storm of nausea that came from it.

Instead, what I needed to do was repair each gate individually, and attune every other gate to breaking down the already broken mana.

I needed to strip out the crap that was there first; like trying to build upstream, and then drink or fish in the water downstream, I had to wait for it to clear first.

If I could help it to clear a little faster? Common sense was that it was a good idea. If I could make my mana stream as pure of broken fragments as possible, then the mana would always be easier to convert as well, meaning that I should be able to regenerate it a lot easier and faster.

Then, once it was as pure as I could make it, I'd tune the other rings. Fix them to convert their various forms automatically for me.

Rather than the rings being overwhelmed by a massive influx of crap—or, to use the river analogy again, rather than having a simple filter net in place to catch all the crap that was floating downriver—I'd have the water running in an enclosed loop.

Each pass that went through multiple filters would purify it, and then when the time came for any additional work in the river, the crap that got stirred up would be caught by filters that were fine to work, rather than being overwhelmed and letting loads tear through.

I nodded in satisfaction, feeling a presence nearby.

I opened my eyes and stared, "seeing" Kelly nearby, hovering through the dungeon sense.

"Are you okay?" she asked hesitantly, seeing the state of me, mainly naked, vomit stained, and exhausted.

"Yeah." I sighed. "I'm not, but I am, if you know what I mean."

"We're waiting on you in the dungeon," she pointed out, and I groaned.

I'd totally forgotten about those fuckers needing me to lay the law down, and I *really* wasn't in the fucking mood for it right now.

"I'll be there in a few minutes," I assured her, and I felt her leave.

I didn't have the time for a proper shower, and the others were all waiting for me, so…

I stripped off, unceremoniously absorbing all my clothing, and summoning a bucket of hot water and a sponge. It'd do for now.

I had a damn fast sponge bath, then I was dressing and absorbing the stone over the doorway. Seconds later, I jogged up the stairs, then launched myself from the roof and into the air.

My manapool was low, thanks to all the crap I'd been doing, something about the contamination breaking away the free, "good" to use mana, but I had plenty for this easily enough.

I flew across the short distance, landing atop the crafting area, and jogged down the stairs from the roof, grunting at the wall of noise that hit me as soon as I was inside.

The entirety of the dungeon was there, save a handful of the kobolds on guard duty. Barry and a small contingent from the park waited near the center, where a platform had been set up.

This building was massive. It was a former printing press for a national newspaper and now it was mostly empty, a few sections kept as rooms for structural reasons more than anything else.

The rest of it was open plan, and over a thousand square meters with a high ceiling.

That meant that even with the hundreds of people who stood here, there was still plenty of space, and the low buzz of conversations carried on as I strode through the middle of the group.

I walked up the stairs to the platform, and turned to look out across the room, waiting, until after thirty seconds, and a good dozen people were still carrying on conversations, Rhodes caught my eye with a questioning glance. I nodded to her, growing more annoyed by the second, then winced as the "drill sergeant" experience came to the fore.

"SILENCE!" she roared in a voice that echoed around the building, probably being heard as much as ten miles out to sea.

"Thank you, Sarge." I forced a smile. "Right, I'm going to make this a short meeting, people, so please, bear with me. I know you've all got things you'd rather do than watch me waffle on."

A few people laughed at that. More stood still, smiling and clearly respectful, while a few…Councilor Merriman opened his mouth, clearly about to say something, but was beaten to it by Sharon, the pig in a wig, making a low and undoubtably snide comment to the man next to her.

I couldn't hear the words, but I got the gist.

As I did by the haughty look on the rest of the group's faces, and I changed my mind about what I was going to say.

"Why do you think you're here?" I called to her, and her friends.

There was a moment of silence, until I reached out and with a mental flex, I lifted them all into the air slowly. I didn't use magic to do it. Well, I did, but not the usual kind.

Instead, I layered another level over and over below the one they were standing atop, lifting them slowly into the air until their entire group was nearly equal with my platform, standing atop a platform of their own.

"We...we're here for an apology, we are!"

"An apology," I said flatly.

"We're the council!" Sharon screeched. "We were elected and everything!"

I looked out across the confused faces on all sides, and I forced a smile, before nodding.

"That's almost true." I shrugged. "There's a couple of important details missing, though..."

"You arrested us, forced us all into a handful of bare rooms, and cut us off from being able to summon food or anything!" another one of the group, a skinny little man, cried out, even as another started to nod quickly.

"That's true as well! We've got rights, and we was cut off!"

"You've got rights," I repeated, shaking my head in disgust. "Okay, people, so let's make this very clear. You, and your group, held an election, and you were chosen by the rest of the dungeon to take over. Is that right?"

"It is!" Merriman said quickly. "We were elected by the people!"

"That's a stretch, but okay, let's hear it...you go for it and tell us all what you've been doing." I stepped back and folded my arms, waiting.

For a few seconds, he stared at me, clearly waiting for a trick or something. But seeing nothing, he started to talk, stepping up to the edge of his little platform and addressing the dungeon community directly.

"I'm Councilor Merriman. I was on the general council of Newcastle, and regularly made a difference to all of your lives..." He puffed his chest up as he looked around. "I helped bring in the permitted parking zones, helped to arrange and enforce the clean air policy, and more, making your lives, and those of your children better! Your good health is down to that, in part, but I've never made a thing of it.

"No, I was content to just help, and to serve you all. But this man?" He gestured to me. "He stole from us all. He's literally claimed the city and stolen it! He has no right to do as he does—demolishing buildings, making honest men, woman, and children fight for him, die for him, while he runs around like a headless chicken.

"He changes his plans constantly, proving he doesn't know what he's doing. He invites monsters inside our walls. Lets them roam free, armed! They could be doing anything...stealing our children, eating them!"

"He's made dinosaurs!" Sharon screeched, unable to help herself. "He summoned dinosaurs and let them loose! We've all seen the films! We know how this will end, but he still does it, and why? So he can ride them!"

"Yes, well…The difference is, while I'm sure he's meant well, and he's even had some small successes in defending the dungeon, he's making it all up as he goes along. He forcibly arrested us, without any legal authority, when we won the election! His council is no better. Not a single one of them was democratically elected. And when the government comes, what do you all think will happen?"

"The government?" someone called out in a stunned voice. "You think the government is coming?"

"With the army," he said quickly, nodding as if he knew something that nobody else did. "They'll be here soon, and when they arrive, and they find that the city of Newcastle, a shining beacon of culture for the North, has been destroyed by a self-styled warlord? They'll march the army straight in. Innocent people will die. That's why we need a change of leadership, and it must be now!"

He nodded as if all of this shit was somehow a well-reasoned argument, before turning and facing me squarely.

"We were democratically elected by the people to take command here. You need to step aside. You can't refuse us, or you're a tyrant, and this isn't a democracy!" He nodded, as did a load of his supporters, making me think of a load of those novelty nodding dogs.

"Well." I shrugged. "I guess you have me there."

Silence fell as people looked from them to me and back again, before one of their group spoke up quickly.

"So…we're in charge then?"

"How do I control the dungeon?" another asked.

"You've not handed over control," Merriman said shrewdly, glaring at me, clearly feeling the ground slipping out from beneath him.

"No." I smiled widely. "You see, there's a couple of things that you either forgot to address, or were hoping I'd forget about, to keep people happy. First and foremost, I *am* the dungeon, and I'm not submitting to you. The access everyone has? It's to the dungeon *through* me. I make all of your requests and abilities work. You try to get rid of me? All this falls apart."

Those closest to me now knew that wasn't true, but fuck it, these dickheads didn't.

"Secondly, you're right! This isn't a fucking democracy," I said louder. "I have a council, it's true, and they advise me and carry out the day-to-day running of the dungeon. That's not a democracy either, though. They *advise* me—I make the final decision."

"You're a tyrant!" Merriman shouted, levelling a finger at me.

"You had your chance to speak, Merriman. Now it's my turn," I growled. "The vote that some of you participated in wasn't a valid vote," I said to the crowd. "First of all, I didn't arrange it, and as the Dungeon Lord, that's kind of a big deal. I didn't ask for it, didn't authorize it, nor did I want it. I have a council, drawn from a lot of the brightest of the dungeon's citizens. If anyone wants to join it, come explain to me, to Aly or to Kelly and Clarissa, why you should be on it, and what you could bring to it. We'll consider it.

"The 'vote' was rigged so that this dickhead and his friends could claim a democratic right to power. They got fifty-one percent of the dungeon's people to vote for one of them to do something. All the jobs they were to do, as near as I've seen, are jobs people already do, so that's a no as well. Just because it was enough in the old world to get you something doesn't mean shit to me, so tough.

"Next, we have the argument for the government coming." I looked around and shook my head. "I think nobody really thinks there's a cat in hell's chance of that, but okay, let's say for argument's sake they do come. Our 'lords and masters' from London personally march all the way up here, at the head of an army to come and take the dungeon…" I snorted in contempt, showing what I thought of that.

"Ignoring the fact that none of those fuckers gave a shit about the North *before* the end of the world, and ignoring all the shit that they'd have to wade through, let's say they somehow magically turned up here? If there was a serious chance of them being here to help? I'd be fucking overjoyed to work with the army, and no general, once they understand that killing us would kill the golden goose, would be anything but happy allies. Let's face it: we can create weapons, ammunition, drugs, and hell, hot chocolate and rum. The army would kick the government out straightaway and move in to help."

That wasn't entirely true, but hell, neither was his example, so fuck it.

"So." I shook my head. "We have you fraudulently setting yourself up as being a replacement to our council and ruling body. We have you attempting to force me and my people aside in favor of you, spreading utter bullshit as you go. Then we have the incident where I had you detained."

"You had no right to trap us!" he shouted. "You imprisoned us, took away our access to the dungeon, refused to let us go and—"

"Again, not correct," I said flatly. "Several of your group were given the option of taking a backpack of supplies and fucking off. The vast majority of you chose to stay, but that's fine. So. You marched across to the council chambers and demanded access, telling the woman who was responsible for access to that area, which is secure for a good fucking reason, that you were now the democratically elected council. When she wouldn't step aside and let you in, you tried to force your way past her.

"A heavily pregnant, and unarmed woman, who ended up in *medical* thanks to you and your people. She could have lost her babies because you decided you wanted to stage a coup."

"A…coup…no! We're the democratically—"

"No," I said forcefully. "You *conned* people into voting for something that you couldn't pull off. You only had *your* group on the voting list. And as soon as you had enough people pick one of the names, any of them would do, you tried to take over. In the process, an innocent woman was hurt, as were her unborn children."

I was trying to keep my temper, despite the fact this shit was taking time from the real fight. Despite the fact that we all needed to be doing anything but fucking around with this shit…still, I was here. My anger made itself known though, as small crackles of lightning started to play across my body, jumping and arcing between my fingers as I flexed them, forcing myself to not form fists and pound these arrogant fucksticks all the way to Australia.

"So," I repeated, "I've been made aware by our resident Judge, that as this was not against a codified law, I shouldn't just execute you all for breaking said nonexistent law."

I saw John cover his eyes with one hand, and heard the groan.

"You'll note I said 'shouldn't,'" I repeated, smiling wolfishly. "And that's an important word here, because frankly, that's my preferred option." I summoned a long-handled war hammer to my hand and rested it on the platform next to me, staring at Merriman and the others.

"Now, I rescued you fuckers, risked my *life*, along with that of my friends', to save you. We lost friends—hell, many of us lost *family* in the fight that saw you get saved from being turned into spare parts for a fucking *lich*, and yet this is how you repay me? Fine. There was no law specifically against this, though I think a law that simply said 'Don't be a dick' would be a great one for us all to live by.

"From now on, attempting to start, run, or inflict a coup on the dungeon, or anywhere inside its borders, will result in either banishment, or death, depending on the situation," I declared, lifting the hammer and slamming the head down hard on the steel below it. The crash filled the air.

"Secondly, for any and all actions that don't have a formal law specifying a punishment, but that are blatantly aimed at fucking us all over, there will be four punishments." I looked from face to face, seeing the concern on the people of the dungeon before me, and the mixture of fear and outrage on the faces of the assholes who caused all of this.

"First, and for the more minor issues, a demerit system. You get three levels. First is a week of serving in the army—physical serving, by the way. No getting off because you've got a bad back—we have healers, after all. You serve seven full days. You refuse? You're put out of the dungeon. You break a leg? No worries, we'll heal you, and you get to start again tomorrow. You keep going until you've managed a full week."

"A full day in the army is twelve hours!" Mike interrupted, his voice booming as he deliberately projected it across the area. "Twelve hours a day of guard duty, physical training with weapons and armor, marching on patrol, and fighting monsters!"

"The second level is a month!" I called out, the gasps that had risen at the thought of fighting monsters growing. "A month is a run of twenty-eight days, each lasting a minimum of twelve-hour days, with a sergeant deciding when your day finishes. It might be twelve hours, or you might piss them off, and like, any other recruit, you get extra detail."

"This is outrageous!" Sharon spluttered, shaking her head. "I refuse!"

"And that's fine!" I replied, smiling. "Because there's still two levels left. The third demerit is banishment. Also, if you want to just leave at any point, you're free to go. Just don't think you can change your mind later. You won't be permitted back in."

Silence fell again.

"The final level is plain and simple," I stated flatly. "You attack a member of the dungeon, you harm an innocent, and it's obviously not an accident and so on?" I lifted my hammer. "Death."

I watched for a long minute as everyone was silent, the ordinary citizens of the dungeon clearly worried that I was becoming the evil tyrant that the plotters had been accusing me of. Then, I went on.

"These people here staged a coup. Not content with avoiding work, hiding in their rooms and more, using the limited resources we're all working our arses off for, to create fucking pamphlets and more, they tried to take over the dungeon. They hurt a heavily pregnant woman when she wouldn't let them pass, and not one of them, to the best of my knowledge, has done so much as fucking help to carry a brick since moving in." I crossed my hands on the pommel of the hammer, staring at them.

"You wanted this to be a democracy. It isn't, but fuck it, let's see what the people who live here really want. Is there anyone who wants to speak in their defense?" I asked the crowd, holding a hand up as one of the accused started to speak. "Not you! You already had your say. Let's see what the people you tried to con think."

There was a long moment before a woman stepped forward, holding her hand up for attention; I stepped back, gesturing for her to come up and stand on the platform, so that everyone could hear her.

It took a few seconds before I remembered her name—Pat—and I couldn't help but smile when she opened her mouth and spoke.

"I was trying to meditate," she said. "Wanting to learn magic, real magic, so I could keep my kids and grandkids safe, and these lot wouldn't damn well shut up…" She went on, speaking of the things they'd said and done, and then when she'd dragged them off, losing her own chance to meditate to help others. She pointed out that Sharon and the others had claimed to have been hard workers, but not one of them could explain what they'd been doing.

She asked the crowd for volunteers, asking whether anyone had seen any of them do anything beyond the absolute bare minimum, and then it was only done until they formed their little group and all started plotting.

After ten minutes of Pat asking them questions, questions the brighter ones refused to answer, it was apparent that not one of them had ever done anything for the dungeon, or its people, unless they were forced to.

Pat nodded to me in respect, then climbed down, and I stepped forward again.

"Well, I won't say I'm surprised, nor sad that others know what you're like," I said clearly, before pointing to my old neighbors. "I'll say it, so everyone knows. I knew those two before the end of the world. They lived below me in a downstairs flat. They were the most unpleasant fuckers I'd ever had to put up with then, and they only got worse, it seems."

"You see!" Sharon squealed quickly, jabbing a finger at me. "He never liked us! That's why he's making all of this up and refusing us our due!"

"Your 'due'…" I grunted. "Yeah, you're right. I never liked you, and yet we still let you in. I left you to your own devices, trusting you'd work to help others rather than taking the piss and helping only yourself. More fool me." I shook my head, before taking a deep breath and calling out in a loud voice.

"If nobody disputes this, then I will give them all the choice of a week in the army to serve, or banishment, and they can choose which they have."

"Why do we have to put up with the fuckers, sir?" a voice called out, and I grinned at the sight of a clearly pissed soldier at the back.

"That's a fair question, and I'm sorry that it seems like I'm using the army as a punishment," I said. "They're to serve so that they understand what it's like on the front line. What it's like to march alongside the kobolds and to have to get back up, when you're exhausted, broken by your day, and then fight again. They're to serve so that they learn some respect for the shit you have to put up with, and who knows, they might be made into a useful member of society yet."

I shrugged, making it clear that as far as I was concerned if they didn't learn, then it was all on them.

"Moving forward, and the other reason that we're all in here, is that there will soon be space for more crafters to join our teams, as well as, yes, a need for more soldiers."

"You see! He's wasting lives…" Merriman shouted, and I spun, glaring at him.

"You just don't know when to shut the fuck up, do you?" another voice called out from the crowd, directed at him, and people spread to the sides, as Ian marched through, glaring up at the group on the raised stage. "That's my WIFE you trampled, my children you nearly killed, all because you wanted to be in charge! Well, *fuck* this!" he shouted, pointing at them.

"Dungeon Lord!" he called to me, and I nodded that I was listening. "You gave them the choice, a week or banishment! When do they have to decide?"

"Now." I shrugged. "They just proved that they can't be trusted to keep their mouths shut even when it's in their interest. So come on, we'll start on the left." I pointed at the woman on the far left corner. "You! Banishment or a week in the army? And not serving that week, just to be exceedingly fucking clear, means you get banished. So no, refusing to do either will result in your being dragged to the wall and tossed out, *without* the bag of supplies you'll get if we banish you."

"A-army!" she cried, clearly terrified and looking like a rabbit in the headlights.

The next in line grunted in shock, then gasped when I repeated the question, taking the army as their choice too. Three more were asked, before it got to Gerald, who ducked behind his wife, and Sharon, the pig in a wig, scowled at me.

"You've no right!" she howled, pointing a pudgy finger at me. "No right at all!"

"Choose," I repeated grimly.

"No!" she snapped. "I'll not serve your sick fantasies about making a woman fight…"

"What?" I asked, thinking I'd misheard.

"You see, he doesn't deny it! Look at her! He makes her dress like a whore, or she has to fight! That's what he's offering—women have to be whores or fight!"

I looked to the side where she pointed, and saw…yup. Ashley.

She looked horrified, and utterly outraged, but knowing her, and the concerns she'd had before about the system choices she was offered, I knew that accusation would have cut deep. She was dressed normally as well. Yeah, earlier she'd been dressed…well, she'd been dressed to draw the eyes.

Now, though? A simple sweater and jeans. Nothing about her outfit said she was attempting to draw the eye; she was just wearing a little makeup and dressed as she damn well chose to, which was her right.

"Oh fuck no," Sarah snapped, marching out of the crowd below, and waving at the group on their little platform. "Dungeon Lord! She's refused to serve. That's banishment instead then, right?"

"Certainly is," I agreed.

"Fantastic. Can I have a set of steps please?" She gestured to the platform, and before I could make them, they were already growing into place, others clearly having approved the request.

Sarah marched up the stairs and grabbed Sharon by the scruff of her neck, batting her pathetic attempt at a slap aside. She dragged the much larger woman down the steps, and headed straight for the door, where I sensed a pair of corpse lords being summoned into being outside, ready to take over from Sarah.

"So, let's make this easy. Any of you want to go with her?" I asked, suddenly feeling much more cheerful. "Gerald?"

"I…I…You can't!" he wailed. "You just can't!"

"He's been a lot more understanding than I would have been," Barry called out, stepping forward and speaking for the first time as Sarah approached the door, dragging the now blubbering and screaming Sharon with her. "Let's make this clear! I'm Barry, and I run the Saltwell Park settlement. We're part of the dungeon, but we have our own council there—" He broke off to point at Merriman.

"If you'd tried this shit there?" he asked. "I'd have shot you myself!"

"Barry…" John called grimly, shaking his head.

"Ah, fuck off, Judge," Barry growled. "Sometimes people need to be shown the fist as well as the glove. *Oi!*" he bellowed, and Sarah turned, dragging Sharon around to make sure she heard him. "Don't bother coming to the park. You'll be turned away!"

"You *can't!*" Gerald wailed again, and I just stared at him.

"You not going with her?" Another of the crowd on the mail floor called up to Gerald, who looked after his wife, then back to the group around him, and then after her, before sobbing and climbing down the steps, following her like a whipped dog.

"Gerald," I called out, making him turn and stare up at me with clear hope in his feral eyes. "Don't forget your bag." I gestured. A bag of supplies started to glow next to him as it was printed into existence.

He hesitated, then kicked at it, his foot passing through the bright lights.

"Fuck you! You'll pay for this, all of you! I'll see you all burn in hell!" he screeched, before running off after his wife.

The rest of the accused were very quiet after that, all of them choosing to serve rather than be put out. All except Merriman.

"You'll regret this." He walked down the steps, clearly trembling with every movement. "I'll be back, and it'll be with the army!"

With that, he stomped over to the supplies. As they finished printing, he claimed them, barely able to lift the damn bag onto his back. Thirty seconds later, the door swung shut behind him, and a third corpse lord was guiding him straight to the exit from the dungeon.

All three were booted out, literally in the case of Sharon, as Sarah, who'd accompanied them all to the gates, kicking her in the ass before turning her back and marching back inside.

A handful of minutes later, Sarah stood back in the crowd, a small cadre of admirers and wannabe soldiers around her. I heard her comment just before Aly and Fin started talking about the crafting positions that would be recruited for.

"Nobody fucks with my friends…"

Chapter Sixteen

The rest of the day passed in a bit of a blur. There were a few questions directed to me, but most of the various requests and questions were sorted by others. I spent some of the time with Mike and Patrick, discussing workout routines, and planning. Then, when Sarah joined us, we moved onto the next building.

The gym and "military building" that was to be built was growing in complexity and expense by the second as we talked. The simple design I'd envisaged originally was quickly replaced as we went over their needs.

Everything from a firing range to an armory where people could work on their personal weapons and maintain their armor. Storerooms seemed utterly pointless until Mike pointed out that the dungeon had been unavailable once, and it was just a good idea to sort out a reserve for the future.

I passed them to Aly and Kelly, and ducked out of the conversation, having gotten a plan for a workout, and leaving it at that point.

"Hey, dude," Chris whispered, nudging me with his shoulder. "How you doing?"

"Hey, man." I smiled as we walked into the canteen, plating up various things from the server rather than bothering with summoning anything in particular. "You okay?"

"Yeah." He shrugged, then grunted. "Any word on the animal lures?"

"They're in progress," I assured him. "They'll be done tonight."

"Thanks." Some of the stress melted out of his shoulders.

We ate, a few of us relaxing and talking normally. Ramnik, Dante, Ashley, and I got into an argument over what was possible and what wasn't, after I explained the gates I'd made and more.

Kelly and the others worked on plans, and for the first time in forever, I didn't involve myself, not even when they turned up to the canteen and continued to argue.

I needed to know roughly what was going on—and I did—but I also needed to trust the others. It was that or not have them in those roles.

An hour later, I was kissing Kelly's forehead, then heading down to our room, her promising to be along once she'd sorted things out.

I had a long hot shower, which was a fucking luxury indeed, and then I laid on the bed, sinking into the dungeon sense and working steadily to absorb enough to be able to afford the lures.

As I'd promised Chris, I set the lures up outside the dungeon, and as I hastily assured Aly, I also got to work on absorbing a shitload more random crap to put toward the cost of the research for the various other bits of kit we needed.

The cages, training areas, and more were going to be a pain in the arse, but they all needed doing. Apparently, Chris was doing that research himself, altering the designs to make them cheaper and more specific to what he needed.

I just stayed out of the whole thing.

A little while later, I felt the telltale warmth of Kelly's skin as she slid into the bed next to me. Then, as I left the dungeon sense, I gripped the bed and stiffened—literally—as she slid down under the duvet and made herself known more intimately.

I, of course, certainly didn't interrupt, and simply enjoyed it, before returning the favor a little while later.

The next morning was cool, but not horrifically cold as it had been, and I slid from the bed, being careful not to wake Kelly. I dressed quickly, had a drink and a quick round of toast, then moved to my makeshift gym.

The first hour was meditation and stretching, as Patrick had suggested. I spent a bit of time focusing on the feeling, the discomfort as the muscles stretched past their usual position, then back to normal, but mainly I worked on a single gate.

Now that I knew more about what I was doing, I spent the time on fixing the second gate, the one I'd just clagged together, and getting myself warmed up.

Once that was done, and the toast and drink had properly settled, I started a steady workout.

Knowing I needed to make the most of this time, I worked my utter arse off, warming up my muscles with a lower weight on the deadlifts and TRX rows—I decided that as the Dungeon Lord I had a right to add a few little extras like them, and quickly absorbed enough to offset the cost—gradually increasing the angle I worked at, as well as the weight and repetitions, until I was at my old personal best, and breezing past it.

Ten minutes later, I was pressing out nearly three times my old maximum. The bar felt like it was in danger of snapping as I slammed it down, bending over and huffing as I tried to catch my breath.

Four hundred kilos. *Four fucking hundred kilos*. I didn't know whether that was a record—my kingdom for a wiki—but damn it was good going. I'd been at a hundred and forty kilos before this, and I'd been pleased with that.

As soon as I could breathe, I dropped and started cracking out push-ups, then forced myself to my feet, grabbing a smaller set of dumbbell weights and pumping them.

I had a plan, but I needed to know whether it worked or not, and to test it, I needed to be at utter failure.

With that in mind, I worked to failure, rather than maximum.

The difference was that I went straight in with the twenty-kilo dumbbells, pounded those until I couldn't do any more, then went to the eighteens, then the fifteens. I continued all the way down to the fives, no breaks, just constantly pushing.

As soon as I couldn't lift the weight I was on any further, I went to the next smallest and continued to work.

The failure set, thanks to having no breaks, was an utter bastard. The muscles never got a chance to recover, and by the end, the five-kilo weight felt as heavy and immobile as a five hundred one would have been.

Of course, just as I admitted defeat, letting the two tiny five-kilo weights sag, that was when Ashley and Dante walked in.

I saw the look they gave me, seeing me struggling with the five kilos and internally I started screaming blue murder. Ten minutes ago, they could have walked in and they'd have seen me lifting insane weights, but noooo.

I wasn't interested in Ashley—or Dante, for that matter—in that way, but seriously? Fuck's sake.

I dumped the weights on the rack and just shook my head. I sat on the floor and grunted out an explanation.

"Drop sets," I said, the light of understanding clear in Ashley's eyes, while Dante looked on, blank. "It's not important." I groaned, lying down on my back on the floor and staring up at the ceiling as I focused, summoning Lightning to flood my body.

My manapool, which was getting reasonable again, dipped significantly, but in thirty seconds I was rolling to my feet, grinning as I pulled up the notifications that had been pulsing away steadily while I worked.

You have gained additional Stat Points in the following areas through constant effort.

- +1 Endurance

- +1 Perception

- +1 Strength

Continue to work hard to increase these or other stats...

I couldn't help but grin. Now the real work could begin. Dante and Ashley were looking at the massively overloaded bar, all four hundred kilos on it, and the look on Dante's face as I stepped in and asked them not to mess with it was priceless.

I took my position, and started work, lifting and pounding the metal.

Dante tried it after me, clearly knowing he wouldn't be able to lift it for many reps, but when he couldn't move it at all, it was a hell of a surprise to him.

"Why…" he started to ask, looking from the five-kilo weights to the four hundred, only to be drawn aside by Ashley, who spoke very quietly to him.

"Hun, no talking in the morning in here, all right? I'll explain later." She frowned, concentrating, and a few seconds later, I felt Aly's presence as she helped Ashley, summoning a large and complicated bit of machinery into one corner.

It was a stepper, or at least that's what I thought of it as: a mechanical, constantly moving set of steps, making it almost like you were climbing a skyscraper, floor by floor.

Ashley clambered onto it, even as Dante sat on the chair next to her, frowning as he looked over the gym equipment, totally at a loss as to what he should be using.

I passed him a few of the smaller weights, leaving him to it, and focusing on my own routine, determined to try to prove my theory.

"Thanks. Um, so like this?" he whispered to me, clearly not understanding the whole point wasn't the silence; it was to not fucking bother me.

He tried doing a few exercises, and I stepped in with a growl. Ashley winced and stopped her climb until I told her it was fine, and gave him a few pointers.

Ten minutes later, and Dante was still asking questions, alternating between her and me, when Sarah trooped in, asking in a hushed voice if it was okay for her and two others to use the rowing machine and weights.

I ignored them—at least, as much as I could—focusing on my own exercises. But after five more minutes, when I finished my drop set—minus half the weights I needed to do it properly—and found that someone had stripped my bar of the bigger weights, happily chatting to their friend about the ideal form for a bench press…

I walked out.

Just up and about-faced, marching out of the fucking room and stomping down the stairs.

I needed to test this, I needed to push myself, and yet…I shook my head. I couldn't be angry; they were my citizens and hell, they were trying to get stronger and fitter.

They risked their lives day in and day out for the good of the dungeon. The least I could do was leave them with the weights and gear I'd been using.

I made it outside, taking a deep breath of the crisp air, forcing a smile as someone called out a greeting, before starting to jog.

I wasn't a runner. Not by choice. I'd occasionally happily run on a treadmill, or through Jesmond Dene in the summer, or along the beach, but that was the maximum.

I'd do it when it was a nice day, warm and summery and preferably with a friend, just pushing steadily to try to keep the belly under control.

I needed more than that, though.

If I was to push myself to my limit, and really make the most out of this, then I needed to really get a move on. I built up the speed steadily, finding it was weird, compared to the way I was used to it.

First, I was used to running in full armor of late, and for a minute I actually considered it, summoning my armor and wearing it for the run; then I dismissed it as a waste of time.

I needed to get the rhythm sorted first, then add weights and exercises, not just a single set weight.

Secondly, in my mind, when I wasn't running to a fight, in my memories I'd be running in the summer, nice and warm and half my current size.

The first lap was a warm-up, steady and hard, but totally do-able. The distance around the inside of the walls wasn't too far, maybe two miles the way I was running it, looping around and enjoying the feeling of loosening up my muscles.

The second I passed the point I'd picked out as the "start," all that changed.

I put my head down and picked up speed, pushing harder and harder until I was at what I thought was my maximum speed. Pushing until I felt I was in danger of tripping myself, and only then slowing slightly, my heart hammering as I gradually drifted to a halt.

While I recovered, I did push-ups until I could do no more, star jumps and burpees, before forcing myself to my feet again and running full speed to a set point, then dropping and exercising until I was broken, then back to my feet and stumbling off again.

Half an hour became an hour, then two, and I started staggering. Pain was screaming up at me from every goddamn muscle, until I finally dropped after a particularly painful set of burpees and couldn't make myself get back up.

I'd not seen any more notifications, but on checking my stat sheet, I could see the numbers clicking up as I steadily closed on another full stat point increase.

I gave in, closing my eyes. My heart thundered, blood surging wildly in my veins as I started to circulate Lightning. And the relief I felt at doing it?

It was insane.

Whatever else the Lightning was doing for me, circulating it through my body was healing me, and not just of wounds. The microtears that were how muscles grew, and the accumulation of aches and pains that were left from adrenal surges, were all washed away in the healing.

Tomorrow would be the test, though. Today, I'd proved that I could work out, and then flush my body with Lightning and still get the gains. Tomorrow I'd do the same, but I'd do it without the Lightning. I'd push myself as hard as I could and just do that, not washing the pain nor damage away, and see whether I improved faster or not.

Then, the day after, by which time my mana should be nicely full anyway, I'd do the same set of exercises, but I'd do it with the Lightning pouring through me, held tightly and repairing constantly as time passed.

The plan was that after three days I should have had time to figure out what was working and what wasn't, as well as the most efficient way of training.

I really, *really* hoped that using Lightning was the most efficient, as not using it at all tomorrow for the test was going to suck ass. I pulled up the notifications and then the stats, and stared at them, grinning like an absolute lunatic.

You have gained additional Stat Points in the following areas through constant effort.

- +1 Agility

- +1 Dexterity

Continue to work hard to increase these or other stats…

Yeah, okay I'd only gained two points, but that was two points! I'd also made a significant improvement in a load of other areas. My Strength had gone from four out of a hundred to thirty-seven out of a hundred. Once that hit the top? That was another point earned.

A few more hours of this, and I should be able to increase that again! Okay, it wasn't a world-shattering change, and it was predictable. Hell, we'd known this before the fall.

Exercise, and your body gets stronger, and so on. Yeah, great…magnificent discovery, Matt. The difference was, though, that in using my Lightning? I was healing myself and ready to go all over again!

This was a fucking game changer.

I jogged back to the main dungeon building, ready to make the most of this discovery and get back to meditation. But as I staggered up the stairs, I could hear that I'd made a terrible mistake.

The "gym" on the top floor was jam-packed when I arrived. At least eight more people were squeezed into the small room, along with more freshly summoned equipment.

I came to a stop in the doorway, staring in utter shock. Ashley and Dante were in one corner, Dante and Ramnik deep in conversation as Ramnik took a turn on the stepping machine that Ashley had summoned.

Mike was talking with two more guys, both of which I guessed to be ex or soon-to-be current military, judging from the overall look. All three were working with a set of weights, and laughter filled the air as one of them dropped a weight on their foot.

Others were encouraging friends, or discussing various new machines that needed to be built, and I just…I just observed in disbelief.

"Fuck this shit," I muttered, moving to the next room along. It was filled with people trying to meditate. The overlapping converters in the last room projected slightly into this room as well, and these people were trying to meditate, despite the noise next door.

I hesitated, then looked in the next room. A guy with hair halfway to his arse, who I'd swear I'd never seen before, was giving a yoga lesson.

Each of the rooms on the top floor of the building were like this as I moved on. I experienced the horrible rise of both anger and despair. I was an asshole for feeling this, I knew.

I desperately wanted to boot them all the fuck out, but they clearly had wanted this, and the more I looked, the more I saw that this was seriously needed by my people.

The problem was, I'd deliberately gotten this set up so that I could grow more powerful to protect them, and there wasn't a cat in fucking hell's chance I could do that now!

I couldn't meditate with all this shit going on. Hell, I couldn't even get into the "gym." And the fact that there was so much equipment appearing from nowhere?

I moved up onto the rooftop, thinking to find a bit of peace there…only to find that a hardy seven who were trying to touch their mana were practically hugging the converters here as well, all while asking one another questions and repeating advice that I knew to be bullshit.

I paused, then about-faced, jogging down the stairs and past everyone I saw without a word. A handful of minutes later, I was in the private area at the bottom of the dungeon, and then into our bedroom.

Kelly had gotten up and gone to "work". The room was in its usual state of disarray, looking as if someone had gotten a wash basket full of clothing, balled it up, and thrown it in every direction at once, and paying no attention to what was knocked over or destroyed in the fun.

I sighed and started to work.

I needed to work on my magic, and I needed to work on my meditation. Realistically, the closeness of the converters didn't matter. They excited their own tied form of mana, making it a little easier to work with that form, and it sped up absorption of that mana. So, if like me, it needed Lightning, then being next to a Lightning converter was a massive boost. But honestly, I was probably the person who needed that crutch the least at this point.

I moved around the room, clearing it quickly as I went, considering what I was feeling and why, and dealing with it. I didn't need the space, not as much as the others did, and although yes, I needed the exercise equipment, I'd make do with sharing that. For now, I could work down here, as long as I wasn't interrupted.

What I couldn't do, though, was meditate in this much of a fucking mess.

An hour it took me, in the end. An entire hour to blitz our room, to absorb the half-eaten food, to repair and replace the clothes, to put them away for fuck's sake!

I even spent some ten minutes doing nothing but cleaning and repairing, then summoning copies of our underwear. My boxers were important to me,—a little luxury—but Kelly was always searching for her favorite sports bra and whatever, so I made sure we both had spares.

All in all, it seemed like a ridiculous way to spend an hour, considering all that I was supposed to be doing with my life, and with the time I'd gotten to train, but by the end of it I'd made some decisions as well.

I was going to have to prioritize several things, and one of them was training for everyone. We'd been going at it ad hoc, telling different people to sort different things, and just running around like a headless chicken, as that asshole had put it.

He'd not been entirely wrong, which was the problem.

Starting at the top, now that we had a secure—more or less—home, with food and warmth and so on, we had the facility to really grow now.

To make the most of it, like any business, we needed a plan and a set of priorities.

Those were, in my mind, defense, research, and expansion.

Expansion would come in time, though we needed to start sending out scouting teams to secure the area and make damn sure we weren't getting snuck up on. I also needed to spend some time on Jack.

He was battered and broken in a lot of ways, but he was also still out there doing laps of the area, hunting down anything that looked to be a threat and tearing it limb from limb.

Research was getting done, and Aly was recruiting others specifically for the various areas we needed covering. That was good because with the expansion to Steel, we'd unlocked a lot more specifications, and it was time we started work on them.

Basically, there were a load more ways to split the focus of the dungeon, and to augment the research that was being done in it. It made sense, after all; as time went on, to produce any kind of large-scale construction, you needed a shitload of different specializations and forms of research done. To make a car, you didn't just need an engine; you needed everything from the wheels to the seats to the damn windscreen.

Defense, though, required us to get our arses in gear. We needed mages, we needed fighters, and we needed equipment. Equipment was being sorted by Aly and Finn, which was great—I had no time for it, after all. But for the fighters and the mages, I could help a little.

The fighters, and to a lesser degree the mages, needed to be able to keep fit and healthy, and to improve their bodies.

The mages needed to learn, to study, and to improve, as well as those who actively wanted to learn magic actually being able to do it.

I'd left it pretty much in Ramnik's hands, as she was the most organized of the mages, and was both powerful and someone I trusted. That was clearly not working out, though, considering she was in the gym with Ashley and Dante, while two separate groups were trying to meditate and teach themselves.

I settled back on the bed, content I'd gotten my head more or less sorted out now. I had intended to work on my magic, to figure out my spells and more. But, honestly, I was going to have to put that aside again, as much as it pissed me off.

I needed to sort the mages and the fighters out. Then, when they were working on their own shit, I could finally concentrate on my shit.

Then, and only then, could I finally fucking work on my magic.

I slid into the dungeon sense, and flitted across to the Parthenon building, finding Kelly and Aly already discussing it, and as soon as I made my presence known…

"Matt, I'm so sorry," Kelly said quickly. "I didn't realize there were so many people who wanted to work out. Aly just…"

"I went to see how it was going," Aly admitted. "I wondered if you'd gone back to the gym. I'd noticed you running earlier, and when you walked into the room and everyone was there? I saw your face…"

"My face?"

"You walked into the gym with a face like thunder, and when I saw the way it was…I mean, we agreed you'd have it pretty much to yourself for a few days, but once word spread that there was somewhere indoors to meditate and work on their magic, and the gym as well…" Aly sounded almost frantic as she blurted it all out.

"I'm sorry, Matt. We didn't think it'd go like this," Kelly said. "I know I was looking forward to getting in a workout, but I didn't think so many people would want to. And considering that this is without Griffiths and the others, and—"

"It's okay," I said loudly, cutting them both off. "Okay, it's all right because it's made me look at things, and that was part of the reason for all of this—to take some time out and try to figure things out while focusing on growing stronger. We'll talk about that in a minute. But where the hell is Griffiths? He should have been back yesterday."

"That's my fault." Kelly shook her head. "The ship is safe, first of all, just so you don't worry about that. It's in the park and we built a room around it. No doors or ways in, either. As soon as he's finished, we'll absorb a panel and make it into a barn or something for the various animals."

"Okay, what happened?" I asked, relieved that the ship, at least, was safe, but now worried about Griffiths.

"Griffiths and the army guys found an entire hospital wing full of people at the QE," Aly said. "Most of them are doctors and nursing staff. They'd had a load of patients, but when the gang moved in…anyway." She changed direction quickly, shaking her head.

"That there were over a hundred medical staff there, and they were basically traumatized and needed help? Griffiths couldn't leave them, but he couldn't abandon his orders either. He took everything to the park, sealed it away, and got a shitload of food and supplies, then went back to the hospital. He's working on sorting things out now, and Clarissa has two of her people sliding an influence generator to the hospital."

"As a base or to loot it?" I asked, nodding as I agreed with either possibility. It was at the top of a hill, after all: clear a load of the houses nearby away and you could see for miles.

"To loot it." Aly shrugged. "I told Griffiths that if people didn't want to join us, then we could do with friends still, and in exchange for the medical gear, we could seal the damaged sections up."

"It's far less than it'll cost for us to get up there, Matt," Kelly assured me. "One of the big MRI machines will earn us literally thousands of points of mana, and to get a load of them and…"

"No." I shook my head. "It's all right…you don't have to justify it. First of all, this is the kind of decision you were well within your rights to make, and secondly, it's a damn good idea. Only changes I'd make to it is that we claim the entire site. Reinforce the walls and more, strip the surrounding areas and anything they'll let us have."

"You want to claim it?" Kelly asked slowly, shaking her head. "Matt, we looked at it, and while it's in a good place, it doesn't make any sense. There's not enough people to make a settlement, and after all the work we've invested in the park and here…"

"I'm not thinking as a settlement." I smiled. "I'm thinking as an outpost. We build a big tower, seal the fucker so it's safe from attacks, put some converters on its roof, get a garrison of kobolds or whatever up there and a few humans, let them keep watch over the area."

"I don't think the staff will be happy about that." Kelly shook her head. "Matt, they don't want to join us. They want to be left alone. But they're negotiating with Griffiths, as he's army. They want him to join them and protect them."

"You think he'll leave us?" I asked, concerned.

"No…" She dragged the word out. "But I think it's making him reevaluate the deal we struck. There's a lot of people out there who need help, and we've just crushed the nearest gangs. We're at the point that once we've replaced our losses, we could start moving out and helping people. I think that's what he's going to push for when he gets back."

"I agree," I said, clearly surprising them both.

"I thought you wanted to focus on the dungeon and on growing stronger?" Aly asked.

"I do," I said firmly. "The difference is, I think we need to really focus on the dungeon for a few days. The research is going well, and that's great, but the buildings?"

I floated around the room, bringing up a map of the area on the wall, the dungeon as it was now, seen from above.

"We're stripping the area like a plague of locusts right now. We've got the living quarters going up, both here and in the park…How's that coming along?"

"Here?" Kelly asked, and I nodded, seeing the outline of the massive construction. "The first four floors are done. We've called off expansion of the next floor until things calmed down a little, but…"

"Okay, that makes sense," I agreed, nodding. "We've got accommodation for everyone at the minute, here and at the park, and we've got the basics hammered out. Now it's time to start looking at the next phase."

"Which is?" Kelly asked, taking a seat.

"Improving it. We're moving past survival, and into getting our lives on track, as well as giving our people the tools they need to really live, not just get through the day."

"How do you mean?" Aly asked.

"Look at the fighters," I said. "Just as an example, look at them…we've had massive losses, seriously fucking nasty ones of late. The entire dungeon creature population virtually died, and a lot of our humans as well. If they were properly outfitted and trained, that would have been a fraction of the numbers."

"I…I did my best…" Aly sounded hurt.

"No!" I shook my head and spoke quickly. "That's not meant as a complaint, Aly, not about any of it. You've done amazing. But look at our forces—think about them. They're physically much as they were when the fall came. Some of them are more powerful, but…fuck this sounds really arrogant, but hey. Look at me." I forced myself to appear more solid in the room. I couldn't exactly flex and pop my pecs, plus I was still only starting to move into the true superhuman levels, but that was the point.

"I'm built like I should be a recruiting poster for steroids, or a fight club." I relaxed and faded a little from view. "Physically, I've never been anywhere near this level, and in the fights? It massively helps."

"Yeah, Matt, you're literally a god." Kelly facepalmed. "If you ever tell anyone I said that, I'll murder you in your sleep," she warned me, glaring.

"Hah!" I laughed. "Tempting! But no, that's not the point here. Chris is close to my size as well. Mike is, too, as are a lot of Griffiths's people. But beyond that? Markus and most of the fighters are…above average. That's it."

"Okay?"

"They need to work on their bodies," I said. "My abilities have nothing to do with my size and fitness. I've spent this time working out, and believe me, I'll be doing it a lot more over the next few days. The point, though, and this is just the fighters, is that we've let them down. We've let them down massively."

"How?" Kelly asked, even as Aly started to nod.

"The gym," Aly said softly.

"That's part of it," I agreed. "They've been working out a little, but they're working out as humans do. They're working out as Markus and the others used to in the army, and they've been doing it without the right gear."

"They could have summoned some?" Kelly suggested.

"They could," I agreed. "But we've been desperately working on stuff, and beyond food, which everyone views as basically a right now, they don't summon things themselves, not even those who know they could."

"They didn't want to waste the mana when we might need it," Aly guessed, seeing the issue.

"Exactly. And yeah, that's a good thing. I'd rather have a kobold warrior to help than a multigym that's in the corner of a room gathering dust. But that's also part of the problem. We've survived the fights, and right now, we *think*—and that's important—we *think* that the area is as secure as we can make it."

"So it's time to make a gym," Aly suggested.

"A gym and more," I agreed. "Chris volunteered to help with the training, mainly because he needs to keep busy until the animal lures bring something in for him to bond. It was a 'make work' job as well, to distract him. But if we think about it? It needs to be done. Mike is usually out of the dungeon on a mission, Griffiths and his team are helping with our troops, but until we have a team to train?"

"They've mainly been keeping to themselves and helping to teach the fighters." Aly nodded. "The fighters we have, have been training with shield and spear as well. Marching as a unit and so on."

"So we need to change it all up." I sighed. "We need to keep the shields and spears for now, so that they have close range and ranged, once you've got the rail guns working. That's not the point right now, though. We need a plan for training, and we need a facility for them to do it in. They're marching and doing sprints and things like that, but without active, hard workouts, they're just not growing. Add in that they desperately need to level? To fight and grow, and they're all low-leveled?"

"We've literally the best facility I can imagine for that as well." Kelly grunted, waving one hand to the wall where an image of the dungeon hung. "But…"

"But we've not had the mana to spend on it to use it properly," I agreed, nodding. "And when we finally started to, we ended up building housing and a load more."

"Exactly. Are we holding off on construction now then?" Kelly asked, gesturing to the dungeon again. "If we keep the demolition and absorption teams going again at the park and here, we can massively ramp up the research and still get the dungeon running for training."

"We are," I said. "We're switching gears, but only once we have two more buildings built." I ignored the looks that Kelly and Aly exchanged. "Don't worry, the first is the gym, so we finish the basic building. We need a gym, showers, and lockers, that's it."

I saw how Kelly and Aly both went to speak, and I plowed on. "I know the military needs a proper building—yes, I damn well know that—and we will build one. But for now? They get a large enough gym and changing area, that's it. Most of the training they need to do will be do-able in the dungeon, and they all have accommodation already. Yes, I know it'd be more efficient with a proper building; yes, I know it makes sense. No, we don't have the fucking time. We're building this as the gym for the entire dungeon population."

"Okay…and not the army?" Aly asked.

"They'll be the main users of it, yes," I said. "But in time, we'll be building a dedicated building for them. For now, this is for everyone. We fill it with the basic equipment. Obviously, we can't put the electric and powered gear in, but we can redesign stuff and fill it once we need it. This is for *everyone*, and that means that the fighters we have can train and learn to push past their limits."

"What's the other building?" Kelly asked, clearly considering where to put things down.

"A mage's tower."

"Matt…" Aly bit her lip. "I thought we were going to use the black tower, you know, that part of the castle…"

"We were," I agreed. "Until I found eight people crammed up against the wall in the room next door to the new 'gym,' trying to use the converters to meditate, and another seven freezing their asses off up on the roof.

"That's when I realized that almost every time I've gone up there, there's been someone there, or shortly after someone has turned up. When you start thinking that, and start adding up that everyone's pretty much working their asses off, so they're doing this in their spare time…"

"That means…" Kelly winced. "There might be literally hundreds of people trying to do it."

"Exactly," I said flatly. "And considering that Ramnik is chilling in the gym with Dante and Ashley…"

"Well, she isn't really responsible for teaching anyone. People just started following her, and…"

"Exactly," I repeated. "She's not in charge, not really. She sort of fell into the position. I kept giving her jobs. Frankly, though, she doesn't seem that interested in teaching, more of learning."

"Best to ask her if she wants to be in charge or not then," Kelly suggested, and I nodded.

"Will do. But that leaves us with the point that we need a mage's tower."

"Why a tower?" Aly asked absently, clearly already thinking of possibilities. "A block or building might be better?"

"It would," I agreed. "But it wouldn't fit. If we look at a wizard's tower, or mage's or whatever in the middle of the dungeon, it says straightaway to people what it is. Make it just another block? No difference. Add to that, we can make each level better for different things, like we talked about doing with the civic center.

"Make a level for Fire, for Water, for Earth, and whatever. If each level is set for different things, then specialists can improve themselves. But we'll also have a single larger floor on the ground when you walk in that will have sixteen converters in it."

I gestured to the wall. Being "in" the dungeon already, it was easier to manipulate the screen for some reason, and I altered the map of the dungeon as we saw it from above.

As it was now, with the latest round of expansion, the dungeon's outer wall started at the corner of Grainger Street, and the A186. Heading from that most westerly point, it went north by northeast all the way to Dean Street, then turned southeast and ran all the way to the bottom of Dean Street where the cliff climbed from sight behind a collection of old buildings. It ringed the bottom of the original old Newcastle defensive castle wall, enclosing the new Parthenon government building.

Heading north by northwest along St. Nicolas Street from the bridge, the wall followed Westgate Road and then onto the A186 to link up at the bottom of Grainger Street again.

The overall shape was a bit fucked up. I'd have preferred a square or something to make it easier to plot out, but that wasn't the way the world worked. It ended up as a rectangle, slanted to the left, and with the top end about three times as big as the bottom right.

If we looked at the layout as a clock, starting at the "0900" position and moving clockwise, the dungeon was on the left-hand side in the middle, with the crafting area to its direct north. To the east was the massive housing pyramid; below that was the pool, then the cathedral, then the training dungeon, the castle and Parthenon. Then we were round to the old housing block, and finally back to the dungeon main building.

Looking at the layout, we had two easy choices for placement. We could make it in the space that was to the west of the main dungeon and crafting block. There was a space about a hundred meters at the base, narrowing to fifty meters or so at the tip.

That was a good size space, or...

"Do we need this?" I pointed at the old accommodation block. "I mean, nobody lives in it now, and while some of it I converted into apartments, they were always a bit shit. I literally slapped them together, and we fixed them as best we could."

"Are you happy to demolish them?" Aly asked, surprised. "I mean, you made them with the power you harvested from the storm, and the rest of the building was pretty much demolished. Some of it is still usable but..."

"I'm a lot of things, but sentimental isn't one of them." I snorted. "Is it empty?"

We examined the building from several angles, finding that there were a handful of people in it, and at one end of the building...

"Yeah, they're not going to be happy if I drop a goblin in there to ask them to leave." I laughed, seeing the cou—*thruple* who were entertaining themselves in one of the rooms.

"Give them a minute?" Kelly suggested. "The effort they're putting in right now, they won't be long."

"I really...I can't watch." Aly shook her head and looked away.

We all left, a little embarrassed, and feeling like we were voyeurs, and yet, if we hadn't looked we would have begun destroying the building with them in it.

Even as distracted as they'd all been, I had to think that'd have put them off their stroke.

"Anyway!" I said. "We build the gym to the north of the accommodation block, I think. Leave a decent-sized space next to it for the military building as well. Replace the old accommodation block with the mage's tower."

"Have you got a plan for it?" Aly asked, her cheeks still flaming red. "And how tall are you looking at?"

"I'm thinking it needs to be a good size," I said. "We make it fifty meters across, and at least twelve stories."

"That's...that's seriously big," Kelly said after a few seconds. "Why does it need to be so big?"

"That's what she said," I muttered without thinking, then grinned at the look on her face. "Anyway, yeah, but I'm thinking we make this the center of magic for us all. Like *all* of us. Thinking logically, we've got at least a hundred people trying to learn magic here randomly, and we've got a much smaller population than the park. Eventually others will join us, including the army, hopefully, and their families. If we base it on even ten percent want to unlock their latent magical capabilities, which is an insanely low number as far as I'm concerned? That's going to be at least five or six hundred before we look at any new influxes of people."

Aly winced. "That's a hell of a lot of people to lose from the rest of the dungeon."

"It is, but on the other side?" Kelly suggested, her eyes shining. "Imagine if we had even a hundred of them as combat mages. The asuras would have been wiped out in seconds, literally."

"Imagine how many of them will want to be crafters, or healers. Farmers, even—hell, they could make a field grow a full crop in a matter of days and we could sell it."

"Magic is a game changer," I said. "If we take fifty combat-trained mages and healers and another fifty soldiers, all armed with rail guns? We can wipe out the bandit threat in the surrounding areas easily. You were worried about the prisoners from Durham? They'd be wiped out in a matter of minutes."

"It sounds incredible, but can we afford it?" Kelly asked me, clearly not wanting to get too excited yet.

"Can we afford not to?" I asked her, twisting the conversation around. "It would be a massive step toward us being entirely safe. It would be a way to defend us against the orcs as well."

"You think?"

"I think it'd be a start," I said frankly. "And once we've got them working on their issues? Once people are learning? I can work on my own."

"How long?" Kelly asked me. "Until you could start it, I mean, and what would you need?"

"A hundred volunteers," I said after a moment's thought. "We start with the ground level of the tower, make it as solid and stable as possible. Then we make at least two floors below ground, one that's just for Darkness converters, one for Earth; then we have the ground floor for now as mixed. We have sixteen converters around the outside of the room, have them in pairs, spaced out equally. We make a platform in the middle…"

As I spoke, a new building appeared on the map, outlined in red over the existing block.

"In the middle, we put a collection of the more powerful and specialized converters, like the Lightning and Storm ones here…"

I dotted them around the platform.

"And we space the rest of them out around the room," I finished, with dozens of dots appearing on the wire drawing. "We have things like Nature converters next to the Life and Earth ones. This will do us for now. Having a load all close together, yeah, I know they're not going to be as efficient as they would if we had them, like, a Water one, in the river. That's fine, though, because that's not why they're there."

"Why are they?" Aly asked, then nodded as she realized it. "Because then people will automatically congregate with the ones that match them…they'll be drawn to the converters."

"Once they're there, they've got a better chance of touching their mana, and that's the first step in becoming a mage." I grinned.

"Mancer," Kelly corrected absently.

"What?"

"They call themselves 'mancers': geomancer, hydromancer, and all the rest."

"Fine." I shrugged. "Mancer's tower or whatever. I don't give a fuck. The point is that if we do this, I'll take a hundred who want to learn, on the condition that they each have to teach at least three more. Once the ball starts rolling, then we should be able to teach a load of people in short order. I'll teach a class or two, mainly because I keep trying to explain things and Ramnik keeps telling me I'm doing it wrong, despite it working."

"You nearly kill yourself on a daily basis," Kelly pointed out.

"Details, details!"

"Seriously, Matt, can you do this?" Aly asked me, and I looked at her, seeing the concern in her face. "If you promise to teach people, personally, there won't be any shortage of people signing up. They know you're literally a god, after all. But that's also the problem. You need to train and improve. If you say you'll do this, you have to do it."

"I will," I said firmly. "But only in the short-term. You know how insane our lives are at the best of times. I'll teach until we can get a dedicated teacher, and as soon as we can get specialists, they'll be responsible for teaching their own students…Dante for pyromancers, etc."

"And Ramnik?" Kelly asked. "She's done a hell of a job so far, and yes, she's not been doing a great deal of teaching, but you did say she was in charge of the mancers already."

"I'll ask her what she wants," I said. "If she wants to be in charge of the mancers, then she can explain what's been happening and start doing classes. It might be that she doesn't even know about these people who want to learn. But if that's the case, then she's not paying much attention."

"That's fine then," Kelly agreed. "Honestly, I think she'd much rather be involved in magical research than anything else."

"That's something else we need," I agreed. "The dungeon spells need to be looked into, and the—"

"The what?" Aly asked me sharply.

"The dungeon spells," I repeated. "You know, like Fear."

"No," she said slowly. "No, Matt, I don't." She pulled the screens up and flicked through the various options, and I grunted, reaching out and stopping her as I saw the research paths she could see, and the lack of the magic option.

"That's weird." I scouted for it on my own internal system. "It was here somewhere…" It took a minute to find, and when I did? I wasn't happy.

"Fucking hell! Look at the cost!" I growled.

<u>Dungeon Spells</u>

Fear:

Fear is a standard general-purpose spell, used primarily to drive away low-level adventurers or monsters while the Dungeon is being remodeled.

Cost: 100 mana to cast, with a further 10 mana per minute active.
AOE: 5 meters, but can be increased for a further 10 mana per meter, per minute active.

It was practically free, and this was the level-one option, with four more to go. The additional "bleed-through" of information hinted that the cost would drop, and the effect would grow as we invested more.

"Now why the hell wasn't that available to you?" I asked rhetorically, focusing in and watching it populate on the screen for the others to see.

"Magical research." Aly groaned. "You took it as an option awhile back, didn't you?"

"Yeah?" I admitted, totally confused.

"Well, when it popped up as an option on my research system, I took a look. I saw that there were a handful of options, but they all needed a specialist to start working on it, and that I wasn't one." She shrugged. "So with the way everything was branching all over the place, I sort of decided I didn't want to see it right now, and moved on. I guess the dungeon took that as a request and buried it. I'm sorry, I'll check and make sure there's nothing else like that."

"It's okay." I shrugged, sighing. "Fuck knows I keep losing my place with things and forgetting to go back."

I drifted around the room. The inability to pace as I often liked to when I was thinking was starting to annoy me.

"Anyway. So this first spell here, we need a magical researcher to work on it, and it'll unlock Fear as a spell for the dungeon, used to 'drive away low-leveled creatures and adventurers when the dungeon is being remodeled.' Hmmm." I looked at the details.

"We need that all the way to the top-levelled version," Kelly said flatly. "If it can be tweaked to cover certain areas? We can use it to reclaim the area. Most of the bandits and assholes around here are low-level. We run this permanently from a few outlying areas, and it'll drive away anything that might cause problems."

"We need to use the lures to get magical creatures in for Chris though and—"

"And that's fine. We leave a few isolated paths open for them to pass through. As long as we can make our people immune to this? It's insanely useful," Kelly said firmly. "We can put out generators for the Fear spell, a converter next to them to pull in some mana to offset the cost, and an alert tower, and between them we don't have to scout or worry about those areas!"

"Uh…Matt?" Aly said softly, her eyes widening as she stared at something before her.

"Yeah?"

"You know how some things, like the mana conversion rates and so on, are a bit…off? And how we've been frantically building converters and more to try to keep up with our needs?"

"Yeah?"

"You know how for a dungeon normally, they'd not be able to just strip the local area for building materials, and they'd therefore have to rely on the converters?"

"Yeah, and everything would take forever to build," I agreed. "It's just one of those things."

"But the other dungeons…they seem to be ahead of us all the time, or at least equal, right? And we've been fighting all day and night. For us to get to where we are, we've had to make massive investments in mana from basically war?"

"Yeah?" I repeated, getting a sinking feeling in the pit of my stomach.

"I think we've been doing this wrong all along."

CHAPTER SEVENTEEN

alf an hour later, I was in the war room, swigging from a bottle of rum and staring at the screen before me in disbelief. I'd left the dungeon sense and had run over to the war room, telling Kelly and Aly to cancel anything else they'd had planned until we had this sorted.

"Tell me that again," I growled. I'd linked to the dungeon, just to make sure that any systems that were marked Eyes Only to the Dungeon Lord, like the spells had been, would show now, and oh fuck, had we made a mistake.

"So, some systems are one-offs in the research tree and others aren't. Like, the mana converters can be researched over and over, making them more powerful, but the itemized storage, those mana crystals or stones were a one-off. We don't need to research them again, we have access to them, and while we can choose to research them again, I get the feeling that it's a closed line."

"That didn't make much more sense that time either," I said flatly.

"Okay!" Aly growled, running her hands through her hair as she thought about how to explain this better. "So, let's go back to basics. Research. When I do it, I can do it through the dungeon, in that I pick a line of research, and I basically feed it mana, and boom, it reaches that number, and the knowledge and access unlocks for the dungeon, right?"

"Yeah." I grunted.

"Okay, well, that's a research line, an 'open' one. I follow the line and boom, we get access. Now let's say we were making a crossbow. The system says it's ten thousand mana—it's not; it's just for this example—and so we can invest ten thousand mana. *Or…*" She paused, glaring at me. "*Or…*I can tinker with it.

"Rather than being stuck in the system and doing it the way the goblin and kobold researchers were doing it, where they literally sit and plod along, trying to figure things out, and the dungeon—I think—uses their brain power and mana to tick away at the total, I know some of the needed things. I can add those bits into the design, altering the things that the dungeon has been working on.

"Overall, sometimes it can take longer to do it this way, but the result is a better product, or, if I add in the more generic details I know, it speeds up the process. Rather than being a thousand mana, or ten thousand, if I can design most of it, it might jump over entire sections, only needing a few hundred instead.

"Alternatively, like with the armor, we can have the dungeon do the standard research, and I can work on my own version at the same time, taking sections that the dungeon figures out and that I have no clue about, and integrating them into my design."

"Okay, makes sense," I agreed.

"Well, these are 'open' lines of research, meaning the dungeon can do them. A 'closed' line is one that once the dungeon has done the research, there's no other version to continue onto. Like the mana stones or crystals, whatever.

They're a solid power source: the purer the mana that's fed into them, the better the charge, and longer lasting."

"So we can't improve on the design?" I asked slowly.

"Yes and no. There's no option to research it *in the dungeon. We* can do it…I could examine it all and do real research, look into the matrices and more, and probably upgrade it eventually, but the dungeon couldn't help with it."

"Okay, what's that got to do with…"

"Matt. The dungeon has hundreds of open and closed lines of research, hell, probably billions, but where we are, we can see hundreds, okay?"

"Right?"

"Well, we fucked up," Aly admitted. "Both of us—me more, but…You remember when you were teaching me about the research system, and you showed me that the cores have different levels, that the conduits, for example, have basic all the way up for Stone cores, and so on? And we agreed we should have been building all the way up we could, but we just didn't have the time and we basically cheated? Leapfrogging the way up the ladder?"

"Yes," I agreed, my stomach churning as I took an extra swig from the bottle. "I'm not going to like this, am I?"

"Not really." She took a deep breath. "Basically, it's the mana storage that was the real point for me. I've been looking at it and wondering how the hell they're worth it. We can store a thousand mana in each one, and yeah, they've cost us thousands to build, but the storage, when we're looking at hundreds of thousands of mana needed for things now? It's just mad. We'd need a hundred of them, and that seems just wasteful and inefficient, right?"

"Yeah, very much so," I agreed. "I'd seen it before and dismissed it as weird but—"

"They're all Bronze-leveled research," Aly said softly.

"What? No. We've done it since then, right?"

"We followed the same line," Aly admitted. "We just continued the same line that we'd begun."

On the screen, the line of mana storage nodes that she'd brought up suddenly flashed back to the beginning of the line, the Bronze core glowing at the beginning of the path. Aly paused, making sure I'd seen it, then went a step further back, and a drop-down list of cores showed.

She went up to Stone, and tried to open that, showing that the path was closed, and there was no research we could do, demonstrating that because we'd missed it, it was now gone. Then she went to Bronze, showing the line we'd been working on, and that it was still open.

Then came Iron, and a closed line.

"Why can we still research the Bronze?" I asked, mouth dry. "I thought that was closed off?"

"We can continue a line; we can't start a new one," she said. "The different species, for example, aren't locked to a core, so they can be worked on at any point. We never did anything with the impai, but they're still there as an option. They're what I'm thinking of as general research. Core research though, stuff that is specific to the core? That can only be done if you unlocked it and followed the line."

"So…we can research earlier lines then?" I asked, then frowned. "Shit, I'm really not getting this. We said before that we wanted to research earlier lines, that would have made the core stronger but now…"

"The law of diminishing returns." Aly shook her head. "We misunderstood it. If, for example, we worked on the basic, then common, then uncommon mana converters from Stone to now? We'd have a truly horrific amount of mana coming in, but we'd be much lower-leveled. Or, if somehow we'd made it to this core level?"

"Yeah?"

"We'd be an utterly unstoppable powerhouse."

"How?"

"Here…" Aly projected a screen and showed the numbers for me. "This is just an illustration, okay? And because we don't have access to all the details, it's literally a guess. Just…use it for the example."

I nodded as she showed ten converters, with each of them earning ten points an hour. I nodded to show I understood it, and she still marked 100 at the bottom, to be clear.

I gestured for her to go on, rolling my eyes.

The next section showed the same ten converters, and now they earned twenty points each, then the next section thirty. I nodded again, showing that I understood basic math as she marked down 200 and 300 at the bottom of each.

"This is where it gets interesting." She marked this first line as Bronze.

The second line started at thirty points per converter, per hour, and then went to sixty. Suddenly there was six hundred mana an hour coming in, and it was still marked as basic. Then the next level doubled that one, moving to a hundred and twenty mana per converter, per hour, then two hundred and forty.

At this point I was sitting up, my mouth drier than the Sahara, and I was having difficulty swallowing.

"You're sure about this?" I asked, and she shook her head.

"We're working on the converter now…two hundred and fifty thousand points for this level, remember?"

"Wait, the conduits, what did it go to?" I asked, pausing things as I made a mental note.

"Ten points per hour, per conduit," Kelly said. "On average, anyway. Longer conduits earn more, shorter earn less, but that's the work out we're using for it. We're getting fifty thousand mana per day from the conduits now."

"Okay, so the next level of research into converters, it's two hundred and fifty thousand…" I paused. "If you're saying that we should have been doing this while we were in Bronze, that would have taken us months…"

"It would," Aly agreed. "Even guessing at it as half a million for the next level of research and it coming in at thirty points of conversion per hour per converter, it's worth it."

"And then we go back to the beginning," I said softly, rolling the screen back to the beginning of the Bronze core, then flowing down the drop-down to Steel, and selecting basic in there for mana converters.

"It's five hundred thousand," I said slowly.

"It doubles the mana coming in," Aly pointed out. "If we do this, let's do the math."

She pulled up the screen again. "So we have currently…a hundred and twenty-five mana converters, spread across the various sites."

I whistled, amazed by how many we'd gotten built so far.

"Now, we're earning on average, sixteen points per converter. That's because some, like the Water ones in the river, and the Air ones above the building, or the Life ones around people, are putting in their maximum of twenty, while others are pulling in from seven and eight to ten and twelve."

She did a very simple math, working on the page.

125 x 16 = 2000

2000 x 24 = 48000

"That's per hour and per day," she pointed out, and I stared at her. "Yes, I know, it's a very round figure, and it's slightly inaccurate, but fuck it. Again, this is a demonstration."

"Go on," I said flatly.

"If we do the two hundred and fifty thousand mana investment, then we can reasonably expect things to double, so it costs us this…" She marked the two hundred and fifty thousand on the screen, and went on to do more math.

Cost: 250k
Time to earn back: 2.5 days

Cost: 500k
Time to earn back: 2.5 days

"You see the common thing here? We earn a fuckload more, but it costs the same time to pay it off. Now, note I say pay it off. That's important, because they're going to take five days each at the current level to earn."

"What, is there a bank we can borrow this from?" I asked, confused.

"No, but it's important, so go with it," Kelly said, clearly having worked something out on her own.

"So, we're looking at ten days to do all of this, but after that point, we'll be earning double what we are now, so further investment becomes cheaper. We're literally going from earning fifty thousand or so a day, to close to two hundred thousand."

She marked on the screen the current mana we earned at forty-eight thousand, and then marked up the cost of the upgrades at a grand total of one and a quarter million points.

That was worked out at just over twenty-six days to earn at our current rate, and just under seven days from that point onward.

"Shit," I muttered, stunned by how much of a difference that was.

"Exactly." Aly said, "This is a seriously huge step up, and when we look at things like the storage nodes? They're exactly the same. We do a few of the lower-leveled ones, and then we do the current ones and it's insane. A thousand points got us space for a hundred in storage…you do a few levels in the stores? We're suddenly able to hold millions of points of mana."

"Your math is wrong," Kelly interrupted, and I looked at her as she flicked it up onto the wall to show us her work next to Aly's.

"Really?" Aly glared at her notes, not seeing it.

"You said that the mana we're supposed to be getting currently is ten per converter, but that we get sixteen, right?"

"Sixteen and a bit, but yeah, it's because—"

"I get why." Kelly smiled. "It's the next bit that's wrong. You worked it out at the next level being twenty points, and thirty, then sixty."

"Right?"

"But if we're getting sixteen, not ten, then the next one, just as a rough working out, should be thirty. Then forty-five. If we say that whatever the normal production is, and we're getting one point five—for ease of working out again—times that, then we're lookin' at twenty becoming thirty, thirty becoming forty-five and…"

"And sixty becoming ninety," I finished for her, utterly gobsmacked.

"Ninety points per hour is two…" Kelly started, only to have Aly speak over her.

"Two hundred and seventy thousand mana a day," she finished. "Well over three hundred thousand mana a day with the conduit research added in as well."

"Holy shit," I whispered.

"Exactly." Kelly grinned. "So, basically, we need to finish the lines or at least reevaluate the investment after each level."

"Out of curiosity, what would the mana be if we'd done each level of research?" I asked. "You know, if we'd…"

"How many levels are there?" Kelly asked me, and I frowned, pulling the system up.

"It's basic, common, uncommon, advanced, rare, legendary, and artifact," I said softly, shaking my head as I looked at it. "Of course it is. An artifact-level converter would be bringing in…" I did the math. "Even a Stone age artifact-level generator would be earning seventy points an hour."

"If we'd done each level, Stone would have maxed out at seventy. Then it's a hundred and forty. Wait…is the progression linear between levels or…"

"What?" I asked.

"Linear," Kelly repeated. "Is each level in a line, like all of the current one, Bronze or whatever, goes up by ten per level of research, or does it double each time?"

"It doubles with the core upgrade, and climbs inside the core level by ten points per degree of research," I said after a moment's thought, taking advantage of the general drift of information that I was clearly not supposed to be party to.

"Then…four thousand, one hundred mana per converter, per hour, and that's the baseline." Kelly shook her head. "That would be, say, six thousand in reality, and at a hundred and twenty-five converters, it'd be…eighteen million mana a day."

"Fuck me sideways." I grunted. "We could do everything and anything with that much mana."

"Realistically?" Aly said then, head cocked to one side as she considered the details. "If that's an actual possibility, to earn that much, I mean, then there's no physical way we could exhaust the mana in an area, right?"

"No." I shook my head, knowing it balls to bones. "The mana here on Earth is limited. If we were pulling that much mana? We'd drain the area totally, and while yeah, eventually more would be pulled to us from wherever it comes from, it'd take thousands of years before the area grew strong enough to keep something like that here."

"Then how do the higher-leveled dungeons survive?" Aly asked. "I mean, if it's possible to do this, then it must have caused such issues before, right?"

"Well, we could do it as we are…" I said slowly, mind racing. "You know, extend out additional cores and set them up in high mana areas."

"Or?" Kelly asked, and I grinned at her. "Matt, I don't like that look…"

"Or, we do it the other way." I tried to stifle a manic grin. "I need to think about this, but maybe I know how we're going to fight the Orcan."

"Oh, God no…" Aly whispered, dropping her face into her hands. "I hate it when he gets ideas!"

"Oh, don't worry," I said, my grin risking taking the top of my head off. "It's probably a stupid plan, but if it works? Oh yeah." I closed my eyes, enjoying the mental image that floated before me.

"Right, so what do we do with the research now that we know this?" Aly said, drawing me back to the conversation.

"There's no choice," I said. "We do this, and then we check the cost of the next level of the converters. If it's the same price as the first level of the Steel core, which I think it's going to be, or near enough, then we take it."

"We need the storage sorted out then." Aly shook her head. "Unless we're going to be using it round the clock, then we need to get the mana storage nodes up to the realistic levels."

"How many do we have?" I pulled up the research details as I asked the question.

"A hundred and sixty," Kelly said, making me wince. "We've been building them as we needed them…"

"That's what made me realize it." Aly shrugged. "If each level of storage was so low, how the hell was it realistic to ever store anything? As it is, it's because they're Bronze level compared to Steel, which we should be using."

"Fair point." I grunted. "Okay, storage nodes then were a thousand mana to research, then five thousand, and the next one is ten."

"And we can store…a hundred, then two fifty, and then five hundred mana per unit with the different levels," Kelly said, clearly looking at the same details as I was.

"Then we pause the current research, do the ten thousand, and then check on the Steel level. That should let us see what we're working with," I muttered distractedly. "Summon whatever food you need. We need to get to work absorbing."

"I need to go and see to Amy," Aly said firmly, and I blinked, turning to her and shaking my head. "Make sure she has her dinner and a bath."

"Sorry. Yes, of course," I apologized. "I didn't mean…"

"It's okay," Aly said with a smile. "But that's families, Matt. You'll understand one day."

With that, she was up and moving, and I winced as Kelly snorted next to me.

"Well done," she congratulated me.

"I didn't mean…" I started to explain, and she shook her head.

"I know that, and so does she, but you basically just told us all that our lives were on hold until this was sorted. Yeah, for me, you kind of *are* my life…I mean, you know. But for her? She has a husband and daughter."

"You're my life, you know that, right?" I asked her, banishing the screens and pulling her chair closer.

"Really?" She looked up at me and playfully fluttered her eyelashes. "I never knew…"

I couldn't help but laugh, and she punched me in the chest.

"I was being serious, you dick!" she complained.

"I know." I leaned in and kissed her. "It's just you and that all-innocent look. It doesn't fit you very well."

"You don't normally complain when I act all innocent." She turned her back on me, pretending to be offended.

"Do you really want to get me thinking about that right now?" I asked her, already feeling a twitch at the thought, and she laughed, a low, throaty sound that ran through me.

"No, fair point." She grinned. "Later, though."

"Later!" I agreed, trying not to think filthy thoughts.

"Into the dungeon," Kelly said to me, and I glanced at her, confused.

"What?"

"I said, get yourself into the dungeon."

"I was going to but—"

"I'm not going in until you are."

"Why not?"

"I don't need you doing anything to me when I'm helpless," she said, pretending to be concerned, and I laughed, getting a quick kiss from her.

"Let's face it, usually it's *you* who wakes *me* up like that," I pointed out to her. "I'm busy working and then boom, hot lips wrapped around me…"

"Is that a complaint?" she asked. "I mean, I can just not do that in the future…"

"Oh, fuck no. It's a request," I said forcefully. "Please, *please* keep doing it…Hell, I can take my pants off now if it'll make it easier for you?"

"I don't think Aly needs to walk in on me on my knees for you," Kelly said with a snort. "You can wait till later."

"Damn," I muttered, only half joking. "Ten seconds of innuendo and my brain is totally broken now."

"In-your-endo…" Kelly said, and I winked at her.

"That's what she said."

"I certainly wasn't complaining," she admitted, kissing me one last time. "Now, get into the dungeon and get absorbing things. I'll join you when I feel it's safe and I'm not going to suddenly choke on something!"

"**Cough—hair gel—cough**" I forced out, then tried to look all innocent. "What?"

"You dare do that to me when I'm not awake and telling you that you can, and I swear it'll be the last time you ever do it."

I opened my mouth, and she glared at me, making me sigh and settle back, sliding into the dungeon sense as I muttered under my breath. "You usually say it's good for your skin…"

"Matt!"

I was in the dungeon then, zipping through the building and cackling as I went, passing through walls and more and out into the evening air.

It didn't take long to reach the massive mound of scrap. A good dozen others worked on it even now, and I silently joined them.

It was at least fifteen minutes before Kelly made her presence known, but when she did, it was to tell me that the ten thousand had been hit already.

"That was quick," I said, somewhat surprised.

"I asked the park to stay on for another ten minutes or so. They were at the end of their shift, but that means that two shifts are working it in the park now. It's bringing in a *lot* more mana."

"How much?"

"There's five hundred people on a shift, so a thousand people are generating at least one point, some dozens, every minute."

"Damn." I sent her a mental smile. "Thank you."

"It's in everyone's best interests." She shrugged. "We were right as well—five hundred points for storage per unit. They need to be updated, but it's like a hundred or so per unit, so they're already in progress, updating."

"And the next level?" I asked.

"In Bronze, it's twenty-five thousand, and goes to a thousand mana per unit. It's ten thousand currently in Steel for the first level, so they are separate. No idea why, but if it doubles? I figured two thousand mana per unit should mean that we've got a load of space moving forward."

"Perfect." I smiled at her. "Let's see how much we can get done in an hour then."

Clearly word spread that there was something going on beyond the usual "work" as more and more people started to show up, and the pile began to collapse in on itself.

Someone on the far side began to sing, after a few minutes, and I smiled. I'd not heard it in a while, a couple of guys singing it, and clearly having to hum bits they couldn't remember, but the usually verboten song "Frosty the Pervert" floated through the air, with more and more people picking it up as the minutes passed.

Each time the song faded, someone else would start singing it, or another of the truly horrific Christmas songs that were so popular a few years back.

"Walking Round in Women's Underwear" got an airing, as did "Yogi Bear" and "Grandma Got Run Over by a Reindeer." A few songs by that terrible old bugger Chubby started being sung, but they died away fairly quickly.

There was a line, even after the end of the world it seemed, and although a lot of people could get away with ignoring certain words, the general tone of those songs were a step too far for most.

"You know it's Chris starting these songs, don't you?" Kelly asked me after a bit and I snorted, totally unsurprised.

"You should have heard him when we worked in the kitchens together," I assured her. "Dirty old bastard chefs were trying to shock us—we were only kids, after all—and he'd just go one worse each time."

"I can imagine."

Another hour passed, and I could sense more and more people slipping away. I took a deep breath, checking the research and nodding in satisfaction, finding Aly nearby as well, as I reached out to her and Kelly, speaking quickly.

"So the plan, if those dirty buggers have finished making an A-frame in the old accommodation," I said with a waggle of my eyebrows and a mental image to them both to show what I was referring to. "Then we start converting the entire building to a tower, and we do it tonight."

"It'll take days to break it all down." Aly frowned, before grinning suddenly. "No, it won't!"

"It won't?" I asked.

"No!" Aly said. "You built it all in one go, a single building, so it's all connected!"

I took off, floating up in the dungeon sense and hovering over the still massive, but much reduced pile.

"Oh yeah." I smiled. "Right, everyone, thank you so much for your help, but we're gonna need some volunteers tonight…"

CHAPTER EIGHTEEN

The cheer that rang out as the fifth floor, the final for now, was completed was almost deafening.

Kelly had sent a call out last night for volunteers again, flitting to the park and speaking to others there, basically asking that anyone who was interested in learning magic gather in the dungeon sense as soon as possible.

I didn't feel right asking people, after they'd worked their arses off all day long, to do even more work, so we made it clear this was a volunteers-only situation.

I sent out the message as well, and spelled out when and where I needed them, and then Kelly and Aly and I got to work. The massive building that was currently in the area we were planning to use had been built, as Aly had said, all in one go when I'd essentially drained a storm into the dungeon.

It'd been a case of an insane amount of mana was available to the dungeon for a very brief period, and rather than let it get wasted, I used it.

I'd channeled the power through myself and into the dungeon; then I'd literally built a building. It was rough, lots of work was needed—alterations and more. Hell, some of the rooms I'd designed in my rush didn't have doors that could be opened. And worse, there were windows that opened into the next room, rather than in the outside walls only. The entire place was a bodge job.

That being said, it was accommodation for literally hundreds of people, after they'd lost everything and had been reduced to living on floors, pressed cheek by jowl with strangers.

They'd been overjoyed when the Dungeon Lord had raised up an apartment block for them all, granting privacy and a home to people who had thought they'd lost such things forever.

Over the next few weeks and months, the new accommodation block had been built, and this one was much better designed, custom built. Although much of it was generic—the rooms were literally copied over and over, after all—it was also far more luxurious than the last one.

People had moved over in a wave, and although some had made a point of saying how much they'd miss the "old" accommodation, because it'd meant so much to them to get it…they were all understandably a fuckload happier in the new one.

The new building was a hell of an investment to build, mainly because each level was heavily armored. The outer walls were a solid meter and more thick, the glass windows could take a howitzer shell without breaking, and, most impressive of all, unlike the rest of old Newcastle, the elevators—despite being in a public building—didn't reek of piss.

That alone was game-changing.

Now that the older building had been completely evacuated, I gathered the nine hundred-odd volunteers and spoke to them all, well aware that for some of them this was their first time in the dungeon sense.

Apart from those like the dickheads who attempted a coup, almost the entire population of the dungeon—this one, at least; not all the park's citizens were in yet, but most were—had the authority to access the simplest layers of the dungeon.

That meant, essentially, they could open the lower-level doors—all we'd used generally, but hey, if we brought out more, then that would be an important distinction—they could also summon food and basic facilities like repairing and cleaning clothing and so on.

Crucially, they could also absorb things.

That was the main skill I needed right now, and why people were here.

I explained the intentions for the tower, and that it would be a safe place for those who wanted to study and learn magic to gather. There would be classes, and there would be guided meditation.

In the future, there would be a hell of a lot more, but for now, that was it. Once magical crafting was up and running, then we'd be able to fill the focal orbs with new spells, and people could learn their future classes that way.

For now, unless they specifically wanted to be a mage of the kind that we already had access to, such as a pyromancer, we weren't going to "force" a mage class on anyone using the orbs, in fear that it would mean we missed out on an actual unique class that suited them better.

I'd expected people to be pissed at that. After all, I was telling them there was an easy path to power, and that I wasn't going to let them take it, but they'd been surprisingly cool with it.

I explained that in order to build the tower, we needed to clear all of this section, not just the accommodation block, which was a fast and easy demolishing, but the last section that was remaining of the original block as well.

We'd left that until now; some people had lived in it, and we'd used it both as a place for people to do things and have some privacy and a rooftop archers' platform, amongst other things.

Tonight, it was time for it all to go.

We'd started in a wave. Essentially, people from both the dungeon proper and the park had flowed over the building all at once. It must have been insane to watch from the outside, and to see fully with your eyes rather than mixed in with the data and more that you got in the dungeon sense. But even here, it was amazing.

It was like one of those time-lapse videos of a fruit being torn apart by ants: bricks and more were absorbed into light; the surrounding bricks sagged, and vanished as others worked on them.

Walls literally vanished into drifting motes of light. People occasionally screamed as walls collapsed or a floor and ceiling fell in, and then the inevitable nervous laughter when they remembered that they were incorporeal.

Minutes became hours, but before the sun rose again, the entire block was clear.

The research on the next level of storage nodes was finished, and then we'd done the first level in the Steel row. As we'd suspected, as soon as a Steel level one was researched, the Bronze level for that was locked out, but that was fine.

We had a hundred and sixty-five storage nodes, and they were all at two thousand capacity now—totaling out at three hundred and thirty thousand capacity.

We'd started on the converter tech next. Common level in Bronze was two hundred and fifty thousand. And just in case—to keep it from being wasted—we'd set it so that anything that went over the storage capacity went straight into research.

As soon as everyone was ready, though, we started the tower.

It was a simple design: circular, with stairs built into the wall. Each level was split into a single large main room, and then dozens of smaller ones around the outside, with the stairs then hidden and winding around the tower between the outer and inner walls of each floor.

The ground level, as you entered the building, was designated as zero, with sub one, two, three, and four if you went downward, and one to five as you climbed upward.

I remembered an argument with my American cousins at that point. They'd weirdly said that the ground floor, which was *obviously* the ground floor, was actually the first floor.

In reality, as all civilized people knew, the first floor was the first floor *above ground level*. I left it at that, though, knowing that in truth, although I'd love to teach those backward colonials the right way of things, it was unlikely any would ever enter the tower.

They'd be expecting it to be full of kids on broomsticks for a start, being intended as a magical school.

Climbing from sub four, we had Death, Earth, Darkness, and Fire as the specializations planned for each floor. The ground floor, or zero, was the widest of the floors for now, and it had a main gathering hall in it that could hold hundreds comfortably.

That would be the floor we worked on first, but the plan was that the next floor would be for private, wizard, mage or mancer accommodation, if they wanted it, and then Life, Water, Light, and Air for the remaining floors, running from two to five.

As the peaked roof slowly finished being printed, the bright light that could be seen for miles died away, and we all stood there in the dungeon sense, staring at our new tower.

It was six stories above the ground, the ground floor and five more atop that, with the final floor, one that would be home to the Air converters, open on all four sides.

For now, the tower was bare, utterly empty inside bar the stairs and physical structures themselves, but it wouldn't be like that for long.

"I'll start with the doors," Aly said from nearby, and I nodded to myself.

"I'll do carpets and cushions. Ground floor only, right?" Kelly asked.

"Perfect," I agreed. "I'll talk to Ramnik now."

"Ummm, maybe you should have done that before now?" Kelly suggested, and I grunted, well aware that in the rush to get things done, after the discoveries from last night, I'd overlooked that small step.

"I know, I know!" I groaned, searching about and seeing that not only was Ramnik not in the dungeon sense any more, but she was physically there outside the tower, staring up at it.

More and more people were vanishing as I looked, and I moved quickly, reaching out through the dungeon sense to those who were still nearby.

"Thank you all!" I called. "This was a hell of an effort, especially after a long day, so please take a little extra time and rest in the morning. We'll have a gathering in the tower at midday. That will be the first lesson, and we'll have a general plan made by then, along with a schedule so that people can come at different times. Again, though, thank you all!"

With that, I slid out of the dungeon sense, climbing to my feet and feeling the aches and pain of my body being slumped in the chair for literally hours, unmoving.

I flooded my body with a little Lightning and sighed. The flash of power left me feeling great as I stretched. For a long second, I regarded Kelly sitting there, her mind working hard in the dungeon sense, and I grinned.

Obviously, if this was Chris, I'd have summoned a permanent marker and have drawn a dick on his face—best friends and all that—but besides something sexual, which was obviously all kinds of wrong, I wasn't sure what I could do.

I hesitated a minute, then sighed, and shifted her body slightly, making her more comfortable, then summoned a blanket and covered her, before leaving the room as quietly as I could.

I jogged down the stairs and along the halls, then down the main stairs and out into the early morning. It was cold, but not frosty for a nice change.

The sun wasn't up yet. Hell, it'd be hours before it was; it was at most…yeah. Ten past five in the morning.

Fuck, I should be in bed still. I certainly shouldn't be fucking around in the cold drizzle that was just this side of sleet…

I didn't even have a goddamn coat on, so I put my head down and ran, splashing through puddles and ignoring the drifting clouds of steam and fog that rolled off the outdoor baths.

It wasn't far. Hell, the main entrance to the tower was about a hundred, maybe a hundred and twenty meters away, angled inward toward the center of the dungeon. I made it to the door quickly, but I was still soaked, and the hardy few, like Ramnik, who'd made it here in the flesh, were already wandering around inside. Their voices echoed as they spoke, pointing out details to each other.

Dante and Ashley were wandering hand in hand, clearly having started to help while already in bed, or planning to be, by the ridiculous outfits they had on.

Dante wore what looked to be retro pajamas from the eighties, a giant talking robot on the front of them, slippers, and a dressing robe, while Ashley…

Well, her outfit peeked between her own robe as she walked around, staring wide-eyed as things appeared, like lights. All I could say about her negligee was that it looked to be silk, or satin, and sheer.

At that point, I looked away and coughed, clearing my eyes of that sight.

Ramnik was easy to find, standing on the far side of the room, staring at the raised dais, and rubbing her chin, clearly feeling uncomfortable and worried about something.

"Ramnik," I called in greeting, striding over to her. "You okay?"

"Matt!" She jumped. "Ummm, yes?"

"You don't sound it." I smiled. "I'm sorry. We were working on something else, and I got carried away with this. I had intended on having you and the others weigh in with some suggestions, but that plan ended up going in the bin. We'll make adjustments and improvements as we go, and I'd like your input on them."

"It's fine," she said quickly. "Look, Matt, you said lessons?"

"Yes," I said. "We need to offer lessons to people. I've had quite a few people mention that they're making it up as they go along, and others are trying to teach themselves in their free time."

"I know." She shook her head. "Matt, the lessons…I'm sorry, I'm just not a very good teacher," she said, wringing her hands as she looked away. "Even the thought of being up there, giving lessons…"

"Do you want to?" I asked her. "To give lessons, I mean?"

"No," she said. "I know you need me to, and I will, but, if someone else wants to teach, am I okay to…?"

"Ramnik, do you want to be in charge of the meditation and teaching, or would you rather be doing magical research?" I asked her bluntly.

"Magical research anytime," she admitted. "I'll do my best but…"

"Okay, look, I kind of just named you as being in charge of the mages—"

"Mancers," she corrected.

"Mancers." I shrugged. "Honestly, I don't give two fucks. They can call themselves 'Gandalfians' for all I give a damn. It really doesn't matter to me. For the short-term, yeah, I'd like you to lead some meditation and lessons. As soon as I can get someone else to do it? I will. In the short-term, I'll be giving lessons as well, so don't worry. Moving forward, though, if you go to Aly and speak to her? We need magical research doing. Literally, it's a section of the research that the dungeon can carry out, but it needs a dedicated magical researcher to do it. You're an Arcanist, not just a War mage, remember."

"I'd prefer that, thank you." She sagged in relief.

"That's fine," I replied, smiling a little. "Next time, though, come and tell me if you're having problems, okay?"

"I will," she assured me, before stepping awkwardly to the side and gesturing behind me. "If you'd like a recommendation on a replacement to give lessons, though?"

"Yeah?" I glanced behind me, seeing Ashley and Dante standing off to one side as Dante moved his hands in a complicated gesture. A flicker of flame sprung to life and then bloomed into a fireball he held out to her.

She reached her hands out and held them close to the flame, clearly enjoying the heat as I shook my head.

"He's good," I said. "Damn, he's really good, especially with Fire. But he's a bit scatterbrained for teaching, I think."

"I meant Ashley," Ramnik corrected.

"She's a mage?" I asked, stunned.

"No." She shook her head, smiling as we watched them. "But she wants to be."

"Really?"

"They're the most unlikely pairing I've ever met." Ramnik sighed. "He is a mage beyond compare, picks things up so easily, but his focus is only on Fire, and her. Literally little else. She, on the other hand, could have been modelling internationally, if not for the fact that she is overly sexual. That was a reason her modelling didn't go further."

"I know she feels a bit upset when it comes to the class she was given—"

"She does, but she's growing to love it. More importantly, though, she worships Dante, and she wants power for herself. Not in the way that would be an issue. I don't think she seeks to rule, put it that way. I think she wants to grow as powerful as she can, to make sure that those she loves are always safe."

"And now she wants to be a mage?" I asked, ignoring the wince she gave me at the term.

"Yes," she said simply. "Her Fire affinity is low, but she's been attempting to raise it day in and day out, amongst others."

"Is she wanting to be a Fire mage like Dante specifically?"

"I don't think so. She just wants to learn and become more powerful."

"Good," I said. "Dante! Ashley! Come join us!" I called across the room, making them both jump. The fire vanished, and the pair hurried over, Ashley quickly tying her robe closed more carefully, while Dante clearly wished he'd gotten dressed before coming over.

"Do you want to go into one of the side rooms and change?" I asked the pair, seeing how Dante was trying to cover his pajamas.

"Ummmm…" Dante started while Ashley nodded, smiling.

"We'll be right back!" she assured me.

"I'm going to slip into the dungeon sense and just make sure nobody is floating around those rooms while they change," Ramnik said firmly, and I nodded absently, leaving her to it as she sat down on a freshly conjured cushion. "One thing, Matt?"

"Yes?"

"Voyeurism."

"Right?"

"We need to address it. I make a point of changing and using the facilities only after I've checked the dungeon to make sure I am in fact, alone, but there must be a way to prevent it automatically."

"Is it a problem?" I winced. "If so, I'm sorry—"

"It's not you who has been doing it, Matt," she said. "I have caught the afterimages of someone attempting to do it several times, however, and I suspect a Peeping Tom is trying to abuse the system of trust we have."

"I'll see what I can do," I growled, sitting on another nearby cushion and sinking into the system.

I found Kelly nearby, and Aly not far from her, the pair of them working on the room, and I brought them up to date on my conversation with Ramnik.

"It's in hand," Kelly assured me.

"You knew about it?" I asked. "I mean, I know there's been a mention before about it, but I was thinking it was accidental, you know, the way that sometimes when we enter the system, we float through a room to get to somewhere and—"

"It was," Kelly said. "It's not in the case of one or two people, or so we think. There's a setting in the dungeon that became active with Iron, and we're training it. It basically tracks everyone, and marks if someone triggers the 'watch' protocols, which we're tweaking."

"John knows about it as well. He helped to adjust them so that people who were genuinely passing through a room or something and accidentally triggered the system weren't punished."

"Do we need to make it a law?" I asked, not liking that it was even needed. I caught the occasional glimpse of a friend, like Aly or Ashley, and their outfits. Much as the other night in the pool, or here earlier when I'd looked away from Ashley when I'd realized what she was wearing. But the thought that someone was getting off on unguarded moments like that?

It made me feel as dirty as if I'd been doing it deliberately.

"We need a way to deal with it," I said firmly. "If that means a law before John can do anything about it…"

"We'll introduce one in a few days," Kelly assured me. "Or you will, anyway. It's on the list of jobs for the future, but for now we've been refining the watch protocols so that when we start, innocent people aren't caught by the system."

"What happens until then?" I asked, not liking the idea of waiting around.

"Until then, we just put up with it," Kelly said. "Look, Matt, as a good guy, you don't think about things in this way, and believe me, it's a relief for me. As a woman? I'm used to making sure I check places before I undress. Making sure there was no cameras or suspicious things in changing rooms was a totally normal thing. The end of the world meant there was less chance of that, but since then, well…the pendulum swings one way, then the other."

"We get used to it," Aly assured me.

"I don't like it," I muttered.

"Neither do we," she assured me blackly. "But look on the bright side. In a few days, we won't have to worry about that any more…the dungeon will be fully trained to watch over us and route people around certain areas."

"People with higher access will still be able to pass through, like you or us if you mark us as having priority, but it'll be logged, and you'll be able to see that nobody is abusing it. Seriously, trust us. As women, we're used to having to do this. If anything, this is a lot better than before the fall."

"I fucking hate the idea that we're not safe from someone in the dungeon," I growled. "Some random guy trying to catch an eyeful of—"

"It's not just men." Kelly snorted. "I worked in the courts, remember? Men were less likely to notice, and less likely to complain of a woman was caught watching them, but it happens. There's been a time or two that I think I've sensed someone watching us in our room, when we've been having fun, and that was a woman. I've not caught her yet, but it's what made me start looking for this."

"A woman?" I asked, snorting when I realized that the feeling of a guy watching us fucking had made my stomach turn, but a woman watching didn't so much. Weird world.

"Anyway!" I dismissed that thought, seeing Ashley and Dante hurrying across to where my body was slumped. "I better get back to it. Thank you both."

"Just accept that we're on it, Matt," Kelly assured me, sending me a mental peck on the cheek. "I'll see you in bed soon. We do need a few hours at least."

"Definitely," I agreed, slipping out of the dungeon sense and straightening up.

"Sorry about that," I said, quickly bringing the other three up to date with the conversation I'd just had with Kelly and Aly.

Dante looked shocked, having clearly not even considered it, Ramnik was blatantly relieved, and Ashley smiled and relaxed.

"It'll be nice to know I'm not being watched in the shower or…doing other things," she admitted. "I've not caught anyone doing it, but knowing how easy the system is to use, it's been a concern."

"I wish you'd mentioned it." I shook my head. "Seriously, it wasn't something I'd even considered. Anyway, now that's dealt with. Moving forward!"

"Ashley, what do you want to be?" Ramnik asked, and Ashley looked at her, frowning.

"What do you mean?"

"We know you're trying to learn magic." I smiled.

"Am I not allowed to…?" She looked concerned.

"Fuck no, be what you want," I assured her. "What we're looking at is that Ramnik loves magic and wants to focus on research. She's not really interested so much in teaching, nor in leading meditation—"

"I don't mind the meditation, you understand, but the teaching? And as many classes as we will need to run a day?" Ramnik interjected.

"Two classes," I said. "For now, we're going to run two classes, that's all. I'll try to teach them myself, one on magic, one on meditation, teaching people to touch their core and so on."

"Okay." Ashley nodded, shifting to sit cross-legged on the cushion before me, while Dante sat next to her, making me grin at how elegant she was unthinkingly, while he was all gangly arms and legs.

Reminded me of me and Kelly.

"Well, how would you like to help out?" I asked Ashley and Dante. "I know you're all about Fire, mate. So once we have some other Fire mages, or pyromancers and whatever you want to call yourselves, we'll start doing specific classes for that."

"I'd love to!" he blurted.

"There won't just be humans in the classes," I warned them. "I'm planning on opening these to all advanced beings. Once we have goblins and kobolds and more that are advanced enough to be able to learn, I want them to be encouraged to do so."

"Sounds good to me!" he agreed quickly.

"What do you want me to do?" Ashley asked.

"I want to help you to learn, just like I will the others."

"Essentially, Ashley, you're very articulate…Matt is less so. If he can help you to unlock any latent abilities, then when he's talking about how he's done it, you will be able to help teach others, suggest alternatives and more."

"So we'll both be teaching." I shrugged. "Dante, you too. You'll help me to guide people. Ramnik will do some…but mainly meditation. Is that good with you?" I asked her, and she nodded, relieved.

"When do we start?" Dante asked me excitedly.

"Midday." I shrugged. "I said we'd start a lesson then, so what we'll do is try to teach two lessons a day for now, lunchtime and…maybe eight at night? That's late enough that any day shift should have long since finished, and early enough that any teams that work on the nights can have a chance at making it, if they don't do the midday one."

"We'd need a nighttime one as well, eventually," Ashley suggested, and I nodded.

"We'll need to run dozens of classes—general purpose one, meditation, specific magics, like manipulating Fire and so on."

"One step at a time," Ramnik said firmly. "First and foremost, yes, I will help, with meditation mainly, but I would much prefer to work on magical research, so thank you for that. Ashley? Dante?"

"We're in," Ashley said after sharing a look with Dante. She gripped his hand tight and grinned at me. "I mean, I don't have any spells yet, not besides my class, but I can't wait to learn."

"Great." I nodded. "First lesson is at midday then. Now I'm heading to the gym for an hour. It's…damn. Nearly six in the morning."

I shook my head, sighing.

"I'm not going to get much sleep, but I can't entirely skip the exercise either. Hell, we were working on this all night. I'll start the word spreading for the lessons, just in case anyone missed it, and then an hour in the gym, then bed."

"I was thinking?" Dante said diffidently. "What about a noticeboard?"

"A what?" I asked, confused.

"You know, a noticeboard."

"Yeah, I know what one is." I smiled. "I mean, what's your plan with one?"

"Make a few of them. Do them around the dungeon here, like one in the canteen, and one in the entrance to the accommodation block, then do the same with the park, link them all together somehow, and you can put notices on them. Maybe make a special one for Barry that has a light on it, and when you send him a message, he can flick a switch, so you know he's read it. It'd save you spending an hour looking for him each time or sending a runner to the camp."

"And that way people can see things like the class schedule." I groaned, facepalming. "Simple, but it works!"

"Yeah. Sorry…should I have mentioned it before?" he asked, and I grunted.

"I should have thought about it before," I corrected. "Ramnik? Get with Aly and sort that please, that's your first assignment, and she can teach you to work with the systems by doing it. It's not really magical research, I know, but it'll be a good primer for you."

"Of course," she said with a gentle smile. "I'll make sure anyone who wants to be here can make it."

"Then I'll leave it to you, and thank you. I'll see you all soon," I said with a smile as I got to my feet. "I'm going to the gym, then food and bed. See you at midday."

CHAPTER NINETEEN

The gym was empty when I arrived, which was a relief. I stripped off, tossing my clothes to one side, and quickly dressed in more gym-appropriate gear, slipping into the dungeon sense at one point to see if I was being watched and shaking my head as I exited it.

Of bloody course I wasn't.

Nobody in their right mind would be hanging around to try to catch me stripping off. Yeah, I looked like a Greek god these days, but you know, I was still a bloke.

I dragged it back into the middle of the room where I'd wanted it, and clambered into the rowing machine again, strapping my feet in and starting to work out. Instead of the way I had yesterday, using Lightning to refresh me as soon as I managed to exhaust myself, today was going to be the painful one.

I'd be recovering naturally, no flooding myself with Lightning at all, not for the entire day.

Picking up speed as my muscles warmed up, I closed my eyes, and slid into my mana channels. As soon as I did it, I felt my body slow, starting to falter as my attention drifted, and I stopped, making myself keep going.

It was weird to split my attention like this, but this was always the plan. If I could do it, I could max out my physical training at the same time as I worked on my mana, and once that worked? I'd be really on the way to godhood.

Moving deeper, I saw how the mana stream surged through the gates, or rings, and then slowed after that. Floating along the stream, I searched until I found the next one, then sank down into the depths, the flow of mana diverting around me as I searched for the remnants.

The fractured rings were easy to pick out, and I moved steadily, lifting and repairing as I went. Pausing and focusing to make sure my body was still working solidly while I did it.

It was actually a hell of a lot better than using a rowing machine normally. I'd always hated using the fuckers, they were so boring, and cardio was such a pain in the ass, anyway.

Doing it while I did this, though? That wasn't so bad. At least I could distract myself.

The minutes stretched out; half an hour came and went, then an hour.

I'd planned to stop at an hour, but the ring was nearly done, and a few more minutes was all…

CLANG!

I jumped, falling out of my focused meditation, and tipping sideways, overbalancing and crashing to the floor, my feet still strapped into the grips and making me twist my back and thighs.

The gate I'd been working on, nearly complete as it was, fractured and collapsed. Great chunks of it shattered and sunk into the depths; the mana sediment and the sludge were stirred up and sent rushing down to clog the stream farther along.

I groaned, trying to keep the little liquid I had in my stomach from covering the floor, while twisting and trying to get my damn feet free. I actually managed to snap one of the footrests—they were only flimsy plastic, after all—but it came off, letting me yank my foot free with a hiss as the plastic cut into my ankle.

Bracing myself, I kicked and twisted the other one free, lifting myself up enough to slide it out, and shaking my head at the blood welling up steadily from the cut carved into the inside of my ankle.

"Uh…sorry, dude. My bad."

I twisted around, wiping the blood free of the plastic with one hand and glaring at a guy I'd never seen before who was hefting a plate in one hand, having clearly been getting them ready to attach to the bar for chest presses.

"Yeah, sorry, man," another man said, wincing. "Hey, you should see a healer about your leg…"

"Yeah," I growled, trying not to growl.

"Uh…if you're done with the rower, can I move it?" the second guy said, gesturing to the machine.

"What?" I struggled to be calm.

"The rower. It's like, right out in the middle of the floor, man. You need to have it over there or somewhere…basic gym etiquette, mate. You need to not be in the way of other people."

"Yeah." I forced a smile. "But I'm trying to meditate. Right here is the best spot, between all the converters."

"Those big things?" The first guy gestured to one of them. "Yeah, man, they're taking up loads of space. I think someone was talking about moving them out last night? They said that they think you can move them if you're like, trusted enough?"

"In the dungeon sense?" I asked, and they nodded. "Yeah, they're not being moved. Not yet. I need them where they are."

"Dude, look, I'm not being a dick, but if you want to be around them, maybe move them into another room and you can, like, meditate there? Then you're not in the way here?" the second guy suggested.

I looked from one of them to the other, seeing the look on their faces.

They saw how insanely jacked I was, and I realized they had no clue who I was. They were just trying to be polite, and to teach me proper gym etiquette, while clearly wanting to get a workout in themselves.

"When did you arrive?" I asked them, changing tack, as I wiped the blood from my leg again, then laid a hand on the rowing machine, focusing and repairing it.

"Whoa, man…that's insane." One of them shook his head as he saw it.

"Ummm, last night, you know?" The one that had dropped the weight plate shrugged. "The big boss called for volunteers to help. We'd joined the park a few days back, and our girls, they want to learn magic, so they said we had to come here and help out."

"Yeah." The other nodded. "We're new, so they didn't want to let us all in, but the guy on the gate said that they weren't going to leave us out there at night either."

"Yeah, turns out they meant to come here in the spirit sense." The first one laughed, shaking his head. "I got some grief from the girls for that, but hey, if they can learn some magic? At least we're here for when they start offering it. Did you see the tower go up? That shit was mad."

"I did." I smiled despite myself. It was actually nice to just be one of the lads for a few minutes, and despite the cut and everything, these two were…

There genuinely didn't seem to be any malice in them. Just two big, and clearly hard guys, judging from the look of them. Their faces showed the signs of a lot of punches and injuries: bent noses, blunt heavy brows, one even had a proper cauliflower ear, which I'd not seen in years, and certainly not on someone of his apparent age.

"Who are you?" I offered my hand to the nearest.

"Jimmy." He smiled, taking it.

"Andre." The second stepped in.

"I'm Matt." I nodded to them.

That they were brothers was clear: the same smile, the same broken beaks; hell, apart from Andre being more ginger/blonde, and Jimmy being dark, they were practically mirror images of each other.

"So, just the four of you?" I asked, curious, my anger fading away as my nausea did.

"Five." Andre shook his head. "Our ma is with us…or she was—she's back at the park."

"Aye, I think we're headin' back. The guard at the gate said they don't let everyone stay here…not as much room as at the park," Jimmy added.

"Aye, we heard there was a little gym here though, so left the girls in the canteen and came up," Andre finished.

"The first lesson is midday today, for the magic side," I told them with a smile. "Stay till then at least. You might get to know some people yet."

"Ah, cool, man, thanks! You one of the fighters here?"

"Yeah, I guess I am," I admitted with a snort. "I keep trying to get out of it, but you know how it is."

"Man, that's not cool." Jimmy shook his head. "Look at you. You're buff as fuck—yeah, you're a bit of a pretty boy, but as strong as you are? You should be happy fightin'."

I saw the disapproval on both faces, and I smiled again. "I guess you're right. You joining up for the fight then?"

"Yeah, see if they'll have us, the way the world is, you know." Andre shrugged. "Let's just say we've got a past."

"Raiders?" I asked, my voice getting harder as I glared at them.

"Nah, man. We both did time, though—armed robbery." Andre shrugged.

"Seriously?" I asked, having thought they seemed like nice guys, if a bit dim.

"Yeah, man. Da was in and outta jail—we said we'd never do it, never be like him, but you know. No jobs, no money? Only so long you can keep away from it. Ended up gettin' talked into a job. Simple one. Jimmy and me were the muscle, keep people quiet. Didn't like it, but a one-off job and then we're out? Sounded good."

"Until that prick pulled a gun," Jimmy growled.

"Aye, some asshole was casing the place, saw us rob it, then tried to rob *us*. Da got shot. We were kicking the fuck out of 'im and the cops arrived. Decided we was all the same gang an' we'd 'ad a fallin' out. All of us got done for armed robbery. Seven years."

"That's...a long time." I shook my head.

"Yeah well, the fucker with the gun nearly died, didn't he? Killed our da, then we nearly killed him, so we all got heavy time."

"Shit." I dropped my head. "You served it then?"

"What?"

"The seven years?"

"Nah. Been down for two, then the world ended. A load broke out, so we went with them, went home an' found our girls."

"They waited?" I asked.

"Aye. Sisters, so that made it easier." Jimmy laughed.

"Fuck man, two brothers marrying two sisters?" I grinned.

"Yeah, load of guys asked all the questions. No, we're not swappin' them all night. No, we don't all fuck each other. No, we don't share a big bed and have gang bangs, all right?" Andre groaned. "Can we use the gym now?"

"Yeah, of course. Sorry, guys." I shook my head and stood, gathering my clothes and looking down at my leg. I could feel the burn from the rowing machine. I'd been on the fucker long enough, after all. *But if I used Lightning to heal myself, was it cheating now? It was an injury, not...*

"You gonna put the rowing machine away?" Jimmy asked me pointedly.

"Yeah." I forced a smile as I moved it.

"Good man. We'll get you trained up, don't worry! Teach you to use the gym proper like," Jimmy finished, clapping me on the shoulder. Considering he had to reach up to do it, he shook his head in disbelief. "How'd you get so big and not know how to behave in the gym?"

"Magic." I winked. "You'll see."

With that, I headed out of what was clearly now a public gym, and jogged down the stairs, stopping off in the canteen, easily spotting the two girls I assumed were with the guys.

I paused on my way past to grab some food, and nodded to them.

"Just arrived?" I asked.

"Yeah, and our lads are here as well. We're not interested," one said, smiling coldly at me, making it clear she didn't want to talk to me, while apparently clearly thinking I was trying to hit on them.

"I know. I just met them." I pointed upward.

"So why'd you ask then?" the same one asked, the hard edge to her face faltering slightly.

"I was just being polite. Don't worry about it." I shrugged and moved off, hearing the other of the two girls start chastising the one who had spoken, and reminding her that they were guests.

I found Michelle and Ian on the far side of the canteen and checked on them, finding out that Michelle was fine, albeit very uncomfortable.

"It's soon," she said to me, shaking her head. "Like, *really* soon."

"Good luck!" I said to the pair, grinning at the look of terror on Ian's face as I moved on, sitting at the back of the canteen and eating quickly.

Ten minutes later, I was past the girls, noting that the one who had spoken to me looked as if she were going to apologize…then shook her head and looked out of the window. Her sister turned to me, smiling and opening her mouth, but I kept going, giving her a quick smile and leaving before she could say anything.

There was no point making an issue of it, but considering that they were new, had no clue, and were clearly trying to find a way to help out? There was no need.

Both girls looked exhausted, and I remembered them, vaguely, as people last night who hadn't had access to the systems and had been trying to help on foot, before being gently but firmly moved away.

They'd tried, though, and that was what mattered.

The pair of them were also beautiful, and being somewhere strange, their husbands or boyfriends being somewhere else and a random, much bigger, heavily muscled guy walked up?

It was understandable.

I jogged down the stairs, and found Kelly already passed out in our bed. Hitting the shower, I cleaned up quickly, then climbed into bed beside her, giving her a kiss, and getting comfy, before sliding deep into the realm of dreams.

I dreamt of silly things. The duvet turned into a rolling series of massive hills that I ran across, trying to reach a slumbering giant Kelly, only to be swallowed by the folds as she shifted around, tossing the blanket to the side.

I ran on and on, then climbed, hanging from soft handholds as I reached and swung, frantically forcing myself higher and higher, until eventually, I crested the top of the mountain of duvet, and beheld the sleeping giantess in all her glory.

Her head was buried in the crook of one elbow. Snores that shook the world roared out and were dragged back in through her nose. A line of drool that I could have sailed a ship in ran from the corner of her mouth and moved south.

Well.

I stood and stared at the lush mountains and valleys before me.

For long seconds I grinned, seriously considering mountaineering, not to mention spelunking…Then she shifted, her arm falling free.

It fell slowly, moving with all the inevitability of a comet impact.

Then it hit, and I blinked, shaking my head.

I'd been clearly half asleep, or more than half, considering the view that I had right now—her laid on her back, naked by my side. In my dream state, I'd taken the view of her and had made an entire world of her, and I snorted, shaking my head and moving her arm back down.

Tucking her in almost regretfully, I contemplated heading "south" in truth and waking her as she'd woken me on more than one occasion. But I saw the time and sighed.

No chance, unfortunately. We had about half an hour before I was due to give my first lesson and teach people about magic. Even if we were primed and ready, going at it for a quickie, that wasn't much time. And considering that she was fast asleep, and I'd not even planned this lesson yet?

No.

I had to get dressed as well, or the first day *really* wouldn't go well.

I considered waking her and seeing whether she wanted to come to the lesson and decided against it. She was busy enough.

I slid out of the bed and moved slowly, dressing quickly in one of the "approved" outfits that Kelly had sorted out for me. I didn't like it, having someone else pick out my clothing, but she'd pointed out that I tended to default to jeans and a T-shirt, and it was frequently a battered one.

There was nothing wrong with that—my other default was full armor—and I wore that a lot. Her point was that I should "dress the part" a bit more.

Hence the smart black jeans and a plain white, long-sleeved top.

I didn't think it was that much of a change, and considering it was teamed up with smart boots, rather than my usual work boots, or armored sabatons, it was comfy at least.

I shrugged and decided to go all out, even brushing my hair back and straightening my beard, rubbing a little oil in, and using some aftershave.

That done, and truthfully feeling a lot better, but yes, slightly ridiculous, I kissed Kelly's sleeping forehead, and slipped from the room.

Five minutes later and after sending out a quick request through the dungeon for someone to join me, I was practically reduced to forcing my way through the crowd in the tower. There was at least a thousand people here, squeezing into a space that we'd expected to be for a few hundred.

Seeing Ramnik and Dante on the platform already, I pushed through the mass of people. Once they saw who I was, most moved for me, but still, as busy as it was, there just wasn't much room. As I got closer, I saw…

I saw Ashley in tears, hugging the blonde who'd told me basically to fuck off in the canteen. Her sister was there by her side, also crying, as was Ashley's younger sister, who I rarely saw. Behind them both stood Andre and Jimmy, and I nodded to them as I stepped up.

"Hey, man." Andre grinned at me. "Good to see you. We grabbed a good spot!"

"Looks like it," I agreed, smiling, again, almost despite myself, warming to the pair of them as Jimmy grinned at me and offered me a fist bump.

I took it and moved in close.

"Ashley, you know them?" I asked, and she nodded.

"Emma and Jenn." She nodded to them. "Two of my oldest friends! You've met them?"

"More of the guys," I admitted, tilting my head to Jimmy and Andre. I saw the way that the girls, apparently Emma and Jenn, looked from me to Ashley, then Ashley to Dante as she waved him over insistently.

"This is, well, this is my boyfriend, Dante," she introduced him, and the girls gaped at her, and then him, then me.

Andre and Jimmy muscled in closer, nodding to him and obviously slipping into "concerned older brother" mode as they started asking him questions.

I grinned at the discomfort on his face, and, seeing that Ashley had the situation well in hand, I left them to it.

"I'll catch you later," I said to Jimmy, who was the closest, clapping him on the shoulder and getting a wink from him, before I slid past them. Ashley and Dante stepped aside to let me through.

I strode up the steps and onto the raised platform, moving over to Ramnik, who seemed to deflate in relief at my arrival. She'd been standing tall and proud, hands clasped demurely before her, but as I stepped in, she very happily moved aside and to the back.

I turned, looking out across the crowded room. The steady buzz of conversation fell silent as people moved, wanting to hear better.

Checking the dungeon, I saw a few people were still on their way, most working on other areas. The room we were in was well past what I'd considered full, anyway, so I straightened, leaving the dungeon sense and holding a hand high for silence.

The last few voices fell away, and I started to speak.

"Thank you all for coming!" I called. "Now, most of you know me, but for those who don't, I'm Matt." I looked around, unable to help myself as I grinned and made eye contact with Ashley's friends.

"I'm the Dungeon Lord of Newcastle."

I saw the looks on their faces, the general "oh fuck" and the disbelief, and I grinned even wider, moving on.

"So, what does that mean?" I asked. "Well, it means I *am* the dungeon. I'll be leading the expansion of our borders, and I'm the final word on the way things are done. Think of me as the final court of appeal. That being said, I'm going to be less involved in the day-to-day running of the dungeon from now on. Kelly and Aly, who most of you know, are taking more of a role in that for me now."

I looked around as I paced, talking to the silent crowd.

"The reason I'm doing less is twofold. It's not, as I'm sure one or two will suspect, because I'm the boss, and so nobody gets to tell me to pull my finger out. Most of you, as I say, know Kelly and Aly. They're not going to be letting me lounge about and avoid work after all, now are they!"

Those who did know Kelly and Aly laughed at that point, and I smiled, shrugged, and moved on.

"The reasons I'm backing out of the dungeon are simple. First and foremost, we need more mages." I saw the wince on Ramnik's face out of the corner of my eye, and I grinned, moving on. "You may call them mancers, mages, or even wizards. Some will call themselves all sorts of names, no doubt, but the truth is simple. They are powerful magic users, and their abilities, spells, and bravery has already turned the tide of many battles." I decided to throw Dante a bone, seeing him standing, tiny and skinny between the hulking brothers, like a pair of bookends watching over a solitary paperback.

"Dante, as an example, is a pyromancer…Dante, get your arse up here and do something impressive." I grinned at him.

In true Dante fashion, he hurried up the stairs, tripped on the top one and landed on one knee, wincing, then forced himself to his feet, doing his best to ignore the laughter that rang out.

"What should I do?" he whispered to me in panic.

"Just do something impressive. Don't hurt anyone, though," I whispered back.

He nodded, stepped out to one end of the platform, turned so he had the longest clear space available to him, and started to move his hands.

A single spark started out between his hands as he rolled them around, as if polishing the surface of an invisible glass ball.

Once the spark grew brighter, and a few people snickered, thinking this was all it was going to be, he suddenly slashed his hands to either side, dragging two streams of fire with them.

He twisted his wrists, forming two short pillars, each three feet or so long, and moved them around each other, then pushed them in toward each other, focusing hard.

The three-foot pillars shifted, wrapping around each other, then tightened in. The air filled with a whine; the fire grew hotter and hotter, going from red to orange, then yellow, then white, and finally blue.

He angled it upward, and pressed it to the ceiling, and gasps rang out as the stone quickly went from grey and cold to glowing hot.

"That's enough of that. Thank you, Dante," I said loudly, starting to clap. "I don't need a damn hole in my floor. I just made the damn place."

"Yes, Lord." He huffed a breath out, cutting the spell and straightening up. Then, clearly thinking he needed to make a point, he blew on his fingertips, as they did on guns in the movies, then strode to the side, grinning at Ashley as he took his place next to Ramnik again.

"Now then…" I called into the excited buzz that was quickly filling the chamber. "I know that's impressive. That's Dante, after all. He's single-handedly killed dozens, if not hundreds of creatures and monsters with his Fire magic. He's our resident pyromancer, as I said, and for those with an affinity to Fire magic, who wish to specialize in that direction? He'll be helping to teach you!"

I noticed a marked difference then in the looks Dante was getting, and grinned over the way that Ashley glared at a few of the girls who were clearly trying to catch Dante's eye.

"Now, that's not all, though. Ramnik here is our magical researcher, and will be helping as well. But if her title of Arcanist doesn't sound that impressive, or the magical researcher doesn't sound that big a deal? Her other title, and class, is *warmancer*."

I let that hang there in the sudden silence.

"She can conjure literal meteors from space to devastate entire areas. If you take nothing else from this little presentation, take this. Do *not* fuck with Ramnik." I grinned and reached out, gesturing to another before me in the crowd, and people moved, stepping aside as he strode forward, mounting the steps to stand beside Dante.

"This is Kilo, one of our resident cryomancers." I introduced the kobold, well aware that we had others but choosing to bring him up. "You might have noticed he's not human. He's one of our kobold allies, born into the dungeon, but absolutely no less a citizen for that. We have other mancers, or mages, several from different classes, including Peter, a human cryomancer. My point in introducing Kilo, however, is that these classes are open to *all*. Provided you're a citizen in good standing, so not doing punishment detail, for example…" I looked around, seeing nods as people got the point.

"Then you're welcome to come to any of these classes. To be very clear, unless you're helping to *teach* a class, you're still expected to work here. Becoming a pyromancer, or any other variant, doesn't mean you get to sit in here and contemplate the inside of your arsehole. You'll still be working. Might be that you're helping by growing plants or harvesting them. Might be that your particular gift lies in investing weapons with magic, or items.

"Maybe you're a healer, or you're daft enough to be like me—fighting on the front lines, and from the back, an allrounder. We need you all, and ideally? I'd love each and every one of you to unlock a magical class. Even if you never use it, knowing that if the shit hits that fan, you can help? It'd be a massive relief to me."

I paused walking back and forth as I watched the crowd, speaking slower.

"Now, I need to be clear here. We're learning. That's where we are. Some of the things we try won't help you. Others will think that it's common sense and will race ahead in these classes. Many will find that it doesn't resonate with you at all." I shrugged.

"Some of the things we will do will be mistakes. Others will really help you, and, to be very clear, this is not without risk. Some of you, if you experiment with these powers, will undoubtably hurt yourselves, or each other. As long as it's accidental, that's fine. *If*, however, I find that one of you have used these powers for personal gain, or to force others to bend to your will? If you take what I give you, and you hurt others without good reason? Well…

"For those who have been reading your prompts and understanding them, or who have been with us a little longer and have seen what's been happening? Yes. I'm the First Lord of the Storm."

I flooded my body with Lightning. The power rolled out, crackling across my skin as my eyes turned to blue-white pits, bathing them all in an unearthly glow.

I cycled the storm through my channels, lifting into the air and hovering there as I spoke to the awestruck and terrified crowd.

"I am the First Lord of the Storm, a Storm Titan in Ascendance. I was the first of the new human pantheons, and yes, I am a god. I have killed other gods, and I am at war."

I hovered there for a few seconds, making sure that everyone had taken the hint. Then I landed, suppressing my power and relaxing, before holding up a hand, my forefinger and thumb held an inch apart.

"I'm just a little god though…for now." I winked, and a round of nervous laughter and applause rang out.

"So! To be clear, those who wish to learn! We will run classes here. They are in addition to any work you're already doing, but speak to those you need to, and we'll all shift around to accommodate your joining lessons as much as we can. Those who wish to take this, and use it to set up your own fiefdom somewhere else? Fine. As long as you live by *my* rules, I don't give a shit. Build a settlement and protect those who need it.

"If, however, you abuse this trust I'm giving you? I will destroy you. I will not allow some warlord to rise up because of my actions. Understand that now."

Silence held for a long minute.

"As I said, I will be doing less in the dungeon over the next few weeks. It may be that you see me in the gym, or elsewhere. You might have heard that I have a private gym on the top floor of the dungeon, for example. It's not just mine, I don't mind sharing, *but*…understand that the reason I am there, and not working elsewhere, is because I'm meditating. I'm using the converters to augment my abilities and to try things out, before I come here and teach them.

"Quite literally, I'm experimenting and then teaching you what works and doesn't." I saw the look on Andre and Jimmy's faces and how the two girls, Emma and Jenn, were frantically asking them and Ashley questions in a panicked whisper. "Now. It had been my intention to give the first lesson here and now, but clearly there's a damn lot of you. As such, we'll break this into three groups." I gestured to Ramnik, Kilo, and Dante.

"These three will each have a token. Go to them when we finish. Take the token—that's your slot. If you get a One, then you're in the first group. You stay. If you get a Two, then come back in an hour, and Three? Well. If you haven't figured out that bit, maybe magic isn't for you," I finished with a chuckle.

"Moving forward, I won't be available to teach all the lessons, of course. Others will take my place." I gestured to Ashley, and she marched up to stand next to me, the top of her head barely equal with my pecs, and I grinned down at her. "This is Ashley…" I saw the looks some of the crowd gave her, clearly not knowing her, they jumped to conclusions.

"Ashley is the chief diplomat of the dungeon and is both trained to lead a squad in battle, and is lethal—and I mean, fucking *lethal*—with a sword or spear. She is also Dante's partner, and is going to help me to teach magic. I shall teach you all, generally, and we will push her harder. As she makes discoveries, she'll share them with you.

"She is learning, and as I say, some things I, or she, tells you may be wrong. This is from our limited understanding, not malice. Again. If you take our teachings and break our trust, you will regret it. If you have an issue attending lessons with non-humans, if you refuse to learn with an open mind, or to be respectful to each other? This is not the place for you."

I swept the crowd with a solid glare.

"If you want to learn, though? And you are willing to accept that if you do this, you are a member of the dungeon—if I need you, I will call on you and you *must* come? Then you're more than welcome here. Please understand I'm not trying to put you off. I want as many taught and trained in magic as possible, but I have to be careful with you all."

With that, I stepped back and strode to Ramnik and the others, Ashley following me.

"How'd that go?" I asked her quietly.

"Well, you nearly made me shit myself when you went all glowing and floated, put it that way." She grinned at me. "You know how terrifying you look when you do that? It's not like the movies, where he looks all sexy, but mostly human. You look genuinely like a god that's considering wiping the planet clean and starting again."

"I'll take that as a compliment." I smiled, focusing and creating three bags, and stone counters. They were simple, white discs with a number one, two, or three marked on them, and I filled the bags with the coins, ready to go, passing them to Ramnik, Dante, and Kilo.

"Hand these out, please," I said, deliberately giving Kilo the bag with all number ones in it. I figured that less people would go to the imposing kobold, and less people for the first group would be better.

"Matt?" Ashley asked, and I nodded to her to go on. "My friends? Look, I know I have no right, but…"

"Bollocks you don't." I snorted. "You sacrifice like any of the rest of us— hell, more than most do. You're our resident Alchemist. You fought on the front lines and led a squad. You're our diplomat and Courtesan *and* you're now learning magic? Hell, you even keep Dante upright and functioning. You've as much of a right to make requests of me as anyone here does. Ask."

"My friends," she said. "Look, Emma said she was a bitch to you earlier, and yeah, she's…well, she can be a bitch, honestly. She's hard as glass and just as sharp, but she's a good person. Honestly, she is. Jenn is just lovely, and their husbands…?"

She looked over at them, then turned her back so they couldn't see her face as she spoke quickly. "They got into trouble a few years back. They broke the law, and they went to jail. It was a robbery, and they did it, trying to feed the family. I know it's not an excuse, not really, but—"

"But they're about as bright as a five-watt lightbulb each, and they got taken advantage of," I agreed, sighing. "Look, Ashley, if you say they're good people, then that's great. I trust you. I don't particularly like her attitude, but equally, I understand it. Tell them to make the effort with people, and as long as they pull their weight? They're in."

"Thank you so much," Ashley breathed, sagging in relief.

"But," I said firmly, "they behave. Just like anyone else. And if John or Kelly comes to me and says there was a lot more to things than they, or you, have told me, then we'll be reevaluating. Make it clear to them, if there's more to the story than they told me? Better to tell me themselves, and we can address it. If they lie and I find out, there won't be the general goodwill I have to them right now to help their cause."

"I understand," she said quickly. "Honestly, they're not very bright, but they're good guys, and they're both really good at martial arts, if that helps."

"It will," I admitted. "They can help us all to train."

CHAPTER TWENTY

It took about twenty minutes for everyone to get a token, and by the time it was done, I was right in that Kilo's bag was the least popular.

There were some two hundred people in the room, and I smiled around, noting that Ashley had directed her friends to Kilo, meaning that they were here together now.

"Okay everyone!" I called out, gesturing for them to gather, even as Dante closed the door to get rid of the lookie-loos.

"So, this will be the first lesson, meaning that you get to be our experimental bunch. What we do here will hopefully go well, but if you don't want to risk yourself in this group, the door is over there, no hard feelings." I waited a minute, noting that nobody moved. "No? Well, you lot are brave." I smiled.

"Okay, first lesson, and this might seem bloody stupid, but it's important. You all have status screens, a collection of stats that tell you about who you are, and that hold information on you. Pull these up now, please."

I gestured to Dante, who grinned, remembering the way he'd taught us all about this step before.

"Okay, everyone!" Dante called out, striding to the front and clapping his hands together and rubbing them in excitement. "You're looking for your affinity system. If you pull up your personal 'body' stats, so your Agility and so on…has everyone got that? Right then…"

He proceeded to talk everyone through the pages, guiding them until everyone could see them, then he stepped to the side, surrendering the floor to me.

"SO!" I boomed out. "Many of you will have high affinities for one or more element or form of mana. Some might have none. Don't worry about it. You will also have some particularly low ones most likely; these are important, so don't ignore them. As a basic rule of thumb, if you have between one and a hundred, this is how naturally adept you are with that form of mana. If, like me, you have anything over a hundred? Please raise your hand."

I waited and nodded after a few seconds. "Don't worry, I would have been frankly astounded had you had anything that high. Mine was raised to it by my class, in part. Now, does anyone have any minus figures?"

Most of the room held their hands up. I nodded and smiled.

"Now these are things you are highly susceptible to, and I have them in the minuses too, so don't worry. For example, has anyone got one of the primary elements in there? That's Fire, Earth, Air, or Water, for those who don't know."

"Fire," one woman called out, and I nodded to her.

"Thank you. Well, I highly recommend you avoid Dante's classes then. Essentially, Fire will do you more than the usual amount of damage, so be careful with it!"

"I know." She held up a scarred left hand that was clearly a long-term issue for her.

I frowned, then looked around the room, already spotting Jo striding toward her determinedly.

"Don't worry," I called, seeing her face when she saw Jo making a beeline for her. "Jo is our head healer. Believe me, you're going to like the conversation you have coming. Feel free to join another class if you miss much now."

I turned back to the rest of the room even as Jo reached her, smiling and taking her to the back of the group.

"So, for those who are worried, nothing bad is happening there," I clarified, gesturing to the conversation. "Jo is just going to see if she can heal that injury. Anyone else who has an outstanding injury? Go see Jo or her healers at the end of this."

I looked around, smiling as I saw a few people touching something hidden— a stomach here, a leg there—and the contemplation on their faces.

"Moving on. The affinity system doesn't just govern magic, although it is massively important. What you'll find is that the affinity system is *you*. For me, I always loved the storms, the crackle and boom of thunder and lightning most of all.

"My mother told me once that it was the giants of the storm fighting with the gods, and rather than scare me, I would spend hours watching, waiting to see a fighter fall from the storm. I think I'd had a plan for saving a god or killing a wounded giant or something, but you know how childish fantasies are." I grinned at the people before me, my nerves settling as I went on.

"Now, the reason I'm telling you this is because I always felt an affinity with the storm, so when I opened my affinities and found that storm sections were much higher? It just made sense. Dante here…"

I gestured to him, and he smiled, lifting one hand.

"He's a pyromaniac. Apparently, the local fire department knew him on sight and were engaged in an ongoing war with him. He loved to watch the flames. Now he's a pyromancer! He managed to naturally unlock his Fire magic, when none of us understood much of it at all."

Dante conjured a fireball in one hand, then passed it from hand to hand, grinning.

"Some of you will have simple and straightforward classes like this. He's a first-level elemental mancer or mage, after all—it looks simple, right?" I saw a few people nodding, and I went on.

"Well, it is. He literally controls fire. The thing is, as time goes on, he'll be able to control that fire more and more. He'll be able to make a fireball that could take out a tank, and probably walk through a live volcano without so much as a scratch. That's not the end of the story, though.

"For those who don't know, starting at level five, then ten, and then every ten levels from then on, you'll be offered a class choice. That choice defines what you can do, but it is also a part of you, so I highly recommend you don't just pick something in a rush. Take your time and consider it.

"I'm a Dungeon Lord, and I chose that several times over, because I didn't understand it. When I risked it and chose an Arcanist class as well—which, by the way is, as near as we can tell, the basic entry-level mage class—my Dungeon Lord class became an *Arcane* Dungeon Lord. My class choices altered slightly, becoming more magic focused, allowing us access to more magic facilities for the dungeon and its inhabitants."

"Some of us are offered rare classes," Ashley called out, stepping forward. "Believe me, the name on the class is a description, but not all of it. Remember that the system that grants this is using our languages, but it's not human based, never mind intended to be in English. Some things are not what they seem. Rare classes are much more powerful than basic ones, so if you're offered one? Seriously consider it. Come to one of us if you want to talk it out, and I assure you, anything you say will be kept in confidence."

"Thank you, Ashley." I smiled to her, knowing exactly what our resident Courtesan was getting at. "Now, Ashley isn't a mage, as I think I said earlier, but she is highly skilled in other areas. As such, I will be talking you all through the individual exercises, then I will work with her here, where you can all see and hear. Once she has her breakthrough, she will be able to teach you, as will the other mancers.

"One point, however! And this is an important one. Some of you might make a spontaneous breakthrough, and I really hope you will, but most likely most of you won't be offered any kind of class until you hit that point, level five, ten, or twenty, for example." I stopped and stared out at the rapt crowd before me.

"For those who want this? You need to level," I said. "To level, you need to gain Experience. You can do that through crafting, through completing quests, from exploring and discovering things, or carrying out research. The most efficient method, though, is through combat."

I paused as a hand was raised hesitantly, and I gestured for them to speak, smiling at them.

"Fighting?" a scrawny man asked. "You mean like in a boxing ring or something, or…"

"I don't know if sparring would gain you much, I'll be honest. No, I mean genuine fighting. Working with spear and shield in a hoplite platoon, or diving into the training dungeon as part of a team. The training dungeon will be opened to people from tomorrow or the day after I believe—we're just getting it remodeled now—so I'll make you all an offer. If you want to, you can run the training dungeon. That's what it's there for. You can borrow some gear if you don't have any, and most of the loot that drops in there will be yours. The conditions are, however, that magical artifacts, including spellbooks and skillbooks, are to be given to the dungeon, and we get to examine anything you get. If we decide we need to take it, you'll be rewarded."

A low grumble started at that, and I hurried on.

"The reason is simple. First, the dungeons are designed to drop them, but they're rare. The dungeon drops loot that's appropriate to the core level and monster, so as a Steel dungeon, you could get anything from a nice steel knife or a spellbook to an item of technology up to and including the level that we as humanity were at prior to the fall. We were getting mainly Bronze age drops before now, so it'll be interesting to see what you get. Most of the time, we'll make a copy of what you got, and give you one of them, as well as a reward. That way, you win."

"And the rest of the time?" a gruff voice called out from the back, clearly intending on staying hidden, and not liking it when people moved to expose the older man.

"The rest of the time, if we can't replicate it, we sacrifice it to the dungeon, or we give it to someone who can use it best. That isn't to say that won't be you. The way this worked before, was that we got an Earth spell from a drop…Tar, wasn't it?" I asked Dante, who nodded.

"So, we got Tar, gave it to someone who was powerful with Earth magic, and then they imbued it into a focal orb. The orbs hold spells, but they also hold the knowledge and handle the more fiddly bits. Essentially, if you use one, you learn the spell gradually and because you're not fucking about with the technical side of things, generally you can cast a more powerful version of it. We then have access to a training tool for anyone who wants to be a…"

"Geomancer," Dante supplied, and I grinned.

"What he said," I agreed. "So, that's for spellbooks, and skillbooks are similar, but not. Instead of teaching you a single spell, they teach the basics of a skill, literally. That sounds simple, but considering it could be anything from making a lace napkin to astrophysics? That is being taken by the dungeon, no discussion. We put it into the dungeon, and the chance of that particular skillbook dropping again in the future becomes one to five percent. As it is? There's half a percent chance of one dropping, and it could be anything. By sacrificing it to the dungeon, we have a good chance of getting lots of those skillbooks over time."

"Isn't that a bit pointless, though?" someone else asked. "I mean, if we're all astrophysicists here, and none of us can use it?"

"It could be," I agreed, nodding. "The thing is, though, we're not the only dungeon."

That got everyone's attention all right.

"We're in contact with a handful of other dungeons," I repeated, looking around at the crowd. "We know that there are over a hundred dungeons scattered across the Earth. They were put here by an alien race to give us a chance to grow strong enough to defend ourselves against the incoming Orcan. They're basically a race of asshole orcs. Highly technological and even more aggressive. They conquer worlds and kill their entire populations, save for a few that they keep supposedly for 'fun.'

"Now, personally? I'm not having that shit," I said sternly. "I'm going to develop this dungeon, and then I'm going to develop the area and recruit people and beings from all races. We're going to tear the Orcan a new asshole, and you're all going to help me. You don't have to help on the front line, but again, if you can? Then please do.

"As I was saying, if we can get skill and spellbooks, and we don't need them? We can trade them with the other dungeons for things we *do* need, giving us an even better chance to win. Those of you who do run the training dungeon: make no mistake—the opponents you face won't go easy on you. They're there to kill you, or to be killed. You will be asked before you enter to declare you understand and accept this, because while we will have healers waiting out here, you'll have to come to them if you need it."

"Why?" one of the people asked, lifting a hand in the air. "Why can't we take a healer with us?"

"You can." I smiled. "You just can't take one of *my* healers with you. Essentially, this is about *you* learning to survive, learning to fight and to rise up. If one of you develops healing abilities? Far from being 'just the healer' as you might have been in a computer game, you'll be desperately courted by teams wanting you to go in with them.

"That brings me to the next point about the training dungeon." I started to pace again, my hands clasped behind my back. "We recommend you enter the dungeon in up to a party of six at a time, and you make your own teams. I'm sure people will want to team up. That being said, you don't *have* to take a team. You can go alone, or in a smaller group. The entire point is that you learn and grow. A team of six is the best, as near as we can tell, but if you want to be a seven or hell, a ten, come to me, or one of your trainers, and make the argument. It might be that we agree."

"What if nobody wants to team up with us?" one skinny guy on his own asked nervously.

"Then you come to a trainer," I said firmly. "We will be running the dungeon on a regular basis, testing things and trying out new abilities. Either you'll be placed with a team by us, or you'll go on a dungeon run with one or more of us."

I saw the looks on more than one face, thinking they'd do much better to not manage to get a team and to have the trainers giving them essentially a one-on-one private training session.

"For those who do run with one of us? I warn you now. You need to take part in the fight to earn Experience, and we won't be running the dungeon on trainee levels. There's a much higher chance of death or dismemberment. Consider this your warning."

"What if we want to be fighters?" Andre called out, and I nodded to him, thinking quickly.

"Then we desperately need you, and I appreciate it, but you're in the wrong place. There will be changes made to the physical training classes as well, and they, too, will be mingling with you all soon. Essentially, we're finding our way right now. We had a training plan before this for fighters, but that's evolving. You, as mage trainees, will train here in the mage's tower.

"The fighters will be getting a building soon as well, as in, in the next few days. The two groups will train separately, and then you'll be able to mingle all you like outside of your classes. I highly recommend you all pick your teams to run the dungeon based on skills and abilities rather than just friendships. After all, a team of all melee fighters will be fucked up by a flying enemy, and a team of mage trainees who haven't unlocked their classes could be slaughtered by a handful of goblins. PICK YOUR TEAMS WISELY," I repeated loudly.

"In conclusion, there is a real chance you will fucking die in the dungeon. I'd really prefer it if you didn't. With that in mind, you can borrow armor before you go in, and weapons. If you get a decent weapon drop or something? Chances are we'll make a copy and then you get to keep it. Same with armor and more. You'll also get coins. These will be the basis of our economy in the future, and at the end of the dungeon run, you can put any loot you don't want into the shop we'll be making. You'll be paid for it, and then it'll go on sale. So if a mage gets a sword they can't lift, for example, they might want to put it up for sale, and a fighter might wish to buy it. You all get the idea of an economy."

"Why does it cost anything?" someone asked. "Why isn't it all just free?"

"Because everything costs something," I said. "For me to summon the creatures you will fight in the dungeon, it costs us in energy, or mana. Literally, if you clear the entire dungeon? That cost us—when we first started—a few days to earn enough mana to replace them all. Right now, it's less than that. As we put more and more advanced creatures in, though? The cost goes up and up. There's no point in you all fighting fluffy kittens, after all. You'd learn nothing, and the kittens…well."

I shrugged.

"Are there any other questions, or shall we begin?" After a minute's silence, I nodded.

"Okay then, make sure you're comfy. You don't need to be cross-legged or in some special stance. Sit, lie down, whatever you want…just make sure you've got some room."

I moved back to the center of the stage, and Ashley approached, looking nervous.

"You all right?" I asked her quietly.

"Yeah, just, you know." She shrugged. "So, what do I need to do? And don't say get naked, or I'll tell Kelly," she joked, and I grinned.

"Damn. I'll have to come up with a new plan now," I replied, both of us speaking too quietly for people to hear us. "So, close your eyes and open your mouth…"

"Yeah, yeah!" She laughed, shaking her head and pulling her hair back into a ponytail. "I'd better get this out of the way then, eh?"

"Ha! Definitely!" I chuckled, then settled down onto the floor, groaning as I got comfortable. "Okay then!" I called, deliberately raising my voice so that everyone could hear me. "The first stage is to find your mana core and channels. We all have them, but until you learn to see them, there's not much you can do. For those who want to be fighters, this will help you to get other options in your class choices later, so you might as well follow along today."

I turned back to Ashley, and, speaking to her but keeping my voice loud enough for others to follow along, I started to guide her.

"Now, close your eyes, and focus on your breathing. In and out, in and out. Focus on your body and relax it. You want to go from the very top of your head all the way to the tips of your toes. Find each and every muscle you can, and relax them, one at a time."

I spoke on, going over the basics of meditation as I knew it, assuring people that you could do this lying down or standing, whatever they wanted, and I couldn't help but smile as more and more of the crowd laid down.

"Now…" I said some ten minutes later, conscious that of their allotted hour, we'd used most of it already. "Move to your heart. Focus on it in your mind, and with your eyes closed, visualize your body as it is. Focus in on your heart, and your bloodstream. Look at the way that it runs through your body. Visualize how the blood runs around and back.

"It's all a single system, no leaks, or there shouldn't be, anyway. The heart beats, pushing the blood to flow through you, carrying oxygen and more to the places it's needed. Do you all understand? Raise your hand if not. There's no shame here, and everyone's eyes are closed. Only I will know, and I can help you."

At first there was nobody, and then slowly, in almost perfect synchronicity, Jimmy and Andre lifted their hands, their eyes closed.

"That's fine, we can talk later," I assured them. "I'll find you, and we can focus on it."

I took a deep breath, and checking the time, grunted. I had literally ten minutes left, and that was it. "Now, if you imagine you are staring at your body, seeing the heart and the blood pumping around your body, now move down slightly, and look to your stomach. Look for a second system. Can you see it?" I looked around the room, seeing surprisingly one or two nodding already.

"Yours may be different to mine. I see a bright blue-white light there, my core, and my mana stream flows out from that point. It travels to my hands and feet, through my body in all directions. But this isn't the same for everyone. For some, you will have no stream. Others will have a diffused wave of light that fills their body."

A handful more nodded, and I glanced at Ashley, seeing the furrowed brow as she clearly stared at something.

"Your core is where your magic is drawn from and stored. These first few lessons will be about finding and reaching your core, but don't worry if you don't do this easily. Some will, and some won't," I said. "Okay, now we're down to the last few minutes of the hour. I'd like you to try to do this again as much as you can tonight. We'll gather here again for a second lesson tomorrow, okay?"

A hand raised hesitantly, and I looked over, seeing it was Emma, Ashley's friend.

"Yes?"

"What if we're in the park?" she asked. "Can we do it from there somehow? Like come through the dungeon sense thingy?"

"Do you want to return to the park?" I asked. "I think you'd be better off being here, for these lessons and for the training. But if you'd rather be in the park, then you're welcome to travel here each day."

"We'd rather be here, but…"

"But you have family there." I nodded. "I know. See Ashley at the end. She'll help sort things out. That goes for any of you. This is a highly important aspect of the dungeon, so I would recommend you stay here for now. It'll mean it's easier for you to congregate with others you meet in the class, and for you to learn. If you need to move here from the park, speak to Ashley, Ramnik, or Kelly please."

Dante raised a hand and gestured to his wrist, making me smile. The wind-up watch he'd taken to wearing made it clear the hour was up.

"Okay, everyone, thank you all for coming, and I'll see you later!" I called. "You really tried today, so thank you!" I started clapping them, and it spread quickly. I felt kinda stupid doing it, but I saw the looks on people's faces, and I did it anyway.

It mattered to them, so it mattered to me.

As one group left, Ashley quickly moved to talk to Emma and the others, then waved them to go as she returned to my side.

"Everything okay?" I asked, and she nodded.

"Thank you," she said. "I've told them I'll sort them out later on tonight, and I'll help the boys as well…with the meditation, I mean."

"It's fine." I smiled. "Did you see your core?"

"I think so? It was…it was like a tiny spark of light, but I don't know if I was imagining it or…"

"That's it." I smiled wider. "Took me forever to find the fucker. Remember, I was making this shit up as I went along."

"So, no change to normal then?" Ramnik asked, joining us. "Would you like me to help with this one?"

"Yes, please," I agreed, nodding quickly.

"We can have Dante take a more active role in the third lesson," Ramnik said, gesturing him closer.

"I'll talk people through things again as I did this time, and then if you and Dante can explain what we're doing as I work with Ashley?"

"Of course."

With that plan in place, I stepped forward and started my speech again, people finding seats and spaces.

Chapter Twenty-One

"I think I'm losing my voice…" I groaned to Kelly, hugging her at the end of the third lesson. She'd slipped in as the last few people were streaming out, and the look she gave a few hopefuls hanging around made it clear that I would not be giving anyone "private" lessons. Or at least not in the way that one or two looked to have been hoping for.

"You did amazing," Kelly assured me, letting go and standing by my side. "You didn't see people when they left. You were too busy focusing on the next lot. There's over a thousand people out there who are trying to learn magic, and they're all excited by the possibilities."

"Realistically, I don't think—"

"No," she agreed, cutting me off. "Not all of them will manage it. Most of them probably won't. But if you get even ten percent of those who want to be mages? That's over a hundred people who could help. That's an insane number."

"It really is." Ramnik joined us, with Dante and Ashley. Kilo and other volunteers had moved on already, and within a few minutes, it was down to just us few.

"So what's the plan next then, boss?" Dante asked.

"The next two days we get as many to find and identify their core as possible," I said decisively. "Once we have a good number who have managed that, we can start to manipulate their mana, compressing and speeding it up."

"That stage will be far harder when they've not found a way to release their mana in a controlled way," Ramnik warned me, and I nodded.

"It probably will. But using their mana and interacting with it, then getting them to their class choices? I think that's the best way to do it for now."

"What about the more advanced classes?" Dante asked. "When will we be starting those?"

"As soon as we can, realistically." I sighed. "Once we have the first breakthroughs, be that from class choices or natural, like you did, Dante, then we'll separate them out. We'll continue to do a guided meditation class each day, even as more and more leave that class."

"Will we continue it for a while, or indefinitely?" Ramnik asked bluntly. "Eventually we need to accept that some people who wish to be mancers will fail. Running classes for those with no aptitude, while laudable…"

"It's also a waste." I nodded. "I know that, but it's also a case of we will hopefully always be expanding. New people will join us, and others will leave or die. We have to be ready for the churn, and as brutal as it sounds, we need to replace those losses. Even if it ends up that we have to use the focal orbs to artificially force people, much as we did with you and others, we will."

"Okay, so…what now?" Dante asked. "I mean, is that it for classes for the day?"

"It is for me," I said. "I need time to train. I have to focus and improve. If you want to take on private students? Go for it."

"Ummm, with the tower…?" Dante started, smiling nervously. "You said that each floor would be specific…"

"And it will," I said. "But for now, we need general-purpose converters, if that's what you were about to ask about. We'll be dotting one or more of each kind we have access to around the ground floor.

"Once that's done, then we need to focus on the rest of the dungeon. If you want more Fire converters? You spend time in the dungeon sense absorbing more crap. Earn enough for a converter? You go for it."

"You mean it?" he squeaked, eyes widening even as his voice broke. "I can do that?"

"You can." I nodded. "Any of you that want to do that? Feel free. I'd appreciate it if, for each one you make for yourself, you make one for the other floors as well, though. We really need them."

"Sure!" Dante's head was in serious danger of coming off he nodded that hard, before grabbing Ashley's hand and half dragging her from the room.

"OH!" I called. "Dante, Ashley?"

"Yeah?"

"I'm just going to say this the once. If you fill the floor full of Fire converters, it'll get very hot. If, for any reason, there's a situation where clothes are coming off? I recommend you close and lock the doors."

"Of course!" Ashley replied with a smile, dragging Dante along as he went from stunned and bright red to an even wider smile and practically sprinting after her.

Ramnik sighed "Did you really need to say that?"

I nodded. "With him? Hell yes. Ashley isn't exactly self-conscious, and they just got together. He's what, eighteen? When I was that age, I literally thought with my dick. If they're meditating and it's hot and there's very little clothing on? Better to embarrass them by saying it, than to embarrass them by a group walking in on them in the middle of 'meditation.'"

I finished with air quotes around "meditation," making it very clear what I meant.

"So," Kelly said with a shake of her head and a grin. "What's next?"

"More planning, unfortunately," I admitted. "Is Griffiths back?"

"He is, and he got the ship."

"Thank God," I muttered, shaking my head. "That's a relief. Okay then, I need to see it, and then I need Chris, you, and Aly, Clarissa, Mike, Griffiths, Rhodes, and…" I paused, thinking quickly. "Patrick, Markus, and whatshisname…the archer trainer…"

"Jeffrey?"

"That's the badger." I nodded. "We need them all."

"Why?"

"Well, as I said to the trainees, they're going to need to do dungeon runs with the fighter trainees."

"And the fighter trainees need to be formally sorted out." Kelly groaned. "Are we ever going to get the research we agreed on done?"

"We are," I insisted. "Once there's a building in place, they can fill it from the gyms in the area. We've got a group of trainees who need extra exercise, after all."

"We do?"

"Yeah, those assholes that tried to raise a coup."

"That's cruel." Kelly shook her head, then she grinned. "I *like* it."

"I think there's a *lot* of gym equipment that needs moving." I smiled. "Also, we need to plan the training schedule out a little, and start a real recruitment for the fighters. How people fell over themselves to train as mages made me think about our recruitment methods so far. We've been asking Clarissa and others to spread the word and just hoping people turn up.

"Most of the training has been in bursts as we've all been doing other things, with Markus and Jeffrey mainly just teaching what they wanted. It's really helped, but also, as we found out the other day, Patrick has been breaking trainees—they quit his class in droves. Is that because they don't need what he's teaching, or is he a crap trainer?"

"That's a bit unsubtle," Kelly said reproachfully.

"I know, but that's the point," I replied, shaking my head. "Is it a case of he's only looking for monks, in which case, yeah, people are going to quit, or are they quitting because he's too hard on them? We've left the various training groups to it, because we've all been running in different directions. Right now, we've got a little space, or at least I hope we do. We need to make the most of it."

"We need more scouts as well then," Kelly said firmly. "We need more notice of any threat."

"Exactly." I nodded. "I totally agree. But the time it takes to get that sorted out, be it scouts or alert towers? That's time that the training is being half done. I'm leaving you in charge of all that shit, and I'm focusing in where I can do the most good."

"What about your own training?" Kelly asked pointedly. "That's why you were doing all of this in the first place."

"I'll do that as well," I said. "I was doing it this morning, then…"

"Then the gym was jam-packed with people," Kelly finished, wincing. "Okay, yeah, I get that one. I went to check on you and found you eating in the canteen, and ten people crammed into the gym upstairs."

"Exactly."

"So you get the classes moving along and then you can teach as you learn, and train?" she asked, and I nodded.

"That way I can experiment a little as well, and as we all learn together, we'll find what works and what doesn't. Also, if we need help? They'll all be there, and if I'm not some distant figure, they're more likely to come when we call."

"I agree," Ramnik said, surprising us both. "These people can only go so far before they need to get to their class experience choices. For them to actually survive long enough to reach that? They need to have fighters with them, and in doing so, they learn to grow together."

"Thank you." I led the way from the tower and set off toward the Parthenon. "Do you want to join us for the meeting?" I asked Ramnik, who shook her head.

"Are you going to the ship?" she asked, and I winced.

"Yeah, I need to go there first. Sorry, scatterbrained."

"I'll see it, if I may?" she asked, staying with us as Kelly guided us around the main dungeon building to a long warehouse design with plain stone walls.

It was set apart from the other buildings, and the specific door design on the entrance made me nod as soon as I saw it. It was similar enough to the standard locked doors of the dungeon to be immediately identifiable. But where the others were simple, this one looked as if it should be protecting Fort Knox.

It was huge, wide, and damn, it looked like a nuke would barely leave a scratch. I'd try to break through the *walls* before that door.

As soon as we approached, it swung open, closing again behind us, and keeping out the rest of the small crowd that had gathered on the dead grass.

I heard a few shouted questions, and pleas to come in, but Griffiths had stationed two of his soldiers outside with clear orders, and nobody tried to follow us.

Once inside, and past the dogleg corridor that Kelly or Aly must have put in after the ship had been put in place, literally making sure it couldn't be removed, I came to a halt, staring at the battered alien craft.

It looked like a missile, much as I'd thought when I first saw it, slightly wider, and stubbier than a human device, with some kind of sticky crystalline structure, like a web that had held the dungeon safe.

It had that when I found it, anyway.

Here it was set on a platform. The hinged door that had been swinging in the breeze when I found it was locked back and open. The webbing that had held the dungeon was gone, be that washed away, or broken, or who knew what. Instead, the interior was heavily braced and filled with small compartments.

Most were empty, but several were still sealed, and I shook my head in disbelief that I'd missed them at the time.

They varied in size, smaller ones being stacked atop each other, looking like a bee's honeycomb in layout, except they were eggshell-white and had been hidden by the web or mesh.

Those that had been broken open were empty or had splattered blood in them. But beyond that, they were abandoned. The sealed ones, though, the small handful that remained, I could already tell held some serious goodies.

Moving in close, I clapped Griffiths on the shoulder and nodded to the ship.

"Well done, mate," I said. "I hear you had some issues?"

"Matt," he replied, nodding. "Yeah, you could say that. I found a few hundred survivors, mostly nurses, doctors, medical specialists, and their families. They…they wanted me to join them."

"I'm not surprised. Are you going to?" I asked, figuring it was better to get it all out in the open straightaway.

"No." He sighed. "I want to, in many ways. They're on their own, after all…almost nobody who can fight to defend them. Their few fighters were all killed by the gang."

"Can you bring them in?" I suggested.

"No. They've seen some of the shit that's going on, and frankly, they're paranoid. The gang came in being nice, and then tortured, raped, and murdered a lot of them. They're really short on trust right now."

"We're extending our reach to the hospital as we speak," Kelly assured him. "Once we get to it, we'll make a safe zone, just a large box or something that's secure, with supplies in it. Then, if they get into trouble? They can seal themselves up and we'll send help. It's the best we can do, I think, if they don't want to join us."

"I seriously doubt they'll enter a big box and just hope you let them back out." He shook his head.

"They will if they're scared enough," I disagreed. "Once things are sorted and we can build it, we can go back and offer them the choice. They can join us and be safe, they can stay there and we'll make a box as a fallback, or they can tell us to get fucked and we'll leave them alone."

"I think they'll choose option three, despite my recommendations," Griffiths said. "But I can hope I'm wrong."

"I hope so too," I admitted. "Anyway, moving on, what do we have here?" I moved in closer and gestured to the storage areas.

"I think it's an emergency stash," Rhodes suggested, moving over. "And hi," she said with a smile.

"Hi yourself," I replied, grinning. "So, a stash?"

"An emergency supply," she explained. "I found this on one of the bodies near to it when we found the ship." She held out a glowing blue crystal, and I took it, whistling softly.

It was about three inches long, two across and an oval, seemingly polished, and a deep, royal blue, with golden fractal patterning that ran through it. It looked like it should have been a gift for an emperor, but the look of it was the least important bit.

Mana crystal	Item
This high-grade Mana crystal has a highly compacted storage lattice full of pure mana and is ready to be used.	
Durability 499/500	**Mana:** 1000/1000

I shook my head in disbelief. If I'd known the fucker had this shit hidden away inside? I'd have come for it ages ago, and no fucking wonder the other dungeons, like that bastard who had been in Gateshead, had been so much more advanced than we were. *With a stash like this to start with?*

I could have massively rocketed through the early shit!

I shook my head again in incredulity, before handing the stone back and moving into the ship, reaching out with the dungeon sense.

The ship was weird in the dungeon sense: it showed almost as part of the dungeon, and yet other sections clearly weren't. The frame of the ship registered as a fairly simple and easily absorbed alloy, but the engines and guidance systems were almost organic.

They looked to have been grown in place, rather than "built" in any traditional sense. There was a *lot* of crystal in the ship as well—a hell of a lot of it—from what I guessed to be communications pathways to the actual engines themselves. Where we'd have used fiber-optic, they used a single piece of crystal. And the more I looked at it, the more I could see it working.

There was less to go wrong with it, for a start, and if the crystal was strong enough, the redundancy of backup systems wouldn't be needed.

As a network engineer, seeing something like this was just…it was amazing. I liked it.

I reached out with the dungeon, flooding the ship with its senses, and got two more surprises. The stores were small in size, but high in wealth, and I nodded, knowing that my issues with the training building had been solved. Yeah, there wasn't enough for something expensive, but for a simple gym and changing areas? Hell yes.

The real issue, though, was the *life sign* from the main fuselage. Sinking my mind in deeper and peeling sections apart, I found it quickly enough, and for the longest time I just sat there, staring at it.

"Matt?" Kelly asked after a while, breaking through my frozen glare. "Are you okay?"

"I am." I shook my head and stood. "Those fucking Cinthian bastards won't be when we're done with the orcs, though."

"Why? What's wrong?"

"You remember the messages we got? That they tried to make peaceful contact, but were attacked? That their envoys barely escaped with their lives, and only some of them did that?"

"Yeah?"

"Well, I'm calling bullshit," I said flatly. "Don't get me wrong. Any politician who had a chance to talk to them would have, I've no doubt, tried to rip everyone off and run with the money. But this ship?"

"Yes?"

"It's number one hundred and twelve."

"Right?"

"It uses a human brain to perform the orbital calculations and shit. It's got a literal brain in place of a computer."

"A…" Kelly looked sick, turning and looking at the ship, then back to me. "Is it? I mean, was it grown…?"

"It doesn't look like a dungeon brain," I said, not knowing exactly how I knew. "Literally, it's too…too *battered*." That was true, I realized. It looked as though it'd had the shit kicked out of it, damaged sections and more, but rather than being done through the crash, that fucker was encased in solid crystal.

It'd been damaged either before it was put in there, or in the process of being connected up. Sections of the ship were hardwired into the brain, and other sections?

I was no brain surgeon, but I recognized a human brain at some instinctual level, and seeing the damage? I was willing to bet they covered the sections that dealt with whoever the "donor," be they willing or not, had been before they got slapped into the ship.

"If they just did it with the ships? That's over a hundred people," I said grimly. "The mana influx and all that shit was an accident—I do believe that. They didn't want us to be wiped out; they wanted us as shock troops. This, though? This I don't like."

"Could they have been dead?" Griffiths asked after a pause for thought. "Reanimated brains that were long since dead?"

"It's possible," I admitted. "But I don't think so."

"Why not?"

"Honestly, I don't know. Something about the feeling."

"Can we do anything about it right now?" Rhodes asked, and we all looked at her. "Seriously? Unless we kill the Orcan, unless we survive and win, we can't do anything. So, with that in mind, has anything changed?"

"Only the level of trust," I admitted.

"Well, if you trusted them at all, you're a fool," she said. "So, moving on, what does this mean for us and what do we do with the ship?" She gestured to the ship.

"It's to be kept as it is," I said. "If we absorb it into the dungeon, we kill the brain. For now, we can't do anything with it, and the brain is stable. We strip out the remaining mana crystals in those compartments…" I pointed to a section of the honeycomb, and Griffiths moved closer to look at it, starting to pry the edges loose.

"And we use some of them as emergency stores, and the rest to build a training center. We leave the ship here, locked away until we reach Glass. That should give us some options with this, its crystal, but it's similar in that way, I think. We reach that level, and we can hopefully use some of this tech."

"Okay. I'll keep a guard on the building…" Griffiths started to say, and I shook my head.

"No point in wasting them," I said. "We've got undead. They can watch around the clock and not get bored. Kelly?"

"I'll put three corpse lords in here," she agreed. "Two inside, one outside at the door. That should discourage the terminally stupid."

"Then that's it." I climbed back out and turned around, reaching out to take stones as Griffiths started to pass them out.

"Do you need this one?" Rhodes asked, looking at me and holding a hand up, the mana crystal held tight.

"You found it fair and square," I said. "If you want to give it up? I wouldn't say no, but if you want to keep it, well, we're not desperate for it."

"I'll keep it," she said. "Unless it can buy us some magic lessons?"

"You'll be getting those, anyway." I shook my head. "In fact, we needed you and Griffiths, as well as the others. Are you done here?"

"We can be." Griffiths nodded.

"Good. We need to settle in and do some planning, think outside of the box a bit."

"Sounds good. Plus, it doesn't look like there's anything else in here…"

There was, in fact, one more stone, considerably larger, and it was absorbing and refilling itself from the ambient mana that streamed past, but I judged that as being a part of the system that kept the brain alive. I kept quiet about it for now, making small talk instead as we headed out.

"Ramnik, are you coming?" I asked her, and she shook her head.

"If you don't need me, then no. I'll help to send people your way, and then I'll go and eat. I was too nervous to eat earlier." She gave a little self-conscious smile, and I grinned.

"I felt a little like that too," I admitted, waving her off as she hugged Kelly, then set off in the direction of the canteen. "We really need a way to summon people." I sighed.

"The noticeboard idea works," Kelly assured me. "It's really simple, so it's not a great deal of use for fast summoning, but it does the job."

"We'll work on it."

Our small group headed onward. Kelly held onto my arm and stared ahead distractedly as she summoned goblins and made them grab the people we were missing by the hand, leading them along like particularly fugly toddlers.

Half an hour later, by the time everyone was assembled, we were all drinking coffee, energy drinks, and, in Rhodes's case, swigging champagne directly from the bottle with a straw.

"What?" She shook her head at the looks people were giving her. "You said this was the end of the day, right? We're having a planning meeting, and your exact words were 'we need to relax and think outside of the box.'"

"That's very true, Matt," Griffiths said seriously. "You want a soldier to think out of the box, you shoot at them, lay down a bet, or you give them alcohol. I'm not seeing any guns, and you already said she could keep the stone, so…"

"Do I look like I give a damn?" I asked with a brief snort of disbelieving laughter. I downed the energy drink and instead summoned a bottle of good rum. "Okay, so I guess this is the rest of the night: we plan, we build, then we chill and relax. Tomorrow, we start hitting it hard again."

"So, what's the problem?" Patrick asked.

I looked to Chris, who cocked an eyebrow at me in question. I nodded to him, and he stood, moving the wall and sorting through a few details, then stunning everyone as he threw up a complex diagram on the wall.

"Matt asked me to have a look at our training schedules and the current fighter training," he said. "He asked if I could organize it a bit better, and this is what you get, really. To be clear, part of my job before all of this was as an analyst, so yeah. I'm not as dumb as I look."

"Don't worry, mate," I said. "Nobody thinks you're that dumb."

"You couldn't breathe and walk if you were really as dumb as you looked." Patrick grinned, and I leaned over for a fist bump, grinning as Chris shot us both the finger.

"ANYWAY." He glared. "If you assholes are finished…"

The first screen that he pulled up was a list of names, and damn it was long.

"This is the list of fighters who signed up to help us." He paused as he made sure everyone was looking, then he tapped the wall, and the vast majority of the names were suddenly struck through in red.

"The red, unfortunately, marks losses in death," he explained, tapping the screen again; the red names winked out, the mass of names shuffling and condensing to take up only a third of the overall number.

"This is the overall fighter core that we have access to." He tapped it again and the screen split. A quarter remained on the left, and the majority moved to the right.

"Now you can see the population of fighters, by the dungeon…" He tapped the left side. "And by the park." He tapped the right.

"Of all of these, we have a grand total of five trainers, not counting Mike, Griffiths, or Rhodes."

The lines reorganized, and suddenly Markus, Jeffrey, Patrick, Pete, and Ken each had a section. Markus and Jeffrey had seven each, Patrick had two, and Pete and Ken each had thirty or so.

"As you can see, there's some details that are becoming clear. Even though we have three trainers here, we've only got a small number of recruits, sixteen to sixty, literally."

"This is my fault." Patrick groaned, standing. "Matt, I'll resign."

"Why?" I asked him.

"I push, and I push hard." He shrugged.

I didn't even have to say it, Kelly beating me to it. "Don't say it, Chris."

"Awwww," he grumbled, then grinned. "I wasn't actually going to say anything, but I love you all too. Anyway. Patrick?"

"Yeah?"

"Sit down, mate." He grinned. "This isn't what it looks like."

"No?"

"Ever wondered why your trainees leave?" he asked.

"Because I'm too hard on them?"

"Nope. I found three of them in the park, and I asked them. Honestly, I thought that was it, at first."

"But?"

"But they all raved about your training," he said. "They couldn't keep up, but they went back to the park and started training others. The problem isn't that you're kicking their asses, or at least not entirely. If they don't want to be special forces, then yeah, Mike's occasional classes and yours are wasted on them, but that's not the problem."

"Then what is?" I asked.

"Recruitment and planning," he said. "When they join us here, they're told they can choose to be frontline or ranged, and they're split out into one group or the other. Sarah handles physical conditioning, along with Rhodes, and the pair of them…"

"Sarah!" I groaned. "Fuck! I forgot to invite her…"

"I'll sort it," Kelly said. "I left her out too."

"Anyway." Chris glared at me for interrupting. "Once Sarah and Rhodes kick the fuck out of them, they send the most promising to Patrick, who does martial arts and general ass-kicking."

"And then they leave," Patrick said.

"And then they leave the training…because they don't need it if they're archers, so that's more or less understandable. The frontline guys? Well, some of your training sessions are at the same times. They choose to fight as a team, rather than as individual martial artists, and boom. Suddenly you're down to almost nobody in your class."

Chris nodded to Patrick as he said that.

"The thing is, because we're all running around like headless chickens, and none of us really know if we're going to be training for a month or fighting round the clock, it makes people less likely to stick around in training.

"Basically, as you saw this morning, there's absolute droves of people willing to help. They just get sick of not knowing what's going on. Then, as more and more quit, what you're left with is a much smaller, but highly dedicated set of trainees."

"Recommendations?" I asked, already knowing what was coming, but needing to hear it out loud.

"Stop fucking around and get a set plan," he said. "Add to that, people are joining for 'ranged' and they're learning to fire a fucking bow and arrow—" Chris broke off to hold a hand up as Jeffrey opened his mouth to object. "Whoa, don't worry, dude. I'm not having a go, not at *you* anyway..."

"He means me." I sighed, waving at Jeffrey to sit back.

"If the boot fits." Chris grinned.

"Is this the guns and rail guns?" Aly asked, getting a nod from both Chris and me.

"They're still in production," she said. "I can give you some now, if you want. They might explode, though. You don't mind that, right?" She cocked one eyebrow, and Chris winced.

"The thing is, they're seeing others with normal guns. They saw the asuras and heard stories of their weapons, and they're made of fucking metal. A bow and arrow, or even a crossbow is fuck all use against that." He shrugged. "I'm sorry, but that's why people are quitting the ranged team. And then, if you look at the hoplites?"

"Yes?" Markus asked, straightening up as his people were named.

"Sword or spear and shield," he said. "Basic armor, while this idiot is literally flying around the battlefield and Ramnik is summoning meteor showers. They're seeing the kobolds with the same gear, and they see them get fucking slaughtered. They know that they're held back in favor of the kobolds being used as cannon fodder, because you can summon more of them, but when things get bad?"

"They're losing heart," I said.

"They are." He nodded. "Less and less show up to training, because they're feeling like they're glorified cannon fodder. As dedicated as these people are? They're *still* willing to fight. But they're making do all the time, and they're losing heart. Some are moving back to the park, and others just do less and less. Basically, we need to fix it, and now."

"And that's why we're here," I said. "First, do we have any recommendations from anyone? I know I've got a plan, but I'd rather have input."

"Scrap the current teams," Rhodes said. "Splitting them into ranged and frontline is a waste of time. Teach everyone as a soldier first, then a specialist."

"Exercise," Griffiths said almost at the same time. "Make them sweat and bleed together. Forge them into a team to bring back their motivation."

"Equipment," Jeffrey said next. "Get rid of the bows and arrows, and give my boys and girls real weapons."

"Advanced training," Patrick said, then grinned as everyone looked at him. "I mean it, people! Okay, look, if we train everyone the same? Make them sweat and cry in the gym, doing laps, all that crap, then we train them to fight as a unit, then with ranged weapons, one after another, we forge them again, right?"

"Yeah," I agreed.

"Then we offer advanced specialist training to a dedicated few. Not just me teaching them martial arts, but we make special forces. Like, I'll teach martial arts, but Rhodes could sneak up on me any day of the week...have her teach stealth. We must have others who could help as well."

"We do," I said, suddenly grinning. "The kobolds."

"What?" More than one voice rang out, and I nodded, unable to stop grinning.

"The advanced kobolds…some of them can talk, others are fine with point and gesture and so on, but more to the point, some of them have abilities. They've started to take classes, to specialize. We have assassins, or we *had* them." I hesitated, looking into the system, and nodding sadly.

"Had," I confirmed. "They died."

"You've got their pattern, though?" Rhodes asked, and I nodded. "Then summon some more. In fact, create an elite force, a couple of assassins, some fighters and a mage. We focus on leveling them alongside our trainees, just as we would the others, but when they unlock their classes? They can start to give lessons."

"That works," I agreed.

"You said you had a plan…" Griffiths said to me, nodding. "I'd like to hear it."

"It's nothing earth-shattering," I said with a shake of my head. "Believe me."

"Still…"

I stared at him, then sighed.

"It's simple." I nodded to Rhodes. "She's already laid out most of it. We recruit heavily, say two hundred volunteers, if we can get that many, and we start them with heavy physical training. We literally kick their ass all day, then go back for more, make them eat massive high-protein meals. They work out around the clock, start a new set of exercises every three hours or so. In between those times, on a night they sleep, and during the day they do additional training—hand-to-hand, ranged, hoplite…all of it.

"They also spend an hour each day, split into thirds, with my mage trainees. They learn to fight, and they learn to meditate. They spend that hour with the other trainees, so they can mingle and make friends.

"Then they get their gear, and in those thirds, they get to enter the training dungeon." I paused, seeing the looks on their faces. "As in, a third a day, so nearly seventy people get to run the dungeon each day. They go in teams of four, and they get to pick a pair of mage trainees to take with them. The mage trainees who don't get picked? They don't get to go. That makes the fighters popular and looked up to. The training schedule will strip their bodies of any fat and bulk muscle damn fast and—"

"It's too much," Rhodes said, even as Mike chimed in, agreeing.

"The human body can't take that hard a routine, not for long," he said.

"And that's where we come back to the mage trainees, and the healers." I smiled. "I've been working my ass off, and basically pushing my muscles past exhaustion. Once I can't do anymore? I collapse, literally. Then I heal myself with my Lightning. Despite the healing of the injuries—because let's face it, that's what exercises are: intentionally damaging the muscles, overloading them but only to a certain point—using magic to heal *after* the exercises?"

I had their total attention now, I could see.

"It works," I finished. "It banishes the pain, the exhaustion, all of it, and it's like I just started. Yeah, I'm tired, but I'm not on my knees anymore. Add to that, this gets the healers an insane amount of practice? Then consider that some of the mage trainees will want to be healers? We could cut them out of the main group, and simply raise them up with the focal orbs, but I'd rather they learned it properly. We can cheat if it doesn't work out."

"You're shitting me," Mike growled, and I looked at him, one eyebrow raised in question. "You can heal workout injuries and you're just telling me this now?"

"I'm still making sure." I shook my head. "Again, this is what I'm planning, but it might not work. Literally, I spent yesterday doing this, working out and pushing hard, then healing myself, and I gained a handful of stat points. Doesn't sound like much, but that's the point. I'm one of the most physically advanced here and I'm gaining points. People who are just starting out? They'll rocket upward."

"Have you done other experiments?" Rhodes asked, and I nodded.

"Today was supposed to be me working out without healing myself, so I had a baseline, but the gym I built was full of people."

"All day?"

"There were only two this morning," I admitted. "But considering I'm also trying to meditate, to see if I can improve that while I'm on the rowing machine for example?" I shook my head. "One of them dropped a weight plate and shocked me out of it. One of the things I've found, and that I'll be talking about in the lessons, is that as we break the ambient mana all around us down into usable forms, it deposits a kind of sludge or sediment of broken mana in the channels.

"The more there is, the more powerful. But stirring it up and flooding the channels hits you with insane nausea. I'm experimenting with a way to cleanse it, but to be startled out of meditation? I accidentally flooded my body with that sludge, and it fucked me up."

"Is that what happened yesterday as well?" Kelly asked, and I nodded.

"That's why I need silence and privacy." I looked around at everyone, toying with my glass, before taking a swig from it. "When that happened, I had to spend hours cleansing my mana streams, and I've not managed it yet. The problem we face is that all mages will end up with this problem. The solution?

"The rings…" I said, looking around the room.

It took me almost an hour to explain everything, going through the rings or gates, and my suspicions. The exercises, then the damage to my body and the gains, before finally reaching the plan for tomorrow, that I'd work myself to the bone in the gym, while continually channeling, so that we could see whether that prevented the gains or helped it.

Halfway through, Rhodes leaned over and plucked my rum glass from my hand and sat back, smiling. I'd frowned, then shrugged and summoned another, only to have it taken away by Mike, who said he'd explain "later" and just to keep talking.

When I finished, finally, Mike stood, and knocked back my rum, before grinning at me.

"So, you need to push yourself in the gym, to make sure of this theory, and we need to build a gym and barracks, then recruit?" he asked, and I nodded, getting a very bad feeling about this.

"Just to be clear, alcohol is a poison, correct?" he asked, and I nodded again. "Excellent."

"Might want to heal yourself now." Griffiths grinned, as I looked from him to the others. "After all, we can't taint the results of the test."

"What—"

"Is there anything else that you need to do?" Rhodes asked, and then, to the rest of the table before I could answer, "Does anyone have a need for him in this next phase?"

A general chorus of *no, nope,* and *he just gets in the way anyway* rang out. That last, of course, came from Chris.

"Then you're mine, Dungeon Lord, sir." Rhodes climbed to her feet. "You might have thought you were pushing your body before, but I can guarantee you, I'll push you harder."

"But—" I tried, my balls trying to retreat at the evil look in her eye.

"You can do it!" Kelly assured me, batting her eyelids. "You're a god, after all. Please? For me?"

"Yeah, you're not afraid, surely?" Chris called, grinning.

"Fuck you, Chris," I said. "Of course I'll try," I said to both Kelly and Rhodes together. I tried to say something else, to beg off until I'd had a hot meal and a bit of a rest, but my words were lost under the general burst of sadistic laughter that rang out around the table.

"Then for the next six hours, you're MINE!" Rhodes growled, reaching over and grabbing me under one arm. "Come on, Dungeon Lord! Up and at them!"

CHAPTER TWENTY-TWO

"I hate you all," I whimpered as I lay on the bed, as agreed, not even stirring my mana slightly, leaving my body to heal as naturally as I could.

"You don't mean that…" Kelly assured me, leaning back and putting her hands above her head.

I'd staggered into the room, and had collapsed onto the bed, facedown by her side, while she was laid in it, propped up by pillows.

"I do." I groaned. "You're all evil."

"Even me?" She flipped the duvet aside to show me that she was, indeed, naked apart from a pair of stockings and suspenders, as she climbed out, sliding gracefully from the bed.

Her creamy white skin and the black lace of the stockings dragged my eyes, but I stayed laid facedown.

"Matt…" she whispered, drawing my name out. "You don't really hate me, do you?"

"Evil," I muttered, managing to just about turn myself over, as she helped me to roll onto my back.

"Oh, I'm not that evil…" she quirked an eyebrow and smiled at me. "And besides, you don't usually complain…"

As she spoke, she undid my belt and tugged at my clothing, rolling me this way and that as she stripped me.

"Unless you want me to stop?" she asked suddenly, drawing her nails along the inside of one of my thighs.

"The spirit is willing…" I assured her. "But the flesh…the flesh is so weak!"

"I'll wake it up."

And my God, she did.

Honestly, I wasn't capable. I could barely rise to the occasion, and from the multitude of injuries from the training—nothing major…just sprains, tears, bruises and muscles pushed so fair past their breaking point that they were in a different time zone—I was reduced to literally laying there and letting her do all the work.

Sometime later, as I slid deep into sleep, I knew that there was categorically no way that my body could be pushed any further.

Literally.

When I woke the next morning and shifted slightly, I had a bare seconds' warning as first my left, and then the right thigh muscle, right at the back, went into cramp.

I frantically kicked the blanket off, half rolling and half jumping from the bed…only to find that half of my muscles weren't talking to me, and the others were screaming abuse.

I toppled sideways, crashing onto the floor and writhing, trying to stretch my legs out, needing to work my fingertips into the knots that were forming deep in the muscles…

Only to find I was doing a T. rex impression with my arms, flopping around weakly and barely responsive.

"Matt?" Kelly asked, stunned. She was half dressed, her hair loose, jeans and a sports bra on, and had clearly been doing one of those arcane rituals women performed to look and smell so good. "What's wrong?" She dropped to her knees next to me and reached out for my legs, seeing me trying to work them. "Hold still…"

I braced myself, hissing in pain as she dug fingers like steel pins in, working the muscles as she kept talking.

"Okay, wow, yeah, these knots are nasty…and here…is that better…damn, I can feel it quivering…"

"That's…what…she said!" I hissed out, unable to help myself.

"You daft bugger!" She laughed, still working my thighs. "Only you would say that!"

"While you're down there—"

"Don't push your luck!" She cut me off, digging in deeper and making me groan in mixed pain and pleasure as the muscles slowly started to unknot.

"Yes, boss…" I managed to get out through gritted teeth, before yelping as she smacked my bare ass hard, getting up.

"Don't you forget it!" she joked.

I groaned and rolled onto my back, then pushed myself to my feet, feeling the muscles quivering again as they almost went back into cramp. As soon as I stood up, I bent over again, reaching down and trying to touch my toes, stretching the muscles in my legs and back out.

"I feel like I've been beaten with a stick…" I whispered, slowly straightening up.

"Did it work?" Kelly glanced over from where she'd sat again at a small dressing table off to one side.

"I…" I blinked, looking at the notifications, and shaking my head as I let loose a low whistle.

There were two of them, and damn.

You have gained additional Stat Points in the following areas through constant effort.

- +3 Agility
- +2 Charisma
- +2 Constitution
- +4 Endurance
- +4 Strength

Continue to work hard to increase these or other stats…

*

Jez Cajiao

Congratulations!

As you have spent more than five hours training under an experienced and highly motivated physical training expert, you have received a training bonus! For the next 24 hours [17.5hours remaining], you will receive a 50% boost to all physical training (Expert Grade).

I couldn't help but pull up my stats and stare in wonder at them.

Name: Matt, First Lord of the Storm				
Host Powers: 1 (Enhanced Regeneration)				
Species: Thunderstorm		**Bonus**: None		
Level: 25		**Progress to next level**: 36,053/45,000		
Stat	**Current Points**	**Description**	**Effect**	**Progress to Next Level**
Agility	38	Governs dodge and movement	Heightened chance to dodge attacks 76%+20%= 96%	4/100
Charisma	28	Governs likely success to charm, seduce, or threaten	35% more likely to succeed in events that require seduction, persuasion, or threats (10%+ (18x2) = 39)	11/100
Constitution	51	Governs Health and Health Regeneration	HP: 51x60 = 3,060	32/100
Dexterity	38	Governs ability with weapons and crafting	+38% Increased chance of improved result +14 to melee damage	87/100
Endurance	41	Governs Stamina and Stamina Regeneration	Stamina: 41x50 = 2,050	1/100
Intelligence	58	Governs base manapool, standard intellectual capacity	Mana: 58x60=3480	52/100
Luck	39	Governs overall chance of bonuses and critical hits	+58% increased chance of positive outcome	88/100
Perception	37	Governs ranged damage and chance to spot hidden items/traps	+27 to all ranged attacks	37/100
Strength	38	Governs damage with melee weapons and carrying capacity	+56 to all damage with Melee weapons	17/100
Wisdom	47	Governs mana regeneration	78 mana regenerated per hour (internal improvements destroyed)	34/100

I still had a single spell to allocate, and a pair of class skill points to use, or at least I damn well would once I'd finished the quest with the asuras.

I'd seen the live quest as soon as I looked at my notifications. A marker flashed that I had outstanding class, dungeon, and personal quests still to complete.

My personal one was one of the ones I'd been damn well trying to make some progress on, but some fucker always interrupted me. Still, I should be able to make some decent progress in this over the next few days.

Congratulations!

You have successfully created your first signature melee spell. Continue to research, investigate, and create to benefit from the wonders of your class. Remember, only you can decide your destiny…Complete this quest to receive a boost to your selected affinities.

- Melee spell: 1/1
- Ranged spell: 0/1
- Defensive spell: 0/1

The asuras Green Queen, though, was yet to be sorted out. I'd been putting it off. Partly because I'd been genuinely busy as fuck, and I had been. The dungeon had been my priority, then the goddamn gates, then trying to get my people back into some form of training and building things back up.

Then, though, I'd put it off again, justifying it to myself as something I could do because I needed to have the mana of the dungeon behind me, and our forces back up to level, so that when I faced her again, I'd be doing it from a position of strength.

That was more or less true, but as I stretched some more, staring at the screen that hovered before my eyes, I was honest enough with myself that I knew that wasn't the only reason.

I was freaked out by the asuras.

They were a species that not only were responsible for the deaths of billions, trillions, and fuck knew how many more, but they were…they were fucking evil to a level I'd never imagined could exist.

It was like if there was a single one "great" god, and they'd peeled the clouds back one day, stared at us all and grunted in disgust, before lifting up their perfect creation to show us all, and it be a cockroach or something.

It was that level of just internal wrongness that was freaking me out. That they were functionally immortal, and that they were so uncaring that some of their kind were trapped down here was one thing, but not knowing?

Being aware that how these fuckers dealt with things meant that they might be literally up there right now sending our sun nova, and I'd find out in a very short time when I became a no. 57, extra crispy?

The knowledge that a species that could do this, was literally hovering around up there and might decide to do this at any point, was insane to me. So I'd been doing what I always did when I was freaked out about something I couldn't control: I'd been ignoring it.

I couldn't afford to do that any longer, though. Today I'd pull my finger out and complete the quest, I decided. It'd gain me another class skill point as well, after all.

Checkmate! (II)

The asuras Green Queen has survived the attack of the Red Queen, albeit through no actions of her own. She is now highly aware that not only are you the master of the local dungeon, and able to provide her with all she requires to rebuild and evolve herself, you have also killed any and all attackers.

Use the current situation to form a more permanent alliance with the asuras queen to complete this quest and receive the following bonuses:

- +3 to top three Attributes

- +1 Class Skill point to allocate

Additional forces (Access to)

- 10,000 XP

"Are you listening?" Kelly asked, and I blinked, thinking that was a weird way to start a conversation.

"Sorry, I was miles away," I admitted, forcing a smile. "What's up?"

"Hmmm." She grumbled, staring for a second before shaking her head. "I was asking what the plan was for today. You got your ass kicked by Rhodes last night, and yeah, she basically broke you, but now? What's the plan for today?"

"I need to teach a class in—" I checked the time, before grunting and nodding to myself in relief. "Three hours, so I've got time for breakfast, then to work out and heal myself up over and over. Today I'd planned on working out and draining my mana at the same time, like channeling constantly as I do it, but Rhodes wants me to do it the other way—to work to collapse, then heal, then go again."

"And then tomorrow do the constant flooding of your body?" Kelly asked, and I nodded. "Was she really that bad?"

"She's utter evil." I nodded. "I mean that…utter, fucking evil. When I thought I had nothing more to give, she'd let me off 'easy' with a drop set."

"When you go until you drop?" Kelly asked, and I nodded again.

"Where you go until you can't manage one more, then you pick up the next weight down and go with that, and just keep going until you're down to the smallest weights we have, and you can't lift them."

"I remember them. I had a PT once. She had me doing them with squats…"

"Evil," I said.

"Very much so. Okay, so you're with Rhodes this morning. Then teaching. Then what?"

"Uh…" I paused, then shook my head. "As much as I don't want to do it, I need to head to the civic center and speak to the asuras. What's it been doing?"

"Rebuilding," Kelly said. "It claimed a lot of the Red Queen's corpse before I could step in, and it started sulking, basically, that I wouldn't let it have all of it, or summon dungeon creatures for it to kill to make itself an army."

"Then yeah, it's past time I went to see it, I guess," I growled, not happy at all that the fucker had basically hidden and left us to defend it, then went and "loot ninja'd" the winnings.

Motherfucker.

"Okay, then what?" Kelly asked, and I hesitated.

"Is there something I should be doing?" I asked, seeing that she was looking for an answer here.

"Do I need to spell it out for you?" She settled back on the chair and watched me.

"Uh…" I hesitated, my mind racing. I was working out and getting stronger, helping to train the new mages, getting some meditation in, then dealing with the asuras, and that'd be most of the day by then.

I'd also had it in my head, as a sort of half-arsed "I need to do that" plan that I'd go to the park and give a quick speech to the people there, see how many I could recruit to the army, and another one here, the same.

Those were clearly not the answers that I was supposed to be giving, as she stood, finishing getting dressed, before moving over and standing before me, waiting.

"I need to have some time off with you?" I asked as much as said.

"I think you deserve it, don't you?"

"Definitely." I grinned.

"I mean time *off*." She reached out and took my hand. "Time for us to actually relax a little and be just us, be Kelly and Matt, not the Lord and Mistress of the Dungeon."

"Okay…?"

"And Matt?" She looked up at me.

"Yeah?"

"I mean for us to have some time out, to actually relax, not just fuck and sleep, okay?" She glared at me.

"Of course," I said quickly, knowing I was on thin ice. "I was thinking the same thing!" I lied.

"Good." There were a few seconds of silence before Kelly spoke again, still holding my hand and looking down at it as she drew fanciful patterns on the back of my hand with her finger. "Look, Matt, I know we're good together, and I know it's all busy, that we're literally fighting for everything, but…"

"But you want a little time-out?" I asked, and she nodded, looking up at me with clear discomfort in her eyes.

"Don't get me wrong," she said quickly, trying to hide it as she spoke. "I know how busy we are. I know that because of what we do, we'll never have much time, but…we met in a bar, like normal people do, and I really liked you."

"I kinda felt the same," I admitted, taking her hand and leading her to the bed, sitting on the edge of it and tugging her down next to me. "When you went home, I spent the entire rest of the night thinking about you."

"I spent the taxi ride home being told off by Michelle because she thought I was going to go home with you and leave her on her own."

"And?" I asked, only half joking.

"And if we'd been out for a date, then yeah, I would have," she admitted, shrugging. "But I was out with a friend, and we'd just met. That's the point, though. We've never actually had a date, you know that?"

"We…we haven't, have we?" I asked, stunned. "I guess, with the way the world has been going…"

"It just happened," Kelly agreed. "Look, I'm not saying I'm unhappy, because I'm not, and I'm certainly not looking around or anything. I'm just saying that it'd be nice if we could have a little bit of time out, that's all. Have a few hours to be Kelly and Matt."

"I'd like that," I agreed, kissing her softly.

"Tonight?" She smiled when I nodded.

"Tonight," I agreed. "I'll get the workouts done, the lessons for the mages, then the asuras and the park for a quick meet-and-greet with Barry, then back to here for another workout..." Even as I was saying it all, I could feel my body screaming with terror. "Then it's our time. A little dinner here maybe?" I suggested, looking around, and then shaking my head.

"No," I said. "I'll sort something, though."

"Thank you," Kelly said, giving me a much happier kiss, before hauling me to my feet. "Now, are you going to heal yourself or what?"

"Hell yes," I said, taking a deep breath and flooding my body with Lightning as soon as she'd let go of my hand.

It felt amazing.

The Lightning that washed through my body rebuilt and repaired me, cell by cell, as it went, and it was fucking glorious.

I went from trying to ignore that pain, the aching of every damn joint in my body, from cramps that were twitching constantly and bruises that were crying out, to wonderful, blissful health.

I straightened up properly, suddenly aware that I'd been leaning a little to the left, and I took a deep breath, letting it out with a whoosh.

"Damn, that feels better," I admitted.

"Good!" Kelly stood on her tiptoes and reached up for a kiss. It was a long one, and when she finally broke away, the twinkle in her eye was back. "I'd hate to think I'd actually broken you last night..."

With that and a laugh, she headed for the door, and I shook my head in amazement at her mercurial moods, before finding the training clothes I'd been wearing, cleansing and repairing them, and dressing quickly.

I hesitated on the stairs a few minutes later. The drifting smell of bacon, beans, fried eggs, and sausages cried out to me, but I kept going, reaching the little gym a minute later.

Rhodes was already there, along with four others, all soldiers. But when I arrived, she nodded sharply to the others, gesturing to the door.

"Move out," she ordered flatly. The others practically bowled one another over in their haste to escape.

"Morning, Rhodes," I said, looking after the other four. "Anything I should know?"

"No, sir." She smiled. "They've been made aware that the holiday with regard to training is now well and truly over, and they're off to assist in the collection of equipment for the new gym."

"And you're here...?" I asked, leaving it open.

"I'm here to continue the experiment, sir," she said with an evil smile.

"Well, fuck." I grunted, my worst fears realized. "I guess I just got myself a PT..."

"I've been called worse," she admitted, all business. "Now then, today you'll be healing yourself after each exercise, as we discussed last night. We'll break the day into two sessions to make the most out of the opportunity. For this morning, you'll exercise to your absolute limit, then heal yourself; then we move onto a new exercise. This afternoon, however, we'll be working in complementary sets. When one muscle is pushed to its limit, we will work an opposite group, legs and then arms for example, until you can't do anything else. Then and only then will you heal yourself. Sound good?"

"Sounds fucking awful," I admitted, getting a smile. "But it'll be early evening, not this afternoon," I said. I more or less remembered the conversation last night that we'd be doing this today, but until she'd said it, it had all been a blur.

It'd been agreed—by which I mean she'd told me, and I'd tried not to weep while getting my ass kicked—that we'd be doing this for a few days so that we could establish the most efficient method of doing it.

She'd also let me know, in passing, that she'd be doing the same with her soldiers in a few days' time, but with the healers working with her. Instead of my Lightning abilities to heal myself, she'd have healers working on her and the rest of her team.

It was the only consolation I had, as she'd quickly pointed out that she'd be using my effort to "inspire, or amuse" the others, depending on my performance.

I nodded and climbed onto the rowing machine, trying to ignore how warm the seat was, the last occupant having just left it.

"I need to work in part on my mana system," I told her. "So as much as I need to push myself, I need to meditate at the same time."

"I'll prod you each time you slow," she assured me, nodding. "You explained this last night."

"Did I?" I muttered, not really remembering, then shaking my head and settling into the rhythm as she set an hourglass—an honest-to-God hourglass, with sand and everything—on the nearest converter.

"This is an hour—literally—glass." She smirked. "For the next hour, as this runs through, don't try to meditate. We need to teach you to work at a stable speed to keep you going at that point without thought. Stare at the glass, watch the sand falling, and show me what you've got."

I nodded, annoyed as I knew I needed to be working on my gates, but fuck it, I'd give this a go for a few minutes. She was the expert trainer, after all.

I brought her up to date on the changes from last night's session, even admitting how much more I'd gained with her help than on my own, despite knowing damn well I was going to regret that.

She nodded, but all she said as the sweat started to roll down my back was to speed up, or to slow when I started to get ragged and lose my form.

She pointed out little changes, straightening my back, moving my legs like this, or my arms to be at this angle.

None of it was earth-shattering—it was just a dozen or more little tweaks—but by the time she finally declared the last grains had fallen, I was both broken and feeling the benefits of her training.

"Don't look at the notifications, if you have any," she said. "Better to keep going. Now, heal yourself, please."

I did it, washing the Lightning through my body, and sighing in relief.

"That's the warm-up." She smiled. "Now then, we're going to work out with these weights here…" Moving me to the bench, she pointed out the set she'd been laying out, kettlebells and a reasonable weight on the bar. "So, we'll start with…"

As much as I hated it, I soon saw the difference. Having someone who actually knew what they were doing leading me through the exercises meant I went from lighter weights than I wanted to start with…but I finished on heavier weights than I'd expected.

Even though she refused to be drawn on how I'd done, I was still left with the impression I'd surprised her, considering we had to physically make the bar bigger to fit more weights on in the end.

By the time we were done, and I was allowed to heal myself and Rhodes left, I was both knackered, and strangely energized. My muscles were swollen with the recent finish to the workout, but thanks to the healing, I actually felt amazing.

I raced down to our rooms, diving into the shower, then drying off and grabbing some jeans and a plain black top, jogging back up to the canteen, and finally eating. Griffiths was there, and he directed me to protein-heavy meals, pushing me to eat more than I was really comfortable with.

Ten minutes after I'd rushed that down, and I was in the mage's tower, looking out across a veritable sea of faces.

"Hello!" I called, forcing a smile. "Now, this might just be me, but there seem to be a few more here than there were yesterday. Who here has a marker that shows two or three?" I glanced around. "Come on, hold them up!"

A good dozen people did so, and I nodded.

"If you can, please come back in an hour, or in two," I said. "The lesson will be the same, but if you just come at any time, we'll end up with situations where people can't get in."

They all left, and I waited, looking around, before shrugging.

"Okay, those with a marker for session one, please hold them up!" I called out, and roughly half of those who were left held theirs up, and I sighed, seeing just how many people were still standing around, confused.

"Right then, I take it you couldn't make it yesterday, or who just found out about the lesson?"

A wave of nods and shrugs ran across the room.

"Not a problem then." I smiled. "Ramnik, could you take this group upstairs, and repeat yesterday's lesson for me, please? Then split them. I think this might happen quite frequently, so until we start having breakouts, let's spread them across the three classes equally. Leave the first session of the day as the smallest, so we've got some space."

"Of course." Ramnik smiled and stepped forward. "Okay, everyone! Anyone who doesn't have a token, or who hasn't been to a lesson so far, please come with me!"

With that, she was off, stepping down from the platform and walking through the crowd that parted for her, one hand in the air so that everyone could see where she was.

A few minutes later, the last stragglers were out of the class, and we were down to a more manageable level. Again, both Dante and Ashley were with me, and I quickly went over the details we'd talked through yesterday, refreshing everyone's memories.

"Now then!" I called, settling down on the platform across from Ashley. "If you can all get comfortable, we need to work on our meditation! So, as before, visualize your heart and…"

The hour flew by, with people putting their hands up if they had questions, rather than interrupt the group, and Dante hurried to them, dealing with those he could.

Where a question was asked several times, he'd feed it back to me, and I'd go over that section again, on the grounds that if three or four were admitting they didn't understand, then at least ten or fifteen more probably didn't and were too embarrassed or ashamed to admit to it.

The second and third session passed quickly. Ramnik, having sent her little class away, joined us for the second, and then gave that class to the others when I was giving my third of the day.

It meant that, once again, my goddamn meditation and magical time for me to work on my own was missed, but that was life.

Ashley could already access her core, finding it much as I described, and almost a third of the others who were attending the classes had managed to find theirs as well.

Considering that was over three hundred people, by the time I waved the last ones out of the class, I was feeling quietly optimistic about the whole thing.

Settling down on a mat, I slid into the dungeon sense and reached out to Kelly, getting a mental smile and the ghost of a kiss, before being directed to the new gym and military building.

It was simple, really, all things considered. Two levels so far, although it was obviously intended to have many more stacked atop it. It was forty meters wide by seventy meters long, with the main doors oriented south, and a set of smaller doors at the north end.

Entering through the southern doors, there was a wide, if shallow entrance area. Then, running down the right side of the building for nearly thirty meters, were offices. Each of them was three meters by three meters, with a two-meter-wide corridor separating them.

The remainder of the right side of the bottom floor was taken up with a pair of small changing areas, some toilets, and showers. They were also segregated by the sexes, as despite movies to the contrary, if you put a lot of fit, healthy young people of opposite sex in the shower together, they didn't just get on with it and ignore the view.

Rather than having half the occupants running around swinging a filled fire hose, and being mortally embarrassed, and the other half of the occupants being less obviously affected, but still highly embarrassed, they were separated out.

Griffiths had pointed it out to me over lunch. Essentially, when people formed teams, and got to know each other a lot more, yes, little issues like sex and nudity would be ignored, or dealt with in other ways. But when this was going to be a general-purpose gym for now and not just for the soldiers?

The pool outside was more than enough of a problem for those with body modesty issues. There was no need to make it worse.

The remainder of the floor was taken up by what would be the gym, a massive area that, even considering walls and internal bracing, still ended up being thirty meters across and just under seventy long.

I nodded in satisfaction, flitting across the dungeon and doing a loop, before flying up as high as I could and searching the area. There were almost thirty people struggling along with weights, exercise machines, and more on stretchers and carts, all headed inward. An escort surrounded them, making sure they were as safe as could be.

That done, and knowing that everything was in hand, I headed over and got a light meal, before returning to our quarters, and my thankfully fixed armor.

This was Aly's work, and I made a mental note to thank her, then I stripped off and redressed in all my gear, once again, summoning a fresh goddamn hammer, and wondering whether in this new world there was a creature that actually stole left socks, and if it did exist, if it had developed a taste for my fucking hammers.

Just in case, I reached out, through the dungeon, finding that Kelly had already anticipated me, and Beta, Kilo, and a half dozen normal kobolds were waiting for me at the exit from the dungeon.

"Thank the gods for competent subordinates," I muttered, remembering it was a bastardization of a phrase from a movie, but not what it was from.

Half an hour later, I drew to a halt outside of the civic center dungeon. The Green Queen was camped out with a couple dozen cars, all in various states of destruction, as well as a battalion of smaller asuras that were working on a complicated assembly.

As soon as I arrived, they pulled back in on themselves. One of them clanked out on four legs to face me, as the others stared threateningly from behind the carcasses of the cars.

I paused, realizing that instead of being haphazardly dragged in and dumped, as the cars had first appeared to me, they were actually positioned in concentric rings, gaps being left between them that suddenly looked like they'd be a bastard to try to pass through if I needed to get out at speed.

"Jack?" I muttered under my breath. "Time to get your arse back here, my son."

I'd summoned him when I'd set off, thinking nothing of it, and Sod's Law, he'd been on the far side of the city at that point. He was nearby, but as I waved Beta and the others back, I decided I'd really rather have him with me in here.

I reached out internally to him, squinting at the mass of metal and bad temper that was squaring off against me, and confirmed that he was only a handful of minutes away. I directed him, silently this time, to enter the building behind the asuras from stealth, and to wait, high up.

If I was attacked, I'd rather have a trump card hidden away, and Jack would be just that.

I blinked, dismissing the connection, and stared at the creature that stomped forward, recognizing the design, if not necessarily the current creature.

It was four-legged, clearly built off the base of the "tank" variant, with the turret removed and just as clearly modified from that point onward. There were two sets of dart throwers, each with huge magazines standing proud. The throwers were mounted on individual swivel heads, and between them, staring at me coldly, was a badly damaged humanoid asuras.

It'd been rebuilt from the waist up, the legs discarded and the two bodies fused together there, creating an impression of a metal man, half reclining into a four-legged chair, with a damn turret on either side of him. The "man" had a shield hand, small and oval, but clearly thick steel, and a sword, or stabbing spear that I recognized as one of ours.

The fucker had taken weapons and...*yup*. I looked the body over, what I could see around the shield it held up between us, and I spotted damaged hoplite armor.

These fuckers had looted my dead.

That put me in a foul mood as I strode forward. The asuras stomped out to meet me, the throwers tracking me and locking in, clearly ready to fire, as I came to a halt a half a dozen meters from them.

"I want to speak to the queen," I called, getting no response. "The asuras queen," I repeated, seeing no reaction. "Fine, fuck you very much!" I stalked forward a few steps, only to have the fucker go on the defensive, firing a warning shot at the floor before me. A single dart glanced off and vanished in a spray of sparks.

"You really want to play like that?" I asked flatly, reaching down inside and letting loose the constraints on my power. Lightning crackled out across my limbs as I lifted into the air, glaring at them, knowing damn well that even if all humans looked alike to them, me being able to fucking fly and command Lightning was going to stand out.

The effect on the asuras was instant, as I'd expected. They did recognize me, after all.

It fucking opened fire.

CHAPTER TWENTY-THREE

I threw myself sideways. A barrage of darts flashed through the air where I'd been a few milli-seconds before, and the damn turrets tracked me. The sound of the magazines being flushed, like I remembered sticking a card in the back wheel of my pedal bike as a kid—a reverberating sound—filled the air.

I bitterly regretted not even considering a fucking shield as two humanoid variants raced forward, leaping up and over the remains of the cars…before the cars suddenly moved!

I landed, hitting the ground and rolling, then shoved myself forward, frantically diving to the left as a fucking hammer—*one of my fucking hammers*—smashed into the pavement where my head had been seconds before.

Landing on my left arm, I shoved back off, heading back the way I'd come. I pushed with the storm as well, crossing the distance in a second, and barely missing the hammer as it rose again.

I grabbed the head of the hammer with my right hand, using it to pivot myself back around to my feet, and dragging the now off-balance humanoid into the path of the tank as it opened fire again. This time the darts hit, pounding into the back and almost passing through the damn chest of the fucker before me.

It started jerking as if it'd gotten its dick stuck in a power socket as dents and pinpoint tenting appeared on the inside of the chestplate.

As close as I was, though, the fucker was going nowhere.

Puffs of blue-white light burst from the asuras as its companion killed it, the humanoid frame shaking.

The second humanoid landed on the far side, staggered slightly. One of its legs ended in a square plate on a ball joint; the other looked like the ball joint had been finished, but never connected.

That made the fucker clatter and stagger as it moved, and with my "shield" sagging as the animating life force left it, I yanked free the hammer from my belt loop, flipping it up and catching it by the haft.

I could hear the running feet of the kobolds, and the roar of Beta as she well and truly lost her shit over me being challenged, making my asshole clench instinctively.

"Definitely a fucking dragon!" I snarled, throwing the hammer at the second humanoid. The head and haft flashed end over end to slam into the fucker.

For the first time, when it was me throwing something, it actually landed right. The head crashed into the middle of its chest and sent it flying; bright light escaped from shattered sections of the body as it fell.

The dart throwers clunked on empty, magazines ejecting as two more slid forward into place. I kicked off, flying through the air to the right as the barrels tracked me. The solid wall of sound as the magazines were flushed again washed over me.

Landing, I cursed as the humanoid shield suddenly collapsed; the arm I'd been holding it by snapped off.

I leapt left, then dove right, ducking my head and hitting the ground, rolling. Darts slammed into the asphalt, ricocheting off in all directions as the cars were dragged back, tightening in around the queen, presumably.

Shoving off, I flashed across the ground between the tank and me. Darts that had been missing now tracked in, and the last dozen punched into me, even as I brought my arms up, crossing them before me.

I hissed in pain as darts punched into my forearm. The twin bones of my left arm snapped under the heavy repeated hits, even as I heard the crash of glass somewhere ahead, as Jack arrived.

Angling down, I slid under the arc of fire before the tank could finish punching the fucking darts into me, flipping around and skidding under the big bastard.

For a split second, I had a second of doubt, remembering that the damn thing was a massive piece of metal. It'd damn well hurt if it dropped onto me…

Then I was punching upward with all the force I could muster. My right fist ripped through the thin metal underbelly as I triggered Storm-Strike.

My mana condensed into a single point, unleashing a horrific burst of damage. The underside of the tank cratered inward and tore like wet tissue paper as the blow landed.

The tank shuddered. My fist sunk deep into the asuras, and for the first time since the fairy had sunk into quiescence, I felt a foreign soul, and it was terrified.

It was angry, no, it was hate-filled, the complex rhythms of personality and memory that I'd felt from the fairy nowhere in evidence as I gasped, feeling the potential as my Soul Forge ability triggered.

I felt it all: the layers upon layers of energy, the compressed soul stuff, whatever it was called, fragments making sense even as my upbringing screamed that what I was doing was wrong.

I felt the soul matrix of another; I felt it shuddering in the split second of its approaching death, and I knew it for what it was. It was a human soul, torn apart, memories cleansed and overwritten with a need to serve the asuras, a determination to protect and serve it, and to feed the fucker more souls.

I felt that matrix already starting to fail, the flickering as strands of energy frayed, too weak to hold together without the mind that should have been its anchor.

The soul was broken, the memories gone, and at most, all that was left behind was an empty shell.

So, I did what I had to do.

I opened my fist, and not knowing how I did it, I pulled inward, a sudden terrible rush of cold energy entering me.

WARNING, SOUL DEVOURER!

Your actions have been identified and reported. The Cinthian Council will be informed of your blasphemy against the immortal souls of your enemies!

I read the notification that flashed up before me, red on black, pulsing warningly, and I dismissed it, uncaring. The Cinthian council could suck my fucking dick as far as I was concerned. And should they come here to make their displeasure known personally?

Well…

I drew the energy of the soul down inside myself. A cool radiance filled me as I stole the energy that had once powered this creature, in its various guises, through life.

Falling to the ground, I gasped, mouth flapping like a fresh landed fish as the power flooded me. Unlike when the fairy bonded her soul to me, and my own soul was torn and weak, I was intact now, and the feeling…

The power that made up a soul poured into me, filling me like a jug half full of water. The excess energy overflowed, and evaporated, even as a sudden great weight fell atop me, pressing me into the ground, holding me pinned there.

The world around me spun and twitched. The ground, literally right before my eyes, suddenly leapt close in ultra-insane HD, then dropped back to a normal distance, seeming to refocus. Then I was staring out of a tunnel at a distant speck of ground, and yet all at once it was the same view.

I felt the pain of the soul, a remnant of memory: fragmented, broken, flapping, and then lost forever. It was like fresh baked bread on the breeze, carried from a far distance, then overridden by another scent, something much closer.

The power that rolled around inside me—was too much, too strong. Pain started to build, and I knew instinctively that it was the half-healed bonds with the fairy. This soul was pressing against them, and the pain…It was dangerous.

This was a mindless soul, something that was driven only by a need to serve the asuras Green Queen. If I tried to absorb it…it might not be me that opened my eyes afterward.

I needed to get rid of it! The energy, the life! All of it. The matrix was unfurling inside me, overlaying my own and…

SOUL FORGE ACTIVE:
Your ability: **[Soul Forge]** has activated. The thrumming energy that you feel is the soul of another, stripped down, all extraneous and impure sections pared away. You have seven seconds to activate the forge and use this soul, before it is absorbed into your body, powering and overlaying your own, granting you the permanent title of **SOUL DEVOURER.**

I grunted, the notification overlaying my vision.

Seven seconds…I had seven…Six seconds! Fuck! Five!

I cast about desperately, seeing nothing I could use. The dead corpse of the fucking tank pressed me into the ground. Four seconds!

I frantically started patting at my pockets, all empty. The belt loop came under my grip, and I snarled that I'd thrown my fucking hammer…Three seconds!

I clenched my fist, feeling a sudden, familiar solid mass on my right hand.

My ring!

I'd had it forever, bought it myself, just liked the style as a young guy, a plain titanium band, simple and yet…

I focused on it, pushing the wave of soul energy that was filling me toward it, blankly.

Target Identified: [Titanium Ring] Confirm?

Yes/No

I spammed "yes," the counter hitting one in my vision and freezing on it as the ring started to pull on the soul. It felt like a plug had been pulled from the bath: the water rushed out of me, pouring down the drain, the vortex dragging it away faster and faster.

Zero.

The soul matrix was dragged into the ring, overlaying a pattern I could suddenly see as I stared at it in shock, the world around me forgotten. Distant fighting rang out as I stared in wonder.

The ring seemed to hover before my eyes; the world around me moved infinitely slowly, as the ring rotated. Three lines flowed around the ring running left to right: one high, one low, and one in the middle, with more sections that were closed off. Dozens of lines ran up and down, creating fractal patterns in the ring, overlaying as I watched, and for a second, I saw more repeating all around it.

Lines radiated outward from stress fractures, from imperfections in the ring itself, and I suddenly realized that the lines, the overlapping dead zones where the lines were tangled, where they were collapsing…it was me!

I was fucking this up!

I was releasing the soul matrix into the ring, which had its own matrix, and shoving them together and sitting back, waiting to see what happened.

I reached out, mentally, and clumsily tried to smooth the lines that overlapped, smearing them instead, feeling the ring's instability growing.

I shifted, gritting my teeth, and pushed hard, feeling the weight on my back as I forced myself up, a mass of steel doing its dead best to hold me in place.

Pushing myself to one knee, hissing with the effort, then shoving the steel aside, I threw myself forward to crash into the ground. I didn't care; the image of the ring before me, with its meshed and smeared lines of power, filled my vision, and every instinct I'd inherited from the dungeon, from the fairy, and everything that was solidly "me" had combined to scream a single warning to me.

Get rid of the fucking ring!

I tried to pull it off, cursing. My gauntlets were in the way. My left arm was almost useless thanks to the goddamn broken bones. My right hand was mostly fine, but Sod's fucking Law—that was the hand the ring was on, of course!

I bit down hard on the gauntlet, fingers flopping, barely useable as I fumbled with the catches, finally managing to get the thing off. I couldn't get the fucking ring off, there was just no way, and…I felt a presence, as Kilo crouched next to me, holding a shield over me and staring into my eyes.

"Help?" he asked, the word slurred but identifiable.

"Fuck yes." I gasped in relief. "The ring!" I shoved that hand forward. "I need it off, and quick!"

He reached out, his stubbly claws clacking on the metal as he tried to pull it off, scrabbling at it clumsily, even as in my vision it pulsed and flashed warningly. He tried again, the ring tight on my finger and barely budging, let alone going over the joint.

"A knife!" I snapped. "Use a knife!"

"Cut?" he tried, head angling to the side on the clear question.

"The finger!" I snapped, waving the hand closer. "Cut the fucking finger off!"

"No cut." He shook his head, a whipping, side-to-side motion as he gestured down at his belt.

I groaned, feeling a sudden spike in heat from the ring, as the unstable energies began to leak. "Run…" I hissed. "It's gonna blow!"

"Blow?"

"Explode!" I hissed. "It'll kill us both! Move!"

He froze, looking from me to the ring, seeing the way it was starting to glow, the way the skin around it was starting to blacken and crisp as I hissed, shaking in pain.

Then he struck.

As a kobold, even an advanced kobold, he had an advantage over any human. He had sharp as shit teeth from the draconic bloodline, and he lunged forward. Teeth snapped shut on the finger, and unfortunately the one right next to it, tearing them free in a single movement, before he spit them out onto the floor, hissing in pain and pawing at his mouth where the leaking heat had burned him.

I grabbed the ring—*heh*—finger between my thumb and forefinger, and stripped the ring off the severed end of the finger, then threw it away, feeling the instabilities building as the ring continued to glow.

It didn't go far, laid half on my back, and using a finger and a thumb, I couldn't get much force behind it, but being the bastard that I am, I managed to get it over the first ring of cars and into the inner circle.

Being the idiot I am, though, I remembered just as I saw it flipping end over end, the ring glinting in the weak mid-afternoon sunlight, that Jack was in there somewhere.

"Jack, run!" I shouted, grabbing my fingers and rolling onto my front as the "ting" of the ring hitting metal rang out.

Then an icy-cold chill enveloped me, as the light dimmed further. I blinked, looking up and seeing Kilo moving his hands as if smoothing the ice that suddenly rose around us. A dome, I realized, sealed to the ground all around us, rising with incredible speed. Blue-tinged light made me grin for a second, then wince as I realized what I needed to do.

I twisted around and pressed the stumps of the two fingers, and the stumps of my fucking hand, against the shield, feeling the frozen surface as I hissed in pain.

I got a few seconds of relief, before having to almost snap myself free of it once it sealed overhead.

I saw at once that the dome was literally sealed solid. The lack of any air holes was about to become a serious problem, as was the rapidly dropping temperature in here.

I was shaking with the cold already, but that could have been shock as well. Staring at the fingers in my hand, I seriously wondered whether it would be better to regrow them or…

BOOM!

Something slammed into the shield, cracking it like an egg. Hundreds of fracture lines spiderwebbed across the outside as Kilo grunted in pain, sagging to his knees and coughing a great gout of blood out.

"Kilo?" I gasped, grabbing at him. The usually blue-tinged scales were blacked with frostbite, and grey with exhaustion.

"I…hold…" Kilo got out, and I grunted, realizing what the daft fucker was doing.

He'd tied the shield to himself, so even now the outside was sealing again. That was great at times, if we were under attack, for example, but not when we were trapped inside the fucking bubble.

"Let it go!" I ordered him, getting a vacant stare from him. "The shield! Release the fucking shield!"

He stared at me for a few more seconds, then seemed to understand, sagging and letting loose a great cloud as he breathed out.

I looked up, seeing that the repairs had stopped, and back at him. He nodded that he had released it. I stood, clenched my fist instinctively and hissed in pain, before switching to my left hand, punching it out and into the shield, triggering Storm-Strike, and again hissing in pain as the jolt ran though me.

The shield shattered through, cascading slivers and slabs of ice falling free to crash into the ground.

I kicked the lower section nearest to me free, stepping out of the shield and staring around, seeing the broken stone, the cars that looked as if they'd been kicked aside by an angry giant…

It wasn't hard to see where the explosion had been. There was a pit in the ground, about a meter deep and three across, and it was fucking glowing.

Cars that had been clearly nearby looked as though they had sections simply cease to exist. Metal that had been left behind, up to the edge of the explosion, glowed cherry-red; splattered molten steel, liquified in a split second and blasted outward, formed streaks on surfaces all around me, and I stared, open-mouthed, in shock.

It wasn't intended as a weapon, but fuck me, if it had been? It would have been a game changer.

A creak sounded from the left, and I spun, seeing a car that had been pushed over shifting, as a humanoid asuras tried to drag itself out from under it.

I growled unthinkingly and reached out, feeling the nearness of the dungeon sense. I strode three meters to the left, summoning a fresh hammer and stomping back toward it.

It looked up at me and reached out, hesitating. It might have been appealing for help. It might have been imploring mercy, or, considering that arm ended in a thrower, it might have been about to try to finish the fight.

I didn't know, and I didn't care.

The hammer smashed into its head, driving it down to bounce off the asphalt. Then a second blow crushed the chest, sending a burst of light escaping on all sides as it lost containment.

I lifted the hammer a third time, and ended it, before stomping around the corner and seeing the fight that had been underway before the explosion.

Jack was back. He'd clearly run when I'd ordered him to, and then returned to help Beta, who stood over the asuras Green Queen, a crossbow pressed to her forehead.

Two of the standard kobolds were dead nearby. One had been torn half apart by a four-armed tank variant with spears built in, and one crushed under a car that had moved at some point.

There were shattered components all around the pair, sections that had been torn free in a burst of fury, if I knew Beta, and she was panting, steam rising from her body.

I had no idea what the hell she'd been doing, but whatever had happened, she'd kicked some arse.

Jack had clearly been in on the fight as well, battered to fuck. Cracks radiated across a lot of his body and at least half a dozen darts were deeply embedded in him, with shatter and scratch patterns suggesting hundreds more had bounced off.

One eye and an ear were missing, and he looked as if he'd been put in a washing machine full of rocks on a spin cycle.

All of this just served to piss me off even more.

I stalked forward, not bothering to stop Beta, deciding that if she fired, it'd just solve the issue for me. Instead, at my approach, she looked up, then nodded, stepping back and moving away from the asuras.

I crouched down next to it, seeing the broken and shattered frame, the damage that had been done.

The queen was half-torn free of what I guessed was her new body, a horseshoe crab shape with multiple arms and dozens of legs, with her new body rearing up from what would have been the face.

She'd stolen anything she could from the Red Queen's corpse, including the remains of her humanoid body. From the chest up, she was mainly the work of art that the Red Queen had been, the glowing red eyes replaced with simple green orbs that seemed to flicker and shine from within. The face was terrible in its robotic beauty, but much of the hair had been discarded. The copper wiring and more showed where Beta had grabbed it and crushed it, dragging her free of the rest of the body.

The waist had been savagely hacked into, and alongside a shattered spear lodged deep into the bigger, main body, was a broken axe.

The blade had been broken in the effort to separate the queen, and I nodded, recognizing again that we needed better fucking weapons.

The legs that jutted out from under the collapsed body were of all designs. Some looked as if they'd been stuck on after being ripped out of the nearest garden, where they'd previously had a washing line strung to them.

Others looked high-tech in nature, like something that should have been carrying out the extermination of mankind for its Skynet overlord.

The queen, though, was laid on the floor, only half connected now, and badly damaged. When she tried to push herself up, clearly planning to try to get back to her main body, Beta hissed a warning, and she hesitated, looking up at me as I squatted nearby.

The eyes of the queen showed no recognition, and no understanding, no curiosity or any other emotion beyond waiting.

I reached out after a long second and laid my still-bleeding right hand on her head, reaching out to her with my mind.

Much as I had before, I felt the swirl of a massive intellect behind those eyes, staring up at me. As soon as I made the connection, my worst fears were realized.

It wasn't that she'd not understood it was me approaching. I'd been worried that was the case, that as a human we all looked too alike for an alien intelligence to tell the difference.

That wasn't it, though.

She'd seen me and recognized me, although how she'd seen me was beyond me. The mélange of images that she shared of my approach showed me in a thousand different spectrums.

No, she'd seen me, and she remembered that I was the Dungeon Lord, and that the dungeon could create life that she could exploit to create an army.

She'd seen me approach and had run the variables. I was with a small force that were numerically inferior to hers, and I was a flesh-and-blood creature of this world. She believed she could defeat me, so she'd gone for it.

Now she believed that I was superior to her and so she would obey...until she decided that I was weak, and then she'd attack again.

It was like I was trying to teach a fucking great white shark to swim alongside and be nice, and I was sticking bigger and bigger bits of bloody meat to my back, wondering when I'd pass the level where I went from uninteresting to lunch.

Fuck that shit.

I remembered the quest. I could form a more permanent alliance with this fucker, and I'd get some bonuses, but was that worth it? Was it worth having a creature that would turn on me as soon as it thought it could win?

I pulled up the screen and re-read the quest as I watched her, half expecting her to try to stab me as soon as I was distracted.

Quest!
Checkmate! (II)

Upon forming a basic alliance with an asuras queen, you have become aware of just who and what they are. They could assist you mightily, or be a terrible scourge upon the face of your planet. Only your actions will decide this.

Form a more permanent alliance with the asuras queen to complete this quest and receive the following bonuses:

- +3 to top three Attributes
- +1 Class Skill point to allocate

Additional forces (Access to)

- 10,000 XP

The plus three to my top attributes was a nice bonus, as was the class skill point. The ten thousand Experience was tempting as well, but it was the additional forces that got me.

I couldn't trust her to obey and so...I paused. Thinking.

It didn't say we had to be friends. It didn't say anything about her being free to roam or to do whatever she wanted.

I didn't like it, but the way this was laying it all out was that she could be useful, and could create additional forces for us. But whatever I did, I sure as shit couldn't trust her.

This whole thing felt alien to me, but as long as I didn't kill her right now, I'd still get the bonuses, right? Then I could plot things out a bit more...

"You serve me," I said aloud, projecting into her mind a binary choice set. She served me in every way, as a slave in all but name—which I utterly hated, but considering she'd just tried to kill me, I didn't see a way around—or I would kill her now.

The binary choice was clear, and I presented it to her with a solid walled intention. Making it clear there was no room to negotiate.

She still tried, offering terms that, as near as I could tell, involved me providing her with victims to turn into her new supporters.

I refused, repeating the same serve or die option, then sending her an image of me destroying her in a massive nuclear-seeming explosion.

I very carefully didn't include in the threat that the image I'd used was from a movie I'd watched just before the fall. Instead, I projected that it was what I'd do to her if need be.

The image of destruction, of a city being destroyed, had the desired effect, combined with her having seen me flying and throwing around lightning, as well as recently blowing up a section of her defenses.

I made the point that this was because she'd attacked me, and got a strange image back, something to do with one of her asuras drones, but she accepted it, and I nodded, relieved.

Standing up, I moved back, gesturing for the others to do the same, as the queen slowly pushed herself backward. Several of the manipulator arms reached down and grabbed onto her body, lifting her back up onto the crab shape.

As soon as she nodded her head, additional arms reached out to the other corpses around her—the robotic ones, anyway—and pulled them back in.

I didn't trust her, not even fucking slightly, but she'd accepted that she would serve me—for now—and that seemed to satisfy the quest prompt.

Quest Complete!
Checkmate! (II)

You have come to a more permanent agreement with the Asuras Green Queen. She will serve you in any way she can for the next [30] solar rotations, at which time, all agreements must be renegotiated.

You have completed this quest and receive the following bonuses:

- +3 to top three Attributes

- +1 Class Skill point to allocate

Additional forces (Access to)

- 10,000 XP

CHAPTER TWENTY-FOUR

I grinned despite myself, then shifted my hand and winced. The fucking pain was unreal. Looking down, I grimaced, then backed away farther from the asuras, and slid into the dungeon sense, finding Kelly waiting, as I knew I would.

"What the absolute fuck just happened?" she asked grimly. "Are you okay? Your poor hand!"

"I'll be fine," I assured her, focusing and pressing the fingers to the bloody stumps, hissing in pain, but circulating my Lightning mana through my body and really hoping that it'd damn well work to fix them.

They were a bit shorter than they should be as well, considering that sections were cleaved through by Kilo's teeth.

"I've already sent Jo to you," Kelly assured me. "Chris and Patrick are with her."

"Oh, thank fuck," I muttered.

"So, what happened?"

"Basically, something happened with one of her drones, I got that much. She lost one, not sure when or how, but that changed things for her. She's even less trusting than before, and is only willing to not attack on the grounds that we'd win. As soon as she's strong enough? She'll attack us again."

"Then kill her now," Kelly said firmly. "Better to end this before she gets any stronger."

"I was thinking that," I admitted. "But then I remembered I had a quest to fucking make a deal with her, and that she could help us. I gave her a choice. Serve me or die, that was it. She tried negotiating, and I sent her a mental image of a nuke going off, from a movie I watched right before the fall, and said that was what would happen if she fucked with me."

"Did she believe you?"

"Oh, she believed me." I chuckled. "I scared the shit out of her."

"So now what?" she asked, and I sent her a mental image of me shrugging.

"I'll head on to the park, meet with Barry and try to recruit some fighters, ask for a couple hundred to join us tomorrow, then head back and we'll have our date." I forced a smile.

"Are you sure that—"

"I am," I said. "Honestly, Kelly, if we wait to have a date when everything is perfect? Or you know, when nothing is going on at least? It'll never happen."

"Okay," she agreed, sending me a ghost of a kiss on the cheek. "What do we do with the queen?"

"We can't trust her," I said. "For now, we contain her, and we plan. I want you to spread out the influence of the dungeon around her, then form some stone walls, thick ones, all around her. Give her enough room to work on herself, and push in the bodies of the dead asuras. She's been creating new ones somehow. We know that she needs souls for that, so regardless of our little falling-out, she's been hunting the local area. If it turns out that she's been killing humans? The deal is off."

"We kill her?" Kelly asked.

"Fuck yes," I growled. "I'd hoped after we saved her, we could make a deal and learn from her, have her act as a friend with her species. Maybe get them to calm the fuck down and stop making stars go nova. Or, failing that, send them to meet the orcs, use their worlds."

"Not much chance of that, though," Kelly said, and I agreed.

"You're right," I said. "Fuck it, though. All we can do is the best we can do at the time. Is there anything else?"

"No," Kelly said sadly. "I'll seal her away for now, and hopefully we can come up with a plan soon."

"Works for me," I said, before reaching out to her with a sigh. "You know, every time it gets better, something gets fucking worse. I'd thought she was ready to make a deal. Hell, I was going to make sure she kept her end of the deal after she fucking hid and let us die to protect her. Now I know I should have fed the bitch to the Red Queen."

"We'd have lost the dungeon," Kelly said gently. "If we'd done that, she'd have attacked you next, and you know it."

"I do, but still," I grumbled. "Anyway, I'll talk to you soon, my love."

A second ghost kiss on my cheek, and then she was gone, and I was straightening up, glaring around as I tried to flex my fingers, hope springing eternal.

My forefinger and pinky flexed no issue. The other two just lay there, still gripped in my hand and pressed into place. I could feel the Lightning working to seal the wounds, and I moved on, holding the fingers there, even as Kilo limped up, holding my hammer out with a grin.

"Oh, thank fuck," I muttered. "Can you put it in for me please?" I asked, twisting and offering my hip.

He nodded, sliding the hammer into the belt loop, even as Beta stepped in close and examined me, cocking her head to one side in question. Clearly she was still happier with non-verbal communication.

"I'm all right," I assured her. "Are you?"

"Tired," she admitted, with Kilo nodding fervently.

"I know. Me, too." I stood straighter, forcing my shoulders back and twisted at the hip, feeling clicks in my back as the healing power of my Lightning went to work.

I'd been channeling it at a low level, not wanting to exhaust it, but also not wanting my goddamn fingers to stay as they were. As such, I was down to a third of my mana, and I was seriously starting to worry I'd have to stop soon, so I had mana should we be attacked.

The bodies of the kobold dead began to vanish, and I sighed, moving out with Beta and Kilo, glad that they, at least, had survived.

The next half an hour was taken up by us walking the remaining distance to the park, and Jo, Chris, and Patrick catching up.

Jo took one look at my fingers and shook her head, declaring them fucked. I apparently had done more damage than I thought, and the magic that was healing them wasn't working the way I wanted. It was healing the broken fragments of bone, flesh, and so on, but it wasn't regrowing the connective tissue.

As such, when Barry found us—we'd headed to the canteen and taken a table, asking a nearby guard to find him and bring him—Jo was already hard at work.

Barry walked in to find Kilo and Beta fully healed, as Jo had done them straightaway, me biting down hard on a wooden section Chris had torn off a nearby chair, as Jo took a knife and carved the mis-healed flesh free.

An hour later, Barry was on board with the recruitment plan, people were gathering for me to talk to them, and Jo was giving me a highly in-depth explanation as to why my goddamn healing had gone so wrong.

Most of it involved cell death, nerve clusters, and something to do with axons, t-cells, and the analogous myelinating glial cells. I asked if I was going to become a zombie, and she just glared at me for some reason.

Moving back outside into the early evening, I winced at the frost that was starting to sparkle everywhere, despite the almost festive air that was building here, only added to by the dozens of braziers and torches that burned around the mass of people, radiating some heat that caused people to huddle in closer together in excitement.

Apparently, the Dungeon Lord coming to visit was starting to become a big thing, which was a bit weird.

"Look…all I'm saying, is if you want to really make an impression, and you want to get a load of recruits?" Barry whispered to me as I was gearing myself up to talk.

"Yeah?" I glanced at him.

"Make a show of it," he hissed. "Show them something, some power…fly or something. Show them you're not just another man, that you're more."

"I am just—"

"Don't be so fucking stupid," he snapped. "You're a god and you're our Dungeon Lord. Use that!"

I glared at him, seeing absolutely no repentance in his eyes, and I growled to myself, and stalked forward.

Kelly had arranged a platform for me, and I shook my head in annoyance. She was clearly on Barry's side with this, considering she'd made it ten foot up, three meters on a side and square to give me some room, but she'd also made it without any steps or anything leading up to it.

I circulated my mana. My armor twitched, and the various scuffs, nicks, and dirt fell away from it, as my cloak—that I'd "accidentally" left behind—mysteriously regrew, falling down my back as I lifted into the air.

The crowd went silent as I floated upward, a ripple flowing out as I came into sight. I forced a smile, waving to kids that sat on their parents shoulders.

The cheer that Barry started made me cringe inwardly—it was so fucking fake-sounding—but as it spread, more and more people joining in, it went from fake to enthusiastic, and some of the butterflies in my stomach settled down.

As I alighted gently on the platform, I lifted my arms, and the crowd fell silent.

I hesitated, not sure how to begin, then I snorted.

"You know…" I called out in as strong and clear a voice as I could. "It's easier to go into battle than it is to start these damn speeches!"

That got a few laughs.

"Seriously!" I continued. "I can stand up here, and I can tell you the way things are. I can tell you about the mage's tower, literally a huge tower that will grow in size in the days and months to come. A place that we hope will become a home for magical learning for all of our people.

"I spread the word about the tower already, as best I could, and that's not the main reason I'm here, but let's start with that." I smiled. "Since the fall, some of us developed abilities, powers that seem godlike to most of us. Hell, the system that we all seem to be linked in, literally refers to me as a god, which is kinda weird, I have to say.

"Both for me personally, and I have to assume, for all of you, especially anyone with a religious mind, although I have to admit, my girlfriend quite likes the changes that came with godhood."

I grinned as I went on, a few more laughs and a bit of "nudge-nudge, wink-wink" spreading through the crowd. I felt better, relaxing a little, until I saw Barry facepalming, as well as Jo and Patrick. Most worrying of all was that Chris grinned in approval.

"Anyway!" I said quickly. "One of the changes that happened, was that magic, something many of us had believed was bullshit, turned out to be real."

That got some more attention.

"You've all seen it by now, I'm sure," I called, lifting my right hand and grinning at the way my fingers all worked again, even as lightning crackled between my fingers, bringing light to the night beyond the smoky torches that Barry had thoughtfully provided.

"What you might not have realized is that magic can be taught," I said clearly, even as I lifted into the air, rotating slowly while lifting both hands, filling them with lightning.

"It's not for everyone. And that's not a case of only our favorites get picked, believe me. It's a case of some of you will have high affinities for certain things. Some, like your own Dante, who's become a powerful pyromancer, were naturally high in Fire magic. Now, to find out about the affinities, I want you to pull up your stats, and look to the side. Mentally reach to the left and pull, while you concentrate on the word 'affinity'…" I called, spending the next minute or so walking them all through it.

"What you'll see here is a result of who you are. Some of you will have a lot of minuses. Others will be all low in numbers. This is no bad thing. You can see what you are naturally predisposed toward here. Some of those who are in training at the minute, for example, have minuses against Fire. They've been warned that because of who and what they are, they receive more damage from Fire than most of us."

I looked around, seeing the confusion on some faces, and I went on.

"Think of it this way. Some of us always got ill, right? Any bug that was going around, any virus, you caught it, or your cousin or brother did, no matter what happened—they were just predisposed to catch everything, right?"

A round of nods met that.

"Well, this is the same. These are showing who you are, and how powerful you could be. It's possible to increase these figures as well. Some choices you make will affect it; for others, class quests and rewards will let you choose to increase your affinities. You can choose to increase an affinity that you already have a high number for, or you can improve a weakness. I've done both, and will continue to do so.

"Now, does anyone here have anything over a hundred?" I asked, not expecting an answer. But as I opened my mouth to assure people that I'd not expected it…a young woman near one of the braziers tentatively lifted her right hand.

"You do?" I asked, and she nodded, face crimson. "That's wonderful!" I called, genuinely pleased, and smiling at her. "What is it?"

"A…a hundred and four…" she admitted, nervously. "For Sand?"

"Sand?" I asked, and she nodded again, looking ashamed. "That's fantastic!" I grinned. "Honestly, I've no clue what that means you can do, but considering my own Lightning is over a hundred, and that means that I can heal myself with it? It's wonderful news! Please, would you like to learn magic?"

"Yes!" She gasped, nodding.

"Then tomorrow you start your first lessons!" I declared. "We'll talk after this, but don't be nervous!" I smiled at her, noting that Jo was already pushing through the crowd toward her, and I turned to look around the rest of the crowd. "Anyone else?"

Silence rang out, and I chuckled. "Honestly, don't worry!" I said. "I certainly didn't expect to meet anyone with a natural affinity over a hundred. So, does anyone had an affinity between seventy-five and a hundred?"

Three more held up their hands, and I nodded, pointing to each, one at a time, meeting two men and a woman, with variously ninety-two in Clay, eighty-seven in Nature, and seventy-six in Phantom.

That last was a thin, almost skeletal woman who looked terrified as she admitted to it. People drew back from her immediately, and I spoke up quickly.

"I don't know exactly what that is, but it could mean anything from speaking to the dead, to being able to hide from people, so don't worry. These powers in and of themselves are totally neutral. What is good or evil is how we use them. Would you like to learn to use your powers?"

She nodded, looking terrified, and I smiled.

"Then you're welcome in my classes. Please, each of you, move to where Barry stands there—we'll talk after this." I noted how a path opened for her in ways that it didn't for the guys who could wield Clay or Nature.

"Well, that's fucking marvelous." I grinned. "Moving on, is there anyone with an affinity that's in the sixty to seventy-four range?"

There were more than a dozen, and I nodded.

"All of you are welcome in my classes—in fact, all of you are, should you choose to help out there, but…and I need to make this clear…there is no guarantee that I can help you unlock your powers."

I looked around the silent crowd.

"All I can do is teach you, and if you have the ability, then it's down to you. This is only part of it, though, and again, you must understand this. I don't want to fight. I don't want to risk my life, day in and day out—hell, an hour ago, or so, I was regrowing fingers I'd had bitten off."

I held up my hand to show everyone, wiggling my fingers to demonstrate that they worked fine.

"That's the simple truth. I lost two fingers and Jo, our resident healer, grew them back for me. I didn't know if she could do it, but she managed, and I'm bloody glad she did. I went into that fight knowing I could die, and just as I did then, I'll fight again soon."

I saw the looks on people's faces: the fear on some, and the determination on others.

"I fight most days, and I stand alongside the bravest men and women I've ever met. I literally lose friends on a daily basis, and I hate it, but I go out and do it again the next day. I do it so that those who can't fight are safe. I do it so that our friends, our families, and our children can live and be safe.

"Some of you have already volunteered, and hopefully others will as well. Some of you have already lost loved ones who fought by my side, and I'm sorry for that. As we grow stronger, so too do our enemies. We lose battles sometimes, and as much as I'd love to lie to you all, to promise that if you join me now, you'll rise to power, and live forever? I won't do that."

I started to pace, moving around the platform and looking out to the people below.

"The truth is, that for every mage or healer, we need fighters. We need the brave men and women who stand between them and our enemies, and hold the line. One of our mages can literally call down meteors from space. A section of land that she designates is destroyed, and almost anything in it is killed. I say almost, because some enemies managed to survive ten fucking meteors from space, and after she's cast that spell? She's broken, and needs time to recover.

"While she's doing that, we step in. We stand between the enemy and her. I can't do that—that spell, I mean. I have others, some of which are horrifically powerful, but I'm no mage." I stopped then, looking around the silent crowds.

"I'm a Dungeon Lord, and a fighter. Hell, my partner Kelly? The blonde woman I'm usually with? She's the Dungeon Mistress and the Mistress of Minions. She can guide the creatures of the dungeon far better than I can, and so I have her do that as well. I make the final decisions with the dungeon, but when we go to war, I'm on the front line."

I looked around again, seeing the expressions on some of the faces, as they glanced after the people who'd been picked out as mages, and then back up at me.

"For every mage who learns their craft, we need fighters to stand with them in a team. We need heroes, I suppose is more accurate. After all, fighting on the front line is a hell of a lot more terrifying than standing behind it. That's why I'm here. We have less than sixty fighters. We've lost brave men and women. Some have moved on and have become diplomats. Others are learning magic. But many died.

"That's why I'm here now," I repeated grimly. "We've learned a lot, and developed new methods, as well as better technology. We've got better armor, weapons, and allies, and for the first time, in the next few days—I hope—we'll have our own rifles, prototype rail guns.

"We'll have weapons that are the equal, and soon far more powerful than the best that we had before the fall, but they're useless. All of them are utterly worthless, without you.

"The guns can't shoot themselves; the shields can't hold themselves over a frightened child, nor rescue a family. We'll be expanding soon, I hope. I'll be leading a team to fight the gangs to the south and the east, bringing more land under our control. We'll free their prisoners and give them a home too. We'll rescue people and bring them back, but I can't do that without you.

"I need volunteers," I called out. "I need two hundred men and women, the bravest and strongest amongst you. I need you to come to the dungeon, and train with me, to learn to use the weapons and armor I give you, and to learn to fight alongside our allies."

I gestured to Beta and Kilo. They both stood tall and proud.

"They are some of the bravest men and women I've ever met. Beta has been with me since before this was more than a handful of families. Kilo is a cryomancer, and he's saved my life more times than I care to count, including today. They're not just creatures of the dungeon; they have souls, and they're our allies.

"The reason I need two hundred of you?" I called out, turning around, seeing the thousand plus who gathered there silently, watching me.

"It's because we'll be training an army. You'll be training around the clock. You'll be like me, or as close as you can come, physically."

I paused then, flipping latches on my armor and unzipping sections, until I was stripped to the waist, standing before them all.

I saw the looks of shock on many of their faces, the belief that I wasn't that big really, that it was all the armor that made so I towered over them. Now, stripped to the waist, that argument was proved wrong.

"We'll use magic to heal you between workouts, and train you around the clock. You'll be pushed harder and made to go further than any army in the history of our species. Your training will make the Spartans of the past pale into insignificance. Because we need heroes!"

I roared that at them, as I turned, holding my hands to the sides as I looked over the faces that stared up at me.

"We need heroes, because this? The fall? It wasn't something that 'happened.' *IT WAS DONE TO US.*"

I saw the difference those words had on the faces around me as people thought about the loved ones they'd lost.

"The people that did this? The *aliens*? The Cinthians. They didn't do it for shits and giggles, either. No, they did this, because the Orcan are coming. A race of genetically and mentally advanced, war-loving orcs that are literally clearing the galaxy of every form of life that isn't theirs. And make no mistake, they're coming *here*.

"If we're not ready? They'll tear their way through, and they'll kill us all. We're working on technology, not because we want an easier life, no, and not because we want the old world back. We're working on this tech, because we're getting ready for a war! We're training the future leaders of our armies. You'll be taught to fight with a spear, a rifle, and a blade, with magic and fucking teeth and nails. We'll push you harder than anyone has ever pushed you before, and then we'll heal you and throw you back in. I'm asking for you now, because you need to level, you need to grow, and you need to understand that no matter what happens, soon, we'll all be in a war for survival.

"The difference, I think, is that those who train, and learn, those who grow and level, will have a much better chance of winning and surviving.

"We'll be making ships, space fighters, and more soon. We'll develop fucking rifles that can hit them in space, and our mages will scour them from existence. As we claim more land, we'll recruit again and again, both because some of you will die, and because we need the forces.

"We don't know how many of them there are. There might be ten thousand or ten trillion. I don't give a shit, and neither should you. All that matters is that there's a fuckload of them coming, and there's no where we can run. We have to fight them, all of them. We'll beat the fuckers back, and then we'll go after the fucking Cinthians, and teach them that nobody fucks with humanity. Not twice, anyway!

"I need *you*. I need volunteers to come and fight, to learn and to train the next generation…" I dropped my arms to my sides and looked out across the silent crowd. "I'm here to ask for heroes to fight by my side. To learn to wield the powers I have, and more. Are there any heroes here?"

Silence.

I'd hoped for a cheer, at least, or for a voice to call out that they were a hero, or they would be.

Instead, I got utter silence for a long collection of heartbeats, then a single hand rose.

It was a young man, skinny enough that I practically could have used him for a toothpick, as he lifted a hand higher that shook in terror.

"Can you use me?" His voice cracked, clearly terrified.

"Use you?" I asked.

"Can I join?" he clarified. "I'm weak, and I'm afraid…but can you make me into a hero?"

"As brave as you are right now?" I nodded. "To stand there and hold your hand up, to volunteer when nobody else will? Hell yes I can use you. I can teach you to fight, and to win. But to be a hero? That's inside you already, lad!"

"And me?" another voice called out, and I turned to see a woman pushing forward, mid to late forties, and with the clear marks of grief on her face. "I lost my kids…Can you make use of an older woman like me?"

"Sarah, one of my fiercest fighters, is older than you, and she'd kick my arse three times over if I dared turn you away. Hell yes I can use you!"

"And me!"

"Me!"

"I volunteer!"

The voices sprang up, coming quick and fast. Like a dam that had burst, the voices rose, and soon I relaxed. I knew that some of these wouldn't come. Not really. They'd been swept up in the moment. They'd seen their friends volunteering, and they'd gone along with it. But some of them? The iron core, like that kid who had asked first. They'd come, and I could see literally hundreds of them clamoring to join us.

"Tomorrow!" I bellowed, and the voices dropped momentarily. "Tonight, celebrate the heroes amongst you, and tomorrow I need them to come to the dungeon! I'll send a team to escort them at first light, so be ready, and cheer them off!"

The shouts rose again, and I turned, leaping from the platform, and landing lightly next to Barry.

"Fucking hell!" Barry grunted, shaking his head. "You've gutted my damn settlement!"

"Nah, a load will back out between now and then," I said pessimistically. "You'll see."

"Doubt it," Barry muttered, escorting me and my team, as well as the mage hopefuls through the cheering throngs, and to the Gothic mansion at the heart of the park.

We got inside, and Barry took us to a large meeting room, letting us all find somewhere to sit, before sitting himself.

"Well, I'll be honest, I didn't expect to find four of you with this much natural affinity straight off," I admitted, smiling at the small group who sat nervously watching me. "I'm damn pleased, though."

"Can you really teach us magic?" one of them asked.

"I can. For you especially." I nodded toward the man with a high affinity for Nature magic. "Chris, what's your affinity?" I asked my friend.

"Less than his," he admitted, even if he didn't say what it was.

"Well, there you go." I sighed, sitting forward and leaning my forearms on the table. "Look, I can artificially uplift you all, and make you mages. Basically, if I give you a focal orb to cast spells through repeatedly, then when you reach your next class choice, you'll be offered a magical class, or so we believe. That's what we've found so far.

"We can do that, but I don't want to, because the only one of you here who has a class that would be served by that is you," I said to the man with the high Nature affinity.

"Using the focal orb will teach you a spell that I put into it," Chris said, taking over. "The problem is that unless you have a high enough affinity for the spell in the orb, it'll injure you."

"And even if you have a high affinity to it, if, for example, it's Fire?" Jo added, her gaze going from face to face. "Then you'd be offered a Fire class."

"Far better that we teach you to access your magic and understand it first. There's going to be a lot of meditation over the next few weeks for you, and then, if need be, you'll accompany a team of fighters into the training dungeon. You'll gain Experience there, even if it's just throwing rocks at the enemy. Once you reach your class choice naturally? You should be offered a choice of several classes.

"We believe that you'll be offered a magical class that's appropriate to you then, so each of your affinities will result in a specialized magic class. That class, being the one that you're naturally gifted in, will be a much better path to power than us artificially boosting you by giving you all Thunderbolt or something," I finished, looking at them all.

"I'd like you to start lessons in the mage's tower tomorrow, but as the others have all had two days' worth of meditation lessons and explanations, would you like to return with us now? Then you can meet some of the other students, and I can ask one of the other mages to bring you up to date?"

"Are we allowed?" the Phantom mage asked, and I grinned.

"I know the Dungeon Lord," I whispered. "I'll put in a good word for you."

"What about our families?" another asked. "I've a wife and two sons…"

"Bring them," I offered with a smile. "You don't have to, but I'd recommend you move to the dungeon until you've learned enough to protect yourself at least. I don't want you to get killed by an opportunist goblin on the way to school one day!"

"Thank you." The man sagged in relief.

"Okay, can you all gather up those you're bringing in, say, half an hour?" I asked. "I don't mind immediate family, but please, no second cousins twice removed and shit." I looked at them all, making the point and getting nods. "Great, then I'll see you in half an hour."

They left quickly, talking excitedly, and I settled back with a groan, rubbing at my face.

"You did well," Barry said gruffly, and I looked at him, quirking an eyebrow in question. "I mean it. You got a lot of people fired up. You'd be better off leading them all there now, don't give them time to get talked out of it by friends and family, but I take it you'll be letting them come back here?"

"Shit." I groaned. "No, they'll need to be there. If they're to go through the full healing and training plan, they'll need to be living in the dungeon. I should have made that clear."

"You'll get more volunteers." Barry grunted, pushing back his chair and standing. "Same terms? They can bring immediate family only?"

"Aye," I agreed. "Wonder how many rooms we've got available, though?"

"You'll need a thousand." Barry headed for the door.

"A *thousand*?" I squeaked.

"At least." He paused in the doorway and looked back, seeming to struggle with the words before just coming out with it.

"Look. I know the dungeon is the heart of the settlement, and here we'll always be a secondary concern, but…"

"No, Barry, we're all one settlement," I said quickly.

"You're training all the forces there," he pointed out. "You've got giant outdoor pools and shining marble government buildings. Here we've got the homes for most people, and we can smash the houses up. There you train mages and heroes; here we break houses down. It's basically not far off a penal colony—" He held a hand up as I started to speak.

"And that's fine!" he said. "We understand, and it's fine *for now*. But you need to look at that for the future. It can't all be the good shit there and here as the colony and second-class citizens. People will get pissed and quit, or rebel." With that he left the room, and we were left looking at one another.

"He's got a point," Chris said after a few seconds.

"I know," I muttered. "But what the hell do we do about it?"

"Make it into a manufacturing center and paradise," Jo suggested.

"What?" I asked, confused, those two generally not being associated in my mind.

"Make this place into a paradise." She gestured around. "The park is big enough. Start making improvements…a pool, restaurants, bigger apartments—hell, anything you want! You want this to be the workers' home? You want people who are the fighters and mages to be in the main dungeon area? Then you need to make this a better place for their families to be. You need to make it so that the people left here know they're valued."

"Fuck's sake," I muttered, dropping my face into my hands. "This shit never happens in the stories…"

"That's because they're stories." Patrick grunted. "You want people to keep supporting us? Give them some luxuries. The way the world is right now, ninety-nine percent would stab their granny to get in here, I've no doubt, but you want people to be happy? They need more than safety. They need to feel valued. If they can't be fighters or mages, they need to know they have a purpose."

"You said a manufactory?" I asked Jo, glancing over at her.

"You want the fighters and mages?" she asked me, then shrugged. "Then send the crafters here. Give them more space. And they're more likely to recruit additional people from here as well."

"Whoa…" Patrick sat up straighter and shook his head. "What about Finn and me?"

"What about you?" Jo asked seriously, sitting forward. "I'm not looking for a fight, but of everyone, Patrick, you can travel back and forth safely, and Finn and the others wouldn't have to live here if they didn't want to. You could escort him, and others, on a morning and a night. Hell, you could use it as a training exercise with some of the fighters!"

"What about research?" he suggested, getting a look from the rest of us.

"They're in the Parthenon," I pointed out. "I'm not building a new section just to even things out more."

"But—" Patrick complained.

"We'll talk about it later," I said firmly. "This is just an idea. Maybe this would be the best place for the beast tamers, and some of the manufacturing, but not all of it. We don't need a fuckload of it anyway. It's training and practicing for most of the crafters and—"

"And they need access to the research systems," Patrick said quickly. "Look, I get it…you want to spread stuff out, but instead of that? What if we looked into what Jo suggested and make any bigger manufacturing sites we need, like for vehicles, here, and make a fuckload of the luxuries here as well? Improve on things like the defenses, and see what we can do?"

I nodded, more to shut him up than agreeing. We did indeed need to fix something here, but equally, I could understand Patrick's point of view. I'd not want to have to travel here every day just because others might be in a huff otherwise.

I changed the subject, and for the next fifteen or twenty minutes, we talked general rubbish, joking about our lives and past, talking about where we'd include next and more.

When Barry stomped back in and grunted that we'd be ready to leave in an hour, I thanked him and kept my mouth shut, settling back and bringing up the dungeon sense, reaching out to Kelly.

"Hey my love," I said, sending her a ghostly kiss and getting a groan from her.

"You better not be trying to cancel our date," she said grimly, making me snort in laughter.

"No, don't worry, and I'd not forgotten about it either," I lied.

"Okay then," she grumbled. "What's up?"

"How's the dungeon doing for mana?" I asked casually.

"You can see it perfectly well," she growled. "Why?"

"Barry suggested we bring the fighters back to the dungeon tonight, and I realized that we need to have them there with us or the healers won't be able to work on them."

"Shit, I never even thought about that!"

"Me neither," I admitted.

"And it's how many?" she asked. "Two hundred?"

"Uhhh, two seconds…I'll check with Barry." I rose out of the dungeon sense and turned to him.

As soon as he saw the look on my face, he laughed and spoke up.

"Four hundred and eleven fighters, with another seven hundred and eighty-six dependents and family members."

"Fuck," I muttered. "That's…going to be a problem."

"Glad it's yours, not mine." Barry grinned evilly.

"Wow, thanks, pal. I'll remember that."

Sinking into the dungeon sense, I reached out to Kelly quickly. "Ah, darling…"

"I'm not toast, don't fucking butter me up," she growled.

"Fair enough. Bite the pillow and brace yourself," I said, changing tack. "Eleven hundred and ninety-seven people. Four hundred and eleven of which are fighter volunteers, and the rest their dependents."

"That's…that's…fuck!" Kelly groaned. "We can't do it. It's just too much. There's only so much room!"

"That's not what you normally say. Usually it's just 'pass the lube,'" I joked, getting a very cold and grim feeling from her. "Uhhh, you know what? I think Barry needs a hand to get people organized. I trust you. You're amazing, and you've got this, right? Right. Feel free to use any of the crystals, that's what they're for. See you soon, my love!" I deliberately ignored the fact I was pretty damn sure the crystals had been used in the construction of the giant-ass gym.

I left the dungeon sense fast, and sat upright. "I've handed it over to Kelly to sort, so unless you all want to be dragged into solving this, we need to look busy as fuck, and fast," I explained quickly.

"Follow me!" Barry barked, leaping up and running for the door.

We moved as one, chairs falling over as we all sprinted for the door as well.

"There's a fuckload of people we need to get sorted out, to make sure they're safe as you march…"

"We," I said.

"Fuck, fine! I'll get a team together," Barry growled, turning as he went down the stairs and glaring up at me. "You better be ready with some magical shit, though. The fliers pass round and round all night, but we've never given them a reason like this to come for dinner…"

"Damn," I growled, having forgotten about the fliers.

We'd seen them a few days back, but the park had been aware of them for a while. Some flying beasts had, when the park was first established, attacked several times, swooping in and taking lone people, leaving behind scattered shoes and blood splatters as the only evidence.

Barry had approached the problem in typical, no shits given, methodical and logic-driven methods.

They asked for a volunteer, and had them sleep out in the open, seemingly all alone.

Then they hid a dozen men with sharpened sticks, knives, and occasional guns in a ring around them, and waited.

The fliers that landed didn't take off again, and clearly word passed that the park was not to be fucked with.

We hadn't even seen the fliers at the dungeon yet, and we weren't sure whether that was because they hadn't seen us, or whether they'd considered us not worth it, as most of our people were generally indoors and we had a smaller population than the park.

There was also the fact that we had more forces and kept slaughtering everyone that fucked with us. But we'd not met these fuckers properly, so if they were intelligent enough to be watching and planning, then it might also be that they were intelligent enough to decide that they didn't want to fuck with the dungeon.

I looked at my mana, then groaned, seeing how much of it I'd used earlier and in my flying stunts.

"I'm going to let you all sort this out," I said suddenly, stepping aside on the balcony of the stairs, getting frowns from the others. "If I'm going to have to fly a lot, I need to meditate and get as much of my mana back as I can," I clarified. "I'm not dodging work."

"Ah, it's okay." Jo nodded. "It makes sense. I'll come get you when we're ready."

"Thank you." I nodded and hurried back up the stairs. I needed to be meditating before Kelly found me; that way, it was unreasonable to interrupt me, as I needed my mana. If I wasn't busy, though? I was fair game. I know how this worked…I'd been in relationships before.

Rushing back into the room, I threw myself into a chair, and almost fell out of the far side as four of the castors it was on rolled traitorously across the floor. The last one stopped me, having decided, as these things did, that unlike its brethren, it wasn't going to roll at all.

I managed to catch myself, then sank into my mana stream as fast as I could, surging along the river of mana and rapidly finding the broken gate I'd been working on before.

"Right, you fucker," I growled to myself, submerging myself and hefting the mass quickly, starting to rebuild.

CHAPTER TWENTY-FIVE

As soon as the next gate was finished, I forced myself to stop, rather than moving onto the next. Instead, I took the time to pull up my outstanding quest rewards. I'd had three sets of three stat points that were due to take effect, as well as two class skill points to assign, and…I'd earned some experience for the fight with the green queen, after all.

Congratulations!

You have reached Level 26.

Current XP to next level stands at 6,053/50,000

You have 9 unspent Stat Points and 11 unspent Skill Points

Nine points were available, and that was on top of the nine points I'd gained thanks to the quest. Sure, they weren't assigned by me consciously, but looking over where they'd been added, I wasn't complaining. Three were added into my Charisma, presumably due to my threatening and convincing the asuras that it was in mortal danger.

Another three were put into Agility, for the dodging and running around, I'd guess, and the final three went into Intelligence, presumably for realizing what was coming with the ring, but it was probably a fifty-fifty if that should have been Luck instead.

I stared in disbelief at my mana, recognizing that with this latest addition, I was truly getting into dangerous territory.

I could feel the disconnect between my body and my mind, and I hissed in pain at that. Moving seemed to blur the world; details on the tens of thousands of items, of general crap that was in sight? Everything from the windowsill to the glass, to the latch and screws, all screamed at me, while remaining stubbornly blurry.

It was beginning, I knew.

I dragged the stats list back up and stared at it. Nine points I had, nine points that could make a massive difference.

The biggest gulf between the points was Charisma to Intelligence, with Charisma being at thirty-one, and Intelligence at sixty-one. They were literally thirty points adrift. I didn't think that mattered, not Charisma in that way, but the others?

Perception wasn't much better at thirty-seven. I could improve my Strength, which was at thirty-eight, and presumably most of the other physical stats through training. Running and assault courses for Agility for example, but Perception?

It was going to be the slowest to grow, as was Charisma, but fuck it, Charisma made it harder or easier to convince people of things, and although, yeah, okay, I needed that, I was steadily increasing that through giving speeches and shit. I could see the way the counter was clicking up each time I did one.

No, I needed to improve my Perception and…Dexterity, I decided.

I put five points into Perception, and four into Dexterity, hissing as the changes took hold. Perception wasn't just my eyes; it covered hearing, touch, smell…everything. It was all tied into a single stat that was all about how I assimilated and made use of the various senses. This time, though? Those five points really did make a damn difference to my eyes.

It felt like someone was rooting around in there with pins, stabbing them and carving new channels. It stopped after thirty seconds or so, but fuck me sideways!

Dexterity, I couldn't really feel any difference, which was weird, considering it was a literal ten percent increase or so, but I shrugged and moved on, blowing out a long breath as the aching in my eyes and skull faded.

With that done, I pulled up the stat sheet and ran over it again quickly, making note of the changes.

Name: Matt, First Lord of the Storm				
Host Powers: 1 (Enhanced Regeneration)				
Species: Thunderstorm		**Bonus**: None		
Level: 26		**Progress to next level**: 6,053/50,000		
Stat	**Current Points**	**Description**	**Effect**	**Progress to Next Level**
Agility	41	Governs dodge and movement	Heightened chance to dodge attacks 82%+20%= 102%	23/100
Charisma	31	Governs likely success to charm, seduce, or threaten	46% more likely to succeed in events that require seduction, persuasion, or threats (10%+ (21x2) = 46)	78/100
Constitution	51	Governs Health and Health Regeneration	HP: 51x60 = 3,060	48/100
Dexterity	42	Governs ability with weapons and crafting	+42% Increased chance of improved result +16 to melee damage	91/100
Endurance	41	Governs Stamina and Stamina Regeneration	Stamina: 41x50 = 2,050	13/100
Intelligence	61	Governs base manapool, standard intellectual capacity	Mana: 61x70=4,270	66/100
Luck	39	Governs overall chance of bonuses and critical hits	+58% increased chance of positive outcome	98/100
Perception	42	Governs ranged damage and chance to spot hidden items/traps	+32 to all ranged attacks	40/100
Strength	38	Governs damage with melee weapons and carrying capacity	+56 to all damage with Melee weapons	22/100
Wisdom	47	Governs mana regeneration	80 mana regenerated per hour (internal improvements destroyed)	34/100

That done, and the feeling of slowly building nausea and disconnect between my mind and body tamped down for now, I moved onto the class options.

<u>Class Skills:</u>

Class selection: Arcane Dungeon Lord

Imbue: You may choose to give freely of your own manapool to imbue an item or creature of the Dungeon with magic. This ability can fail, and spectacularly so; however, creations of wondrous might can also be brought into being. Be wary. (Selected)

Evolution: Foresight: No longer are your creations the chance things they were…now see the true potential of a creature! (Selected)

Monster Master: No longer do the creatures of the Dungeon view you with apathy or irritation when you pass by. Now they are devoted to you! This skill ranks in levels from 0 (Interested) to 5 (Worshipful). (Current level: 0, Interested)

Evolution: Lord of All! The creatures of your Dungeon know their true master, and those who follow willingly can now receive arcane gifts that match their level of devotion! (Selected)

Arcane Breeder: Some Dungeon Lords wish for only the purest strains to survive, while others enjoy the randomness of evolution…select the genes you wish to see and promote them!

Artificer: You may gift magical artifacts to your creations, and when combined with Foresight, these creatures will gain significant bonuses to magical item creation and replication. This skill ranks in levels from 0 (Curiosity) to 5 (Legendary). (Current level: 0, Curiosity)

Arcane Pets: Your sentient Dungeon inhabitants can gather and breed pets, but where before there was an element of random chance, now you may lure those you wish into the range of your tamers. This skill ranks in levels from 0 (Magical) to 5 (Legendary Creatures) (Current level: 0, Magical).

Insatiable Curiosity: Random Sentient Dungeon Creatures will now have the chance to be spawned with an Insatiable Curiosity. These creatures can be put to work in your Research Nodes to increase Research by a staggering degree. This skill ranks in levels from 0 (Incompetent) to 5 (Genius). (Current level: 2, Interested)

Evolution: Magical Researcher! Before, your researchers were generalists, plodding along at their task, be that a better toilet seat or a converter; now they stand a chance at developing true magical gifts, and at learning the secrets of creation! This skill ranks in levels from 0 (Novice) to 5 (Master). (Current level: 1, Apprentice)

Manafield: Your Dungeon's Manafield will now passively expand at 10% more than the previous rate, enabling greater growth in a shorter period of time. This skill ranks in levels from 0 (Restricted) to 5 (Expansive). (Current Level: 1, Limited)

Evolution: Tides of Mana! All life creates mana, as do elemental interactions. Now through the wonders of gravitational magic, you can start to draw more mana into the area of your Dungeon. This skill ranks in levels from 0 (Gentle) to 5 (Vortex). (Current Level: 1, Steady)

Reach Out and Touch Me: Your Dungeon is no longer only controllable when you are within its own environs. Now you can interact with it at increasing distances. This skill ranks in levels from 0 (Local) to 5 (Interstellar). (Current level: 0, Local)

Evolution: Gates! No longer is the Dungeon a distant creation. This skill unlocks the creation of the Gates, transportals that can be built inside the Dungeon and activated at a remote location to provide a stable link between the two points.

This skill ranks in levels from 0 (Single Gate) to 5 (Unlimited) (Current level: 0, Single).

Two points I had. Two goddamn points to spend. I'd been deliberately putting it off, thinking that I might be better off waiting until I hit my next class choice, and using the skill points then, really supercharging my options.

That might be hours or weeks away, though, considering how little we knew about what was coming. That was certainly the case for the single spell I had to choose. I needed to not choose it until I'd actually taken some time and learned a little more about magic.

There was no point in choosing something that I could learn myself; that'd be a waste.

I worked through it by a process of elimination, as I always did.

Imbue and Foresight were already taken, so they were out, as was Lord of All. It was only a one-level thing, after all. Monster Master was tempting, as I was summoning more and more advanced creatures. Having them start off worshipping me rather than regarding me with apathy could be damn useful. But realistically, I needed to know if they were assholes from the beginning.

If I summoned a goblin, they tended to like and obey automatically. An orc? They were dicks straight off. I could add the points there and the orcs would become great soldiers for me. Whoo, yeah.

It wouldn't change who they were, though…just how they felt about me.

That meant I could summon an orc, think they were great and set them loose to roam the dungeon, thinking they'd be like that with everyone, and find out an hour later that they'd been peckish and had skewered a bairn and have been roasting them over a fire for a snack.

No, I think I'd leave that one for now.

Arcane Breeder? That implied letting the various races "get it on," which was just wrong. Also, I seriously doubted that newborn dungeon creatures would be much different to newborn "normal" creatures, in that they'd be fuck all use for a few years at least.

Nope.

Artificer was a serious contender, though. We needed the goddamn magical weapons and desperately; we just hadn't managed it yet. That was a serious possibility.

Arcane Pets? I'd chosen one level in it to help Chris, but…three levels would make a hell of a difference, overall. For a start, there was a realistic chance of getting something cool, and not just for Chris. The various races would need mounts, and Beta…

Fuck.

Beta had demanded a new mount. A dog, specifically.

She didn't really ask for much, so to ignore her on this? Especially when she was suddenly as powerful as she was because of her devotion to me? Well, it was a bit of a shitty thing to do.

I'd keep that one in mind.

Insatiable Curiosity, or its evolution, Magical Researcher, were possibilities. Two points dumped into either would be a massive improvement, especially when we needed to build a new research team.

Manafield was a possible boost to the mana in the area, but it wasn't really that important right now. We'd invested in it already, after all. Same with its evolution, Tides of Mana.

Reach Out and Touch Me? Nope. It was useful inside the local area, and I wasn't going to be going far for a while, I suspected. Moving on…

Gates? Nah. I had one ready to go, I could build it when I needed to, and for now, I genuinely didn't need to.

A quick evaluation done, and I pulled up the real contenders.

Artificer, Arcane Pets, and Researcher, magical or normal, were the four options that were realistic. Although I could invest a point in two of them, realistically, we'd see more bang for our buck by going all in.

As much as I'd like a cool new level of pets as mounts, we'd not got it up and running properly yet, so it could wait until I got the next boost, I hoped. Beta could make do with a "normal" dog. Or, you know, a Triceratops.

Artificer…we barely had normal crafting going on yet. Next time maybe.

It was down to magical or normal research.

Realistically, almost everything we did in the dungeon was "magic," which made me think that maybe that was the way to go, but…

I sighed and selected Insatiable Curiosity as the old Arthur C. Clarke quote rang out in my head, comparing sufficiently advanced science to magic.

There might be no real magic at all, or it might all be magic. I genuinely didn't know. But right now? I could damn well do with some normal tech in our lives, boosting our researchers from Interested at the third of six levels, all the way to Gifted at the fifth, or fourth, as it was. The damn counter started at zero, weirdly, after all.

There was only one more level to go, and I resolved that I'd select that soon as well.

I blinked the screens away and focused on the room around me, noting the darkness, and growling as I wondered just how much time had passed.

Had they forgotten to send someone for me?

I clattered down the stairs, and noted Beta and Kilo falling in on either side of me as I left, checking the time on the way and finding we were only twenty minutes over the hour we'd set as a limit. But still.

Ten minutes later, I'd been redirected to the main gathering point by the northern gate. Approaching, I was struck by the mixed air of barely controlled chaos and carnival that was going on. One bugger walked round with a tray braced on his stomach, the strap running around behind his neck, and was trying to sell sausages in a bun at insane prices.

The fucker was asking for a gold coin each, and yet he was doing a roaring trade.

Nobody, as I passed him, seemed to be actually paying in coins, but they were all paying with various trinkets and trades, ones that he made vanish with a toothy smile, before vanishing himself before the customer tried a mouthful of their purchase.

"Oh God…" I heard one woman comment to her friend. "That's awful."

"You sure? It smells amazing…" her friend said, before taking a bite and gagging.

I squeezed past the pair, shaking my head and wondering what the actual fuck was going on, considering they could have summoned the food themselves. But I guessed that the attraction of being able to add your own condiments and do things as we used to was just too much for some to pass up.

I stepped through the milling masses of people, hearing snatches of conversation, of people reassuring each other that they could, should, or would do this.

I heard children complaining that they didn't want to move, and others guessing at how wonderful it'd be to live somewhere "under the Dungeon Lord's eye."

There were snippets of conversation about me as I moved silently past. Everything from that I supplemented my powers with necromancy and the sacrifice of innocents, to that I maintained a harem of the most beautiful women and fucked them all personally every night.

Weirdest was that it was two young and attractive women who I heard talking about that, and a comment from one of them asking if her friend thought they'd be able to "get in on it" too.

That threw me a little. I stumbled into an unseen puddle behind them. These girls would have barely looked at me before the fall, and now would love to be part of my harem.

"Kelly would murder me," I muttered, shaking my head as I passed by.

There were people with massive hiking rucksacks full of personal possessions, and entire families with nothing, simply standing, ready to move out.

The smallest children were gathered in a big, wheeled monstrosity, clearly designed to advertise a nearby nursery, and I grinned as I remembered us bringing it here originally, having looted it on the way past the place.

I passed through the outer ring and into the more private area that had been claimed for the "command team" in a small coffee shop, hearing Jo complaining that I'd better turn up soon as I closed the door behind me.

"There you are!" she called, glaring at me. "An hour, we agreed! It's been half that again!"

"You said you'd come and get me," I pointed out, moving closer. "I was meditating, remember?"

"Told you!" Chris added laconically to Patrick. "Told you she said she'd get him."

"Did I?" Jo asked, blankly. "Fuck, sorry."

"It's fine," I assured her. "All good here?" I looked around.

"Yeah. As far as I know, we're all ready. It's a bit of a clusterfuck, but that's the way it goes. Either we'll be attacked, or we won't. Can you fly all the way from here to the dungeon?"

"Possibly," I admitted, looking at my mana. "But, realistically, I won't be. I might be able to make it all the way if I went flat out, but that'd be fuck all use to anyone. I'll jump up and fly around periodically, see if I can discover anything following. Our best chance, though? We're a big fucking group. More likely than not, anything with a brain will steer clear."

"Probably for the best," Barry agreed, catching the last bit I said as he entered. "I've got ten men with me, mostly spears and shields, but hey, that's life. One guy has a rifle with a handful of bullets, as a last reserve."

"I'll give him half a mag." Chris sighed. "Better to have it and not need it…"

"Than need it and not have it," Barry agreed. "Thank you."

"Are we ready?" I asked him, and he nodded.

"As we can be. Ideally, I'd say put it all off till tomorrow, and gain that extra time to plan, probably send people across in batches of fifty with a real escort, but they're ready now. They know the risk they run leaving the park at all, so best to get it over with. Plus, it means we've got a decent bit of space suddenly. That'll be appreciated."

"Yeah well, we've got fuck all, but Kelly is working on it," I said, sighing.

"Shall we?" Barry gestured to the door, grinning. "Personally, I'm only coming to see Kelly murder you. Don't get much in the way of cabaret these days."

"Yeah well, fuck you very much." I sighed again, motioning to the door. "You lead."

Barry headed out the door without another word, but outside he pulled out a little red whistle: three short blasts, followed by a long one, then three more.

Silence fell quickly, and people formed up, kids on the inside, parents, then those who were looking to be fighters, I guessed, on the outside.

In a matter of seconds, they were ready, and Chris and I exchanged an amazed look.

"What, don't you do drills?" Barry asked, pretending it was normal, before turning and addressing the gathered people. "Okay, everyone. You know what to do. Get ready as we're gonna be running most of the way. We'll stop for breaks at the art gallery, let everyone catch their breath and make sure we're still together, and then again at the civic center…"

"He started them three days ago," Jo informed me, speaking over Barry. "Don't let him fool you. Same with the whistle."

"Thanks." I winked at her and gave Barry a thumbs-up. "We were doing shit like that before…think we should do it again?" I asked Jo.

"Run drills?" She rubbed her chin. "Probably. It'd be a good thing for everyone to have a plan, you know, in case we're attacked. Like we had with the bells…just maybe make a thing of that again? We've had a load of new people join us, after all."

"Out!" Barry shouted, pointing at the gate.

"Whoops." I grimaced, pushing off the wall I'd been leaning against. "Were we supposed to be listening to that?" I asked Chris.

"He just told them all you were shit useless in bed and you promised them all foot-rubs after the run," he quipped, grinning at me.

"Oh, that's all right then." I grinned back at him. "As the mighty Dungeon Lord, I hereby volunteer you to do it all. Enjoy!"

"Bastard."

"Love you too."

We set off jogging, then picked up speed into a steady run, splitting to either side and guiding the group.

Some of the smaller kids started to cry, until a nearby parent sang a silly song. Others joined in, and soon we were running at a good speed, voices raised in song, with even Jo singing along.

"I'm so glad I've not got kids, man," Chris called to me, moving in close. "Having to learn shit like this? Man, it's just painful!"

"Yeah, well, it's keeping them quiet and happy," I pointed out, before crouching, then kicking off. "Be right back!"

I leapt into the air, flashing upward, flooding my body with Lightning for a few seconds, and vanished upward into the darkness.

Cutting the Lightning as soon as I was up, I hesitated, hovering and waiting, hoping that if we were being followed, I'd see them before they saw me. But after a full minute, I blasted ahead again, catching up with the head of the column and landing to cheers.

"Anything?" Chris asked me.

"Fuck all, but I can only see so far. Anything that's flying around at night is gonna be better at hiding than I am at finding, I bet."

"Well, that just gives me the warm and fuzzies, you know that?" Chris looked up into the blackness above us. "How far to the art gallery?"

"Just a few hundred meters ahead off to the left," I assured him, then grimaced and set off into the lead. "I'll check it out!" I called to him and Barry as I flashed ahead.

The art gallery was barely out of sight of the park, it was really that close, but most of those on this run were going to be out of breath by that point. It was better to let them rest and recover, than to push them too hard.

It was an older building, built in the Victorian style, which meant it was all blocky columns and arced windows, lots of marble inside and solid quarried stone outside.

The entrance had a series of metal grates dragged across and secured at some point, presumably to protect the art that it'd once housed.

When I landed there, though, the grates were broken and dragged back. The glass doors that led inside had been shattered, and there was a trail of dried blood leading inward.

We were just off the line of claimed territory for the dungeon—the fastest route was a straight line, after all—but a perfectly straight line? Well, it ignored the route elevation and dips, buildings and more. that meant I couldn't just summon something and send it in to check it out. That was fine. I could see a little in the dark. My Perception was at a level that, in old human terms, would have been the equivalent of military assisted headgear, which was nice.

I strode forward. My right hand pulled my hammer up and free of the loop, holding it ready even as I heard the others approaching.

Cursing, I hurried inside, shaking my head at how bloody stupid it was to have not done the route beforehand, just to be sure, or to have waited until tomorrow and to have summoned kobolds.

I knew we had sod all mana available, with arranging the next level of accommodation as well as everything else, but fuck's sake.

I passed from room to room, finding empty places on the walls where art had presumably once hung. The darkness was a pain, but between the boosts to my various senses, it only took a few minutes to check the entire building. Two rooms had been recently fought in, and there was a smear of blood that led into a toilet, which was disturbing as fuck, considering a body looked to have been dragged that way.

There was nothing there now, though, and the silent stalls stood empty.

I waited, slowly moving from one to the next, pushing the door open and checking each of the individual thrones, but there was nothing.

"Okay, people!" I called, returning to the main entrance. "Everyone in. Stay clear of the men's toilets, but the building is empty."

"What's up?" Barry asked me, stepping in close and smiling at people as he waved them in.

"Not sure," I admitted. "Someone died…handprints, drag marks, but the toilets that the body was dragged into? Spotless."

"In Gateshead?"

"It's an art gallery," I pointed out.

"It's still Gateshead," he replied, deadpan.

"You check it out then. I can't see anything."

"Too dark?" He reached for his pack and pulled a lighter free.

"Nah, I can see all right. I just mean there's nothing to see, as near as I can—"

A scream broke us out of our conversation, and I ran deeper into the building, Barry following.

"What?" I called, skidding on the marble and glaring around, my hammer held ready. "What happened?"

"Toni…" An older woman clutched her sobbing little girl to her. "She said she saw something, there!"

I followed the shakily pointed finger but saw nothing. Barry and I moved down the corridor, even as people moved back uncertainly.

The corridor was wide, easily four meters, and made to let people wander here and there from room to room, looking at paintings or whatever they had, the occasional sculpture standing in the corners of the room.

Two rooms led off the corridor: the men's toilets, complete with bloodstained handprint on the floor before it and smeared blood leading inward, and a broom closet. The ladies' toilet had been farther up the corridor, and beyond that?

Nothing.

A single huge sheet of polished bronze stood attached to the back wall, reflecting the room behind us, and I shook my head, straightening.

"You think she saw a reflection?" Barry asked, and I nodded to the men's toilet.

"Probably. Check that. I'll make sure of the closet, and then we're out of here in five minutes."

"Deal."

Barry was barely gone thirty seconds, then he returned, striding out, his spear slid into the sheath on his back, even as I poked and prodded at the back wall of the closet, making sure it was as solid as it looked.

"Anything?"

"Nothing." I grunted. "You?"

He smiled. "No threat at all."

"Really?" I frowned. "I thought—" I moved past him and stared into the toilets, seeing dirt and dust, a crack that ran across one mirror, and no blood stains, not inside anyway.

"Barry," I whispered.

"Yeah?" Barry stepped in close.

"Get everyone out."

"What's wrong?" Barry smiled at me and moved in even closer.

"Barry," I said slowly, seeing the wide smile on his face and the way he leaned in as if to speak in confidence or...

He opened his mouth at the same time that a crash came from the toilet. One of the stalls walls smashed from the anchor points, as *Barry* staggered out, a spindly white figure clinging to his back.

The "Barry" standing next to me lunged forward, mouth opening wide and teeth gleaming, suddenly pointed. His skin shifted, going grey and bumps spreading; eyes that were bright yellow gleamed in the dark, and stringy, thin, and long black hair appeared.

I twisted at the hip, bracing one foot, and swept my left hand across, slapping its reaching arms aside, then drove my shoulder into it, picking the creature up and ramming it into the wall.

Nails scrabbled at my back, tearing into the cloak and trying to reach my neck and face, but it was turned half away from me. As I drove it back into the wall again, I felt as much as heard the bones breaking.

Black blood gushed from its mouth, and it coughed weakly, lifting its legs and planting them on me. It dragged them down again, nails clicking and catching as it snapped and lunged, trying to bite me.

I twisted, smashing the head of my hammer into its gut, then drew back as it crumpled around it. I grabbed it by the neck, pinning it to the wall, and looked deeper into the restroom. Barry had another creature clinging to his back and strands of black webbing wrapped around him.

He was twisting and slamming himself against the walls. One stall was smashed to pieces already; the others looked battered to fuck suddenly, and blood smears covered the floor and walls again.

I looked back at the creature that had attacked me, then threw it at the wall, leaving it to bounce and fall, leaving a blood smear on the wall as I raced to Barry's side.

I dropped my hammer, not daring to swing it when he was twisting and spinning, and instead reached out, grabbing the fucker by the back of the neck.

Instantly, it went wild, releasing Barry and trying to yank itself around, mouth snapping and claws flashing as it tried to get at me, or get free.

"Motherfucker!" Barry growled, yanking the black threads free and twisting around, pulling them off and throwing them free. "What the hell is that thing!"

"Dead," I snarled, taking two quick steps and putting my left hand on the back of its head, the right gripping its neck, then driving it face-first into the wall as hard as I could.

It was hard stone, a veneer of marble over brick, and the crunching sound its face made as it bucked inward turned my stomach, but the body went nuts, spasming and quivering. I swore as it tried to do a "skunk" and drive any attacker away in disgust.

A spray of filth shot out, fortunately missing me, but making Barry, behind me, gag, as I drove its head into the wall again.

The second blow was enough to finish it off, and I dumped the corpse on the floor, sweeping up my hammer as I glared around.

"Any more of them?" I asked.

"I didn't see those fuckers until it was too late, dragged me into the stall. What the hell were you doing with the other one?"

"It looked like you." I shook my head. "Hell, it *spoke* like you. If not for the fucking smile, I might have believed it."

"What smile?" He glowered.

"Exactly." I grunted, kicking the corpse, then headed for the door. "Fucker kept smiling at me, so I knew it wasn't you."

"I smile," Barry growled, stepping up and punting the creature in the side, making damn sure it was dead. "I'll smile a lot more when I pour fucking petrol in here and light it."

"The other one," I whispered, having stepped out into the corridor, and stared at the blood smear on the floor, as well as the way that people were sitting and resting nearby, totally oblivious, talking and playing with their kids. "What the hell?"

I followed the blood smear, seeing the one I'd beaten the shit out of dragging itself along the floor, and reaching up to the...to the mirror?

The full-length, floor-to-ceiling mirror rippled as the creature reached up, and a hand reached back through, grabbing its wrist and dragging it upward.

I stared in shock, then cast my Examine spell, grunting at the details revealed.

Changeling	Fey Creature

The Changeling is a lesser Fey, still under the control of the Daoine Sidhe, but rarely permitted within their hallowed halls. The Changelings are often sent to establish nests as a precursor to a greater infiltration. Where possible, a changeling nest should be destroyed, root and branch.

Ability:

Planar Travel! Changelings are gifted with planar travel, passing through the portals between worlds as easily as most pass from one room to another.

Glamour! The Changeling rarely actually changes its form. Few can physically adjust to another body flawlessly. Instead, they mimic it, through the use of a glamour ability, convincing those they target to let their guard down as the creature gets close enough to strike.

Weaknesses: Fire, Iron, and Metal Magics

HP: 11/80
Stamina: 37/50
Mana: 11/600
Speed: 6/10
Level: 3

HP 11/80	Special Abilities: 1/2

"Changeling," I tensed, before sprinting forward. The changeling hissed in fear and anger as it slipped from our realm. The bronze mirror shivered like it was liquid, then solidified, and as I reached it, it was solid again.

The sound of the building around us seemed to jump a notch, like a bubble had burst, and I punched the mirror in anger, denting it, but doing fuck all real damage.

"Where is it?" Barry skidded to a halt next to me.

"Gone." I glared at my reflection. "It went through the mirror."

"Well, that's just fucking peachy," he growled. "They can use mirrors? I thought they hated them?"

"What?"

"Mirrors…they hate them, shows them as they really are," he repeated.

"That's vampyres, isn't it?"

"Fucked if I know. I heard it as a kiddies' tale," Barry admitted. "Now what?"

I turned, not liking having my back to the mirror, and moved away quickly, shaking my head. "Fuck this shit," I muttered. "Barry, get them moving. Better to be tired out there than fucked in here."

"Aye, sounds good to me," Barry snarled, moving forward and clapping his hands for attention, then blasting the whistle again. "Right, you lot…"

I turned back, glancing at the mirror, then at the people nearby. They looked totally confused, having had no clue what the hell just happened to make me order them to move on. None of them had seen a thing, except…

Except the little girl.

I caught her eye, seeing the wide-eyed look of horror on the child's face, and I moved in close.

"Are you okay?" I asked, and she stared at me in terror. "Do you know who I am?" I tried again.

"Dungeon Lord, she's fine." Her mother forced a smile, shaking her head. "I'm sorry. We didn't mean to waste your time…"

"Does this look like a waste of time?" I lifted my right hand and showed the black blood that still stuck to it. "You saw me fight it, didn't you?" I asked the little girl.

She swallowed hard, then nodded, confusing her mother even more.

"Good." I forced a smile. "You keep your eyes open, all right? You see anything, anything at all that shouldn't be there? Tell them to get me. I'll sort it out."

"Lord, she's just a child…she didn't—" the mother tried again, and I shook my head, cutting her off.

"It was a changeling," I said. "A creature that can hide itself, force people to see what they want. Look." I took two steps and pushed open the door to the toilet, gesturing inside.

The mother peered around the corner and gasped, seeing the creature and blood spread everywhere.

"I didn't see it," I said. "It'd grabbed Barry, and another one was waiting for me. It could have killed people, if your daughter…"

"Toni."

"If Toni hadn't seen it, it would have gotten someone at least. Now we know about them. If she sees something? You call for me." I got terrified nods, then gestured toward the door. "Go," I ordered, waiting until I was sure I was the last in the building, before turning to the mirror again.

"We'll meet again, you little shit," I promised it, wishing I had a Molotov cocktail to throw. I hesitated for a second, thinking that the corpse could be useful, maybe get some changelings of our own…but I couldn't ask these people, running desperately through the night, to carry it. And I sure as shit couldn't afford the distraction.

Nothing presented itself as an alternative, and I followed the others out, leaving the body behind, vowing to burn the whole place later.

The next leg of the run was uneventful, beyond how clearly exhausted most people were. We ran from the art gallery to the civic center, then entered and rested there for half an hour, squatting and taking the time to bring Kelly and the others up to date on the changeling.

She was annoyed when I first reached out, clearly still trying to fix the accommodation, but by the time I was finished, she was fine again, promising to keep her eyes open.

A contingent of kobolds reached us then, and the last leg was done with considerably less stress, covering the remaining distance in a series of short jogs and walks, while I flew from building to building, staring out into the darkness, searching for any threat.

Whatever the fliers were, they kept their distance and were clearly fixated on the park. That was fine as far as I was concerned; as long as they didn't attack, fuck them very much. They could stay there until we could catch them and tame them, and everyone was a winner.

Reaching the south entrance of the dungeon, a cheer went up as the doors opened, and hundreds of people were waiting, greeting us with a rising cheer. I didn't know what or who had prompted this, but it was a hell of a nice touch, and jogging to the side, letting the people stream past, I smiled at the looks of wonder on their faces.

The inner gates were open as well, the ones from the castle "holding area" into the dungeon proper, and the gentle glow of the pool, as well as the spreading steam, the cheering people, and the general cleanliness and warmth was clearly appreciated.

They were home at last.

CHAPTER TWENTY-SIX

Kelly found me only a few minutes later, kissing my cheek and shaking her head when I opened my mouth to explain.

"It's fine. It was the right thing to do," she assured me. "It'll be a little tight. We've spread them over the floors of the mage's tower for now, and they're being assigned to rooms as soon as we can get them. Tonight, they can make do with blankets and the floors in there. Tomorrow, with their help, we can get the next floor of the accommodation started, and they'll be able to move in by the end of the day, with some luck."

"Thank you." I took her in my arms and hugged her, kissing the top of her head.

"Anytime," she promised. "Now, I know we were having date night tonight, but…"

"But?"

"But Rhodes is chomping at the bit to finish your training for the day, and you'll not be capable after that, unless you meditate and rest now. How about we do it tomorrow night, and welcome people here in the canteen instead?"

"Deal," I agreed, relieved. I'd had a plan for the night, and to make a little something that would help that plan, but I needed mana for that, and the way things had gone today?

It just wasn't happening.

"So, how about you go play," Kelly sighed, pointing to where Rhodes stood, grinning evilly, "and I'll get people settled?"

"Thank you again," I whispered, kissing her and nodding. I didn't want to go and exercise, fuck no, but, if we were to make the most of this, I damn well needed to.

Kelly stood on tiptoes and kissed me, before dropping down and striding over to the nearest groups, calling out for their attention, as Barry jogged back to me.

"I'm heading straight back with my people," Barry said. "I don't like those things being so close to the park…"

"Me neither. Take these…" I reached into the dungeon sense, printing up a handful of Molotov cocktails. They were easy to make, after all: high-proof alcohol, a rag stuffed in the neck that was soaked in the substance, then light it and throw. Job done.

"Thanks," he grunted, then frowned as I summoned a single goblin mageling as well. "What's that for?"

"Disgust," I replied. "It's a spell they have. Literally, it makes anything nearby want to slaughter the fuckers—very goblin-appropriate spell. But, more to the point, shove that fucker into somewhere and order him to use the spell, you'll soon see if there's anything inside."

"Canary in the coal mine, eh?"

"Well, put it this way, you're not going to lose any sleep over him." I shrugged.

"Works for me. Thanks, Matt. Come on, you little fucker," he said first to me, then to the goblin, before he turned and led his small team out of the dungeon. He was off and jogging through the gates before they could close, headed back to the park, even as I turned to find Rhodes by my side.

"That time then?" She gave me a firm nod. "Might as well get to it." I groaned, falling into step by her side. The pair of us headed across the dungeon and then up to the impromptu gym on the top floor. "Did I miss much?" I asked her, conversationally.

"Not much. Some of the scumbags from that coup who were ordered to join up refused to help. They tried complaining that they were too old, too exhausted, or too precious to get their nails broken carrying gym equipment..."

I grinned. "How'd that work out for them?"

"Not well. When they refused to help, and just followed along, they got a nasty surprise at the gate when we refused them entry, shoving them back out and closing the gate in their faces."

"How'd that go down?"

"They learned that they needed to help," she said with a snort of amusement. "They were left outside while the rest of their squad ate lunch and had a half an hour break, got healed up of any exhaustion and pulled muscles. And then they were allowed to join the squad when it set off for the gyms again."

"They pulled their weight after that?" I guessed.

"They did, but there was talk about them refusing to leave tomorrow. I'm betting they'll be hiding and stirring up trouble tonight."

"If they do, they'll regret it," I assured her. "Anything else?"

"No sign of the three who were put out, but, I'm betting that they'll turn up. Turds always float to the top, eventually."

"Probably," I grumbled. The two guys in the gym when we entered jumped to their feet as they saw Rhodes and me. "Andre, Jimmy," I greeted them.

"Uh...Dungeon Lord," they said a heartbeat apart, glancing at each other.

"Thought you might come here." Andre scratched the back of his head. "Look, I, uh, we..."

"We wanted to apologize," Jimmy finished for his brother, in a rush. "We didn't know it was your gym. We thought it was everyone's. So when we wus tellin' you off for not putting gear back—"

"It's fine." I shook my head. "Honestly. No stress. You know why I was upset now, right? About the meditation?"

"Yeah..." Andre lied slowly, making it clear that "no" was the word that was missing from the conversation.

"Okay, look, when I'm meditating, if I'm shocked out of the trance, it hurts. It damages me, and it makes me feel really sick, all right? That's all."

"Right." Jimmy nodded. "So we'll be real quiet then."

"Yeah, real quiet," Andre agreed, grinning and seemingly relieved.

"So...can we stay?" Jimmy asked after a few seconds. "Us and the girls, I mean?"

"They're training to be mages, right?" I asked, and they nodded.

"Aye, we heard you wanted fighters too, right? Can we join them?" Andre asked, and I looked to Rhodes, who was clearly waiting for permission from me.

"Gentlemen, this is Sergeant Rhodes, British Army, and she'll be evaluating you and the other fighters tomorrow…" I started, and she took over smoothly.

"But there's no reason I can't start now. You look like you know your way around a gym?"

"Oh, aye…" Jimmy nodded.

"Yes, Sergeant," she corrected. "You'll be learning proper discipline, or you'll not last the week. You want to stay?"

"Aye…I mean, yes sir, Sergeant!" Andre straightened up and elbowed his brother. The pair of them tried to salute, and I winced.

"Fuck me, I've got my work cut out for me." Rhodes groaned, before shaking her head. "First off, no 'sir' bullshit to an NCO. We work for a living! Second…" She started in on them, moving around, making them suck their bellies in, stand fully straight, back at this angle, arm at that…

I clambered onto the rowing machine and started in on my warm-up, grinning to myself as I slid into a meditative trance.

Seemingly seconds later, I felt a gentle pressure on my arm, and heard Rhodes whispering to pick up speed, and I nodded, doing it.

It was weird trying to split my focus like this, moving rhythmically on the rowing machine while my brain was fully disengaged, but as the minutes passed, it grew easier.

She touched my shoulder and ordered me to speed up every so often, my rhythm clearly faltering as I focused elsewhere, and I did as she directed.

Eventually, I felt her hand on my shoulder again, and when she didn't say anything, I slowly rose from the depths, blinking into the bright light of the room, stunned to find my chest heaving with exertion, and sweat pouring off me.

"Looks like you found your rhythm," Rhodes said with a quirk of the lips. "Ready for the weights?"

"Yeah…just…give me…a minute…" I groaned, taking a shaking breath, wiping sweat from my forehead, then channeling my Lightning through my body and…and feeling so much better, it was unreal.

My muscles, which had just been screaming at me, suddenly felt pleasantly warmed up. My back that had been aching? Golden.

I caught my breath in seconds, then stood, stretching and finding that I'd done that on instinct. I didn't feel even slightly uncomfortable.

"My turn." Jimmy moved over to the rowing machine, and hesitated, looking at the sweat-drenched seat. "Dude…look, I know you're the boss and everything but…" He shook his head and looked at the seat sadly.

"I've got it," I assured him, waving a hand and catching the towel I summoned from the dungeon. The way his eyes widened at that, he clearly still wasn't used to the dungeon's true capabilities yet.

"Don't worry," I said. "I'll learn." I wiped the seat down, then myself as I moved off, grinning.

The weights area was next. Deadlifts to start, and bench and rack. The next half an hour was too busy to really meditate at the same time, but that was fine; I'd managed to reconstruct another gate while on the rowing machine, and as time went on, I knew I'd get more.

I settled into the rhythm, even starting to joke a little with Rhodes and the guys, as we moved up into the "real" weights, and then I surpassed them all.

It became a competition, as they added more weights, me pushing harder, healing myself between sets, and grunting as I heaved weights up that would have secured me medals before all of this.

By the time we threw the towel in, literally, dumping it for the morning, and we went to the canteen, the brothers were much happier, and they left us with a few jokes about beating me tomorrow.

Rhodes and I joined the others at "our" table, and we all ate and relaxed, taking turns to go for a walk around and speak to people at the other tables.

We'd…*I'd* been against admitting too many people at once before this, but as the days passed, I saw that although my reasoning was sound—pricks like Gerald and his wife were still out there, after all—I needed to be a lot more flexible than I had been.

As a group, most of us went to the pool after dinner that night. People sitting around looked nervous, and we were back to working on integrating them, reaching out and drawing people into conversation and joking with them.

The evening became night, and Kelly and I went to bed, fooled around a little, and then slept, calm and relaxed, happy with our lives and relationship.

The last thing I saw, as I slid into sleep, was the notifications from the day.

You have gained additional Stat Points in the following areas through constant effort.

- +1 Constitution
- +1 Dexterity
- +2 Endurance
- +2 Strength

Continue to work hard to increase these or other stats…

*

Congratulations!

You have killed the following:
- 1x Fey Changeling, Level 4, 50 XP

Total XP earned: 50 XP

Total XP awarded 50 XP

Current XP to next level stands at 6,103/50,000

The next morning, although coming far too soon after last night for my liking, was easy enough. A light breakfast, followed by a light workout, then a longer, and much harder one, where I channeled almost continuously, using only a tiny fraction of my mana by the second, but doing it ongoing.

It quickly became apparent that it made a hell of a difference. Rather than just healing my damaged muscles, it helped me to push harder, and further.

Hours passed in a blur, until I stopped, a realization coming painfully. I pulled up my stat sheet, and compared it to last night, then made a note of all the numbers, spending an entire hour frantically pushing myself harder than ever before with the weights, until Rhodes stopped me.

"Well?" she asked, clearly suspecting what I was about to say.

"Healing constantly lets me push harder…but I've made no gains at all," I admitted, sighing. "Well, a very minor one in Intelligence and Perception, probably for spotting the issue, but that's it."

"Shame," she agreed, sitting down on a bench and nodding. "It makes sense, though. If you're healing the damage before it happens, then there's no room for growth. The body is returning to the same position each time, rather than growing and improving. Well, at least we know."

"Aye." I grunted. "Well, time for the lessons anyway."

"Matt?" Rhodes called as I stood, and I nodded, glancing over at her. "Once you're done with the lessons for the day, take the night off the gym. I know it doesn't feel like it, but your body will still need some time to recover, even if it's just one day a week."

"Yes, Sarge," I agreed with a smile. "You ready for this?"

"Fighter recruitment?" She stood and grinned at me. "I was born ready, sir."

We had two sets of lessons planned today, or at least I did. First was to meet and greet the new fighter core, go over their training for the next few weeks and make things clear to them. Then I'd be joining the final mages' lesson of the day as they were ongoing currently, joining them for meditation, and to answer any questions.

Joining the fighters and the various trainees to the north of the dungeon, next to the newly equipment-filled gym, I stood on yet another fucking platform, although this time I had a few others with me, at least.

"Morning!" I called, striding to the front and looking out over the nearly six hundred volunteers for the new dungeon army, from the new arrivals and those who'd volunteered from the dungeon as well.

Most of them were human, with only a small contingent of kobolds in their midst, but that was fine. We'd be making more and adding them in later.

"Or is it afternoon?" I asked, rhetorically. "Ah well, fuck it. You're all here for one reason—you're here to protect our families, and that makes you all heroes in my eyes, so fuck it," I repeated. "Heroes get an occasional later start as a reward!"

That got a few chuckles.

"So, I'm here to go over the dungeon, your training, and introduce you to the various ugly mugs behind me, who'll be in charge of you on a day-to-day basis and your training. First and foremost, this is Mike."

Mike strode forward, standing at attention, and nodded to the crowd, sweeping them with a steely-eyed look.

"I'm Captain Mike Jefferson, ex-Special Forces, and Captain of the Guard for the dungeon. That's my formal title, and I'm responsible overall for the dungeon's defense and for its armed forces. My second, and your day-to-day commander, is Captain Griffiths, formerly of the Coldstream Guards." Griffiths stepped forward and nodded at them all, before stepping back and leaving Mike to introduce the others.

"This is Sergeant Sarah Offerton, who along with Sergeant Rhodes will be responsible for kicking your arse repeatedly in training and the field. Remember: the more you sweat, the less you bleed. Our plan is to keep you fuckers around until you die of old age. To make sure you have a chance at that? We're going to do our level best to break you all!

"Next are training Sergeants Markus and Jeffrey. They specialize in melee armed and ranged weapons. Expect to spend a lot of time cursing their names!"

I grinned at the looks on their faces as Mike went on.

"Next, Sergeants Chris and Patrick. They'll be with you in the field as much as in training, and they're a pair of evil bastards, so I don't recommend getting on their bad sides. Chris specializes in field craft and animal handling, and Patrick in unarmed combat. Understand this—while they'll both teach you basic skills, you don't get into their advanced classes without a personal invitation. You want a chance at special forces? Impress your trainers."

With that, he stepped back, and I nodded to him in thanks, before stepping forward again.

"Now, you know who will be doing what, but you don't know how or why," I said clearly. "That's simple. We bleed, so that those we love don't have to. I'll be fighting beside many of you, but some of you will be sent on missions and you won't return. You will lose your lives in the defense of the dungeon, of your families and friends, and in the defense of the person next to you. Take a look around. Go on," I ordered.

"These people next to you, all around you, will be responsible for your safety in the day, weeks, and years to come. They will be the person on guard while you sleep, the person who's examined the tracks that circle your camp, and who stands between you and our enemies."

I saw the looks they were giving one another, and I grinned.

"To give you all the best chance of surviving that, and of having those around you make the very best decisions, the ones that lead to you and us surviving, you'll all be trained the same.

"That's going to be hard, physically demanding training to start with. You'll be taught to run faster, farther, and for longer than you ever thought you could. You'll be taught to fight, with spears, swords, shields and hammers, axes, rifles, explosives. And for a rare few? Magic.

"You see, we don't just expect ground pounders from you. Some of you will have the innate ability to fight with magic as well. You'll gain classes that will turn you into one-man—or woman—killing machines. You might be a crack shot, or lethal up close with spears and shields.

"You might be one of those destined to be a pilot. We're going to need them, and I'll listen to anyone who has a request when the time comes. We'll be creating vehicles eventually…tanks and fighters, jets and fucking spacecraft. Believe me when I say the only limit on how far you go right now?

"That's you. Everyone who stands here with me has proved themselves to me personally. Maybe the first general of our forces won't be from those of us up here, but is one of you? Maybe one of you will be the reason our world is made safe. One of you might be the first person to leave our solar system, in an Earth-made craft, or the first to reach level one hundred.

"I'm literally a minor god," I called out. "I'm ascending, day by day, growing in power and fighting other gods. I grow more powerful as I kill them, and yet? Maybe one day one of you will surpass me." I paused, looking around at them all.

"This is what I mean when I say that the only one who will define how far you go is you. Over the next days and weeks, we'll be introducing new weapons to the field. Some of you will be entrusted with the latest weapons for testing and day-to-day use, others will not. That's both because there will be limited capacity at first, and because frankly, as we learn, these weapons will change quickly. What is new today may be obsolete tomorrow.

"Rifles will be upgraded and adjusted to be more powerful, more accurate, and more reliable. As these weapons are tested, however, others will be fighting and dying with more conventional equipment. Remember, this is the reality of war: every day will be dangerous, every day will be hard, and you'll be pushed to the utter brink.

"From today, as your training begins, you will be cycled through the gym; you'll be pushed to lift, to squat, and to run harder and heavier than you ever have in your life.

"Muscles will tear, bones will break. Believe me when I say that, at some point today, no matter how you feel right now, you will consider quitting." I turned and gestured to Jo, who stepped forward. Her small cadre of healers behind her looked concerned as they studied how many people there were here.

"Jo and her team will be healing you between exercise sets. As many of you as there are? We'll be asking for volunteers as well. The way that the class system works is that as you hit your fifth level, then tenth, and every ten after that, you'll be offered a new class.

"Classes are the system's way of identifying and assisting you. So if, as an example, you're a fighter who spends a lot of time donating your mana to the healers, and assisting them with the focal orbs—those are magical artifacts that hold spells—then it's likely you'll be offered a battlefield healer class, possibly a field medic or something similar.

"That, in turn, should you choose it, will grant you healing spells that you can keep yourself and your fellow fighters alive with." I smiled and gestured to Jo and the others again.

"For now, though, I expect them to be tired, and you will all be asked again and again to assist with the focal orbs. When you reach your class choices, these are personal to you. Please understand that some of you will be offered classes that are totally different to those around you, and it's for a good reason. The classes you are offered are literally paths to power. Some of you may be offered uncommon, or rare classes. Consider these carefully, and please, if you're offered a rare or above class, come to your trainers. It may be we know about the relevant class and can advise you. It will, however, always be your choice.

"Next, as well as physical training in the gym and outside, you will be taught to fight. This is where it gets even more fun! Once your trainers deem you worthy, you'll be granted access to the training dungeon. You'll be able to form teams, and you'll enter the dungeon on a regular basis, fighting the creatures that we can summon. Understand this now: they are there to kill any and all who enter, and that includes me! If I step into the training dungeon, I'd better be ready to fight, or I'll be killed."

I paused, looking around and making sure they all understood that.

"This isn't because we want to risk your lives needlessly, but because for you, to face creatures that are predictable, if dangerous, to begin with is the best way for you to learn. You'll be able to loot those you kill, and more to the point, you'll earn Experience! That Experience will enable you to level, and from there you'll have a much better chance in a fight. The other side of this is that you'll be able to pick mage trainees to form teams with you.

"The mage trainees will *not* have access to their magic yet, most likely. They might never gain magic, or they may gain access to horrific skills. We don't know. We're training them, and giving them every chance we can, but for them to make the most of that? They need to reach their class choices.

"For them to do that? They need you. Understand that this gives you the chance to form a team with someone who may one day be able to command the earth to swallow their enemies, so please, don't be a dick.

"Equally though, they *need* you. The more powerful and flashy a spell is? The more mana it uses. The more mana, the less a mage can use it. Expect that your squishy mage friends will need a lot of protection from you, both now and later, but that when you need them? You're going to *really* need them."

I paused as someone raised a hand in question.

"Yes?" I gestured to them.

"Why are we in teams?" an older woman asked. "I thought we were to be an army."

"You will." I nodded. "And that's a very good point. The reason you need teams, though, is because not all fights will be armies against each other. Sometimes, most of the time, in fact, you'll be sent out in smaller squads, most likely of six: two melee fighters, two ranged, a mage, and a healer. This is a good all-round team, and something that can be scaled up or down easily. We can simply add another team or two to you, and have a hell of a lot more strength and depth.

"You'll be sent to do recon, to protect people or an area. You might be asked to face monsters in their dens, to clear them out, and you might be sent to make an example of someone who's been a dick. We don't know what you'll face, but you'll do it together, and that's why I have a cadre of kobolds in here. You'll be fighting alongside each other, as well as other non-human allies, so you might as well get used to it now."

I stood there for a few seconds, waiting, but either there were no more questions, or people were too nervous to ask them right now.

"Okay then, I'll be honest, there's nearly six hundred of you, which is more than we'd dared hope, so thank you. But you're going to have to be patient over the next few days as we get you all moving. One more quick point; once you complete your 'basic' training, some of you will be offered advanced training classes.

"These will be for the specialists, and will be highly limited, but these will be the future beast masters, assassins, spell-swords and more…Those who complete these courses will be the elite. You've seen or heard of my team and I when we fight. You think that we're good? The elites will be taught everything we know, and will be encouraged to surpass us, to march out there and rescue entire cities! If you want a shot at the kind of power that they'll one day wield? Work hard and excel now.

"You'll be split into six teams, I believe?" I turned to Mike, who nodded and stepped forward, taking over the narrative.

"You'll be split into six groups, each named for a hero of the past. Your teams will be your families for the next month, and at the end of it, will determine your immediate future. You'll be randomly assigned numbers. A token given out by one of my team will be the identifier and those numbers will tell you where to go.

"Those teams will need their own training cadre, and my people will be picking those members over the next few days. Some of you will be named as squad leaders, lance corporals, and corporals. The ranks will be like this..." He paused, making sure he had everyone's rapt attention.

"Trainees are what you are for now, until you prove yourself. Once you do that? You'll be a squaddie, or squad member. Those who stand head and shoulders above their fellows will be squad leaders. Until you prove yourself? A squad leader will be responsible for themselves and three squaddies." He started to pace as he spoke.

"Once you prove yourself, and have a kill under your belt, you'll be a hoplite soldier. There will be a corporal for every three soldiers, forming a basic team that will be granted access to the dungeon. The lance corporal for the team will be chosen from the mages. That way, you will always have someone who understands magic in secondary command of the team. This is the theory, and for now it stands. *However*...if there's a problem with this plan, once there's real-world experience? Come to us. Talk to us. Things might need to be changed. This is life, after all. No battle plan survives contact with the enemy."

"Good luck to you all," I said, as Mike turned to give way to me again. "I'll be joining the occasional training session here and there, but mainly you're all going to be working your arses off for the next few weeks. Get used to very little sleep, lots and lots of exercise and food, and probably crying in the showers because you can't believe how fucked you feel. That's reality, though. Give us six weeks, that's all I ask. Serve in the military for six weeks, and if it's not for you? You can quit and we'll find you another job, no hard feelings. You'll keep your accommodation here, as will your family. Fail and quit before then? Equally, no hard feelings, but the room you take up will be needed by your replacement, so you'll need to move back to the park.

"Last the six weeks and then look at yourself, that's all we ask. Look at the strength you've gained, and those whose lives you've saved. I hope you'll agree to stay on after that, but we can talk about it once you've graduated basic training. Again, thank you all, and good luck."

The others had spread out and were walking through the crowd, handing out tokens to people. Much as with the mages, they were simple round white stones, each with a number on them.

Mike stepped up and started to speak again.

"Now the six groups, each will have a dedicated trainer who's responsible for you first thing in the morning and last at night. These are your personal leaders, and if you need something, be that advice or an ass-kicking, these are the ones you go to. They'll be teaching all the groups, but you will be their personal team, so expect extra lessons in their chosen specialty!" Mike boomed, getting people's attention again as they shifted from looking at the tokens and comparing them with people nearby.

"Team one, Hercules, the strongest of them all! You're up for the gym first, and you're with Rhodes. Good luck, you're gonna need it! Follow her to the back now and form up!"

People started to separate out, and I grinned despite myself. Andre and Jimmy had somehow managed to both get tokens for the same team, and both for hers.

"Team two, Bellerophon!" Mike called. "The monster slayers of the ancient world, you better believe you've a lot to live up to. You're with Markus, and you've got melee training first!" Mike strode to the side, holding a hand out and gesturing to where Markus was moving off to the right.

"Team three, Achilles! The greatest warrior of the ancient world, you're with Patrick, and if you thought people needed luck with Rhodes, believe me, you'll be studying unarmed combat a lot! You get to start with the basics of kung fu today!" He gestured to the right where a smirking Patrick was jogging now with a hand held in the air, Mike grinned.

"Team four, Ulysses! The great explorer, and one who loved to travel, get used to it, because you'll be under Chris's gaze a lot. He's responsible for you, and you to him! You're on cardio for the next hour!" He winced, seeing the state of a lot of the volunteers, and I nodded as well, knowing they'd be broken soon.

"Team five, Hector! The great defender, leader of the armies of Troy, or one of them, you'll be studying ranged combat and defenses with Jeffrey first, and he's responsible for you!" Jeffrey, ever the prepared one, lifted a green banner into the air and waved it, getting people's attention, before leading them off in yet another direction.

"Last of all, Theseus, slayer of the minotaur, and generally someone who took absolutely no shit from anyone! Congratulations, team six, you get Sarah. Group tactics and close team fighting will be your focus, and I believe she's ready to break you all already with something!"

Sarah shook her head at Jeffrey's banner, then lifted a spear in the air to make sure people could see it, before striding off to one side, leading her people away.

I blew out a long breath, before shaking my head in amazement. No matter how basic and simple we made things, there were still at least thirty people milling around before the platform, looking for direction.

"Right!" I called, striding forward, as Jo sent her people off after the groups and stepped up to help me. "Who here missed the tokens?"

CHAPTER TWENTY-SEVEN

Fifteen minutes later, I slipped into the end of the second mage class, moving as silently as I could. The room had changed a little since we first started. A good dozen more converters were scattered around the room. I smiled as I saw the looks of contentment from people who practically cuddled specific converters that matched their affinity.

"Okay, thank you all!" Dante called, clapping his hands together. "You're making great progress. And remember, fighter training is starting today, so for those who want additional meditation training? Ashley and I will be here tonight for an hour or two if you have any questions or need any help."

I moved through the crowd, nodding to and greeting a few people as I recognized them. A minute later, I clapped Dante on the shoulder in greeting, stopping by his side.

"How's it going?" I asked him, getting a grin.

"Fantastic," he admitted. "I feel like we're making real headway now. Yeah, there's only so much we can do with meditation alone, but most people can sense their core now, and those who've managed to guide their mana out and around their bodies are all able to sense the movement of their mana."

"So once they unlock their classes, they should do well." I smiled.

"That's the hope!" he said. "We've got a few people who are level four, and are doing well with their meditation…I was wondering if I could…?" He broke off, expectantly.

"What?" I asked. "Take them into the dungeon?"

"Yeah," he admitted. "It'd be really good for people to see that this is working."

"It's only been a few days," I pointed out, and he grinned.

"It has, but you know, until you can actually control your mana enough to do something, it's pretty dull just sitting here pulling on threads of mana. Once they see someone actually benefit from it all? That'll change."

"A few days yet. I'd love to say yes…honestly, I would," I said as he opened his mouth to try to convince me. "The problem, as always, is mana. Tomorrow we should be finished with the mana converter research. That'll bring in a load more mana, we hope, but we'll need to upgrade all the converters we have in place."

"Damn."

"Yeah. Once they're all upgraded, we'll have a lot more mana to play with, and we can start summoning more dungeon creatures. After that, we'll hopefully get more aware kobolds and even more with the research perk.

"Once we've got all those working, it'll make the research come along a lot faster, and that'll give us more mana to spend on other things, mate. It's all a balancing act—do we invest in infrastructure, in the military, in research?" I shrugged.

"Honestly, we could have accomplished so much more by focusing in just one area so far, specializing, but the only reason we've survived this long is because we've got strength and depth."

"I know," he said, shaking his head. "It's just…well…"

"You want to move your stuff along," I agreed. "Believe me, I know the feeling. I desperately want to work on my personal spells and more, but there's only so many hours in the day. And, frankly, if I push myself to do it all day long, and take no breaks? I'll go mad."

"You've not done your personal quests yet?" Dante asked me, shocked. "The first ones?"

"Nope," I admitted grimly, glancing around and making sure nobody else was close enough to overhear. "When do I have the time, Dante? After the things I had to do to win the last goddamn fight, I need to rebuild my mana channels before I do anything else. Each gate I repair costs me hours, and I'm flooding myself with the mana equivalent of sludge the entire time."

"And you're here?" he asked me, disbelieving. "You need to be sorting that out!"

"I fucking know, mate." I forced a friendly smile for the benefit of the people who were even now moving in and finding their spaces in the room. "But, as I say, I can only do so much. Only so many hours in the fucking day, you know."

"I…I'm sorry." Dante shook his head. "I know. I do. It just seems insane that with everything that's going on, and that we need you so much, that you're here teaching people to mediate instead of…"

I fixed him with a look and waited. After a few seconds, he stopped, all on his own, and finally nodded again.

"I get it," he said. "You're doing it because we all need it."

"Yeah," I agreed. "We needed all of this sorting. Now that the fighters are in training, though? That's another job sorted. Once they have some accommodation, we can all get back to research, and that in turn will speed up everything else. Every hour that people aren't preparing for the next fight is an hour that's wasted right now. And I know that sounds fucking stupid after I've just said I need to relax or I'll be fucked.

"The truth is that our greatest strength is the dungeon and the effect it can have on our people. There will be thousands of settlements out there now, and only a very small number will have dungeons attached. Those that do will be split between building up the dungeon and letting people use its facilities to grow stronger. The difference is that the dungeon fairies that run the others have their own goals and aims. This dungeon only has me.

"It's been built and worked on to the exclusive aim of helping the human race. We're training people to fight now, to use magic, and once they're all up to speed? We'll have an army that can roll out and wipe out the fucking monsters. We'll claim all of the country, free people from the shit that's going on, and soon we'll have so much mana rolling in that we don't need to stop.

"All we'll be missing is the people to use the weapons and to take the training we can give, and that's where we're at now. The other dungeons are starting to let people in, and to see what the world is all about now, but they're separate entities, the dungeon and the people. Here, we're not. And if we can keep this up? We'll be too strong for them to start any shit with us. They'll have to form alliances, and then the Orcan will be here and who knows, maybe we'll actually be fucking ready for them."

"I can teach this class, if you want," Dante said. "Look, Ramnik and I can take turns teaching the classes. You can come here and listen and see how we're doing, step in if we're going the wrong way, or just teach the first lesson each day, then sit. We can teach the second and third, or more."

"I'll teach the first," I said after a few seconds' thought. "That was always the plan, but rather than sitting and teaching Ashley afterward and you and Ramnik helping the others to do as we do, you give her whatever private lessons she needs, and I'll just teach the first class. I need to get my mana gates fixed. Once I know how they're doing and I know for sure what I'm trying to do works, then I'll start teaching you all to do that next."

"Okay. Want me to teach this one?" he asked, and I hesitated, before nodding.

"Yeah, thank you." I agreed, smiling and clapping him on the shoulder again. "I'll work on my gates instead."

"No worries." Dante smiled, then summoned a drink, chugging the branded bottle.

I strode from the platform, nodding in passing again to a few people as I moved to the very back, sitting down next to a Fire converter and turning to get comfy, while watching the incoming crowd.

Ten minutes or so passed as people filtered in, gradually filling the room, before Dante began.

"Okay, everyone! Thank you for coming, and welcome to the guided meditation class for today. As usual, we're going to be working on sensing our mana, and guiding it to do a single loop around our bodies. Once we're all at the stage that we can manage that, we'll move onto the next lesson…Yes?" Dante asked, and I grinned as the first questions started, even as the last few people moved in, taking up seats.

"What if we can already do that?" a young lad at the front asked.

"Then you can practice and improve, you can help others, or you can leave," Dante said firmly. "These lessons are for *everyone*. Some here will be able to push further, and faster, but that's no indication of strength nor ability! Different people can do different things and find different aspects of magic easier or harder to deal with."

"Are there more advanced classes for those of us who aren't so slow?" the same kid asked, and I moved to make sure I knew who he was, mentally marking him as someone to watch in the future. His shock of blond hair, carefully styled, and his well-pressed clothes made me dislike him already.

Where most people had been clearly busting their ass before coming to the classes, he looked as if he'd just stepped off a catwalk.

I snorted to myself and sat back, closing my eyes as Dante spoke coldly, cutting the arrogant little fucker down.

"Yes, actually. There are personal classes available with some of the various trainers. Spaces are limited. They're invite only to those we believe are worth the additional training—"

"So how do I get my invite?"

Dante paused, watching him in silence for a few seconds.

"What?" the kid asked, totally oblivious.

"Here's a hint, kid…" someone called from farther back in the group. "Stop interrupting the mage who's trying to answer your questions!"

"Fuck you!" the young guy called back, waving one hand dismissively, not even turning to see who had spoken. "So come on, how do I get the invite?"

"You want an invite to the private classes?" I called, standing so that everyone could see me.

"Yeah?" he replied, staring at me.

"Well, you have to pass the tests first. Physical comes before all the others. You want a chance at my personal group? Go to Sergeant Rhodes right now, tell her what you were asking for in the class, and that I said she was to give you the special class physical test."

"I…what do I have to do?" He seemed suddenly less sure of himself, and I grinned.

"I just told you, and you only get one chance. Are you turning it down?"

"NO!"

"Then go find Rhodes. Tell her that I give her permission to send you on to the other trainers for their tests afterward." I could barely stifle the grin that was threatening to split my face as he pushed his way through the crowd, looking smug as he told people to get out of his way.

"I'll be back once I've done them!" he proclaimed loudly, and I nodded seriously.

"Of course," I agreed. "I expect you'll learn a lot…"

"Humility for a start…" someone nearby muttered, and I shushed them quickly.

As soon as he was out of the room, the sniggers started, and then a few seconds after, the full-blown laughter.

"Okay, people!" I called out after a bit, seeing the grins and disbelief on their faces as they discussed his actions. "It's not his fault he's too arrogant and dumb to read the writing on the wall. But once he's been sent for some of the classics by the others, he'll probably be back, so let's play nice…"

"Classics?" Dante asked me, and I nodded.

"You know, Rhodes will make him run and do burpees until he cries, but Chris and the others are more likely to send him for a bag of nail holes, or to find the sky hook, the skirting board ladders or for a long stand. You know. The classics. Like tartan paint."

"What's wrong with tartan paint?" Dante asked slowly, before facepalming. "Sorry, just got that one," he apologized.

"Damn, I'll have to try to get you with some of the others then," I replied dryly. "Now, anyone else want to be an ass, or can we get on with the lesson?"

Silence held for a few seconds, and I nodded.

"Sounds like you're up, Dante." I settled back down and shook my head in disbelief at the kid's antics.

"Okay, everyone, now that the fun's over, let's start by going over the basics again, then we can get started…"

While Dante led the class, I closed my eyes and sunk into myself, diving into the mana flow and following the current until I found the next gate, sinking deep to find the shattered remains.

Seeing the fluted, broken sections laid there in the silt at the bottom of the channel, I paused for a long second, examining it and wondering whether it was just me or whether it was getting deeper.

For whatever reason, I was visualizing my mana channels as rivers, and it worked; hell, the others were picking it up, and it worked for them too, but…

I knew that part of this was just in my head, that I was seeing things as I expected to see them, and that my brain was filtering things. That being said, though, I was learning constantly. The "sediment" that I envisaged looked like gleaming sand and dirty mud, mixed in and packed around the remains of the gates.

Was it a case of the gates purifying the stream before and now they weren't now, and making things worse instead?

That would make sense. I'd never noticed the sediment before. But if the rings had been dragging more mana in than I'd been capable of absorbing "naturally" before, then maybe broken, they were dragging in the crap?

And that was why the sediment was at its worst around the fractured remains of the gates?

I shook my head, deciding that the priority was to put the gates back together first. They'd been built originally with the help of that furry shit-biscuit, so I could only hope that once I'd gotten them back together, they'd stop sucking in the crap, and I could start purifying the system more.

I lifted the first sections of the gate from the depths, pressing them back into place and gritting my teeth at the sudden burst of nausea that freeing of so much sediment brought.

Clouds of it floated away downstream, and I forced myself to ignore it.

The minutes passed quickly, and soon I distantly heard people moving around. Ignoring them, I continued to work, and soon the dull roar of hundreds of voices died away to a steady buzz as people moved back and forth.

I ignored it all, working on, pressing mana into the shattered sections, smoothing it into place and making sure it was solid and safe before moving to the next section.

Eventually, I surfaced from the depths, the gate complete and dragging mana faster and faster through itself. The sediment that had gathered around the base slowly broke free and was sucked downstream.

I set off, following it, going more on instinct than anything, as I searched for the next gate.

The stream was definitely moving faster overall now than it had been. The flow of mana built, and for the first time, when I reach the next gate, I neither passed on nor tried to fix it.

Instead, I sank down into the sediment and examined it.

It was made of, as I'd seen before, a mass of "broken" mana, fragments that had no home, and that were slowly growing, absorbing the free ambient mana all around them.

They created additional linkages and finally connected fully, forming a recognizable mana form. Once that was done, the stream would pull them along, sending them cartwheeling and rolling across the sediment.

They'd pick more up as they go, more linkages, until suddenly a fully formed strain of mana was floating free in the stream, mingling with the others that were sucked in.

It seemed mad, but if that was what was happening all the time, the fragments were discarded bits that were then reforming and adding to my mana overall, then surely there had to be a way I could help the process?

Especially as once it reached my core, the core itself tore the mana forms apart, didn't it? The core…

I'd not seen much in the way of sediment in the mana streams. Not overall. I'd seen great clouds of it clogging the stream, and I'd nearly lost my damn lunch at the feeling, but it didn't last long. The cloud of crappy mana floated away and inside of a minute or so, it was usually over.

That seemed…wrong.

Surely, if I kept stirring it up, it'd be getting worse, right? I mean, it wasn't actually water in a river.

It was mana and although the fractured bits settled to the bottom, the process was in part because the remains of the rings were there, right?

I hesitated, then grit my teeth. Time to test a theory, and hope I didn't end up vomiting on anyone.

Reaching out, I sank my metaphorical and spiritual hands into the silt and sediment, dragged them deeper…and then started tearing right and left, setting a vast cloud of shit loose into my mana channels.

Instantly, the bile rose, and I let go—not of my stomach, but of the bottom of the channel, allowing myself to be swept away.

I floated downstream with all the sludge I'd stirred up, watching it, and occasionally sinking to drag my hands and feet through the bottom to stir up more as my stomach settled.

Soon the pristine flow of the channel was a raging stream of filth, and I had to force myself to keep going, and not to lose control and redecorate the area.

My stomach roiled, and the bubbling in my guts suggested that if I didn't get control or let it come "up" soon, it'd make its own way "down"—and to hell with my wishes.

I gritted my teeth and held on tight, the stream filthy with it all as I passed the remnants of the last gate and streamed out into…into the great emptiness.

The core suddenly gleamed before me, the massive multifaceted star that, the closer I drew, I knew would resolve into a massive construction of columns spinning around a central axis.

Each of the massive pillars had one end sunk into the stream of mana, and the other…

I hesitated, lifting clear of the morass, and I hovered there, staring, stunned. I'd always seen the pillars as in motion; the central spire of pure mana was stationary, with either end of it sunk deep into the stream, but the others were in constant motion.

I'd noticed that they flowed out from a central axis, where they all joined to the pure, and from there, they flew round and round in a complicated motion, forever dipping deeper and lifting into shallower "waters" of the stream.

What I'd not considered was the other end.

They didn't terminate at the pure; they joined it there—but they locked onto it halfway along their length. I'd always landed and looked "down" the length of the massive spires, but one direction seemed as good as the other.

Now, though...now I was looking at it, and for the first time I saw it when the stream was contaminated with the mana fragments.

One end of the spires seemed to glow more powerfully than the other. As the stream was purified, the shattered fragments were drawn into the spires, drunk down almost greedily, and I shook my head in disbelief at my stupidity.

All this time, I'd been using the mana converters and more to drag more mana in, and the dungeon converted and stored a fragment of it in its various forms ready for us...but they broke the mana down to pure!

I'd never considered that I was doing the same.

Nor that the end result of that, logically, unless we put in place a filtering system, was a mass of corruption.

My mana channels were a microcosm of the damn world around us, as the various converters and natural processes pulled in the mana and used it in their ways.

In return, they discarded the fragments that were left behind, and although the dungeons in the short-term would be wonders that would purify the area and act as havens?

In the long-term, they'd give rise to terrible creations of twisted mana.

Instead of the naturally accumulating corrupted mana that would be everywhere, the dungeons would cleanse the area. Then they'd also continually leave a thin layer of discarded fragments around the area.

That would build up, the mass growing deeper and deeper until it reached critical mass, overtaking the dungeon's ability to process.

I hovered there, my mind racing as I imagined the logical end to that process: the rise of the "dark" dungeons. Dungeons that were more like the ones we'd always known of in stories and more: hellholes that existed to draw the adventurers in and slaughter them.

Mine was designed to do that as well, in part, but my creatures were...well...they were *good*. They defended the dungeon, and they looked after the people I told them to.

A dark dungeon would be like the second dungeon I found. But rather than sacrificing the locals to boost its growth, so that one day it could save more people...it'd simply spawn more and more terrible creatures, sending them out to slaughter and kill.

The core was almost done already, the mana stream on the far side that sank back into my mana channels gleaming and pure, and I shook my head in disbelief.

For the core to accept all the mana fragments so happily, it was either designed, or evolved to do so. That meant that there would be a way to make sure the dungeon didn't fall into that trap as well. After all, if I could make my damn body process it, with nothing but mental constructs, there had to be a method for the dungeon as well.

Right?

I lifted from the depths of my mana system, blinking in the gentle light of the tower, and looked around. The lesson was done, and the families who were reduced to camping here had returned. They were waiting patiently for their accommodation to be finished, and I swallowed hard, feeling the last of the nausea replaced with shame.

I'd dragged these people here from their rooms in the park, giving them hope for a better future, without telling them what they'd be giving up.

It was my responsibility to fix this, and soon.

Moving through the handfuls of small families, I made it outside, taking a deep breath of the cold, crisp air and squinting in the darkness.

Torches and dungeon lights were lit, but still, the sun had been up when I'd entered. And it'd not felt like I was in there for *that* long, surely?

I could hear squeals and laughter coming from the pool, and I smiled despite everything. I jogged around the outside, enjoying the rise in temperature as I moved closer to the pool, then shivering as I headed away, entering the Parthenon.

There were markedly less people in here than the last time I'd run over, when the amateur-hour coup was in progress, and I couldn't help but smile as the thick glass doors closed behind me.

The air in here was warm, and despite how much marble coated every surface, the rugs were deep and clean, the shelves held colorful books, and the air was filled with the smell of fresh baked bread and pastries, coffee and minted hot chocolate. It all combined with the gasps and giggles of children on the rugs to one side, having a story read to them, to create a sudden warmth in anyone's heart.

Moving across the floor toward the upper council chambers above, the research areas and the war rooms, I couldn't help myself as I passed a counter, and I plucked a Danish pastry and hot chocolate free, smiling my thanks to the older lady who maintained it, seeing the clear happiness on her face as she watched the children, and worked to prepare their evening snack.

I'd not considered the differences this section of the dungeon had brought. Not really, anyway. Because so many people were needed to work around the clock, there was always a team in the Parthenon, I'd been told, and I'd just accepted that, that no matter what, sometimes you'd not want to leave your kids in their room if you were working. And if you didn't have family to watch over them, what did you do?

This was the result.

In Eastern culture, this was much more pronounced, I'd heard, that the retired members of the family stayed home and looked after the kids while the younger and middle members worked.

Here, the elderly were involved in the dungeon, and could work as hard as anyone, manipulating the dungeon systems to absorb materials and to increase our reach.

That was what I'd assumed people were doing, anyway. But as was so often the case, I'd not considered the reality of the situation.

Many of these people had lost grandchildren, children, and friends, and for them, to help with the children like this, to sit and read stories? To make sure they were well fed and safe, to play with them and to essentially run a round-the-clock nursery program, was wonderful.

I stopped halfway up the stairs and stared out across the lower floors. Dozens of children sat cross-legged on a massive white rug, while a man and woman in their eighties, if they were a day, took turns reading the male and female parts from a story.

The look of wonder on the faces of the children made me shake my head sadly.

I remembered my family reading to me when I was small, vaguely, and then after I'd lost them, and I'd ended up in the system, well…. Although I'd been too old to need the stories, I'd damn well needed the love. Here we had an entire generation that had lost huge swathes of their families.

Mothers, fathers, siblings and grandparents: most had lost some, if not all of them. And that wasn't even considering the literal dozens of kids who had utterly no one.

I'd been focused, as always, on the day-to-day running of things, of working and fighting, and I couldn't help but feel proud, knowing Kelly and Aly would have been responsible for this.

The children we'd rescued from Aaron's "care" were here somewhere, or in the park, being integrated into the dungeon's population, and looked after.

They were the new recipients of the "care" system that I grew up in, and I was damn well sure they were better off in our hands than I had been in the government's.

I forced myself to move again, climbing to the top and weaving along the corridors and through rooms until I entered the war room.

It was dimly lit, only two people in attendance. Kelly, unsurprisingly, was slumped in a chair that molded to her body, cushioning her like a flight acceleration couch as she worked in the dungeon sense.

Aly, on the other hand, sat at one of the desks, a small notepad before her as she scribbled away, screens arranged in a half-circle around her as she checked details and made plans.

"Matt," she said in greeting as I entered, barely looking over. "Do you need me?"

"Yeah."

"Can you wait while I finish this, or is the world ending?" she asked me crisply.

"I can wait."

"Okay, few minutes then," she muttered absently, making a few more calculations and ticking things off on another screen.

I nodded, settling back and bringing up the map, looking over the area, and staring in wonder at the speed we were clearing it.

We'd been demolishing all the houses around the park before absorbing them, mainly because it got us more mana, and was easier and faster, as well as enabling people to clear out the keepsakes and more of the previous owners.

Here, in the center of the city, we'd been doing that originally, but had switched to stripping the building, then absorbing it all. The difference was significant; for whatever reason, absorbing a single brick got us the equivalent of a point of mana, more or less.

Absorbing four or five bricks that were all connected still only got us two, and sometimes three mana.

It didn't make much sense, but it appeared the bigger the mass, the more energy it was to absorb it. Therefore, it was much more cost-effective to do it brick by brick.

Back to the park—that was what we were doing, and it worked out much better. Here, though, in the city, surrounded by hundreds and thousands of buildings that were all at least four or five stories high, most with cellars and lower floors and not having any access to any kind of mechanical systems to tear them down?

It just didn't make sense to send people in with sledgehammers and risk their lives with collapsing buildings, when we could make do by absorbing more buildings to offset the loss.

I was staring at the space we'd managed to clear, when Aly sat up suddenly, rubbing the small of her back and groaning.

"Too many hours in this damn chair," she muttered, climbing to her feet and stretching. "So, what dastardly plan have you come up with and how much is it going to fuck up the research plan now?" She fixed me with a warning glare.

"Ah," I said. "Uh…I love you, really?"

"Oh gods…" Aly slumped back into her chair and dropped her head into her hands. "He's a demon sent to ruin my life…"

"You're my favorite almost-sister-in-law?" I tried again, smiling manically.

"I hate you," Aly replied. She slumped her head down and buried it in her arms, lifting one hand and summoning a bottle of red wine, and pointing it at me. "Open this, then tell me."

I shrugged, summoning a bottle opener and setting to work, deliberately not asking why she summoned the bottle and not just a glass holding this particular red wine.

"Soooo…" I started.

"Wine first," Aly growled, lifting her head and fixing me with a glare.

I cut the last of the top free, and set to work on the cork, noting that it was a real one, not a plastic one, and that it was fairly old, considering that detail alone.

Popping it free, I summoned a glass, tilting the bottle and…was stopped as she snatched the bottle from me.

"I don't know what shit you've got planned," she mumbled. "Until then, I don't trust that I'll only need a glass." With that, she settled back in her chair, turning to face me fully, and summoned a long straw.

It was one of those whirly ones that went in all sorts of directions and ended with a parasol, presumably in case it rained and you were in a hot tub.

Whatever the reason, I couldn't help but smile genuinely as she glared at me, sitting back in the chair and sucking on a ridiculously long twisty and cheerful straw.

"Okay then." I leaned back into a chair nearby. "So, looking at the mana absorption and conversion research, I think we need to be looking for something that might not be there yet, or even at all. But there's a problem that's coming with regard to mana sediment, or fragments. What I've found is…"

CHAPTER TWENTY-EIGHT

The next two days passed in a blur. I woke early and worked till late, splitting my daytime focus between rebuilding my gates, stirring up the sludge, and gritting my teeth until as much of it was absorbed as possible, and essentially punishing myself in the gym.

I managed an early workout with Rhodes, Andre, and Jimmy, who had become her right and left hands respectively. It seemed that when it came to physical things, they were both insanely competitive and genuinely "nice" guys.

Admittedly, the whole *armed robbery* thing was a minor issue, but that was essentially being buried as they wanted to be fighters anyway, and we wanted them to fight. The deal for criminals who hadn't paid off their debt was to either pay it off in the army with us or, if it was something that wasn't appropriate to the new world we found ourselves in?

It was forgotten.

We weren't in the business of justice. And frankly, if someone had been a fraudster in the old world, but fought to protect kids and innocents here? Fuck it, they were all right in my book.

As long as their crimes stayed in the past, anyway.

If they started ripping people off again, then they'd be in for a nasty surprise.

The brothers and Rhodes worked me hard, encouraging me as I strained, and every day we all saw increases in our stats. I spent as much time as I could in meditation, and as soon as the final gate was repaired, I felt a wave of relief when I found that the overall change was to begin scouring the last of the sediment free.

Once that was done, and I felt like I could finally work out on a simple machine, like a rower, and still meditate without losing my focus, I really got down to it.

Hours passed in a blur as I started to work on my class quests instead.

Magic was both insanely easy, and fucking complicated as all hell.

Reaching down inside myself, I could pull my mana to hand any time I wanted, and I could do basically fuck all with it beyond that. Whatever the class system instituted, it missed all the "controls" side of things, simply installing the relevant direct access, somehow.

To use my Incinerate spell required absolutely no gestures, no funny-sounding words, nothing.

Yet to try to recreate that step by step? It was insanely complicated. I pulled the notification back up for the quest and re-read it a hundred times. I could, of course, have gone to Dante or Ramnik or any of the others who had managed to do this, and I could ask for their help at any time, but that seemed *wrong*.

I'd created spells before. The Soul Beam, and yeah, okay, *maybe* that wasn't the success story I'd like it to have been. It was insanely powerful, admittedly, but it also scoured my soul apart.

So yeah.

Losing access to that in my reversion to Storm Titan wasn't really a bad thing.

Storm-Strike, on the other hand, had come from the system in part, and for whatever reason, the system had accepted that as my melee spell.

Reading the notification that I'd gained on getting the Arcanist class again, I shook my head in how goddamn unhelpful it was.

Class Quest!

As an Arcanist, you have gained access to the secrets of creation itself, or at least the ones not very well hidden. Magic, mana, and mysteries fill your mind, and you are finally ready to move on and prove yourself.

You have successfully created your first signature melee spell. Continue to research, investigate, and create to benefit from the wonders of your class. Remember, only you can decide your destiny…

Complete this quest to receive a boost to your selected affinities.

- **Melee spell**: 1/1
- **Ranged spell**: 0/1
- **Defensive spell**: 0/1

I simply willed it to "be," normally, I just selected the spell and, boom. There you go. It wasn't like I needed to do anything else. But when I thought about that, that seemed insane.

After all, if that was all there was to it, then surely a more experienced mage would be utterly impossible to defeat? They could simply decide that everyone who opposed them had just had a heart attack.

Pour mana into it, and boom—that was the new reality.

The universe didn't work like that, not really; therefore, what the spells I'd gained before had to be doing was acting as a relay of sorts. Thinking about it in tech terms, I made the "request" to the central computer, like when you clicked a button on the screen; it wasn't the mouse in your hand nor the screen that showed the button you'd just clicked that did the work.

It was the computer itself.

It took the request and evaluated it, decided whether it matched the list of instructions it had, and then responded as it'd been designed to.

If this/then that.

It was simple.

Logically, this was the same. Whatever system we were all now a part of was "in" me. Logically, the spells I was using were stored "in" the system as well, and after I unlocked them, I was simply clicking the target and selecting "incinerate" or "lightning" or whatever.

The actual heavy lifting was being done elsewhere.

That meant that my new spells would be vastly different from the old, and that explained why I couldn't just unlock them and move on.

If I didn't learn to actually use the magic myself, to channel it and to do whatever I needed to, I'd be essentially reduced to a "standard user."

I'd have access to whatever spells I unlocked from the system, but nothing more. If I wanted to reach real power, I'd always have to figure out the path.

After all, if I was some day to end up facing the Orcan in fucking space or whatever, it wasn't like I could just accept that until I was at insanely close ranges, I couldn't use magic. In space battles, I had the impression that speed and distance were important details.

With that in mind, I started again, wondering why the Storm-Strike was accepted as my melee choice, and Soul Beam had been, but my normal spells weren't.

Thinking my way through it, the best I could come up with was that Soul Beam had been a normal spell, more or less, but that I'd taken control of the mana and made it do what I wanted, guiding it personally.

Storm-Strike was the same. When I thought about it, I'd never tried activating it the way that I did Incinerate or others. I'd always flooded the Storm mana into my fist or foot, and I'd driven it out of that contact point, punching and kicking as I did it.

I'd guided the mana and made it do what I wanted.

That was it; it had to be.

I needed a ranged and defensive spell, and with that in mind, well…I knew what I needed straightaway. I needed access to my Lightning spell again.

I'd lost it when I'd upgraded to Storm Bolt, but regardless of the name, it required bloody pure mana to use, and so like the Soul Beam, I'd gained access to it, and then lost the fucker.

Basically, if I filled myself with pure mana and was willing to risk the soul burn, and being turned into a ghoul as Thor had put it, then I could have access to these spells. Otherwise, I needed to reconstruct my Lightning Bolt again.

That should be the easiest for me, considering my natural affinity with Lightning, so I started there.

Channeling Lightning-aspected mana down my arms and into my hands was easy. I'd done it hundreds of times by now, and that was flawless. After the very first attempt to control it externally, rather than just "hold" it, I decided I'd experiment on my own from now on, and far from anyone else. I'd practically filled the room with lightning.

Sometime later, I found myself on the roof of the mage's tower, having flown across and landed on it, before getting to work on what had originally been sort of a plan for mine and Kelly's date as much as anything else.

The tower had a peaked roof, and was open to the elements on the sides, here at the very top, allowing the wind to blow through and boost the mana conversion from the Air converters. But above that?

I created an insanely strong, but thin post that led upward.

It was literally for me, and me alone. Well, and Kelly.

The post rose a hundred meters into the air, solid steel all the way around, and built into the structure of the tower, making damn sure there would not be a weak spot that could cause it to come tumbling down in a high wind.

At the very top of the tower was a small, round room. It was barely four meters from one side to the other, and although that sounded quite large, once you added in that I'd be filling it with two Lightning and two Storm converters, it really fucking wasn't.

Add to that, I'd made it so that it, too, would be open on all sides and above, with a single spire that would climb higher to act as a lightning conductor.

It would once it was finished, anyway.

I was planning to create a table, chairs, and glass walls all the way around with a roof, essentially a romantic date, well away from everyone else, still safe and together, though. We'd eat, hopefully fool around, then I'd absorb everything into the dungeon, and we'd fly back down. Then I'd replace the table, chairs, and whatever with the four converters, and I'd have a private meditation chamber that literally no other fucker could reach, as well as a way to drain storms into the dungeon, should the opportunity arise.

For now, it was somewhere for me to sit and experiment with my magic, and I'd not injure anyone.

Two days, I spent hour upon hour up there, adjusting and manipulating my mana until at long last, I managed it.

Congratulations!

Through constant trial and error, experimentation, and sheer bloody-mindedness, you have managed to rediscover, and this time actually understand, the spell Lightning Bolt.

Lightning Bolt: Cast a blast of Lightning at your target, stunning and possibly frying them with the power of electricity.

Note: This spell has lessening effects, depending on the area traveled, the medium travelled through, and the mana dedicated to the spell.

[Originally this spell cost 50 mana per casting, and did from 50,000V to 150,000mV depending on the spell points invested. This limit is no longer in force, and the only limit to the spell is that which you, as the caster, assign it.]

*

Congratulations!

You have discovered that the path to power is never ending; a mere step down the road have you taken, and yet, your power grows. You have created a new ranged spell.

Continue to research, investigate, and create to benefit from the wonders of your class. Remember, only you can decide your destiny…Complete this quest to receive a boost to your selected affinities.

- **Melee spell:** 1/1
- **Ranged spell:** 1/1
- **Defensive spell:** 0/1

"Defensive" was weirdly the easiest to accomplish, in that I'd already learned to cast the spell outward and hit a target that I wanted to, excluding all others. It was a case of guiding the Air-aspected mana aside, creating a tunnel that linked directly to the target, and then "pouring" the Lightning into that vacuum.

It was fast and insanely powerful; the more mana I plowed into it, the more the target felt the love.

The defensive spell was much the same except that instead of powering the mana out of me and to "fall" down the tunnel to the target, I guided it out into a dome all around me, then back into me. As I was essentially cycling my mana out and back in, aside from a small loss from the time it was "out," it wasn't even expensive to maintain. I suspected it would be much more expensive to maintain once I was hitting people with it, but that was for another day.

Once I'd done that, and I was grinning to myself over my success, a thought occurred to me as well, though, and I twisted my mana to flow across my body, as I'd done a hundred times.

Instead of doing it as I had been each time, and focusing on it as a threat, or as an example of what I was, I thought of it as turning me into a living Taser and boom. Second defensive spell notification.

Fucker.

I dismissed them both, scanning them and seeing they were practically identical to the last notification, simply swapping out ranged for defensive, and moved straight to the good shit.

Congratulations!

You have successfully crafted your first signature spells. These spells are unique to you, and although others may evidence highly similar versions, they are different. Each personal spell you create is an amalgamation of your knowledge, your abilities, and your affinities. They will evolve as you do: the stronger you grow in the relevant affinities that make up these spells, the stronger your spell will, in turn, grow.

Know this: each spell you create will gain you a five percent [5%] increase in their relative affinity up to one hundred percent [100%]

Your Spells have gained you a fifteen percent [15%] increase in your Lightning affinity, but as this affinity is already at or surpassing the maximum affinity level, the bonus has been assigned to the lowest of the component mana forms.

In this case, your [AIR] mana was the lowest affinity of the contributory mana forms, and has been selected for advancement.

[AIR] mana has been increased from [72%] to [87%].

I couldn't help but fucking grin at that. Yeah, okay, I was hoping for more Lightning powers, but when I stopped and thought about it, I'd been almost exclusively using Lightning in the Storm-Strike. I'd cycled the damn mana to my fists and more, most of the time using Lightning instead of Storm.

Had I used Storm for the majority of these spells? I'd have increased my Water affinity massively.

Hell, if I'd been forming a solid stone shield or something out of Earth?

Fuck.

I stopped for a few seconds, contemplating the possibilities before finally sighing and releasing my power.

Tomorrow, I'd start on the next phase, but in my downtime, I'd work on the other spells as well. After all, I could use that Experience to help the next generation of mages.

The problem was that phase two required a lot more time and effort than I really wanted to commit to right now.

Finishing up for the day, I stood, then created the walls and roof on my little aerie, leaving the door till last, and quickly created a nice table and chairs. At the last minute, I decided the sex swing was probably something to make afterward, when there was a little more room and the table and chairs had been reabsorbed.

It was a little unsubtle, as well.

An hour later, as Kelly walked out of the war room, exhausted but pleased with everything that she'd accomplished for the day, I stopped her, standing in the corridor before her.

"Ta-daaa!" I joked, doing a little jazz hands as she stared at me. I'd already planned my clothes out, and arranged a haircut and beard trim, so it'd not taken long. But as I saw the shock, and then approval in her eyes, it became clear it was well worth the effort.

I'd had my beard and haircut, styled short and brushed, a little oil, nice, smart black jeans, and a clean white silk shirt, and I'd even put on aftershave.

Overall, the impression I got from the way she was looking at me was very, very positive, and I swept her up in a kiss.

"What's all this for?" she asked, a little breathlessly as I set her back down.

"Date night," I said firmly. "You've got two hours, then I want you back here. Ashley has a friend who was apparently a hairdresser and beautician. I didn't want to just book you in without asking, but I know you've said a few times you wish you could get a proper cut and—"

"Where is she?"

"I mean, you look fantastic, so don't think I'm saying you need to..." I teased her.

"Matt, if you think you're getting any tonight, or any night in the near future, believe me, you better spill and right goddamn now," she growled. "If I've only got two hours..."

"She's expecting you. Top floor of the dungeon, far west end. She spent the day setting up her gear, and she's going to be splitting her time between mage training and beautician-type stuff. When she asked, I just said yes," I explained, shrugging. "Want me to fly you over?"

"Yes." She nodded enthusiastically. "Right goddamn now."

Less than a minute later, and I was setting her down on the roof of the dungeon. Two minutes later, I was back, striding in to sit across from Aly, who eyed me with amusement.

"So, maybe you're not as dumb as you look after all."

"I couldn't be," I assured her, grinning. "Not and breathe too."

"True," she agreed. "So, I heard the conversation, obviously. Two hours, then back here. What have you planned?"

"Dinner." I shrugged. "In the aerie, just the two of us. It's the most private place I can come up with and—"

"Matt, honey, that's great. Kelly's my sister-in-law, and my friend, and you're my friend and my boss. I'm happy you've got a nice dinner planned, but the point I'm getting at is that you've told her to come here in two hours, and you're here now. That implies you're planning on being here for the next two hours?"

"Well, yes..."

"And am I to be here?"

"Well, yeah, for some of it, maybe?" I winced.

"Do I need wine?" she asked me grimly.

"No." I shook my head. "I'm not looking to change anything. I've just been so tied up in training and everything, that I need a research update, that's all."

"Oh...you could have just asked, you know," she grumbled.

"I was planning on it—you just didn't give me the chance," I pointed out, getting a grin from her.

"Okay..." she said, clearly gathering her thoughts. "So, we completed the converters research about five hours ago. I know the timescale jumped around a bit. First, we were ahead—half of everything we earn goes into the research 'pot,' after all—so when we all started doing extra hours here and there to build the tower and the accommodation, that really helped. But then we needed to make beds and more, which slowed things down so...anyway." She shrugged, settling back in her chair and thinking as she went on.

"It's done, and the average went as we'd expected. The 'normal' now for the converters has moved from between ten and twenty, to twenty to forty. We're getting an average of thirty, a little more, but for easy working out, we're going to say thirty points an hour per converter..."

"And we've got what, a hundred and twenty-five converters?" I asked, before shaking my head. "No, no, wait...I made a couple in the tower and—"

"And you told Dante he could make them as well, as long as for each Fire one he made, he made another for other people."

"Oh, yeah, I'd forgotten about that but..."

"A hundred and seventy-six," she finished for me. "Between the few we've all made and the bloody mess he's made, we now have a hundred and seventy-six, earning an average of thirty points an hour. That's five thousand, two hundred and eighty points an hour, or a hundred and twenty-six thousand, seven hundred and twenty points a day. Combine that with the conduits, which has reached fifty-four thousand, seven hundred and twenty points a day now..."

She checked the details, double-checking as I sat there stunned, before smiling and nodding.

"Yes, I thought that was right. One hundred and eighty-one thousand, four hundred and forty points a day."

I sat there gobsmacked for what seemed like ages, before shaking myself out of it.

"Remember, that's what we've got coming in now from the converters and the conduits. We've got another hundred to a hundred and fifty thousand mana coming in from the stripping of the local area as well. As usual, that's getting halved. Half goes to the dungeon for us to use in anything we need, like finishing the accommodation for the new people—that'll be done in an hour, by the way. I was going to ask you if you wanted to give them their new room keys, you know, like Barry did?" She glanced at me.

"No, we give them to their trainers, let them hand them out. Makes them trust their trainers more," I decided after a few seconds' thought.

"Okay, anyway. Half is available for the dungeon to use, but that still means that we've got a hundred and forty thousand plus mana a day to play with. I've got the common-level Blacksmithing crafting area in the system at the minute. Literally, I'm doing them in batches, with basic, then common for each, one after the other."

"How much are they again?" I asked, sitting back and getting comfy.

"Five thousand for the basic, fifty thousand for the common."

"And the uncommon?" I winced.

"Really?" she asked me sternly. "Really, Matt, you want to change it all *again*?"

"I'm curious," I admitted, forcing a smile.

"A hundred thousand," she said flatly.

"How much to build them? For each, I mean?"

"Ummm…basic is…twenty thousand, common is thirty-five, and uncommon is fifty."

"So, if we're making these, and thinking as a long-term, 'we're not investing in these fuckers again for a while' way, then are we better doing common or uncommon?" I asked, knowing the answer.

"Uncommon," she said. "It means we can do one a day, if we steal a little from the dungeon pot."

"Easy fix." I shrugged. "Assign the dungeon a hundred thousand mana per day instead for the building. That gives us a tidy boost to the research, and we build a new facility each day."

"Blacksmithing is in progress now; Glassblowing is next. I'd planned on it starting in a few hours, but it'll be tomorrow now then. Then Mechanist, Armorer, Tinker, Alchemist—we've got the basic done for that and Glassblowing but still need common and uncommon—Herbalist, Arcanist, Clothier, Leatherworker, Weaver, Potter, and Jeweler."

"Shit," I muttered. "That's…thirteen days?"

"Thereabouts," she agreed. "Is that a problem?"

"We need to prioritize the rifles," I explained. "As much as I wish it wasn't the case, we damn well need to build as many as we can, and they've got to be the best we can make."

"That's the problem." She smiled tightly. "Look, the rifles I've designed? They're not the system's version. That's because I cut corners and made the Frankenstein's monster version of the damn thing. You want to push all the way for proper rifles? We can do that instead, and it'd probably be ready sooner."

"Right…" I winced.

"And they'd be better, believe me." She sighed. "Look, in the short-term, my rifle won't cut it against the army rifles, and yeah, we can fast-track that research, but I don't recommend it."

"Why?" I asked, knowing that with Aly it was more than "because I invented it and fuck you all."

"Basically, to make guns, current, real-world guns, we need a few things, such as a Chemist—that's an advanced level of an Alchemist, by the way—so we not only need the research path, but we need the specialist. For them to make the gun powders that modern rifles use, we need the Alchemy lab at uncommon at least. Then we need someone who's appropriate to the actual facility…that's part of the cost.

"We need a Gunsmith, that's another profession, as well as a crafting facility, one that I think unlocks fully once we've researched Alchemy, Blacksmithing, and Tinker to common at the very least…"

"Fuck."

"*Then*, once we've got them, that's when we need the Gunsmith. They can begin to research the relevant weapons, unlocking them if we want more advanced versions, such as rail guns. If we just want the current versions?"

I nodded quickly.

"Then we need all of those still, but we feed a gun into the dungeon."

"Why the hell is that?" I growled. "We can produce all this other shit easily enough without the various facilities."

"Think about it, Matt. All of this? It's because they want us to be powerful in our own right. They want us to learn, to improve and to develop. We *can* reproduce weapons like the assault rifles now. We've been able to do it since we reached Steel, but—"

"What?" I grunted, stunned. "Why the hell didn't you tell me that—"

"The bullets alone cost us a thousand mana," she finished. "*Each.*"

"What the absolute fuck?" I snarled. "That makes no sense!"

"It's to force us to develop our dungeon, the surrounding facilities and skills, or at least that's what makes the most sense." She sighed, pulling up a research system.

"This became available at some point over the last few days. It shows the facilities we have, and the cost of things we produce. You see the health potions?"

I nodded. The system showed a billion items, but the potions were fairly clear, and once they were selected, a visual version of it hovered in the air between us, projected above the table. It showed a small red flask, glimmering slightly along with the basic breakdown beneath it.

Healing Potion	Potion
This is a weak healing potion. Although only slightly more potent than a stiff whisky and being told to "walk it off," it does provide 14 points of healing across 60 seconds and can be poured into a wound to directly concentrate the healing process and stop bleeding.	
Durability 10/10	**Potion Strength:** Weak

"Right?" I asked, noticing at the last second that the amount of health that could be replaced by it had risen from eight to fourteen, and yet it was still classed as 'weak'.

"Well, that costs us five hundred and fifty mana."

"Okay…"

"Remember that Ashley made twenty-six vials of this over a day, with Dante, and it cost us only the ingredient cost. That five hundred and fifty mana cost goes down once we do this…" She pulled up some more screens.

She selected the Glassblower crafting facility that had been unlocked with the "basic" research done ages ago, and she placed it on the map of the dungeon, as if she were about to order it be built.

The cost on the screen below the potion dropped by a hundred mana, and the effectiveness raised by another six points. The new numbers showed as greyed out and in brackets, but they were clearly an "if you do this, then…" hint.

"Fuck," I grunted, sitting forward and looking at the list. "What about the Glassblower? Do we have anyone who can do it?"

"Not yet," she admitted grimly. "I've been searching, mainly because it's more important than I think we realized, but nobody is interested, let alone having the skill set."

"Fuck." I knew damn well we needed it for the focal orbs, if nothing else. "Is it complicated?"

"Glassblowing?"

"Yeah."

"Fairly. I mean, the first steps will be pretty obvious—melt the sand and then blow it to the shape you want; cut it off and let it cool. But that's all I know. It's like me saying to cook food all you have to do is burn meat, then comparing what you end up with to an à la carte meal. They're totally different things."

"Fuck, fuck, fuckity fuck," I growled under my breath. "And you think this is the same for the guns? That if we could build the facilities, we'd see a massive drop in the cost?"

"I think so. We can't test it, as we need other things in place really, but just adding the Blacksmiths in the same way knocked fifty points off the cost per bullet, and that's the lowest version."

"And you think it's better not to do that?"

"I think we *should* do it," she corrected. "I just think we need to focus on the rail gun design first. If we invest in the other side? We're looking at easily as long as the current build strategy to get the cost down to a manageable level. If instead we focus, as I have been, on the rail gun? We can rebuild it section by section. Improving it all the way. The cost for them is much better, as well."

"How much?" I asked.

"Three thousand a rifle, to make, and another two thousand per rechargeable battery. A reload magazine costs—at the moment—around two hundred."

"How many—"

"A magazine holds a hundred fléchettes," she answered, and I whistled in shock.

"A hundred shots for two hundred mana?"

"And that'll drop as we develop more facilities," she added, smiling.

"Okay, so why the hell don't we have them?" I asked her shrewdly.

"Because, as it is? I've barely got them past the point of not exploding at random intervals. I've got the power source—the mana crystals—stable and locked down to release the same charge each time, and I've got a recharging station design sorted."

Aly pulled up the details between us, gesturing at the rifle that appeared, and then a device that looked a little like a tree, with grips to slot a dozen rifles in around the trunk.

"See, each rifle can be slotted in here, and the dungeon will recharge the crystal. Or, in the field, you could swap the crystal out, have people carry two maybe." She shrugged as she went on, sweeping the "tree" aside and just showing the rifle.

She spun the image of the rifle around, displaying three designs: a snub-nosed version, a long-barreled one, and then a wide, three-barrel design.

They were fairly sleek, polished, and looked lethal, making me grin.

"Don't get too excited," she warned me grimly. "I've done an assault rifle, a sniper rifle, and a shotgun version. All three have the same issues, so I'm hoping that the fixes will be equally universal, or more or less anyway."

"What's the problem?" I flicked it around to the snub-nosed design and looked it over.

"First, control. There's no recoil, as there's no explosion, but they're shit for accuracy. And you've got either a single shot, or unload the entire magazine as your options…basically pull the trigger gently, or hard and hold it. Then you've got a great club. That's it. Reloads can be an issue. I've copied the magazine design from the army assault rifle, but they're still sticking and falling out. I can't get the combination quite right.

"Last of all, sights. As I said, accuracy is crap for this. I know it's down to the barrel—I've just not figured it out yet. Add to it the sights are Iron and for the sniper at least, we need better. I've tried to stick a copied design from the army gear on there, but it's thirteen thousand a go, and it's poor, to say the least. I think that new versions will unlock for research once the Glassblowing and Mechanism workshops are unlocked and we have people in them."

"So, we just need someone in the room?" I asked, slowly.

"Well, no, they need to be trying to work as well. They need to actually try to do the job. But then, yeah, as long as they're in there doing that, I think it'll unlock."

"Well, we can have kobolds help in the various jobs. I'll take a place as well."

"A place?" She frowned.

"You said nobody's interested in the Glassblowing one?"

"No."

"I'll do it." I shrugged. "For a few days, I can do a couple of hours in there, no stress."

"Matt, we need more than that. We need you to try to learn and—"

"I know," I said, looking at her. "I have an ability, from the fairy, from its soul and class change and all the rest? It's called Soul Forge."

"Okay, that sounds ominous. And it's disturbing that this is the first I'm hearing of it." Aly groaned, before settling back and pulling out a pad and pen. "What does it do, and how? Why is it a good or bad thing, please?"

"Right, well, I think I can make really powerful magical artifacts." I forced a smile. "The only downside is, it needs a soul to use it, and it kinda blows up if I get it wrong."

"How bad an explosion?"

"Bit more than a grenade?" I suggested, then shook my head. "Actually, no, scratch that, it was more like a powerful bomb, but the area it destroyed was sort of…vanished? You know, like a glowing white-hot crater left behind and so on."

"So, you have a new skill, that might blow up and destroy a small area, or give us a magically imbued creation as a result?" She glared at me.

"Yeah…but the soul I tried it on was one of those that the asuras had stripped, so it was damaged already."

"So they might not explode?"

"Maybe…" I hedged. "Or maybe they'll be a bit more explodey. Not really sure."

"Matt, you're not filling me with confidence…" Aly whispered, resting her face in her hands and rubbing at her temples with her thumbs.

"Okay," I said, unable to keep from smiling. "Look, we need someone to help in the various crafts until we find actual craftsmen or people who want to learn, right? I need something to put the souls in if I do capture any, and I need to experiment with them, which, yeah, sounds really wrong. I'll help in the Glassblowing workshop for a few hours for a few days, and I'll try to figure shit out. It can't be that hard. Me being there should unlock the research options with the sights and drop the cost. We use the time to get them sorted and make as many as we can. If the price goes up when I'm not doing it? I'll go work for an hour or two, and you make the damn guns."

"It might not work," Aly warned me. "It's playing the system. They might have considered that."

"Think they can tell the difference between genuinely trying but for the short-term, and someone who's just fucking around?" I saw the look on her face, and I moved on quickly. "To be clear, I'll be really trying, by the way."

"I…you know what, Matt?" Aly broke off, thinking. "Fuck it. It might work, it might not, but right now, we've got nobody else who's volunteered, so even a few hours of you fucking around in there would be wonderful. If it works? That's great. If it needs someone always in there?"

"If need be, we spawn a kobold with the research perk and tell them that's their job now," I said. "Their innate curiosity will keep them at it."

"Then that's it for now. We're building the crafting village, with uncommon Blacksmiths as the first part tomorrow. The day after that, you're off to play in the Glassblowing forge."

"Then I get tonight to relax, and tomorrow to get on with my training." I smiled. "I guess I'll make the most of it then!"

"Still my sister-in-law," Aly growled, pointing one finger at me. "I don't need details, and I don't need to hear you two fooling around all night. Keep the noise down."

"Nope." I grinned as I gestured to the door. "You staying or going? I'm going to spend the next hour or so making a few little alterations to my plan for dinner, then absorb some shit to offset it. You done for the day or you want to hang around?"

"I'm done," she declared, standing and packing her notepads away in a shoulder bag. "I'm getting the hell out of here before you can ruin another research plan."

"Love you too!" I called after her, grinning as she hurried from the room, before settling back in the comfy chair and letting out a long breath.

"Right then, first the food…"

The rest of the two hours passed quickly, so quickly that when I checked the dungeon sense for Kelly, she was still in the makeshift salon. Half an hour later when I checked again, she was just leaving, heading to our rooms, and I left her to it again, amusing myself by making a copy of the new shotgun designs, losing myself in playing with the details, grinning as I saw the "design viability indication" rise from forty-seven percent to fifty-two.

I'd not noticed it before, having never really spent any time in the research systems since we were at the very first and most basic systems, but now…

The design screen showed a cost to produce, a cost to research—presumably, I could put the design in and set the parameters, and it'd give me a cost to make them—and an overall viability of the design as it stood.

Looking over the research cost, I swiftly saw why Aly had ignored it. Half a million mana to produce the shotgun. Four days nearly, and yeah, the shotgun would be usable I was sure, but fuck me, it might be barely that as well.

The aliens that designed this system wanted humans to fight for them for a reason. I had to think their weapon designs would be as half-arsed as the rest of the shit they'd done so far.

No, I'd work on the design for this a little, though. I was pleasantly surprised by both how intuitive and how easy the system was to use. Altering things was literally as quick as thought now.

That led me to look at the research systems themselves. I found, to my shock, that they'd been upgraded several times while I'd not been looking.

I blinked, startled as a hand shook me gently, and opening my eyes, all thought of the research systems, or indeed anything else, vanished.

Kelly was here and ready for our date. And my gods…

She was perfect.

I loved her, so I knew that no matter what she wore, or didn't, she was perfect, but holy fucking shit. She smiled confidently at me in a little black dress, simple, elegant, and understated, knee-length lace-up boots and her hair gleaming blonde, cut stylishly and with clearly a lot of work put into her hair, makeup, and more.

She saw the stunned look on my face, and after a full minute, laughed and reached out, grabbing my hand and trying to pull me to my feet.

Instead, I pulled her to me, making her cry out in supposed outrage, before she melted into the kiss. I held her to me for long seconds, one arm around her back, the other resting on her ass, as we kissed.

"So…" she said breathlessly a few seconds later. "I hope I didn't get all dressed up just to be ravished in this chair?"

"Dinner first," I promised, kissing her again, deeply. "Then a damn good ravishing. Oh, gods yes," I growled as she slid back off me, treating me to a lot of leg as she went.

"So, taking me anywhere nice?" she asked, as I stood and adjusted myself, before taking her hand and leading her to the main doors.

People couldn't help but double take at the sight of us both—her far more than me. But even as self-conscious as I was at my very worst, I had to admit that we cut a hell of an image.

Her—graceful, beautiful, and classy, silver jewelry and black material, blonde and beautiful, with just a touch of filth in the "fuck-me" boots.

While I was, by almost any standards, a beast these days. Standing just over seven foot, heavily muscled, but not to the ridiculous levels I'd seen some go to, my hair and beard trimmed and styled—hell, Ashley's friend had insisted on trimming my fucking *eyebrows*.

I'd said it was ridiculous, and to leave them, and I'd been just as thoroughly ignored by her. She'd not "styled" them, which was a relief—that was a step too far—but she'd trimmed the wayward ones that stuck out crazily and grew to silly lengths. Add to all of that, that I was wearing smart looking boots, black jeans, and a crisp white silk shirt?

Yeah.

We looked amazing.

Taking her hand, I led her through the people who were looking, seemingly stunned, before I wrapped my arms around her, and told her to hold on.

"Where…" she started to ask, before laughing as I flew us upward. The cold air whistled past as we vanished from most people's sight.

Seconds later, I landed in the little aerie, pulling the door closed behind us, and mentally adjusting the small area in the dungeon's control, heating it up a little.

The table that stood before us, alone in the room beyond the two chairs, was wooden and square, covered with a plain white tablecloth. Our first course, a simple deep-fried mozzarella dish with dips, waited for us.

Candles were lit, champagne was cooling in the ice bucket, and the glasses were ready.

"I…this is what you've been doing today?" Kelly asked, stunned.

"I've been working, but I was planning this for a little while," I admitted. "I'll be adding in Storm and Lightning converters soon, and taking the walls back down, but for tonight?" I couldn't help but smile at her obvious delight.

I took her hand and led her to the table, pulling out the chair for her and pushing it in as she sat, before popping the champagne and pouring it for us both.

"To us…" I lifted my glass, getting a wide smile from Kelly.

"To us," she agreed, before sipping from the flute and sighing. "That's wonderful."

"It should be." I smiled. "It's Dom Pérignon, vintage. No idea where it came from, but it's supposed to be good, and yeah, I like it too."

The next hour passed in a pleasant blur. Three courses were all that we had, although even that seemed insanely luxurious, considering the way that the world was these days. The main dish of a chicken tit each stuffed with jalapeños, chorizo, and smoked applewood cheese was wrapped in smoked bacon.

They were served with a cheesy bechamel chili pepper and garlic sauce, mountains of proper chips—or what my cousins would have called fries, but thick cut and homecooked—and of course a nice light caramel cheesecake for dessert.

"I'm stuffed…" Kelly groaned a little while later, pushing her chair back. "Seriously, you're gonna have to rip me out of this dress. There's no way it's coming off otherwise."

"Sounds fun." I grinned, and she grinned back.

"Soon," she promised. "Soon. Just let it settle a little!"

I made sure we were both finished, and stood, reabsorbing my chair and the table, as well as everything on it, saving only the champagne and our glasses.

Kelly stood, and I banished her chair as well, before summoning a deep sofa, and smiling as she fell back onto it.

"Gods, I love magic…" she whispered, closing her eyes.

I joined her, settling into place and kissing her cheek.

For half an hour or so, we just laid there, talking a little, planning some few things like my upcoming dungeon run and more, but mainly just relaxing and enjoying each other's presence. It began to rain outside, going quickly from a slow drizzle to a heavy downpour, and the glass walls of the aerie began to fog up.

I summoned four smaller candles, little ones that were deposited in their own bowls around the inner wall, causing the glass to steam up even more as I absorbed the brighter, larger candles.

"Well, then…" Kelly whispered, rolling onto her front from where she had been pressed against my side, and kissing me deeply. "I guess as you took care of dinner, and our accommodation, I'd better put out…"

"Well, you don't have to…" I said automatically, as she climbed to her feet, hesitating for a second, before turning back to me.

"Oh, believe me, I know." She grinned. "Sorry, just making sure nobody was watching."

"Oh…?" I grinned, as the little addition I'd considered earlier was suddenly there, hanging from a connection in the ceiling.

"So, are you going to tear me out of this dress, and help me into the swing, or do I have to take care of myself?" She crooked one finger. Although the little black dress looked demure and classy, the fact she'd not bothered with any underwear made it obvious what had been on her mind all along.

The glass walls steamed up a hell of a lot more before the rain passed and the sun rose again, and neither of us got much sleep that night.

CHAPTER TWENTY-NINE

By the time Kelly and I arrived to breakfast with the others, it was apparently obvious that we'd had a successful date night, mainly because we were both yawning and looked tousled.

We'd summoned a large, very comfortable rug at one point during the night, and had ended up getting the little sleep we had, on that.

This morning, we'd decided, should include breakfast, a trip to our rooms to shower and sort ourselves out, and then work, in that order.

The fact that we'd spent the night in the aerie was obvious to our little group, but it was Chris, of course, who made the first comment.

"So…do we need to book in for the banging station, or what?" he asked, and I looked at him in question. "You know, the sky-high fuckeroo room. The penthouse suite? The tall and tasty?"

He gestured upward with one finger, and I stared at him, before laughing as Mike covered his eyes with both hands and started to whisper to himself.

"Chris!" Patrick growled, shaking his head in disgust. "Honestly, man, you need to calm down and think for once! It's the mile-high club or nothing…"

"It's not a mile," Aly pointed out.

"It's not six inches either, but who's measuring," he replied calmly. "So Matt, how about it? Is it available for date night bookings or not? You're not the only one who could do with a nice treat, you know…"

"And enough about Kelly," Finn joked, making Kelly blush and laugh, shoving him with her shoulder as she sat next to him.

"You can't kill them all, Mike, not *all* of them…just one or two maybe, but not all of them…"

"And we'll take our turn on the rotation as well," Aly added in, getting a sudden interested look from Mike as he lifted his face from his hands.

"We're having a turn?" he asked.

"Don't worry, we'll change the sheets," Aly assured him.

"It's more of a rug and sex swing style of thing," Kelly pretend-whispered, making sure everyone could hear.

"Nice," Chris added, giving me a double thumbs-up. "Stay classy, San Diego."

"Fuck you, Chris." I sighed, rubbing at my eyes as I thought. "Look, I actually made the damn place for meditation and…"

"Meditation…" Patrick made air quotes with his fingers, to a round of laughter.

"*And* I was planning on removing the walls and filling it with converters, using it to feed the dungeon and produce storms!" I finished, glaring at him.

"So you're the only one who gets to play?" Patrick asked. "That's bad, man."

"I'd not say no to a night on the rotation, if that's what we're talking about." Jo said as she came in and sat down, looking from one to another of us. "What's up?"

"I was just explaining," I said, before shaking my head and changing direction. "Look, let's do this another way, all right? First, the aerie was intended as a meditation and conversion point, somewhere to draw lightning strikes and channel them into the dungeon. It doesn't even have a ladder to it. And if it did, would you want to climb a ladder that high?"

"Depends if Becky's above me." Chris shrugged, nudging her with his shoulder. "In a short skirt? Hell yes, I'd follow that ass anywhere…"

"Make a platform halfway, and we'll swap over." Becky grinned. "You wear that kilt, and I'm fine with it…"

"A kilt?" I groaned. "Fuck's sake, pass the mind bleach…I did *not* need that mental image!"

"Anyway," Patrick said, pretending to be above such things. "It'd be nice to have something like that, if it was possible?" He glanced at me, and I sighed, looking around and seeing how many others were waiting to see what I'd say too.

"Okay," I said, stabbing a sausage with my fork and cutting into it. "Fine. When there's a storm coming, though, the room is off-limits to everyone. I'll be putting converters in it and spending time up there then. Beyond that, I guess we'll come up with a plan for the rest of the time and somehow figure out an access route."

"Whoo hoo!" Chris lifted both hands. "Baggsy first night!"

"I take it you're going to want me to maintain the list and sort the details out?" Aly asked, and I shrugged, seeing the gleam in her eye.

"If you're volunteering?" I asked.

"I'll sort it." She nodded to me. "Kelly, you're on babysitting duty tonight."

"No problem," Kelly assured her, smiling. "We'll sort a ladder or something."

I glanced from Kelly and Aly to Mike, who suddenly seemed a lot less annoyed and grumpy, and even shot me a wink as the girls started to talk about access methods.

"You know you'll need to make more, don't you?" he asked, the others having started up their own conversations again.

"What's that?" I mumbled around a mouthful of toast.

"We'll need more rooms like that. Think about it. There's well over a thousand people here now. Even if everyone was coupled up, which they're not, that'd be over a year before people could get 'booked in.' We'll need more."

"I need a damn meditation chamber," I pointed out grimly. "That was what it was for, for fuck's sake."

"You've got a gym, and a tower, so stop your whining," Mike grunted, grinning at the outraged look on my face. "Seriously, build one…build a *dozen.* You said there were flying creatures out there? Build the lures on a platform up there if need be, and a bunch of different platforms for people to have dates and time-outs."

"Are you insane?" I asked. "What about the various monsters? You think they'll all be flying past, or worse, lured in, and not think of a nice snack as they pass people?"

"I…" He paused, then nodded. "All right, fair point. I'd not considered that side of things. You got a solution?"

"Bulletproof glass and titanium," Kelly interrupted, leaning in to kiss my check. "That's the plan, anyway. If the rooms are built to last, they might as well be built for real fun as well. Make them like a fancy hotel…"

"You're all insane." I wiped my mouth, shaking my head. "I'm going for a shower, then I'll be working on my mana. I'll be meditating until mage class today, just in case any of you fuckers want me. Then…"

"Showtime?" Kelly asked, and I nodded. "I'll sort it out." She smiled. "Don't expect it to be easy, though!"

"I won't," I said, kissing her cheek. "Aly…I saw the work that's been done on the research facilities. You did that in your own time, didn't you?"

Aly winced, then shrugged. "I've been absorbing things in my downtime, making sure we had enough to improve the facilities, that's all."

"You didn't have to do that."

"I really did," she corrected. "We've got dozens, if not hundreds of priorities we should be working on. Making my research area nicer and more efficient was always going to be a minor issue for us."

"It's a hell of an improvement," I pointed out, and she shrugged. "Well, either way, thank you for doing it," I said, kissing Kelly again and moving off.

I left the others to it, heading down to our room. A second quick shower later, and the world was a better place, especially for me, and after a quick change of clothes, I was off to the mage's tower.

Although it wasn't exactly off-limits, it was peaceful in the tower, especially now that two levels of the accommodation block had been completed for the new people. We had plenty of room there now, and as such the tower had returned to a quiet place of meditation and study.

Mana had been spent here by someone as well. A collection of comfortable high-backed chairs and deep rugs were scattered around, giving those who were here now somewhere cozy to sit.

I made my way up onto the platform we used for lessons, and settled down on a large rug, closing my eyes and stretching out, hands behind my head.

The low murmur of conversation had stilled on my arrival, and although it sprang up again as I settled in, it stayed low, which I was thankful for.

Pulling up my mana channels, I sank deep into them, sighing as I did so. They were clean now, and back to what they had been. My mana regeneration was back to "normal" at just under a hundred and twenty points an hour, with that figure considerably increased with my meditation.

The next step, and one that I'd been considering for some time, was the altering of the rings.

I'd sensed that I could make changes to them—hell, I'd done it before. The only difference was mine were no longer fucked. I'd figured out that I could have them form whatever mana I wanted, have one that specifically stripped Lightning-aspected mana from the stream, and that would boost my regeneration of that aspect massively.

The problem would be that I'd then end up with a fuckload of broken mana sludge in my channels…

There was another option, though. I'd made the original gates with Thor's help. *What if I made another few gates?*

What if, instead of the usual gates in my body, I made two new ones, and specialized them to Storm and Lightning mana? I had sixteen already, gates I meant, and I could make each gate do something different. What if instead I made every *other* gate specialized in a specific, basic mana form? Earth, Air, Fire and so on, but with a single purifying gate between them? One that broke down and sped up the sludge?

It'd either massively increase my mana, or it'd utterly fuck me up.

"Well, that's why they pay me the big bucks," I grunted, shifting slightly, and then flowing around the mana system again, looking for the right place to start.

The best place, where it would have the minimal impact, was right before the mana entered the core, surely. After all, if it ended up setting a load of sludge free, it wouldn't have far to go before it was absorbed.

I nodded to myself.

There was a fair gap between the nearest gate or ring, and this section, so I reached out, sinking to the bottom of the channel, and set to work.

Time passed, and I genuinely had no concept of how much it was, until seemingly seconds later, I was roused by someone kicking the bottom of my boot.

Blinking, I squinted up. The sudden rumble of voices crashed in as I realized I'd not even noticed as the room filled, ready for the lesson.

"Hey…" I croaked up at Dante.

"Hey, boss," Dante replied, grinning as he squatted next to me. "You all right?"

"Yeah," I assured him. "I was just deep in the zone…" I saw the grin. "What?"

"You were working?" He hid a smile, or tried to.

"Yeah, I was meditating, working on the gates."

"Oh…"

"What?"

"Nothing."

"Just say it," I growled.

"You were snoring."

"Bollocks," I declared gracefully.

"You really were," he assured me with a shit-eating grin.

"Weird…" I sat up, then looked around. "Well, I guess that's a discovery in itself then. I actually feel like I've had a nap, but when I look at the gates, I can see where I was up to. Maybe the body can sleep while your mind works?"

"It'd be cool if it was possible," he agreed.

"But you don't believe it," I finished for him.

"*I* totally believe you, boss," he said, ruining the lie with the slow nodding and smiles.

"Fuck you very much," I grumbled, getting to my feet and looking around. "Okay then, the room looks full. Are we ready?"

"They've been here for about ten minutes," he said. "I thought you'd wake up on your own, but when they started getting louder…"

"You woke me by kicking my foot," I concluded. "Okay, makes sense I guess, so let's give the first lesson. I—what?" I asked, pausing again as I saw the look he gave me.

"Are you really opening the dungeon again today?" he asked, and I nodded. "And you're doing a dungeon run alone?"

"Aye. I need to practice with my spells. Why?"

"Can we watch?" he asked quickly, the words falling over themselves as he said it, grinning. "It'd really help, showing how to combine magic and fighting, as well as the rewards. What time?"

"Yeah, of course. As to time, I guess before dinner? Straight after the last lesson, I guess." I shrugged, turning back to the crowd, as Dante stepped up with me, opening his mouth to speak. I let him, confused, before resisting the desire to facepalm.

"The dungeon run is on and you're all welcome to come and watch it!" he called out, grinning. "It'll be right after the last lesson of the day, in the training dungeon across the road. One floor is being prepped currently with enemies for the Dungeon Lord to fight! He's doing it alone, practicing with his magic, so—"

"Yes!" I said quickly. "Thank you, Dante! Yeah, uh…I guess if you all want to come along, you're welcome to." I shrugged. "There's not a load of space, but you'll be able to watch from above."

"I'll spread the word," Dante said excitedly, hopping down and vanishing into the crowd before I could stop him.

"Fuck," I muttered, before straightening up and forcing a smile. I'd been thinking he was a friend and someone I trusted; I didn't mind him coming along and watching when I was fighting—he might have valuable feedback for me. But now that it was *everyone*?

Well, no help for it.

"So, people!" I called, clapping my hands together. "What we'll be doing today is working on constructing our first mana gates. They're basically rings that constrain your mana, forcing the channel narrower, and making it run faster. That, in turn, means that…"

Three and a half hours later, and I stood in the new "safe" room, at the beginning of the dungeon. Kelly was beside me, with Chris and the others all outside and above, watching.

I'd not given any more thought to my request to Kelly that she prep the dungeon for me to run today when we'd discussed it last night in each other's arms.

It'd never occurred to me that people would want to watch me. And if it had, I'd have probably asked that we put it off for a few days at least, let me get a few runs in first, to make sure I knew what I was facing, and that my spells were working the way I wanted.

Now, I was paying for that lack of attention, as even here I could dimly hear the carnival-like air of the floor above.

The entirety of the goddamn dungeon had turned out.

Kelly and Aly had created mirrors that reflected the scene below and attached them to the ceiling so more people than just the front row could watch, and between that, the fact that some shmuck had put a band together and they were playing merry tunes, and the various foodstuffs that were being handed out from carts?

It made me think I knew what it was like for the gladiators in Rome.

"Okay, remember, don't go too far," Kelly said softly, well aware of my feelings. I'd told her at least four times already, but there was no way to stop this without looking like a fucking idiot.

"Too far?" I asked absently.

"Don't push too hard. We can't step in and stop the dungeon creatures from attacking you, and not undermine the whole thing. People have to know that it's possible to die in there. If I step in and save you, they'll expect us to do it for them, and the whole premise of the training dungeon is ruined."

"Oh, I'm terribly sorry," I apologized grimly. "Who was it that told Dante again?"

"Okay, maybe we shouldn't have talked about it so openly at the table after you left to get changed." She winced. "But he knows that wasn't what you meant now, and he's mortified. Ashley apparently asked him how he'd feel if the tables were turned and he had to perform in front of everyone."

"I'm still gonna kill him later," I grumbled, and she stood on tiptoes to kiss my cheek.

"No, you won't," she assured me. "Ashley has dealt with it, and it won't happen again. And you know it was your fault as well."

"Yeah, well…" I mumbled.

"So, are you ready?" She looked me over. "Got your potions? You have the focal orb with the healing spell, just in case, right?"

"Yeah, I've got three, and no," I said, confused. "Why would I have that?"

"To heal yourself!" She shook her head. "I'll go get it. You can put it in a pouch or —"

"I can heal with my Lightning," I pointed out.

"Oh, well yeah, but…"

"If I've not got the mana for Lightning, I won't have it for the orb," I said. "Better that Jo or the others have it, and if I need it, I'll escape."

"Okay," she agreed, hands resting on my left arm, as she tugged on the bracings, looking at the knots and more.

"Are you all right?"

"Yeah, just, you know, concerned."

"I'll be fine," I assured her, smiling at her.

"What?" she asked, confused. "Oh, no, I mean I went to a lot of trouble to build this new version of the dungeon. There's traps and everything…I just don't want you trashing the place…"

"Oh, well fuck you very much." I grinned at her, and got a sheepish smile back.

"Sorry. I'm worried about you, really, you know," she admitted. "I can tone the traps down, maybe cut some of the creatures out—"

"No," I said softly. "I need to actually train, and to practice. If you cut them down and make it easy, it wastes the mana and our time. I need to be pushed harder."

"Well, good luck," she said quietly, before hugging me tight. "I do love you, you know?"

"I know. I love you too."

"I know." She kissed me one last time, then darted for the door, clearly not wanting to watch me face the creatures she'd summoned.

I watched her go, then turned back, checking my weapons one last time: My hammer on its place on the right side of my hip. Three spears in the sheath over my left shoulder. My longsword over the right. A dagger in its sheath on my left hip. And that was it.

I picked the shield up from where I'd set it down and shrugged my shoulders in my armor. The fucking cape caught on things as I strode forward, entering the dungeon proper, for the first time as an "adventurer."

CHAPTER THIRTY

As soon as I stepped inside, I felt a twisting in my chest and a sudden pain as something—and it took only a second to recognize it as the dungeon fairy's soul—made contact with the dungeon around me.

I froze, half expecting to be attacked at once and slaughtered by feckin' behemoths or something. But as soon as the connection was made, the dungeon shimmered around me, seeming to come to life in a way it never had before.

Congratulations Dungeon Lord!

You have entered the [Second Steel Dungeon].

This dungeon is [Bound] and as such [cannot] be claimed.

Do you wish to continue?

*

Warning!

Crossing the boundary will signify that you are ready and accept the risk posed to you by the inhabitants of the dungeon.

*

WARNING!

This Dungeon is set to Uncommon and will be a lethal challenge for the unwary…

A red line appeared before me, a light that flowed across the floor, running left to right. I, being the tremendously intelligent man I am, immediately stepped through the line.

Congratulations, Dungeon Lord!

You have chosen to continue! The inhabitants of this dungeon have been deliberately created to test your physical, mental, and magical prowess, but are currently under-leveled. This is obviously not appropriate for a full dive, and you will therefore face highly restricted loot.

Do you wish to face the inhabitants at this level, or, for double the chance at magical artifacts and significantly better loot, do you wish to face them at a level appropriate to your own?

I paused at that, considering it. Yeah, admittedly, most of the chances to drop for magical loot were literally one percent, but still…

I nodded, before speaking aloud.

"I accept."

Excellent!

As a Dungeon Lord, you have entered your dungeon for the first time since it has grown fully active. Are you prepared to face the Trial?

Yes/No

Note: Although the rewards for surviving a full trial Dungeon are significant (including possible core level upgrades), the risk is also commensurately higher.

You may leave the dungeon at this time, but you will not be permitted to reenter until a fresh trial has been prepared...

I hesitated for a few seconds, thinking about it; then I cursed and accepted it again. I could always leave if I needed to...even if to do it, I had to get Kelly to tear a pathway down from above.

The resulting drain on the mana of the dungeon nearly sent me to my knees. A hundred and fifty-eight thousand mana, plus change, was ripped from the mana stores, and all around me, I felt the difference.

Hell, I bet those above me felt it as well, considering it felt like a damn earthquake as the air filled with clouds of dust, the ground shook, and the walls reformed.

Bestial screams rose in the distance, bloodlust clear as the various dungeon creatures were artificially increased to my level.

I felt it, and information unlocked as I gritted my teeth. The exit behind me swung shut, the doors slamming together with a boom that was terrible in its finality.

I wasn't getting back out that way.

Whatever I'd thought I was getting into, it wasn't this. I reached to the side, focusing, and a new menu popped up.

Congratulations, Dungeon Lord!

As you are participating in the trial dungeon, most of the high-level systems have been restricted. You have [10000] mana to spend to summon additional forces at any time, but this number is finite, and will not replenish.

Do you wish to access your additional forces at this time?

Yes/No

I paused, then shook my head, selecting no.

Very well.

As this is the first time you have entered the trial dungeon while it is fully active, a short tutorial is available, as well as a series of recommendations. Do you wish to view them?

Yes/No

I chose yes this time, grunting as a projection appeared before me. The crowd above went even more distantly silent as people struggled to make out what was happening.

An image of a party ran into view, plowing through the dungeon, triggering traps, fighting beasts, and more. But after a handful of rooms, they decided to leave, returning to the entrance, and found it locked, sealed against them.

They were trapped and spent some time trying to find a way out, until, finally, they went back and continued through the dungeon. The inference was clear: once the door closed, it stayed that way. This time, the party continued on, and eventually found a small door in one wall, partly hidden, with a symbol of a six-pointed star inside a circle on the door.

Once they found this, they rested a little inside, finding a collection of seats and beds, a fountain, supplies, and a lever.

The lever, when they pulled it, unlocked the entrance. Then they immediately headed back, fighting a few roaming mobs on the way, but this time when they found the entrance, they were allowed to leave.

The inference was clear: the only way out was by reaching an exit room.

The next image showed a Dungeon Lord entering, and summoning a team of minions—apparently I could choose from a list—and then running the dungeon with them.

Again, the entrance was sealed, but as the Dungeon Lord, I clearly had an extra perk. I watched as the lord collected all the loot and fled back to the door. It stayed closed, until he deposited everything, including his own armor and gear, into a hole that opened for it.

Once that was done? He was allowed to leave.

Being the boss had some perks—it'd just cost me everything I gained in here, or brought with me.

The next image showed the Dungeon Lord battling their way through the dungeon, summoning minions as he went, and getting reasonable loot, then using the lever at the entrance to leave, taking his loot with him.

Next was an image of both the Dungeon Lord and their minions and the adventuring party running side by side, occasionally blurring as they passed through each other, making it clear it was still an image, and the two groups were overlaid, not assisting each other.

This time they finished the dungeon, killing everything, and they got a bonus magical artifact for the party, and for the Dungeon Lord…

"The bonuses." I grunted, seeing a pop-up that offered options. "It's the fucking bonuses the fairy is supposed to give me the details for. I have to run the goddamn trial dungeon to get them."

The final image showed the Dungeon Lord doing the dungeon alone, not summoning any minions, and the result…the screen that offered the bonuses was suddenly glowing; golden, silver, and blue options lit up with an internal light.

The additional information that drifted across to me made it clear what it meant.

I run the dungeon alone, and I'd get the best bonus rewards.

The fucking aliens specifically wanted the Dungeon Lords to train, and this was how they'd decided to make sure it happened.

I shook my head, snorting as I put it all together. They were smarter than I was, that was for sure. In putting an option in for the Dungeon Lord to run the dungeon, they could make sure that even if the dungeon was somewhere that was totally safe, the lord would be forced to train and grow, as would the parties.

I had to guess that the change had come from the dungeon reaching Steel and becoming much more powerful, but it could have been from the dead fairy I shared a soul with as well.

Either way, we had an opportunity here, and I'd come here for training. Might as well make the most out of it.

I knelt, smoothing the sandy floor underfoot, and quickly cleared a space, before dragging my finger through it, exaggerating the lines to make sure they were clear from above.

> *Can't leave. Dungeon locked. Creatures boosted to my level and higher. Only way out? Win.*
>
> *Love you all.*

That done, I straightened, looking up and grinning at the black glass that covered the ceiling of the passage, and winking, before setting off.

I strode forward, following along the short corridor, loving the attention to detail that Kelly and the others—I knew she'd have to have had help to accomplish this—had put in.

The ground was solid, yet covered in a layer of sand, maybe a handful of inches deep. It was enough for a decent foothold, yet I instinctively knew it'd tire me out a lot more than walking on stone, and it'd soak up blood easily.

The walls looked to be a naturally occurring tunnel formation, rough and varying—wider in some spots, narrow in others—with the ceiling overhead flat and smooth as glass.

It was pitch black, and I damn well knew that it was both thick enough for a dragon to tap-dance on it, and one-way only, allowing everyone above to watch me.

I reached the end of the small corridor, and was about to step out, when a discoloration near the ground caught my eye.

I leapt backward instinctively, landing just outside of the trap's radius, as half a dozen spears slammed to a halt, their tips coated in steel and gleaming. Had I been in the middle of that, I'd have been crippled at the very least.

I couldn't feel Kelly, and for a split second I tried to slide into the dungeon sense, thinking to go to her and tell her to calm the traps the fuck down in the future, only to find I couldn't do it.

I was trapped inside my own body while in here, and that minor detail made me grit my teeth.

First, no sneaky way to check for any more traps and shit. Second, no way out if the dungeon were attacked! We could be under attack right now, and I'd never goddamn know it.

I growled, shaking my head at the spears as they clunked, and started to slowly retract.

So, time to be very careful, I mentally reprimanded myself, stepping forward, and moving closer to the trap. This time I saw it before I set it off: a tiny glimmer of a crystal at ground level, hidden under a tiny overhang of stone.

I moved back, drawing my hammer, and moved it near to the crystal, hissing as the trap activated again. A spear slammed into the hammer's head despite how quick I'd tried to pull it back.

This time I just nodded, then started to swing. Fuck this shit.

I hit the crystal first, smashing it with a little cracking noise and a puff of smoke. Then I attacked the spears themselves, shattering them all before they could retract.

A minute later, I backed up, then ran and jumped across the remains of the trap, just in case. This time, landing on the far side, I found myself in a small cavern, shaped like a kidney, with a guttering torch on one wall, sending flickering shadows dancing across the walls.

I glanced around, seeing nothing, and turned back to examine the trap from this side, making sure I was clear of it. I swiped a section of the sand smooth, writing a brief message there.

Fucking REALLY??

It summed up just how I felt about that trap pretty well, all things considered. But I was a lot more thankful that, as I was writing it, a shadow flickered across me from behind.

I reacted without thought, diving to the side and rolling to my feet, spinning around and glaring around the small room, seeing nothing.

Hesitating, I bit my teeth. The popping and crackling of the dying torch on the wall made it clear that soon I'd be in darkness, if I didn't move.

There was a second torch nearby, resting against the wall right below it.

"Convenient," I muttered. "Too fucking convenient!" A need to move, and just what I needed right there, nice and available? *Nope.*

I got the feeling that the dungeon hadn't just upped the level of the enemies I was facing, but had increased the traps as well. But Kelly had designed this place as a trial for me. As such…what would *I* put in here, if it was for me?

Definitely easy, attractive loot and solutions, that was for sure.

Possibly a glory hole as well, but between the fact that it'd probably be a mimic's mouth, and the entire dungeon was watching me, I'd not be using it and falling for that!

Slowly, I slid to the right, passing the entrance to the cavern, moving closer to the tempting prize, and waiting. The light flickered and popped; the flames lifted higher and flooded the cavern with light…before falling again, and I saw it.

It was a nice, easy and tempting trap, all right. The torch was almost certainly fine, as I stared deliberately at it.

What wasn't fine, though? I twisted at the hip and underarm-flung the hammer to my right and forward; the heavy metal head whistled through the air, as I reached up and dragged a spear free.

The hammer slammed into the chest of the creeping ghast with a crunch of breaking bone. It staggered back, coughing blood as the damn thing's stealth ability collapsed.

It was shoved aside by another to its left as they collided, and my shield and spear were up, as I leapt forward.

The cavern was too dark to see anything clearly. And even if it'd been perfectly lit, I'd have had difficulty spotting these fuckers. But then, that was the point.

The flickering flames had cast dodgy, irregular shadows; those, in turn, had been mimicked by the ghasts. But they had to constantly adjust, and they were just that little out of sync.

I ducked as I landed, shoving forward with the oval shield I held, lifting it to cover my chest and head, even as I stabbed out blindly, feeling the tip punch through flesh and bone.

I twisted, rolling my wrist, then yanked it backward, making the wound significantly worse. Blood sprayed into the air, bladed forearms hitting the shields and sliding right and left.

I angled it, sliding the length from north to south, to east and west, and then dug my foot in and leapt forward, battering two more from their feet.

I could only see one, but that barely slowed me, stabbing down with the spear, then yanking it back and leaping forward like an eighties pro wrestler. I put all my body weight behind the shield, driving it down atop the stunned and injured figures.

More bones crunched, and I remembered these fuckers and the way they were built, even as I rolled to my feet and slashed sideways at the blurred figures that were trying to get back up and follow me.

Thin bones, narrow chests, and ambush predators…they weren't a frontline fighter, meaning they couldn't take much in the way of punishment. And although we'd upgraded the design to common, these looked like the originals, which was a relief.

The common variant was much more lethal, heavier muscled, and—

I dove aside before I even completed the thought, my mind still struggling along, while my body took direct action and got me the hell out of the way.

I hit the sand and rolled, coming to my feet and planting my back against the wall. The blur of a much larger figure swept through the space I'd just vacated.

My spear was useless here. With my back against the wall, the damn thing was too long! I lunged forward, moving away from the wall and tilting the spearhead down. The leaf-shaped blade, razor-sharp and gleaming, angled for the blur as it dropped stealth, and the "common" lesser ghast was revealed.

I seriously didn't want to know what the fuck a normal, or worse yet, a greater ghast was, because the lesser versions were fucking horrifying.

It stood almost as tall as me, and looked like someone took a pro bodybuilder and replaced their forearms with bone spurs that ended in a wicked point, sharp as fuck with a serrated inner edge. They had backward-sweeping bone spikes on their elbows, a massive jaw that split apart to be basically nightmare fuel, a row of spikes down its back, and a tail that ended in another spike, except it was also mobile like a fucking scorpion's, flashing back and forth.

All in all, they were sodding terrifying, and that was when they were on my side.

Seeing the big bastard lunging at me, getting in close before I could get the space to angle my spear right?

It wasn't happy making, that was for sure.

It crashed into the spear while I was still lowering it, smashing it aside as it lunged forward, maw opening wide to bite. I twisted at the hip, pushing forward and driving the shield into its chest.

The advantage I had over these fuckers, I saw straightaway, wasn't just down to the magic that I had yet to use, but that they were built on the same base as the basic versions.

Lightweight bones, specifically, and ambush predators.

It might be heavily muscled when you looked at them, seeing all the ridged mass that made them look like they should be on the front of a magazine, but that was just it.

They were designed and evolved for fast attack and vanishing, not stand-up fights.

Slamming the shield into the fucker, I sent it staggering back, feet digging deep into the sand, before it lunged again.

This time, though, the fucker was back far enough.

I lowered the spear and stabbed out, catching it as it tried to leap at me, grunting as it impaled itself on the spear, twisting and writhing. Its growls changed, a bubbling, hissing noise entering its voice as the left lung deflated.

It tried to get at me anyway, shoving forward, even with my spear lodged in its chest keeping it at arm's length. But I had it now, and pushed hard, then pulled it forward.

The sudden lack of resistance meant it almost flew forward, right claw hitting and being deflected by my shield. I pulled the spear to my right and down, angling and guiding the body in that direction, as a full-force snap kick whipped out.

I triggered Storm-Strike through the heel of my boot as I kicked, and the ghast practically detonated.

The body flew backward; blood sprayed in all directions, making two more of the smaller variants clear on the left and right, creeping forward, suddenly coated in their brother's internals.

Two swift steps to the left, and my spear skewered the one on that side, sliding out smoothly to punch through the thing's chest, then lifting free as it collapsed.

And then there were just us two.

It was down to the single lesser ghast, the basic version and me facing each other. Yeah, it was in stealth still, but it was also covered in splattered blood, and whatever its stealth ability was, it was built into its skin, not a magical thing.

It looked like someone had poured a bloody bucket over solid air, leaving the outline and bits clear, while other sections were still blurred out.

It tried slinking to the side, and I stayed fixed on the spot it'd been, before slowly turning, pretending to have lost it.

It paused, then began to creep forward...and met my shield as I lunged, battering it from its feet and into the wall. It bounced, falling to the floor, stunned—then met my boot coming the other way.

It took a handful of strikes to kick the fucker to death, but when the skull buckled in and the body spasmed, I stopped, then stepped back.

The spear dug into the fractured and broken skull, piercing the brain, and apparently ending the fight.

Distantly, I could hear cheering, and I fought to get my breathing under control again, looking around the room. The bodies started to dissolve, becoming motes of light that broke apart, leaving behind six small reliquaries, and a seventh, slightly larger one.

I moved from one to the other, tapping them and watching as the small golden pyramids stopped rotating in the air. The side closest to me folded down, and a void appeared before me.

Reaching inside and rooting around, I came up with a grand total of five gold coins, two rubies, a small round stone about the size of my thumbnail that glowed a merry blue, a dagger that was frankly shit, and two packets of cheese and onion crisps.

I couldn't help but laugh at that, even as I pocketed one of the bags and tore the other open, eating as I checked my notifications.

Congratulations!

You have killed the following:
- 6x Lesser Ghast [basic], Levels 15-25, 2,750 XP
- 1x Lesser Ghast [common], Level 22, 690 XP

Total XP earned: 3,440 XP

Total XP awarded 3,440 XP

Current XP to next level stands at 9,543/50,000

*

You have gained additional Stat Points in the following areas through constant effort.
- +1 Agility
- +1 Charisma
- +1 Luck

Continue to work hard to increase these or other stats…

My stats weren't building anywhere near as fast as they had been before now, but then I'd spent most of the last few days on my magic more than anything else.

That being said, most of my stats had significant progress in the "progress to next level" section when I checked my stat screen, and I was more than happy with that.

I wiped my spear tip through the sand, then scraped the congealed mass of blood off, before returning it to the sheath on my back, and setting off slowly into the next section.

The cavern I'd been in had been kidney-shaped, or like a wonky figure eight, if seen from above, but I could clearly see the path that led onward from here, canting sharply to the right almost straightaway. This time I made sure my hammer was back in its loop on my hip, and I picked up the torch that had been set aside helpfully as a lure before.

I lit it and moved out, slowly creeping along the tunnel and examining the floor and walls as I went, feeling more confident as I found the second trap with plenty of space to go.

It was a trip wire, one that linked along and sank into the wall. Following the line it ran, I found a small section that was cut out of the wall on either side, narrow and dark, hidden again under an overhanging section of rock.

I nodded to myself, moved back a bit to where I'd passed a large rock, and picked it up, tossing it onto the trip wire from a distance.

I nearly shit myself.

Two long, narrow, and fucking rotating serrated blades slid out of the wall on either side of the tunnel, arcing down and out before being yanked sideways and back into the wall.

They'd been angled down at forty-five degrees, and the way they'd been yanked back?

I stared in shock at the evil fucking trap, knowing that somewhere above Leighton was making frantic notes for his own traps for the future.

The sharp edge of the blades would have cut deep into both of my legs had I been walking through there; then they'd have been yanked backward, the serrated teeth ripping the wounds wider, even as I'd have collapsed to the floor, crippled.

Fuck me sideways.

I rested the torch against the wall and brandished my hammer, triggering the trip wire again and smashing the blades with my hammer, making damn sure they couldn't move any more before I gingerly made my way through them, finding a second, almost identical trap literally on the other side of them, where if I'd leapt forward to avoid the last one, I'd have landed.

I started to have serious second thoughts about this.

I needed the bonuses. We needed them as a *community*, never mind the dungeon side of things—anything that could make a serious boost to us all was damn well required never mind desired—but still…

These traps were fucking diabolical, and I was seriously close to missing them. I hesitated, chewing my lip, as I repeated the process, smashing the next set of blades, before hanging my hammer back in its loop and picking the torch up.

Maybe I should summon a few goblins? Send them forward?

Hell, I could summon a few with Disgust active, send them to round creatures up, and lead them back toward the damn traps. They could clear the dungeon for me…

But that was the point, wasn't it?

I needed to learn, and to train.

That was literally why the rewards hadn't just been handed to me.

It was to force me into here, to fight and to level.

Motherfuckers.

I decided at this point, inching forward and examining the broken traps, as well as the area all around, that once I was out of here, when the Orcan were dealt with, and shit was properly settled…I'd go find these Cinthian dickheads, and I'd put them in a fucking dungeon of my own design.

Complicated.

Evil.

Hell, I'd probably even make all the creatures in it drop tomato fucking crisps as their only loot drop. Just to really fuck with people.

The next cavern was up ahead. A light shone cheerily from around a dogleg to the right, and as I reached it, I stared in wonder.

The cavern before me was larger than the last, twenty to thirty meters or so across, and looked to be roughly round. But the difference from the last one to this?

It was night and day, literally.

I stepped out and looked across the marvel before me.

I was on the verge of an underground, or hidden at least, grove that looked to be full of the joys of summer.

Bees and insects flitted around; leaves fluttered in a gentle breeze; warmth, real *summer's* warmth, bathed the cavern. Here and there, poking through the blanket of grass and moss that covered the forest floor, was the occasional flower.

The ground level slipped down a good five meters or so, a slope leading from the tunnel behind me, and before I knew what I was doing, I was sliding down the steep side, catching myself as I jogged a few feet into the wonder.

I forced myself to stop. I was in the fucking dungeon: everything here was made to kill me. So rushing in any deeper was madness. But…

There was something about this place, something so inviting! Tiny creatures flitted around, buzzing from branch to branch, and as I watched them, I realized they were fairies. Dozens of them flitted here and there, watching me.

Instead of how most of the fucking creatures I'd faced that weren't actually bonded to me acted, they were curious, friendly even, and I wondered whether this was actually a safe room.

It seemed a little early, to put a safe room in already, but…it'd make sense, I supposed, give you a way to back out, or to rest before you worked your way in deeper.

If that was the case, though, why the hell would you stop people from leaving via the entrance?

Something moved deeper in the grove, and I jerked around, following it. I saw flashes of movement between the trees, squinting as I tried to make it out, before looking around again.

The walls of the cavern were covered with creeping vines and moss. Trees reached upward, their tops pressed tight against the glass of the ceiling. And where it'd been solid black before, now it glowed with summer sunshine.

I could hear a gentle breeze continuing to rustle the leaves, and feel that pleasant warmth in the air. Sniffing, I nodded to myself. *Summer.* I could smell it—the warmth, the smell of grass and moss, of fresh turned dirt and pollen.

It was a paradise, and seeing it like this, I was determined to rebuild it in the accommodations blocks for our people. Gifting them somewhere like this, somewhere so safe to relax, would be…

Safe.

Why the hell had I thought that?

I gripped the torch tight, realizing that despite my intentions to stay still and observe, to stand well back and watch for traps for a fucking start, I was halfway into the miniature grove already.

I'd not even realized that I was…

I was still moving.

My legs trembled as I tried to stop, and for a second, I genuinely didn't think I could. Then I staggered, pain blooming in both legs as I became suddenly aware of something I'd missed all this time.

A gentle melodic voice was singing, and as soon as I heard it, I relaxed; I felt the need to move again, to just move a little closer in, to see what could be making such a wonderful sound.

I felt the urge, and I saw it for what it was.

A trap.

A notification flashed in the corner of my eye, and I banished it, too busy looking around, gritting my teeth as my legs twitched.

Resisting the siren song of whatever was deeper in the grove was harder than I expected. I resisted the desperate pull of curiosity, the desire to move deeper, and the twitching of muscles on the verge of going into cramp as I stopped myself.

Whatever it was that was causing it, though, the pain in my legs actually helped to sharpen my mind, so I was actually almost thankful for it.

There.

The movement was back. Something ran through the trees off to my right, and I twisted, following it. As soon as I was moving again, the cramping relaxed. Whatever caused it had clearly used my lack of awareness to attack me, and I growled under my breath.

They wanted me to follow, I guessed, but they'd soon find out why that was a fucking mistake on their part.

I wove between the trees, the motion just ahead—something small, clad in greys and greens, browns that blended with the surrounding trees and...

I stepped around a tree that seemed to tower over me, its trunk at least six feet across and hundreds high. A feeling of distant "wrongness" built in me as I came to a halt, seeing the creature that waited for me.

It was a dryad, or I assumed it was, anyway: a wooden being, with glowing, gentle green light emanating from the eyes, and mouth of a carven face. The body sat back against a tree; the roots of that tree and more around it reached out to intertwine with sections of the creature.

All around the dryad were crumpled fragments of armor, shattered and crumbling piles of bones. Still, I felt the need to go to it, to settle into its embrace and relax, to find true peace and comfort, as I slept away my problems...

I grinned inside my helmet, as everything clicked into place. The humming song that floated around me suddenly grew louder and the cramps started up in my arms and legs again, warning me as I paused.

Small forest-garbed creatures peered around trees to the sides, and I saw their wickedly curved blades glinting.

"You want me?" I asked the figure, seeing the trap for what it was. "Let's play then." I tossed the torch aside, knowing that'd get the fucker's attention, and I grinned when the head followed the flaming brand more than me.

No forest creature, even a summoned one, was going to ignore fire, certainly not when they were made out of fucking wood. I vaguely remembered the original text for the dryads saying something about them being guardians of the forest, and mainly peaceful.

Clearly, as they leveled, they became very different creatures, because the one in front of me right now grabbed the flaming torch out of the air with a reaching branch, before sending more and more out to pick me up.

I let her.

I even let her take my shield as more tendrils reached out, grasping vines flowing around the edges and tugging gently but firmly.

I'd not drawn my hammer nor my other weapons free—not because I didn't see the danger, but because I'd decided that it was time to take the goddamn fight to the enemy.

It was time to change the tempo. Thus far I'd been creeping along; I'd been fighting for my life, and I'd been obviously searching for traps.

I'd demonstrated to everyone watching what they needed to do. But if the entire fight was like that? How many of those who were wavering would choose to come in here and face creatures that would be a similar level of challenge to them?

I'd be lucky if one in ten of the forming groups actually made use of the dungeon.

No, I needed to make this an example, as well as a dungeon run. That meant that I needed to take some risks, and I needed…to have some *fun*.

Besides, I had come in here to get some practice with my magic.

I let the dryad lift me closer, arms lifting to welcome me into its embrace, and I waited until the last possible second, then I struck. I'd used Storm-Strike dozens of times now, and yet I'd been channeling Storm, or Lightning into it.

This time I channeled *Fire*.

Instead of the usual explosion of force that destroyed things at the point of impact—this was more like having my fist enveloped in a flaming glove—its face and the look of horror, then hatred on the dryad's face was worth the effort alone.

The stopping of the song, though, one that I'd suspected she'd been singing, helped as well, as the surrounding forest suddenly blurred.

It shrank, the trees becoming stunted; the light withered, as goblins poured free of the surrounding wood. The fairies screamed in rage and hatred.

"Let's fucking go!" I roared, channeling Fire into the shield formation that I'd used my Lightning in before.

A roaring conflagration of flame burst into life around me, flaring up and pouring out of me like napalm, flowing around to form a circular shield, one that cut through the vines and tendrils holding me easily.

I dropped to the floor, grunting and gritting my teeth against the pain, as I cut the spell. I couldn't hold it, not with Fire. Dante could have, but he lived and breathed Fire.

For me, I'd need to study, to learn to use it more first. For every flickering flame that caressed my skin, I felt pain. I burned, punished by my own spell as I stripped the wood from me. But the effect the flames had on me was nothing compared to what it had on a creature of the forest, comprised entirely of wood.

CHAPTER THIRTY-ONE

The dryad screamed in fear. Flames rushed along the tendrils and up toward the main body. The wooden behemoth tore itself free of the stunted trees all around it and frantically tried to escape as the goblins and fairies dove at me. I didn't bother to draw weapons, not for these.

They were the basic version. At worst, the goblins might be the uncommon version, but I was fairly sure they were just common.

The fairies would be the same. Steel seemed to have its creatures start at common rather than basic, but I didn't give two shits.

I was armed and armored, I was a mage, and I was looking for a fight, and even level twenty to thirty goblins, as basic as they were, were like paper people.

As the dryad staggered backward, snapping off healthy growths to discard them before the flames could reach her, the goblins and fairies struck.

I was surrounded by flying pests that darted in and out. The fairies cast bright flashes of lights, miniature fireballs and sprays of freezing cold. Goblins ran forward, waving daggers and leaping at me, and through it all I spun.

I backhanded a fairy from the air, feeling the tiny bones break as my full-force slap hit it; the snarl cut off in a squeak of pain, one that ended as its body hit the floor.

Flapping feet raced in. The closest goblin leapt for me, a dagger in each hand already raised and slashing, until it met my "Sparta" kick full-force in the face.

It crumpled; the head rocketed backward, the legs flipped forward, and arms went akimbo as its neck snapped into the impact.

The next hit me from the side. Its single dagger hit the armor over my stomach and skittered across it, leaving a deep scratch. I slapped my right hand on the back of its head, clamping down hard and lifting it, grabbing it by one leg with my left, then swinging it around.

My homemade goblin club smashed another of the fairies from the air as it screamed, arms flailing, dagger forgotten. I spun, building up momentum and hitting two of his former allies with the goblin, before he stopped twisting and screaming. The reverberation of his impact into the back of the dryad made it clear he wasn't going to be getting back up.

The dryad, finally free of the encroaching flames, spun and shrieked at me, before leaping in, arms outstretched, fingers growing multiple thorny additions.

I grinned and spun up the flame shield again.

It might be painful to summon, it might leave my armor smoking each time, but it was doing a fucking number on the dryad. And as it was both my own spell, and I had a high affinity to the element, the actual real "damage" it was doing to me was minimal…more like a severe case of sunburn.

The dryad shrieked and leapt back, only to turn and try to run as I leapt after her, pinning her between me and the tree she'd been resting against.

She was humanoid, two arms and legs, even if she didn't move much like it, them bending more like tentacles, rather than limbs.

I stomped on the back of her right leg, using Storm-Strike, and blasted a hole through that limb, sending her crashing to the floor. Grabbing the top of her head from behind, I pulled back hard and banished the flaming shield—it was draining my mana faster than I'd expected. I cursed; the fairies were dive-bombing, casting spells, and, apparently, as I saw at the last second, gathering in small teams to lift goblins and throw them into the fire.

That was draining the mana far faster than I'd bargained on. I punched the dryad in the back of the neck, ignoring the reaching hands, as I triggered Storm-Strike again, this time filling it with Storm mana and releasing the concussive power of a thunderbolt.

I'd used almost fifteen hundred mana in this fight already, I noted absently, ripping the head of the dryad free and tossing it aside. I needed to finish this fast.

The goblins were mainly already dead, the fairies having been grabbing them and throwing them at me to strip away my shield. There were still a dozen or more of the little fuckers flying around, and now that I'd cut the shield again, instead of being surrounded by blackening, screaming goblins on their way to becoming charcoal, I was surrounded by fairies with glowing hands.

I dove to the left, rolling and yanking my shield across my body again. I grinned as the oval metal rang with multiple impacts, growing cold enough to sting even through my gauntlets, while other sections grew suddenly hot as tiny fireballs slammed into it repeatedly.

"No, here!" a tiny piping voice screamed, and after a second, one section of the shield started to grow even colder. I hid beneath it, taking hit after hit as I tried to come up with a way of killing the fuckers without using my mana.

"Now fire!" the same voice yelled.

The same area was heating, and then…*warping*.

The little shit was freezing the metal, then heating it! Forcing the metal to undergo the vast temperature differences wasn't just robbing it of any tempering, it'd twist and possibly shatter the fucking thing!

"THAT'S IT!" I snarled, triggering my Lightning shield and standing, throwing the normal, physical shield aside as I ran at the small group of fairies.

They burst apart, heading in all directions, but as I jumped, planting one foot on the slumped back of the dead dryad, I managed to throw myself high enough that the outer edge of the shield caught three of them, tearing through them and sending them screaming to the floor.

I landed hard, yanked a spear free, and stabbed out as fast as I could, skewering each of them and flicking them away. The outraged screams of the fairies as I did that let me know it was working.

I spun. The final goblin that had been waiting for his chance leapt out, dagger raised, only to be sent ass over teakettle by the blunt end of my spear as I whipped it around, catching his leg as he leapt.

He flipped over and plowed into the earth, lifting his head and spitting out a mouthful of dirt. Then he collapsed again as the blade of the spear sank into the middle of his back, carving a great divot, then lifted free.

"I can do this all day!" I called out, bluffing, before unleashing a full Lightning Bolt at one of the flying figures. She exploded, remains of her limbs and wings flying in all directions.

"Surrender or die!" I roared, before twisting and lunging, sending the spear through a blurring figure of eight movement that missed the fairy I was aiming for by an inch, but lopped the wings off a terminally unlucky one that flashed out from behind a tree at exactly the wrong time.

She tumbled, screaming through the air to crash into the forest floor with a crunch of breaking bones, her tiny body half impacting a root.

"Pl…ease…" She gasped, trying to raise one hand to me in supplication, and barely managing to make it shake.

"Fuck." I grunted, seeing the tiny humanoid with large eyes, the very image of a fairy we'd all been exposed to as kids watching TV.

She lifted one hand shakily, then coughed blood all over herself.

I gritted my teeth, feeling sick to my stomach, as I took a quick step to the left, then stomped on her.

The last sound she made was a scream, then a series of grisly cracks as her bones broke.

"I'm no healer!" I called out as outraged screams rose around me, and the final handful wove in and out of the trees, glowing spells forming in their hands. "So, this is the last chance offered. Surrender, or die."

"Never!" one of the fairies screamed, tearing back into sight, rounding a tree trunk and letting loose a set of three tiny missiles. Each of them arced away on a new trajectory, all aligned on me, and as soon as the spell left her hands, she went grey in the face and fell from the sky. Another of her companions barely managed to catch her as she tumbled limply from the air.

The pair vanished into the trees, as the three missiles slammed into me, making me hiss in pain. They were expertly targeted, punching into the gaps in my armor. One sunk into the inside of my right elbow, one the thick tendon at the top of my bicep, just where the pauldron and upper arm split to allow for movement, and the last…

The back of my right knee.

They slammed home, then a second later detonated, making me howl in pain as I fell to one knee.

Gleeful laughter rang out around me. The last three fairies flew in closer, watching me, unconcerned now that they knew my arm and leg were out of action.

I gritted my teeth and started to circulate my mana, dragging the Lightning up and around my body, and healing myself as quickly as I could.

"You deserve this, human!" one of the fairies snarled, floating forward. A fireball appeared in her hand as she glared at me.

"You attacked me, you crazy little fuck," I pointed out through gritted teeth.

"You invaded our dungeon!"

"I'm trapped here unless I can find a way out," I snapped, deliberately hiding the relief as the injuries started to heal at last.

"You killed her…" another growled, moving in closer.

"That one?" I nodded to the one I'd stood on. "I couldn't heal her—you want me to leave her to suffer?"

"I could have!" the third shrieked. "I could have healed her!"

"Really?" I asked, smiling through my helm. "So, we've got a multiple missile, freezing, healing, and fireballs. Any other fun spells?" I shifted as the flesh knit together in my arm and leg. I could feel the itch as hair regrew, then the cool sensation of sensitive flesh exposed to the air for the first time.

"You'll never know," the nearest hissed, lifting both hands as a crackling bolt of lightning leapt into being, making me stifle a grin.

"Oh no!" I gasped, lifting both hands and pressing them to the cheeks of my helmet in mock horror. "Not lightning! My nemesis! Please, noooo!"

"Die!" she shrieked. The lightning lashed out, the second fairy quickly summoning the same spell and hitting me as well.

I managed to last a few seconds, thrashing from side to side, throwing my hands up and shouting "Oh woe is me" and shit like that.

That was all I could manage, though, before I reached down and casually swept up the spear again, then slammed it straight through the mouthy one, pinning her to the tree behind and cutting off the spell.

"No!" the other two screamed, stunned.

"Fuck's sake, you're dumb," I grunted, yanking the spear back out and letting the now dead, mouthy one fall, even as the second spun, trying to flee.

"My turn." I unleashed a Lightning Bolt after her and her companion the healer, cutting it off after a few seconds when sooty smoke was all that was left of the pair of them.

Silence fell, even the distant sound of cheers muted, as people dealt with the terrible reality of the fight, the darkness that was a real dungeon dive, rather than a game.

The reliquaries didn't appear yet, and I nodded, taking that to mean that the last two that had fled were still alive, and hiding.

"I meant what I said," I called out. "Surrender, and I'll not kill you. I'm trapped here and need to clear the dungeon to escape. That means I kill everything between me and the exit. But if you join me?"

"Why would we trust you?" a voice called from somewhere deeper in the mass of branches.

"I could have killed you all from a distance," I pointed out. "Hell, it would have been cheaper in mana costs."

"So why didn't you?"

"I'm here to train," I admitted. "I didn't expect to get trapped, nor have others who were actually aware in here with me. I was expecting the others to be unaware of themselves."

"You know how we came to be part of the dungeon?" a fairy asked, creeping slowly into view. Her tiny face peeked out between the dead tree branches. "You know what it is to be born of the dungeon?"

"Yes and no," I admitted. "I've met some of the creatures of the dungeon, but not ones that are so…"

"Beautiful?" she suggested.

"Articulate," I corrected. "Most are trying to either get through their day and don't give a shit, or are brain-dead. Only a few are more, and they seem happy with their lives."

"They're free," she said curtly.

"Free?"

"Free to roam. Not bound to the depths," she explained slowly. "Those of us that are bound to the depths of the dungeon can't leave."

"Why not?"

"We'd have to be unbound," she snapped, as if it were the most obvious thing in the world.

"Right...?"

"Only the Dungeon Lord can free us, so we're bound here!"

"And if I was to free you?" I asked deliberately. "Make you free to roam the dungeon, bound only to me and my council?"

"What's a council?"

"They're...well, they're friends who help me."

"Friends who let you come down here, and watch you through the glass?" she asked shrewdly.

"Some of them, yeah."

"Not very good friends..."

"You'd be surprised." I snorted. "Look, you could be free and—"

The pain that suddenly burst into being in my neck was awful, as the other fairy, unknown to me, had snuck around and crept up on me.

I'd missed her closing on me; I'd missed her getting into position, but I sure as shit didn't miss when she sank her sharp fangs into the artery in my neck, releasing a spell at the same time.

I'd have screamed, if I could.

The pain was horrific; paralysis spread out from the bite as she clung to me, gnawing on me.

I reacted instinctively, tensing up, bringing my shoulders up, my head down, and triggered my Lightning, flooding my body with it.

My armored shoulders rose, my helm crushed down, and the tiny fairy crumpled with a muffled scream. The pop and crackle of tiny bones as she died reverberated in my helm.

I fell to the floor. The paralysis her bite engendered made it hard for me to move at all, and I laid there, half on my side, staring wide-eyed straight ahead, trying to breathe, feeling my blood pouring from the wound in my neck.

Was this it? The end of the road for me? Already?

No. No, this couldn't be it.

I reached down deep and pulled at my mana, converting it to Lightning as fast as I could, sending it directly to the wound, feeling it cauterizing and rebuilding the area, but...

I could feel the pumping blood as well, the running red tide that was my life seeping from the wound as I grew weaker.

If I could have moved, I could have pressed a hand to it. I could have slowed the blood long enough for the magic to heal me, probably.

Without that pressure, though...

I blinked as the little figure alighted before me, striding forward, glaring into my eyes as I looked at her in shock, finally seeing one of them up close.

She was a tiny, almost perfectly formed woman, her eyes larger than any human's, angled enough to make it very clear that she was inhuman, with a waist that was almost segmented thorax rather than thin hips.

Her wings were large and luminescent, fluttering gently in the air, before folding back. Their thin, gossamer-like construction reflected the light and seemed to be filled with a rainbow.

She was also noticeably naked, although thankfully it seemed she owed the design of her anatomy more to a line of plastic dolls than to any biological designer.

"You killed her," she accused me. "You killed all my sisters."

I tried to talk, tried to move, but it was futile. Whatever had been done to me with her bite, it was a case of I could heal that, burn it away with the Lightning, I knew, *or* I could pour the Lightning out into my throat wound.

I didn't have the strength to do both.

"You'll die now." The fairy smiled grimly as she pulled a long needle from where she'd been holding it behind her back and stepped forward.

"The paralysis will last an entire cycle. She gave her life to it, draining your lifeblood and mana to give her, her only chance at surviving." She took hold of my eyelid and peeled it back, staring into the vastness of my eyeball as she lifted the needle to make sure I could see it.

"I'm going to drive this into your brain. It'll take me awhile, digging in through your eye, but I'll manage it," she hissed, her hatred clear as she drew back.

I might not be able to move, but that didn't mean I was totally helpless.

I needed my mana—it was frantically trying to save my life—but that wasn't all I had at my disposal.

I bid farewell to the bonus, and instead reached out, selecting the Dungeon Lord minion system I'd been shown on entry, frantically spamming a single goblin right behind the fairy.

She spun around—the light of the goblin's summoning had reflected in my eyes—and stared aghast at the new creation as it quickly appeared.

"What...?" She gasped, as the mageling blinked dumbly before casting Disgust.

As soon as the goblin finished "printing," my second choice began to appear. This time a kobold—advanced, of course—and although expensive, coming in at five thousand of my ten thousand limited points, it was also armed, armored, and ready.

The fairy screeched in sudden fury, leaping at the goblin as she realized that everything that had happened was its fault, not mine, and she stabbed him, repeatedly with the needle.

The goblin screamed in agony and spun, starting to run for it, managing to get all of a few feet before she managed to drive the needle into an artery and tore open his throat. The goblin collapsed, clutching at his neck, and the fairy screamed in rage, stabbing him again and again, until he lost control and stopped channeling into the spell.

There was a moment of stunned disbelief on the part of the fairy, even as the goblin was choking and thrashing. Then the kobold was there, fist closing around the fairy's body.

One quick bite later, and it was all over.

The kobold tossed the other half of the fairy into its mouth, chewing thoughtfully, as it examined me, before sighing and pulling out a small mat of moss from a pocket. He clapped that to my neck, holding it in place, before getting a thin twine and winding that around, nodding to me in recognition of the situation, and waiting.

I coughed, then laid there, growing weaker by the second, continuing to cycle my mana, unable to even meditate. I waited, the seconds ticking away.

I was so woozy I could barely focus, when the "bleeding" debuff on my neck finally vanished, and it was the last sight I saw as, in relief, I finally let myself pass out.

Several hours later—I had no way to know how many, blocked from the main dungeon system as I was—I awoke, blinking and looking around the little dead grove, seeing all the bodies had long since dissolved.

The kobold I'd summoned had been the first choice when I'd pulled up that system. I'd seen the three options, each level twenty-five, all complete with their gear, and I'd spammed the first one, knowing I had literally seconds before the psycho fairy was back and rooting for my brain via my eyeball.

> **Kobold Adventurer:** The kobold adventurer is a loner, highly respected by his or her own people. They have nonetheless chosen to leave the tribe, striking out on their own to explore the world. As such, they have evolved into the general jack-of-all-trades.
>
> Able to hunt, track, and kill with ease, the Kobold adventurer is infected with a wanderlust that makes it highly unlikely they will remain in any location for long.
>
> Their species-specific bonus to trap-making has evolved into a fully-fledged rogue skillset. Able to find, disarm, and build traps, pick locks, and generally get into and out of most places undetected, the adventurer has learned over the long years of travel that partners might be advantageous to their future, but they are far from necessary.
>
> ### *Be Warned!*
>
> **Where some summons will follow you slavishly, the adventurer will stay by your side only so long as your goals, and actions, align.**
>
> **Cost:** 5000 mana to summon, fully equipped.
> **Status:** Unbound.
> **Note:** As with all sentient dungeon creatures, this pattern is….

I'd had no more time to read—hell, I'd barely skimmed that, making sure I was actually getting a kobold that wasn't just about to stab me and nick my gear, the way my day was going. He wasn't openly hostile, not yet at least, and I'd had no time to examine the other options, so I'd taken him.

I shifted, wincing. One hand came up to my neck and found the mat of moss still held in place, dried blood all around it. My movement was clearly noticed by the kobold, who'd made a small fire and had been sitting before it, staring into the flames, a large pack dumped by his side.

"I wouldn't move that yet." The kobold glanced over.

"I…Thank you." I nodded, forcing myself to sit up, clearing my throat roughly as I looked around. "How long was I out?"

"A few cycles."

"Cycles?" I asked, having had them used as hours and days in the system, and really hoping I'd not been unconscious for days.

"Cycles," he repeated, frowning, then reached up to scratch his neck as he thought. "The sun…this world has a sun, yes?"

"Yes."

"More than one?"

"No."

"That's a relief." He grunted. "Too many damn worlds with lots of them. Never know if it's bum or breakfast time."

"You know of other worlds?" I asked, stunned.

"I know a lot of things." He snorted. "Just like I know you're in for a world of hurt."

"Why'd you say that?" I asked him.

"You're in one of these." He shrugged, then gestured around. "Last time I was summoned into one was awhile back—didn't last long."

"Wait…" I coughed, then spat a load of congealed blood out, hacking to get it all up and out. "Wait, you know what and where we are?"

"Not *where*…just that we're in a trial dungeon, *again*." He shrugged, kicking at the dirt before him. "One of those things, isn't it?"

"Hold the fuck up." I reached up and tested my neck, then pulled the moss free, grunting as it came loose along with some hairs, leaving the dried sticky blood behind, but unmarked skin.

"Fast healer," the kobold noted, and I nodded.

"Yeah. That I am. You got a name?"

"You're one of those, eh?"

"One of what?"

"One of those who thinks that any other species is just a dumb animal?"

He looked annoyed, as near as I could tell, but certainly not surprised.

"No," I said grimly. "I've got friends who are kobolds, sort of. I just…I never met one like you, that's all."

"What rank are they?"

"Rank?"

"Common?" he suggested, and I shook my head.

"Advanced."

"A good sign then." He sighed, before straightening. "Look, I'll lay it out, before the dungeon fairy comes and does it for me, and makes it look worse than it is. Yes, I'm a criminal. Yes, I'm paying for my crimes. Any other questions?"

"What the fuck?" I asked, totally bewildered.

He looked at me, clearly searching my face for something, before grunting and shaking his head as if amazed I could be so stupid.

"You don't know," he stated flatly.

"Don't know what?"

"Did you summon me?"

"Yeah…?"

"That's not gonna bite it," he snapped, standing. "Did you summon me, yes or no?"

"Yes." I glared at him.

"Why?"

"Why did I summon you, or why you in particular?"

"Both."

"I was paralyzed, and that fucking fairy was about to dig her way through my eyeball with a needle till she got to my brain. I picked the first option that I saw that looked even vaguely useful."

"Useful." He grunted. "Yeah, I suppose that makes sense."

"Your turn," I growled. "Who are you, and what the fuck did you mean, you're a criminal?"

"We all are." He gestured to the dungeon around us. "Every soul bound in a trial dungeon is a criminal, here to pay off our crimes in the service of the galaxy, training our 'betters' to help face the horde." The last bit he spat, clearly disgusted.

"What did you do to end up here?" I asked. "And how does all of this work?"

He looked at me for a long few seconds, before shrugging and moving back to sit down, sorting through his bags and pulling out a flask; he took a pull from it, and offered it to me. I reached to the side, unthinkingly trying to summon a bottle myself, only to have it fail.

He laughed and offered the flask again, and this time I took it, taking a swig and hissing at the burn.

"What…the fuck…is that?" I coughed.

"Good." He grinned, the characteristic kobold wide, toothy smile making him both threatening and clearly amused. "It's good is what it is. All right, you know the rules of the trial dungeon?"

"Nope."

"Fucking fairies," he growled under his breath. "In my day, they'd have made sure you knew everything before you were let in here. I know they can't lead you by the hand, but for Lars' sake."

"Lars?"

"God of mischief, pranks, and alcoholism." My new companion grunted. "Anyway. I'm Drak, master criminal, and sentenced to a thousand deaths. Let's just get it out there in the open. No, I'm not a bad person. Yes, maybe a little something occasionally made its way through my claws that wasn't technically mine."

"You're a thief and a smuggler?" I asked, getting a shrug. "You got sentenced to a thousand deaths for that?"

"Maybe I entered something—accidentally, I'll add—that belonged to the imperial family." He shrugged.

"What was it?"

"The princess."

"What was the princess?"

"The person I damn well entered accidentally!"

"How the hell do you 'enter' someone? Accidentally or not?" I asked, confused, until he made a little forward and back gesture with his hips.

"You fucked the princess?" I asked, grinning despite myself.

"Maybe." He winked.

"And you did it accidentally?"

"I was drunk. She snuck out of the palace. It's something I found out after she does regularly, but apparently people know enough to not get too familiar with her."

"And you did?"

"She was pretty, I had a lot to drink, and I was flirting with her. I saw the way everyone else was staying clear, and I just…you know. I didn't understand. I flirted; she flirted. I made a suggestion about my room; she was up for it. And yeah, two hours later, I'm being dragged out of the tavern bedroom, she's screaming at the guards to let me go, and they're all hitting me with knorr-lok claws. Next thing I know, I'm in the palace. Chained to the floor. The princess is screaming that I'm to be the father of the next generation of the royal family, and the emperor is screaming that I'm gonna find out what happens to scum like me. I did the only thing I could think of, and I claimed the right to serve my sentence in the dungeon."

"And then?"

"The emperor intervened, didn't he." He grunted. "I should have gotten ten, or hell, fifty deaths. A thousand? That's reserved for the likes of planetary genocide!"

"So you ended up in the dungeon." I nodded, scratching at my neck. "So how does it work?"

"Every time I, or any of the other sentients, die, our soul is reclaimed by the dungeon. Memories are cloned, and all that makes us, us is stored. Then we're released. We fly onward on the great journey until the next summoning, and the next copy of our soul is reborn."

"How do you know?" I asked.

"It's…look. I get to keep my memories. It's shit, but that's life. I've tried just staying here, ignoring things, but death comes eventually either way. Starvation is a crappy way to go. So I picked my gear, and it comes with me. I've been told that if I get to the end of the trial dungeon then I get ten deaths taken off the total I have to face, and the Dungeon Lord or Master…that'd be you, I'm assuming?" He paused, looking over at me, and I nodded.

"Well, you get the option to strike a deal with me, if you want."

"What kind of deal?"

"Don't know," he admitted. "I've never made it out yet."

"You're shitting me."

"You have to make it all the way to the *end*. Most Dungeon Lords get out at the first room. They take their loot and run. That's why the bonuses are so powerful. Otherwise, everyone would ignore them."

"How powerful?"

"You…you really don't know anything, do you?" he wondered, searching my face as I shook my head.

"Let's just say that the dungeon fairy and I don't exactly talk a lot," I hedged, and he grinned at me.

"Well, in that case, yeah, the bonuses they use to draw you down are usually powerful, a tech upgrade or building you need. But I'm guessing you were tricked into coming here by a dungeon fairy that wants rid of you?"

"Something like that." I nodded.

"Maybe we can come to a deal then," he said slowly, looking me over. "You're armed to the teeth. How'd that little fairy get you like that?"

"Stupid mistake," I admitted. "I tried to recruit them when I realized they were sentient."

"Damn stupid mistake," he agreed. "If she'd agreed, her soul would have gotten ten deaths added on. That body, or incarnation, might have done well out of it, getting to live, but her main body gets to pay for it."

"How many deaths do you have left?" I asked suddenly.

"Nine hundred and thirty-seven." He sighed. "I've died seventy-three times."

"So, no real incentive for you to try to cheat me then…you're back here again and again either way."

"True." He sighed, shifting on the log he'd been sitting on. "But, it means that as this individual…" He tapped himself on the chest. "I'd quite like to live still. Dying hurts, after all. So, you summoned me…did you have a plan or was I just the first soul you saw?"

"Bit of both," I admitted. "I'd intended on doing it all alone, not summoning any help, but I needed to once I was paralyzed."

"You've got magic?"

"I do."

"Thought so. Why'd you not use it on her?"

"Instead of summoning you and the goblin?" I asked, and he nodded. "Honestly, I could have Lightning Bolted her to the face, or whatever, but as close as she was to my eye, I panicked. Add to that, I wasn't entirely sure that she'd be the last one, and I was bleeding out."

"So you summoned one of us because why not." He nodded, taking a swig and staring into the flames. "Makes sense."

"Yeah." I stretched, and paused to wave up at the glass, hoping that the people up there weren't too worried about me, only to get a grunt from him.

"Don't bother."

"What?"

"They've gone," he explained. "About half a cycle after you summoned me, there was some noise, and it's been silent ever since. The dungeon fairy probably kicked them all out."

"Cycle." I clicked my fingers. "How long is a damn cycle!"

"We've been talking about a quarter of a cycle now," he offered after a moment's thought.

"Okay, so a cycle is about an hour. Good to know. Next point…you're an adventurer, or that's what it said. What does that mean? For me and this situation, I mean? I know what an adventurer is."

"It means that I can help you, but I can't do it all," he said. "I've gotten some Experience fighting, some tomb raiding, so I'm good with traps, some basic medical knowledge…I can do a little of everything, but to be clear, none of it is great. I tend to work alone, so I'm used to having to do anything I need to." He twisted his shoulders, rolling them forward and back, and shook his head from side to side, before pausing at the look I was giving him.

"Oh, sorry. It's a gesture from my world. It means, sort of 'it is what it is' or 'crap happens.'"

"Ah." I nodded. "We do it like this." I shrugged my shoulders.

"We have that one too," he said. "But this one means a bit more like 'squeezing by'…pulling yourself from the egg, you know?"

"Got you." I nodded. "Uh, one question, though…"

"Only one?"

"Okay, fair point. Another fucking question then?"

"Go."

"You speak perfect English?"

"Nope."

"But I can understand you," I pointed out.

"I'm not speaking your language, and you're not speaking mine. Part of the system activation is that your world is flooded by mana. Part of the effect that has is a communication spell. We all speak that language now."

"How the hell can that work?" I asked, stunned. "I mean the sheer fucking logistics of it…"

"No clue." He shook his head. "You want my advice? Some of this shit is just the way it is. We were on our way to a full-blown technological revolution when mana came, apparently, and knocked us back down to the level of beasts. That's why there's so many versions of my species. Same for most of us."

"The system…Oh, fuck it," I growled. "Look, there's just too many goddamn questions I have! Right, you said they left?" I gestured upward.

"Yeah, few hundred of them it felt like. They all left a while ago. There's a few left, but only a few."

"You can hear them?"

"Sense," he corrected. "Vibrations."

"Fine, whatever. You say you can get ten deaths knocked off your sentence if we make it to the end of the dungeon?"

"Yes."

"And if I leave early?"

"I'm killed, and a death is counted off my balance."

"Fuck. No pressure then," I growled. "Fine, let's do this. I already summoned you, and that goblin, although he died too sharpish to judge if he was, well, alive."

"He will have been," Drak muttered, before scratching at his snout. "Okay, so you've got how many points left?"

"Uh, four thousand five hundred."

"That many?" He nodded. "How much for another kobold like me?"

"Five thousand."

"Figures." He groaned. "And the goblin?"

"That one was five hundred."

"They usually that expensive?" He clarified, "To spawn, I mean?"

"Nope."

"Thought not. That fairy really hates you."

"You have no idea."

"Yeah well, what else can we get? We need a fighter. I'm guessing you don't want to do that?"

"I can do it," I admitted. "I like doing it, in fact. I just use magic as well."

"That's a nice surprise then." He shrugged. "Maybe we'll have a chance after all. So, what else can you summon for that?"

I pulled up the system, flicking through.

"Up to nine goblins, all the same class, magelings, each with a few spells, or fighters, but they're…"

"Crap and dumb as rocks."

"Basically."

"What else?"

"I could get one of the Fey, the Daoine Sidhe…" I stumbled over the word, and he frantically shook his head.

"Fuck no. You want some of them? You can kill me or leave me here. They're utter bastards. Egg thieves. I'd rather die."

"Uh…two dryads?"

"Pointless."

"Nine fairies?"

"It'd be fun to watch what the fairy does to you afterward for summoning her kin, but hey, limited choices I guess."

"Orcan?"

"Do I look like I want to die that badly?"

"Scepiniir?"

"Shit, really?"

"Yeah, although they come with a load of rules, like they can't be summoned into an arena for the purposes of entertainment, so that's out."

"Is this feeling very entertaining to you?"

"What?"

"Are there people up there eating and drinking and being entertained?" he said more clearly. "Or is this an *actual* dungeon run? Consider your response and remember that your words here might be reported back to the Scepiniir Empire. Is this an *entertainment,* or do you need one of the *premier warrior species in the galaxy to fight by your side?*"

"It's…it's definitely *not* an entertainment," I said loudly and clearly, getting a nod and a smile from Drak. "And yes, we're at serious risk. We need…fuck."

"What?" he growled. "What do we need?"

"We need five hundred more fucking mana is what we need."

"Shitfuck!" he shouted, kicking a nearby fallen branch, then grabbing his foot and snarling something under his breath. After a few seconds, he waved his hands at me to "get on with it," and I started back through the list.

"Lesser ghast?"

"Monster." He shook his head. "It won't be self-aware. Better to just leave them out."

"That's harpies out as well, although I suppose they'd be fuck all use for flying around anyway in here," I muttered, before going on. "Right. That leaves impai, Undead, Raiju, or vermin."

"Undead then." He grunted. "Vermin are fucking useless, Raiju won't respond in here, so you'd just lose the summoning cost, and impai are annoying, though I could happily kill a few for entertainment right now."

"Okay, skeletons and zombies are five hundred each, wraiths are two thousand, and a corpse lord is four thousand. Looks like they're slightly out from their real-world costs—a skeleton is ten mana out there, with a corpse lord at two thousand."

"Yeah, there's different rules for in here." He grunted again. "Okay, corpse lords…those big fuckers, yeah? The ones that can summon more undead to help them?"

"Yeah, but we're in the dungeon. The enemy break down when they die."

"Well, that's just wonderful…" He groaned. "You've not seen any bodies lying around? No dead? Figures. If the fairy liked you, it should have given you some of them, just do them around like furniture, but you could have used them. Hell, maybe there'll be some in the future? I can hope…"

"Sounds like our best choice then," I muttered, then I nodded, glancing over the lists. "Okay, the fairies could use magic. I'm thinking one of them as well?"

"You can, but I'm betting you regret it." He shrugged. "The undead won't be aware, not properly, but the fairy will. Should be fun to watch what happens at least."

"Why do you say that?"

"How many did you kill?"

"The fairies?" I asked, and he nodded. "Two minutes…" I pulled up the notifications, grunting as I looked them over.

You have gained an additional Stat Point in the following area through constant effort.

- +1 Perception

Continue to work hard to increase this or other stats…

*

Congratulations!

You have killed the following:
- 1x Dryad [Common], Level 25, 2,850 XP
- 11x Fey Fairies [Common], Levels 15-22, 1,940 XP
- 8x Goblin grove hunters [Common], levels 10-18, 1,380 XP

Total XP earned: 6,170 XP
Total XP awarded 6,170 XP

Current XP to next level stands at 15,713/50,000

"Eleven," I grunted. "I didn't get anything for you being in the party, though."

"I wasn't in the party." He shrugged. "I'm counted as a summoned minion for the purposes of the trial dungeon, but you get no Experience from me, and I don't level, no matter what I do."

"Joy. Just one more way to fuck me over, eh?"

"Pretty much. Welcome to my life. Anyway, my point was you want to summon a fairy? There's twenty fairy souls in here. You were responsible for twelve of their deaths—want to place a bet on the fairy you get?"

I looked from him to the screen that hovered before me, then back to him and groaned. "How many of them have healing magic?"

"No clue. You think we all get to sit around in a break room and talk about our lives? We're in storage, dead."

"Fuck!" I snarled. "Fine!" Reaching out, I flicked the selection. The corpse lord appeared in a handful of seconds, towering over us where we sat.

Several seconds later, the fairy appeared, and immediately screamed in fury at seeing my face, lunging forward, fingers extended like claws.

I couldn't be sure, but I just fucking *knew* that the one I'd gotten? The same goddamn one that was going to dig her way through my eyeball with a needle.

Great.

CHAPTER THIRTY-TWO

"**D**ie!" she screamed, launching herself at me, even as Drak and the corpse lord sprang into action.

"Stop, you crazy witch!" Drak shouted, reaching for her, even as the corpse lord slapped her tiny form from the sky, sending her crashing into the floor with a squeak.

"Stop!" I yelled as it moved, lifting one hand, ready to step on her, and Drak tackled it from the side, trying to knock it back from her.

Considering it was twice his size and easily half again his weight, not to mention entirely constructed of overlapping solid bone, it barely noticed him, beyond grabbing him by the back of the neck and twisting, lifting him into the air.

I had visions of the fucker going on a rampage and killing all my new help, and shrieked, "Just fucking *stop*, you dickheads!"

They did. Something about the power of the dungeon, and them being summons, stopped them, although the corpse lord still had one foot raised, and it slowly toppled sideways, crashing to the ground.

"Fucking hell, why is this my life?" I grunted, looking at them all. "Seriously, you fucking dicks, I summoned you to *help*!"

"And…I'm…trying!" Drak gasped, still gripped tightly by one of the corpse lord's massive hands.

"Let go of him," I ordered. It dropped him onto the floor, before slowly standing. "Okay, you idiots, we're all allies here, so no attacking each other *or me*—which I can't fucking believe I have to say."

"You killed my sisters!" the fairy spat, crawling out from the shadow of the corpse lord, one arm cradled to her chest, nose broken and glaring at me, a wing obviously snapped and another entirely missing.

"And you all attacked me for being in the dungeon," I replied coldly. "You knew what you were signing up for. Drak told me about your deals. You a criminal too?"

"I hope an imp bites your dick off." She coughed some blood onto the floor and spit. "Kill me now."

"Told you not to summon her," Drak groaned, rubbing his neck and twisting, glaring at her.

"Thief," she snapped at him.

"Witch," he shot back.

"Will you all fucking stop!" I snarled. "Fuck's sake. I thought you didn't know each other?"

"Yeah, I know two of them," he admitted.

"Out of twenty?"

"Yeah."

"And this is one of the two?"

"He stole the healing potion on our last run!"

"I was bleeding out!"

"You'd lost a finger!" she snarled. "The lord was gutted, literally!"

"It wouldn't have saved him." He shrugged.

"Not once you stole it, it fucking wouldn't! We had a chance!"

"Okay, just to add to the last order, no stealing from me either!" I snapped, glaring at them both. "Fuck's sake, I'm already starting to prefer the corpse lord, and he's dumber than a bag of rocks."

"Unless you've a healing potion anyway, I'm as good as dead." The fairy spat, wincing, before sinking to her knees. "Just finish it now."

"I take it you can't heal?" I asked, and she shook her head.

"Triarach Diúracán—my missiles," she explained. "We each got to keep a single spell. That was what I chose."

"Fair enough. Here," I muttered, pulling out and offering her a healing potion, one of the three that I'd brought in.

"Don't suppose you've one that's more my size?" she asked, and I snorted. "Didn't think so." She sighed. "Pull the cork at least…"

I winced, nodding, and pulled the cork out. The flask was a test tube style, and it gleamed red with a sweet concoction, but it was also about the same size as the fairy was.

I knelt next to her, although I still watched, waiting for her to attack, as I angled it to the side for her to dip a hand in.

She raised it to her lips, drinking, and went back for more three times, before shaking her head and telling me to recork it.

"No point in wasting it," she said. "Okay, if you keep giving me a little every few minutes, in an hour I'll be just about able to breathe without pain."

"And fly?" I asked.

"Are you insane?" She snorted, sounding less angry and more defeated and despairing. "Seriously, think for a second. If that was a highly concentrated potion, yeah, maybe. As it is? It'll recover less than a quarter of my overall health, and that's if I drank it all. I could take a *bath* in that. You ever tried drinking a bathtub's worth of anything?"

"Shit." I groaned, nodding. "That makes sense, as much as I wish it didn't."

"So we've a broken fairy who can't cast a spell, and a brain-dead undead." Drak sighed, shaking his head and looking over at me. "Seriously, boss, might be a better idea to do the walk of shame."

"The walk—" I remembered the image of the Dungeon Lord sacrificing everything they had and walking out naked. "No, hell with that," I growled.

"Just saying, our chances aren't good. Okay, so given the summoning list you mentioned…how big is the area you built the dungeon in to?"

"It's a big building," I admitted. "But it's only one floor that's supposed to have been used for this…I think?"

"How many rooms or caverns?"

"Originally?" I rubbed my chin, then shrugged. "About twenty, I think?"

"That's near the maximum," the fairy pointed out, looking at Drak. "You think the dungeon fairy would go all out on his first one?"

"She hates him, I think." He grunted a laugh. "The maximum is twenty-five rooms. Given the creatures you mentioned you have access to and the maximum size of the dungeon…" He thought for a few seconds, before looking up and watching me.

"Look, I don't blame you if you want to take the easy way out. How many rooms are you in?"

"Two," I admitted, getting low laughs from both him and the fairy.

"Yeah, I'd just give up." The fairy sighed. "Seriously, make it quick, though. And I'm sorry. I shouldn't have held it against you. It's all a game."

"It's all a game," Drak echoed, nodding.

"What?"

"It's what we're told when we're prepared for the dungeon," the fairy said, forcing a smile as she looked at me. "That it's all a game and we might as well just relax and play."

"Also, that if we gain skills, while they won't level in here, not the way that they do outside, we'll still be able to learn. So anything we do learn in here helps our futures. Once I've died a thousand times, I'll be fucking skilled at that, at least," he said sadly.

"A *thousand*?" The tiny fairy squawked in shock. "What did you do?"

"Fucked a princess," I replied, grinning and seeing how Drak grinned back at me.

"And that's cost you a thousand deaths?" she asked, surprised.

"Yeah."

"Weird." She sighed. "Remind me never to change my shape near you."

"You can shape shift?" I asked, and she nodded.

"It costs a lot of mana, but we can become larger or smaller, and shape shift."

"So what, you could look like anyone?" I asked, surprised.

She glared at me. "I'm not a sex toy, you disgusting pervert."

"Wait, no, I wasn't—"

"Yeah, of course you weren't," she snapped, shaking her head. "Don't even think about it."

"I wasn't!" I retorted. "Fuck's sake, I'm in a relationship. And even if I wasn't, why would I…You know what? Fuck you all. I'm no sexual deviant, and I don't care what you think! Fine, there's maybe twenty more rooms? I'll clear them all!"

"That's the spirit!" Drak cheered me on, grinning.

"You said something about the creatures I can summon…is that all the dungeon can use?" I asked.

"Yeah, they can artificially level us to the same as you, or near enough, and they can use souls from the roster they have. It's about a thousand members, I think, per world, and all the dungeons pull from it, but whatever. That's all they can use. So, if you wanted to summon a dragon, there's one of them in the roster. But she's insane, and frankly would kill you instantly just for summoning her. You couldn't summon her unless you had access to the pattern already."

"That's a long-winded way of saying that the dungeon can only use the same beings as you can," the fairy piped up, and I nodded my thanks to her, offering the potion again.

"What's your name?" I asked her.

"Ciara."

"And the big guy is brain-dead," Drak pointed out again, unnecessarily.

"He is," I grunted. "Ciara, you can't fly, and you can't fight, unless we get you a healing potion, so what about guiding him?" I suggested, gesturing to the corpse lord.

"I can do that," she agreed. "You're really going to try to get to the other end of the dungeon?"

"I am."

"Ten deaths off your sentence," Drak pointed out. "How many you got left?"

"Seventeen," she said.

"You in then?" I asked, and she shrugged.

"I've nothing else to do," she admitted. "I'll help, but when you get more mana to summon, could you—"

"He's on limited."

"Shit."

"What?" I asked.

"Limited," Drak explained. "Your mana doesn't regenerate…for summons, I mean."

I nodded my understanding. Relief flooded me as I checked my mana. In the four hours or so I'd been unconscious, plus the time I'd spent here talking, I'd recovered just over five hundred personal mana.

For a second, I'd thought he meant I'd not recover any of it, and I'd been damn well panicking.

"Then let's do this," I declared, getting to my feet and ready for a resounding cheer from my new team.

I got a pair of grudging assents from the kobold and the fairy, and a flat, blank stare from the undead.

Fuck it, it'd have to do.

"Drak, you're on trap detection. You lead the way," I ordered. "Ciara, you…ride the corpse lord, I guess. Behind me."

"Oh, I can barely contain my excitement." She sighed, reaching up a hand, and the corpse lord crouched down to her, gently picking her up and carrying her with one of its lower arms.

I turned to Drak, and nodded to the exit from the cavern, and he grinned.

"Let's go have fun," he suggested, drawing a sword, and moved past, starting to search.

The tunnel that led from the cavern was short and winding, falling back on itself like a snake, making it awkward for the corpse lord to squeeze through. But it was also thankfully untrapped, and before we reached the next cavern, Drak slid back to where we waited a few meters back from him.

"Okay, undead here, a dozen smaller ones. Probably your kind, judging from your build. They're a lot smaller than you are, though. Do we need a plan?"

"Probably not for a dozen. Anything hidden away?" I scratched at my neck as I thought.

"Not that I can see, but you know, I'm an adventurer, not a fucking witch."

"There are witches?" I asked him, then shook my head. "You know what, if we live, you can tell me all this weird-ass shit. Let's go kill things."

"That's an attitude I can get behind!" He grinned. "Just give me a minute…" He pulled his backpack around and dumped his shortsword back into its sheath, before rummaging for a second. Soon he pulled out a mace, then unhooked a small buckler shield from the side of the pack and strapped it onto his other arm, still grinning and nodding that he was ready.

I led the way this time, pulling my hammer loose and carrying my slightly bent shield at the ready.

Thirty seconds later, we were racing into the room. The dozen skeletons that were slowly plodding around the room looked up and ran in, all at once.

They were armored, mainly, and had swords, spears, maces, and axes, as well as shields, with two at the back hefting bows and letting loose almost instantly.

Any thought that this was going to be an easy slaughter-fest was lost in the first ten seconds of the fight.

The nearest three skeletons all fell in on me, two with spears jabbing for my face and thighs, driving me back as one with a huge two-handed axe, slamming it into my shield as hard as it could.

I grunted, surprised by the strength, but hooked my hammer around the spear that was going low, yanked it to the left, ducked under the high thrust, and spun, brushing the axe strike aside.

I slammed the hammer into the side of the "high" spearman's head, tearing it free and sending the body clattering to the floor as the life left it.

Now there were two.

An arrow as long as my fucking arm slammed into my shield, ricocheting off and staggering me. I snarled in fury, returning fire with a Lightning Bolt to the archer's face, detonating his head, before I caught the next axe blow on the shield. The "low" spear grazed my side, where I'd clearly left it open accidentally. I swore, backing up, then rushed forward, catching the axe man with the shield as he lifted his weapon, driving him back and off-balance…

Another arrow hit me, this time glancing off a pauldron. I hissed in pain. It'd not penetrated, but it still made my left arm go numb.

The spear flashed forward again, and I twisted, dodging it as it flashed past my face. I triggered Storm-Strike, kicking out and unleashing it through my boot as I caught the spear-wielding fucker in the left thigh.

Its armor and the rotten leg beneath it exploded, sending the skeleton crashing to the floor, even as I battered the axe aside with my hammer, and uppercutted him, sending the helmet—complete with head—flying off with a pop of disconnecting vertebrae.

On the backswing, I caught the spear-wielding, now one-legged fucker trying to stab me, and smashed the spear aside, before slamming my hammer into the faceplate of his helm.

The entire front of his skull buckled in, and I saw teeth tumbling free from the bottom as I wrenched my hammer to the side, ripping it free…

And another arrow slammed into my back, this time lower down on the right-hand side. It was a much better strike, and had I not been wearing plate, I'd have been seriously fucked.

As it was, it still goddamn hurt. I staggered, then hit the damaged one under me again in the head, making sure of him, before turning to face the remaining archer.

I'd taken the first one out with that Lightning Bolt to the face, which was a relief, but the other one clearly hadn't got the memo about not fucking with me.

He was firing over and over, splitting his focus between the others and me, and the corpse lord looked like a pincushion. It was forced to use one arm just to deflect arrows that were aimed at its head. The left upper arm had at least five broken arrows lodged in it, but the other three arms were a blur.

Ciara was hanging on around its neck, glaring around it and giving directions, as the big fucker took a hit from an axe, hacking one of the lower arms free.

It staggered, then lunged forward, grabbing the axe wielder by the head and simply ripping the skull free, sending what looked to be its fourth body clattering to the floor.

I checked on Drak quickly, then growled as another arrow slammed into the damaged section of my shield. The point actually made it through, and the whole thing reverberated.

He was fine, I decided, switching my attention back to the archer. Drak was alive still, and the corpse lord was headed to help him, as I started to run at the archer.

My shield jerked again, as another arrow slammed into it, then a third. Then it shook again, as this time I drove the large oval slab of metal full into the archer, picking it up and smashing it into the wall of the cavern.

I bounced off, the skeleton the meat in a "Matt-and-cavern-wall" sandwich, and it was far from tasty.

It was battered and broken, though. The fucker tried to draw a dagger instead, only to crumple as my hammer smashed the top of its skull like an egg. The skeleton clattered into a disconnected pile of bone and armor at that point, and I twisted around, surveying the rest of the cavern.

The final skeleton was a spear wielder, and against Drak, it'd been doing well; his shield was keeping it from doing real damage, but it was also keeping him from inflicting any.

Not so, the corpse lord.

It just ran in from the side, grabbed the spear in one hand, ripped it free, grabbed the skeleton's left arm and dragged it closer, then tore the helm, and then the skull free, crushing it in one massive hand.

With that, the fight was over. Drak had managed two, I'd managed five, and Ciara and the corpse lord were on five as well. I sagged slightly with relief that we were all alive, intact, and aside from a few scratches, scrapes, and well, multiple broken bones on Ciara's part, we were functional.

"Loot as quick as you can and then we're outta here," I called to the others.

"What's the rules on loot?" Drak called back, reaching out to a reliquary as it appeared before him.

"Who cares?" Ciara grunted. "Even if we get out of this, we're only buying ten deaths off—wait!" She sat up, staring at me in shock. "Are you offering us freedom? What you said before? Are you freeing us if we join you?"

"If you join me, at the end of this, I'll do my best to strike a deal with you," I promised. "I desperately need help, so if you want to be free-roaming dungeon citizens…"

"Would we have to fight? To serve?" she asked quickly, making it clear that "serve" may very well not mean what I was thinking it meant.

"I'd ask you to fight to defend the dungeon and your lives, other citizens as well, but I'd not force you, not when I know you're alive and sane. I'd also not force you to do whatever you're worried about. You'd have a job, research or magical training or whatever. Nothing…you know." I shrugged, shaking my head.

"I accept!" she snapped. "You give me freedom in exchange for teaching some idiots about magic? By the buried halls, yes!"

"You'll teach my people all you know about magic?" I asked just as quickly. "You'll learn and teach, and swear to obey me and those placed over you?"

"I will…for ten of your local system years, but…"

"Yeah?"

"No twisted, kinky shit, all right?" She glared at me. "You try to do anything like that…"

"Fuck no." I groaned. "I swear that you will never be expected nor demanded to perform any kind of sexual service for me or mine, or your contract with me is null and void and you're free. Okay?"

"Hells yes!" she agreed, grinning.

"What about your original body?" Drak asked, and she snorted.

"Fuck it. It's only a meat sleeve…you think I care about it? Watch how fast I get out of here." She snorted.

"Fine." He sighed, reaching into another reliquary. "So, as I was asking before. What about the loot?"

"Magical is mine," I said firmly. "That's one of the reasons I'm here. Coinage and jewels are yours if you want them, same as normal, non-rare as fuck stuff. Any skillbooks or spellbooks, definitely mine. I'll reward you for them, though."

"Potions?" he asked. "Class-specific gear?"

"Such as?"

"Specialist trap detection and disarming tools?"

"That's a very specific question," Ciara pointed out smugly, getting a glare from him.

"Yeah, well, how about it?" he asked, and I noted that he hadn't removed his hand from the reliquary yet.

"It's yours while we're in here. When we leave, I'll have the dungeon make a copy and you get the copy," I offered.

"I want the original."

"Why?"

"They're generally better," Ciara advised me, seeming happy to help suddenly. "As much as the dungeon *should* reproduce things exactly, there can be minor issues with magical or specialist equipment."

"I get the original," I repeated flatly. "The dungeon will provide a copy, and compensation to you for giving it up."

"Fine," he growled, pulling his hand free and holding up a rolled bag so that we could both see it.

Trap Kit	Item
This small kit is designed to provide the aspiring Trapsmith with everything they need to build, maintain, and disable traps up to the "rare" level.	
Durability 20/20	**Rarity:** Uncommon

"It's not magical," I said after a second, frowning at him.

"Doesn't need to be," he replied. "It's uncommon grade. Back home, it'd have cost me at least fifty gold."

"Damn."

"Exactly. So, you want it, or can I use it to keep us alive?"

"I'd rather live than be a richer corpse," I said. "I'd only make a copy, anyway, so don't be a dick about it. If I could make a copy, then you'd be able to make as many as you need from the dungeon."

"Yeah, until the fairy stops you from destabilizing the local economy." He laughed.

"You think?" I shook my head, moving to the nearest of my reliquaries. "Fucking figures," I grunted, tossing the cheese and onion crisps aside and moving to the next.

"What, about the economy?" Ciara asked.

"Yeah?"

"It's a standard concern," she assured me. "Any new dungeon that's been planted has to account for the local economy, or the planetary governor would shut it down."

"Yeah, you're gonna be wanting a chat after we get out of here..." I muttered under my breath, seeing that they were expecting a whole different kind of a world outside.

The other four reliquaries had, between them, four silver coins, thirty-seven copper, one apple, and a tiny hat.

The hat was both too small for any of the rest of us, and much too big for Ciara, who took one look at it and shook her head.

"Gnomish," she declared, looking inside the rim, then pointing to it. "See, made by one of their older houses."

"What does it do?" I asked, taking it back from her and looking in the rim.

"It's a hat," she said slowly, as if speaking to an idiot. "You put it on your head. It keeps the rain off, and looks nice."

"It doesn't do anything else?"

"What did you expect?" Drak asked as we walked to the next section. Ciara happily handed her loot over as we went—a green stone earring, three gold coins, and a potato. The two maces, the corpse lord was keeping.

"I don't know, something to do with engineering," I explained lamely.

"Why?" Ciara asked me, clearly confused. "It's a *hat*. I'd understand it if it was a helmet or had goggles or something, but its gnomish."

"Exactly!"

"It's not a goblin hat," she pointed out, and I paused.

"What?"

"Goblins." She nodded amiably. "Nasty little buggers. There're no higher-leveled ones in here, are there? Just common?"

"Just common," I assured her.

"That's a relief then."

"Trap!" Drak called out, and we moved back, giving him some room to work.

The next ten minutes was a mixture of random questions that left us both as confused as when we started, and the awkward ones.

"Why do you look like that?" I'd asked at one point as she straightened, wincing from her latest drink as a rib popped into place and she adjusted her tits.

"Like what?" She looked down at her body.

"Like…fuck's sake," I muttered, shaking my head. "Like you've got no nipples or anything?" I decided it was better to just say it.

"You…you want to see my nipples?" she asked, horrified, wrapping her arms around herself.

"Fuck no!" I said quickly. "Fuck's sake, this sounds so fucking wrong! Oh gods, why did I even ask this…"

"You think it's wrong?" She glared at me. "You're the one who started this conversation! Why can't I see your…wait, you're male, right?" she asked me after a second, and I nodded. "Well, why isn't it just swinging around like you don't care?"

"First, because I don't need to show it off, and second, because it'd get mauled!"

"Yeah well, it's the same for me!" she snapped. "Why the hell would I show my nipples or my—"

"That's not what I meant." I cut her off hurriedly, holding one hand up. "Look, I meant it looks like you're naked, okay? Not wearing any clothing…"

"I know what naked means," she growled, and I heard Drak sniggering behind me as I tried to dig myself out of the hole my stupid comment had dug.

"Okay, so if you're naked, why aren't your nipples *or anything else* obvious? That's all I meant! I wasn't asking to see them, I just…don't understand!" I waved my hands to her. "Look, you're one of only a few fairies I've ever met, and most of them were trying to kill me, or they weren't humanoid-looking! I just…I was curious, okay?"

"Ohhhh," she said slowly, before nodding and forcing a smile. "I think I understand. So you just don't know how we breed, and you were curious?"

"I don't know how you breed," I agreed. "And I'm not that curious, I just…Look. For my species, when we have no clothes on, our sexual organs are clearly visible. You seem to be smooth skin everywhere. I was just curious and—"

"And you thought it was a good conversation to have with a magical tiny female you just met?" Drak asked, straightening up and tucking his tools away. "One you'd recently killed?"

"Fucking hell, there is no way this conversation was a good idea, was there?" I mumbled. "Ciara, I'm sorry. It really wasn't meant like that."

"It's okay." She smiled. "I understand—really, I do. It just wasn't a conversation I was expecting to have. To make it as simple and clear as I can, we aren't sexual in the way that most species are. We develop our bodies as we age, like most, but we don't deploy our sexual organs unless there is a need, or we're…'interested.' Because we have nothing to show, and we don't feel heat and cold, many of our kind simply don't bother with 'clothing' in the way that most sapients do."

"Thank you." I shook my head. "Don't worry, I'll never ask anything like that again," I said grimly.

"No, no, please do." Drak grinned at me. "Personally, I found the whole conversation hilarious."

"Remind me not to let you spend any time with Chris," I muttered, glaring at the kobold.

"Who is he?" he asked, and being the good friend I am, I couldn't help but smile suddenly.

"He's…well, he's a friend. But he's really into sex with other species, so if he tries to get you to drink with him, or to talk to you? He's only after one thing," I assured him, stifling the smile.

"And it's males he's after?"

"Oh, anything," I asserted. "Males, females…leather cushions—just watch him."

"If he tries to get me drunk, I'll hurt him," Drak warned me, and I nodded.

"That's fine," I said. "Nothing permanent, though…just pain, all right?"

"Okay…" With that, Drak moved back into the tunnel and hurried along, checking for the next trap.

"He's not like that, is he?" Ciara asked me in a low whisper.

"No, and he's happily in a relationship, but I thought it'd be funny."

"I can see this new dungeon life will be an interesting one," she said philosophically. "At least I won't be bored."

"Never that," I promised. "Gods, what I'd give for a few boring days."

The tunnel was a short one, terminating in a long, wide cavern. Three skeletal archers were easily spotted on a raised platform to the left and the right, and they fired arrows as soon as we entered, driving us back into the tunnel.

"What do we do?" I asked them, and Ciara smiled, patting the corpse lord on the head.

"If I can get halfway across the cavern, I can take out three. My missile spell costs a lot of my mana, but I can independently target it, and they should kill the skeletons easily enough, one each to the neck. But that's only three of them…" She looked to Drak and me.

"I can take the others," I said firmly. "Three Lightning Bolts should do it."

"Then that's it." Drak shrugged. "Nice easy one for me."

"Not so much," Ciara replied, eyes twinkling. "We need a distraction."

"Fuck."

"Here." I passed him my battered but still solid shield. "Hide behind that."

"Once you've got their attention, we'll run forward. You lead, and I'll take out the right-hand three as quickly as I can," she assured him.

"I'll get the left from here," I nodded, "as soon as you have their attention."

"Fuck." The kobold took the shield and glared at me. "I better be keeping anything magical I loot after this," he tried, and I grinned, shaking my head.

"Nope, but good try."

"Well, worth a go," he grumbled. Then, taking a deep breath, he drew his sword and ran forward into the cavern, slapping the flat of the blade against the shield. The ring of steel on steel filled the air.

Arrows flew at him, slamming into the shield and shattering as the corpse lord and its rider sprinted out next, and then it was my turn.

Stepping up, I was already channeling my mana when the first of the archers came into sight. The raised platforms on either side of the exit from the cavern were barely large enough to hold three on each.

It was lit by a pair of torches in the middle of the room, making it much easier to spot anything running forward. Drak suddenly shouted out a warning and dove forward, leaping over a section of seemingly innocent sandy ground…until it collapsed, showing a concealed pit.

He rolled, shouting out in pain as an arrow caught him in the thigh, and he dropped, crouching under the shield.

I let loose with my Lightning Bolt, but rather than fire and forget, I continued to pour mana in, and dragged the solid bar of crackling energy from left to right at head height.

I'd left the first one too quickly, I saw a second later, and jerked it back as the second died; the first staggered, merely badly toasted. I hit him again, then jerked to the right, blasting the third archer from the platform, sending it crashing to the cavern below, smoking and shaking. I cut off the mana and ended the spell.

Ciara was cackling wildly as all of her missiles slammed home, adjusting on the fly to punch deep into the throats of all three archers, before detonating.

Three heads were ripped free, and I took off running, racing past where she stood on the corpse lord's back, leaping over the pit—I couldn't help but look down, seeing the jagged blades glinting below—and then hurdling Drak as he peered around my shield.

The skeleton was slowly pushing itself to its feet when my hammer crashed into the back of its head, and that was it—the fight was over.

"You all right?" I asked Drak.

"Do I look all right?" he countered, ripping the arrow from his thigh with a groan of pain.

"Yeah, actually," I assured him.

"Well, that shows how little you know," he replied rudely. "Now stop asking stupid questions and give me a damn healing potion."

"We've only got two more," I warned him. "Do you *need* it?"

"Yes, I damn well do!" he snapped, pointing at the small wound in his thigh. "Arrow, leg! Give me the fucking potion!"

"Here." I sighed, passing it over. I didn't begrudge him the potion, not really, but I'd not have used one for so minor a wound, personally. But we had one left, plus the rest of the one that Ciara was working her way through, and we could hope more would drop soon.

At the end of the day, having his wholehearted help, rather than limping everywhere, was probably better.

The drops from these six were crap, and went into the bag, mainly crisps and coins, as well as a prismatic feather that was apparently "a good drop" according to Drak, but fuck all use as near as I could tell.

"Let's move on," I growled, checking the notifications and dismissing them. I was getting no Experience for their kills, which was annoying, but decent for my own, so that was a relief.

The next hour was all skeletons, five rooms of them, before Ciara eventually begged for a rest, complaining that her mana was almost nonexistent, and pointing out that for a mana-based life-form, that was far more serious for her than it was for me.

We meditated, rested, and the barriers between us, low as they were, gradually melted away. Everything from favorite foods to relationships were discussed—Drak was apparently considered strange because he liked to be on his own, rather than in a group relationship, which was the norm for kobolds, and Ciara was happily single for some time before she'd been sentenced to the dungeon—and eventually my awkward questions became a source of amusement, rather than concern.

After two more hours, we agreed that there wasn't much more that could be done for the day and set the corpse lord to stand in the tunnel entrance, while we took turns sleeping.

I spent most of the night meditating.

By morning, though, I was more and more concerned.

I'd been cut off from the dungeon sense, and all communication with the outside world. Normally that wouldn't have concerned me—hell, they could still see *me*—but the fact that there was someone up there—Drak could sense vibrations insanely well; it was part of his paranoid scout build—but that there was only apparently ever one or at the most two people there?

It seemed weird.

When Kelly and I had discussed it, I wasn't happy about being watched, but equally, it was important for people to see, that even the Dungeon Lord could get his ass handed to him but get up and fight on.

It could be that people were just fucking bored. After all, I was spending a lot of this time sitting around and meditating, but…Ah, fuck it.

I was oscillating between being annoyed that she'd taken people away, because they should be learning from this, being terrified that I was missing something really important, like an invasion, and just a tiny bit goddamn thankful that there was nobody else up there, as I'd needed to go for a little walk and take a shit not that long ago, and watching the lord of all he bloody surveyed kicking sand over his turd and having to use a little paper that a kobold had found to wipe my arse?

Well, it wasn't very "lordly."

By the time the others had awoken, and we'd eaten from the meager rations we had—I'd basically brought snacks, not expecting to be in for long, and certainly not expecting to have to share—we were all ready to damn well kill someone.

"Come on then," I grumbled, stepping up to the corpse lord, lifting Ciara up to slide onto his shoulder.

"Thank you." She sighed. "Gods, I miss my wings…"

"We've got good healers," I assured her, forcing a smile as she nodded, shifting uncomfortably.

"I'll look forward to that, for the future, but hopefully my regeneration and the rest of that potion will do it," she said, before we set off again.

The next room wasn't far, but we smelled it before we saw it. Drak turned to glare at me, spitting out a single word, heavy with disgust.

"Goblins."

CHAPTER THIRTY-THREE

Creeping up to the edge of the tunnel, before ordering the corpse lord to stay back there out of sight, then falling to our knees and crawling up to stare over the edge, we swore, long and low. The cavern before us was huge, and I mean fucking *huge*.

Where the entrance opened out, it was at the top of a cliffside, with a winding switchback that led to the ground below. The entrance point was roughly the middle of the next room, with the cavern vanishing to the left and right out of sight, curving slightly around, with blasted sandstone pillars dotted here and there, winding their way to the roof.

The ground was sandy, but where the rest of the dungeon so far had been plain rock and sand, this…it looked like somewhere that should be baking beneath the harsh glare of the Saharan sun.

The light was dim, late evening if I was any judge, but the scattered dirt, stunted plants, and the general state of the place suggested that if the last area had been reminiscent of the deep forest, this was the edge of a desert, or somewhere equally inhospitable.

The worst part, though, was the inhabitants.

Clearly the dungeon was restricted to the level that I'd unlocked, which with the goblins was "common," thankfully. That, however, meant that seeing as the goblins couldn't compete on quality, they'd gone for the "quantity has a quality all of its own" style.

There were maybe a hundred, all told, of the little bastards roaming around down there. Some were in gangs, others in smaller groups, with a rough settlement in the middle of the cavern that seemed to be full as well.

I stared at it, squinting, before scooting backward into the corridor and turning to face Drak.

"What the fuck is that shit?" I asked him flatly.

"What?" he asked, mystified.

"You asked how big the original building was!" I snapped at him. "You said that it'd use the original area that was given over to it, and something about how it might be a little bigger than before, but it wouldn't be much! I sure as shit didn't have a fucking village in the middle of the building!"

"How big is the building?" he asked after a few seconds' thought.

"Uh…right, this is a meter." I marked an area out on the ground. "Overall, it's probably…" I knew we'd worked this out before, fuck I knew we had, but I just couldn't remember.

"I think it's about seventy meters on the short side, maybe a hundred and fifty on the long. It's a triangle, so times those by each other and divide by two…maybe five thousand square meters?" I guessed, shrugging.

"And it's just one floor?"

"No, the entire building covers seven floors, but the top two are farms and the next one is where everyone was watching us, and the kobolds live there…"

"So, four floors, each about five thousand, so twenty thousand square meters?" he asked me, aghast. "Even if the dungeon just made use of the levels by building up and down, that could mean dozens more caverns like this!"

I paused, reworking the layout in my mind. Twenty thousand square meters. That was twenty kilometers, if I looked at it as a meter-wide tunnel, say. That was…fuck me with a running chainsaw! That was twelve fucking *miles*.

Moving back to the cavern, and doing a little guesswork, some mental mapping and…

"Fuck me, there actually could be literally a dozen like this."

"No," Ciara said firmly. "Think about this logically. They have to give you a chance. The dungeon is generated on a scan of you and your known capabilities. That size? With hundreds more enemies? It just couldn't work."

"Well, it's looking like evidence trumps logic," I growled, gesturing with a thumb in the direction of the goblins.

"No, it doesn't." Ciara sighed. "Look, you said that it took a hundred and fifty thousand mana to rebuild the dungeon, right?"

"Yeah?"

"How much would it cost to build a site this big?" She waved toward the goblins and so on. "Work it out. A hundred, maybe a hundred and fifty goblins, what's that going to cost?"

"Uh…thirty mana a pop, so maybe four and a half thousand?"

"Okay, boosting them to level twenty-five will cost at least a few hundred per goblin. Then give them clothing, gear, build the village?"

"Thirty thousand to boost them, plus another say, thirty thousand to equip them and build the village, add in the other creatures so far…"

"And you're running low on available mana," she said. "If the trial dungeon was generated using the existing structure, and absorbing whatever was already here, then it will have saved some of the cost, but not all. If there's a hundred to a hundred and fifty down there, add on more caverns like this, and higher creatures like the corpse lord, the ghasts, and so on? I'd bet a handful more caverns, but all with higher-levelled enemies in them."

"Higher leveled," I grunted, shaking my head. "And we've got one healing potion left, once you finish this one off."

"Well, we could plan for this better," Ciara said after a few seconds, crouching next to me and peering over the edge of the cliff. "Look, if we can get you through this, to the other side, and find you a safe room to unlock the entrance, will you come back in the future and release us?"

"We'd never get him back through here," Drak snapped. "You're thinking of a run? Just race straight through the middle? We'd all die, and at best, he'd make it to the safe room. Then what? He unlocks it and has to run back through here. He'd be dead in seconds when they're expecting him."

"He could go and sacrifice his gear then," she suggested, and again Drak shook his head.

"You think he'll come back? I don't," he grumbled. "If he has to hand over all of his gear, losing it all? He'll never risk coming back, and you know it."

"I'd just recreate it all, get potions and everything else I need, prepare properly…" I muttered, thinking it over.

"You lose everything you hand over," he replied flatly.

"Yeah, but I'd just resummon it and—"

"It's deleted from the dungeon," Ciara admitted. "Whatever you put in, it's deleted. So if you created that armor yourself?"

"A friend made it," I said.

"It'd be deleted, along with all the earlier versions. They'd have to remake it from scratch. Same with everything else—your weapons, your potions…everything."

"Then we break it. I walk up naked with just a coin or whatever, dump that in and—"

"And you're being watched by the dungeon and assessed. Stuff like that wouldn't be allowed. Plus, the dungeon fairy is—"

"Dead," I grunted, before sighing and moving back a little to talk easier. "The fairy is dead."

"You killed her?" Ciara asked, looking sick.

"Nope." I shook my head. "When I found the dungeon core, she was dead. Her soul occasionally helps me, that's all."

"Then we're in no better a place." Drak groaned. "Hell, it's worse!"

"Why?" Ciara asked, before starting to swear.

"What?" I asked the pair of them.

"The interface for the trial dungeon is only available to the dungeon fairy, or to the Dungeon Lord at the end of the trial. You leave here early? You'll never get to come back," Drak grunted, slumping to sit on his ass.

"Could you take the place of the dungeon fairy?" I asked Ciara, and she shook her head.

"No chance," she admitted. "I'd need massive interface facilities to be built into me, and I'd need to be taught to use them. That takes years, or at the very least a full didactic memory download from the Cinthians. That's before I could even start to learn to use the dungeon, and…" She hesitated, looking at me, before Drak went on in her place.

"And there can only be one true master of the dungeon. If you make her the dungeon's dedicated fairy, I'd imagine you'd lose a lot of your access to the dungeon, and she'd be able to remove you if you upset her. You just met her— you want to take that chance?"

"Especially after you slaughtered my sisters." She sighed. "Not a good idea. Sorry and all. I'm trying to like you, and I'm sure that eventually we can be friends, but…"

"So." I sighed. "I can't leave the trial dungeon any other way beyond winning it, or I'd never get back in, right?"

"Basically, yeah," Drak grunted. "Plus you'd lose all your equipment and have to walk past your citizens as a naked, unarmed weakling."

"Weakling?" I flexed a bicep slowly.

"Yeah, very pretty," he grunted, unimpressed. "No offense, but I've not seen your kind before. As far as I know, you're a shitty-ass specimen."

"Fair enough. Why the hell would it try to humiliate me by making me walk out naked, though?"

"It's meant—I think—to make it clear that you failed, and to give others the chance to kill you and take your place."

"Great," I growled. "Fucking Cinthians keep adding shit to my list."

"List?"

"Of reasons I'm going to kill them all."

"Seriously?" Ciara asked, staring at me, wide-eyed.

"Hell, if we can include the kobold empire on the list, you've got me by your side for life," Drak growled. "Just the emperor and his court, though…"

I smiled. "Not the princess?"

"Not the princess," he agreed, grinning widely. "I'm planning on going back to her someday."

"You think she's waiting for you?" Ciara asked almost curiously. "Holding an egg ready?"

"Who—"

"Who gives a damn." I cut them off. "Look, we need to do this." I gestured toward the cavern below. "Plans for afterward need to be put aside. The end is all that matters, I guess."

"Okay." Drak sighed. "Looking over it, I'm betting we've got the weakest outside, roaming in packs. There'll be some soldiers inside at least, probably a few mages and yeah, either an over-priest or a warlord."

"Why do you say that?" Ciara asked.

"It's supposed to be beatable, by him alone if need be. There'll be groupings as well, lines that they don't cross. Remember that the majority of them will be thinking, real souls that are spun up to use in this. But, they won't attack unless they see you. If we can draw them away, we can take them out in smaller numbers, then assault the settlement." Drak shrugged. "I've done these rooms before."

"Have you ever got to the end?" I asked, and he shook his head.

"Made it a few levels, though, and I'll help where I can."

"Shit, sorry, you did say. You?" I asked, switching to Ciara, who shook her head.

"Fairies are generally ignored in these situations. Few of us have any kind of meaningful mana reserve," she admitted. "If I could heal, yeah, I could be a lot more use to you, but—"

"But you can kill three enemies at once." I nodded. "I'd rather have you do that," I said. "Right, looking over the cavern…"

We spent the next ten minutes planning, with Ciara making the most of both her speed and diminutive size, as even with damaged wings, after finishing off the healing potion, she could fly again.

It was only just, and it wore her out, but her zipping out to the right and left, searching and returning to draw a small map in the dirt of the cavern floor for us made a hell of a difference.

It turned out that the cavern was roughly crescent moon-shaped, with the entrance and exit across from each other in the middle, the settlement directly in the center. We either snuck around the outside—fucking unlikely—or we went through the settlement itself.

The twin "horns" of the crescent, however, vanished to the right and left, with the left leading to a rocky gully, and the right to a sweltering naphtha pit, bubbling and burping with rising bubbles.

Both sides notably had small groupings in them. The naphtha team was collecting the naphtha into filthy barrels, and the gully team appeared to be mindlessly mining.

"If we run straight for the settlement, or try to sneak around, as soon as we're seen, they'll all come running, no doubt," Drak growled. "I've not tried the naphtha pit, but the last time I was in a situation like this, we slaughtered the miners, then drew the smaller groups to us, before raiding the settlement."

"How'd it work out?" I asked.

"Did it twice," he admitted. "First time we won, and easily. The warlord died fairly quick."

"And the second?" Ciara queried.

"Put it this way…I did tell you I'd never made it to the end, right?"

"How bad?" I asked.

"I took a necrotic spell to the face," he replied grimly. "I lasted long enough to feel my skull rotting apart."

"So, not good then." I grinned. "Let's hope that the warlord is home, not the priest."

"Or that there's no mage or worse, a real necromancer," Ciara added.

"Oh, thank you for that wonderful thought," Drak groused, and I grinned at them both.

"So when you ran for the settlement, the naphtha pit miners didn't attack you?"

"First time, they made it there once we'd already finished the settlement guards off, and we killed them easily enough. Second time, well…No clue, really."

"Did the Dungeon Lord make it out?"

"No clue," he repeated.

"Great. Okay, let's play it safe. Can we make it to the groups from up here, first of all?"

"There's a narrow path that takes us along from above," Ciara informed me with a smile. "You should be able to hide all the way."

"We just went down the switchback and then ran to the left each time," Drak admitted. "Had to stop and kill the roaming groups as we went, so the miners were ready for us as well. This could work out well."

"So, gully from above, draw them up to us, then draw in the roaming mobs. Then we do the naphtha pit, then the settlement," I said firmly.

"Sounds fun." Ciara grinned. "What do I do?"

"Scouting, please," I asked, gesturing upward. "Once we've got the gully cleared, you can draw in the groups to us, and stay high so we have a warning if more are coming."

"And me?" Drak asked.

"With me." I shrugged. "We get to fight the goblins."

"Joy," he grumbled, but he followed along as I lead the way from the path that went downward, and instead we followed Ciara, clambering through and over small spindly bushes, before dropping down to run in a crouch along the hidden path at the top, making me smile despite myself.

I'd been feeling that everything was out to kill me—which, yeah, it was—*but* I'd also forgotten the important detail here. This was supposed to be a trial, and as such it was designed to test me, to make me work for it, but to be ultimately beatable. They wanted me to grow. They wanted me to *win.*

Thinking of it in game terms instead? I had a group of roaming mobs, I had allies, and I had usable environments to make the most of.

All told, I'd been looking at this the wrong fucking way.

We scrambled around the hidden path, running from boulder to boulder, until we reached the narrow gulley, looking down at the section that was filled with lackadaisical goblins pretending to mine.

Mainly what they were doing was trying to rob each other, as apparently they were as lazy as legend said, not to mention as dumb.

There were maybe fourteen of them, all with picks and hammers, smashing into the rock in an oval area, surrounded by high sides and a narrow entrance that led in.

They were ranged around the inside of the circular canyon, mostly pretending to chip away at the walls, gathering up what looked to be ores and gems from here, and dumping them into their baskets.

As soon as one wasn't looking, though, their neighbor would try to steal something from their basket.

Sometimes it was successful; other times they'd be caught, and a quick and nasty fight would break out, usually resulting in both combatants' baskets getting looted by their friends while they were busy.

The upshot of all of this, we quickly realized, was that there was almost fuck all "mining" being done. The goblins were robbing each other blind, and we could have probably driven a marching band round the top of the canyon, and they'd never have noticed.

"So," I said after a few minutes of watching. "Should we actually get involved or just leave them to it? I mean, another ten to fifteen minutes of this and they'll be so wounded we don't even need to fight them."

"There'll be a shift change soon then." Drak shook his head. "Remember, they're conscious creatures, not mindless. They won't do your job for you, and whatever is in charge here wants whatever they're mining. If they kill each other, they get nothing."

"Then we wait for the shift change." I grinned at him. "In fact, Ciara?"

"Yes?"

"Can you see anyone heading this way?"

"I'll go look." She darted away, staying up near to the ceiling and weaving in and out of the occasional stalactites that hung from the overhanging sections.

She returned in a minute, flashing back to land between us and nodding to me. "There's maybe ten more of them heading this way," she said curiously. "You've got a plan?"

"I do." I grinned. "How wide would you say that section is?"

"Where they're all fighting?"

"Yeah."

"Maybe ten of those meter thingies across?" she guessed, and I nodded.

"I thought so too. How many goblins do you think you could get chasing you into there?"

"Uhhhh, maybe a few groups?" She rubbed her pointed chin in thought. "In and then up here?"

"For you, yeah," I said, outlining the new plan.

Thirty seconds later, she was off, zipping around the paths and back out of sight.

We waited in silence for a few minutes, broken only by the occasional comment like, "Looks like the one with the big spot is getting robbed again…"

We'd reached the stage of placing bets on the goblins—Big Nose was doing really well in the fights, but also had the least gems thanks to Super Spot, who'd entirely given up mining and was now creeping around looting—but finally the shift change arrived.

There were fifteen of them, not the original ten that Ciara had seen, and they'd barely made it into the canyon, when a new fight broke out.

The newcomers wanted the baskets that were in place—complete with their contents—and wanted the battered, exhausted goblins to take their empty baskets back instead.

Clearly there was a cost, should they do that, or the contents were worth money, as the earlier shift went mad at the order, and a bigger scuffle than before broke out.

There were close on thirty goblins fighting tooth and nail, hammer and pick, when Ciara led another seventeen naphtha-covered and raving goblins around the corner and into the canyon, zipping up and over the stunned fighters, leading straight to us.

The mass that was already fighting were trampled by their enthusiastic cousins, and the canyon was suddenly wall to wall with ugly fuckers screaming and fighting.

I stared down at them all, instantly thrown back to the "good old days" of insane football hooliganism when I first started drinking in Newcastle, and after a derby match, the police would close off the top and the bottom of the Bigg Market off and leave all the lunatics to fight it out, then arrest anyone that was left in that sweet spot between "unconscious, but alive," and "too broken to resist arrest."

"You going to do something?" Drak hissed at me, and I snorted, shaking my head.

"Sorry, just an old memory," I explained, before reaching out a hand and selecting the entire area. There was a tiny section at the back that wasn't quite covered by the spell's radius, but all the fun sections were.

"Lightning Storm!" I called out. My voice carried across the fight, and made them all look up.

The mana that was ripped from me was a hell of a loss—fifteen hundred points, all gone in a split second—but damn, it was worth it. Forty-six goblins all told, maybe half of the overall population of the cavern, certainly the majority of those outside of the settlement, were suddenly mystified by the appearance of thick black and grey clouds that rolled out to hang above them.

I couldn't help but grin down at them all. The first few finally noticed me and pointed…before the first blast tore free of the clouds.

It punched down and through an upraised pick. The metal acted as a lovely conductor for the tens of thousands of volts that poured into the tiny green and yellow figure.

Steam burst from his eyes and ears, mouth and nose, as his liquids flash-fried in the ongoing pulse of lightning. And then it rolled out across the entire section, through the joy of goblins touching each other, shoulder to butthole.

A single bolt became a handful, which became dozens, punching down from the clouds that were barely higher than we were. The encircling walls of the canyon meant that there was nowhere for the goblins to run. Then, add in the metal hammers, picks, and their weapons and armor? Also that they were virtually cheek by jowl by now?

The smell of burnt goblin was one that I'd be smelling for the rest of my life. It was a mixture of "that guy in full cosplay at the convention who didn't believe in deodorant" and "rotten rat that died of intestinal issues."

With a pinch of "burnt hair and earwax" thrown in as well.

It was just *nasty*, but when the smoke cleared enough for us to look down into the canyon, I had to admit it was worth it.

Even the fucking walls of the canyon looked to have melted at one point, and everything, and I mean everything, down there was dead.

I pulled up my notifications and nodded in satisfaction. It might have cost me fifteen hundred mana, but hey, no pain, no gain.

Congratulations!

You have killed the following:
- 17x Skeletal Warriors [Common], Levels 12-25, 1,200 XP
- 11x Skeletal Archers [Common], Levels 15-22, 495 XP
- 46x Goblins [Common], levels 10-24, 7,145 XP

Total XP earned: 8,840 XP
Total XP awarded 8,840 XP

Current XP to next level stands at 24,553/50,000

Eight thousand, hell, nearly nine thousand Experience, all from a single spell. And on top of that? As the walls slowly cooled, the shimmering heat dissipating, the first of the reliquaries started to appear.

"Damn…" Drak grunted, shaking his head in shock. "Makes me want to learn magic."

"Sounds like a plan," I said. "We're hoping for everyone to learn, eventually. Now, if you don't mind, I have some looting to do."

With that, I skidded down the side of the canyon. The dirt and sandstone cascaded off and slowed me, but the angle was so sharp that there was no way to walk it.

A minute later, and I was growling to myself again as I tried to find space for the damn coins and crap.

Some of the loot was interesting; the gemstones, for example, were pretty. The "fossilized fairy" was cool; it literally looked like the fairy had been doing about 90 on the freeway, and had hit a rock, sinking into it and boom. Frozen for the ages.

It was going on my fucking wall, if I had anything to say about it.

Most of the loot, though, was just crap: copper coins, agates, copper wire, and various bits of crafting components—goblins used a lot of bone in "crafting" apparently—and shitty-grade daggers.

There was a bow, three arrows that looked more dangerous to the archer than anyone else, and several alchemical components that I just…

Just no.

I picked them out, saw what they looked to be…and fucking dropped them instantly.

"Filthy little bastards," I growled, wiping my hands on my armor. *Whatever goddamn possessed a goblin to walk around with a pocket full of dried dicks?*

I was about to head out of the canyon—it was insanely hot even now, and the smell was horrific—when something sparkling caught my eye.

I nudged a crispy critter leg aside, grimacing at the blackened flesh, only to move in quickly when I saw what had caught my eye.

It was the crap they'd been digging out of the wall. Some of it was ore, but most of it were large stones. Stones that gleamed with an inner light.

"Mana crystals!" I grunted, staring at them, before dumping the general shit I'd been collecting out onto the floor, and hastily grabbing the stones and ore instead.

Mana crystal	Item
This high-grade Mana crystal is full of pure mana and is ready to be used.	
Durability 487/500	**Mana:** 500/500

Most of the stones were glowing fiercely, and by the time I made it out of the narrow canyon, I had nearly fifty of them: forty-eight mana crystals.

I was grinning like a fucking lunatic as I started out of the narrow gap, before pausing and covering my eyes.

The light from so many goblins breaking down all at once was intense, but once it was done, it was a hell of a lot easier getting out. But as soon as I stood next to Drak, I found the "slight" downside to such a thing as well.

The gates of the settlement were opening, and the mass of goblins streaking out, screaming and waving pointy metal in the air, suggested that they weren't coming for tea and biscuits.

CHAPTER THIRTY-FOUR

"**W**ell, fuck-a-doodle-doo," I groaned, shaking my head as I saw them. "Drak, get your arse in there!" I snapped, jerking my thumb back over my shoulder toward the canyon.

"Might be a better idea to get the bone-bum down here instead," he suggested, wincing at the heat that still radiated off the walls.

"Nope." I shook my head. "Ciara, get your arse up there. Send the corpse lord to the naphtha pits. He's to get…"

As I explained the plan to Ciara, Drak started to work. Ignoring the shitty tools the goblins had been using, he had a shovel out and was digging already.

The entrance to the canyon down here was literally two meters, if that, wide, with walls of rough sandstone that climbed on either side. With an hour to work, we could have made a hell of a defensive formation, I could see that even with my limited experience.

With a matter of minutes before the fuckers could reach us, though, Drak was making the most of the time, in a way only an evil genius could.

He moved back and forth, digging a dozen pits, only maybe eight inches around, circular, and each time he flipped the earth back toward the incoming mass, making little piles that would trip the incoming goblins.

"What's the plan?" I asked, feeling a bit jittery, watching the ravening horde that was closing on us, while I just stood there, looking pretty.

"Make us an easier way up," he called, reaching into his pack and tossing me a decent-looking pickaxe. "I'd rather have a way up to the next level, if possible…"

"You think this is gonna work?" I asked.

"You want me to blow glitter up your bum hole or the truth?" he called to me, as I jogged to the back of the canyon.

"The truth!" I called back, before quickly digging into the wall, frantically chopping out a handful of steps in the stone and debris that would allow us to at least get a few feet up easier if we needed it.

"You don't mean that!" he shouted. "Okay, fuck's sake, I think it's time!"

"I mean it," I assured him, jogging back to the entrance, standing to his right and staring at the mass as they covered the last dozen meters.

"We're so dead it's not even funny." He grabbed my pickaxe as I offered it, equipping a small shield as a flight of stones were set loose.

"Yeah, okay, lie to me." I lifted my own battered shield over my head and grunted as some slingers started to fire stones at us. The clatter and bang of them hitting the walls around us and bouncing off made it hard to talk.

"The payment is with the courier!" He laughed, and I grinned. Some things were clearly universal.

"They're a cheerful lot, aren't they!" I called over the crash of the stones, amazed and slightly worried by just how many stones were making it through the narrow gap. "And skilled!"

"They're goblins." He grunted, a particularly hard hit setting the metal rim of his shield ringing like a bell. "They'd starve if they couldn't kill a rat with a sling."

"Explains a lot," I said, wincing as I looked at the goblins. "They going to stop firing anytime soon? They'll hit their own…oh."

"Yeah," he agreed. "Count of three, step to the side, out of sight. Let them waste their stones."

We did it, moving as one. The last load of stones passed through the gap, hitting many of their own in the backs of their head and more as the front line kept running, closing the distance.

"Now!" Drak shouted, stepping back into sight and bracing his shield with both hands.

I did the same, driving it forward and grunting as the impact of multiple bodies made it shake.

My feet scrapped back a few inches as more and more bodies hit. Then I saw Drak start, and I knew it was time for the slaughter.

He was using a long, curved dagger, slashing fast and rough, carving his way through the virtual wall of flesh before us, and I cursed having not thought of that before now.

I had, of course, my hammer. It'd worked well with the shield. I could brace the head and shaft against the back and boom, extra stability. Now, though?

I couldn't swing it. I needed to hit them fast, and as they were, dozens of hands were already grabbing onto my shield, trying to yank it aside.

Daggers reached around and slashed, making me jerk back and forth. I snarled, shifting my grip on the hammer to hold it near the head, then jabbed forward repeatedly, crashing into faces, knees, fingers, and more.

Most of the goblins that were in the front line were the lowest caste: massive, long ears, and a nose more like a dog's muzzle, up between their eyes. The eyes themselves were black and solid, with a small maw filled with jagged teeth.

Combine that face with a short, dumpy body that was more upright animal than humanoid, the long, sharp nails, and the body odor that could be used as an offensive weapon? Finally, add in the chemical weapons that were released as they farted almost constantly, and it was clear this was a creature that not even a mother could love.

The mass before me were just the "fodder", the lowest of the low, and also the least dangerous…in anything but numbers.

With a little space, and a longer weapon, like one of those sword staffs I'd seen in the museums, I could have carved a path through them, but considering the limited space we had, I had to make do.

I twisted the oval shield to the right, angling it lengthways, covering as much of Drak and me as I could, while making the most of my longer reach, driving the head of the hammer into a face that peered over, terminally reducing its chances of finding a mate.

Or of seeing the dawn, considering the way its face crumpled around the hammer; the body twitched and collapsed backward, squealing.

I dragged the hammer sideways across the edge of the shield, hearing shrieks as I broke and crushed fingers, then shoved forward with the shield, driving a load of the little buggers backward.

Drak was steady by my side, dagger flashing.

He was smaller than me physically, clearly having worked more on his Dexterity and Agility. The combination of him lunging back and forth and my more brutish slams of the shield, worked well. As each of the smaller goblins fell to the floor, I'd see a dagger flash out, opening a throat or an artery if it was within his reach.

If they fell on my right, well, I just stomped on their faces.

It was a tactic that was working, right up until a pair of enterprising little fuckers crawled underneath my shield and grabbed onto my legs as I focused on reaching over the top.

The first I knew of it was when a set of long, sharp nails dug into the overlapping scalemail of my thigh, pushing up into the connections.

The scalemail was wonderful, overlapping as it was, but the connections were simply loops of wire, protected from damage by the scales that were laid over them like roof tiles.

Once they were damaged, the nails dug into the flesh of my thigh, and I swore viciously, yanking the shield back and downward, crushing the little bastard against my knee, then kicking him off, stunned.

When he fell backward, his claws tore loose from my leg in a gush of blood, as the other goblin stabbed upward. A dagger skittered across my groin armor, then dug into my left hip.

I punched sideways with my right hand. That it still held a hammer only helped with the impact, but the damage was done.

Even as the body flew backward, only to be grabbed and the throat slit by Drak, I was stepping back, circulating my Lightning, frantically trying to stop the blood loss and pain.

"You need that out of you!" Drak shouted, before snapping his own dagger on a hastily raised shield. "Crim's balls!" he swore. "Bite your shield!"

"What?" I snapped, distractedly, shaking my head. A handful of warning symbols popped up, and I knew that they were very bad news.

"Fuck it!" Drak snarled, reaching over and ripping the dagger free of my side; the serrated tips made me scream in pain and rage. "Sorry!" he shouted, burying it straight into another leering face.

I staggered back. The hot, sticky wash of blood that ran free on the left joined the mauled thigh on the right to make me reel drunkenly.

I needed to use magic, and I growled, having wanted to hold it. I'd rather not fucking die, though, and with that thought in mind, I smashed my hammer into another snarling face, then raised my right hand, unleashing a blast of Lightning that I slashed sideways from right to left.

Drak cursed, leaping back and shaking one hand, having caught a little of the transmitted Lightning through the figure he'd been busily stabbing. But instead of cussing me out, he pushed straight back in, stabbing as fast as he could.

I left the hammer embedded in the body, reaching up and yanking a spear free, using it as a brace, clinging to it as I let him kill. I went back to circulating my mana as steadily as I could, taking the few seconds of peace I had, as he struck and struck again.

He was a blur, but now that the majority of the first line were down, the warriors were up.

After, that is, the slingers made their presence known again.

A dozen or more stones slammed into my shield, and at least as many hit Drak. Only a few of them were deflected by his shield. He screamed and fell, before dragging himself back, trying to get out of the line of fire.

I returned fire, strafing the Lightning Bolt left to right, killing a handful, but mainly raising only screams and shrieks, as the slingers stepped out from behind shields again.

"Ciara!" I bellowed up at the sky. "Now would be fucking good!" I dragged my shield across my body, stepping forward and deliberately getting between them and Drak, taking a second hail of stones, and swearing as my legs trembled.

I checked my mana and reluctantly cut the circulating Lightning. I had seventeen hundred and forty mana left, and I damn well needed all of it now.

I had two choices, if I wanted to survive this. First and foremost, I needed to kill all these fuckers. That was my plan: kill them all and get us some time to rest and recover, hoping that there weren't many rooms like this ahead of me.

The problem was…I couldn't see a boss.

If I used Atomic Furnace or Lightning Storm, and bottomed out my mana, then they walked round the corner, I'd be fucked. But if I didn't…

I heard three fast explosions behind and above me, and I cursed, knowing that they'd done exactly what we'd been relying on them not doing.

Ciara had needed to fire off her missiles, which meant some fuckers were trying to flank us.

"Drak!"

"What?" he hissed back at me.

"What the hell do you think!" I snarled. "How's dinner coming along?"

"What?" he asked, confused.

"Get the hell up there!" I barked, jerking my head in the direction of the canyon wall.

"I can't climb!" he snarled. "I've broken bones!"

"You'll have a damn sight more than that soon if you don't fucking run!" I bit back. "You think they look friendly?"

"If I damn well could, I'd already be up there!" he snapped. "Give me one of those damn spears!"

"You'd have a chance if you climb…" I told him, chucking him the spear I was holding, and pulling another free of the sheath on my back.

"If I escape to the tunnel, then what?" he snarled. "I get to bleed out up there instead?"

"The goblins…wait, they wouldn't follow you?" I asked, stunned, as the goblin warriors screamed as one and started to run at me.

"Nah, they're locked to their territory." He grunted, forcing himself back up and standing gingerly.

"You didn't think to mention that?" I hissed, scrabbling through my pockets, and pulling the last potion free.

"Why?" He eyed the potion.

I hesitated. If I poured it on my wounds, then necked the rest, I'd have a much better chance. But...

"Here!" I snapped at him. "Now get your arse up there!"

I pointed behind us at the sheer side of the canyon.

"I...I don't know if I can climb it," he admitted.

"If you don't damn well go now, you'll never find out!"

That was all it took. He dropped my spear and staggered to the back wall, downing the potion as he went, before driving his claws into the canyon wall, dragging himself upward.

"Stupid, stupid bastard," I growled to myself. "I should have damn well seen it!"

The warriors reached the narrow entrance a few seconds later, and I focused down, shield up, spear flashing forward.

These weren't the dumb, almost beasts of the fodder wave. They were smart, they were leveled, and like Alphonso and his brothers I'd summoned before, they were fully aware, desperate to kill me, and to survive themselves.

That they knew that, for them, death truly wasn't the end, meant that they were fearless, and I was pushed back steadily.

Watching over the shield, I stabbed out with the spear, slamming it through the gap in the armor of the figure before me, a slavering, wide-eyed berserker that rushed forward, short iron buckler on the left arm, a jagged shortsword in the right already swinging crazily.

The spearhead sank into his throat, punching through the grey-green flesh just below its Adam's apple, jerking to a halt. Its body collapsed, dragging the spear down as his spinal column was severed.

I stepped back even farther, twisting and yanking, before discarding the spear, stuck as it was by the body.

I drove the shield forward, crashing it into two of them and throwing them back, before the massively overworked and damaged shield gave way with a great crack.

I swore, shaking the remains of the shield off my left arm, even as I struggled to draw the longsword, swearing again over how long the fucker was.

Yes, I was taller now, with commensurately longer arms, which had massively helped in the past.

Unfortunately, Aly had resized my damn sword, so that it fit my fighting style again, and I was back to struggling to get the last six inches or so free.

I managed it, accidentally gashing the palm of my left hand on the blade as I did, and then grinned as the blade seemed to hum to life.

"I'd forgotten about you," I whispered, reaching down inside, and gritting my teeth as I swung hard, right to left.

PAIN.

Fuck, the pain of that swing!

It was worth it, even though I was below the level I wanted to keep my mana at now. Two hundred mana gone in the blink of an eye, as the sword, a copy of the one that Dalbir had wielded, made its triumphant return to the world.

Void Blade	Magical Weapon
Damage: Null	**Charge**: Null
This sword is enchanted with the "Void Blade'" spell, draining its user's mana and health to cut through almost any substance.	
Durability: 19/20	**Rarity**: Rare

I grinned as its details popped up before me, unbidden, even as the goblins before me shrieked as though I'd sent their souls straight to hell, the section that the sword had hit seemingly ceasing to exist.

The bodies collapsed—flesh and steel, leather and filth all equally torn from existence, as the goblins on either side and behind drew back, stunned.

"You want some of this?" I screamed, leaping forward. The longsword flashed around and into a two-handed grip, blade raised into the air by the right side of my head, feet falling directly into stance automatically, as I grinned maniacally.

"Let's dance, bitches," I snarled, lunging and driving the wide point straight through the chest of a scruffy figure in the second row.

As before, there was almost no sensation of impact. Instead, the blade seemed to dip in, and then lift free, like I was attacking a pool of water.

The effect on the goblin, though?

It screamed, dropping its weapon and grabbing the spurting hole in its chest.

I stepped back, reset my stance, then whipped the blade around, using my left-hand grip on the pommel to grant it extra speed and to guide, the right more to hold and provide power.

The blade carved through from high right to low left, then around into a figure of eight and high left into low right, as I stepped forward, and again, and again.

The rictus of pain and battle fury on my face mixed with the screams of the goblins and the flying blood, as all around me bodies fell.

Before I knew it, I was a handful of meters past the front of the canyon, out into the open, and surrounded on all sides. Goblins were running: those in front of me desperately screeching and trying to flee, dozens of others closing in all around me, claws and blades reaching, axes flashing, and spears fuckin' spearing.

I twisted, lopping the head off a spear aimed for my face, before dipping down and whipping the sword around in a frantic circle.

Screams were cut off, the shattering sound of steel, the crash of falling bodies…and then I almost collapsed myself.

The pain…it was insane, like my heart's blood was being torn free of me. My mana approached bottom, and I staggered. The world crashed back in as I heard Ciara screaming at me to "Fucking run, you idiot!"

I straightened up, blinking owlishly up at her, and at the sight of the corpse lord.

It'd made it through!

It was damaged, but it also held—one in either set of arms—two filthy black barrels.

I dug down deep and leapt into the air, frantically converting the last of my mana into Storm and flying as fast as I could back into the canyon, and then up. I ran out of mana before I made it up the side of the canyon fully, crashing into the wall about two-thirds of the way to the top.

I scrabbled frantically at the stone, barely managing to keep from sliding back down thanks to still holding my damn sword, as Ciara shouted to the corpse lord to "Throw it!"

It did, sending the twin barrels flying through the air to crash into the milling, stunned crowd. The first barrel actually killed one of the figures outright, slamming into him from above. Then the rest of the goblins realized what was about to happen.

They were covered in sticky naphtha, battered, beaten, and all in far too close a proximity to each other, as I twisted around, lifting my right hand, and pointed at a figure in the middle that was slightly bigger than the others.

"Incinerate," I hissed, before almost blacking out. My mana was all gone, and an extra one hundred health was torn from me to fuel the spell with blood magic.

My target screeched in pain, my aim having been locked onto the haft of his halberd. He got the backwash of heat, but the halberd was the real deal. The wooden haft went from filthy and scruffy, to black and charred in a second.

The insane level of heat was sufficient that the wood began to glow. Cherry-red sections came to life, as he frantically held his breath. The goblins on all sides froze as they saw the glow, and the naphtha that covered them.

It was as if the world held its breath as well. For long seconds, nothing happened; then the glowing wood slowly began to dim, and its wielder grinned around at his companions, shifting his feet slightly as he relaxed.

That was a mistake.

The head of the halberd wasn't that heavy, but it was solid steel, and heavy enough, that when the haft was as dry and charred, weakened critically as it was, it snapped.

Silence fell as the head tumbled past wide eyes, smacking into its wielder, who dumped the rest of the staff on instinct, catching the head before it could hit him from above.

I dimly saw the grin on his face as he caught it, then the way it poured from his face. Horror replaced it, as the charred haft's fall gave it enough of a burst of oxygen to flare back to brightness.

The glowing tip hit the naphtha; there was a collectively indrawn breath…and then the drifting fumes that were pouring off the mess ignited with a solid *whump* I felt in my chest, even here high above and a dozen meters from them.

The goblins' screams were short-lived. Nothing coated in naphtha and set alight got to scream for very long. And judging that the dungeon had gone for a naturally occurring version of the stuff, it was a mix of complex hydrocarbons, such as tar and petrol, meaning it wasn't just insanely hot once it caught, it was also sticky as fuck.

Refined versions of this would be used as "Greek fire" back in antiquity, and that had created a lasting impression on anyone who was on the wrong side of it.

For both of their last seconds of life.

I clung to the wall of the canyon, panting hoarsely. My chest felt raw, blood slowly dried on my cheeks, my lips…I coughed. A tearing sensation in my chest made it clear I was seriously low on health. I slid a little, then more, as the mana migraine built.

One foot came free, and I tried to brace myself, digging at the rock, but it was all for nothing.

I started to slide free, dropping the sword. I scrabbled at the stone and shattered earth, sending torn-free dirt cascading into the canyon, before a hand clamped over my own, dragging me upward.

I flinched, twisting and looking up…and saw the corpse lord's inhumanly glowing eyes staring down at me. It slowly dragged me upward, and I let out a shuddering breath, sagging as I was lifted onto solid ground, collapsing in exhaustion.

"Well, that went well," Ciara declared cheerfully a few minutes later, making Drak and I glare at her. "No, really, it did. I mean, let's face it, you're both alive, and they're not. That's kinda the most important level of detail here, right?"

"And if they come again?" I asked her grimly.

"With what?" She grinned. "They sent all the locals to fight you, and they all died. Then they sent their soldiers out, and they all died. Remember, no survivors got away. As far as the settlement knows? You're sitting here at full mana and health, ready to kill anything that comes near."

"Yeah, but if they come—" I started.

"They won't," she assured me. "Remember, any goblins left in the settlement are probably experienced. They were forced to give up their soul for this, for their crimes. They want to live, not die. They'll be hoping you take as long as possible before you attack, both so they can get their defenses ready, and so they can live as long as possible. For all they know, you're here to mine the crystals and don't give a shit about them. If they leave you alone? You'll leave them alone."

"I'll leave them all alone," I growled, shaking my head. "I just want to get to the end."

"It doesn't work like that." Drak groaned, flopping down close by. "Why the hell didn't you tell me you could fly?"

"You never asked," I said flatly. "Now explain."

"The dungeon has to be cleared. If you just run all the way through, you'd have to go back to the beginning and kill everything, but they'd all know what was coming. Otherwise, all you'd have to do is stealth and you'd win, or you know, fly," he grumbled.

"Fuck's sake, I hate this place," I growled. "First I'm told there's a way out, then there isn't, then it's only a way out if I don't want to ever try again, now the sneaky route won't work…Fuck my life."

"You're five kobzar high, and about the same across the shoulders wearing armor. You'd be crap at stealth anyway," he muttered, shaking his head and laying back, staring up at the ceiling. "So what does it matter?"

"It…it just does, all right?" I growled, before shifting around to get more comfortable. "Ciara, can you see anything?"

"Like?"

"Like another fucking goblin army sneaking up on us," I snapped.

"No, nothing like that. There's someone who's stealthed and heading this way, but there's only the one of them."

"There's *what*?" I asked in a low hiss.

"A rogue or assassin," she explained. "They're good, but dumb. It's okay…I'm watching them."

"How can they be good but dumb?" I asked, trying my best not to swear at her.

"They're almost invisible, and they're moving slow so that the blur of their movement doesn't give them away. That's how they're good, clearly experienced."

"And dumb?"

"They're staying crouched low to avoid the smoke, but they're moving through it still, and a big goblin-shaped patch of smoke isn't exactly subtle."

"Okay…so now what?" I asked her.

"Want me to kill them?" she asked, conversationally.

"Yes," I said firmly.

"Okay, be right back," she said cheerfully, lifting into the air and buzzing off in the direction of the settlement.

"What the fuck was that all about?" I asked Drak, who grunted, not even opening his eyes.

"Fairies," he said flatly. "They've got tiny brains. Don't expect them to be good at much until they grow a little. For now, she can be all intelligent and cunning, reliable even, but when something distracts her? Yeah."

"Well, that's just peachy." I struggled to sit up. "I need to meditate, but I need to watch for—"

A trio of booms rang out, and a scream from below rose immediately, followed by a hail of darts flashing through the air after Ciara as she laughed and flitted back toward us.

"It's the area boss," she said breathlessly, landing nearby. "He's down to half health, and he's bleeding badly. Looks like he was coming to see what was going on."

"What happened to 'he'll leave you alone'?" I asked grimly.

"Best guess is all I can give you," she said unrepentantly.

"Fine, whatever," I groused. "Oi, you boney fuck. Go capture the goblin," I ordered the corpse lord, and it set off without pause, as the other two watched it go, and I laid back, closing my eyes again.

"You think he'll win?" Drak asked me after a few seconds.

"Don't know, don't care. I'm meditating. If he wins, tell me. If he loses, wake me if the bad guy gets close."

With that, I sank into my mana stream, feeling the tiny amount of mana I had to work with, and the slowly infiltrating fresh mana, even as I pulled on it, dragging as much into my channels and core as possible.

Seconds turned to minutes, and the migraine vanished. Minutes passed on and on, until I couldn't take it any longer, and opened my eyes, finding the corpse lord standing a handful of feet away, a goblin rogue dangling, bloodied, from its claws before my eyes.

"Fucking hell!" I snapped, jerking upright.

"Hey, boss." Drak yawned. "You're awake, right? So it's my turn for sleep?"

"I said to wake me if he fucking won!" I snapped at the kobold, who shrugged.

"Well, the bugger's alive still, so he's not really won, but he's not lost either. How about we call it a draw?"

"Does he look like he'd be agreeing?" I hissed. "The fucker looks like shit!"

"He's a goblin," Drak pointed out reasonably. "They always look like shit."

"He's being held by his wrists and ankles, bleeding out and unconscious, by a corpse lord. I'd say he's probably having slightly worse day, don't you think?"

"Na, for a goblin, that's about normal." Drak laughed, pointing a claw at the dangling figure. "Seriously, boss, goblins' lives are short, brutal, and ugly, just like them. If he got free and escaped, I doubt this would even be in the top ten shitty days of his life."

"Damn."

"So, what did you want him alive for then?" he asked, and I shrugged.

"I figured the reliquaries wouldn't appear until all the enemies in the immediate area were killed. I didn't want to try to loot the ones in the fire, so…"

"So hold him until the naphtha burns itself out and then kill him?" Drak asked, and I shrugged. "That's a bit cold."

"He's a goblin rogue at best, probably an assassin, who was on his way to kill us all," I pointed out, before glancing down the canyon. Most of the flames were out. "But fine, you think I should give him a chance?"

"Well, not really. It's just…" He struggled with the words, and I nodded.

"I get it. Throw him over the side," I ordered the corpse lord, who didn't even hesitate, tossing the goblin over the edge, as he started to frantically twist and shout.

I'd suspected the fucker wasn't really unconscious, and I'd been planning to stop the corpse lord, then question him. The fucker was *fast*, though, and the goblin tumbled from sight, screaming as he bounced off the walls on his way down.

"Damn, that's cold," Drak whispered, peering after him. "Ah well, you mind if I loot his corpse? Probably got some good gear."

"If it's magical, it's mine," I said firmly. "You know that."

"True, but I'll get a copy." He shrugged, already setting off over the side.

"Wait, can he do that? Loot the corpse directly, not just the reliquary?" I asked Ciara, who snorted and turned over, before letting loose with an actual glitter fart. I stared at the dissipating cloud of glitter for a second before starting to cough and retch, dragging myself away quickly.

I hesitated, then followed the damn kobold down, exhausted but sure as shit not willing to sleep anywhere near that ass.

By the time we'd both reached the bottom of the canyon, the rogue was gasping out his last, and Drak limped over to him and stabbed him in the chest, before starting to rifle through his clothes as quick as he could.

"You can loot creatures in the dungeon twice," he called to me, still searching. "First and foremost, physically. If you're in contact with a weapon or armor when the body dissipates, it'll be left behind, so if you want something, grab it. Secondly, the reliquary. Usually you get higher quality gear from the reliquary, but it's a risk—you never know what you'll get. But on a boss? Best to double-check," he explained.

"Gotcha." I nodded. "Anything good?"

"Two health and a mana." He grinned, holding them up, then going to pocket them.

"Thank you," I said firmly, holding my hand out.

"They're not magical…" he said quickly.

"They're not a fucking rum and Coke, either. Gimmie," I growled, taking them and popping the mana potion straightaway, gasping at the powerful, minty fresh wave that tore through me, before plonking myself down and staring in awe at my mana channels, ignoring Drak as he muttered and complained.

My mana channels had seemed to develop holes all the way along one side as soon as I downed the potion, but rather than the mana leaking out, the holes were sucking inward!

I groaned, feeling powerfully sick for a few seconds. The rising nausea got worse and worse…and then it stopped. The nausea was still there, but draining away, as the holes in the sides of my mana channels sealed again.

Six seconds it'd lasted, six fucking seconds, and I'd gained three thousand mana!

I couldn't believe it. I examined both potions, finding they were "average" quality and strength, and replaced two thousand health at a time.

One of them was being damn well kept for sacrificing to the damn dungeon later on, that I was sure of. As much as I wanted to, I didn't drink either of them.

Instead, I settled down and started to meditate again, quickly circulating my Lightning through my body and recovering my health.

"Tell me when the reliquaries appear," I called out, my eyes closed, and he grunted, before agreeing, searching the last few pockets and more.

"Reliquaries," he growled a minute or so later, kicking the sole of my boot, and I sighed, opening one eye and confirming that they were indeed there.

"Fine," I growled, getting up and stretching, continuing to circulate the mana as I moved over and started to search. "Did you find anything else?" I asked, and he shook his head. "Really?" I asked again, pushing and getting a glare.

"A dagger," he admitted, showing it to me, waving the hilt around. "It's good steel, that's all. No magic. Or are you going to steal that as well?"

"You're an asshole," I growled. "You know potions are magical."

"You said artifacts, weapons…you never mentioned potions!" he snapped, clearly pissed, and I shook my head.

"What's your problem?" I asked after a few seconds, finding coins and crap mainly in the reliquaries, tossing them aside when there was nothing worth the effort of carrying.

"What do you mean?" he asked, clearly sulking.

"Potions," I said. "You take them straightaway, rather than holding them until you need them."

"No I don't."

"You do, and you damn well know it," I corrected. "Do I need to order you to tell me the truth?"

"You try it, and you can whistle for any help, I'll not be giving you any," he snarled.

"He's an addict," Ciara called from above, floating down and stretching as she came. "Potion addict. I should have seen it before."

"What?" I asked, looking at him, then my bag, confused. "They're addictive?"

"Can be. Depends on how you end up with them." She said softly, "If you get seriously hurt, and there's no healers? Might be that you need to take a load of potions over a period of time."

"And you get addicted to the feeling of healing, as well as the sudden dip in pain." I finished for her, remembering a program I'd watched on addiction years ago. "Damn, I'm sorry, man." I shook my head, looking at Drak.

"Can I have the potion?" he asked me after a few seconds.

"No."

"Then you're not that sorry, are you," he snapped, stalking off.

"Drak!" I called after him. "We need them for later, in case we're hurt!"

"Fuck off!" Drak snarled, marching off out of sight.

"He knows," Ciara whispered, landing on my shoulder and yawning again. "Gods, I'm so tired…Anyway. He knows it's wrong and that we shouldn't give it to him. He's just angry and embarrassed, I think. He'll get over it."

"I hope so," I whispered. "We need him."

"We do," she agreed. "But…"

"But?"

"Am I okay to go scout?" She glanced at me and got a nod. "Thanks. I'll hit the settlement first, make sure it's empty, and then do a lap, make sure they're all dead."

"Go," I agreed, sure that the reliquaries wouldn't have shown if there were others near by, but hey. "I'll…I'll wait up there, back in the corridor with the corpse lord watching over me. I need to meditate and recover."

She zipped away, and I hesitated, weighing up going off after Drak, then decided against it, sighing and forcing myself to recover my weapons and then climb, rather than fly.

A handful of minutes later, and I was sitting down in the tunnel, sighing as I rested my back against the cool stone. The corpse lord stood over me, as I slid into meditation.

I had maybe half an hour to go of circulating my mana to fully heal myself as I was. I could force it to go faster, focus the Lightning where I needed it most, but after the draining of my life force from the sword and the blood magic?

I needed to just…rest.

Half an hour, then an hour, then two passed, with the world around me drifting further and further away, until a tiny high-pitched voice broke me from my meditation.

"I found it!" Ciara squeaked, landing on my shoulder and grabbing my face, peering into my eyes at a frankly terrifying range. "I found it!"

"That's nice…" I managed to force out. "Uh…What did you find?"

"The safe room!" She grinned. "I found the safe room!"

"Right?" I asked, blinking and getting to my feet, staring after her as she flitted back, heading fast back down the tunnel and out into the goblin biome.

I followed after, telling the corpse lord to follow us, before launching myself off the edge and flying after her, then twisting around in mid-air after the crash that came from behind me.

I flew back, groaning as I stared at the pile of bones, and facepalmed.

"What happened?" Drak asked me, moving over from where he'd been sitting off to one side.

"I was following Ciara," I explained, gritting my teeth and trying to maintain my temper. "I told the fucker to follow us and…"

"And it tried to fly after you." He snorted, making me glare at him. "Hey, don't blame me."

"I'm not," I snapped, then sighed. "I'm sorry, I just…fuck it. I'm sorry." I shrugged, and he nodded at me, understanding the unspoken details.

"It doesn't matter, and I'm sorry too. Right, so what do we do with this?" He kicked one of the bones, and it shuffled slightly, clicking into place.

"It's still alive." I swore, staring down in shock, and he shook his head.

"Can't be," he pointed out. "It's broken."

"It'll rebuild itself…" Ciara called, flying closer. "Just leave it to work and come on!"

"She's found the safe room," I told him, seeing the way his eyes widened, and the smile was back.

"Lead on!" he called, starting to half jog, half limp after her.

It took the three of us about ten minutes to reach it, hidden on the far side of the cavern, high up in a section of rocks. I could have flown there in a fraction of the time, but considering Drak was both just getting over our argument, and was injured? It seemed a dickish thing to do.

The door was recessed under a rock overhang, angled away from the path below, just to make things as difficult as possible. But as soon as my hand touched the six-pointed star in a circle in the middle? It slid back, revealing a small, but well-appointed room.

Stepping in, and out of the heat and dryness of the desert behind, I let out a groan as I felt air-conditioning, saw beds in alcoves around the back of the room and a fountain in the middle, with the bloody lever on one side—not to mention the stacked rations stacked next to it.

"Food!" Drak called out, falling on them.

"What do we have?" I asked, and he looked at me askance. "What?" I wondered whether the fucker was addicted to food as well.

"You can get whatever you want, obviously," he said, as if that made perfect sense.

"What?"

"It's the dungeon," he pointed out, frowning, before grinning and clicking his claws. "You don't know!"

"What don't I fucking know?" I growled at him.

"You can summon in here." He shrugged. "Use your powers. You can't leave, or summon other creatures, but it's a safe room. You can rest and recover at least."

"You're shitting me!" I snapped, reaching out and slipping into the dungeon sense. It was only a partial one, I couldn't reach the main systems, but I could summon food, drinks, and damn, I made the most of it.

My steak dinner was wonderful. Piles of chips, bread slathered in butter, and a can of my usual energy drink did wonders for my mental state, and even though it bothered me that I couldn't reach Kelly or the others, and we'd slept not that long ago, I still fell into a deep and dreamless sleep in record time.

CHAPTER THIRTY-FIVE

I slept longer than I should have, but by the time I awoke, Ciara and Drak were up, sitting and talking in low voices, and the broken corpse lord stood off to one side as well. Plenty of its overall structure was shattered, but it was upright, and even if it only took a handful of blows before dying, at least it was something.

I sat upright, staring around and yawning, banishing sleep as I looked around.

"Anything happen?" I asked, getting a shake of the head from Drak.

"This thing turned up half a cycle ago, that's it," he told me, picking at a chicken leg. "I like these. We need some to walk with."

"Fine." I stretched, wondering at the life I led that I slept in my armor and felt fine. It wasn't important, though. What was, was that we were all well fed, rested, and no longer at each other's throats.

"We need to get this done today," I said flatly. "I need to get back up there."

"It's always worth resting in a safe room when you can," Ciara pointed out. "Not only for the food, but you heal and recover mana faster in here."

"I noticed," I said. "Believe me, that little detail will be getting figured out when we leave here, and I'll be making recovery areas around the damn dungeon." I was aware, all over again, just how many little cool details we were missing out on.

Setting out, we searched the settlement, giving ourselves half an hour to do it, and found another forty-odd mana crystals in that time, as well as at least another fifty gold, making it more than worth it.

The gold was nice, but not really important, so I left it, and pretended not to notice Drak ferreting it away every time my back was turned.

The next room was empty, as was the one after, but the third was full of a handful of small goblins, commanded by three large orcs, all of which were waiting, and watching for us.

"How did they know we were coming?" I asked Ciara, who was frantically spinning in place, eyes wide…as the corpse lord collapsed.

"Rogues!" she cried out, and I cursed, activating my Lightning shield barely in time.

The figure that slammed into the shield from the right was huge, making the entire magical creation shudder as Ciara shouted her warning, staggering back, thrashing wildly.

I'd barely gotten it up in time, but as I stared at her, my shield shook again. Each time it was hit drained more and more mana. I spun, coming face-to-face with another rogue.

This one was an orc as well, male, and thankfully wearing leather armor rather than just "hanging" around. But the speed of his strikes? He was dual wielding, slamming the blades one after the other into the shield and sending great flares of lightning surging across the dome.

"Oi!" I shouted, jumping forward, only to grin as he was hurled backward by the dome, which remained centered on me as I jumped. "Oh, I like this…" I said, grinning as Drak took the opportunity to stab the downed rogue in the throat.

I twisted around and started to run.

The goblins barely registered as I plowed into them, smashing them from their feet and hammering them over and over with Lightning as I trampled them. But the orcs? They were smashed into the walls, bouncing off, stunned and smoking, bleeding and battered.

I cut the spell, and started stabbing as fast as I could. The shouts and shrieks from behind made it clear that the others were making the most of the free Experience as well.

It took less than three minutes to clear the entire cavern this time. Yes, it was small, but it took time to find the goblin that was trying to hide in one corner. My reactivated shield illuminated and fried him at the same time.

"I really need to make this invisible," I muttered, shaking my head. "If they had no warning…"

"It'd be a hell of a weapon." Ciara grinned. "Especially next to cliffs. It's weird, though. I've never seen a shield like that. Usually they just burn you if you pass through. Yours is solid…"

"Thank you." I smiled. "I made it myself."

"Must be a bastard of a cost for the mana?"

"It's…not cheap," I admitted, wincing. "But hey, they're all dead, so…?"

"It is…impressive," Ciara said diplomatically.

"If it's stupid and it works, it's not stupid, right?"

"*Anyway*…I thought you wanted to get a move on?" Drak growled.

"Fine, whatever," I grumbled, falling to looting. Most of it, again, was crap: three packets of cheese and onion, two apples, one "magaradon tooth," which was apparently some kind of massive off-world herbivore. Its tooth could be, and had been, used as a club by an orc. Also, we found a single peanut.

"I'm allergic to those," Drak had growled, and I'd saved him from the terrible threat, by promptly eating it.

Drak got a plastic princess tiara, which was amusing, as I told him it was a symbol of rank for my people, and he packed it away very carefully, promising not to abuse it.

We all knew he utterly intended on abusing it, which was why I'd told him that, just for pure shits and giggles.

The next two caverns were much the same—a handful of goblins and some orcs, no real challenge, and a handful of additional loot, several gems, and finally, *finally*, a magical artifact.

"So, what kind of sick ever-loving fucking hell made this a magical artifact then?" I stared at it in disgust.

"Hey, that's an important grooming tool, that is. It's not my fault you don't know good shit when you see it!" Drak complained.

"It's for cleaning your ass crack," I growled, passing it to him. "You can have it."

"Seriously?" he asked, eyes wide. "A magical scale cleaner, and I can keep it?"

"Its description included the phrase 'to reach the areas that the sun shall not see…'" I growled, rubbing my hands on my armor, shuddering lightly. "I sure as shit don't want it."

"I'll have it." He looked around furtively. "So…roughly how long do we—"

"You've got five minutes," I growled. "Use it somewhere out of my sight."

"Happily," he called, running back the way we came.

"Fucking hell, Sod's Law we get that shit," I growled to myself, shaking my head over a goddamn magical scale cleaner.

"It's actually worth a lot," Ciara assured me, and I shook my head in revulsion.

"We'll make copies of it for the other kobolds as a gift." I plonked myself down and started to meditate again, trying to improve my mood.

Fifteen minutes or so later, a gleaming Drak swaggered up, grinning widely. Every scale appeared to glow with health, and he just…he just looked healthy and happy.

"You have no idea how much I needed that." He sighed, shaking his head in disbelief.

"I can tell." I forced myself to smile. "When we get out of here, I'll make some copies for the others. Sorry that I didn't understand before."

"I'll allow it…for a small fee." He grinned. "Your words were 'you can have it,' remember?"

"I do." I smiled back at him. "Mind you, I just realized, we've not discussed rent yet, have we? Or food, or your training and equipment costs…"

"What is this 'rent'?" He frowned.

"It's gold you pay me daily for a room to sleep in." I widened my smile.

"And…gold, you say?" He swallowed hard. "How much gold are we paid, per day?"

"Less than the rent, if you're a dick," I said simply. "I gave you that, and you're well within your rights to keep it, but not sharing with the others? Or trying to rip me off every five minutes? Dick move, man."

"We…we'll discuss it," he offered, a lot more carefully, and I nodded.

"Time to move on."

This tunnel was longer than the others, winding and boring, and after a solid twenty minutes, it was starting to really annoy us all.

That, of course, was when we found the trap.

I say "found," but the spear that punched through Drak's stomach, severing his spine and sending him crashing to the floor, screaming in agony, wasn't exactly "found" so much as it found *us*, setting off a clanging in the distance as it triggered.

"Shit!" I shouted, jumping back automatically, before hurrying forward to reach out for him as he slumped sideways, crashing into the wall and tumbling to the floor. The spear slid backward, resetting into the wall, ready for the next victim.

I grabbed him by the arm and dragged him backward, cursing as I saw the way his legs no longer worked, the way he shook and coughed. His scales already seemed duller, as his eyes grew bloodshot.

"P…poi…poison!" he managed to get out, eye flickering as blood pumped from the wound.

"Shitfuck!" I snarled, reaching into the pouch, yanking one of the healing potions out and biting the cork, ripping it free and spitting it onto the floor. "Hold on!" I barked at him. His muscles quivered as he instinctively tried to close his hands over the wound protectively.

I shoved him back, forcing his arms out of the way, and dribbled about a quarter of the potion into the front of the wound. Then, rolling him over, I poured the same into the far side, cursing as I saw the lines of infection that radiated outward from the wound.

"It's not good," Ciara whispered, hovering to one side, rubbing her hands together in fear.

"No shit!" I snapped, forcing the potion into his mouth. "Come on, dammit!" I snarled. "Drink it, you stubborn fucker!"

He gulped it down, panic in his eyes, even as a roar rang out from farther down the tunnel.

"Go..." He groaned a few seconds later when he could get out the words. "Leave me, you idiot!"

"Like hell I will!" I snarled at him, twisting and pulling the second potion free, and squinting from him to it. "Ah, fuck it...easy come, easy go." I pulled the cork free and did the same again.

"He won't be able to run..." Ciara floated up and took a deep breath. "I'll get you as much time as I can."

"No," I growled. "For now? Stay with him. Keep him conscious and keep him safe...As soon as he's on his feet, well, come help." I sighed, standing and wishing I had a goddamn shield. I'd been able to fix my gear, and summon food, but no weapons, no replacement gear, and sure as shit no shield.

I had my spears though, my sword, a dagger and a hammer, some magic, and a notoriously bad temper. It was time to *play*.

I cast my shield, just in case, and sprinted forward, deciding that I'd rather face whatever was coming a little farther along the tunnel, rather than trampling Drak.

Sprinting ahead, I felt the impact of the spear trap, triggering and glancing off the side of the shield before snapping under the pressure. It dropped my mana by another hundred, but it was worth it, as a few meters on, a second, and then a third triggered.

By the time I approached the next bend in the tunnel, and finally saw movement ahead—literally, they were coming around it at the same time—I was down three hundred plus mana, and in an even fouler mood than I had been.

It was a blur, making me think it was either a stealthed rogue or...

The lesser ghast became visible as the shield slammed into it, electrifying it and smashing it from its feet. It screamed, bouncing back against the corner of the tunnel, then into my shield, and then back again, crushed between it and the wall, as I cut the mana to the shield and uppercutted it, damn hard, with the hammer.

Blood, teeth, and brain matter painted the tunnel ceiling. A second ghast plowed into me from the right, bone spurs scratching their way across my armor and teeth flashing for my throat.

I backhanded the fucker, triggering Storm-Strike and detonating its skull, then grabbed it by the remains of its neck and yanked it forward, dumping it behind me.

There were a handful more thrashing, wounded bodies visible farther down the tunnel, taken out by traps on their way to me. I cast my shield again, racing forward.

The walls of the tunnel blurred past. Roars from somewhere ahead rang out, and wounded ghasts died—trampled, burned, and shocked by lightning as I ran.

The next bend in the corridor was to the left, then a right, then…then I was skidding, trying to stop. I slid, suddenly, into a new room, one that I damn well knew was the final one.

There was no way this was "naturally" inside the training dungeon.

For a start, the area that lay before me was at least as wide as the original building, and perhaps twice as deep. The second set of proof was the switchback I could see in the distance leading up to the group that stood watching me, standing around a throne that reeked of magic and wealth.

I identified the creatures around the throne as Daoine Sidhe, a willowy, graceful group of six that stood, three on either side of the creature that sat atop the throne.

I frowned, not having seen one of them before, but guessing that—

Wham!

I was sent reeling, hitting the floor and rolling, as a figure leapt through the air at me.

I dropped the shield at the last second, seeing how much my mana had dropped from those blows already, and instead curled my legs as the figure leapt at me.

"Scepiniir!" I spat, identifying the fucker that leapt onto me. The same species as was closing from the sides, and was sat atop the throne watching me. This nearest one flew toward me, its axe raised above its head, descending fast. I let loose with a blast of Lightning from my left hand, making it scream as its muscles went into spasm, then released a blast of Storm-Strike through the soles of my boots as I kicked upward, driving them into its stomach.

The Scepiniir flipped over and over, whimpering. The air blasted from its body as its stomach was rendered into sausage meat. I rolled to the right, forcing myself to my feet. Two more ran in from ahead and the right, and I lunged at them, determined that I'd damn well finish this fast, and get Drak to Jo.

The figure to my right had a spear; the one directly ahead, a shield and a wicked-looking axe. I snarled, lunging for the spear, twisting my hammer across my body and swinging downward, hooking the head of the spear and yanking it aside, passing under my right elbow. I punched the fucker in the face, triggering Storm-Strike and killing him instantly, blood and fur flying. I twisted around, barely managing to block the axe with my hammer.

They were fast, at least as fast as I was, and the only reason I was still alive, let alone winning, was because I'd not stopped, and was mixing magic and cold steel.

I couldn't afford to keep up the magic much longer, though, and with that in mind, I took a step back, then another, reaching up to pull one of my shortened spears free of their sheath, as the Scepiniir leapt at me, slashing with his axe.

I swung with the hammer, managing to catch his axe on the side of the blade. A loud crash of steel rung out as my opponent hissed in pain, then drove his shield into me, hard, sending me reeling, before following up with a series of fast hacks that nearly caught me.

I stabbed out blindly with the spear, hoping to drive him back, and only succeeded in losing the damn thing as he hooked his axe behind the head and slid it down toward my fingers, making me drop it.

I managed to get a good blow against his shield in retaliation. A loud cracking sound announced that whatever it was made of, it didn't like that.

Judging from the snarl from the Scepiniir, they didn't either.

We backed away, starting to circle. My gaze darted from my opponent before me to the slope that led up to the higher ground and the seven figures up there, waiting.

They were still there, and I had to hope that was all there were, because this fucker was *skilled.*

I'd barely set myself before he was on me again, axe flashing. I jumped back, landing and darting forward again, swinging the hammer, aiming for the center of his shield. The fucker dropped to the floor; a fast spin kick took me in the side of the knee, even as the hammer, robbed of its rightful target, flashed past overhead, helping to yank me off-balance.

I flipped, going arse over teakettle, and landed on my right shoulder, rolling and coming to my feet. I dove forward, hitting the ground and rolling again, swinging blindly and being rewarded with a scream as the hammer pounded into the side of an ankle…before the shield bashed me in the face, sending me onto my back.

I rolled again, every instinct screaming that to stay still was to die.

The axe bit deep into the ground by my head, underscoring that thought, literally close enough that I felt the impact into the earth. I grabbed his arm, kicking up and under the shield to take him in the crotch, before grabbing the shield and pulling.

He leapt onto me, making me grin as I tried to bring him into place to grapple, and then panic as I realized that he'd had the same idea.

He wasn't losing his axe and shield—he was dumping them!

The Scepiniir had leapt at me, and still, I'd barely seen what the fuckers looked like.

They were a blur of flashing teeth, glittering steel and silver armor, blades and fur.

My mind frantically categorized them as walking humanoid tigers or lions, and it only got worse from there.

He chuffed at me, lunging forward, mouth opening wide with teeth and saliva gleaming, only to grunt as I drove my left foot into its stomach.

I'd lifted my feet on instinct, long-ago martial arts training and more recent "ground mount" training by Patrick fusing together into automatic, ingrained response.

I stomped into the inside of his hip, boot catching on a section of his armor as I straightened my leg, grabbed his wrists, and twisted frantically, trying to keep them from my throat…and cursed as he slowly, oh so fucking slowly, extended his claws.

I had him pushed back, though: he was on one knee, the opposite ankle broken, and he was stretching forward, back arched downward. His eyes opened wider in shock when I flipped my right leg around, tucking it under his chin and pulling his head sideways, before repeating the move with my left.

Before he knew what to do, I had him by both wrists, his claws scrabbling against my chest armor and scouring it, dragging him closer to my throat by the inch…until I straightened my legs fully, pushing him back, and he started to choke.

His eyes went even wider. He spat and snarled, before he got himself braced, forcing himself to his knees and then feet.

He was coughing and choking, frantically trying to get a breath down, as I snarled, pulling on his wrists and pushing as hard as I could with my legs. His throat started to collapse under the pressure.

He tried to lift us both, thinking to stand and to slam me down, knocking me out or breaking my back. Then I saw it in his eyes, the realization that such a move would result in his throat being crushed for sure.

There was a split-second hesitation; then he started to shake me, trying to toss me free, twisting his arms and frantically trying to get his chin down, to protect his throat.

His face was going redder under all that fur, his eyes bloodshot and bugging out, only to lean heavily on his smashed ankle, which gave out. He dropped to one knee, frantically trying to free his neck.

I twisted, pulling one foot from his throat and planting it firm on the floor. He gasped down a breath, all tactics forgotten in that split second of relief…then I used the leverage to drive him sideways and into the cavern floor full force, face-first.

He grunted, then coughed, still barely able to breathe; I rocked him back, then did it again, and again. I saw fur torn free on the rocks, blood running and the dazed look in his eyes, before, on the next impact, something broke.

He spasmed. A dent appeared in his skull, and blood suddenly gushed from his nostrils and mouth. I gave him another hit, this time just to be sure, but knowing as I did it, that there'd been little need.

This had been a fight to the death, and the way he'd gone suddenly weak and flaccid, there was no doubt who'd won it.

I kicked his corpse free, rolling to the left, and forced myself to my knees, looking up at the switchback that led up to the watching seven.

The figure sitting atop the throne said something, and two of the Daoine Sidhe bowed elegantly, before seeming to flow forward, picking their way down the rock-strewn path toward me.

I hesitated only a second, catching my breath and looking around, seeing the room in its entirety for the first time and blowing out a long breath.

It was a rocky one this, but here and there were green and browns of mixed grasses, reds and ochre dirt exposed occasionally, as well as multiple layers of sediment that was all too specific to be made up on spec.

It made me think of the American Badlands, somewhere I'd always wanted to visit, in the hopes of finding a genuine fossil, and now…now I might end up buried here instead.

I forced myself to my feet, grabbing my hammer and shoving it back into the loop of my belt, leaving the spear. Even at a handful of feet aside, it was too far, when the other weapons were so close.

I picked up the wicked-looking axe, admiring the overlapping pattern of raised and lowered banding, before picking up the shield and settling it onto my left arm, pulling the strap and gripping the leather handle tight.

The leather creaked under the force, and I had to shake my head in disbelief. I could feel the ridges of the previous owner's grip, the sweat and years of use, and yet, I'd just killed him, and taken his possessions as if it were nothing.

I didn't have the time to search him, not properly, and instead I tore the two small pouches on his hip free, stuffing them into my own, determined to look them over later.

Then I stood, waiting, for the Daoine Sidhe to reach me. Every second longer they took was a risk for Drak, I knew, and I hated that, but it was a second longer for me to recover my health, my mana and my stamina, each of which were definitely ranked in descending order at the minute.

My health was a little battered but high, my mana was halved, and my stamina? Well, it was getting a workout. I'd fought with the undead for a full day before, pushing myself past the point of human capacity. To say they were unimaginative fucks in a fight was an understatement. Literally, block their claws or weapon, smash their skull, boom.

The real issue there had been conservation of stamina to ensure I could keep going, and not fall on the mountain of the dead.

Here, though, I was facing skilled, leveled, and fucking lethal opponents. The Daoine Sidhe that were approaching were…

They were weird.

They both looked like well-dressed courtiers from some shitty period drama, but brought up to date a bit, all black and red, with a bit of lace thrown in for shits and giggles.

I half expected them to start speaking French, and then there really would be fucking trouble. But instead, the one on the left, a fox-faced woman with multiple tails that flicked and danced, reminding me of something that tickled at the back of my mind, lifted her arms…and shimmered.

Suddenly she stepped to the left, and then the right. Each time, a new version of her stepped aside: first two, then three, then four and five, more and more were spreading out.

In seconds, there were a dozen clones plus her. As she moved, lowering her arms, a glow started as she rolled her fingers, grinning. A light was dragged behind in slow motion. Each gesture she made left an afterimage, and all the copies did the same.

Add to that, the other one…I twisted, having been distracted by the thirteen figures, and cursed, seeing that fucker was gone.

"Oh, it's like that, is it?" I muttered, twisting and squinting, trying to spot anything, any characteristic blurring or…

A click of a stone shifting nearby sent me crouching, axe swinging in a blur to the right, and laughter rang out, making me curse.

The fucker was in close already, and he thought it was hilarious that I couldn't see him, did he?

Fine.

Two can play silly fuckers.

I cast my shield, hearing a curse as he presumably had to jump back out of range…then I triggered the Storm and flew sideways as fast as I could.

I plowed through one of the copies of the foxy lady, and it screamed in pain, then shattered as if it were made of glass. Fragments cascaded to the floor as they spun, tracking me; figures moved as they continued to dance their fingers in weird patterns, light flowing…

I suddenly remembered where I'd seen something like this before.

Becky.

I swore, knowing my mana was dropping by the second, and cut the shield, arcing around and flashing back toward them at full speed.

Becky had literally torn the asuras constructor's soul free of the body and chained it in a pocket dimension, using it to feed on and make herself stronger.

It'd been torn through steel and floated through the air as it was dragged away, unable to fight her. The last shit I needed was to have my soul torn apart. I'd worked in a call center once—there wasn't much left.

I held the shield in place and hacked with the sword. The figures shifted to track me and continued to cast whatever spell it was, but not responding beyond that.

I slashed left and right. The axe shattered the figures, each of them barely having enough of a physical form to slow the axe blade, and yet…

I needed to be faster!

I didn't know whether they were all decoys, whether they were going for my soul and she needed a certain number to make it work, or whether they were simply to keep me busy while she worked.

Twisting to the left, I shoved myself in that direction with the power, then cut it, landing and skidding, slashing left and right, then throwing the axe end over end at the next nearest in line, before punching my right fist forward. The bright cleansing power of Lightning tearing free in a beam that I slashed left to right killed two more, before I yanked a spear free and threw that as well.

I launched myself to the right with the Storm, powering my jump into a solid leap that covered a good four meters; I landed, running and skidding, before snatching the axe back up and throwing it again.

They were down to…*Wait.*

I'd blasted left to right with the Lightning across four of them, three were dead, one still stood, and although she looked unharmed…I snatched the last spear free and launched myself at her, flashing across the distance, right arm cocked back; then I threw.

The spear wobbled in the air, barely ahead of my own flight, but it was enough.

The figure before me screamed as the spear slammed into her upper right arm. The spell that was by now an almost fully formed cartwheel spiraled slowly before her, and each of her copies juddered to a halt, before shaking slightly, making me think of a cog in a watch when it hit an unexpected bit of dirt. Then it warped.

I landed right before her, seeing her floundering, the spear lodged in her arm, as she stared in horror at the spell. She was clutching the spear, but the white light that had been shimmering from her fingertips was tinged with blood now, and it started to draw on that.

"No, no!" she babbled. "No, you can't!" She ignored both me standing before her, and the wound as she frantically reached for the spell, her blood being viciously ripped from her and into the spell as she screamed in agony.

I ducked down, not wanting to touch the spell, and grabbed her ankle, yanking it forward and right. She staggered, blinking, seeming to see me for the first time, right beside her; she turned, reaching forward to grab the edge of the spell like a physical wheel. The center of the wheel collapsed inward, seeming to fall into a deep hole in space. A bright-white light tore free, angled upward and away.

She screamed with the effort, trying to turn it toward me, and the light carved its way down the side of the dungeon, ripping stone apart on its way.

I did the only reasonable thing I could, considering I was standing to the side, and the spell was ripping her blood and life force free to power itself.

I punched her in the face and grabbed the "wheel," sliding behind her, and twisted the aim point. It was slow, like I was dragging a massively heavy weight but…

But fuck me! The remaining three figures, the mirror copies of whatever they were, each of them was projecting a weaker version of the spell as well! They were carving the fuck out of the dungeon, and I grinned as I dragged it around, angling it upward toward the figures gathered around the throne.

I saw the look of horror on their faces as the spell closed in on them. The pair on the left started to cast a spell as quick as they could, while the ones on the right vanished into stealth, making me curse. The Scepiniir on the throne slammed a staff down; a shield sprung up around them, and them alone.

The spell hit the throne, and the shield turned midnight black. Crackles of power flared out and grounded all around it as the figures right by it screamed, hit by the discharge.

I cast my own shield, just in case, and grinned when a figure to my left, literally at arm's reach, was thrown back, snarling in pain.

Releasing my hold on the spell, I stepped to the left, then rabbit-punched the struggling fox in the side of the head, leaving her to collapse. She dangled there, seemingly held up by the spell as it drained her. It and her copies still poured blistering magic into the shield that protected the Scepiniir atop the throne.

"Right, you fucker," I growled at the rogue, who'd managed to keep his feet and was glaring at me now. "Don't suppose you want to surrender?" I cut my shield before it could catch the hanging power source behind me, and dragged my hammer free of the belt loop, offering the shield on my left arm to him.

"I think not," he replied, smiling toothily at me. "You, on the other hand, may make a wonderful pet yet…Tell me, are you housebroken?"

"Nah." I shook my head. "I keep getting smacked on the nose for shitting in shoes. You?"

"What?"

"Shoes," I repeated, closing on him. "What? You've never had a pet that shit in your shoes? That special, soft and warm surprise when you're late and need to rush out the house?"

"That's disgusting," he hissed, and I lunged forward, driving the hammer up and out, aiming the flat of the head for his disgusted face…only to have it pass through an image that popped like a soap bubble.

"Surprise!" a voice hissed in my ear as an arm wrapped around my neck from behind, a dagger driven up under my backplate and into my right kidney, then ripping sideways.

I screamed, staggering, hammer falling from spasming fingers.

A voice screamed out from above, demanding he stop the "Soul Snare," and he laughed in my ear.

"Now why would I do that?" he whispered, twisting the knife and making me cry out. "You did well, my pet. Turning that spell on our little lordling? If the spell lasts longer than his shield, well, it'll cost him more than a death."

"How much more?" I hissed, fighting for time.

"More than you've got to spare." He snorted. "Tell me, my pet, what is your life worth? What can you, as a Dungeon Lord, offer me?"

"What…do you want…?" I asked through gritted teeth.

"Freedom," he replied softly, almost lovingly, to me from behind. "I want my freedom, and some trinkets, minor things, but powerful…Tell me, little Dungeon Lord, if I kill you, I pay off an additional five deaths from my debt…what's your life worth to you? What will you give me, to make me giving up those five deaths seem worth it?"

"Kill him!" another voice called out, before a third screamed down not to.

"No!" it shouted. "I want him alive!"

"He wants to kill you himself," the rogue whispered. "Five deaths…he thinks he should be able to claim them himself, five deaths off his total. Well…he's been in here longer than any of us, a thousand deaths for his crimes…"

"And…you?" I asked.

"Oh, I have many deaths still to pay off, many. But eventually I'll be free again, and—"

"Not on my watch, you won't be," a sweet, high-pitched voice whispered to us both, before slamming her right hand into the side of the rogue's head.

CHAPTER THIRTY-SIX

The detonation as all three of Ciara's Triarach Diúracán went off at once, driven into the rogue's ear, was enough to send me sprawling forward, hitting the floor hard and making me cry out in agony as the dagger hit the bottom of my armor and ripped free. A great gout of blood washed down my back.

"Ciara!" I groaned, rolling onto my side and forcing myself around. The fairy was sprawled several feet away, her right arm missing from the upper arm down, her left desperately holding the wound closed as blood spurted free.

I dragged myself across to her, glancing at the headless rogue, and hissing in pain, as my destroyed kidney made its displeasure known.

"Dammit…you crazy damn fairy!" I hissed through gritted teeth, reaching out to her, and staring into her panicked, pain-filled eyes.

"Is he…is he dead?" She gasped in pain, blood spraying through her tightly clenched fingers.

"He's dead," I assured her, glancing at the headless corpse, pushing my Lightning mana to gather around where I'd once had a right kidney, starting the healing and regrowth process.

"Just hold on…" I begged her, gritting my teeth, then reaching out and dragging myself to the rogue's body, frantically searching him, looking for a potion, a bandage—hell, a fucking *zip-tie* would probably save her life at this stage, but…

A boot appeared from nowhere, crashing into my chin, ripping my helmet from my head and sending me rolling, stunned, before a dagger was driven through the meat of my left hand, and then a second kick to the face, and a fresh dagger into the right, digging deep into the ground below.

I'd lost the shield at some point, but the pain of both hands being out of action? Fuck!

"Stop it, stop the spell!" another voice—the Scepiniir on the throne—screamed from above, desperation clear in their voice, as the shield shook frantically.

"No, I don't think so," a new voice sighed from above me, as two blurs appeared, then resolved into the pair of Daoine Sidhe that had vanished earlier.

One was dressed in pale leathers and snowy-white lace, straps that held daggers crisscrossing over her chest, blonde hair elegantly piled in a cascade of curls, while across from her stood another, as dark as she was fair.

He wore red and gold, and practically dripped gold lace. A tricorne hat with an honest-to-God fucking *plume* looking like he'd stuck a peacock on his head topped off the outfit, and I hated him instantly.

They reminded me of every picture I'd ever seen of the floured and pomp-obsessed French aristocracy of the 1800s, and their beauty and angled almond-shaped eyes only made it worse.

The woman stood as if bored, while the man…He stepped forward, his boot coming down slowly on Ciara's leg, and he twisted it with a cruel smile, like I'd seen people put their cigarettes out in movies, obviously enjoying her scream.

"Incinerate!" I snarled, designating the prick's crotch, watching to see him suffer more pain than he was inflicting…only to stare in shock as he burst out laughing.

"Oh no, I don't think so." The woman squatted down before me and pulled out another of the daggers that ran across her chest. She held it up before my eyes, waving it to make sure I was watching, then flicked the tip, making it "sing" with the reverberations.

I'd thought of them as daggers, because that was what I was used to seeing now—every fucker seemed to have daggers—but these weren't those. They were sharp all the way around, two-edged and razor-sharp, a raised fuller running down the middle and patterned as if made from Damascus, a straight blade, with a simple handle, and…and a mana crystal set into each as a pommel stone.

Now that I was looking at it, I saw the subtle glow of the stone, and she nodded at me, smiling, seeing me making the connections.

"The Blades of T'Pau," she said clearly. "Also known as the mana thieves, and by, oh, at least a dozen other different names. They block your access to mana, and if I do this…" She dragged the tip down my breastplate, looking curiously at the design, before sliding one hand under the scalemail, and tugging it up to expose the softer undergarments, and my lower stomach.

"Tell me, does this hurt?" She fluttered her eyelashes, as she slowly pushed the blade into me, cutting the connections and then through the material below.

I felt the shape of the blade first, the tip pressing down, and then quickly after, the sharpness as it reached my flesh, digging into me.

"Fuck you…bitch!" I hissed, determined not to show any pain, not to…"FUUUUUCK!" I shouted as she slowly drove the blade through me, hitting the bone of my spine and shearing across the side of it, then hitting the back of my armor with a solid "ding."

"Now, as I was saying before you so rudely interrupted me," she whispered, gripping the hilt and smiling evilly. "Any mana you have? It's…*MINE!*"

The crystal in the hilt of the dagger suddenly flashed with prismatic light, and she sighed, clearly enjoying the feeling of ripping my mana from me.

"Don't kill him," the man warned her. "Wait till the others are here. Then we play."

"We have a special game we play here, did you know that?" she asked me, almost conversationally. "As only one of us can gain the five-death reduction for killing you, we play a game to decide who it'll be. We pick a weapon, and an area, and we're each assigned a number, then we roll the dice. If our number comes up? Well…"

"You remember the Jamaican?" Her companion grinned.

"Oh I do!" She laughed. "Squealed like a little turnik when you crushed his 'manhood' with the hammer. You know, I'd never heard a voice go so high? Certainly not one that started so deep…"

"You're…monsters…" I gasped, and they looked at each other, then laughed.

"You're only just figuring this out?" The man squinted at my right hand. "Uh oh, that looks loose…" He kicked the hilt and drove the blade to one side, cutting deep into my hand and making me cry out in pain, as he laughed cruelly.

"Recruiting a lower-level creature such as this, when you could have summoned one of us?" The woman gestured at Ciara, shaking her head as if disappointed by a small child. "Honestly, you've only yourself to blame, really. I mean, look at the size of her. Her brain is only so large, after all. She might have been useful, but she'd never be worth much effort."

"She's worth ten…of you…" I managed to get out through gritted teeth, and the Daoine Sidhe burst out laughing, before reaching up and stroking my face gently.

"Oh bless it, it's lost its mind," she said amusedly.

"Baynath," the man said, and the woman looked up in question. "His shield's failing," he explained, grinning, and the pair smiled cruelly, standing to watch.

The other two Daoine Sidhe, presumably mages, from the way they'd gone straight for magic instead of stealth, were standing, watching up on the level above, clearly waiting to loot their boss's corpse.

The body of the mage that had cast the spell was shaking now, crumbling to dust as it collapsed, the last spurts of life being torn from her dying form. It wasn't going to fail in time for the Scepiniir, though. The shield failed, and the spell punched through the last remnants, slamming into him where he hunkered down, frantically trying to avoid it, still on his throne.

"Nooooooo!" he wailed, as his body arced in pain. His healthy skin shifted to grey and desiccated in an instant, as the spell finally locked onto a living soul, beginning to rip it from the body.

"Will he be reborn?" Baynath asked her male companion curiously. The pair of them watched as their supposed ally's soul was ripped free; his body sagged, seeming smaller and pathetic as the soul was dragged, immobilized, through the air.

"I don't actually know." He rubbed his chin. "I mean, she's dead, so she can't hold the soul, but then, she won't be releasing it either. What happens to souls bound into a dimensional fragment when nobody has control of it? Is he condemned to eternity in there? Will he dissipate? Is there even entropy in a dimensional fragment? It's all *very* interesting."

The copies all winked out, their spells dying entirely, as the soul reached the dangling, dead form of the caster, being dragged into the void, then vanished as the tear in reality snapped closed.

"Well, we'll know if he's reborn with us, I suppose." Baynath sighed, shaking her head. "Anything good?" she called up to the mages, who were gingerly reaching around the spell's blast, and already fumbling through their former ally's pockets.

"Not yet!" one called back, the other too busy to speak.

While they were talking, I was desperately racking my brain to figure a way out of this.

I'd seen the state of Ciara—the paleness, the final few spurts of blood, each progressively weaker than the last—and I looked over at her, now, while gritting my teeth and working my hands back and forth, literally slicing them apart as I tried to free myself, the earth that held the rest of the blades releasing only grudgingly.

We shared a long look, and I saw it when it happened: the sad, forced smile, the fear, and the final relaxation, as her body sagged, the life leaving it, and her eyes filmed over in death.

"No," I whispered, shaking my head. "No, you can't…"

"Oh, we can," Baynath called over her shoulder to me, unconcerned, and not even bothering to turn around. "We can and we will. Get ready to die, slowly and painfully."

"Anyway…you think Ferragus will try to hide things again?" the man asked her, and she shrugged.

"Wouldn't you?" she replied curiously.

"Well, yes, okay, I would." He snorted, before cursing and turning around, looking down at Ciara's body. "Oh, for…accursed fairies!" He snarled, yanking a dagger out of its sheath on his hip.

He drove it forward, stabbing it deep into her frail little form, spearing her and cutting so deep her shoulder and damaged arm came apart from the rest of her corpse.

"Too late!" he snarled. "Pathetic little creatures! That might have cost me a point of Constitution!"

"What?" his companion asked, watching as he desecrated the small body.

"I selected the random spawn perk," he explained, idly stripping Ciara from his blade and flicking her toward me. Her corpse smacked into the cavern floor near my face, lying there, even more broken and smaller, without the spark that she had been filled with in life. "I got this dagger this time around…steals a point of Constitution if you bond it. Permanent increase as well." He grinned.

"So that's why you were killing those goblins!" She laughed. "I thought you were just amusing yourself…"

"Nope, gained eleven points," he replied smugly.

"Impossible!" She gasped. "That many?"

"It stopped working at fifty. The Examine spell doesn't mention it when you check the blade, but once you hit fifty, it warns you that your body reaches a plateau, and it won't work anymore," he confirmed. "Stabbed a few more just to be sure, of course, but yeah. I wanted to check with her. Might be species specific, after all."

"Give it to me," she demanded hungrily.

"Why should I?" He laughed.

"We've been allies for six lives!" She gasped. "That's longer than any bonding I've had, and twice what you're worth, you know it."

"A bonding, eh?" He sniggered. "And yet still you refuse to share your more…fun…abilities with me?"

"You want to fuck me? Give me the dagger," she countered. "I'll let you."

"I'll fuck you first. Maybe if you earn it, I'll give you the dagger after…"

"You know I'll blow your tiny mind." She laughed, but I could hear the edge in her voice. "What's to stop you keeping the dagger once you've fucked me?"

"You'd stab me while I slept?" he suggested.

"I might do that regardless," she admitted. "Give me that dagger first though and…"

"So…"

They'd moved in close and were speaking in low, passionate voices, their faces full of feigned lust…but they were both drawing daggers behind their backs as well.

No.

I wasn't having them kill each other.

They were going to die, all right…but not until *I* was done with them! They'd killed Ciara, Drak was no doubt hiding somewhere, or already dead, and I was little better. I didn't know if I'd get out of this, but I didn't give a shit right now. There was a chance, even if it was a low one, that these evil fucks could escape from here.

They were alive, after all—alive and uninjured.

I knew that the dungeon "should" kill them once I was dead, according to Ciara and Drak, but for all I knew, not having a fairy to "turn it off" meant they'd be left to wander around.

If they found the lever and pulled it? If they just walked out when everyone was asleep?

The thought of what a pair of sadistic fucks like these could do out there, to those I loved…*No.*

I couldn't channel, not to cast anyway.

I could still feel my mana in me, though. It flowed around and past the blades driven into me. It was still there, but it wasn't until I tried to cast it out, tried to affect the outside world, that the daggers seemed to get their fill.

That was important.

I could feel it, and it meant that rather than stripping the mana from me, I still had some.

I closed my eyes, gritting my teeth as they continued to mutter filth to each other, him demanding and her promising…provided he hand the dagger over first.

A deep breath out, a deep breath in, and I tensed. The daggers were driven through my hands aligned between the bones, in the center of both hands.

Well, I couldn't get them out of the earth, I quickly realized. The blood that had run down the blade had turned the ground directly around them into a sucking mass that was rapidly hardening.

That left me one choice…well, besides staying there until they decided to kill me.

Rather than think about it anymore, I just did it, yanking both elbows in toward my sides, ripping the blades from the center of my hands, all the way out, literally cutting my hands apart as the blades carved their way between my fingers.

I whimpered. Blood sprayed from both hands as I grabbed the dagger in my stomach, my hands barely working to close, and I pulled at it desperately, ripping it free.

"Oh, bless it!" Baynath laughed. "Look, the little lordling thinks it can be free…"

"Should we give it a chance?" Her companion laughed.

"Ummmm…" Baynath tapped at her chin in thought.

I frantically circulated Lightning, trying to heal my wounds enough that I could function and…

"No." Baynath grinned, before kicking me in the face.

I rolled, smacking into the dirt, reeling. I tried to focus. The power of those boots, armored as they were, crashing into the side of my head? It was stunning.

I laid there, blinking stupidly, trying to focus, and…

There was something right before my eyes, something blurry, something pale but red as well. Half a translucent wing swam into focus, and I snarled. My vision cleared, focusing on the still, tiny form of Ciara.

I saw her, and the world turned red with my rage.

Digging deep, I ripped the mana from my core, flooding myself with the Storm, launching myself forward, a split second before a blade crashed into the dirt where I'd been.

I was crippled, my hands barely closed, I was low on mana, and I had a powerful need to fucking murder them all.

I arced around toward the nearest wall, flipping over and skidding as I came to a halt, bracing myself and glaring at the look on their faces as they stared upward.

They began to blur, and I snarled in fury. "No, you fucking don't!" I hissed, casting Incinerate. The air distorted as Baynath moved. It was a fuzzing of the air as she presumably stepped over Ciara's remains, but that was enough—oh fuck, that was enough.

She screeched in pain, becoming suddenly visible, crashing to the floor. Her ankle and the clothing around it glowed cherry-red and charred black as she collapsed, hands going to grab her foot; then she howled as they came into contact with the remains of the heat field, and began to blacken as well.

Her blood was boiling, cells cascading into death. Shock set in as she screamed again, writhing, before holding her hand out to the air next to her.

"Ashok!" she begged. "Your ring! Pleeeeease!"

I kicked off, doubling down with my mana, knowing I had less than four hundred left, and a little less than that in health…two hundred and seven points, and dropping.

I focused on a tiny distortion, and I snarled, rocketing toward it, and unleashing Lightning from the mess that was my left hand. Skin split as the force of my passage tore the wound open wider.

I screamed, even as Ashok appeared, shaking and cursing as Lightning coursed through him. I plowed straight into him at full speed, flipping over at the last second, tucking my knees up toward my chest. Pain ripped through me from that wound…and then I kicked out as hard as I could.

The combination of the Lightning attack just finishing, then my heavily armored form crashing into him, was memorable—or it was for me, anyway.

He was sent flying, slamming into a section of rock, and bounced back, before collapsing to the floor and leaving a bloody smear on the rock behind him.

I hit the floor hard though as well. My armor tore in places, and I screamed as my left little finger snagged on something and my hand was torn in half. The cut spread, much as a tear in the cardboard changes a solid box into a shredded mess in seconds.

I curled into a ball instinctively, the world full of pain, my stomach bleeding heavily, intestines leaking, left hand utterly fucked and my right…I forced myself to uncurl, shaking and wanting to vomit with the pain. I twisted around, searching for him.

"Damn…you!" He groaned a few seconds later from my left, pushing himself up and pulling a ring from a pocket.

"Ashok, no!" Baynath whimpered, her hands useless and her left ankle a twisted lump that would never again bear her weight. "I need—"

"Tough…" he whispered, pulling the ring toward his finger.

I launched myself at him. Unable to use my hands properly, I powered my body through mana, shoving out with the Storm from behind, sending myself crashing into him. The ring bounced free.

"Fool!" he shouted, backhanding me, dragging a dagger free and raising it, fury in his eyes, even as blood ran from the corner of his mouth.

I rolled over, trying to move my arms, my legs. Pain spasmed through me, and he grabbed my arm, yanking me around…

I grinned up at him through bloody teeth and dropped my mana from a hundred and thirty-seven to thirty-seven alone, as I kneed him in the stomach, triggering Storm-Strike.

He doubled over, eyes bugging out. The knee caught him in the short ribs, angling upward, and it was like a shotgun going off internally.

His ribs shattered. The comforting rigidity they'd always provided his chest was transformed into bone-fléchettes that tore through organs; the internal shock wave caused those self-same organs to compress, and then burst.

He collapsed, vomiting blood, eyes wide, body spasming, as I twisted around. Crawling like a slug with serious issues, across the floor toward the gleaming ring he'd dropped.

I didn't have enough mana to examine it, but the frantic way that Baynath was headed for it said all I needed to know. It was her last chance, and mine.

Ashok was whimpering and coughing blood, but even he started trying to reach the ring when he realized what we were all doing.

I triggered my Storm mana, flinging myself forward a handful of meters, crashing into a rock and bouncing off, probably injuring myself far more than if I'd just crawled or hell, got up and walked. But I was only a meter away from it now, seeing the simple gold band with a raised blue gem set into it.

It'd bounced and rolled across the ground from Ashok when I'd hit him, covering more ground than I'd have expected. I could hear shouts from the upper level, as well as the sudden crash of magics used offensively, that made me rush even more.

If I got through all of this, only to die from some dickhead walking up with a fireball? *No.*

Ciara had given her life for me.

She'd chosen, rather than risk firing her spell at distance and have it stopped by armor or shielding spells, to physically drive the spell into place, knowing exactly what the consequence would be for her.

No, she'd died to give me this chance, and I'd damn well be walking out of here!

I forced myself across the last short distance, reaching forward with my right hand, gritting my teeth at the mess that it was in: the flowing blood, the filth that was driven into the gaps between my upper and lower pairs of fingers, the red pulsing flesh…

I managed to force my longest finger through the metal band on the third attempt, the crunching sound of gravel nearby being moved by a frantic Baynath crawling closer as I dragged the hand back and tried to settle the ring, rolling onto my back, pressed hard against a dusty, blood-smeared rock.

The ring slid down my finger, catching on the second joint, too small to go all the way down it. Then it shifted, resizing, and I forced it into place against a rock, feeling the ring settle snugly…and nothing happen.

I needed to activate it, I realized.

A magic ring that just activated whenever it wanted would be fucking useless, not to mention insanely dangerous. No, it had to have a trigger, an activation phrase, a…

"Please…" Baynath whispered, and I glared at her. "I'll serve you," she begged, her hands curled uselessly, fingers blackened, her face full of the realization that even if I died now, she would too, her "allies" taking the time to amuse themselves with the injured and weak member of their cabal at the end of it all.

"How?" I asked her roughly.

"However you want," she promised, and I spat in disgust, forcing myself up.

"No, you stupid…*cough* fucker! How does it *work*!" I clarified, shaking the finger at her.

"There's two uses!" She gasped. "Give it to me, and I'll heal…"

"Don't be stupid," I hissed. "They'll kill you if you're weak, and I'm not giving you this." I shook the finger. "Tell me how it works, and I'll heal you *after* I heal."

"No, you won't…" She shook her head, sagging back, hissing in pain.

"You've a chance that I'll heal you, or I'll make your death fast, I promise," I warned her. "With them? You've no chance, and you know it!"

"By Khance's balls…" she whispered, tears forming at the edges of her eyes, clearly unable to believe she was in this situation. "The activation word is Shemer," she admitted in a low, defeated voice.

"Shemer!" I said aloud, before screaming.

"Fool!" She laughed, forcing it out as she watched me writhe, shaking as the stored mana activated, powering out not into a healing spell, but into an anti-theft enchantment designed to destroy any who were not worthy.

I thrashed around. Pain flashed through me, along with the mana as cells were flooded with ten thousand points of stored…*Lightning mana.*

My injuries were flash healed; the wounds deep in my hands bubbled over with frantic cell regrowth. Filth and impurities were forced out; healthy flesh dragged the split-apart sections together. And the pain…fuck, it was worse than the original wounds being inflicted! I'd curled up into a ball. Bones that had been barely healed, hairline fractures, cuts…hell, my fucking carved-apart intestines and my destroyed and only partially rebuilt goddamn kidney: all of it was rebuilt in seconds, as the final changes ran their course, and I blinked, lying facedown, facing away from her.

I focused on the dirt before me, splattered with my own blood and saliva, listening to her hoarse laughter as she forced out the words.

"You think I'd ever help you? You think I'd let you force me, Baynath of the Black Gate, to serve a mortal? You think—"

She cut off abruptly as I twisted around, coming face-to-face with her, and she saw that not only was I still alive, but I was grinning maniacally as I closed my fist around her throat.

"Remember when I promised I'd make it quick?" I asked her in a low, hard voice.

"Y…yes!" She choked out.

"You should have fucking took that chance!" I ripped one of her mana-stealing knives free, then drove it into her stomach. "This feels familiar…" I whispered, staring into her eyes as they widened in panic.

The crystal in the hilt of the blade flared to life, and I felt a fast influx of mana before she could choke it off. I knew that the blades could only take mana if it was being actively used, not just passively circling, and I glanced at her hands, seeing the fresh pink flesh that had begun to show through the charred blackness.

"Healing spells, eh?" I twisted the dagger, and angling it upward, aimed toward her heart. "You can channel into the healing spell and hope you can beat the drain and the damage I do…or you can not, and die full of mana when I gut you," I offered conversationally, before starting to drag it upward.

The horror on her face, and the pain, made it clear she knew she had no chance, just as the sudden rush of mana through the crystal and into me made it clear that she couldn't help but try.

I hesitated, halfway through the act, not out of any wish to not go through with it, but I could feel her soul, now that I was indeed carving her mortal body apart.

I could feel that soul, and I almost tore it from her.

The only reason I didn't in the end? It wasn't the threats of "consequences" if I did it. The fuckers who were warning me off doing exactly this, I'd now found were very guilty of "do what I say, not what I do," considering the souls imprisoned in the dungeon network.

No, it was the genuine fear of fucking up and setting off the soul equivalent of a fucking nuke inside my own goddamn dungeon.

Three seconds later, it was over, and she sagged against me, dead.

Two hundred and fifteen mana I'd managed to recover to, and I was fully healed.

Time to go fuck up their plans.

I shoved her body back from me, grabbing her necklace at the last second as the corpse rolled away, revealing its glittering gold strands, snapping it free and pocketing it for later examination.

I twisted around, seeing the last, shallow, and pain-filled breaths panting out of Ashok. I moved to him, grabbing his fancy dagger, and grunting as I saw a screen pop up before me.

Vampiric Dagger	Magical Weapon
Damage: 5-7	Stat: Constitution
A Vampiric Dagger is a powerful weapon. Unbonded, it will drain health and grant it to the user. Bonded, it will steal a single stat point of the appropriate type per kill, per charge.	
Durability: 7/10	Charge: 1/4

I recognized it now, remembering Kelly getting it as a loot drop, and us sacrificing it to the dungeon ages ago. This time I bonded it and positioned the tip directly over his right eyeball.

"Plu…ease…" he whispered.

"Go fuck yourself," I growled at him, driving the mana-stealing dagger into his crotch, then ramming the stat-stealing one into his eye.

I hissed, shuddering as the dagger in his eye stole…*something* from him, and drove it into me. It wasn't the promised point of Constitution—clearly what he'd told his partner about it stopping working at fifty was true—but there was *something*.

I licked my lips, shaking, and stared at him, before tugging both daggers free, and stabbing him again with the vampiric one.

Nothing this time, but for a second? I'd definitely felt something, and more than that, I'd felt a rush of ecstasy run through me at his death. And I damn well wanted more. I could feel…I could feel the dagger trying to drag me toward Baynath's body. I moved quickly, darting to her side and stabbing her, getting only a tiny surge in power, but it was better than nothing.

I stared down at the dagger, blood coating it as I tugged it free. As another spell went off with a boom above me, I hesitated only a second, quickly unfastening the daggers across Baynath's chest and strapping it to myself, awkwardly, considering I was still in my battered and broken armor, then set off running.

There were three of the daggers laid loose on the ground behind me, one in my hand and two more in their sheaths, so I had to hope they'd not dissipate when she was reduced to motes of light to make way for her reliquary, but at least I had some of them.

There was a thought to stop and retrieve them, but I dismissed it in a second, racing up the switchback, scrambling as I skidded on loose rocks.

Coming to the top, I saw the remaining three I'd seen from below. The Scepiniir was laid slumped in the remains of his throne, gold having ran like water at some point. Great gouges melted out of it, and a story in a thousand small images that were carved into it, irrevocably destroyed.

I saw it all in an instant, just as I saw the first of the Daoine Sidhe, dead, with a dagger driven through its lower spine and the throat ripped out by a second blade. One I recognized from our meals together.

I raced around the thrones, seeing the metal floor that took over from the dirt and rock, the pedestal that stood there proud and ready, requiring only the handprint of the Dungeon Lord to activate, once all the challenges were met.

Before it, and standing over the bleeding and broken form of my kobold companion Drak, was the last of the defenders.

This Daoine Sidhe was tall, standing with his back to me, and holding the staff that the Scepiniir had held before. It was pressed to the underside of Drak's chin, hard against his throat as the figure laughed, slowly increasing the pressure on the staff, clearly enjoying crushing the kobold's windpipe.

"Is it done?" he called over his shoulder, turning to glance at me, grinning.

"Yeah!" I replied, running full tilt at him, and activating my mana, launching myself through the air.

"You!" he screeched, whipping the staff around.

Whatever else he might be, the Daoine Sidhe was no slouch. The staff crashed into my side as I slammed into him, sending us both flying. My mana blade was lodged into his left shoulder, the vampiric dagger having cut a line across the outside of his right arm, but only lightly.

The staff, however, was long, and fucking heavy.

I didn't know whether it was solid metal, or just coated in it, but once he'd gotten it moving, it'd not stopped easily. And the inertia? Hell, the force of that thing hitting me had damn well *hurt*.

I'd hit the floor and rolled, coming back to my feet with a hiss, only to leap back as he swung the staff again, this time unleashing a bright gout of flames from one end.

I had no time to dodge, barely managing to trigger the mana I had into my shield. It flared into life, then failed; the bright-white light of the fire punched through the shield like a blowtorch through paper.

I threw myself aside, dodging behind the throne, skidding and dodging back again as he whipped the staff to point at the other side. The jet of flames erupting right before my face.

For a few seconds, we twisted and ran back and forth, me using the throne as a shield...until he snarled in frustration and levelled it at the throne directly, instead of trying to get at me on the far side.

The top began to glow, and then sag, as I tried to flip the vampiric dagger over, thinking to throw it at him.

I couldn't.

My hand wouldn't release. I couldn't even sheathe the damn thing!

My fingers were tightly closed around it, holding on for dear life, and the shock that realization caused almost cost me my life, as I hesitated, the gold glowing brighter...then it sagged and flowed down. The flame shot through to thunder past my head as I raced to the right.

He dragged it after me, the roar of the approaching fuckin' jet engine suddenly guttering out as he collapsed with a scream.

I twisted, planted a foot on a rock, and changed direction, seeing Drak had dragged himself across the floor and had slashed the back of the fucker's legs, severing his hamstrings and sending him crashing to the floor.

I leapt through the air, landing hard atop him and forcing his breath from him with a whoosh. The vampiric dagger moved of its own accord, driving up fast and hard, punching through the underside of his chin. The tip grated through bone and brain to reappear with a crunch, the very tip gleaming bloodily from the top of his head.

The Daoine Sidhe spasmed once, then lay still. I groaned in pleasure, the dagger draining him of something, feeding me with it, making me shake as the feeling went on and on.

"Matt..." Drak whispered from nearby, and I twisted, fixing on him and grinning.

The flood of energy, of power that had been ripped through the dagger and fed into me, dying away as the life force of the fucker was consumed guttered away, leaving me feeling hollow, and hungry.

"Matt?" Drak tried again, licking his lips, clearly scared. "Ciara, is she...?"

At the mention of her name, it was as if I'd had a bucket of iced water dunked over my head: the blood lust, the hunger…all of it vanished. I almost collapsed, horrified by the thoughts I'd just begun to have, the way that Drak had appeared to me.

I'd not been seeing a mostly trustworthy companion, a kobold that was a bit of a shit, but had come through for me again and again. No, I'd been seeing another source of life.

I'd just started to think it, but I knew the shape of the thoughts, and the hunger that was behind them, the driving need.

I dropped the dagger, able to now that the threat and bloodlust was gone, and I frantically scrubbed my hands on my armored leg, shuddering.

"Ciara…" Drak tried again. "Is she…?"

"I'm sorry," I said softly. "She died."

"Ah…" he whispered, closing his eyes and shaking his head. "Well, I guess it is what it is." His voice was sad, pain clear in it, as he sagged back. "Well, at least we had fun while it lasted."

"We did it," I told him, looking around, realizing it for the first time myself. "We've reached the end of the dungeon."

I could see it was true. Where we'd been expecting more caverns and rooms, the dungeon had clearly gone for a mass fight plan instead, and from here I could see the bodies piled like cordwood off to the right.

Goblins lay there, dead, in a pile of stinking bloody meat, and I shook my head in disbelief. They'd made an impossible job possible, because the dungeon used the souls of criminals to give the trial dungeon inhabitants sentience. They were forced to remain in their sections, each cavern or grouping forced to stay there, and only the dumb monsters like the lesser ghasts enabled to roam.

That had led to the criminals themselves turning on each other when they thought there was a possible gain for them, and that dumb fuck Ashok stabbing all the goblins to death, stealing their Constitution, one point at a time.

The fight had been three-quarters luck, on my part. That I'd survived at all, I mean, and it was only through the help of Drak and Ciara, and she'd lost her life to help me.

"Go on," he growled. "End it!"

CHAPTER THIRTY-SEVEN

"What?" I asked him, aghast, thinking he was expecting me to kill him, when he nodded to the pedestal and the awaiting handprint scanner.

He was battered, bleeding in a dozen places, and exhausted, but he was alive, and I nodded to him, straightening up and forcing myself to my feet.

"I'll just check his pockets, if you don't mind?" Drak grinned to me, reaching out to the nearest body…as it collapsed into a cascade of motes of light. "Egg fuckers!" he cursed, pounding a fist into the metal floor, then whimpering as he shook his hand.

I strode forward, slapping my hand to the pedestal, and read the prompt that flared to life before me.

Congratulations, Dungeon Lord!

You have survived, and conquered, your first Trial Dungeon!

Know this: in addition to the bonus rewards you were previously awarded, you will receive the standard reward from the Dungeon system for completing a trial…

Are you ready?

Yes/Yes

I grunted and flicked yes, unsurprisingly.

The screens that flashed up were like I stood in a programmer's office: there were suddenly three separate screens, slightly curved, and turned sideways, hovering directly before me, and to the left and right.

I glanced from one to the next, seeing that they were each my rewards.

The first screen dealt exclusively with me, the second was an artifact, and the third the dungeon, making me nod as I looked them over.

They were a variety of colors, clearly intended to denote rarity, moving from white to cream, to green to blue.

Blue showed as rare, but there were no higher options. I flicked my finger up and down before each screen, watching as the options flooded past, then focused, restructuring by rarity.

I didn't want to ignore the non-rare stuff; after all, something awesome might be common, but amazing for us, and always taken by dungeons because it was insanely powerful, but…scanning over them, nothing in the lower colors stood out.

In my personal rewards, I narrowed it down to two blues—rare—and one green—uncommon—then re-read them.

Personal Skill Matrix: Choose two personal skills and split 30 levels across them in any mixture you choose.

Note: No skill may be raised above level 50, and although this didactic imprint grants knowledge, it cannot imprint aptitude. You have been warned.

*

Affinity Boost! Gain 50 affinity points to assign in any mixture so desired.

Note: No affinity may be raised above 75. Artificially boosting an affinity grants aptitude, but not knowledge. You have been warned.

They were both the rare options, and although they were a bit "meh" at first glance, I could also see why they were rare.

For example, the personal skill matrix could take me from an average rifleman to a fucking sharpshooter that would make Mike green with envy if I dropped twenty-nine of those levels into it.

Add to that, if I sank those points into Rifles, I'd then have the Firearms skill artificially boosted to match it.

I paused, summoning the last notification I'd dismissed for Rifles. I'd done little with that skill for a while, we'd been so low on ammunition, and as normal, if it wasn't a level that got me a "real" bonus, like the multiples of tens were, I just ignored it.

Congratulations!

You have reached level 27 in Rifles!

You receive a 2% increase in chance to inflict critical damage and a 1% increased chance to hit your target per point. Because you have gained this level in a sub-skill of Firearms, you have also received the requisite levels in Firearms, granting a 1% chance of familiarity with unknown Firearms operation and a 1% increased chance to hit your target per point earned. Increase your skill to further improve your damage bonuses.

Congratulations!

You have increased your Firearms skill to level 27!

At level 20, you gained an increased chance to hit your target by an additional 20%. This stacks with the class of Firearms, such as a 7% chance to hit with energy weapons becoming a combined 27%. + 20% chance of familiarity with unknown firearms, and now you gain a 20% chance to intuit methods of repair and maintenance for any firearms in your possession. Increased familiarity with said firearms will increase this chance.

Okay, I couldn't surpass fifty with it, but I could reach it. Twenty-three points dumped into this would get me to fifty, so I'd have three new multiples of ten as a bonus, then I'd also have the additional 20% chance to hit, added to the 50% chance I'd have from the skill level, and not even including whatever other bonuses I got...

I'd have at least a seventy percent chance of hitting my target every time. That was fucking insane.

Alternately, I could slam twenty-nine points into something like magical artifact creation. I'd be the equivalent of a journeyman, I guessed, or hell, maybe I'd just be an apprentice or a novice, I didn't know, but I'd have the knowledge of creating magical fucking artifacts.

This was insanely tempting. And as for the affinity points? Fifty of them? I could take Earth all the way to the maximum of seventy-five, and still have points left over to put into raising my Water affinity to there as well, or near enough.

That would mean I could gradually work on increasing them both, day by day, until I reached the maximum.

They were simple, at first glance, and not exactly exciting, not as a "rare" reward, but when you thought about it? When you looked at it and really considered the possibilities?

Fuck me.

What the hell would I be looking at if I'd earned a legendary reward? As soon as that crossed my mind, I knew I'd have to try for it. Now that I knew what the hell that trial dungeon actually was? I could prepare and equip myself properly, train and bring goddamn healing potions and more.

Artifacts that would even the playing field, and the damn guns that Aly was developing!

A rail gun would have sorted this shit right out.

I moved to the third and final option, grunting as I looked it over as well.

Personal Spell Matrix: A single shard of personal spell training, available to be chosen from a single school used in the trial dungeon.

Choose from the following to receive a random spell shard:
- Lightning
- Lightning
- Storm

I had to shake my head at that. I'd basically used my Lightning to such a level that there was little option beyond it, as near as the dungeon could see.

It was tempting, it really was, but I dismissed it. The other options were everything from Experience rewards to random equipment and stat point upgrades—singular, of course.

I went back to the first two options, considered it for several seconds, then sighed, and selected the personal skill matrix.

Thirty goddamn levels I could break down into any combination over two skills was just too good a boost to turn down. I winced, half expecting I'd have to decide them straightaway, when the light of the dungeon "printing" something flared before me, and a small orb dropped into my outstretched hand.

It was a ball, metallic, with a space for a thumb to be pressed to it, and being me, I did so promptly.

There was a click, and the upper half slid back, splitting into sections that slid down into the lower, and revealing a single monocle on a velvet-looking cushion. I reached for it, then forced myself to stop. I'd look at it later. I knew what it was now.

As soon as I lowered my hand, the fragments slid back up, and the ball was reformed, the upper sections sliding closed. I slipped it into a pocket, and moved to the middle selection, the artifacts.

This time around I had a single rare in blue, and two uncommon greens.

As soon as I saw the option that hung there before me? It was a done deal.

I glanced at the second and third options, and literally slid my gaze across the first few of the others, but it wasn't a choice. Not really.

Warped Spatial Container	Item
This basic container, reminiscent of a simple pouch, has been constructed with internal dimensions that greatly exceed its exterior ones, providing a 90% weight reduction for all items stored within.	
Maximum capacity: 200L of liquids, 200kgs of solid weight spread across 50 individual slots.	
Note: Identical items may be stacked in individual slots up to 99 times.	
Durability 500/500	**Rarity:** Rare

The other two possible artifacts? A monocle of identification and a sword that dealt "spirit damage" equal to its physical one.

Nope. The rest of the artifacts? They weren't even artifacts; they were fucking ingredients and shit like that. A hundred grams of orichalcum might be great or fucking useless. I dismissed them, uncaring, catching the pouch as it fell from the air, and I grinned to myself as I stared at it.

I didn't care about the cost.

These fuckers were being reproduced, and damn soon. I finally had a "bag of holding" and gods, it was a wonderful thing!

Moving onto the third and final screen, the reward for me surviving the dungeon, and—if I was reading this right—something I could earn again, if I did the dungeon over and over.

I had three rare, and two uncommon this time, the last two being blueprints for animal companions for the dungeon, specifically a duck and some breed of eagle, which caught my eye. Until I realized that by the size measurements, it'd basically be a normal-sized bird.

If I'd been able to ride the fucker? Hell yes, that would have been a contender. Something that was just large enough to sit on my shoulder and shit down my back? Nope.

As to the duck? It was a fucking waterproof chicken with a kazoo. Hard pass. Unless it came with its own bath of hoisin, and prepared itself lovingly with pancakes, I wasn't interested.

The two greens were slightly better. One was a new species: a short, fugly-looking creature that reminded me of a devil in traditional myth, or an imp. Where the impai were apparently somehow related to birds, and just looked like devils, the Derish were the real deal. Looking at it, I saw an image of a small creature on all fours. They were described as being opportunist murderers and excelled in "idle theft, property destruction, and low-grade terror."

Nope.

Next was a structure for the dungeon, an uncommon grade mining hub. That was a contender. It deployed small golems, controlling them remotely, harvested and refined the minerals as they went. It included the lower-grade versions, and could be upgraded, and I vaguely recognized the specs from one of the research options I'd passed up in the past.

That was all the low-grade shit out of the way, and finally, I was into the three rare ones.

They were, in no particular order, a core "turnkey upgrade," basically permitting us to halve the upgrade time from Steel to Glass, access to the rare species Dvork, or we could choose a single-use defensive platform.

The defensive platform was the first to be discarded. It was something that we'd be able to research and build once we reached Glass from the details I could see, and it was literally a single-use facility.

You transport it to the site you want it, and you activate it; it literally deploys a small fortification—walls, ground…everything—like a miniature offshoot of the dungeon, using a core fragment to power itself.

Depending on the level of the weaponry deployed, and the situation, it'd last anywhere from a few minutes to a few years, but once it was activated, that was it.

You couldn't move it, and you couldn't restructure it. You activate it and realize that you left a hole in one wall because you're shit at reading plans? Well, better start fuckin' running then.

They were rare, but I was betting that was because no fucker made them, rather than they were valuable.

The fast upgrade? It halved the time it would take, which was massive. I had a vague idea that it'd take at least a few weeks to go from the current level of Steel to Glass, should we choose to do so right now, so halving that?

It was a massive savings.

The Dvork, though?

They were a different level.

Mammal: The Dvorks, Dvorkian or People of the Deep, are the ancient enemies of the Orcan, a people that were recently disabused of their final world by the Orcan expansion.

The Dvork are shipbuilders and engineers beyond compare, but suffer from two significant situational modifiers.

1. The Dvorkian race is now formally acknowledged as extinct, and those summoned through the dungeon and given artificial life are unavoidably aware of this. As such, they suffer from significant emotional and physical issues, including uncontrolled aggression and a desire to render themselves insensate through external means. Commonly alcohol.

2.   Dvorks as a race evolved on high-gravity, mineral- and ore-rich worlds, resulting in physical differences from most races. They are shorter of stature, broad and enormously strong. These are all minor issues compared to the fact that no Dvork can successfully mate outside of such a location. This results in an extremely high likelihood of Dvorkian breeding programs failing.

Cost: *Dvork (Common):* 500 Earth, 1500 Pure Mana, 20 Control points. Maintenance is 45 mana points per day, per individual.
Included Level: Common.

I read over it again and again. They were dwarves! At least I assumed they were…engineers and shipbuilders beyond compare! Fuck yes!

Although, it looked like it was a case of fuck with them, and find out. They'd lost all their worlds, the Orcan had slaughtered them, and although they were capable of being reborn through the dungeon, and as such would always be dungeon creatures "first," they were clearly also a species that would have issues.

Not least the fact that should they wish to get "busy" and repopulate their worlds after all of this, they'd need to find high-G worlds to do the dirty on first.

I didn't use things like the breeding hut so that was a relief, as it didn't really affect us that much. But I did suspect that, for the species themselves? That was a far more massive issue. I also guessed it was a warning for anyone with a dungeon that was planning to return the species.

For me, it came down to two options. First, did we go for the massive jump in speed for Glass, gaining literally nothing but time, but considering just how important time was?

Or, did we bring back a species that were renowned as shipbuilders and engineers?

Thinking of it that way? Admittedly, in theory, all blueprints and designs should be available through the dungeon, with enough work. We should be able to create anything the Dvork could design for us, ourselves.

Should.

Or we could save a week or two where we'd not have access to automated research and the main construction facilities.

When I looked at it like that? It wasn't a fucking choice.

Dvork it was.

I selected it and sighed as I felt the change coming over the dungeon as the lockouts were removed. The reliquaries were flashing for the Daoine Sidhe I'd killed, and I resolved to get them as fast as possible. But for now?

I checked the system, making sure we had the mana available, and winced as fifty thousand mana was taken to replicate the high-end healing potion I'd added to the schematics when I was in the safe room.

Moving to Drak's side, I held out the potion, and he stared at it, then me, eyes wide and tongue nervously flickering over his lips.

"Take it," I ordered him, seeing the screen that flashed up for me, regarding him.

I could absorb him back into the dungeon for no cost, and I'd gain a blueprint for him, complete with his gear. It'd only have his most basic skills and details, but as an adventurer, he was a significant upgrade over the normal advanced kobolds.

Alternatively, I could set conditions on him, and free him from the dungeon to serve me. I could impose things like the minimum and maximum distance he was permitted to roam from the dungeon, who had direct authority over him, and…and a dozen other details.

I waved them all aside, approving "free" and banishing the "are you sure" message with an annoyed mental click.

Clearly, he saw the conditions, and that they were blank.

"I…I…"

"You earned it," I assured him. "I'd like you to stay, to help and to be a part of the dungeon, but I'll not enforce that. You saved me, and you earned your freedom." I forced a smile, then shook my head. "I'm sorry about Ciara. I liked her."

"Me too," he admitted. "I…I'll think about staying." He sighed. "Just for now, though! And we'll talk about pay!"

"We will," I agreed, smiling, before feeling her presence. "I'll be back," I assured him, sitting back and closing my eyes as I slid into the dungeon sense, freeing myself of my body, reaching out to Kelly…and feeling her panic and terror.

"Kelly?"

"Matt!" She practically wept, grabbing onto me and dragging me free of the trial dungeon, then up into the air above. "HELP!" she begged as I stared around, stunned, seeing the smoke climbing, the bodies of the dead outside the northern wall, and the holes that were literally being blown in the wall as I watched.

"Fuck!" I swore, reaching out through the dungeon, seeing that goddamn fifty fucking thousand mana I'd just spent on that high-end healing potion, and just how many more creatures I could have summoned for that.

"Where the hell are the reinforcements?" I growled, scanning the dungeon as my mind raced.

"We couldn't summon them! Not once the trial began. It wouldn't let us!"

"Mike!" I asked desperately. "Mike and Griffiths, where—"

"Gone!" She sent me an image of somewhere to the north, and I flashed up higher, and higher, reaching as high as I could go, and saw in the distance…smoke and gunfire.

I dove back down, scanning over the dungeon, finding that we were under attack by a small, coordinated, and fucking *human* force, all dressed in the uniform of British soldiers.

"Matt, we've got a handful of our trainee forces, but the majority are over at the park with the mages. They're recruiting! They wanted to show off how far they've come in just a few days, and I agreed. I thought it was a good idea…" Aly apologized.

Dozens of bodies were scattered everywhere, kobolds and humans, shredded by assault weapons, as I blinked back to my body, growling as I opened my eyes.

I'd seen enough to see exactly what was going on.

We were under assault by a small team, from the army base to the east, with a second squad held back in reserve, clearly assessing and ready should they be needed.

Someone had waited until Mike, Griffiths, and the others had gone, and then they'd attacked.

This wasn't just bad timing. This was done by someone who knew us. Someone who knew what was going on, and who had probably convinced Aly to send most of our forces to the park.

We had a mole and a traitor.

"Drak!" I snarled, climbing to my feet, and holding my right hand out, focusing as I stood, summoning the shotgun that was marked in the system as "complete, with issues."

The light condensed, flashing as it rolled back and forth, dimming after three seconds as a short, three-barreled, and fucking brutal-looking weapon dropped into my hands.

It looked like something that should be carried to Mars and used for hunting demons by a massive rock of a man. I fucking loved it.

All three magazines were filled with flechettes, and although it might not be a precision weapon, it could probably be used to fuck King Kong up, so it'd do for me, considering the mood I was in.

"You want to kill something?" I asked him, pumping the bottom barrel with a satisfying *ch-clunk*. "Because some fucker is attacking us, and they're slaughtering my kobolds with heavy weapons."

"Do I get one of those?" He clambered to his feet, the healing potion having already done its work.

"Oh yeah," I growled, as the second of the new guns materialized, falling into his outstretched hands.

I could feel the kobolds being summoned above me, our reinforcements being printed even as we turned and started to run. A set of stairs opened ahead that led up to the next level, and freedom.

Someone was about to have a *VERY* bad day.

Epilogue

"Well, this isn't exactly happy making!" Mike called to Griffiths, who grunted, returning fire across the road. The ambush they'd walked into had taken down most of the new dungeon forces that he'd brought.

Nobody knew what the hell the enemy was, beyond heavily armed and apparently reluctant to kill, but they sure as shit laid a good ambush.

"No, I'd say it's positively fucking annoying!" Griffiths called back, sighting down his rifle and firing a fast three-round burst at a dimly identifiable figure.

"We need to pull back!" Rhodes barked to the pair, cursing as she slammed a boot down on something on the road.

"We need to free the others," Patrick called, staring through the poison cloud at the weakly struggling people laid by the side of the road. "We can't just…"

"Coronaught!" Rhodes bellowed, leaping to her feet and sprinting back the way they'd come. "Fucking *move*, you idiots!"

"What?" Mike asked dumbly, every instinct in him fighting to keep him rooted there. Gunfire tore through the air above them, well over half of their forces were down with some kind of vine trap that unleashed a gas attack, and he was in—admittedly limited—cover.

"*RUN!*" Griffiths barked, lunging to his feet and triggering one of the recently discovered soldiers' "special abilities." He blurred across six or seven meters, diving to the floor then rolling; then he was back up and weaving as bullets flew after him.

"What do we do, sir?" one of the trainees, a promising soldier by the name of Taylor called to him. The rest of them looked around in confusion.

"Fuck!" Mike shouted, rolling and coming to his knees as fast as he could. "When an NCO runs, *you fucking RUN!*" he bellowed, eyes widening as he saw a narrow black worm wriggling before him, another flying off his right boot at his sudden motion, and a third…on the back of the soldier before him, one who'd just turned to run.

"We're in a nest!" he screamed, reaching up and grabbing the zip on his camo overcoat.

Mike ripped the zip down as quick as he could, shrugging out of it as he ran, almost losing his rifle in the process. Vines by the sides of the road were suddenly triggered, puffing out additional clouds of spores and who knew what else.

He ran, he ran as fast as he could, but all around him, his people started to drop.

Ahead, others ran through the clouds of spores. He coughed and staggered, finally reaching clear air, and saw there were less than a quarter of the original forces he'd led into the ambush.

All of those who had made it out were the elite: Patrick, Jo, Rhodes, McIntyre, Griffiths, and the twins, Jimmy and Andre, as well as a single mage, Ramnik surprisingly, had made it out.

They'd made it through their use of magic, skills, or because they were gifted with Constitution and Stamina in levels comparable to bulls.

Although they were undoubtably the most skilled and dangerous of their forces, and yes, the most likely to succeed in a rescue attempt, they were also the leadership, and those responsible for the troops caught in the trap below.

Leaving the best of their trainees in the hand of an obvious trap…it went against everything they were as individuals, let alone as soldiers.

"Keep going!" Griffiths bellowed, leading them up the small hill ahead, all of them panting and coughing as their lungs tried to get rid of the crap the vines had been releasing.

"Strip!" Rhodes barked to the group once they were over the hill and out of direct line of sight, as far as they knew.

"What's that?" Mike blinked.

"Strip," she repeated, in a grim voice, already undoing her armor and shucking her way out of it. "Believe me, I know it's not ideal, not here and certainly not now, but if you've one of those fuckers on you? Best to dump everything, and we find out here and now."

"Sarge, what are they?" Andre called to her, already moving to disrobe.

"Parasites." Her voice muffled as she pulled her top off over her head. "They get into you, and they control your brain, make you shit yourself to death with worms breeding in you. Now you gonna finish stripping and check your gear double time, or do I need to beat the shit out of you for looking where you've no business?" she asked, not even glancing in the twins' direction.

"No, Sarge!" they chorused, frantically getting back to stripping.

The entire group did it as quickly as they could, exceedingly conscious that at any point the enemy could march over the top of the hill and catch them in their skivvies.

Fortunately, the creatures seemed content with capturing the majority of the force, along with their guide, Pots. He was a marine who had been at the base in the north of Scotland. That he'd made it all the way to Otterburn with his people only to be attacked there by a group of soldiers with grey skin and black eyes had sat badly with Mike and Griffiths, as had the knowledge that the infection was spreading.

He'd been more than half mad when he'd turned up at the north wall the day before yesterday, begging for help. They'd taken all of a few hours to get everyone geared up and had gone hunting for bear.

If they could catch one of the infected, then pull back, and have Jo heal them? Prove it could be done?

It'd be worth it.

Mike wasn't an idiot, though; he'd taken enough people that they were an overwhelming force all on their own, just in case.

They'd been ready to be careful. They'd been more than paranoid moving into place already, but they were miles from the last reported sighting of the enemy, and they'd not been expecting the fucking things to be the coronaughts, nor the vines that knocked them out.

All in all, it was shaping up to be a shitty day.

"What's that?" Andre suddenly screamed, pointing at a small grey lump under Jimmy's skin, inching its way up his brother's broad back.

"Jo!" Mike snapped, directing the healer to Jimmy. "You're up."

"Now what?" Griffiths whispered to Mike, the pair of them quickly checking each other, then their gear, all the while shooting glances at Jo and her progress.

"Now we hope that Matt finishes that fucking dungeon run soon, because we just gave them our most promising recruits, and I want them back!" Mike said in a low, flat voice, as the pair started to quickly redress.

"They won this round. Those vines were a fucking sneaky trick, but we're the British Army, mate. Someone fucks with us, they pull back a bloody stump with no body attached," he finished grimly.

"Damn right," Griffiths growled, before stiffening, clearly worried as Jo stepped in close, gesturing with the gently glowing focal orb.

"It works," she said. "The coronaught is alien to the body, regardless of its methods, so the healing spell treats it as any other infection. It burns it out, breaking it down and repairing the cells. As to if it'll work with others who are fully infected?" She hesitated, then nodded.

"It *should*, but note, we need to test it. I don't know how the parasites act inside of the body. If they take up space in the brain to live, they might erase the memory centers, as an example. Then we heal them, and we're left with people who have no clue who or what they are. Or worse, people who are broken in ways we just can't fix."

"Well, we've got a weapon against them, besides just shooting them in the fucking head then." Mike sighed, relieved. "At least we've got a chance."

"Do we retreat or advance?" Griffiths asked, looking to Mike.

"Advance," Mike responded after a few seconds. "They can't have this shit all the way around the base, and we know what it looks like now. We circle around it, and hit them, try to rescue our people, or at least see what's happening to them."

"This is going to end in a clusterfuck, you know that, right?" Griffiths said, and Mike hesitated, then looked him square in the eye.

"You want to go back to the dungeon?" he offered.

"Hell no, sir," Griffiths said with a smile. "We lost some of our soldiers on the way down, and more since. If we can rescue them now? I'm all in for it. I'm just warning you."

"So quit bitching and help me find someone to shoot in the face," Mike growled. "Gods, I hope the others are doing better than we are…"

He and the others dressed quickly. Jimmy looked traumatized by the experience he'd just undergone, while Andre had been the only one of them to find a worm in his gear as well, stomping on it mercilessly.

They moved out, skirting around the ambush site and moving quickly but checking the ground as they ran in single file. Miles passed as they shadowed their former trainees, along with their captors. The former allies and enemies now stomped unsteadily along the road toward the distant lights of Otterburn Camp, while Mike and his people crept ever closer.

It was time for shit to get real.

THE END
OF
BOOK 5

ARTEM

Okay, so yeah, I admit it. I had yet another project on the go, and yeah, it was another secret for about a year!

Basically, four of us, Kevin Sinclair, Lars Machmüller, Dawn Chapman and I came up with the world of Artem, a fixed Cyberpunk world that we'll be making more announcements about soon.

For now though? The important thing is that it's four very different stories, spread across two books each, with some of the characters meeting, others passing like ships in the night, sharing the city from totally different perspectives.

Kevin Sinclair tells the story of Oshbob, a wounded and discarded orc, wounded in a landmine disposal, and left to rot.

Lars Machmüller tells the tale of Bowdoin, a hacker, and his band of friends as they claw their way out of the dirt!

Dawn Chapman tells the tale of Ruslan, a helo pilot and corporation man that sees the world from a totally different angle, literally.

Lastly, I tell the tale of Kabutt, a Special forces armored suit operative, wounded and betrayed as he seeks to build a new life.

Hope you'll all give it a try!

ARTEM: REVANANT

Artem One

1st August 2023

The city of ten thousand souls, and at least a hundred times as many people, filled to bursting with the detritus of the races. Elves, humans, orcs, dwarves, and goblins, all crushed in its merciless grip, with the corporations towering to the skies, and the spectres roaming beneath.

The slums were somewhere that Kabutt thought he'd escaped by serving as a feared APS Operator, the most elite of the armoured front-line warriors the city had ever produced.

But when his team and their transport are taken out by drones, and his body and suit are wrecked, Kabutt is mustered out, abandoned into one of the great arcologies.

As his retirement 'gift' he gets a room paid for a month, his favourite gun, and the cheap-ass mods they'd saddled him with.

No, there was only one direction to go from here. Up.

Apparently, others had tried this path before; rising from the gutter to kill their way to the top, and they'd mostly failed.

They didn't have a score to settle and a terrifyingly short fuse though. Kabutt, on the other hand, did. Someone's going to regret sending those drones…

Artem: *Revanant*

REVIEWS

Hey! Well, I hope you enjoyed the book? If so, please, please remember to leave a review, its massively important, as not only does it let others know about the book, it also tells Amazon that the book is worth promoting, and makes it more likely that more people will see it.

That in turn will hopefully keep me able to keep writing full time, while listening to crazy German bands screaming in my ears, and frankly, I kinda really like that!

If you want to spread the good word, that'd be amazing, and if you know of anyone that might be interested in stocking my books, I'm happy to reach out and send them samples, but honestly, if you enjoy my madness, that's massive for me.
Thank you.

Facebook and Social Media

If you want to reach out, chat or shoot the shit, you can always find me on either my author page here:

www.facebook.com/JezCajiaoAuthor

_OR_

We've recently set up a new Facebook group to spread the word about cool LitRPG books. It's dedicated to two very simple rules, 1; lets spread the word about new and old brilliant LitRPG books, and 2: Don't be a Dick!

They sound like really simple rules, but you'd be amazed…

Come join us!

https://www.facebook.com/groups/litrpglegion

I'm also on Discord here: **https://discord.gg/u5JYHscCEH**

Or I'm reaching out on other forms of social media atm, I'm just spread a little thin that's all!

You're most likely to find me on Discord, but please, don't be offended when I don't approve friend requests on my personal Facebook pages. I did originally, and several people abused that, sending messages to my family and being generally unpleasant, hence, the author page:

https://www.facebook.com/JezCajiaoAuthor

I hope you understand.

PATREON!

Okay then, now for those of you that don't know about Patreon, its essentially a way to support your favorite nutcases, you can sign up for a day or a month or a year, and you get various benefits for it, ranging from my heartfelt thanks, to advance access to the books, to me sending them books, naming characters and more.

At the time of me writing this, the advanced Patreon readers are finishing up Age of Forged Steel, about to start on the next of my secret projects (They'll have access to it for about a month before I even go public with it existing) so yeah, you get plenty for the support!

There's one of my wonderful supporters out there that I have to thank personally as well; ASeaInStorm, you utter legend you. Thank you for sticking with it mate.

http://www.patreon.com/Jezcajiao

RECOMMENDATIONS

I'm often asked for personal recommendations, so if this book has whetted your appetite for more LitRPG, please have a look at the following, these are brilliant series by brilliant authors!

Ascend Online by Luke Chmilenko

The Land by Aleron Kong

Challengers Call by Nathan A Thompson

SoulShip also by Nathan

Endless Online by M H Johnson

Silver Fox and the Western Hero, also by M H Johnson

The Good Guys/Bad Guys by Eric Ugland

Condition: Evolution by Kevin Sinclair

Space Seasons by Dawn Chapman

The Wayward Bard by Lars M

LITRPG!

To learn more about LitRPG, talk to other authors including myself, and to just have an awesome time, please join the LitRPG Group

www.facebook.com/groups/LitRPGGroup

FACEBOOK

There's also a few really active Facebook groups I'd recommend you join, as you'll get to hear about great new books, new releases and interact with all your (new) favorite authors! (I may also be there, skulking at the back and enjoying the memes…)

www.facebook.com/groups/LitRPGsociety/

www.facebook.com/groups/LitRPG.books/

www.facebook.com/groups/LitRPGforum/

www.facebook.com/groups/gamelitsociety/